ALL THE SHADOWS OF DEATH

ALL THE SHADOWS OF DEATH

VALRUE BOOK TWO

COLEY TAYLOR

A catalogue record for this book is available from the National Library of New Zealand:

ISBN (ebook): 978-1-7386244-4-7
ISBN (paperback): 978-1-7386244-3-0
ISBN (hardback): 978-1-7386244-5-4

Dear Reader

I'm an indie author (self-published), so in my spare time when I'm not writing, designing book covers, or coordinating beta-readers and editing, I do all my own book marketing. Marketing is the hardest part!

Reviews are super important for marketing and determining how well a book sells. After reading *All the Shadows of Death*, please consider leaving an honest review on the platform from which you bought it, and on Goodreads.

Thank you so much,
Coley xx

www.valruefantasyseries.com

Instagram: @ColeyTaylorAuthor
TikTok: @ColeyTaylorAuthor
Facebook.com/ColeyTaylorAuthor

CONTENT WARNING

This book contains Adult Only content, including swearing, sex, violence, and deals with the subjects of abuse and suicide.

Contents

DIJAK'S MAP

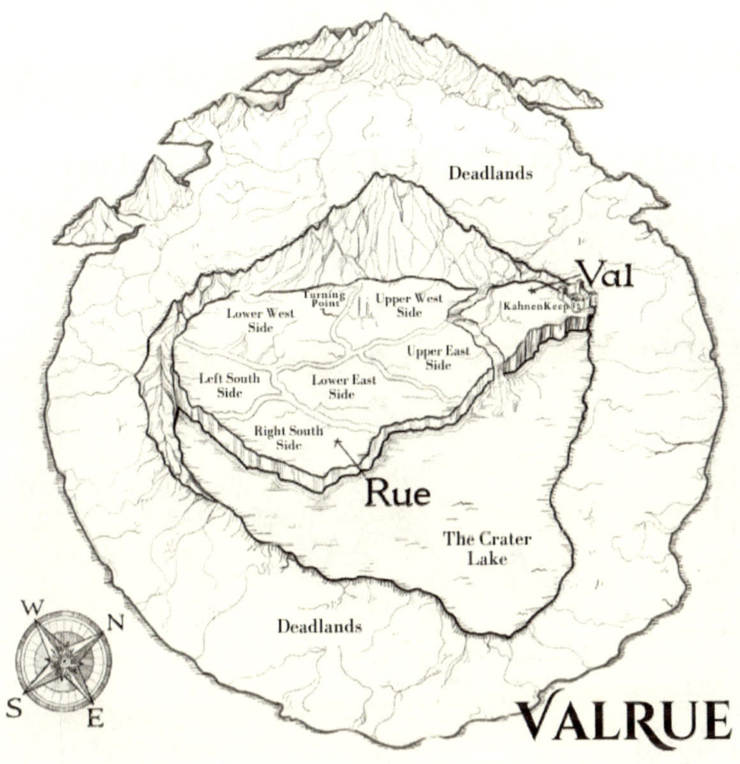

. . . A map of Valrue within her mountain crater. I imagine Rue looks different from how you remember, the streetling gangs having carved out their territories. The Deadlands continue to grow beyond the outline depicted, forming a barren expanse of such scale that no paper in my possession could hope to capture them. I do not envy the Krijen posted out there . . .

From Yours,
Dijak

KIMJIT'S MAP OF THE DEADLANDS

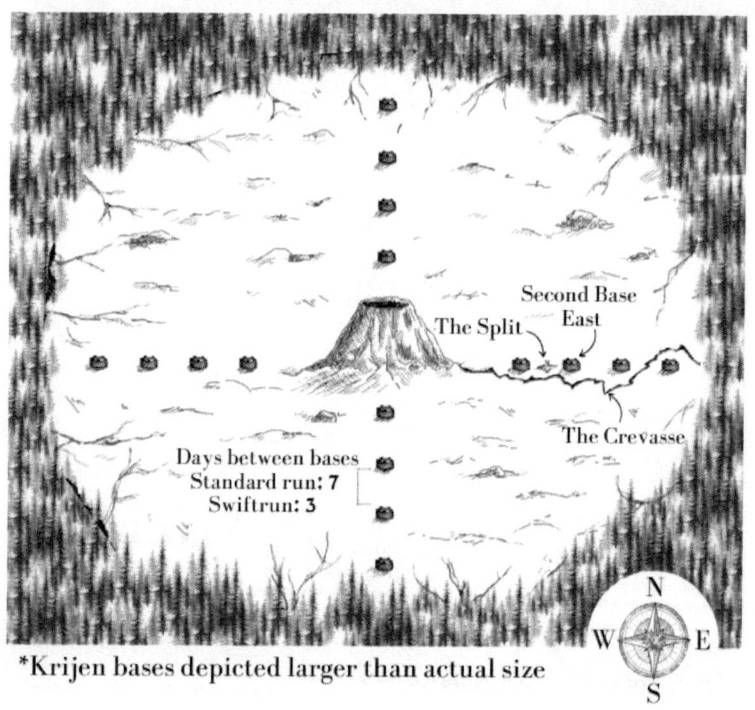

*Krijen bases depicted larger than actual size

CHARACTER MAP

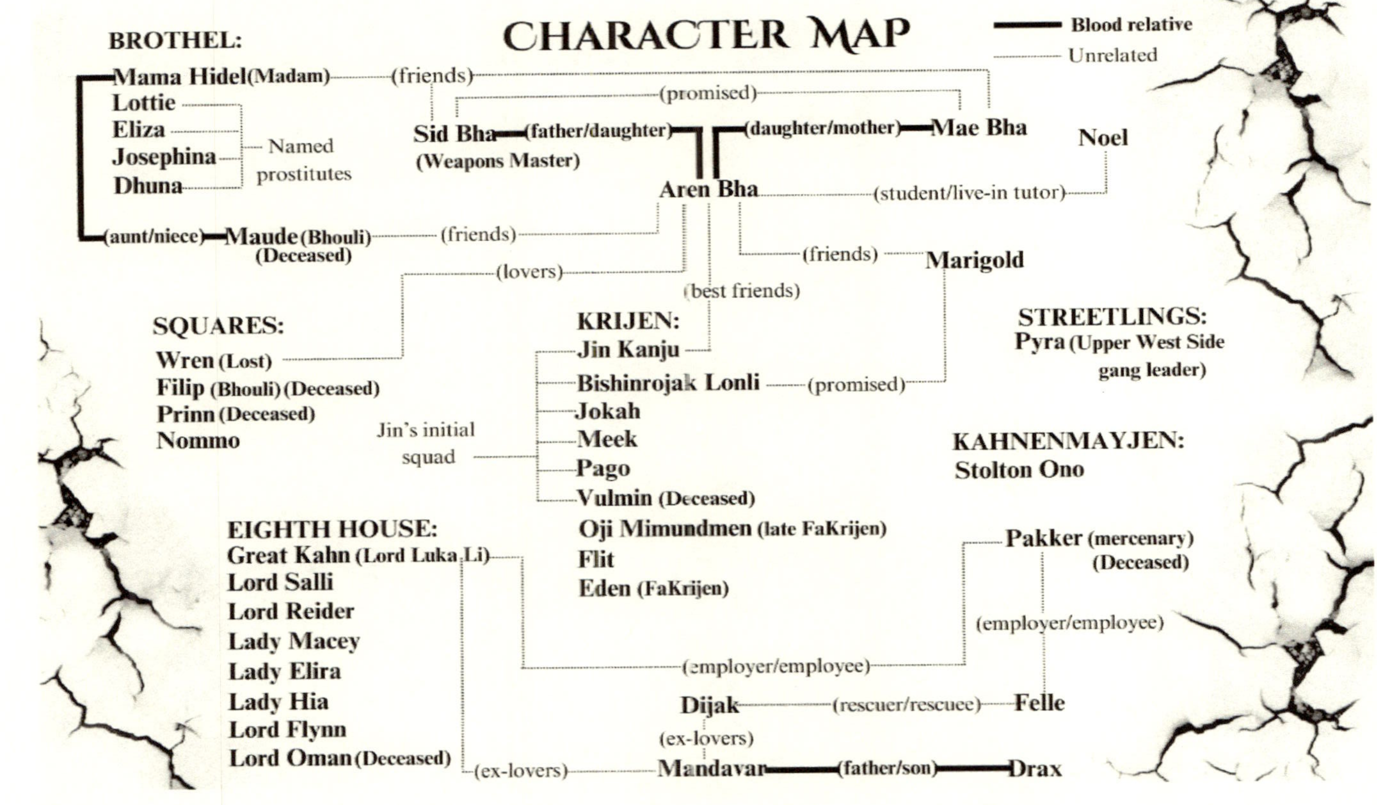

There is an additional character map for Book Two: *All the Shadows of Death* at the back of this book. It contains spoilers and is recommended to be viewed on book completion.

First Glossary

This glossary contains terms from Valrue Book One: *The Dark Side of Happiness*. To avoid spoilers, terms yet to be explored in Book Two: *All the Shadows of Death* are in a separate glossary at the back of this book.

Bhouli (say Boo-lee) – Secretive sect of people

Dancing Ceremony – Ceremonial duelling of the oldest Squares (the Fifteenths) prior to becoming Krijen

Deadlands – Lifeless area surrounding Valrue

Distribution Centre – Stone-walled, mayj-made structure in Val that all incoming and outgoing goods pass through

Eighth House – Ruling government house of Valrue

FaKrijen (say Fa-kree-jin) – Leader of the Krijen

Great Kahn – Prime minister of Valrue

Harnessing ability – One of the two pillars of majik

Making the Cross – Moving from Rue into Val

Mayj(en) – Person(s) with majikal abilities

Nomajik – No majikal abilities (bastardised term)

Lomajik – Limited majikal abilities (bastardised term)

Himajik – Significant majikal abilities (bastardised term)

Kahn(en) – Minister(s) of Valrue

KahnenCull – Colloquial name for the Distribution Centre

KahnenKeep – Government house

KahnenMayj(en) – Person(s) with majikal abilities in the employ of the Kahnen

KahnenMinder – Servants of the Kahnen

KahnenSpeaker – Voice of the Kahnen

Krijen (say Kree-jin) – Warriors of Valrue

Krije (say Kree-jay) – Ceremonial sword used by Krijen in combat

Power – One of the two pillars of majik

Promise – Partner, typically engaged or wed

Skahk – Derogatory term for a mayj

Square(s) – Krijen in training

Squad – Group of Krijen, typically six, with a chosen leader

Streetling(s) – Homeless youths living in Valrue

Swiftrun – The fastest supply run across the Deadlands from forest farms to Valrue

Swiftrunner(s) – Employees of the Kahnen who run supplies across the Deadlands

The People – Voting citizens of Valrue

Turned – To die by harnessing power beyond what one has

Turning – When a mayj starts running out of power while harnessing. The sensation is highly addictive

The Unsettlement – Crisis of majikal and natural imbalance in Valrue where, with humans as a key exception, an excess of majikal power drove almost all living things from the city

The Spells of Weaving:

Can only be cast/ woven by mayjen of the Weaving expression. Significant power is required to Break these bonds.

The Cardonia Spell – Power that is Woven between matter to bind it into a lattice-like structure called cardonite. Durable, particularly against majik.

The Thorson Spell – Power that is Woven into a bond between objects that can be passed through. The bound objects are called Lockstones.

The Du Bellor Spell – Power that is Woven between matter as a means of storage outside the body. It is leaky and burdensome though if a certain 'mass' of power is obtained, the spell becomes self-sustaining. Woven into the crater lake by Mandavar, the Du Bellor Spell caused the Unsettlement in Valrue.

PROLOGUE

Four years ago

T he woman was the real deal, that much the girl knew. She'd seen the woman around, spouting tales of her virtue to the People, to mayjen lovers and haters alike.

'So,' the woman began, 'have you thought about what I said?'

The girl folded her arms. Her parents had always told her that even if you wanted something really badly, you shouldn't let other people know. That way, they couldn't use it to make you do things.

Not that her parents had been good role models by any means.

The girl narrowed her eyes. 'You're sure you'll get voted in?' She added a suspicious tone to her voice to make her sound more reluctant than she was.

'I am already in,' the woman replied. 'But you must be willing to play your part. I cannot pull this off without you. It is important you understand that.'

The girl turned her suspicious look up a notch. The offer was tempting. To trick the Kahnen, put a player in their midst and rip them apart from the inside out after everything they'd done? It would be *so* satisfying.

Had the woman asked her if she was interested only three months ago, the girl would've said no. Her big sister wouldn't have wanted something like that for her, not after what their parents put them through, trying to drag them into a bad world. A world where your uncles and aunts – who weren't really your uncles and aunts – disappeared or died. A world where people would show up in the middle of the night and threaten to pull you from your bed before your father came in to scare them away. A world where women cried outside the door to your house until your mother told them lies to shut them up.

The girl's sister had kept her from all of that. She'd done well after their parents died to make an honest living and to put food on the table that wasn't dipped in someone's blood. But then that horrible, inexcusable thing happened. A Kahn wanting his way had sent in Krijen who wouldn't know wrong if it smacked them in the face.

The girl's sister had always told her to be forgiving and kind because people were usually good at heart even if they weren't always nice. But what had being forgiving and kind got her sister? It got her killed, that was what.

That was when the girl decided she should be more like her parents after all.

'Okay,' the girl agreed, 'I'll do it, on one condition.'

'Yes?'

'I get to decide who I become.'

'Of course,' the woman replied, 'I would not have it any other way. I am not here to tell you what to do. We will be partners.'

The girl wasn't really sure what was in it for the woman. It was hard to understand why, of all people, she would hold a vendetta against the Kahnen. I mean, weren't they just like her? They dressed the same; they talked just as smartly. So what was it that made her dislike them so much? Maybe she had a story too.

One day, the girl would ask her but not today. Today the girl was happy, wrapped snuggly in dreams about her own story and where it would go from here now that it could end in revenge.

CHAPTER I:
AREN BHA

Turning Point was always busiest at dawn. Somehow they always ended up with so little time, rushing to get everything done before Aren had to leave again, back to her dreary life in Val.

The organised chaos of the Point was a welcome distraction for Aren. One month ago, her father, Sid Bha, had left to appeal to the Great Kahn for the release of Mama Hidel and her women from the KahnenKeep dungeon. It had taken him a week to leave after he said he would, finally mustering the courage. It had been hard to watch him go, trembling violently as he'd stepped through the mansion gates, heading to the Keep.

He'd not returned.

Aren found herself wallowing, coming up with all sorts of horrendous imaginings about what had happened to him.

And if she wasn't thinking about her father, she was thinking about Maude, the fourteen-year-old Bhouli girl who was sitting in a dungeon cell, along with Mama Hidel and the women from the brothel.

That was why it was a relief when the sun started to set, and Aren began counting down the hours until she could leave her family mansion for the Point, where she would be kept so busy there wouldn't be time to think about her father and Maude and Mama Hidel anymore.

Aren was thankful she had something to do that mattered. Each week, she watched the familiar, sunken faces at the Point grow fuller, suddenly flush with smiles where previously there were only frowns. She was getting to know some of the regular visitors, having spent many hours in their company. Everyone in the food line at the Point had a story to tell, and Aren frequently got lost in them.

That was probably why she missed the grubby little hand as it snatched a slice of cornbread from the pile in front of her.

'Hey!'

People in the food line cried out and lunged at the streetling boy as he zigzagged past them, cackling. He twisted around as he ran, making a rude gesture at Aren with his hand. She let him go, placing her hands on her hips as everyone turned to watch the streetling flee down the alleyway.

As the streetling neared the mouth of the Point, a dark figure appeared from the shadows and threw out an arm, catching the streetling across the chest. With a whump, the streetling landed on his back on the cobblestones.

The apprehender stepped from the shadows into the light, revealing a young man wearing patched clothes, his long black hair tied up in a knot.

Aren watched with a satisfied smile as the young man picked the streetling up by the scruff of his neck and plucked the cornbread from his hand. '*No stealing*,' Wren snarled. He dropped the stunned streetling on his feet. The boy immediately took off down the nearest alleyway, legs and arms pumping madly to escape his wounded pride.

Wren waited for the streetling to dart around the corner before he spun on his heel and walked up the line towards Aren. A few daring eyes followed him as he went.

Wren was a Lost Square, doomed to disgrace since his defeat at his Dancing Ceremony over a year ago. Social convention deemed him unworthy of acknowledgement in the eyes of the People. Aren didn't believe that though. Although she kept pointing it out, Wren didn't seem to realise he was being seen again even if by only a few. But it was still more than before, and it made Aren happier than she could put into words.

Aren smiled wider at Wren as he approached.

'I wonder when the streetlings will realise it's easier to wait in line,' Wren said dryly, stopping next to her.

Aren laughed. 'Some of them have.' She pointed to a gaggle of rough-looking youths halfway down the food line, their bare torsos slung with belts, their stolen boots three sizes too big for them. They looked supremely annoyed to be waiting with the rest of the visitors to the Point, but they kept their fingers jammed into their armpits as though determined to prove they could do it.

Wren raised an eyebrow but said nothing. Since he'd saved a few streetlings from the Krijen in the aftermath of the Celebrations, some of them had started coming to Turning Point *not* for the purpose of making trouble. But Aren knew Wren still didn't trust them.

Aren waved to the next person in the line, who stepped forward to collect their meal. Aren had put together a huge pot of stew to go with the cornbread, which was going down a treat. *Thank goodness for Noel,* she thought. Noel had been her tutor since she was a young girl and had taught her everything she knew. She wouldn't have a clue how to cook without him. The maids had mostly done it until Noel had given in to her complaints and let her help in the kitchen, for curiosity's sake.

Wren glanced at Aren before taking a bite of the cornbread in his hand. 'Shouldn't you be going soon?' he asked.

Aren pouted, pretending to be upset. 'Are you that eager to get rid of me?'

Wren snorted. 'Getting rid of you isn't possible,' he said, not taking his eyes off his food. 'I tried that before. It didn't work.'

Aren stuck her tongue out at him.

'But seriously,' he said, 'you need to go. I can take it from here.'

Wren's eyes flickered towards the line of hungry people. Everyone was behaving themselves today. They knew Wren would throw them from the Point if they tried anything untoward, especially if they harassed the majikal residents – the Turners – with whom the visitors to the Point had a tense relationship. Luckily the threat of being publically reprimanded by a Lost Square was enough to keep them in line. For the most part.

'I'm still waiting on one delivery,' Aren said.

'Thatcher?'

'Of course.'

Wren scowled. 'Then he'd better be back soon. You know he won't deal with me.'

'You don't give him the chance,' Aren said.

'When he stops trying to steal coin, I'll be nicer to him.'

'We can afford to lose some coin to keep him, Wren. He's a good worker.'

'Not if he's skimming off the top. Don't let him take advantage.'

Aren sighed. Not surprisingly, the streetlings were obnoxious little things, but it was mostly due to boredom. She'd discovered that if you gave them something to do, they latched onto it with a fury. As the demand for food and medicine grew at the Point, Aren and Wren quickly ran out of supplies. There was only so much Aren could sneak from her home without her family noticing. That and Aren wanted to do it *herself*. It had taken a little while, but eventually, Aren figured out how to earn coin.

Rue was a huge, terrifying maze, especially for the wealthier inhabitants of Val, who often had to do business there. There was a demand for things to get done and get done fast but made almost impossible by the fact that unless you knew the streets and their inhabitants, you were easy prey. At the very least, you would get lost, herded into an alleyway and have your clothes and boots stolen at knifepoint. Or in the streetlings' case, nailpoint.

So Aren entered the business of deliveries, her services taken up with sighs of relief by the wealthy merchants of Valrue. Whether it was a package or a secret, Aren and her little team of streetlings got it where it needed to go.

Of course, there were a few issues at the start, and a furious Wren had to hunt down the streetlings who'd run off with the goods. However, the streetlings soon realised that if they actually did the job as asked, they got a coin at the end. Or maybe two if they were naughty like Thatcher.

Just then, Aren spotted him, most notably by the brown, ratty hair that hung to his waist. He bounced up to her on his impossibly knocked knees, holding out a little coin purse, which he dropped into her open palm.

'Thank you, Thatcher,' Aren said with a smile. She dug into the purse and handed him back a coin and a bit of cornbread. Thatcher grinned toothily back at her before stuffing the cornbread into his mouth.

'You're late,' Wren growled. Thatcher pointedly turned his back to him.

Aren frowned. 'Thatcher, what happened?'

'The stupid merchant wouldn't give me the delivery for *ages*,' Thatcher said, bits of cornbread spraying from his mouth.

Aren folded her arms. 'Why? He was expecting you.'

Thatcher shrugged his scrawny shoulders. 'Dunno. It's okay though. After I said I would cut his pinky finger off, he handed it right over.'

Aren moaned and rubbed her temples. *There goes some business*, she thought. 'No, Thatcher. You can't threaten clients. I've told you this before.'

Thatcher stopped chewing. 'Not even a little?'

'Not even a little. If they give you trouble, just tell me. The same goes for the other streetlings.'

Thatcher looked at her like she was crazy.

'I mean it, Thatcher,' Aren warned.

Thatcher swallowed loudly, gave her a thumbs up, and then took off down the street.

Aren opened the purse again and had a proper look. To her surprise, there were twelve coins inside. They weren't short this time. Triumphant, she swung the purse in front of Wren's face. 'Look! He didn't take any! You just need to give them a chance.'

Wren turned his dark monolid eyes on her. 'Aren,' he said, '*go*.'

Aren tucked the purse into her wraps, and before Wren could protest, she'd stood on her tiptoes and kissed him on the cheek. She walked past the line and made her way down the Point, waving to a few of the Turners who smiled dazedly up at her from their nooks and doorways. When she reached the end of the alleyway, she broke into a tired jog, back towards Val.

***

The sun was well and truly up by the time Aren got back to the Bha mansion. She climbed in through her window and hid the coin purse under her bed. She stripped off her tight-fitting wraps, swapping them for a skirt and blouse. She'd given up on wearing a disguise into Rue. No one had ever recognised her, and she didn't care if they did. Wren was the one who was worried about her being seen with him and the delinquents of the Lower West Side.

Aren flopped onto her bed, closing her eyes. She knew she should show her face in the dining room as it was breakfast time, and she should've already been up and sparring. But just this once, maybe they would believe her if she said she had slept in –

There was a knock at her bedroom door.

'Aren? Are you awake? Bish is here to see you.'

Aren dragged herself off her bed, crossed the room, and tugged her door open.

Mae, her mother, stood in the hallway with her heart-shaped face and rosy cheeks, her hand poised to knock again.

'Bish is here?' Aren asked.

Mae nodded. 'In the sitting room.' Her eyes ran over Aren, a little line appearing between her brows. 'Oh, my dear.' Mae held a hand to her daughter's cheek. 'You look exhausted. You can't sleep?' She presumed Aren was kept awake from worrying over Sid.

Aren placed her hand over her mother's, nodding. It was only a little lie, but it made Aren feel guilty. She hated lying to her mother even though it was all she did these days. She'd promised Wren she wouldn't say anything about the Point or about him. Not wearing a disguise was a small rebellion against his wishes, but if Aren were to tell her parents about him, it would be a full-blown betrayal. She would never do that.

Aren made her way to the sitting room where Bish waited in his wheeling chair. He'd broken his back last year in the Deadlands on a supply run that had gone wrong. A bandit mayj had thrown a wagon wheel at him. He'd not been able to walk since.

'Hey, Aren,' Bish said as she entered.

'Hey.' Aren closed the door and hurried to sit in the chair next to him, leaning in so that her mother wouldn't hear. 'Well?'

'He's not in any of the cells,' Bish replied softly. 'I spoke to some of the Krijen guards. There is no one of Sid's description there. I'm sorry, Aren. I don't know where he is.' Bish looked drawn, his cheeks sallow. Combined with his thinning blond hair, he'd aged far beyond his twenty-two years. He hadn't really been himself lately, and he wouldn't say why. Marigold, his promise, was going mad with worry.

'There's nowhere else in the KahnenKeep to imprison someone?' Aren asked.

'Not that I know of. I asked Flit too, one of the Krijen who knows the Keep well. She couldn't think of anywhere he might be.'

'Flit? Is she trustworthy?'

'She won't tell anyone.'

Aren gave Bish a strange look. 'I still don't get why you won't ask Jin –'

'Jin isn't around to ask,' Bish snapped, uncharacteristically harsh.

It was true. Aren hadn't seen Jin since he'd first left for the Deadlands a year ago after their awful argument. But he'd been back in Valrue for over a month, and Aren was worried he'd forgotten about her. She *could* go looking for him, but if truth be told, she was nervous to do so because Jin knew exactly where she was, and he still didn't come. But that didn't explain why Bish hadn't seen him either.

'Has something happened between you and Jin?' Aren asked.

'No,' Bish replied, 'I just have little to do with him. He's the KrijenMayj now. He's busy. And I'm barely Krijen anymore.'

Aren didn't know what to say to that. Because of his injury, Bish wasn't part of a squad nor did he have any Krijen duties, but he'd not been formally discharged. He was in a horrible limbo that was almost more cruel.

Aren didn't like the Krijen. They did unspeakable things like killing children.

'There's something else,' Bish went on. 'While I was there, I asked Flit about Mama Hidel and the women. She says there isn't a Bhouli girl with them.'

Aren gasped. 'You don't think the Kahnen know about Maude's ability? They wouldn't hurt her, would they?'

'I don't think they'd hurt her,' Bish said. 'She'd be too valuable.' For some unknown reason, mayjen couldn't harness around Maude. Aren hoped that Bish was right and that the Kahnen wouldn't hurt her, but she knew they'd use her if they could. Bish purposefully hadn't said it. He probably thought Aren was too delicate to hear something like that.

'Maybe they've got Maude wherever they've got Sid,' Bish suggested.

Feeling restless despite her fatigue, Aren folded her arms so that she wouldn't snap her wrist wraps, clinging to the idea that her father and Maude were both still alive. They had to be. Somehow Aren felt like she'd know it if they weren't.

Aren and Bish dissolved into silence, preoccupied with their own thoughts. After a while, Bish cleared his throat. 'Is . . . is Drax around?'

Bish and Marigold had accepted Drax with little incident possibly because both Mae and Noel were present when Aren explained who he was. That way, they couldn't write it off as some outrageous idea of Aren's to keep him around. Drax had also trembled uncontrollably when Bish pulled out his daggers. It was hard to see the deformed little mayj as a threat even if he had murdered Oji, the late FaKrijen.

'He'll be somewhere,' Aren replied. As she spoke, a scarred white hand curled around the window that faced the inner courtyard. Drax's face followed it, his usually lifeless blue eyes wide. There was more flesh on his bones now, and his hair was washed and cut so it curled around his ears. He stood a little taller though still looked like a boy instead of the young man he was.

Drax eased himself over the stone window ledge and shuffled into the room, his head ducked low. Drax knew he shouldn't listen to private conversations.

'Sorry, Aren,' Drax said, crouching next to the chair she sat in.

'That's all right.'

Drax turned his eyes towards Bish, whose cheeks reddened under the mayj's intense gaze.

'Um . . .' Bish said, 'so I wanted to ask you something about majik if that's okay?'

Drax looked at Aren. She shrugged. 'If you want to.'

'Okay,' Drax replied. He looked back to Bish.

'I've noticed you can build things with majik,' Bish said. 'I've seen you do it with that stone tree in the courtyard. The other day, you took it apart. Then you put it back together again like it was brand new.'

Drax's head whipped around to Aren once more.

'I don't care if you're harnessing, Drax,' she said. 'Please, listen to Bish.'

Bish was twisting his hands together in his lap. Whatever he needed to ask clearly had him tied up in knots. 'I've heard some things about how majik works,' Bish said. 'I was wondering . . . can you heal people?' He swallowed. 'I mean, can you heal *me?*'

'No,' Drax said bluntly. Bish looked crestfallen.

'Drax,' Aren said quickly, her gut twisting in sympathy for Bish, 'can you tell him why?'

Drax blinked at her. 'I don't know how to explain it.'

'Please try.'

Drax wore the tiniest frown. He must've learned to do that recently. He'd only ever had a blank expression before now, a by-product of the life he'd lived in the KahnenKeep dungeons. Aren had yet to hear that story.

'The part of you that is broken . . .' Drax cocked his head in thought. 'Majik cannot fix that.'

Bish's eyes widened. 'So you're saying you *can* heal people, just not me?'

'In your spine, there are little pieces that don't come back. I can't make them.'

'How do you know?' Bish asked.

Drax shrugged. 'It won't work.'

'You won't even try?'

Drax shook his head again.

'I'm so sorry,' Aren said softly. Bish wiped his eyes with the back of his hands. 'Fuck this,' he muttered.

'Are you okay?' Aren asked, regretting it immediately. It was a stupid question. Of course Bish wasn't okay.

'I'm fine,' Bish said. 'I should go. Marigold will be wondering where I am.' He swivelled his wheeling chair around and rolled towards the door.

'Bish! Wait.' Aren rose from her chair, dashed across the room, and threw her arms around him. Bish stiffened at first, but then she felt him relax and he hugged her back, giving her a gentle squeeze. After a time, Aren let him go. 'Did that help?' she asked.

Bish's mouth twitched. 'It actually did,' he said.

Aren opened the door for him, and he wheeled himself through, soon disappearing around the corner and heading towards the main entrance. Aren closed the door.

'Bish is sad,' Drax said.

'I know,' Aren replied. 'I think everyone is a bit sad right now.'

'Because of Sid?'

'Because of lots of things.'

Drax looked out the window towards the peaks of the mountain surrounding the crater lake next to which the city nestled. 'Sid wasn't in the KahnenKeep dungeon,' he said.

'No, he wasn't.'

'The Krijen don't know where he is.'

Aren sighed. 'No.'

Drax turned his icy blue eyes on her. 'I know where he is.'

CHAPTER 2:
JIN KANJU

To Jin's disappointment, there were no loose nails in the Krijen bunks at the KahnenKeep. He lay on his back in the darkness, the perfectly nailed wooden slats just visible above him. Filip stood over him, arms propped against the bunk. Filip's bald head glowed in the dim, a curling trail of white ink smeared from his fiery brows up over his alabaster skull. He never wore his Bhouli headscarf anymore. He'd not worn it since the Dancing Ceremony last year when he'd removed it for their dance right before Jin had killed him.

Save for Filip, whatever he was, Jin was alone in the Krijen bunkroom allocated to his derelict squad. After Jin had become the KrijenMayj, his squad had moved from the Left South Side barracks to the Keep at the request of the Kahnen. That had been shortly after Maude had thrown herself into the lake.

Not that anyone knew about Maude. Jin hadn't yet summoned the courage to tell Mama Hidel that her niece was dead and that he'd seen it happen. That he'd had the chance to stop her.

Filip had no such hang-ups. 'Stop moping,' he said. 'It's done. There's no point crying about it.'

'Should I tell Mama Hidel?'

'Are you crazy? Of course not! She'll never believe Maude jumped.'

'What if I say that man pushed her?'

Filip laughed. 'Fuck no, you *suck* at lying.'

Jin thumbed the tops of his dagger hilts snuggled at his thighs. 'Then why wouldn't they believe me if I told the truth?'

'Because people aren't rational. If you tell them something they don't want to hear, they won't believe it. Just stay away from Mama Hidel.'

Jin was silent. Maybe Filip was right. No one else knew he'd gone after Maude. If he stayed away from the women, no one would ever think to blame him for the death of the Bhouli girl.

'Do you reckon the man who took her was a mercenary? He was trained to fight, but he certainly wasn't Krijen.'

'Without a doubt,' Filip replied. 'I reckon he was in on it with that murdering skahk. You remember how the mercenary reacted when you said the Krijen hadn't caught him? That's why he wanted to cut off your hands. You're too much of a threat.'

Jin's face twisted in the darkness. He hated the streetling skahk who'd murdered Oji. Despite every Krijen in the city remaining on high alert, every home upturned, and every street scoured, the skahk evaded capture. Jin's veins burned just thinking about him.

'What Maude said about the lake . . . do you think that's true?'

'I do,' Filip said. 'Can't you feel it?'

Jin could. Where there was once a heaviness, a nagging desire to run and leave the city behind, now there was nothing but air. Jin could breathe better; he felt more in control. It was because the weight of a foreign power wasn't hanging over him, pulling him down. It felt like he was back in the Deadlands, which made sense if the source of the power had been the crater lake next to the city. In the Deadlands, he had been too far away to feel it.

'Yeah, I can tell there's something different,' Jin replied. 'It's because Maude broke the spell. That's what that torn-out page meant, right? It was a spell that caused the Unsettlement.'

Filip nodded in agreement. 'So who cast it? That skahk is too young.

The Unsettlement started years ago, so it can't have been him.'

Jin pondered this. 'Maybe –'

The door to the bunkroom creaked open, letting in a strip of light. 'Jin? Are you in here?'

Meek, Jin's sandy-haired squad member, stuck his head into the room. He spotted Jin on the bed. 'What are you doing? We've all been waiting for you! Pago is going out of his mind.'

Jin stifled a groan and sat up. He'd been dreading this. As much as he wanted to learn about majik, he didn't like the idea of being humiliated in front of his squad for how little he knew. It made it that much worse that they were all so fucking excited about it.

'Come on!' Meek nagged. 'Pago will have my balls.'

Dragging his feet, Jin followed Meek out into the blinding light of the stone corridor. The Keep cut into the mountain, and the open windows to their right gave a sweeping view of the city. At first, Jin had found it breathtaking. Now it just pissed him off to know the skahk was in his sight, and he couldn't get to him. That, and Jin could see Aren's family mansion from here. He badly wanted to see her, but Bish had warned him to stay away. The threat of what Bish might say if Jin tried to speak to Aren was too great.

Jin had used majik on Bish at their Dancing Ceremony last year. Bish had been bloodied, bruised, and near-blind. He would've become Lost if Jin hadn't intervened. But when Jin had told Bish what he'd done, Bish had thrown it back in his face. He'd said that Jin had made him a cheater, that he'd ruined Wren's life too. Bish didn't care what Jin had saved him from probably because of what happened afterwards. Bish had broken his back, and he was angry and bitter about it. He'd taken it out on Jin. Jin could forgive him for that.

The problem was that Jin couldn't be sure Bish would keep this secret to himself. However, if Bish told people, it would throw his own victory at the Dancing Ceremony into question. Jin hoped Bish wasn't willing to take the risk. Bish knew that being Lost wasn't worth that. Nothing was.

Jin's attention floated back to Meek as he followed him through the Keep. Jin wasn't sure where they were going, not having paid attention to Pago's instructions the day before. Meek walked quickly, eager to arrive. Filip kept close behind Jin, his footsteps thudding on the stone beneath their feet. It sounded terribly real even though Filip wasn't.

Jin's stomach growled loudly enough that Meek glanced back at him. 'How can you possibly be hungry?' Meek asked. 'You were at breakfast an hour ago.'

Jin grunted. Three bowls of that shitty breakfast maize hadn't been enough, and Jin wasn't willing to force down a fourth. He'd been ravenous for weeks now, but he was sick of eating.

'It's because you're harnessing more often now,' Filip said. 'You need to eat.'

'Easy for you to say, you don't have to eat that slop,' Jin muttered. 'And I've barely been harnessing.' Save for the odd flick of his wrist to relieve some of the ever-building power in his chest, Jin was doing his best to avoid harnessing, as ordered by the Kahnen.

Meek glanced back at Jin. 'What did you say?'

'Nothing,' Jin said quickly. He hadn't realised he'd spoken out loud.

They wove through the Keep until they came to a massive grey archway, blue tendrils webbed across its surface. The archway housed two large wooden doors which stood open, beckoning them in. Jin twitched with apprehension as they stepped through.

The polished room beyond was enormous with a high ceiling that stretched up into the peaks of the mountain above them. Every surface comprised the same grey and blue stone. Jin felt a crawl down his spine. He didn't like this room very much.

He disliked it even more when he saw who stood in it. The KahnenMayj, Stolt, was just as foul as Jin remembered, right down to the sneer on his face. Next to Stolt stood seven members of the Eighth House, including the new Kahn whose name Jin couldn't remember. All but one. The Great Kahn was not there.

For once, the Kahnen were dressed like normal people, in shirts and skirts or trousers. It was strange to see them without their glittering gowns on. Jin figured it was because there was no one here they wanted to impress.

The other remaining members of Jin's squad were also there: Jokah and their squad leader Pago. To Jin's surprise, Pago was flanked by Flit, the freckle-faced brunette from the Deadlands, and Nommo, a thick-set Krijen with a snub nose who Jin had been a Square with.

Pago stepped up to meet them as they entered. 'The FaKrijen gave me permission to recruit to the squad,' he said, answering Jin's unspoken question. 'Flit was an obvious choice. As for Nommo, I thought you might like a familiar face.'

Nommo grinned at Jin. It was definitely nice to see him, but Nommo had a loud mouth and pushed boundaries. Jin wasn't sure he would keep what he knew about Jin to himself.

'You've got quite an audience,' Pago said quietly. 'I hope that's okay.'

Just what I need, Jin thought as he nodded. *More people to see me fail.*

'Welcome, Jin,' Lady Macey said, stepping forward. A year into her role, she was the second newest member of the Eighth House though one of the oldest, her neatly pinned brown hair heavily speckled with grey. 'I hope you do not mind us attending today. We are all very interested to see what you can do.'

Lady Macey nodded to Stolt, who looked like he was sucking on something sour, inexplicably rolling what looked like a small stone between his fingers.

'First things first,' Stolt said, looking at Jin, 'we need to figure out what you are. Unless you can tell us?'

Jin had no idea what that meant. He reluctantly shook his head, and Stolt's lip curled in amusement. Stolt stepped forward and thrust a fist at Jin's face as if to punch him, stopping just short of his nose. Jin didn't flinch, resisting the temptation to lunge back. It was uncomfortable to be this close to Stolt. Jin knew why now. That torn-out page he'd found on the mercenary had mentioned it. Mayjen of significant power repelled each other. Jin could *feel* Stolt; he itched to get away from him.

'Hold out your hand,' Stolt demanded.

Tentatively Jin held out his unscarred hand. His other hand still twinged where the mercenary had skewered it with his knife, though it was mostly healed now. Jin had been lucky. The knife hadn't hit anything important. He couldn't imagine not being able to grip his daggers properly.

Stolt dropped the stone he'd been rolling between his fingers into Jin's open palm before quickly stepping back. Jin looked down at the stone. It seemed like a normal stone. 'What's this for?' he asked.

'A test. There are a few simple ways for us to find out what you are. We'll go from there.'

Stolt glanced towards the Kahnen who stood in a row, watching intently. 'This test is fairly redundant given what we've already seen but still has its uses.' Stolt folded his arms. 'Make the stone move.'

Jin gave Stolt a suspicious look. The request was so easy he wondered if the KahnenMayj was trying to trick him.

Jin quickly scanned the room. Every single eye was trained on him, waiting. Their attention was making him squirm.

'Oh, come on,' Filip whined, 'you can do *that*.'

Jin looked down at the stone in his palm and slowly lifted his other hand. He released a tiny flicker of heat from his index finger, lifting the stone until it hovered a few inches above his palm. It was easier than breathing. The creature inside his chest stirred, nudged awake at the prospect of harnessing again.

'Let it go,' Stolt commanded. Jin extinguished the trickle of heat, and the stone dropped back into his palm. Jin lowered his empty hand.

'Crush the stone.'

Jin almost laughed. The number of times he'd pulverised stones into dust in the Deadlands trying to expend a bit of power to stop himself from exploding. Jin raised his other hand again and squeezed it into a fist, warmth flaring in his wrist as the stone sitting in his open palm turned to dust.

'Put the stone back together again.'

It seemed a strange request, but Jin obliged. He wiggled the fingers of his empty hand, the little mound of dust coming together to reform a vague replica of the stone.

A shadow crossed Stolt's face.

'He looks nervous,' Filip said. Jin agreed.

'Let go,' Stolt said. 'Stop harnessing.'

Jin cut off his power to the stone. As expected, with nothing binding it, it fell back into dust in his palm. An alarming grin appeared on Stolt's face.

'That can't be good,' Filip said.

The Kahnen were muttering quietly to each other, also having noticed Stolt's reaction. 'What does that mean?' asked Lord Flynn, the young scholarly one.

'Nothing yet,' Stolt replied, his eyes not leaving the dust in Jin's palm. 'Do it again,' he repeated. 'Put the stone back together.'

Baffled, Jin waved his hand and the dust became stone again. He kept his power flowing through it, holding it together with majik.

'No,' Stolt said, his grin widening, 'you need to Build it.'

'I don't know what that means,' Jin said, growing frustrated at Stolt's gleeful expression.

'He's doing this on purpose,' Filip said. 'He's trying to make you look like a fool.'

It's working, Jin thought. The Kahnen all had furrows on their foreheads. Jin's squad looked equally confused.

'Reach for the pieces of it,' Stolt said, 'and bind them back together.'

'I *am*,' Jin said, feeling stupider by the second. He poured more power into the stone, crushing the dust back into itself. He couldn't conceive what Stolt was asking of him. 'I don't know how to do it any differently.'

'You really know nothing after all,' Stolt said.

Jin wanted to hit him.

'Do it,' Filip egged, but Jin pressed the urge down. He wouldn't dare provoke Stolt like that, mostly because of the Kahnen being there. He wasn't worried about Stolt. Jin was almost certain he could pull the KahnenMayj to pieces if given the chance. Almost.

'Let it go,' Stolt commanded.

With his jaw clenched in annoyance, Jin dropped his hand and the stone poofed back into dust in his palm. 'Are you going to show me what you mean then?' he asked.

Stolt smirked at him. 'With pleasure.' Stolt raised his own hand, flicking his wrist and bringing his fingertips together. The dust jumped together in Jin's palm, reforming the stone. Then Stolt clasped both his hands behind his back, making it mockingly clear he'd cut off his majik.

Jin stared at the stone. It was completely whole again, looking exactly like it had in the beginning before he'd crushed it. Jin looked up at Stolt, astonished. 'How did you do that?'

Stolt gave him a withering look. 'Majik, of course.' He turned to the Kahnen. 'Your KrijenMayj is nothing more than a Breaker.' The Kahnen looked at each other, all sharing the same nonplussed expression. Jin glanced at his squad, all of whom returned blank looks. Flit met Jin's eye and shrugged.

'Explain yourself, Stolt,' Lady Elira demanded. The Kahn had a haughty look on her face, her curly hair piled on top of her head. 'What is a Breaker?'

'In simple terms, a Breaker can move objects and pull things apart but cannot put them back together. A mediocre harnessing ability.'

'I think you're supposed to be offended by that,' Filip commented to Jin.

Lord Flynn frowned. 'How is that possible? We all saw what Jin did on the day of the Celebrations. He is clearly himajik.'

Stolt's smile faltered. 'I'm not finished yet,' he snapped. Stolt pointed to a spot on the webbed blue and grey wall of the room they stood in. 'Break it,' he commanded sharply.

Everyone turned to look at the polished stone surface. Jin hesitated, glancing at Pago, who looked nervous too. Was this a trick to get Jin to destroy KahnenKeep property? That was an arrestable offence.

Stolt rolled his eyes. 'Loosen up, Krijen. It's not like it can't be fixed.'

Pago nodded at Jin.

Jin still held the stone Stolt had given him. He tucked it into his wraps and tentatively stretched a hand out towards the wall, sending a surge of heat from his chest, down his arm, and out from his fingertips. He met a surprising resistance as he pressed against the surface, not what he would have expected from mountain stone. It was exactly like when Jin had tried to harness the webbed shards of the Split, the colossal stone-like structure in the Deadlands.

'It's the same stuff,' Filip said. 'It's made from majik. You felt it when you came into the room. Push harder.'

Jin pressed harder and harder until with a loud crack the wall shattered under his majik, creating a little ring of impact as though he'd punched it with his fist. Jin lowered his hand.

Stolt was eyeing him warily. 'How do you feel?'

Jin felt nothing. 'What do you mean?'

Stolt's nostrils flared as he turned to Jin's squad. 'I want a volunteer.'

Nommo immediately put his hand up. 'I'll do it.' He spun to Pago. 'Can I, sir?'

Pago frowned, uncertain whether or not to give permission. 'What do you want him for?' the squad leader asked Stolt.

'Another test,' the KahnenMayj said unhelpfully. 'It won't hurt, not unless your KrijenMayj is an idiot.'

Pago nodded his head confidently at Jin and waved Nommo forward.

'Are you a mayj?' Stolt asked Nommo. The Kahnen gasped. It was an incredibly rude question.

'Nope,' Nommo replied with a smile, his mouth popping on the *p*. Stolt nodded and turned to Jin. 'Lift him.'

The heat in Jin's chest turned to ice.

'What? That is ridiculous,' Lady Elira said. 'Majik does not work on people.'

'But it must.' Lord Reider frowned. 'We were all at the Celebrations. We all saw what that streetling mayj did to the late FaKrijen.' All the Krijen but Jin lifted their left hands to their clavicles, saluting Oji. Jin was still frozen in place.

'Majik works on people,' Stolt confirmed.

Lady Hia clutched at her chest, her fragile disposition getting the better of her. 'How is that possible?'

'Surely this is beyond Jin's capabilities,' Lord Flynn said. 'You already said he has poor harnessing ability.'

'He does,' Stolt replied. 'That doesn't matter. This is related to power, not harnessing.'

Everyone looked at Jin expectantly. His palms twitched, and his heart picked up a furious pace. He didn't want to use majik on Nommo. He hated the feeling of controlling someone else; nothing good could come of that. He had proof now too, given what had happened with Bish.

'I don't think that's the real reason you don't like harnessing people,' Filip said. 'Regardless, you've got to do it. If you don't, they'll think you're useless. And if the Kahnen think you're useless, who knows what they'll do.'

'Come on, Jin,' Nommo encouraged him, 'try it. I'm ready.'

Jin threw Stolt the most loathsome look he could muster before slowly raising his hand towards Nommo. It felt *wrong* as he drew upon the heat inside his chest, veins boiling as power burst from his palm. He slowly lifted Nommo up. As soon as Nommo's heels lifted off the floor, Lady Hia shrieked and clutched at Lady Macey for support.

'By the Great fu –' Meek swallowed his curse as Pago shot him a look.

'Woah,' Nommo said as he rose, flinging his arms out as though to rebalance himself, 'this feels *insane.*'

Jin adjusted his hand slightly to keep Nommo steady. He soon felt the familiar dulling of the ringing in his head and the dampening of the fire in his chest. Nommo was heavy, heavier than when Jin lifted himself, and the weight of him dragged on Jin's lungs. Knowing where it would lead, Jin began lowering Nommo to the ground, but Stolt hissed at him. 'Did I say you could put him down?'

Jin paused, teeth clenched.

'This is incredible,' Lord Flynn uttered breathlessly. Stolt glowered at him.

'What is the point in keeping Nommo up there?' Jokah asked, speaking for the first time. Jokah was their oldest squad member, having been Krijen longer than Jin had been alive. Jin could feel a bead of sweat trickling down the side of his face, which Jokah's eyes were following.

'Surely Jin's passed this test,' the older Krijen said.

'We need to know his limitations,' Stolt replied.

Jin saw Flit's eyes flash. 'And what about yours?' she asked Stolt.

'I know mine.'

Nommo had finally stopped wriggling, so Jin just concentrated on breathing. Whilst it was effortful to hold Nommo in the air, a disturbing peace soon crept in to accompany it, almost like Jin was floating himself.

'How are you feeling?' Stolt repeated.

Jin smiled at him, knowing it would piss him off. 'Tired.'

Stolt looked satisfactorily angered. 'Put him down,' he spat.

Jin gently lowered Nommo to the ground and cut off his majik, wincing as everything came crashing back to him. He reached up and wiped the sweat from his eyes; his hair was sticking to his forehead. But he was glad to have upset Stolt.

'You've freaked him out,' Filip agreed happily.

Jin's squad were all looking at him in a very un-Krijen-like manner, their mouths hanging open. Jokah alone kept his warrior composure. 'Well done, Jin,' he said.

'He's not *done*,' Stolt said. He turned to Jin. 'Lift me,' he demanded.

Jokah took a step closer to Jin, his stance distinctly defensive. 'The same test?' he asked. 'What will that prove?'

'It's not the same test, you idiot,' Stolt said. 'I'm a mayj. If he' – Stolt jerked his head towards Nommo – 'is telling the truth about not being a mayj, then it will be much harder to lift me. It requires pushing against more power.'

'So you are testing Jin's power?' Lady Macey asked.

'Obviously.'

'So he is himajik.'

'Not the word I would use. But if it helps your understanding, then yes.'

'What word would you use?' Lord Flynn asked.

'He is an Influencer,' Stolt sneered. 'It means he can affect people by overcoming their innate power.'

'Is it rare?'

Stolt's upper lip curled. 'It's not common.'

'Then you already know he's exceptional,' Flit said coldly. 'We're done here.' Her hands were resting on her dagger hilts.

'We. Are. Not. Done,' Stolt snarled, turning back to Jin. 'Lift me, I said.'

'He wants you to Turn,' Filip said. 'But you know you won't. Just do it. I love the look on his face when he panics.'

But what if I do Turn? Jin thought. *What if he's too heavy?*

Filip glared at him. 'What did you say, coward?'

Gritting his teeth, Jin held his hand out towards Stolt, who flinched. Jin wondered if it had been a bluff, and Stolt hadn't actually expected him to try it.

Go slowly, Jin told himself. *If it becomes too much, cut it off.* He felt a little tired from lifting Nommo, but it was like having done a few sprints to prepare for a running race. His muscles were warm, and his power was returning quickly, churning in his chest. Jin raised an arm, sucked in a breath, and picked up Stolt.

The weight of Stolt hit Jin harder than his father punched. Jin staggered, his breath catching. The sudden euphoria he'd felt when he'd lifted the mercenary was back even though the mercenary hadn't been a mayj, unlike Stolt. Maybe it had only been difficult then because Maude had drained him, and he'd run the length of Valrue, and he'd not slept for days.

The huge webbed-walled room spun around Jin, and everything grew blessedly quiet. The Kahnen and Krijen ebbed away into blurry shapes in the corners of Jin's vision. Filip was gone as was the ringing.

But Jin wasn't dead yet, and Stolt's feet were barely off the ground.

It took so much power to keep Stolt in the air that Jin was sure his arm was about to catch fire. He raised his other arm, pouring power down it, spreading the heat across his torso and out from his fingertips until Stolt's feet moved higher off the ground. Stolt was heavier than Nommo, but he still wasn't all that heavy. Maybe Jin could hold him here forever in this tranquil oblivion. It felt *good.*

Jin vaguely heard his name being called. It happened over and over again until someone grabbed his shoulder and wrenched him around.

'*Enough.*' That was Pago.

Jin cut off his power, stumbling as everything came crashing back again. It was the shittiest feeling. Jin absentmindedly raised his left hand to his clavicle, saluting his squad leader. He didn't realise he was leaning on Pago until his squad leader shoved him upright. 'Get him out of here.'

Jin let Jokah, Nommo, and Meek lead him into the corridor.

'That prick,' said Meek once they were out of earshot. 'I reckon he was trying to get you to Turn.'

'That was amazing,' said Nommo, his face flushed with excitement. 'I had no idea you could do majik the whole time we were Squares! Well,' – he made a face – 'maybe I did, but that was just . . . wow –'

'Are you all right, Jin?' Jokah grasped Jin by the shoulders, inspecting him closely. Jin didn't like Jokah looking at him like that. It reminded him too much of Bish, which was painful to think about.

'I'm fine.' He felt light-headed and tired, but nothing hurt.

Pago and Flit trotted out of the doors and came over. 'Well, I think you impressed them,' Pago said. He looked serious. 'They're happy for now, but they're already talking about the next time.'

'That's the point of this, isn't it?' Jin replied. 'I'm supposed to be learning how to use majik.' He shivered. It wasn't cold, but the heat inside him was almost gone with his power drained. It felt nice. But his power would come back.

'Maybe there will be more teaching next time, and less torment,' Flit muttered.

'You sure spooked Stolt,' Nommo said. 'I don't think he can do what you can. And maybe you can't *Build* stuff, or whatever he called it, but what you can do is way better.'

'Absolutely,' said Meek. Everyone else murmured their agreement. Jin flushed at their praise, making Meek guffaw and slap him on the back just as Jin's stomach growled loudly. 'Let's get you some food,' Meek said. 'Surely the Kahnen have some vault stuffed full of sumptuous delicacies to feed their KrijenMayj.'

Chatting happily amongst themselves, the squad made their way down the corridor with Pago in the lead. 'Jin, can I speak to you for a second?' Flit beckoned Jin back to her. He slowed, letting the others walk ahead of them until he fell into step with Flit. Unbeknownst to her, Filip walked on her other side.

'It's great to have you in the squad,' Jin said. Back in the Deadlands, he'd worried he'd scared Flit when she returned so quickly to the city after discovering he was a mayj. Her smile said otherwise.

'Yeah, I'm glad Pago asked me,' Flit said. 'But I was squad leader for so long, I keep forgetting it's not my role anymore. I was a bit pushy in there.'

'I don't think he minds,' Jin said quietly, watching Pago up ahead. 'I'm not sure he enjoys being squad leader. Anyway, what did you want to talk to me about?'

'I thought you might want to know that I saw Bish the other day. I told him where you were. I'm not sure if he came to find you?'

Jin felt a stab of fear through his fatigue. 'No, he didn't. Did he say what he wanted?'

'If I'm honest, he didn't actually ask for you,' Flit said, biting her lip. 'I was helping him with something, and he asked about those women in the dungeons . . . um . . . the prostitutes? I think you know them.'

'Yeah. I know them.' Jin caught himself thumbing his daggers, and he stopped, stretching out his fingers. 'Did Bish talk to them?'

'No, but I told him the Bhouli girl was gone. I don't understand what happened there. I told the FaKrijen because I thought maybe she'd escaped, but he didn't give me any orders about what to do.' Flit shrugged. 'Anyway, guarding the dungeons isn't my job anymore, now that I'm in a new squad.'

Jin was quiet. He hoped Flit couldn't hear his heart pounding. The sound of their squad laughing ahead was probably enough to cover it.

'Is there anything *you* want to talk about?' Flit asked. 'I know it's not my place, but I got the impression that Bish was angry with you. Did something happen?'

'No,' Jin said, not meeting Flit's eyes. It wasn't entirely true. He wanted to talk to Lottie, or Eliza, or Dhuna, or any of the women sitting locked in a cell downstairs. But Flit wouldn't understand that.

'You know, you've got a good squad here,' Flit said. 'And I get why you find it difficult to trust us, especially after what happened in the Deadlands. I'm sorry about that. But everyone wants to make up for it, and we want to help. But you've just got to let us, you know?'

'She's got a point,' Filip drawled.

Jin wasn't so sure. He didn't want to share his secrets with just anyone; they weren't normal secrets. But Flit looked so earnest that he had to give her something.

'Thanks, Flit,' Jin said. 'I'll try.'

CHAPTER 3:
THE GREAT KAHN

The Great Kahn had never known peace like this. Even though the mercenary hadn't come back to tell him if the plan had been a success, the Great Kahn knew it was. He'd been on the tower ramparts when the lake exploded. He'd drowned in the droplets of freedom as they sprinkled across his eyelids even if only for a second. Now all he had to do was wait.

Eventually, the evidence proving the end of the Unsettlement would come. For now, he busied himself with the things that he'd put off for twenty-six years, things that Luka had always wanted to do but never did because he was distracted by Mandavar.

The Bhouli, for one, were still a mystery to him. The girl who saved them had stoked the Great Kahn's interest in his most elusive citizens. It seemed only right that given her sacrifice, he would make an effort to do more for them.

The Great Kahn made his way to the KahnenLibrary, an obsequious KahnenMinder trailing behind. Even the Minders responded to the Great Kahn's new mood. They didn't tremble in fear every time the Great Kahn looked at them anymore.

The KahnenLibrary was a cavernous room shaped like the inside of a bell with a stone core straight down the middle. Rope pulleys attached to little wooden platforms criss-crossed the space so you could slide or climb to and from the core, hunting the shelves for whatever knowledge you sought.

As the Great Kahn stepped onto a platform and grasped the handrail, he made a mental note to burn the majik books and scrolls still hidden in Mandavar's study. He couldn't risk anyone doing what Mandavar had done ever again.

Not that it would be possible. Mandavar had been an extraordinary mayj, one-of-a-kind, the sole exception being his son. But the Great Kahn was not worried about Drax. The boy had spent too long being told what to do. Whatever meagre initiative he'd developed which led to his defiance of Felle, it would never be enough to make him a real threat, especially without a master.

The mercenary had kept the torn-out page containing the Du Bellor Spell, but the Great Kahn wasn't worried about that either. The mercenary wouldn't be so stupid as to give it to someone who could use it. He'd suffer the consequences as much as the rest of them.

As for implicating the Great Kahn by itself, the page was meaningless. It was only the final letter from Dijak that could be troublesome if it fell into the wrong hands. The Great Kahn would've had the mercenary remove it now that the deed was done, but he suspected that if the mercenary hadn't come back by now, he would never return. The Great Kahn would have to get the letter from Felle somehow. However, Felle was rid of the mercenary, rid of Drax, and according to the mercenary, Felle did not know of the truth she held in that letter. She was powerless in more ways than one.

So for now, nothing could ruin the Great Kahn's jubilance.

The minder pulled on the ropes, and they glided to the uppermost section of the bell, swaying gently as they came to a stop. The Great Kahn stepped out onto the thin-railed walkway that wound around the walls and began perusing book titles.

He wasn't sure if there would be any literature on the Bhouli. He didn't know if they had written scripture, or if like many other ancient cultures, they simply passed their knowledge on through stories. Or possibly patterns, in their case.

After half an hour of fruitless searching, the Great Kahn waved over a librarian. The librarian leapt onto a platform and zipped down to him in such haste that the platform swung furiously once it reached its stopper, the librarian clinging to its sides.

Before now, it had never bothered the Great Kahn that people feared him. For some reason, it did now. It was annoying.

'How can I help, my Great Lord?' The librarian looked queasy as he attempted a bow, staggering on the still-swinging platform.

'I am interested in the Bhouli,' the Great Kahn replied.

'The-the Bhouli? I'm sorry to say we have no pieces of literature dedicated solely to the topic despite our attempts to source some.'

The Great Kahn was disappointed. He turned away.

'But-but *wait*!' The librarian stepped off the platform, looking alarmed. 'My Great Lord, we do have something! Follow me.' The librarian hastened along the curve of books, his finger tracing innumerous titles. 'Here it is,' he said, pulling out an enormous dusty volume. 'We have multiple copies.' He held it up so the Great Kahn could see the title, bowing his head unnecessarily.

'*The Founding of Valrue*,' the Great Kahn read.

The librarian wedged the heavy book against his ribs and opened the cover to the contents page, the book's spine creaking in protest. 'Yes, here . . . page three hundred and six.' He riffled through the stiff pages until he came to the right one, holding the book out once more. 'There are some small sections on the Bhouli in this volume,' the librarian explained. 'Of all the literature I've read, these give the most detail though I admit it's still somewhat lacking. We tried, my Great Lord, but given the Unsettlement, we struggle to add to our collections on any topics, let alone the Bhouli.'

'A shame, but not your fault,' the Great Kahn replied. *No*, he thought, *I believe it is mine.*

The librarian looked immensely relieved.

'Have we not been able to gather any information from the Bhouli living in Valrue?' the Great Kahn asked.

'They are incredibly private, my Great Lord. I considered sending a scholar into the city, but if I'm honest, I thought it would be a waste of time. However, if you think it worthwhile . . .'

The Great Kahn waved his hand. 'No, this will do.'

'I should say, there were quite a few references to majik in that book,' the librarian said in hushed tones. 'We covered the relevant words up to save from removing entire pages, but it makes for slightly disjointed reading.' The librarian twisted his hands in front of him nervously.

'Never mind. I will manage.' The Great Kahn would likely have the undoctored pages somewhere in Mandavar's study. He'd not paid much attention to the Bhouli mentions during his time spent delving through the forbidden literature, only the majik. It would be worthwhile re-reading them.

The Great Kahn took the book from the librarian and stepped onto the platform, the Minder following. 'Take me down.' They soared to the bottom, and as the Great Kahn stepped off the platform, Lord Flynn swept into the library in his glittering robes, his stiff collar high about his neck. Lord Flynn stopped in front of the Great Kahn and gave a small bow. He did not need permission to speak outside of the Red Room, but regardless, the young Kahn stared at the Great Kahn until he nodded.

'My Great Lord,' Lord Flynn said, 'I noticed you were not at the training today. It was quite spectacular. I have to say, you made a wise decision to spare that young Krijen's life.'

The Great Kahn's high spirits evaporated. The fact that the skahk still breathed was a reminder of how Oji, the late FaKrijen, had played him. Even after the insufferable man had died, the Great Kahn still had to deal with his hateful spawn.

'I did not wish to attend,' the Great Kahn said in a clipped voice.

'He is both a Breaker and Influencer,' Lord Flynn continued in a rush, his excitement making him oblivious to the Great Kahn's tone. 'Stolt was cagey about what that meant, but we could all tell it was impressive. You know how Stolt can be.'

Both the Minder and the librarian edged away from the Great Kahn as he swelled. 'I do not know what is going on in your head, Lord Flynn,' the Great Kahn said dangerously, 'but you seem to forget that majik is still illegal, by order of your own house.'

Lord Flynn's face fell. 'But-but my Great Lord –'

'*You are not above the law*, Lord Flynn. If I hear you discussing majik openly like this again, you will regret it. Am I understood?'

Lord Flynn bit his lip and ducked his head. 'Yes, my Great Lord.'

'That goes for the rest of the Eighth House. Now get out of my way.' The Great Kahn shoved past Lord Flynn out of the KahnenLibrary, storming towards his chambers. The Minder stumbled after him, trembling again.

Although angry at how short-lived his happiness had been, the Great Kahn knew he couldn't have it both ways. He couldn't expect the Unsettlement to end and not have people clamouring to know more about majik. When word got out that the Unsettlement was over, it was only going to get worse.

But once the Great Kahn had taken a moment to calm himself, he remembered he needn't worry so much.

Lord Flynn was but one man, always shoving his nose where it shouldn't be, a desperate know-it-all. The People still hated mayjen, hated majik. There had always been tension between the majikal and non-majikal communities. The Unsettlement had simply been the oil to ignite the flames. They weren't to know it had been the fault of one mayj.

The Great Kahn knew his own hatred of majik was unjustified. Majik had its uses, and the only reason he wanted it gone was because of what Mandavar had done to him. The Great Kahn had been kidding himself earlier to think he would be free from his ex-lover's clutches so easily. But that doesn't mean that he wouldn't be, one day. He just needed to let go of his hatred of Mandavar, which needed to start with the Weapon's Master.

The Great Kahn had not forgotten about Sid Bha. He was holding onto the man because, like Oji, Sid Bha had played him too. Both men were subtle yet aggravating reminders of Mandavar. Sid Bha's defiance – however minor – was particularly irksome given how perfect a puppet the Great Kahn had presumed him to be. It had been an unpleasant shock to learn Sid Bha had been harbouring abandoned mayjen children with the brothel keeper, Mama Hidel, under his nose.

But if the Great Kahn truly wanted to move on from Mandavar, he had to let go of his hatred not only for Sid Bha but for Oji and his skahk spawn and eventually for Drax too.

But for now, Sid Bha would do.

The Founding of Valrue (Excerpt 1)

The decision to settle within the crater was, in part, because of the noticeable flourishing of the Bhouli, who initially distanced themselves from the early settlers of the mountain. While only a few sightings of them were noted in the initial months of arrival, the Bhouli soon frequented the camps of the early settlers, no doubt intrigued by their visitors.

To this day, it is not known where the Bhouli reside, nor from where they originated. Whilst many civilisations share characteristic likenesses, the Bhouli's vast range of complexions, from alabaster-white to the deepest umber, offer no clues to outsiders. Attempts to seek clarity from the Bhouli were in vain with their lengthy yet enigmatic answers. Of interest, several Bhouli individuals referred to an event called the Great Change. Although the details still evade our understanding, the Great Change seems to have led the Bhouli to an adjustment of a previously nomadic lifestyle to one of permanence.

Considering the Bhouli's aversion to exposing their heads to the sky (presumed from their distinctive white head coverings), alongside their preoccupation with the stars, it is possible the Bhouli reside within the mountain itself. This allows them to be on higher ground to provide the sensation of being 'closer' to the night sky whilst ensuring a physical barrier above them.

In support of this theory, several tunnels were discovered by the early settlers within the slopes of the mountain crater. However, no matter how many were explored, all led to dead ends or looped back on themselves. No Bhouli were ever found within them. An influential Builder of the settler community expressed a desire to explore the tunnels further with majik, but there were concerns the Bhouli would consider it invasive and threaten the symbiosis achieved between the two groups. Thus, the exploration of these tunnels was not enacted until much later and unfortunately, under fraught circumstances.

CHAPTER 4:
AREN BHA

Aren didn't tell Wren what she was planning. He would only try to warn her off, and when she refused, he would insist on coming too. She wasn't having that. It was enough that she needed Drax to come with her. At least she trusted that if something went wrong, Drax could get away.

'You have to promise you'll run, Drax. You'll do that? You *promise?*'

'Okay, Aren.'

His blank face gave nothing away, but Aren knew he must be feeling something. They were about to go back to the place where he'd been raised. 'Tamed,' he called it. She could only imagine what horrors he'd lived through.

'And you're sure you're okay to do this?' Aren asked again. 'Because we can find another way. You're *sure?*'

'Yes, we need to get Sid.' He turned his ice-blue eyes on her, and to Aren's astonishment, he smiled. It didn't quite reach his eyes like a real smile would, but it meant he'd seen enough happiness here to know what it looked like.

Aren struggled with Drax. While he seemed content never to leave the safety of the mansion, he was always waiting at the door whenever she came home as though he depended on her return. During the day, he followed Mae around the house, watched Noel bake bread, or sat outside by the stone tree. Instead of chasing the shade like he used to, he would sit in the sun until he burned unless someone took him inside. Aren assumed he liked the warmth of it.

Aren was careful to always *ask* things of Drax, never to *tell*, because she knew he would do anything for her, whether or not he wanted to, and that bothered her. But she was also learning how to read him. Not all the time, but sometimes, she felt like she could tell what he was thinking. He seemed happy, at least. She figured whatever life he had here must be better than before.

At first, Wren had been wary of him, but after observing Drax from afar for a few weeks, Wren didn't seem worried anymore. Wren still avoided him though, which Aren thought was a shame because, out of everyone, Drax would be the one to accept Wren without question. He didn't understand the treatment of the Lost Squares any more than Aren did.

However, every time Aren suggested to Wren that she introduce them, Wren would shake his head. 'Not yet,' he would say.

Aren wished she could see Wren again before she and Drax left on their rescue mission, but it would only make him suspicious if she turned up unexpectedly at the Point, especially if she were going to get emotional about it, which was likely, given she wasn't sure if she would make it back.

Drax crouched on the wide window ledge in Aren's room, watching while Aren slid innumerous knives and daggers into her midnight-blue wraps. The moment she tucked her cardonite dagger in behind her back felt rather poignant. Her father had given it to her.

To settle her nerves, Aren absentmindedly rubbed the spot on her wrist where her white-ink tattoo was. Maude had done it for her. The circular swirling Bhouli design meant both happiness and luck. Aren didn't enjoy relying on luck, but it couldn't hurt to have extra for tonight. Maybe they would find Maude wherever they found Sid.

Aren tied her hair back and wrapped a dark scarf around her head, leaving an end loose to cover her face when needed. She'd chosen to invest in some scarves after the grubby make-up-and-beggar's-hat debacle. She still felt guilty she'd not returned the hat to the beggar; she'd lost it the night that Pyra had caught her. If Aren ever saw the beggar again, she would buy him a new one.

Aren threw a scarf to Drax. 'Can you please put this on?' Seemingly of its own accord, the scarf wound itself around Drax's face, his hands staying limp in his lap. Aren tried her best to make nothing of him harnessing, which was really, *really* difficult because it was enthralling to watch.

After Bish mentioned it, that afternoon, Aren had watched while Drax melted the stone tree into a puddle on the ground and then made it spring into being again, not a leaf out of place. Noel had seen it too, his expression incredulous, which amused Aren. For most of her life, she'd assumed Noel knew everything, so she took great delight in his reluctant fascination with Drax and his majikal abilities. Noel still wasn't as happy as everyone else to have Drax stay, but he'd come to accept it.

With the exception of Bish and Marigold, no other visitors were allowed into the mansion. The maids were let go, each with a month's wages and outstanding references. Their hurt expressions were hard to bear but a necessity to keep Drax a secret. Aren wasn't sure if Drax was cognisant of the sacrifices made for him. If he was, he said nothing, and Aren said nothing as well. As much as she wanted him to understand the world, she would hate to ruin whatever bliss he found in ignorance. He'd been through enough already.

Yet here she was, dragging him back into it.

'Do you want a dagger?' Aren asked guiltily. As expected, Drax blinked at her and shook his head. He didn't like violence, and his majik would serve him better than any blade anyway.

'Okay then, let's go.'

Drax hugged Aren's heels as they stepped out over the window ledge and crept alongside the stone wall surrounding the mansion. They turned the corner, past the entrance to the house, and started down the pathway leading to the main gate, avoiding strips of moonlight. Aren unlatched the massive gate and hauled it open. She let Drax amble through first before slipping in behind him, turning to latch it again.

'What do you think you're doing?'

Aren nearly jumped out of her skin. She spun to see Noel and Mae, who'd been standing out of sight behind the wall. It was Noel who had spoken, his eyebrows arching up to his white hairline as he surveyed Aren and Drax in their incriminating attire. Mae had her arms folded, her petite face darker on the cheeks, her flush nothing but shadow in the gloom. She looked mad possibly because she'd caught her daughter sneaking out in the middle of the night. However, Aren noted with interest that Noel and Mae stood too far apart to have been having a casual conversation.

'Were you arguing?' Aren asked.

'Don't avoid my question,' Noel growled. 'Where are you sneaking off to?'

Drax was cowering so much that he was practically sitting on the ground at Aren's feet. She stepped in front of him and folded her arms, mirroring her mother's stance. 'What are you arguing about? Why are you out here in the dark?'

'We didn't want to wake you,' said Mae. 'Answer Noel's question, please. And why is Drax with you? He shouldn't leave the house.'

Aren opened her mouth, a lie ready on her tongue, but nothing came out. She was sick of lying to her mother. *No more*, she thought.

'We're going to save Sid,' Aren said, lifting her chin. 'I'm done twiddling my thumbs, waiting for Pa to come home, or worse, waiting for the Krijen to come knocking and tell us he's dead. So we're going to do something about it before I go stark-raving mad. And don't you dare try to stop us because the only way you'll be able to do that is if you barricade me in my room, and I'll just ask Drax to let me out.' It all came out in a rush.

Noel looked horrified. 'That's the most ridiculous –'

'I'm coming with you,' Mae said.

Noel spun to face her. *'What?'*

Mae moved to stand by her daughter. Drax startled and shuffled to the side to give her room.

'The man I love is imprisoned,' Mae said to Noel. 'I'm going to help my daughter save him.'

Aren's jaw dropped. Then she threw her arms around her mother's neck. 'Really, Ma?'

'Yes, dear, I'm done waiting too. I'm in.'

Noel gaped at them, three against one. 'This is madness!' he cried. 'We don't even know where Sid is!'

'Drax knows where Sid is,' Aren replied. 'Don't you, Drax, in the KahnenKeep?'

Drax nodded before flinching away from Noel's furious look.

'You cannot take Drax,' Noel hissed. 'You cannot stroll through the KahnenKeep with the most wanted person in the city and not expect to get caught!'

'We won't get caught,' Aren said stubbornly. 'And even if they catch us, they won't get Drax. He promised to run.'

'I don't care about Drax. I care about you and Mae! You'll both be arrested and charged with treason –'

'Well, maybe they'll throw us in the same cell as Sid, and we can finally be a family again,' Mae said ruefully. 'I miss chatting to Mama Hidel too. We can ask the Krijen to put us all next to her.'

Aren managed not to laugh, but she couldn't hide her smirk. Noel threw up his hands in disbelief. 'This isn't the slightest bit funny! Mae, why are you fighting me on this? Only yesterday you were telling me how worried you were that Aren would do something drastic!'

Mae shrugged apologetically at her daughter before looking back to Noel. 'I know.' Mae sniffed. 'But I've changed my mind. And Aren is a grown woman. I can't stop her from doing what she wants.'

'You are her *mother*,' Noel said exasperatedly. 'Of course you can stop her! You should be ashamed of the examples you've set for her.'

Mae's face darkened. 'What do you mean by that?'

'*Well*,' Noel huffed, 'first, you snuck mayjen children into the brothel and kept doing it even after majik became illegal. Second, you allowed Drax to stay in the house despite my warning of how foolish a decision that was, risking the safety of the entire family. And now this? You can hardly wonder where Aren gets it!'

Mae didn't reply, turning her eyes away from Noel. Aren suspected some of the things he mentioned were a part of the argument they'd been having.

'And I *know*,' Noel continued, 'there is still something going on because no matter how many times you stock up my medicine cupboard, I notice when things go missing! Great Kahn save me from this Bha family!'

Aren was sure to meet Noel's accusatory stare with a carefully perplexed expression. She and Wren had been responsible for the missing medicine, having taken it for the residents of Turning Point. They'd replaced it but obviously not soon enough.

After his outburst, Noel quickly settled, rubbing his temples. 'Sorry, sorry. This is a lot.'

Now that Noel had stopped yelling, Drax peered around Aren's legs. 'It is okay to go, Aren?'

'Yes, Drax, it's okay,' she said. 'So are you coming, Noel?'

Noel dropped his hands, giving her a flat look. 'Yes, I'm coming.'

***

Noel had clearly done something like this before. He followed Drax like a whisper, so quiet that if Aren didn't keep herself within a stride of him in the darkness, she would lose him. Noel had always been so private, so selective about everything he told her. Aren hardly knew anything about him at all. It was a strange thought, considering that most of what she knew about the world had been thanks to Noel's tutoring. Before she'd met Wren anyway.

Nope, don't think about him, Aren thought. Her mind often got carried away with Wren, and it wouldn't do to be distracted now.

Aren glanced behind her, catching her mother's eye. Aren had so rarely seen her mother wearing anything other than a dress that it was bizarre to see her in dark wraps and a scarf. Aren had pulled her own scarf up to hide her face. They all crept along in a row, only the stars watching from above.

Aren wasn't entirely sure where they were. Drax had never seen the main entrance to the KahnenKeep, so that was not where they were headed. She had no idea how he planned to get inside, but he led them with an air of uncharacteristic confidence that settled Aren's unease. She'd been worried he would panic as they grew closer, but it seemed to be the opposite.

It wasn't long before they made it to the northernmost tip of Val, to the distant left of the Keep. They were moving along the mountain face, the city twinkling below them, when Drax stopped and peered at a section of rock. It didn't look any different to the rest.

With a gentle rumble, an enormous chunk of mountain wall pulled away in front of them, perfectly circular. Noel leapt backwards from it, smacking a hand across his mouth. 'By the Great Kahn, Drax,' he breathed through his fingers, 'a little warning next time?'

Drax ducked his head guiltily, and the circular chunk settled down against the side of the mountain of its own accord.

Aren followed Noel into the mountain, stepping into a dimly lit tunnel, candles burning in brackets along the black walls. The tunnel curved so they couldn't see too far in either direction, sending Aren's senses into overdrive. Only now she realised how relaxed she'd become travelling through Rue given its shady streets scared her less than this quiet tunnel did.

Aren jumped at a gentle crunching sound behind them. She spun around, ready to fight whatever terror was upon them, but it was just Drax harnessing the section of the mountain seamlessly back into place. If anyone walked by, they'd never be able to tell. There wasn't a single crack to mark the spot.

Drax began ambling down the tunnel. Everyone quickly followed.

'What do we do if someone comes?' Mae whispered. Drax glanced over his shoulder at her and held out a limp hand to the wall in response, his intention clear. He would just take them back through the wall.

The tunnel curved to the left, heading deeper into the mountain, the candles in brackets along the walls lit the whole way. They wouldn't burn indefinitely. Someone had been here recently.

'Drax,' Noel asked in hushed tones, 'how do you know where Sid is?'

Drax turned his huge eyes back to Noel. 'I was there too,' he said simply.

'So . . . they didn't keep you in the main dungeon?' Noel rarely asked Drax anything. Aren could hear the nerves in his voice.

'Sometimes,' Drax said. 'Sometimes not. The place we are going has no Krijen.'

'Oh?'

'It has KahnenMayjen.'

Noel stopped so suddenly that Aren walked into him. He whirled to face Aren. 'Did you know this?' he hissed.

Aren shrugged. 'You should have asked that *before* you agreed to come. Anyway, Pa said there's only one KahnenMayj left, and Drax can handle that. Isn't that right, Drax?'

Drax nodded, his face blank, then turned back to the empty tunnel. Noel muttered something unintelligible under his breath.

The thick walls sent their footsteps echoing back at them, so Noel held up a hand now and then, stopping to listen to make sure there weren't any other sounds coming towards them.

Aren shivered. It was cold inside the tunnel, and while her blood pumped madly through her body, her wraps were thin.

Eventually Drax came to a stop, staring at another section of the wall. Aren, Noel, and Mae gathered around. 'What is it?' Aren asked Drax.

Drax touched his wrist to the wall. Aren squinted at it more closely. There was a smooth rounded plate sitting flush with the mountain wall, blending into the black rock.

'I'm not sure,' Noel replied, edging in to get a closer look.

'Look,' Mae said, pointing, 'there are more.'

Aren looked down the tunnel. There were two more plates embedded into the walls at wide, even intervals. 'There are more behind us, too,'

Noel said.

'What are they?' Aren asked.

'Heavy,' said Drax. 'I'm going to open it,' he said pointedly to Noel, who took a step back, looking bewildered.

And so beneath Drax's unwavering gaze, the first stone plate began to turn.

CHAPTER 5:
SID BHA

Sid had grown used to his little prison. There wasn't a speck of light, so all he could see was blackness. It was small; it paced five steps in every direction. Sid knew its roundness, and how there was a smoother section of wall around waist height as though someone had traced their fingers along the stone over and over again, walking in a circle as they slowly lost their mind. He wasn't at that point yet, but he worried it might come. He could've been here for three days or three months. He couldn't say. But surely madness took longer than that – years hopefully.

Sid always imagined that solitude would be the worst part of being locked in a room like this, or claustrophobia. But as it turned out, it was the visits from Stolt. Stolt brought him food, took away the bucket he used to relieve himself, and said unhelpful things like 'I don't know what you were expecting, Sid. Did you honestly think the Great Kahn was going to let a bunch of guilty whores walk free because you asked him nicely?'

Sid tried to count the number of times Stolt visited to get an idea of how much time had passed, but he wasn't sure if Stolt visited once a day or once a week. He thought maybe he could use his stomach as a gauge for the time passing, but Sid wasn't all that hungry. He'd never lived on the edge of his nerves like this before. A few times, he was so pent up he couldn't eat. Once he vomited up his meal into his bucket, unable to stop his stomach churning.

The one redeeming thing about Stolt's visits was his reassurances that Sid's family were okay. 'They're fine,' Stolt would say every time Sid asked. 'Stop worrying. I'll tell you if there is any trouble.'

Sid didn't trust Stolt in the slightest, but the KahnenMayj's word was all he had right now. He had to believe that Stolt was telling the truth. One day when Sid was feeling particularly bold after a bout of hope found him, he'd fired a series of questions at Stolt.

'Do you know when I'll be let out?'

'Nope, not a clue.'

'Why am I here and not in the main dungeon?'

'Not sure.'

'Has anyone asked for me?'

'Don't think so.'

After that, Sid slipped into a spiral of misery for a few hours or days or weeks. So it went on like this, loops and circles of thoughts and emotions until Sid caught himself walking in a circle and running his hand along the smooth section of the wall in the darkness. It terrified him so much that he sat down in what he guessed was the middle of the room and wrapped his arms around his knees, squeezing himself into a tiny ball so that he would stay away from the infinite loop of insanity.

Sid was huddled like this when he heard muted voices behind the walls. *Voices*, plural, and none of them sounded like Stolt's deep tones.

'Hello?' Sid called. 'Hello? Is someone there?'

The voices stopped. Sid leapt up and pressed his ear against the wall, listening. He hoped desperately that this was real, and he wasn't finally going mad. The section of wall he leant on moved under his fingertips, and he scrambled backwards, shoving himself away from the orange light that suddenly flooded his little prison because it hurt to look at it, let alone stand in it.

A dark figure wearing a black scarf over its face stepped into the light of the doorway, lingering in silence, leaving Sid trembling until the moment the figure spoke. 'Is there someone in here?'

'Noel!' Sid threw himself at the figure, sending Noel staggering under his weight.

'Oh my goodness! *Sid!*'

Sid clung to Noel as his knees buckled with relief, and Noel wrapped his arms gloriously around him. Sid couldn't see much at all because the light was so bright, but he heard delighted cries just before two other warm bodies pressed against him. He knew them instantly despite their disguises.

'Aren! Mae! Oh my, what are you doing here?'

'We've come to save you, you silly thing!' Mae cried, her voice shrill in Sid's ear.

As Sid's eyes adjusted, her beautiful face came into focus, tears streaming down her cheeks. 'I can't believe Drax found you,' she said.

Indeed, Drax's twisted little figure stood awkwardly off to the side, his icy blue eyes wide.

'Drax, come here!' Mae grabbed him and pulled him into the embrace, which he stoically endured until Mae released him and he shuffled away, crouching behind Aren.

'We need to move,' Noel said. 'Are you okay, Sid? You're not hurt?'

'I'm not hurt. I can walk.'

'Let's go then.'

Noel grabbed onto something behind Sid and heaved on it. The section of wall behind them hissed shut, locking them out of his prison. They hurried down the tunnel with Drax in the lead.

'How did you get in here?' Sid asked.

'We'll explain later,' Noel replied.

Sid held onto Mae as they ran not because he needed support but because he wanted to make sure she was really there, and it wasn't his mind playing tricks on him. She was warm and soft, and she clung tightly back to him. Aren was ahead, and she kept glancing over her shoulder to look at them, the orange glow from the bracketed candles on the tunnel walls lighting up her smile every time.

'I can't believe you're here,' Sid murmured to Mae. 'I just can't believe it.'

'Shush now, dear,' Mae said, but her voice was gentle.

They'd not gone far when Drax paused in the tunnel. Noel raised a hand, and they all came to a stop, listening. After Sid's lengthy time spent sitting in a pitch-black room, his ears had become very sensitive. Now that they stood still, he could hear the rhythmic echo of footsteps up ahead. Someone was walking down the tunnel towards them.

Drax looked back, the whites of his eyes glowing in the dim. Noel waved his arms frantically, pointing to the wall. Drax fixed his gaze on it. With a slight rumble, a chunk of the wall broke away from the rest, hovering just off the ground. It had barely made a sound, but even so, the distant footsteps paused for a moment, then restarted, quicker this time.

Aren darted through the hole in the wall. Mae shoved Sid ahead of herself after their daughter. Sid gasped as he stepped through the hole and his boots tapped polished stone. They were no longer in the tunnels but in a high-ceilinged corridor with webbed walls. Sid looked in both directions. Thankfully, the corridor was empty.

Mae was right on Sid's heels, followed closely by Drax, then Noel. Suddenly, a loud cry resounded with the pounding footsteps in the tunnel, chasing after Noel.

'OI!'

The floating section of rock slammed back into the wall, cutting off the sound. Sid clutched at Mae, his breath catching. 'Who was that? Was it Stolt?'

'It's okay,' Mae replied, 'they won't be able to get through –' The section of wall exploded out at them, showering them with rubble. Aren screamed.

'It's Stolt!' Sid cried as he threw his arms over his head.

'Who is Stolt?' Aren yelled back.

'The KahnenMayj –'

'RUN!' Noel bellowed.

Aren took off in a sprint. Sid and the others dashed after her, running blind down the corridor through the dust and dim. 'Where are we?' Aren yelled over her shoulder. 'Where do I go, Pa?'

'I don't know! I've not got my bearings yet!'

It was obvious they were in the KahnenKeep, but there was nothing to distinguish this corridor from all the rest.

'Well, hurry up and find them!' Aren screamed.

They dashed around a corner and headed down another corridor that, to Sid's alarm, started to curve back on itself as they ran down it. Aren must've noticed too because she came to a screeching halt and dove off to the right, up a flight of stairs, leading to a landing where the webbed walls abruptly turned to wooden panelling. Soft red carpet appeared beneath their feet, sending a fresh bolt of terror through Sid as he recognised it.

Aren darted through an open door into a small empty sitting room with a few books on shelves around them. Everyone bent over, gasping. Noel quickly pressed the door closed.

'We are near the KahnenChambers,' Sid moaned quietly. 'We are so far from the exit –'

'Sid!'

Everyone jumped. Stolt's voice was right outside the door.

'How did he find us so quickly?' Mae hissed.

'You have that skahk with you, don't you, Sid?' Stolt rumbled. 'I can *feel* him, you idiots. You can't hide from me.' Everyone turned to Drax, who shrank down into the carpet.

'Sid,' Stolt's voice continued, 'I don't know what you're doing with him, but it doesn't look good for you.'

The door smacked open, and Stolt stepped into the doorway, his cloak swirling about his ankles, his expression stormy. Noel threw his arms wide, a barrier between Stolt and the room. 'Don't you dare come closer,' Noel warned.

Stolt didn't even spare Noel a glance. Instead, his eyes locked on Drax who cowered at the back of the room. To Sid's horror, Aren stepped in front of the little mayj, her cardonite dagger in her hand. 'You leave him alone,' she said. There wasn't a note of fear in her voice.

'Get out of the way, girl,' Stolt snarled.

Aren didn't move.

'Aren, no!' Sid stumbled as he ran to her, holding his hands out to Stolt. 'Please don't,' he begged. 'This is my family. Please don't hurt them.'

A slow smile spread across Stolt's face. 'Oh, a rescue mission, is it? Wow, Sid, I'm impressed. I wouldn't have thought you'd be worth the trouble.'

'Please, Stolt, let them go. You can take me back to the prison –'

'I don't care about *you*. I care about that skahk right there. What're you doing with him, Sid? What've you got yourself into?'

Sid was trembling violently. He saw Noel eyeing up Stolt's flexing hands. Noel was a mayj, sure, but he couldn't take on Stolt.

'Unless . . .' Stolt said, 'you're his accomplices? It is possible that *you*, Sid, were behind the murder of the late FaKrijen?' Stolt began to laugh. 'You've blinded-sided me, you really have. You were so close with Oji. I would never have guessed you were plotting to kill him. Then again, you've always been quiet. Cowardly actually. No one would suspect someone as mousy as you. The perfect ruse . . .'

Underneath the terror and stabbing distraction of Stolt's cruel words, it dawned on Sid that the KahnenMayj was stalling. He'd done nothing but talk since trapping them in this room.

From the look on Noel's face, he'd come to the same conclusion. Stolt must've alerted someone. The Krijen perhaps or, Great Kahn forbid, another KahnenMayj if what they'd heard was a lie, and it wasn't just Stolt left.

Or Jin.

Noel caught Sid's eye just as Noel flicked his wrist. Stolt bellowed as the tail of his robes whipped around his torso and up and over his head, binding and blinding him. Before Sid could blink, Noel had run at the KahnenMayj, tackling him to the floor.

'*Go!*'

Sid cried out as Aren grabbed his arm and wrenched him forward. He snatched at Mae, and they raced past Noel and Stolt on the floor. Sid twisted around as they reached the doorway. 'Noel!'

Noel leapt to his feet. Drax had followed them to the doorway, and his head whipped around as Stolt staggered upright, dragging his robes from his face, snarling. He raised a hand towards Noel just as one of the plush sofas tore across the room and slammed into him, sending Stolt and the sofa crashing through the wall. The noise was deafening.

'Go!' Noel yelled again. He dashed through the door and together they tore down the corridor, Sid in the lead this time. He led them through the twisting maze of the Keep, using every shortcut he knew, avoiding the hallways where the Krijen would be patrolling. Shouts punctured the corridors, echoing back to them. There was no doubt that the Krijen knew about them now.

Their muffled footsteps exploded into thunder as the carpeted floor became polished stone again, and the wooden panelling turned to webbed walls as the corridors widened. They rounded a corner and moonlight streamed in through open windows in the walls, throwing a glorious blue hue over the corridor, mingling with the orange from the candles. Sid came to a stop in the shadows, gasping and clutching a stitch in his side. 'We're close,' he gasped, 'but it's the main exit. It'll be guarded, I'm not sure where to take us.'

'Pa, where are the dungeons?'

'Not far, down the corridor to the left, then down the stairs to the bottom. But the dungeons will be guarded too. I don't think we should go that way.'

Aren turned to him with a familiar, stubborn look in her eye. *Oh no,* Sid thought.

'I want to get the women out,' Aren said.

Noel groaned. Mae snatched Aren's hand. She knew her daughter well. 'I'm sorry, Aren,' she said. 'I want to as well, but we can't. They know we're here. We must get out while we can!'

Aren pulled her hand from her mother's. 'We can't leave them. We'll never get another chance!'

'No,' Noel snapped, 'there is a KahnenMayj on our backs, and the Krijen are coming – *no, Aren!*' Noel lunged at her, but Aren had already sprinted off through the moonlight strips with Drax scrambling after her.

Mae made to follow, but Sid grabbed onto her arm. 'No!' he begged.

'Get off me, Sid!'

'It's the wrong way –'

'That's our *daughter!*' Mae cried. 'Great Kahn help me, if you stop me, Sid, I'll never forgive you!' Mae wrenched her arm from Sid's grip and ran after Aren. Noel swore loudly, then raced after them. 'Come on, Sid!' he yelled over his shoulder. 'We can't split up!'

This is it, Sid thought as he hurried after Noel. Tonight was the night they were all going to die. He almost wished he was back in his little black prison. Sure, he might've been going crazy, but at least he'd been safe.

CHAPTER 6:
JIN KANJU

'Come on, Jin, tell me how many!'

'I don't know how many.'

'How can you not know?'

'I haven't been counting.'

'Take a guess then.'

Nommo was as persistent as ever. Jin felt like a Square again, getting grilled on mundane topics which seemed to give the others great pleasure, for reasons that evaded Jin.

'I dunno. Forty.'

Nomo's jaw dropped. *'Forty?'*

'What? Is that a lot?'

'Ten is a lot! Forty is ludicrous. You nutter.' Nommo had a stupid grin on his face. 'Fuck, I forgot how inferior you made us all feel.' Even though Nommo was grinning, Jin frowned. He hoped it wasn't true. No one should be made to feel inferior, not because of him.

A slight breeze lifted Jin's hair. The air was cooler up here, pleasant against his hot skin. They were patrolling the upper ramparts of the KahnenKeep, right near the peak of the mountain. The only people who might dare attempt to enter the Keep this way would be mayjen or perhaps some very determined acrobats. It would be a treacherous scale up the side of the mountain to get in this way. But Jin had come to expect anything. This was where *he* would try to get in if he felt inclined to sneak into the Keep.

Despite the threat of invasion, Jin felt almost at ease up here, chatting to Nommo about nothing. Even Filip wasn't bothering him. Instead the dead Square stood quietly behind him on the ramparts, listening to the conversation. Other than the burning creep of his power returning after his majikal exertions during today's training, Jin was well-rested. Life at the Keep was definitely slower than in the Deadlands.

Jin was doing another sweep of the dark ramparts when someone shouted his name. He and Nommo leant over the rampart wall, looking into the dark courtyard below. 'It's Pago,' Nommo said. He cupped his hands over his mouth. 'Above you, sir!'

'There is an escaped prisoner!' Pago shouted up to them. 'Get down here now!'

'Oh, shit,' Nommo said. He and Jin sprinted to the rampart tower and took the steps four at a time as they spiralled down, hands flung out to brace against the wall. They burst through the door at the bottom, and Pago ran towards them. 'Stolt raised the alarm!' he yelled. 'The mayj who killed Oji is in the KahnenChambers!'

It took a moment for Pago's words to sink in.

Then Jin was running.

He poured power into his muscles, moving at breakneck speed through the Keep. He pushed off walls that cracked under him, but he only ran faster. He was so far from the KahnenChambers. *That skahk is going to get away before I get there*, Jin thought desperately. 'These fucking walls!' he bellowed.

Filip ran next to him. 'Just harness your way through,' Filip said. 'Stolt can fix them!'

For once, Jin didn't question the dead Square. He thrust a hand down to the floor, a bolt of power ripping from him. With a bang, the floor fell away, and he leapt down into the space, trailing debris. KahnenMinders screamed as he landed next to them, and he took off again. He thrust out his hands again as he ran, shattering walls in his path and tearing through an assortment of rooms that he fled through so quickly he couldn't tell what they were for, leaving squeals of surprise in his wake.

Finally, Jin burst through the wooden panelling of the KahnenChambers, startling the Krijen gathered on the other side. Daggers flashed as they were drawn. Flit and Jokah were among the Krijen, crouched over a body tangled in a cloak. They both leapt up, daggers in hand. 'By the Great Kahn, Jin!' Flit cried. 'You gave us a fright!' Meek was there too, along with two other Krijen who Jin didn't know. Recognising Jin, they all lowered their daggers.

'Where's Pago?' Jokah asked.

'Coming,' Jin said. He quickly took in the rest of the room. There was a broken sofa, its frame snapped and cushions scattered. Beyond that was a gaping hole in the wall.

'Where's the skahk?' Jin asked. He joined Flit and Jokah by the body. He could feel who it was before he recognised him.

'It's Stolt,' Flit said. 'He's alive, just unconscious.'

'What a shame,' Filip muttered.

Jin could see a deep gash on the KahnenMayj's head. 'The skahk did this?'

'He must've,' Jokah replied. 'He got away.'

Jin growled. 'Which way did he go?'

'There are three squads already combing the Keep,' Flit said. 'Stolt's signal was regarding four intruders and one escapee though everyone is accounted for in the dungeons, so I don't understand –'

'I said *which way did he go?*'

'We don't know. I thought you might have an idea of how to find him.'

Jin was shaking with suppressed adrenalin, power, and heat, and all the mess that came with it. 'Calm down,' Filip commanded. Jin dug his nails into his palms and sucked in air, trying to quash the fire raging inside so he could think straight. It was difficult, but eventually, everything faded to pins and needles.

'Good,' Filip said in approval. 'Now, you can feel Stolt, right? Maybe you could feel the skahk too if you try.'

Jin hadn't thought of that. He stilled, concentrating. He could feel a vague revulsion, but it was familiar. It was Stolt.

'I can't feel the skahk,' Jin muttered. He'd not been speaking to the Krijen, but they looked up when he spoke.

'What?' Meek asked.

Jin didn't answer. He closed his eyes, wondering if it might help.

'The skahk might feel different,' Filip said, 'stronger, maybe.'

But all Jin could feel was Stolt. 'He's getting in the way,' Jin said, frustrated. 'I need to move away from here.'

Jin strode off, heading down one of the corridors. The Krijen called out to him, but he didn't stop. None of them were squad leaders requiring he follow their orders, and none of them could keep up. He needed to move fast if he wanted to find this skahk and rip him to pieces. Vengeance for Oji.

Jin broke into a run again, spooking dazed Kahnen and Minders as they stuck their heads out of their rooms, awakened by the commotion. Jin recognised Lord Salli's broad figure, looking almost comical in a dressing gown as he leant out of a doorway. 'KrijenMayj!' he called. 'What's —'

Jin didn't hear what he said. He was already down a staircase, heading into the bowels of the Keep. Filip was hot on his heels. 'Why are you going down?' Filip asked.

'Because everyone else is up!' Jin replied. Fleeing criminals would not go where there were Krijen if they could avoid it, not even skahks like this one. That, and the stone belly of the dungeons would pose no barrier to escape for a mayj of his abilities.

Jin was charging down another corridor when Filip spoke again.

'Woah . . . you feel that?'

Jin skidded to a stop, his nerves pulsing. He was slightly breathless, more from the crushing weight of his power than exertion from running. Very little other than harnessing tired him anymore.

'Do you feel it now?' Filip pressed.

It was subtle, but it was there, the insidious creep of something that put Jin so badly on edge that it made his teeth hurt. Naturally he wanted to run from it.

'He's moving!' Jin gasped. 'He's moving towards the dungeons!'

'What are you waiting for then? Go after him!'

Jin tore towards the sensation, feeling his body protest, his blood hot enough that it hurt. Then it hit him, a consuming repulsion so strong it felt like was he back beneath the Split in the Deadlands.

'HE'S RIGHT HERE!'

Jin thrust out a hand ahead of him, blasting a heavy chunk of webbed wall straight into the skahk as he fled down the stone staircase on the other side.

Fuck, Jin thought, relishing the skahk's scream as the wall hit him. It sounded good.

Jin raised his hand again, glimpsing a pair of dead blue eyes just before the piece of wall filled his vision as it slammed back into him. Jin cartwheeled through the air, smacking into the ground and skidding all the way back down the corridor.

Jin roared and leapt to his feet. He threw out a hand, snatching at the skahk, but he'd aimed blindly and missed; instead, the whole staircase ripped towards him, caught in his majik. Not that it mattered. Jin *felt* the skahk falling, heard him wail, heard someone else yelling –

The skahk tumbled from the rubble and landed at Jin's feet.

'KILL HIM!' Filip screamed.

Jin didn't think. He just reacted. He reached out and grabbed the skahk with majik, ready to twist his skull from his spine. But Jin didn't hear the satisfying crunch he expected. Instead, he found himself hurling through blissful oblivion. Filip was gone, the ringing was gone, and Jin didn't hurt anymore. The world was nothing now, just some long-forgotten nightmare because he was floating in a dream where there was only peace, a rapture to drown in. Jin loved it; he could stay here forever.

But something told him he needed to let go.

This was not like when he harnessed Stolt. This bliss would come to an end. He just didn't know when, and he wouldn't feel it coming closer because he felt nothing anymore. But escape could not be his. He didn't want to Turn. It would be the coward's way to go. His father would never allow that. He had to let go.

Jin felt for the fire in his chest as it rolled from him in molten waves. He smothered it.

Just as quickly as the world had gone, it came roaring back. There was a cold, hard floor against his face. Filip was screaming in his ear, 'Don't harness him like that, he's too heavy! You'll Turn!'

Jin knew that already. He could feel the difference in his chest, a long-lost fatigue tugging at him.

'*What are you doing?*' Filip shrieked. 'Get up! He's still here!'

Jin's eyes flew open, and he staggered to his feet as the skahk did the same, the effort to deflect Jin's attack having also sent him to the ground. Jin could see the skahk's icy blue eyes rimmed all the way around with white. 'Scared of me, are you?' Jin asked. 'You *should* be scared, you murdering piece of shit!'

The skahk turned and ran. Jin took off after him, anger boiling his blood once more, burning through the fatigue. He reached out with his hands as the skahk spun in a circle as though to get a glimpse of him so he could harness.

A chunk of rubble flew towards Jin and melted into a sphere. It enveloped one of his wrists and became solid, jerking him backwards and almost wrenching his arm from its socket. The sensation was so horrendously similar to what the mercenary had done to him that Jin screamed, tearing at the sphere with his free hand, and when it didn't come free, he found his sense again and splayed his fingers, harnessing it to dust.

Jin looked up just as the skahk skidded around the corner. Jin tore after him, confident he could catch him. Jin was faster, and the skahk didn't seem to move properly as though the evil in him had twisted not only his head but his body too.

Jin rounded the corner into a room of open windows, and he was suddenly sliding on the stone floor that had become liquid beneath his feet. Before he could catch himself, he smacked straight into the wall in front of him. '*What is this majik?*' Jin shouted, cursing his own ignorance for the umpteenth time. He pushed off the wall, spotting the skahk on the far side of the room just as he leapt onto a windowsill. His cretinous silhouette was backlit for the briefest of seconds as he looked down, hesitating. Then he jumped.

Jin lunged towards the window, leaping over the sill after the skahk. The fall into the empty courtyard below was further than expected. Jin smacked into the ground, shock reverberating from the soles of his feet right up into his brain.

The skahk cried out and scrambled back from him, having landed only a few paces away, struggling on twisted legs.

Jin had him this time. He raised his hands towards the skahk, but his fists suddenly jerked away, grabbed by some invisible force. The skahk stumbled, looking dazed. He'd let go of Jin's fists as quickly as he'd harnessed them.

'He can't hold on to you either,' Filip said. 'Keep at it, tire him out!'

Jin reached out again, intending to grab onto the skahk's baggy clothes with majik and drag him back, but the ground burst up around Jin's boots, and he yelled out as he fell downwards into stone that had become nothing but dust, snatching for an edge to cling onto. He sank to his chin before his hands found purchase.

Gritting his teeth, Jin hauled himself over the lip of the hole, spilling stone dust onto the ground. 'This is impossible!' he gasped. 'I can't tell when he's going to do something. He's not using his hands! Is it definitely him harnessing?'

'*Yes,*' Filip said, as he watched Jin struggle, 'it's him!'

Jin pushed himself to his feet, stone dust clouding around him. He hadn't even taken a step forward when his wraps pulled free from his wrists and wrapped themselves together, snapping his arms shut. The material began closing around his fingers.

'Stop him, stop him *now,*' Filip commanded. 'You need to keep your hands free!'

Jin tried to separate his hands but met an impossible resistance. Panic sent another surge of power ripping from his chest. He poured it down his arms, forcing them apart, stretching and snapping the material of his wraps until finally he was free.

But the skahk was fleeing, getting further away, and Jin didn't know what to do except snatch at his baggy clothes, dragging the skahk back a little, but the effort involved was enormous. The skahk was pulling back on his own clothes in the strangest way, fighting back without fighting against him, and Jin could feel the numbness of bliss looming once more. He was so drained. If he pushed too hard, he might end up trapped in it again and start to Turn, and then he would lose the skahk forever.

'I can't fight this thing. I don't know how!' Jin cried, hauling back as hard as he dared, the bliss teasing him as it danced within reach. 'He's going to get away!'

'He's expecting majik,' Filip growled. 'Stop fighting like a mayj and start fighting like a Krijen!'

Jin hadn't bothered with his daggers because he assumed they would be useless against this skahk, but he was desperate and Filip had a point. Jin cut off his majik, releasing the skahk's clothes, and pulled a dagger from this thigh just as something small barrelled into him from the side. It was one of the skahk's accomplices, having finally caught up with them.

Jin reacted, slashing at the body and shoving it aside, not taking his eyes off the skahk, knowing that if he looked away, there was every chance he would lose him.

The skahk glanced behind himself as he ran, and this time he did a double-take. The skahk let loose an anguished scream and skidded to a halt, turning back, his skeletal arms stretched towards his fallen accomplice.

Jin smiled as he raised his dagger, ready to spear it through the skahk's chest.

'*Jin.*'

Jin stumbled to a stop, his blood congealing in his veins at the sound of her voice. He whipped around, dagger still poised in his hand.

At the edge of the courtyard, there was a small crumpled figure on the ground beneath one of the stone archways. The figure raised her head. 'Jin, it's me,' she said as she reached up and pulled down the material covering her face.

The heat in Jin's body was gone, snuffed out. There was no mistaking her beautiful freckled face under the moonlight.

'*Aren?*'

Jin dropped his dagger and suddenly he was on his knees beside her, gathering her into his arms. 'What are you *doing* here?' he cried.

Aren was still tugging at the scarf, trying to pull it off her head. Jin reached up and helped her push it back, her auburn hair tumbling out.

It was her. It was definitely her.

After a year of waiting, here she was in front of him, right when he least expected it, exactly where she shouldn't be.

'Aren, I'm so sorry!' Jin choked. 'Why did you do that? Why did you get in the way?'

Aren gave him a weak smile. 'It's okay, I'll be fine. It doesn't hurt.'

But there was a darkness spreading across her abdomen that said otherwise. Jin's hands were shaking, his brain jammed. He was growing dizzy and he knew why, but he didn't want to believe it.

'Aren –'

'Your hair is so long now,' Aren said, reaching up her hand to hold it just short of his face as though she didn't quite have it in her to touch him. 'I almost don't . . . recognise you. It's so good . . . to see you, Jin.'

Jin grabbed her hand. It was still warm, but her breathlessness scared him. 'Hold on,' Jin said. 'Hold on, I'll get help –'

'No, no,' she said, 'don't go anywhere . . . I want to talk . . . to you . . .' Her hand went limp in Jin's grip.

'Aren? *Aren!* No, no no hold on . . . I said hold on!'

But as always, Aren didn't listen to him. Instead, her smile softened and her head rolled back, and before Jin could scream at her not to go, she was already staring up at the stars with glassy eyes that didn't see.

CHAPTER 7:
SID BHA

Aren was too far ahead of them. Sid watched in disbelief as his fearless daughter reached out to Jin, the shape of his name on her lips.

Jin's dagger flashed and with one swipe he sent Aren soaring straight into the pillar of a stone archway, an impossible distance away. Sid thought he would hear a noise, the sound of her body hitting the stone, but he didn't. He heard nothing, felt nothing. He only had sight left of his senses, and he saw Jin stop and toss away his bloodied weapon as his mouth formed Aren's name.

Sid floundered in the irony of it.

If only Jin had let Aren say his name first, then he wouldn't have struck her. It didn't seem fair for it to be this way.

Noel reached them before Sid did. Sid watched Noel shove Jin aside and grab Aren by her shoulders. Her arms flopped at her sides.

'Aren?' Noel asked. '*Aren?*'

Finally, Sid arrived at Noel's side, his eyes taking in the puckered slit that transected his daughter's chest moments before Noel pressed her headscarf over it and scooped her into his arms. 'I've got her!' Noel shouted. 'Let's go!'

Mae was screaming at Jin, who sat on the ground at their feet, his face whiter than the stone of the Keep behind him. Even in the dim light, his eyes looked red. The combination was rather monstrous, Sid thought. He'd never seen someone look like that before.

Sid grabbed Mae and pulled on her arms until she stopped screaming and turned to him, shaking, and together they ran after Noel.

Drax must have been with them too, up ahead but out of sight because everything in their path evaporated to mist and reformed behind them, enabling their escape and protecting their backs.

Soon they were at the gates, then on the main street of Val, then down an alleyway, and then at a yell from Noel, Drax tore through one of the sleepy shop doors. They entered what looked like an apothecary, the walls lined with shelves filled with bottles and a solid wooden table in the middle of the room that Noel lowered Aren down onto.

Sid slammed the door shut and turned around in a daze to watch the scene before him. Mae was sobbing, pulling at the wet material around Aren's chest, exposing the hideous wound. Noel was everywhere, scattering bottles and digging through drawers. He ran to Aren with his hands full, dumping everything on the table next to her, some of it rolling off and smashing on the floor.

'Check her pulse!'

Noel's voice was steady, but the high notes of it betrayed his terror. Mae pressed a hand heavily on the wound, feeling along her daughter's neck with the other.

Drax was in the way, pushing in front of Mae to get to Aren, sending more bottles shattering to the floor. Noel pulled him away and flung him bodily across the room. 'Sid! Keep him out of the way!'

As Drax lunged back towards Aren, Sid dove forward and grabbed him around the waist, hauling him backwards. Drax fought against him in complete silence, squirming and pushing back at Sid with his useless limp hands.

'I can't find it, Noel!' Mae shrieked, tears dripping from her cheeks. 'I can't find her pulse! Great Kahn, help us, she's not breathing –'

'Here! Let me!' Noel pulled his hands free of the mess on Aren's chest and pressed his fingers around her neck, his thumbs smearing bloody lines across her face. Mae was searching Noel's own face with wild eyes, waiting. Drax still scrabbled at the ground, trying to get a foothold as Sid held him up, both hands wrapped around his bony chest.

'No, oh no,' Noel said. His hands left Aren's neck, moving to her wrists. 'No, no, no . . .' He leant down, an ear to her chest, his hands gripping the bloody folds of her once-midnight-blue wraps. Slowly Noel raised his head. 'She's gone,' he whispered.

The words struck Sid so heavily, so hard, like osmium or like cardonite. Sid didn't realise he'd let go of Drax. He staggered towards his daughter, blinded by tears, fumbling until he reached her. He ran his hands over her arms and her face, his fingers tracing her freckles. Aren's eyes were open just a touch, and as Noel said, she was gone from them. Sid slowly lowered his forehead to hers, which was still warm. It surprised him even though it shouldn't because she'd been here only a minute ago. He closed his eyes. That way, with the warmth of her, it was almost like she wasn't gone. Sid held himself there, hanging onto his daughter, his beautiful little girl who had always brimmed with happiness.

'You get away from her!'

Sid opened his eyes and looked up. Mae was tugging on Drax as he leant over Aren, pressing so close he had her blood all over his front. 'Don't touch her!' Mae yelled.

Noel grabbed Mae's shoulders, pulling her away. 'Wait, Mae,' Noel said. 'Let him near.' He raised a trembling hand. 'Look.'

Mae stopped fighting, wiping tears from her eyes. Sid leant to the side, looking beyond Drax, who'd pressed himself against Aren once more. Sid gasped. As he watched, Aren's shredded wraps brightened, the wetness receding back towards the slash across her chest.

'Is he – what's he doing?' Sid asked. But it was obvious what Drax was doing.

'Help him, Noel!' Mae cried.

'By the Great Kahn . . .' Noel hurried forward, raising his hands above Aren, but he hesitated, looking lost and doing nothing. 'I-I can't help him,' Noel said. 'This majik is beyond me! But wait . . .' He reached in and gently peeled Aren's wraps further back from the wound. 'Can you see, Drax?' he asked. 'Can you see what you're doing? Tell me if there is something I can do!'

Drax shook his head and didn't reply, fluttering his stiff fingers gently along Aren's torn skin. Sid didn't understand why he used his hands now. Maybe he needed them for this.

Mae staggered to Sid and clutched at his arm, her eyes wide. 'Nothing's happening!' she cried.

'It will, it will,' Noel repeated as though he needed convincing himself. 'The wound is deep. It will take time for him to pull it back together. Then he can restart her heart.' Explaining it seemed to calm Noel though it surely couldn't be that simple.

'Is that possible?' Sid asked.

'I think so, as long as he has enough power,' Noel replied, his voice flat now. 'But the delicacy required –'

The floorboards above them creaked. Sid's gaze shot upwards, scouring the ceiling. 'Are . . . are people living above this shop?' he asked.

'Yes, this is Master Harro's apothecary,' Noel explained, still staring intently at Aren. 'We will deal with him when he comes.'

Sid swallowed. Mae squeezed his arm even tighter, her nails digging into his skin.

'Drax, please,' Mae begged. 'You've got to get her breathing!'

Drax was shaking now, his face paler than Sid had ever seen it. He had the same look the KahnenMayjen got when they spent too long working on cardonite. Morbid thoughts raced through Sid's mind. 'What if Drax Turns?' he asked. 'What if he can't do it?'

'Don't you talk like that,' Mae snapped back. 'Don't you say that!'

There were more sounds above them, dull footfalls moving across the floor, then thudding down the walls as though someone was descending a stairwell. The interior door behind them creaked open.

Noel flung out a hand and the door crunched back into its frame. Whoever was behind it – supposedly Master Harro – let out a muffled yell.

Noel kept his hand up, the other braced against the wooden table upon which Aren lay, his jaw clenched. 'I don't want to waste my power,' he said. 'Drax might need help. Barricade the door!'

Sid dashed to the door, throwing his meagre weight against it.

'You save my daughter!' Mae yelled to Noel and Drax. 'We'll keep Master Harro away!'

Mae ran to join Sid, pulling a dagger from her wraps. She turned and flung her back to the door, bracing herself against it, the dagger clutched to her chest. Sid looked down at it, shocked to see Mae with a weapon. 'You-you know how to use that?'

'I know which end to stab him with,' Mae said darkly.

Master Harro hammered hard on the door, every knock rattling Sid's spine.

Noel dropped his hand and ran back over to the shelves, tossing more items around.

Sid yelped as something heavy smacked into the door by his head. 'He's going to break the door down!' Sid cried. Mae shook her head, snarling, and shoved back harder, digging her heels into the floor. Her eyes were fixed on Drax, whose lips were turning blue.

'Hang in there, Drax,' Noel yelled, still digging through drawers. 'I know how to help!' He let out a yell of triumph and dashed back over to the table. In his hand, he held an enormous hooked needle, the sight of it sending terror quivering down Sid's spine. With an impressively steady hand, Noel threaded the needle. Then he leant over Drax and speared the point right through Aren's flesh.

'Wait!' Sid cried as the door bucked behind them again. 'You need to burn it first so it doesn't get infected –'

'*You think she's got time for that?*'

The next bang on the door jarred Sid's teeth. At the same time, Drax staggered and slumped onto the edge of the table.

'It's okay!' Noel cried. 'Just *hold* it now, Drax, I've got this part –'

Something exploded right by Sid's face, and Mae screamed as an axe head crashed through the door between them, showering them with wood chips.

'We've got to go!' Mae yelled as the axe head jerked backwards, catching on the wood and tearing a jagged hole, accompanied by a deep bellow from its wielder on the other side.

'Thieves!' Master Harro shouted. 'Get out of my shop!'

'Almost there!' Noel yelled over the racket. 'I can't run and sew!'

The axe head crashed through the door again, widening the jagged hole. Mae turned her head towards it. 'If you *dare* come in here,' she threatened Master Harro, 'I'll cut you to shreds!'

'Don't you steal from me –'

'*Sid!*'

Sid spun around at Noel's yell. Drax was gagging, one arm flung over Aren's torso as he sank to the floor, slowly dragging her from the table. Sid raced forward and hauled Drax upright. Mae leapt free as the door crunched, and the shop owner forced himself through the hole he'd made, his axe held high.

Mae leapt forward, bringing her dagger hilt down onto Master Harro's head with a crack. The man dropped like a stone, his axe clattering to the floor.

Sid blinked at Mae, whose dagger hand was raised above her head once more, prepared for another blow. She stared down at the shop owner, looking a little stunned herself.

'These stitches will hold for now,' Noel said. 'Let's move!' He thrust out a hand and jerked it back towards him, and the door that led to the street swung open. Noel gathered Aren into his arms and ran out the door.

Sid hurried forward and dragged Drax up from the floor. Mae rushed to help, and together they carried Drax into the street after Noel. Drax was a dead weight. He held his arms out weakly towards Aren, legs dragging across the cobbles, his breathing deep and ragged. 'Quickly,' Noel said, turning to wait. 'Keep him close to her. He needs to be close!'

Mercifully, Val was dark and empty, given the late hour. They hurried across the cobbles, Mae straining to see Aren as they ran. 'Is she alive?' she asked Noel.

'She's got a pulse.'

'Does that mean she's alive?'

'I'm not sure.'

'Is she breathing?'

'Yes!'

'So she's alive?'

'I don't know! I don't know how this works!'

'Wait, *wait!*' Sid cried, having realised which direction they were going in. Noel spun on the spot, Aren's limp limbs dangling from his arms.

'*What?*'

'We can't go home,' Sid said. 'They know where we live!'

Noel swore, then swore again. He bit his lip and stared at the ground, his eyes flickering to either side, a battle clearly raging in his head.

'What is it?' Mae asked.

Sid could tell Noel had an idea, one he was reluctant to share. Mae knew it too. 'Great Kahn, help me,' she said dangerously. 'Noel, if you don't –'

'This way.' Noel pivoted on the spot, changing direction to head down the slope. 'I know a place, but it's far and it's in Rue,' he said. 'And even if we make it, I don't know what will happen . . . Jakki might just kill me on her doorstep.'

CHAPTER 8:
JIN KANJU

An hour later, Jin stood in Aren's bedroom, looking at her open wardrobe. Her clothes were strewn across the floor as though she'd been hunting for something before she left. He'd not been in her bedroom much during their friendship, but every time, it had been a mess. So that hadn't changed in the year they'd spent apart.

It was raining outside, which was becoming more common these days. But it wasn't just rain; it was a downpour as though the sky had sensed Jin's mood and tried to replicate it. And failed.

Nothing could have prepared Jin for this. This ache inside that hurt when he breathed, like someone had shoved an icicle straight into the forge of his heart and left it there to burn as it melted.

It was made so much worse by the fact that Aren was here. She stood a little ways from Jin, wearing midnight-blue wraps, her auburn hair long like it had been when she died. This stood out to Jin. She'd usually kept it short by her chin.

'You killed me,' Aren said to him. 'Why did you kill me?' Her voice wasn't harsh. It was curious.

'I'm so sorry,' Jin croaked. 'I was trying to kill the skahk. Why were you there? Why were you with him?'

'I think he tricked me, Jin. He led me there because he knew you would be there too. He thought you might spare him because of me.'

Jin found it painful to look at her. Like Filip, she didn't have a wound in her chest, where he'd sliced her, but the fact she was whole and unharmed made it worse because it was a lie. Jin knew it was his mind, trying to make it better.

He'd left that dagger in the courtyard. He wondered if someone had picked it up or if it was still there with Aren's blood on it. He didn't want it back.

'But why was Sid there?' Jin asked. 'And Mae and Noel, how could he have tricked all of you?'

Jin knew Aren was too kind, too trusting. He could forgive *her* for falling for the skahk's lies. But Noel was too smart, Sid too scared, and Mae too stubborn to believe lies so easily. Jin didn't understand how they could've let this happen.

Aren didn't answer. But if she were like Filip, she wouldn't speak much yet. That would come later. Great Kahn save Jin when she did. He didn't think he could ignore her as easily as he ignored Filip.

Jin could hear the Krijen moving about the house, no longer quiet. They must have searched everywhere and found nothing. It felt wrong to violate Aren's home like this, the home he'd practically shared with her, but he had no choice. They had to find the skahk, and that started with the people who had helped him.

It didn't even feel like betrayal, not yet. Just confusion.

Filip was watching Aren with his arms folded. He'd said nothing since she had appeared as though he was taking the time to process what she was doing there and what to make of her. Jin didn't know if there would be room in his head for two of them. Time would tell.

Jin looked around Aren's room again. Her bed was unmade, the covers tousled. There was a puzzle in the middle of the bedsheet, the pieces scattered as though she'd left it behind in a hurry. Jin wandered over to it, recognising it by the lines and the colour. It was called Fickle and Foe. Aren always cheated at that game. She used to complain about how good Noel was at it, and it frustrated her.

How you could cheat at a one-player game, Jin had no idea. He'd never actually thought to ask her, but then again, she'd not played it in years. He didn't know why she'd gone back to it. The thought was enough to make Jin gasp for breath. He put a hand on his chest, stumbling over to one of the open windows where the rain pooled on the wide stone sill.

Bizarrely, sitting on the stone, dripping water all over the floor, was a pair of boots. Jin stared at them. They were Squares' boots. The leather tongue of the left foot bore a long slit as though sliced through by a blade, repaired with neat black stitches.

Why did Aren have Squares' boots? They were far too big for her.

The mystery of it terrified Jin. What else had he missed out on in the last year of Aren's life? What stories did she want to share with him but now never could?

Jin's throat tightened, his lungs collapsed, and his vision blurred, but for once, it wasn't his power trying to suffocate him. It was just a regular old panic attack. Because of a pair of boots.

Jin squeezed his eyes shut and slid down to the floor, his fingers dragging his wraps away from his throat, trying to make room for air.

'Jin? Jin, are you okay?' Footsteps thudded towards him, and someone crouched down at his side. 'Keep breathing, son. It'll be over soon.' It was Jokah. Jin felt a hand on his shoulder and he hated it, but he let it go. He was too busy trying to not die.

More footsteps sounded, and Jin felt his squad pressing in, probably looking down in pity and feeling sorry for him. It was this thought that forced him from the floor, up to his feet. He leaned back against the wall and opened his eyes. Everyone but Pago was there. 'Did you find the skahk?' Jin asked, his voice strained.

Meek shook his head. 'No, but we didn't expect to. It's pretty obvious he was here though. You said it's just the family, that tutor guy, and the maids? Well, I can't imagine any of them sleeping outside under a stone tree.' Meek held up a pile of blankets and a rolled mattress.

'He was sleeping in the sparring court?'

'Looks like it.'

Jin took a deep breath, air whistling down his narrow throat. 'Maybe . . . maybe they didn't want him in the house?' he speculated. 'How do we know he wasn't keeping them here, under threat?'

'Jin,' Flit said softly, 'they came together to rescue the Weapon's Master.' She meant that Sid and the skahk had been allies. Or at least not enemies.

'Do we know why Sid was locked up?' Jin asked.

Flit shook her head. 'Stolt won't say why, only that it was at the Great Kahn's orders. It explains why we didn't know about the escape. He wasn't in the dungeon. They kept him somewhere else in the Keep.'

'Why weren't we told?' Jin asked angrily. 'How can we guard a prisoner we don't know exists?'

'That's what the FaKrijen wants to know too.'

'We need some fucking answers!'

Everyone nodded in agreement though no one seemed to share the same fury as Jin. They were still looking at him with concern. He was sick of their faces.

'What's next? What's our plan?'

'Jin,' Jokah said, 'you need to take a break.'

'I don't want a break. I want to catch that murdering, cankerous filth.'

'We all do. But we need to speak to the FaKrijen and the Eighth House. Like you said, we need answers first. Then we will get orders.'

'I'll go on my own then,' Jin said. 'Just come find me when you've spoken to the FaKrijen.'

'No way,' Meek said, 'we're not letting you go anywhere.'

Their commiserable looks were incessant, growing worse. Jin couldn't stand it anymore. 'Why are you all looking at me like that?' he demanded. 'What do you know?'

'Nommo told us who she was,' Jokah said quietly.

That loud-mouthed prick, Jin thought viciously, glaring at Nommo, who didn't look in the least bit guilty. 'I had to,' he said. 'They needed to understand.'

'They didn't need to know anything!'

'It's *Aren*, Jin. Of course, they did.'

'We are so sorry,' said Flit.

Jin's hands twitched. 'Get out,' he snarled. 'Get out and leave me alone.'

'No,' Meek said, 'we're not leaving you alone ever again. Well, at least not until we know you won't do something stupid.'

'That's right,' Flit said, 'you're stuck with us. Come on, let's go. Being here won't help.'

It was her freckles that did it. The ones that were like Aren's. Jin snapped and shoved Flit, just a little harder than he intended so that she staggered backwards.

'You can't order me around –'

'*I* can,' Pago said, stepping through the door. His voice was low, angry. 'You just assaulted one of your squad members,' he said as he strode over, hand resting on the hilt of one of his daggers.

'Sir,' Flit began, 'it's okay –'

'No, it's not,' Pago growled. 'That's sixty cuts, Jin. You know it.' The whole squad stilled, bracing for Jin's reaction.

Jin was quiet. He'd never been punished as a Krijen even though it had happened plenty of times as a Square, and to him more than most. As a Krijen, punishment was different. It was designed to last. But Jin had had worse, way worse.

'Sorry, Flit,' he muttered. He didn't really mean it.

'That's okay, Jin.'

Jin turned to Pago. 'Now?'

Pago shook his head. 'Tomorrow.'

Aren had disappeared, but Jin knew she would be back the second happiness came knocking. Not that Jin believed he would ever be happy again. Anyway, Filip was still there like an ugly scar that glared of a hurt you could never forget.

'Back to the Keep,' Pago commanded. 'Jokah, you're on first watch.'

'Yes, sir,' Jokah said, stepping in behind Jin, who cringed. It was not Jokah's first time on Jin Watch. He'd had to do it in the Deadlands too.

As wasteful as it was for them to spend their spare time watching him,
Jin knew there was no point in arguing. He'd just proven he couldn't be
trusted not to do something stupid. He'd hurt Flit.

'I'm sorry, I really am,' he said to her as they walked back to the
Keep. He meant it this time.

Flit shrugged. 'There's nothing to be sorry for. I can't imagine what
you're feeling right now, considering . . . well. I'm amazed you didn't
hit me harder.'

'You should've hit me back. I deserved it.'

'That's not true.'

Jin didn't answer. Flit was wrong, of course, but he left it alone, for
now.

CHAPTER 9:
PYRA

Pyra was getting sick of cutting out tongues. She knew it was a means to an end, but it was a very gross business to be in, particularly when people expected you to be eating them. She'd tried once and put her foot down.

There was only so far good acting could take you and gagging on sliced tongues was not what she had signed up for. Luckily, it was easy to start a rumour based on half-truths, and that rumour had run like wildfire through Rue.

The plan had been going well, to a point. There had been a few rocky patches though perhaps rocky was an understatement, especially on the day of the Celebrations. She couldn't believe that *freaking*, stupidly tall blond Krijen had turned out to be a mayj and had almost ruined the whole thing. It annoyed Pyra immensely that she'd born the blame for the shambles that day turned into. As if she could have possibly planned for that! Krijen weren't supposed to be allowed to use their brains, let alone *harness*.

To add to Pyra's fury, she'd been told the Kahnen had decided to give the stupid blond Krijen some fancy title – the *KrijenMayj* – which meant that when they formally announced it, he could harness without getting his hands chopped off. It was outrageously unfair. The streetlings didn't get the same treatment, and they weren't messing with the balance any worse, but they still got strung up.

The other thing pissing Pyra off was that the KrijenMayj had killed not only Trigger, her favourite zippy little streetling mayj, but he'd also killed Juno, her second-in-command. It was *so hard* to find a good second when everyone was trying to murder you. It had taken ages to find someone not quite smart enough to determine a decent enough plot to kill her but ruthless enough to put the other streetlings off wanting to try.

That, and Pyra had to be careful with whom she shared the truth. Juno had known everything, and he'd actually been good with it. But she'd spent the better part of a year grooming him before she'd told him, and he'd come from a place where she knew he would understand. Pyra doubted she would be that lucky again.

So far, with the other streetlings, Pyra got away with lies. But this time, a good cover story wouldn't be enough because there was another hitch in the plan, more irritating and unexpected than the KrijenMayj.

It was the Lost Square.

It shouldn't even *exist*. It was nothing, a no one, but somehow it had become such an irksome *pest* that Pyra grudgingly agreed they had to do something about it. Ugh. Even just thinking about the thing made her skin crawl.

She'd come up with a plan, but like most streetling plans, it required a lot of secrecy and a lot of manpower. Or child power. However you wanted to say it.

Pyra was currently nestled atop a roof overlooking an alleyway on the Upper West Side, watching the passers-by with keen eyes. It was hot up here, but Pyra had on her floppy black broad-brimmed hat she'd stolen from some crazy, make-up-smeared creeper last year. It flopped over her eyes, and it was a little sticky and worn. However, it stopped her patchy head from burning.

'Pyra?'

Barrett, her burly ever-faithful-yet-idiotic carrier was prodding her on the arm. 'You wanted to know when that girl left the Point, aye?'

'Yes, she's gone?'

'She's been gone for a while.'

'How long is a while?'

'A few days,' Barrett mumbled. Barrett was dumb, but he was strong, which was useful, especially for wielding crossbows. He was also the only one in the Upper West Side gang Pyra felt would do whatever she asked and not question why. But Pyra knew she needed more brain than Barrett for her plan. That was why she'd asked Rifter to help.

Rifter stood next to Barrett. He was tall and lanky for fourteen, kind of like Juno had been but blonder with an upturned nose. Rifter knew something was going down, but he hadn't yet asked Pyra about it. As perceptive as he was, Rifter didn't have a chance of figuring it out though he was definitely trying.

Pyra looked at Rifter. 'Have you figured out a pattern yet?'

'I thought I had,' Rifter replied. 'The girl comes almost every night, a few hours after sundown. Then she leaves about an hour before dawn. Not on rainy days though. And this has been pretty consistent since we've been watching for the past month. But all of a sudden, she's been gone *way* longer than normal. Like five days longer. And it's not even raining.'

'And you don't know why?'

Rifter screwed up his face in thought. 'I dunno. That *thing* has been acting strange too. I mean, it's usually around all the time. Even when you don't think it's there, it is. But two nights ago, one of the residents tore a chunk out of another, and it didn't show up to sort them out, which was weird.'

Pyra scowled. That *was* weird. She'd not been able to get near the Point for over a year because of that Lost Square protecting the Turners, too majik-crazed to defend themselves. But now they were running rampant on each other, and it didn't show up? It made no sense.

'It was back in the morning,' Rifter said, 'and I've been watching it the whole time since. It seems *really* wound up about something. I reckon something happened to the girl.'

Pyra wished that it had. It would make things easier. Not *easy* but definitely better because this Lost Square was pissing her off more than anything else in her entire life. More than the Kahnen. Why hadn't it wandered into the Deadlands or topped itself like all the other Lost Squares? And *why*, of all the people in the city, did it choose to help the *criminals* of Turning Point?

It was also sad the thing had hoodwinked that poor girl into its twisted schemes, enough that she'd also become a pain in the arse. Together, the girl and the Lost Square were corrupting the whole campaign.

Why me? Pyra thought irritably. *Haven't I had to deal with enough?*

Rifter folded his arms and looked sideways at Pyra as if to ask, *So are you gonna tell me why you're making me stalk this disgusting thing?*

Pyra folded her arms too. 'All in good time, Rifter,' she said. Pyra would tell him when she was sure of the timing. They needed the girl to be gone because she was too good at watching the Lost Square's back.

But should Pyra and her streetlings commence their plan *now* when the girl could show up at any moment? Or should they wait until the girl came back from wherever she'd disappeared to and let her slide into routine again so they could be certain she wouldn't be around? Pyra knew she had to decide and soon. But the only reason she'd gotten this far was because she was cautious, and she wasn't about to throw that to the wind for the sake of getting something done faster, no matter how much pressure she was under. There was too much at stake, not just for her but for the entirety of Rue.

Pyra wished she could do it by herself, but it would be stupid to try. Even with a small horde of streetlings, including burly Barrett and brainy Rifter – once Rifter was in the know – it was still going to be ridiculously difficult to catch the Lost Square.

CHAPTER 10:
AREN BHA

Aren's eyelids were heavy. She tried opening them, but it didn't work. So she just listened for a bit.

'It's been six days. How do we know she's actually going to wake up?' That sounded like her father.

'Drax says she will,' said Mae. She was using her firm voice, the one she used when she was telling Aren off. Only this time, it was meant for Sid.

'She's going to starve if she doesn't wake up soon!'

'No, she won't. Noel's been able to get some food into her.'

'Will she even be the same? How do we know her head's not damaged? She wasn't breathing for so long –'

'Drax said he began harnessing her even before we got to the apothecary. He thinks it will be enough, and that's good enough for me.'

'But –'

'By the *Great Kahn,* Sid,' Mae growled, 'if you say *one more* negative thing, I'm going to toss you off the top of this tower!'

Aren's senses were coming alive. She was definitely warm, swaddled in soft things, like blankets on a bed. It was quiet, save for her Ma and Pa bickering. That in itself was unusual.

There was an ache in Aren's chest beginning to niggle at her. It was getting worse as she awoke, worse and worse, and suddenly it hurt so bad she was certain she'd been torn open.

As the pain peaked, Aren opened her eyes. Her first thought was that the ceiling was closer than she remembered it being. She was not in her own room. The second thought was back to the pain. 'Ow,' she said.

'Aren!'

Suddenly her vision filled with worried faces. Mae, Sid, and Noel were crowded around her left side. Behind them stood an older woman with wild grey curls barely contained by a headband, whom Aren didn't recognise.

'Everything's okay,' Mae reassured her. 'You're okay. You're safe.'

'This hurts,' Aren said, bringing a hand to her chest. Her voice wasn't quite right. It was all weak and squeaky. 'Where are we?'

Aren raised her head off the pillow, trying to get a better look. She was lying on a wide bed in the middle of an unfamiliar room. There were no other furnishings apart from a wooden dresser to the right. There were two doors, an open one to the left and a closed one at the back wall. There weren't any windows, so everything was lit with lamps. But there was sunlight coming in through the open door.

Noel turned to the grey-haired woman behind him. 'Do you have anything for the pain?' The woman nodded and slipped out the open door.

'Aren, listen to me,' Noel began gently, leaning towards her. 'I'm going to tell you everything that's happened, but I need you to stay calm and still, for your heart.'

'For my heart?'

Aren slowly pushed herself into an upright position, wincing. She pressed her fingers into her chest, where it hurt the most. She could feel something, a hard ridge that wasn't there before.

'Now,' Noel said, 'don't panic –'

Panicking, Aren pinched the material away and looked down inside her shirt. Diagonally across her chest from her left shoulder to the bottom of her right ribs was a garish dark red line, raised at the edges. There were neat black stitches along its entire length. Aren felt sick just looking at it. 'What is this?' she cried. 'What *happened* to me?'

Something moved underneath the blankets next to her. Aren screamed and tried to scramble away from it, but she was trapped in the sheets, flailing, until Mae reached forward and pressed Aren's arms down, making shushing noises.

Drax's head appeared from beneath the blankets, his eyelids drooping. 'Aren,' he said, 'stop moving.'

'Drax!' Aren yelled. 'What are you *doing*?'

'Aren, listen,' Noel said quickly, grabbing her attention, 'when we went to the KahnenKeep, you were badly wounded. Drax had to use majik to save you. Until you've healed properly, he needs to hold everything in place. Apart from my stitches. Those are fine.'

Horrified, Aren looked down at her chest again, then to Drax, who was now sitting up next to her, his blank face somehow troubled. 'I'm sorry, Aren,' he said. 'I can't heal you more. So we are waiting.'

Aren stared at him, completely lost.

'What Drax means,' the grey-haired woman said as she entered the room again with a little jar in hand, 'is that he doesn't have enough power to Build your tissue back together because as well as holding all the little bits of you in place until they heal, he's also got to keep your heart going, and that alone is a terrific achievement. It should take about six weeks for you to heal. So we are waiting.' The woman moved between Sid and Marigold, opening the jar. 'I'm Jakki, by the way,' she added. 'Here, put this on it. It'll stop it hurting so much.'

'I'll do it.' Mae took the jar off Jakki and sat down next to Aren, gently tugging away Aren's collar. Starting at Aren's shoulder, she began dabbing a thick salve along the hideous stitched ridge.

'It's only a numbing cream,' Jakki explained, 'but it will help.'

Aren clenched her jaw as Mae spread the cream on thickly. It smelled funny but not something she could put a name to. Drax had disappeared back under the blankets. Aren looked down at the lump that was him. 'Is he all right?'

Noel sighed. 'Drax is –'

'A wonder,' Jakki interrupted.

Noel frowned. 'He'll be fine. He just needs sleep and food.'

An immediate problem sprung to Aren's mind. 'You said he was keeping me alive,' she said. 'Can he harness while he's asleep?'

'He sure can,' said Jakki, folding her arms and nodding. 'Like I said, he's a wonder.'

'I think most mayjen *could* harness in their sleep,' Noel said in the scholarly voice he once used to tutor Aren. 'If you don't actively cut off your power, it continues to flow. The challenge lies in directing your majik once you lose consciousness, though' – Noel frowned – 'I guess this wouldn't apply to Drax. He doesn't use his hands to harness.'

Jakki scoffed at that though Aren couldn't tell if she'd scoffed at the comment about Drax or at Noel.

Noel continued explaining, ignoring Jakki. 'The concern would be whether you would wake up if you were running out of power. You could accidentally Turn yourself. It would be dangerous to try it.'

'I'd like to see you try it,' Jakki muttered.

Aren blinked. Jakki and Noel knew each other. Like *really* knew each other.

'How do you . . . Wait.' Aren shook her head. She had too many other pressing questions. 'Can someone please explain what happened? Did we save Mama Hidel? Did we save Maude?'

The look on Sid's face said it all. 'No. Stolt alerted the Krijen, and they came after us. They wanted Drax.'

'It was Jin, wasn't it?'

It was coming back. Aren remembered the staircase exploding behind her, Jin yelling.

'Yep,' said Jakki. 'He was the one who killed you.'

Noel looked shocked. '*Jakki!*'

'What? You weren't going to tell her?'

'It was an accident,' Noel said quickly to Aren. 'You were in disguise. He didn't see who you were. But all the same . . . yes, Jin killed you.'

Everyone's faces were twisting, Sid's in torment, Noel's in sorrow. Mae's expression was particularly strained.

'Well, I'm okay,' Aren said, unsure how to react to such news. 'Is Jin though? Drax didn't hurt him?'

Jakki raised an eyebrow. 'You're kidding, right? This supposed friend of yours nearly slices you in half, and you're worried about him?'

'Jin seemed unhurt,' said Noel. 'But we can't speak with him. It's far too risky. The Krijen are still after Drax, and they know we're with him. We are all suspects now. That's why we can't go home. Jakki has been kind enough to let us stay with her until we figure something out.'

'*Very* kind,' Jakki said, 'considering you show up on my doorstep after sixteen years with a girl who's been sliced in half and *him.*' She jerked her head towards the lump under the blankets.

Mae finished rubbing salve on Aren's wound and tugged her shirt back up. It felt a little better, but the salve was only numbing the surface. The wound was deep. Aren was thirsty and hungry too. And tired. She was so, so tired. 'What do we do now?' she asked. She wanted to talk to Jin, to let him know she was all right.

'You will stay in bed and rest,' Mae said firmly. 'If you exert yourself, you're going to make it harder for Drax.'

Aren didn't like the sound of that. 'Is it really going to take six weeks for me to heal?'

Jakki nodded. It was a long time. But Aren would do it without complaint for Drax. Speaking to Jin would have to wait.

'What are *you* going to do?' Aren asked, looking around at her family and Noel.

'We aren't sure yet,' Mae replied. 'I'm just grateful we are all alive. But we need to lie low, so we'll stay here for now.'

Mae shot an apologetic look in Jakki's direction, who grunted. 'I could've stopped you at the door if I wanted,' she said. 'You don't need to feel guilty about this. But *you*' – she glared at Noel – 'you should.' With that, Jakki snatched the salve off Mae and stalked from the room.

Noel watched her go before closing his eyes and pinching the bridge of his nose.

'Noel, please go after her,' Mae said. 'She's making a lot of sacrifices for us. I hate to see her upset.'

'You don't know Jakki,' Noel said. 'It's best to give her some time. Aren, can we get you anything?'

Aren was parched. 'Water, please.'

Noel nodded and disappeared through the same door as Jakki. Mae reached out and took Aren's hand. Sid stood behind her, his hand on her shoulder. Mae let out a big sigh. 'We can't believe it,' she said. 'We can't believe you're okay.' She squeezed Aren's hand gently. 'We thought we'd lost you.'

'I'm lucky, I guess,' Aren said. Then she frowned, a sudden thought coming to her. 'Are we in Rue?'

'Yes.'

'How long did you say we've been here?'

'Six days.'

Oh no, Aren thought. She shoved the blankets back and threw her legs over the side of the bed.

'What are you doing?' her mother thundered.

'I've just got to do something . . .' Aren made to stand up, but her world spun and Drax wailed behind her, reaching out a limp hand. Mae yelped and pushed Aren back down.

'What did we *just* say? You must rest!'

Aren flopped back onto the pillows, waiting for the dizziness to settle. Sid looked imploringly down at her. 'What is it? What can we do?'

Aren couldn't tell them, could she? Would Wren forgive her for that? Maybe not. Her mother looked ropable.

'I just wanted to see Marigold and Bish,' Aren lied.

'They know you're alive,' Mae said. 'We'll let them know you're awake. *You* are staying *here*.' She practically snarled it. 'I mean that, Aren.'

Aren nodded. Her mother was rarely so stern as this.

'And *what* is taking Noel so long with getting you some water?' Mae got up, huffing as she walked out of the room, leaving Aren with her father. Aren looked up at him. 'Ma is really upset, isn't she?'

Sid took Mae's place on the bed. 'She is. You gave us all such a fright.'

'Sorry. But I'm fine.' There wasn't much else she could say. 'Pa, can you do something for me, please?'

Her father was quiet, his eyes searching hers. 'You weren't going to see Marigold and Bish,' he concluded after a short pause. Aren smiled. He knew her well.

'No. Can you help me?'

Sid hesitated. 'I'm not going to like it, am I? That's why you waited for your mother to leave.' His voice quivered.

'Please, Pa. It's really important to me.'

Sid slowly nodded. 'How could I deny you anything after what you just did for me?' He looked like he regretted the words even as they came out of his mouth. 'Tell me what I need to do.'

CHAPTER II:
JIN KANJU

It had been eight days since Jin killed Aren, and Stolt still hadn't fixed the cracks Jin had left in the webbed wall of the training room.

'*Again.*'

Jin wanted to punch him. He wanted to see Stolt's pointed nose break and put blood all down that shocking white robe of his.

Pago looked about as angry as Jin felt. 'Isn't that enough?' his squad leader asked the KahnenMayj.

'No, he's not done yet.'

'He's exhausted! We are *all* exhausted!'

'You might be. He's not.'

'Just leave it,' Jin muttered to Pago. Pago folded his arms but stepped back.

The Kahnen weren't here this time, for which Jin was grateful. But his squad were, and they were puffing. Their faces were red, daggers hanging from their hands, looking like the barbarians that Stolt kept calling them.

'Can you please explain the point of this, again?' Jokah asked. Even the older Krijen's patience was wearing thin. He'd been impeccably polite until this point.

'Having seen what your KrijenMayj did to the Keep the other day,' Stolt said, 'and after having spent a week cleaning up his mess, I've now confirmed what I suspected.' He looked scathingly at Jin. 'You fight with no finesse, with no thought. You're wasteful and destructive. Majik is about efficiency. *This* is what I am trying to teach you.'

'You've said the same thing a million times now,' Meek moaned at Stolt. 'Don't grab the person. Grab their *clothes*. I think he's got it.'

'It's more than that! What is it with you Krijen and butchering the most sophisticated majikal concepts? Efficiency is also about cognitive dexterity! A Breaker who only thinks in a linear fashion, no matter how powerful he is, is going to do poorly against a Builder, regardless of his power. Which is exactly why the late FaKrijen's killer got away.'

'So us chucking daggers repeatedly at Jin is going to make him more efficient?' Flit asked.

'It's going to challenge his cognitive process. It's going to make him think about the best way to tackle an impossible task and use majik sparingly but effectively. He needs to learn to *preserve* his power.'

Filip stood a little way off, watching. He laughed. 'I really don't think you having enough power is a problem,' he called to Jin. 'You're practically living with the sun inside you.' He laughed again, the sound winding Jin up even more.

'These exercises will also help your squad practise fighting against other mayjen,' Stolt added. '*Again.*'

Pago sighed and waved his hand, and Jin's squad surrounded him once more. He knew they wouldn't hurt him on purpose, but they'd quickly learned to stop pulling their punches. Not when he was using majik.

Aren was watching too, next to Filip. She'd said nothing since reappearing this morning while Jin was eating breakfast. He'd upturned his whole bowl of maize onto the floor in shock and had to sprint from the room as another panic attack took him. Pago had sat with him in the corridor this time, ordering the others away until it was over. Surely his squad knew he was going mad.

Flit snapped a dagger at Jin, and he side-stepped it, dropping below a coordinated attack from Meek and Pago, who slashed their daggers through the spot Jin had occupied a second before.

Nommo ducked low and whipped his foot around. Jin grabbed Nommo's wraps with majik and flung him away, sending Nommo skidding across the floor. Jin brought his elbow up to Pago's face just as Jokah barged forth from somewhere, and Flit stuck out her foot, sending Jin tumbling.

As Jin fell backwards, he caught Jokah's wrist and placed a foot squarely in the older Krijen's gut. When the curve of Jin's back kissed the ground, he used the momentum to fling Jokah over himself. Flit lithely stepped out of the way as Jokah, like Nommo, went skidding across the room.

Flit and Pago converged on Jin with their daggers. Jin leapt to his feet, and with majik, he wrenched their daggers from them. With a flick of his wrists, he turned the daggers in the air, sending them spearing point first back towards their owners.

Jin heard movement behind him, and he spun around, the daggers soaring with him. He'd forgotten to let go. Jin quickly dropped them, grabbed his own daggers from his thigh wraps and brought them up to parry Meek's attack just as Nommo came barrelling in from the side and tackled Jin to the floor, dagger held to Jin's throat. 'Gotcha!' Nommo yelled, puffing.

Jin raised his head off the floor, looking at Stolt. The KahnenMayj was sucking on his lips with a sour expression. 'You're not thinking laterally,' he said. 'You can't seem to deal with more than two objects at once.'

'Oh yeah?' Jin shoved Nommo off him and stood up. 'Funny that because I only have two hands.'

'Yeah,' Meek said, waving his dagger in the air as the squad gathered around, all of them wiping sweat from their eyes. 'What do you expect him to do, harness out of his arse?'

Stolt ignored Meek's comment. 'You're not even trying,' he snapped.

'I *am* trying,' Jin said. 'When is it going to be your turn, huh? Can you actually do all this stuff, or are you just acting like you can?'

'This isn't show and tell. It's a teaching exercise. I'll not harness because you want to see what I can do.'

Jin muttered a stream of curse words under his breath, all the worst ones he could think of. Skahk didn't really cut it, not for Stolt.

'Decorous as always,' Stolt responded dryly.

'Can I at least use my power on myself?'

Stolt scowled. 'You haven't been?'

Jin paused. 'No.'

'So it's worse than I thought. You're barely able to harness if you're doing anything else. Your cognitive dexterity is abysmal. I shouldn't have expected anything more from a Breaker, even an over-inflated one like you.'

That was it. Jin couldn't restrain himself anymore. He flung out his hand and loosed an explosion of heat, grabbing hold of Stolt's robes. With as much power as he could muster, he tossed the KahnenMayj the length of the room.

Unfortunately, Stolt didn't crash through the webbed stone at the other end. Instead, he landed on his feet, skidding to a stop just before he hit the wall. The KahnenMayj turned around, teeth bared.

'Oh shit,' Filip said. 'What did you do that for?'

Jin's chest rumbled with heat. He didn't care what Filip thought. Instead he looked at Aren, who said nothing.

Jin's squad glanced nervously between the two mayjen. 'Oi,' Pago hissed at Jin, 'what are you playing at?'

Stolt strode back towards them, his face thunderous. Jin was loath to back down, but there was a slight nudge of nerves beneath his fury. He didn't actually know what Stolt could do.

Stolt waved his hands. At once, all the Krijen blades melted from their dagger hilts, dripping onto the floor. Like tiny steel rivers, they flowed towards Jin, who staggered backwards in shock, his palms burning as his tingling nerves ignited.

The rivers collided, forming a flowing steel ring on the floor around Jin. He looked down at it. 'What are you –'

The steel ring exploded over Jin, blinding him, and he threw out his hands to stop it, but there was so much that he couldn't grab it all. It folded over him, and in seconds, the steel had flowed down to his hands, coating them like a pair of gloves.

The flowing steel hardened.

Jin's heart was pumping wildly in his chest. He held his steel-coated hands up in front of him, working to keep himself calm. He tried to move his fingers. He couldn't. Jin had expected worse from Stolt, but there was something about having his hands trapped that sent his fear into overdrive.

'Take them off,' Jin called to Stolt. Stolt kept walking towards him, hands by his sides, no longer harnessing. The steel gloves were heating up so fast from the heat of Jin's palms that his fingers were burning.

'Take them off!'

'No,' Stolt said, stopping in front of Jin and bringing with him that familiar revulsion. This close, Jin could see there was a little bead of sweat dripping down Stolt's temple. Stolt flicked it away. 'You are arrogant and angry,' he said. 'That is a bad combination, especially in a mayj. You wanted to see what I could do. Do you like it? Are you impressed?'

Jin opened his mouth to retort but didn't get there because Aren spoke to him, making him jump. 'It's thin steel,' she said, inclining her head towards the steel gloves that trapped his hands. 'Smash it.'

Not a bad idea, Jin thought. He walked past his stunned squad and slammed one of his fists against the webbed wall. The steel glove shattered onto the floor. Jin did the same with the other, flexing his fingers as he walked back to stand next to his squad.

'Don't you dare attack me again,' Stolt said. 'Or next time I will use cardonite.'

'What's cardonite?' Filip asked.

Jin didn't know or care. He wasn't sure what was worse, the humiliation of being reprimanded by Stolt in front of his squad or that Aren had been there to see it.

With a wave of Stolt's hands, the shattered pieces of steel became a river again and split off into silver tendrils, flowing back to their respective dagger hilts. Meek stared, dumbfounded, at the blade that reformed at the end of his dagger hilt. He ran a finger down it, eyeing it curiously.

Through the mess of anger and embarrassment that Jin felt, a twinge of jealousy peeped through. *Why can't I do that?* he thought.

Filip spat on the ground. Jin looked up at him, shocked.

'Do you *want* to be like Stolt?' the dead Square demanded.

'No,' Jin muttered.

'Let us keep going,' Stolt said. 'Or do you need time to sulk?'

Pago ducked his head towards Jin. 'Hey, it's okay if you want a break.'

'No, sir,' Jin said quickly, 'I'd rather keep going.'

'Again then,' said Stolt. 'Expand your reach.'

Jin wasn't quite ready when his squad attacked the second time, but as the first two blades came towards him, he reluctantly acknowledged that Stolt had taught him something. He didn't know why he'd not done it before; it seemed so obvious.

This time, rather than pulling daggers from the hands of Meek and Nommo, who were up first, Jin harnessed the blades into powder.

'Oh, shit!'

Meek pulled out a spare knife as Jin spun back to him. He grabbed Meek by his wraps with majik and sent him slamming against the back wall, pinning him there. Jin kept his hand up, his majik flowing.

Fighting one-handed was nothing, Jin reminded himself. He'd done it plenty of times as a Square. Their Geni, on occasion, had strapped a hand behind their backs, forcing them to just use the one. Jin just had to make sure he didn't let go of Meek.

With his free hand, Jin grabbed Nommo's boots and pulled them out from under him. Nommo smacked into the ground, making hoarse sounds as he struggled to suck the air back into his lungs.

Flit and Pago stepped forward with fresh daggers, and Jin sensed Jokah coming at him from behind. Jin kicked out, bolstering his leg muscles with power so that he moved lightning fast. His foot connected with Jokah's gut as he simultaneously crushed Flit's dagger with majik and sent the dagger-dust streaking into Pago's face. Pago cried out, his dagger missing its mark as he stumbled, blinded.

Empty-handed, Flit threw herself at Jin just as Jokah came at him once more, his face determined, but one hand was clutched against his ribs. Nommo was rising to his feet again, still wheezing.

Jin spun, twisting his harnessing arm to keep Meek pinned to the wall while bringing his other fist into the side of Flit's head with a little pop of power. She raised her fist to deflect it, but he crashed right through, connecting with her temple. She dropped to the ground.

Jokah leapt onto Jin and wrapped his arms around his neck, squeezing. Pago appeared in front, pulling his hand back to throw a punch. Enduring Jokah's stranglehold and one hand still out towards Meek, Jin caught Pago's fist before it connected with his face, squeezing it with a nudge of power. The bones in Pago's hand crunched, and Pago screamed.

Jin let go of Pago's fist, distracted by black dots appearing in his vision from lack of oxygen. He grabbed Jokah's arm, hauling the older Krijen over his shoulder and onto the ground.

Nommo, having recovered from being winded, lunged towards Jin. Jin brought his hand up under Nommo's chin, sending his head snapping back. Nommo grunted and hit the floor a second time.

Still Jin held Meek to the wall. The trapped Krijen yelled obscenities that echoed around the room in a cacophony. Jin couldn't make out exactly what he was saying.

With Jin's blood pounding the way it was, the gentle nick of a blade at his throat felt colder than normal. An arm was wrapped around his chest. Pago was behind him. Jin flicked his wrist, and the dagger at his neck exploded. He twisted free from Pago's grip, punching through the steel dust. Pago's nose broke under his fist.

Jokah was back up, pulling his cleaver from his wraps, of all things. Jin wasn't expecting it. The sight of the weapon sent Jin screaming back to the memory of that black tunnel, the mercenary kneeling on him, holding Jin's own cleaver high above his head. He was going to lose his hands.

Fear took over.

Heat blazed down Jin's arms and fingers, making his limbs jerk. He didn't think. He relinquished the flow of majik trapping Meek and clamped the cleaver between his hands, ripping it away from Jokah. It spun the length of the room and bounced off the webbed wall with a bang.

Jin hesitated as Jokah's red face, not the mercenary's, filled his vision. Jokah seized the opportunity. The older Krijen grabbed Jin's head in his hands and slammed his forehead into Jin's so hard that Jin saw the stars in the night sky, the ones the Bhouli wanted to get to. Jin's legs gave way beneath him, and he slid to his knees.

Jokah's knee rammed into his face, tossing him onto his back. Meek was there now too, and he knelt on Jin's chest, so heavy that Jin couldn't breathe, and Jin was trapped beneath that mercenary all over again.

Instinctively, Jin reached out with majik. He grabbed Meek, the body of him, and shoved him away, straight up into the air.

Jin's power sighed from him, replaced by that glorious weightlessness that he got lost in. Relishing the feeling, he sent Meek further away, stretching his arm out far enough towards the ceiling that his squad member cried out in alarm as he rose into the darkness above them, above the flickering light in the room, up into the storm clouds that rolled.

Meek was an inch tall when Jin heard Aren yelling at him to let go. He did so, leaping to his feet as Meek began to fall.

Jokah turned his head up, mouth agape as Meek plummeted towards the ground, his terrified cry reverberating off the walls.

'Jin!' Aren screamed. 'Jin, catch him!'

Jin raised a hand. With a burst of majik he caught Meek by his wraps, bringing him to a stop just above the polished floor. Jin lowered him slowly, but Meek was shaking so badly that his legs folded under him and he sat down on the floor, looking dazed.

Jin dropped his hand to his side, taking deep breaths. His arms ached with fire, but his chest had cooled. He felt better for having thrown Meek into the air, as wrong as it was. Jin hated how much he loved that feeling. It was as though he *needed* it.

Filip shot him a knowing look. 'You clearly do,' he said.

Jin growled, looking away.

The ringing silence in the room was punctured by Flit's gentle groan as she slowly sat up, a hand to her head.

'Wow,' Nommo gasped. He too was sitting on the floor, rubbing his neck. 'You hit way harder now than when we were Squares.'

Pago was bleeding all down his front, one hand clasped over his nose, the other hand sagging by his side, looking horribly misshapen. 'You dick, Jin,' he said, spitting blood from his mouth. 'Did you have to?'

Jin wished it had been Stolt. Even so, Jin didn't feel the guilt that he should, looking around his squad, scattered in a broken circle around him.

Meek was as white as a sheet. 'Can we have a break now?' he asked.

'We are done for today,' Stolt said. His voice was stern, but he was looking at Jin was a guarded expression. 'That was better. But I told you not to harness like that. You need to *conserve* power when you fight.'

'Fuck you,' Jin spat. He turned and shoved open the doors, storming into the passageway beyond, leaving his squad behind.

CHAPTER 12:
AREN BHA

Aren was frustrated. For one, the room was boring to look at. She'd counted the marks on the ceiling, the dents in the walls. Well, the ones she could see from where she lay anyway, considering she couldn't get out of bed without waking Drax. She'd picked the blanket so badly that there were loose threads everywhere, and she was dreading Jakki seeing it.

Worse than the boredom was the worry. Aren didn't know if her father would do as she asked. While she figured he'd be the most willing of everyone to pass on her message, he'd also be the least likely to make it back from Turning Point. Sid quivered at the thought of putting his boots on the wrong feet, let alone braving the hoodlum- and streetling-infested alleyways of the Lower West Side. That wasn't to mention the Krijen were surely out in force, looking for him.

Aren felt a wave of fresh guilt, but she shoved it down. It was done. She moaned softly, rubbing her face in her hands. The wait was killing her.

Everyone else had been in the kitchen, which was the room next to hers. They had gone quiet long enough ago that Aren suspected they weren't there anymore. She had no idea how big Jakki's home was, but if it were anything like the other homes in the towers of Rue, it would be an extensive maze of rooms and corridors, enough to befuddle anyone not born and raised there. She'd not seen the towers herself, of course, but had listened intently to Noel when he spoke of them. The homes were distinct from each other within each tower, but apparently, it was not uncommon to have strangers take shortcuts through your living room. Not unless you made an effort to keep them out. Aren suspected Jakki would be one such person. Aren had never seen Noel so put in his place by anyone before. It was rather amusing to watch.

The door to the bedroom moved silently on its hinges, and to Aren's delight, Wren's anxious face appeared. His dark eyes scanned the room before they found her.

'Aren! Thank fuck!'

Wren dashed across the room and threw himself to his knees beside the bed. Aren grabbed his hands in hers, wincing as her stitches pulled. 'Wren!' she cried. 'I wasn't sure if you would come!' She reached up and dragged his face so close that their noses touched.

'I'm so sorry,' Wren said, his breath warm on her cheeks. 'Sid came yesterday, but I couldn't get in here! There aren't any windows in this place, and I had to wait for everyone to leave –'

'I was worried you'd be angry at me for telling Pa about you –'

'I don't care about that! I'm glad you sent him. I thought you were dead. I was waiting for you at your house, and all of a sudden there were Krijen everywhere and then Jin came into your room . . .' He paused, his dark eyes shining earnestly at her. 'Aren, what happened? Sid told me nothing other than that you were alive, so I followed him here . . .'

Wren tensed as Drax stirred next to Aren, the little mayj's curly black hair just visible above the blankets. Wren stared at him, mouth open. Then his eyes darted back to Aren's. He dropped her hands and stood up, backing away from the bed.

'Don't worry,' Aren said quickly. 'Drax won't say anything about you being here if he wakes up.'

Wren grimaced. 'That's . . . that's not the problem.'

It took Aren a moment to realise what he meant. '*Oh,*' she said, 'no, you've got the wrong idea! Drax just needs to be close.'

'*That* close?'

'Yes. Let me explain.'

Wren took another step back.

'*Please*,' Aren repeated, dismayed at the look on his face. Wren slowly sat down on the floor, keeping a cautious distance between them. 'Tell me from here.'

Wren's face was hard to watch as Aren told the story from the point where she'd left home with Drax. It was particularly difficult to describe what Jin had done, but she wouldn't lie to Wren. She tugged down her sleeping shirt to show him the ugly wound. Wren hissed when he saw it. 'That fucking *monster*,' he said, balling his fists in his lap. 'I'm going to kill him –'

'You're not going anywhere near him,' Aren said. 'It was an accident, and I'm fine. No harm done.' She pulled her shirt back up. 'Now, will you come back over here?'

'You haven't explained Drax.'

Nervously, Aren explained that too, sighing with relief when Wren unfolded himself from the floor and returned to kneel at her side. 'He's keeping you alive?'

'Yes.'

'Okay.' He hesitated. 'I'm sorry.'

Aren grinned at him. 'I can't believe you were worried about *that.*'

Wren didn't reply. He gently pushed Aren's hair back from her face, his fingers tangling in it. 'Shit, Aren,' he said. 'So what now?'

Just then, muffled voices sounded outside the door. Wren was on his feet in an instant, his face white.

'It's okay to meet them,' Aren said quietly.

'That's not a good idea.'

'But Pa already knows –'

Aren stopped speaking at the sound of Bish's voice. Wren looked horrified. 'No, definitely not. Not him.' He was looking around the room for an escape route. 'Why are there no fucking *windows* in this place?'

'That's a closet,' Aren said, pointing to the door at the back of the room. Wren sprinted to it, slipping out of sight. The closet door closed with a tiny click just as the one leading from the kitchen swung open.

'Aren!'

Marigold ran across the room and threw herself down on the bed, pulling Aren into a hug. Aren winced as her stitches tugged again. Bish wheeled in after Marigold, his face serious. 'By the Great Kahn, I can't believe it,' he said.

'Sid told us *everything*,' Marigold gushed. 'I'm so glad you're all right!'

It was nice to see them, but Aren was horribly distracted, knowing Wren was hiding across the room. She did her best to smile and keep her eyes on their faces, but it was hard not to let her attention drift towards the closet door.

A million excuses were running through her head about how to get Bish and Marigold out. She could tell them she was tired and they would leave, but she felt guilty about asking them to go, given they'd only just arrived. *Five more minutes*, she decided. They would understand.

Aren nodded along to their chattering, trying to come up with responses to convince them she was listening when she wasn't. She found herself staring at Bish's wheeling chair. 'Noel and Sid helped,' Bish said, noticing what she was looking at. He'd assumed Aren was wondering how he'd gotten up the stairs. Aren blushed, but Bish didn't seem bothered.

'Everyone's here now,' Marigold said. 'They're just in the other room.'

'Everyone?' Aren asked.

Marigold smiled, nodding.

Wren was well and truly trapped. Bish and Marigold kept talking, but Aren didn't hear a word they said. *Maybe there is a back to the closet?* she thought. *Or maybe Wren could rip up the floorboards and get out that way.*

'Aren, you seem distracted,' Marigold said, looking worried. 'Are we bothering you?'

'No! Sorry, I'm tired, that's all.'

Bish took Marigold by the arm. 'We should let her rest.'

Marigold's face fell. She braced herself to stand up off the bed and then hesitated.

'Marigold, *no*,' Bish warned. 'Leave it.'

Instead, Marigold reached out and took Aren's hand in hers. 'Aren,' she said, 'you're not thinking about *it*, are you?'

Aren had no idea what she meant. 'What?'

'Marigold, please don't,' Bish begged.

'Don't what?' Aren asked, looking between them.

'Well . . .' Marigold began, biting her lip, 'your father said something earlier that, frankly, was a little concerning.'

Darn it, Pa, Aren thought. This must be about Turning Point. When Marigold had said Sid told them everything, Aren hoped he'd left out that part. But Aren couldn't blame her father. Knowing him, he would have come back traumatised, and Mae and Noel had dragged the truth out of him. Not that he would have put up much of a fight.

If Aren's heart was working properly, it would be pounding hard, which was probably why she felt calmer than she should.

'What did Pa say?' Aren asked carefully.

Marigold leant forward, bringing her voice down to a whisper. 'Your father said you asked him to find a *Lost Square*.'

Aren made sure to meet Marigold's eyes. 'Yes, I did,' she replied. Even though she'd waited such a long time to tell everyone about Wren, this wasn't how she envisaged it. She worried about what Marigold would say, especially with Wren listening in. The closest door was thick wood, but there was a gap underneath it that Aren didn't trust. Then again, aside from her father, Marigold was the gentlest, kindest soul she knew. Aren just needed to explain. Marigold would get it.

'It's true?' Marigold asked with a strange tone to her voice. Aren leant back, trying to read her face. A furrow had appeared between Marigold's eyebrows. It didn't suit her.

'Yes,' Aren repeated, rubbing her wrists nervously under the blankets. She had no wrist wraps to snap. 'It's true.'

Marigold looked like Aren had slapped her. She dropped Aren's hand onto the blankets. 'How could you do such a thing?' she cried. 'How could you ask that of your father?'

'It's okay! And he's not just any Lost Square,' Aren said. She turned to Bish. 'It's Wren.'

The colour drained from Bish's face.

'*What?*' Marigold's voice was suddenly so shrill it was unbearable, and her rouged lips trembled. 'What does it want with you?'

That was when Aren understood what Marigold had meant before when she'd asked if Aren was thinking about 'it'. She'd not been talking about Turning Point. By 'it', she meant Wren.

Anger flooded Aren in a strange way. She felt mad, but her body didn't react the way it normally would. Next to her, Drax twitched in his sleep.

'We're saving people together,' Aren said.

'You're – what?'

'We're helping people in Rue,' Aren explained. 'I'm doing something worthwhile, for once in my life.'

Marigold just stared, her jaw hanging open.

'He's *that* Lost Square, isn't he?' Bish asked quietly.

Marigold spun to him, alarmed. 'What do you mean?'

'There's been a Lost Square hanging around the Lower West Side,' Bish said. 'Everyone knows, the Krijen too. They just don't talk about it.'

'That's him,' Aren said with a smile. 'Wren helps people that no one else does. He's a good person.'

'The Lower West Side?' Marigold asked, bringing a hand to her chest. 'You mean that place that's infested with those mayjen criminals? Aren, please tell me it's not true!'

'You don't get it,' Aren said. 'I've been to Turning Point. I've met the residents and the people who come for help. They aren't criminals, they just got served a raw deal in life, like Wren did. He lost *one* dance, and everyone condemned him.'

Bish flinched at that. Aren would've felt bad, but Marigold's upper lip pulled up, and an ugly expression twisted her face. 'The Lost Square is using you,' she said.

'What? No, he's not –'

'Listen to me!'

Drax jerked upright, the blankets falling off him. His head flickered between Aren and Marigold. He didn't like raised voices. Aren clamped her mouth shut for his sake, shocked as she was by Marigold's reaction.

'You cannot possibly think this is okay!' Marigold cried. 'Lost Squares shouldn't *exist*. It's wrong that it's still here, just-just . . . *ugh!'*

Aren had never seen Marigold like this before. Her face was flushed and she had a wild look in her eye. 'How did you even meet it?' Marigold demanded.

'He saved my life,' Aren said, indignant. This was her chance to convince Marigold that Wren was good. 'He saved my life *twice*. You know that rally I got caught in last year? Wren pulled me out of the crowd and took me home. I would have died if it weren't for him. Then later, I got attacked by streetlings in Rue. Wren fought them off.'

Marigold's eyes looked like they were about to pop out of her head. 'What were you doing in Rue? It asked you to go, didn't it?'

'No!' Aren snapped, annoyed at Marigold's assumption. 'I went on my own. My point was that Wren saved me, *again*.'

Marigold gasped as though with a sudden, horrific realisation. 'Oh, Aren, you think you owe it something, don't you? That's why you're helping it?'

'I do owe him,' Aren said. 'But it's not like that. I want to help at the Point.' She hesitated. 'I want *him*.'

Marigold froze.

'That's right,' Aren said. She narrowed her eyes. 'I like Wren, and he likes me.'

'Great Kahn, save you.' Marigold raised a shaking hand to her head. 'You can't have feelings for a Lost Square! It's not a person, Aren! It's sucking you into its failure because it can't handle the consequences. You said it got a raw deal in life? That's a lie! It knew exactly what to expect if lost its dance, all the Squares did.'

'But that's not fair!'

'*Fair?* Do you think this Lost Square is being fair to the Fifteenths who won their dances, disregarding their achievement, treating their victories like they are nothing? And now it's forcing itself upon you when it knows it's wrong! How can you want *that*?'

Marigold's rant had left her breathless, her shoulders rising and falling with exertion. Aren was stunned into silence. Drax had sunk beneath the covers once more. Only his blue eyes peeked out, afraid and unblinking.

'Look.' Marigold's voice softened a little. 'This is going to sound bad, and I'm sorry. But the Lost Square would've heard about you from Jin. It would've known how kind you are, about your heart of gold. So it *chose* you. You think it just happened upon you when you needed saving at the rally? Or that other time in Rue? No one is that lucky, Aren.'

Aren shook her head. 'You're making it out like Wren planned it somehow, to trick me into trusting him. That's ridiculous.'

Marigold gave her a pitiful look. '*I'm* ridiculous? When you're the one risking everything while this Lost Square's got nothing to lose? It's manipulating you! It's got you thinking it cares for you when everything it does is for itself.'

'No,' Aren argued back, 'Wren's not like that. He's decent.'

'This is completely *indecent*. It's preying on you and you're letting it!'

'*Get out.*'

Drax placed a hand on Aren's arm. Maybe he could tell her heart should be beating faster than it was. She felt dizzy.

'You know I'm right –'

'I said, GET OUT!'

'Marigold, please, let's go.' Bish had wheeled himself to the door and was looking over his shoulder at them.

'Bish,' Marigold implored, 'surely you agree with me?'

'It doesn't matter what I think. Aren wants us out.'

Marigold gave Aren one last pitiful look before getting up and crossing the room. She opened the door and walked out. Bish watched her leave and then glanced over his shoulder at Aren. Aren didn't understand his expression. But he'd called Wren 'he', not 'it'. Maybe that meant something. Or maybe it was just a bad habit he had yet to break. Wren had been like a brother to Bish. They'd been Squares together for fifteen years. Then Bish had beaten him at the Dancing Ceremony and left him to his fate.

Bish wheeled himself through the door. It closed behind him.

Angry tears welled in Aren's eyes. Drax cocked his head at her. 'You are upset,' he said. Aren looked away from him, using the blanket to wipe her eyes. 'Please, can you go too, Drax? I need a few minutes to myself.'

Drax's blank face was worried. 'It will be hard.' He meant being so far away from her.

'I know,' Aren replied. 'I'm sorry. Just a few minutes, then you can come back in.'

'Okay, Aren.'

Aren slowly stood up from the bed, leaning on the wall as Drax ambled to the door. She closed her eyes, concentrating on staying upright as the room spun. She heard the door close after him. Once the sensation had settled, Aren opened her eyes and slowly made her way along the wall, listening to the rumble of voices in the kitchen. Drax would keep them all away, at least for a short while.

The room swayed as Aren shuffled along, her heart not quite keeping up with her movements. She finally reached the closet door. What were the chances there was a secret back to it and Wren had left, and not heard a thing? With a shaking hand, Aren reached out and turned the handle, easing it open.

Wren stood in the dark at the back of the closet. She could just make out the sharp edges of him, the jagged points of his expression. He was looking right at her, his face full of hatred.

The Founding of Valrue (Excerpt 2)

Given the protection the mountain offered, the appeal of living off the lake life, and the surrounding lush forests, the early settlers set about creating a more permanent home within the mountain crater.

Val was quickly established at the base of the north wall of the crater across the natural river that cut through the tip of the step shouldering the lake. A bridge was harnessed from the mountain stone across the river, and the riverbed and sides were reinforced to prevent further erosion.

Whilst the harsh weather of the mountain throughout the first winter threatened the survival of Val, the settlers used the shallow mountain tunnels in the north side of the crater as shelters to great effect. In preparation for the winter, a storage centre had also been constructed from the mountain stone in the midst of Val by a mayj, proving invaluable for the town's survival. With the growth of the town's population, the storage centre – known today as the Distribution Centre or more controversially, the KahnenCull – was expanded for the next season.

Naturally, the number of mayjen grew with the population of the townsfolk, and harnessing was strongly encouraged. The resulting shift in the natural and majikal balance quickly led to the tempering of the winters, and eventually, the warmth of majik allowed the townspeople to thrive on the surface year-round, no longer needing to retreat to the tunnels during the winter. However, out of convenience, the north tunnels were kept to house the town's officials and eventually widened into rooms. Later on, these rooms formed part of the structure that became known as the KahnenKeep.

The town grew rapidly. The settlers soon erected more buildings across the river and harnessed the stone step to extend further out over the lake. To the bewilderment of the town's inhabitants, a Bhouli mayj by the name of Gosha began visiting daily, persistent in helping construct new homes. When asked why she did it without so much as a coin in return, she responded it was her purpose to give shelter.

After months of interaction with Gosha, the settlers surmised the Bhouli spent their lives seeking and defining their purpose, the meaning more tangible than first understood. Bhouli may have a singular purpose or multiple purposes. They express self-explorations using temporary white ink symbols known as patterns. When a Bhouli is particularly confident with a selected pattern, the pattern is permanently inked under the skin and referred to as a tattoo. Multiple tattoos may be required to fully define a single purpose, and a Bhouli will continue to add tattoos until they feel their purpose has been satisfactorily defined.

Whilst certain patterns have predetermined meaning, most patterns are unique, their meaning determined by the wearer. Therefore, Bhouli with the same or similarly defined purposes may not share the same tattoos.

At first, it was assumed Bhouli youngsters used only temporary ink. However, given several writings of this time describe Bhouli children as young as six having ink under their skin, it seemed age was no barrier to permanently defining one's purpose.

A purpose must first be tattooed before it can be fulfilled. Obviously, a body with only smeared ink patterns and devoid of tattoos indicates both an undefined and unfulfilled purpose. However, a Bhouli with a permanent tattoo, or even multiple tattoos, may have defined their purpose but has by no means fulfilled it. Fulfilment of a purpose is not marked on the body in any way. It is up to the individual in question to acknowledge fulfilment for themselves. Unlike in many cultures, for Bhouli, social recognition of one's achievements is not strongly coveted. This does not mean to say that Bhouli do not appreciate the fulfilment of another's purposes, merely that the opinion of others is not a determinant of whether or not one will go to the stars.

CHAPTER 13:
THE GREAT KAHN

It was disappointing to hear that the Weapon's Master had escaped moments before Stolt turned up to release him. If only he'd waited. The Great Kahn had so wanted to pardon Sid Bha, for Luka's sake, and now the opportunity was lost.

How the Weapon's Master had gotten mixed up with the likes of Mandavar's son, the Great Kahn had no idea. It was possible he was the boy's new master. Given that Sid Bha may not have the feeble disposition the Great Kahn had previously assumed, the Great Kahn was slightly more nervous about the boy being on the loose. Then again, there was no reason he wouldn't be able to talk Drax down again if the Weapon's Master sent the boy to kill him as Felle had done. Additionally, that skahk of a KrijenMayj posed a real threat to Drax now. His single redeeming quality.

Under FaKrijen Eden, the Krijen clamoured with renewed vigour to hunt down Oji's killer and his unlikely accomplices. The Great Kahn went to great lengths to distance himself from their fury at having Drax slip through their fingers yet again. The Great Kahn was worried that if he involved himself in the hunt, he might tip back into the tyrant of a man he'd become, given how much he still despised the boy.

The Great Kahn's tenuous new conscience struggled against the lingering habit of hatred that had dominated him for the last quarter of a century. But it was early days, the Great Kahn reminded himself. One did not become a new man overnight. He'd also never attempted to reinvent himself before. It was proving to be a greater challenge than expected.

The Great Kahn brought his attention back to the present. He was in the Red Room, the stone slab stretched out before him. The Kahnen of the Eighth House sat in their high-backed chairs along its length. Teal, the long-haired KahnenSpeaker, stood behind the Great Kahn's throne-like chair, watching the room with polite interest. KahnenMinders floated around, ready to pounce on orders.

The Eighth House had a new member, a replacement for Lord Oman who'd been killed by streetlings at the Celebrations. For the first time during his rule, the Great Kahn didn't actually care who the new house member was, only that the People had voted him in. His name was Lord Bajeridine, and all he did was listen. Meanwhile the others were more vocal than ever.

The Red Room rang with voices, the velvet walls struggling to smother the sounds of the debate. 'It is far too soon,' Lord Reider said. 'We cannot possibly announce the KrijenMayj to the People. For starters, he has barely begun training –'

'We *need* a dissuasion,' Lady Elira interrupted. 'I have not been able to sleep at night since the Celebrations!'

'Your concerns regarding our safety are valid,' Lady Macey replied in a carefully controlled tone, 'but not a good enough reason to reveal our hand, not if there is a risk of a streetling uprising.'

The timid Lady Hia let out a little cry. 'Do you think that is a real possibility –'

Lord Salli rode right over the top of her. '*Reveal our hand*?' he sneered. 'The whole city watched us soar over their heads! They saw the KrijenMayj with their own eyes! They saw him harness!'

'The People have no reason to believe we indulged him further,' said Lady Macey. 'For all they know, we had him dealt with in the appropriate manner.'

'I think the People noticed we did not execute him,' Lord Salli retorted, 'which I am still not convinced he does not deserve!'

'Lords and ladies, *please*,' Lord Reider implored, 'are we not worried about how this will look to the People? Have you all forgotten that we remain in the midst of a majikal crisis? Sure, the People accept the continuation of the KahnenMayjen because they trust them to harness with great care and necessity. However, announcing a *Krijen*Mayj may not look like strength to the People but a betrayal.'

'A betrayal? *We* are the government,' Lady Elira cried. 'We make the rules!'

'This is a democracy,' Lord Reider said, rising to his feet. 'The People should dictate our rules! I am astounded by the expectation many of you have for our citizens to obey our laws while we flout them frivolously! *If*, not *when*, we announce the KrijenMayj, we must be prepared for a backlash, especially if we are to recruit more mayjen from Krijen ranks. And our solidarity on this is a *must*,' he said pointedly to Lord Salli, who bristled.

The Great Kahn watched with interest. He rarely saw Lord Reider lose his temper. Also, the Great Kahn didn't agree with him. While it was a fair assumption to make, the Great Kahn doubted there would be a backlash against the announcement of a KrijenMayj. Yes, the People had long thought majik contemptible even before the Unsettlement. It was a product of envy, compounded by KahnenMayjen elitism. But even the most downtrodden, despicable citizens couldn't hide their morbid fascination with majik. Who could blame them? People chased power. A Krijen who could do majik would be *most* alluring, the very epitome of a quintessential warrior. The KrijenMayj would have the People on their knees in awe.

How repugnant.

'My Great Lord,' said Teal, leaning into the Great Kahn's ear as the squabbling continued, 'may I interject? There is another piece of news that is pivotal for this discussion.' The Great Kahn nodded and waved his hand. Immediately, the Kahnen dissolved into silence, save for their huffing.

Teal cleared his throat. 'Further to my previous news, today I have received the latest monthly reports from the Deadlands. The Krijen of Fourth Base South spotted something of great importance whilst roaming.' Teal paused dramatically.

'Get on with it, Teal,' Lord Salli snapped. 'This is not a Dancing Ceremony.'

'My lords and ladies, the roamers spotted deer.'

'*Deer?*'

'Yes, Lord Flynn, deer.'

'As in the animal?'

'Yes, my lord.'

Lady Hia gasped. 'What . . . what does this mean?'

'The Base Master reported they have not had a sighting of deer, nor of any living creature, for over a decade. It is highly unusual. Not only have they seen them, but since they first appeared, the creatures have increased in number. I should add that it takes a minimum of twelve days for news of the Fourth Base to reach Valrue.'

The Great Kahn smiled. It was finally happening. Because of him. 'Are you suggesting, Teal,' he began, 'that this is a sign the majikal imbalance is correcting?'

'It is not so strongly worded in the report, my Great Lord, but the Base Master did not specify any other possible reason.'

There was a collective gasp around the stone slab.

'This is wonderful news,' the Great Kahn said. 'Is the FaKrijen aware?'

'He is on his way to Fourth Base South as we speak, my Great Lord. He wished to verify it himself.'

Lord Flynn cleared his throat. 'Have there been any other signs, Teal? Anything else which might give us more confidence that this is really happening?'

'Not yet, my lord, but you have my word that my eyes and ears are searching. I will not hesitate to inform you of any news no matter how trivial it appears.'

'I appreciate that, Teal,' Lord Reider replied, 'but I agree with Lord Flynn. We must not get our hopes up. We need more proof.'

'You just want an excuse to keep the KrijenMayj under wraps,' Lady Elira countered. 'If this is indeed the end of the Unsettlement, then we have no reason to hide him!'

'*If* the Unsettlement is over, it is not an excuse to start advocating for majik. Do we know why it is over? Does anyone have a clue why the Unsettlement might suddenly resolve itself? How do we know it will not happen again?' His questions were met with blank faces.

'You will all keep your heads,' the Great Kahn said quietly. Everyone turned to look at him. 'Speak of this to no one. We will wait until we have more proof. Majik is still illegal, and we will treat it as such. Thank you, Teal.' The Speaker gave a little bow and stepped back.

'My Great Lord,' said Lord Flynn, 'to go back to our first issue, did the FaKrijen leave word on any unrest in the city? While we have had no further threats made against us, as Lady Elira mentioned, the possibility of a streetling uprising seems very real.'

He sounds nervous, the Great Kahn noted. Normally, he would actively enjoy the discomfort of his Kahnen, but it bothered him this time.

The Great Kahn chewed on his tongue as he thought on his answer. The insults made against his democracy by the streetling girl had been a nasty shock at the Celebrations, tempting his anger. But it hadn't bothered him further; he'd not considered her threats against the Eighth House an actual problem. He himself was untouchable, and his Kahnen were nothing but replaceable puppets. However, Mandavar's manipulations had long monopolised his thoughts, rendering him indifferent to their worries however legitimate. Now that he was free from Mandavar, perhaps his Kahnen deserved his attention.

'FaKrijen Eden did not leave word,' the Great Kahn said, 'but we should monitor the sentiments of the People. I will request an audience with the relevant squad leaders while the FaKrijen is away. And if it gives you reassurance, we will increase your protection.'

The Great Kahn's statement met with a mixture of poorly veiled relief and astonishment, the Eighth House unused to him being so amenable. He thought of his interaction with Lord Flynn the other day, how quickly the Great Kahn had returned to threats when Lord Flynn mentioned majik merely to make conversation. While the topic was abhorred, the intention had been pure.

Was that really what he had come to, ruling with cruelty and fear? He had done things in the name of protecting Valrue that he'd never dreamt he would do. He did not regret them, no. But that did not mean he couldn't do things differently, moving forward.

I will not be this man that Mandavar made me, the Great Kahn told himself. *I will not.*

Luka deserved better than that.

CHAPTER 14:
AREN BHA

Aren clung to the closet doorframe, it being the only thing keeping her upright as her heart struggled. She tried not to let Wren's face scare her. He wore that look she hadn't seen in months, the one he had after pulling her from the crowd at the rally. She remembered how nasty he'd been that day and reminded herself he hadn't meant it. That was what was happening now. It was just him thinking he was alone again.

'Wren, I'm so sorry –'

'I didn't want to do this, Aren,' he said, his words biting. '*You* wanted to do this. You were the one who kept pushing me.'

'Really, it's okay.' Aren stretched out a hand and placed it on his chest, putting her weight on him so she could let go of the doorframe. His heart thrummed against her fingers.

'I don't believe any of what Marigold said,' Aren said firmly.

'Why not? It's true,' Wren spat.

Aren snorted in a very Wren-like fashion. 'You mean the part about you devising some convoluted plan to trick me into trusting you? She's only saying that because you're Lost. She's got this idea in her head about what that makes you.'

'You think it was a coincidence I was there both times?'

Aren narrowed her eyes at him. 'I know it was. I know what you're doing –'

'Marigold is right. No one is that lucky.'

Aren thought of the tattoo that Maude had inked on her arm. Happiness and luck, Maude had said. 'I think *I'm* that lucky,' Aren replied.

Wren didn't look any less angry. 'So you're just going to ignore everything she said?'

'I listened. Marigold said nothing that changed my mind. She called you *it*. She was vile.'

Aren really wished Wren would hold her if not for the comfort of it, but at least to help her stand up. Her knees were wobbling. She leaned her forehead against his chest, bracing against another wave of dizziness. Drax was struggling with her heart, even though he was only a room away.

'You said I was a good person,' Wren said. 'I'm *not* a good person. I knew what being a Square meant, the sacrifice I might have to make, only I was too shit scared to follow through with it.'

'That doesn't make you a bad person, Wren. The Squares and the Krijen and the People are wrong.'

'So *everyone* except you is wrong?'

'Yes.'

'Fine,' Wren growled, 'so shoving aside the fifteen years of expectation that I turned my back on, I've done other bad things now too. *Objectively* bad. It's like being Lost makes you do things you would never do, so you eventually hate yourself enough that you want to end it anyway. I stole, I scared people, I forced myself into your life –'

'No, you didn't.' Aren raised her head as much as she dared, still leaning against him.

'I snuck into your room with a dagger!'

'You sneak everywhere with a dagger. And you forget that *I* attacked *you*. You didn't touch me. You didn't do anything bad.'

'The bad part was in my head.'

Aren paused. 'What do you mean?'

Wren lifted his hands to his face and groaned into them.

'Tell me,' Aren said. She sounded confident, but inside she was nervous. Wren had a high tolerance for badness. If *he* thought it was bad, it was probably worse than she could imagine.

'All right,' Wren said. 'I just need to go back a bit to explain it.'

'Go on,' Aren said, hoping she wouldn't regret this.

'Okay.' Wren took a breath. 'When I saved you from that rally, I didn't plan it, no. But Marigold was right in that I did it for myself. I needed to do something decent to justify why I was alive, you know? It just so happened you were the one person in the entire city willing to look at me, instead of through me.'

Aren still had her hand on Wren's chest. Wren reached up and slowly pulled it away, letting it drop between them.

'But I knew that,' Aren complained. 'I knew when you saved me at the rally that it wasn't just for me. But that doesn't make it bad.'

'I'm not done.'

Aren swayed on the spot, waiting for the bad part.

'Like I told you when I first came to your room, I wasn't sure it was you who turned up at the Point. I convinced myself it was a good enough excuse to go see you, to ask. By then, I'd been Lost for months. Sure, the residents at the Point put up with me but only because it meant they could Turn longer because I protected them from the streetlings. So when I came to your house, I wasn't thinking straight.' Wren gazed somewhere off to the side, making his expression impossible to read in the darkness. 'I don't know what I'd been hoping for,' he went on, 'but when you attacked me, I figured that whatever it was, it wouldn't happen. So I was ready to take you away.'

Aren frowned. 'Take me away? Where?'

'I don't know!' Wren said with a sudden sharpness. 'Anywhere! Somewhere I could keep you so that we could talk.'

'Just . . . just talk?'

'Yeah. Even though it would have been very *wrong.* I'm disgusted it went through my mind.' He said nothing more, his face still turned away.

'That's it?' Aren asked.

Wren nodded. 'Yeah.'

Aren wished she was feeling less weak and that she didn't have a broken heart so she could knock some sense into him. 'Oh, Wren! You had me thinking it was something truly awful!'

Wren slowly turned his face back to her, looking disgusted. 'That's not awful enough? Stealing you away because I couldn't handle all the shitty loneliness I brought upon myself?'

'But you didn't,' Aren said. 'You didn't take me. You haven't told me why.'

'Because you insisted the Lost thing didn't bother you,' Wren said, shaking his head as though he still couldn't believe it. 'You said you *wanted* to help at the Point. You wanted to help *me*.'

Aren smiled at him. 'You have no idea how happy I was when you agreed. I wanted something from you, too, and I actually took it. You were my escape. Do you think that was wrong of me?'

'That's different.'

'No, it's not. I understand you. Now enough of this.'

Aren reached towards him again. Wren gently pushed her hands down. 'Hold on. There is one more thing.'

Great Kahn save me, Aren thought. 'What now?'

'There's something that's been bothering me. A lot. Aren't you worried that the only reason I stick around is because no one else will have me?'

Aren bit her lip. She'd considered it vaguely, just once, but she'd brushed it aside. Wren wasn't like that.

But she should probably ask. 'Is it true?'

'No, but I can't prove it.' He sounded frustrated.

Aren thought for a moment. 'Do you love me?' she asked.

Wren stiffened. 'What?'

'Do you love me?'

'You can't ask me that!'

'I just did.'

'Why the fuck would me saying that make a difference?'

'Because many people, myself included, think saying it means something. Proof that you actually care, you know?'

'I don't think that.'

Aren's heart sank. 'Why not?'

'Because they are just words. Words don't mean shit.'

'If that were true, then what Marigold said just now wouldn't bother you.'

'Aren,' Wren said in an exasperated tone, 'I'd have to be made of fucking *stone* for what Marigold said not to bother me.'

'Don't you believe her. *Don't.*'

Wren didn't reply. He was quiet for a long time. Aren ached to put her arms around him, but her heart was still too sore for that. Instead, she laid her cheek on his chest. Great Kahn help her if *Marigold,* of all people, was going to scare him away after everything they'd been through.

'Fine, don't say it,' Aren snapped. 'But you better keep coming back to me.'

To her relief, Wren snorted, like he always did when she said something he considered absurd. 'Of course, I'll come back,' he said as he finally wrapped his arms around her, holding her to his chest. 'If I didn't, you'd probably do something stupid, like threaten Pyra just to see if I would save you again.'

'That's not a bad idea,' Aren teased. 'I'll keep it in mind.'

'That's not funny.'

'Oh, but it is.'

'*Aren –*'

'Okay, okay.'

As Wren rested his chin on the top of her head, Aren mused how happy she would be to stay in this dark cupboard with him forever. But Drax had other ideas.

'Aren?'

Wren stiffened again. Drax had crept inside the bedroom and was peering around the closet door. Aren's heartbeat strengthened at his presence.

'Can I come closer now?' Drax asked. 'This is too hard.'

Drax seemed only mildly curious to see Wren standing there with her. He cocked his head to the side, looking up at the Lost Square with his usual blank expression. Wren dropped his arms from around Aren and took a step back, his eyes wide.

'Drax, you can't stare at people,' Aren gently reminded him. 'It's rude.'

Drax immediately looked down at his feet, sinking his head into his shoulders. Aren scowled. She didn't like it when he acted like that.

'It's all right,' Wren said softly. 'I don't mind you looking at me.'

Drax peered cautiously up at him.

'Thanks,' Wren said, 'for saving Aren.'

Drax went back to his staring, his blue eyes intense. 'Okay, Wren,' he said. Wren jumped at the sound of his name.

'I told you,' Aren said to him. 'Drax will like you.'

'Aren? Are you all right?' Mae called from the other room.

'Oh, fuck,' Wren said, his eyes darting around. 'There's no way out of here. I tried pulling up the floorboards, but it's stone underneath.'

'You can't get out? They're going to see you?'

'I guess so. I can't stay here.'

'Are you okay with that?'

Wren grimaced. 'They know about me now anyway. I just wish Bish wasn't here. Are *you* okay with this?'

'I've always wanted them to meet you.'

'Fuck knows why.' He looked up at the ceiling, closing his eyes at the sound of footsteps crossing the bedroom. 'Ah, shit.'

'Aren?' Mae was just outside the closet. 'Aren, what –'

Aren grabbed Wren's hand and led him into the lamp-lit bedroom, Drax ambling along beside them. Out of the corner of her eye, Aren saw her mother go rigid. They passed her.

They'd made it to the open door that led into the kitchen when Drax grabbed Aren by the back of her sleeping shirt. She stopped and looked around at him. He didn't look good; his lips were blue, and he shook gently.

'Bye then,' Aren said, looking back to Wren. She sensed it was best not to kiss him on the cheek as she usually would. A grateful smile tugged at the corner of his mouth. 'Bye.' He let go of her hand and walked through the open door, crossed the kitchen, and disappeared down the staircase beyond.

The irony of it was that everyone watched him go.

Marigold, Bish, Sid, and Noel were all in the kitchen. Once Wren left, Aren felt their eyes pan over to her, but she didn't want to look at them. Jakki wasn't there, which was a good thing. Aren didn't know how she would react to a Lost Square in her home. Badly, Aren figured.

Aren followed Drax back into the bedroom. Her mother raced forward to help her into bed. Drax curled up next to Aren, one hand across her chest, which didn't bother her. Her heart fluttered madly, but she was unsure if it was because of the look on her mother's face, or if Drax was struggling to keep it going after being pushed for so long. Aren felt guilty about both. But she would not forgive any unkindness towards Wren.

'Aren –'

'Ma, unless you have something nice to say, I don't want to hear it.'

'This is senseless.'

'No. How you're treating Wren is senseless.'

Mae flinched at the name, brushing away a tear before it fell from her cheek. 'I don't want this for you. You'll get hurt.'

'If I do, that's on me.'

'You are so trusting, Aren. You see good in everyone, even when it isn't there. Can't you see how your father and I blame ourselves for that?' She got up and left, closing the door behind her, leaving Aren feeling wretched. As tired as she was, her mind whirred.

'Drax? Can you talk? Can I ask you something?'

Drax rolled over and blinked at her wearily. 'I can talk.'

'It's about what happened with Jin. When he attacked you, you fought back, yes?'

'Yes. I know he is your friend, but he was scary, Aren. He wanted to hurt me.'

'That's not why I'm asking. I'm glad you ran. But I don't understand why you couldn't beat him. Everyone keeps telling me how good you are at majik.'

Drax shifted under the sheets, uncomfortable. 'I wasn't trained to fight,' he said. 'They didn't want that. Jin moved so fast; it was hard to think. I tried to catch his hands, but he was too heavy.'

'Too heavy?'

'Heavy to hold on to. With majik.'

'Heavier than holding on to me, you mean?'

'Much heavier. He is a mayj.'

'But he's different to you?'

'Yes.'

'How?'

'Jin is . . . stronger.' Drax paused. 'I am more . . . detailed? I don't know how to say it.'

'Stronger? As in, more powerful?' The extent of Aren's majikal knowledge was limited to what she'd prised from a protesting Noel over the years. She knew there were two pillars of majik: power and harnessing ability. It wasn't for lack of trying that she knew nothing more about either, other than if a mayj used more power than they had, they Turned. And everyone knew that.

'Drax, I don't know much about majik, but I find it hard to believe that Jin is more powerful than you. I mean, what you did to Oji' – Aren winced an apology – 'Noel seemed to think that was a really big deal, majikally speaking.'

'I could only do that because of the lake,' Drax said. 'But that's gone now.'

'The lake?'

'The lake,' Drax repeated. 'The power that was in the lake. The power Pakker wanted me to use.'

CHAPTER 15:
JIN KANJU

On the thirteenth day after Jin killed Aren, Nommo grabbed him and shook him roughly by the shoulders. 'Jin! For fuck's sake, you're making *me* depressed. Look, I know you loved her and all, but by the sounds of it, she was a traitorous little cunt.'

Jin earned himself another sixty cuts when he punched Nommo in the face, but Pago was fair. Nommo got sixty as well.

After that was done, Nommo and Meek cornered Jin during the evening meal. 'We're going out tonight,' Meek announced. 'It's our first night off in Great Kahn only knows how long, and I plan on getting *very* drunk. You have to come, Jin, because it's my watch tonight.'

Jin had no plans for his night off, and there was no point in trying to lie about it. He grunted and got up to get another helping of food. When he got back to the table, Flit and Pago were there as well. Jin started eating, not really noticing what it was. He couldn't even taste it. The voices of his squad were just muffled noises. Now and then the tempo would change as they told stories and laughed. About what, Jin didn't care. He didn't care about anything anymore.

Nommo's voice punctured his absent mind. 'Shit, Jin, did you even stop to take a breath?'

Jin had stood up from the table again. He looked down at his squad. 'What?'

'You've just inhaled your third plate of food, and it tastes like arse.' Jin didn't know what Nommo wanted from him. He dropped the plate – it clattered loudly on the table – and headed towards the exit. He didn't know where he was going.

Nommo and Meek were suddenly on either side of him. 'All right, you're eager to go, we hear you,' Nommo said. 'But out of those black wraps first. You're not Krijen tonight.'

They marched him back to their bunkroom and threw a pair of trousers and a shirt at him. He ripped off his wraps and boots and pulled on the clothes before sitting down on the bed. 'You look strange in that colour,' Filip said to him. Jin looked down. He was wearing different shades of brown.

'We're coming with you!' Flit said excitedly as she and Pago walked through the door. 'We asked Jokah too, but he said no.'

'The old fart,' Meek said with a grin. Pago scowled at him.

'Sorry, sir,' Meek said quickly, 'but could you please tone it down for our night off? You were way more relaxed in the Deadlands . . . and did I mention it's our night off?'

Flit turned to Pago, raising a questioning eyebrow.

Pago nodded. 'Okay, fine.'

Flit grinned at him in approval.

Aren stood next to Flit. They looked horribly similar though Aren was smaller, her features more delicate. 'I'm right here,' Aren said to him. 'You shouldn't look so sad because I'm right here.' It was the only thing she'd said for days, and she said it over and over and *over* again, and it drove Jin crazy because he didn't know what to say back to her. He found himself wishing it had been Flit who had died instead because she was *really* there, and Aren wasn't.

'Jin, are you ready?' Flit asked. Jin looked away, feeling guilty.

'And so you should,' Aren said to him.

'Put your boots on,' Meek prompted. 'Let's go!'

Jin trudged along beside his squad as they wound through the KahnenKeep and out into Val. He didn't know what day or time it was, but the sky was darkening and the streets were busy, the bars even more so. They passed several windows from which an ear-splitting raucous erupted, dulling again as they moved on. Jin wasn't paying much attention, so it was a shock when he realised where they were going. He stopped so abruptly in the street that Meek walked into him. 'No. Not Fivers,' Jin said.

'What? Why not? Fivers is the best!'

Jin shook his head. The last time he'd been to Fivers, he'd had an argument with Aren. That had been before he'd killed her.

'No, I'm not going.'

'Aw, come on –'

Jin had taken a few steps back up the street when Nommo ran in front of him, his hands up. 'Okay! Okay . . . we'll go somewhere else.'

Jin didn't know where they ended up, but it was just as loud as all the rest. He was staring at a glass bottle behind the bar when someone tapped him on the arm. He turned to look. It was a young woman, her cheeks rouged and her lips red to match. 'Hi,' she said, 'I've not seen you here before.'

'I've not been here before.' Jin looked over her head. Pago was on the woman's other side, yelling an order at the bartender. The rest of the squad were shoving their way towards a corner spot. Jin started towards them, but the woman quickly stepped in front of him. He felt a flare of annoyance. Why was everyone suddenly determined to get in his way?

'I'm Nora,' the woman said.

'Jin,' Jin replied through gritted teeth. He wanted to push her away, but he knew the women at the brothel would be furious with him if he did.

'Excuse me.' He nudged Nora aside as politely as he could. Pago turned around, his arms laden with tankards, the contents sloshing over his sleeves. 'Jin, help me!'

Jin grabbed two tankards and followed his squad leader through the crowd. People moved out of their way. It was busy, but it wasn't as packed as Fivers had been on the night of the Dancing Ceremony.

They got to the booth, and Jin carelessly dropped the tankards on the table. 'Hey!' Meek moaned at him. 'Don't spill it!'

'Sit here, Jin.' Nommo stood up, letting Jin into the booth. He shoved a full tankard in front of him. 'So,' he said, turning to Jin with a sly smile on his face, 'who was that woman?'

'Nora,' Jin replied, staring at his ale. The bubbles that floated around the edges of the liquid were slowly popping, one by one.

His squad had trapped him in the corner on purpose so he couldn't escape. Flit sat on his right side and Nommo on his left, talking so loudly over him that Jin couldn't even hear the ringing in his head, which was fine by him.

Filip leaned against the bar, still on the other side of the room. Jin didn't realise Filip could go that far away. Aren wasn't here. She'd disappeared when Fivers was mentioned. She'd not come back.

'Oi!'

Jin blinked. Meek was leaning towards him, both hands around his empty tankard. 'Your face is sagging more than my great aunt's arse. Either drink or put a smile on that mopey face. Take your pick.'

Jin lifted the tankard in front of him and took a few drags under Meek's watchful eye. It must have been sitting there for a while because it was warm. Once Meek seemed satisfied, Jin put it down and wiped his mouth.

'Say, Flit,' Nommo said, 'what's it like being a woman in the Krijen?'

Flit had been taking a swig from her tankard. She paused, peering over the rim suspiciously. 'Well, that depends on exactly what you're asking me.'

'Now,' Nommo replied, 'don't take this the wrong way, but there's a reason there are more men than women in the Krijen. Because, you know, we are faster and stronger –'

Pago shook his head. 'That's *not* the reason.'

Nommo turned to him with his mouth open in surprise, but Flit slammed her empty tankard down on the table, and they both jerked around to face her.

'Woah, hold up,' Flit said. 'Nommo, do you actually think you're *stronger* than me?'

'And faster,' Nommo repeated.

'I'll have you know,' Flit said, waggling a finger at him, 'that the Square I beat in my Dancing Ceremony was a *boy*.'

'So not a man then?'

Flit lifted her arm onto the table, braced her elbow on the wood, and opened her hand in invitation. 'I'll prove it right now.'

Nommo stared at it. 'You're not serious? I'll destroy you!'

'Try me.'

Nommo smirked. He leaned forward and placed his elbow down on the table next to hers, grasping her hand. 'Move your drink, Jin,' he warned, not taking his eyes off Flit.

Jin obediently took his tankard off the table and leaned back, holding it in his lap, out of harm's way. In spite of himself, he was interested in seeing what would happen. Pago half stood up out of his seat, looking incredulous. 'Are you actually doing this?'

'Yes,' Flit said. 'Ready, Nommo?'

'Am I ever.'

'Go!' Flit yelled. Immediately, their fists stiffened, their arms shaking violently. Veins popped out the back of Flit's hand, and her face twisted in effort. Nommo stuck his lower jaw out, looking particularly brutish.

After a few intense seconds, Jin could see Flit's initial burst of strength wavering. She began losing ground, her wrist bending under the weight of Nommo's.

Jin couldn't help himself. Under the table, he slowly raised a finger from the tankard he held, angling it towards Flit. He knew he shouldn't, that he'd told himself he wouldn't, but there was no way he was going to put up with Nommo's smug face for the rest of the evening.

Jin let a tiny river of heat ebb from his chest, down his arm, and out through his fingertip. He nudged on Flit's arm, a little touch of pleasure accompanying it. It was nothing like lifting someone but enough that he could feel it, how nice it was.

Flit and Nommo's forearms straightened once more. Nommo's face was turning a deep puce. Flit let out a low growl.

By now, spectators had come running from every corner of the bar, jostling the table. They were shouting, sending ale splashing over Pago and Meek, neither of who seemed to notice. Instead, they were yelling their blatant preference for the winner. 'Go, Flit, go!'

Jin pressed a little more power from his chest and looked over at Filip, who was still leaning against the bar. The dead Bhouli was shaking his head, but he had a smile on his face.

'Put him out of his misery!' someone yelled.

Flit almost had Nommo's arm on the table. His eyes were bulging out of his head and beads of sweat tracked down his face. Jin almost felt sorry for him as slowly but surely, the back of Nommo's hand hit wood.

The bar exploded with noise. Pago and Meek leapt to their feet, cheering with everyone else as a pile of people landed on Flit, shaking her shoulders and slapping her on the back. Her face was flushed, her eyes sparkling.

Nommo looked livid. He stood up and moved towards the bar, snarling as people slapped him on the back. He soon came back with more tankards, shoving one at Jin.

'Not a fucking word,' he said.

***

Sometime later, they all staggered out of the bar. Jin was feeling pleasantly numbed. Filip was gone, Aren was gone, the ringing in his head was gone, and his balance and ability to use his tongue properly were gone too.

Drinking ale felt as good as harnessing people but way simpler, and with less guilt. He wondered why he'd never tried it before. Sure he drank but not this much and not all of it, everything at once. 'Hold on,' he said, remembering there was a conversation that he'd wanted to finish, but not had the chance. He spotted Pago ahead of him.

'Hey! Sir!'

Pago turned.

'Sir,' Jin asked, 'why do you think there are fewer women in the Krijen?'

Pago had on a slack-jawed expression. 'Huh?'

'Why –'

'Oh right,' Pago said, 'because women are smarter than men.'

'That's right,' Flit said from next to Jin, rather dopey-eyed. 'How come you know that?'

'I have six sisters,' Pago replied, holding up a hand and an extra thumb.

'*Six*?' Meek cried. 'What do you need that many sisters for?'

Jin was still wading through what Pago had said. 'Hold on,' he repeated. 'Why . . . why would being smarter mean you *don't* become Krijen?'

But Pago wasn't listening. He'd already turned back around, staggering into Meek.

Flit was looking at Jin with a funny expression. 'Your hair is so long now,' she said. 'Do you want me to braid it?'

Jin pouted. He didn't like her talking about his hair. It upset him a *lot*. He wasn't sure why.

'Fuck, look at the face on him,' Meek said.

Flit looked hurt.

'Oh, go on, Jin,' Nommo said. 'It's a Deadlands thing. You have to.' Nommo was walking much straighter than the others. Jin forgot what was bothering him. He grinned at Nommo. 'Who's sulking now?'

'Whatever.'

Steps came up to meet Jin, and he sat down hard. Wherever they were, it was quieter than before, but there was still a rumble of noise around them. Somewhere in Val, he guessed.

Flit sat down on the step behind him and dragged her hands through his hair.

Pago flopped down next to Jin. 'I want a braid too,' the squad leader whined.

'Yes, sir, you'll get your turn,' Flit slurred. 'I have to remember how to do it first.'

Jin craned his head to look at her. She had her tongue stuck out in concentration, his blond hair twisted in her fingers. 'Stop moving,' she said, yanking on his hair. He put his head forward again.

'Say, Jin,' said Meek, 'you know how you threw me into the air the other day –'

'What? When?'

'With Stolt –'

'Oh.' Jin didn't like Stolt. 'Yeah?'

'Well, can you do that to yourself?'

'Sure,' Jin nodded.

'I said stop *moving*,' Flit snapped again.

Nommo crouched down in front of Jin. 'Are you saying you can pick yourself up off the ground with majik?'

'Yup.'

'Shit, seriously? Is it like how the birds did it? Like actual flying? Do you flap your arms? Can you show us?'

'It's not flying –'

'No, no, no, no,' Pago said, swaying and shaking his head. 'No flying. Jin is a secret, remember?'

'Yeah, Valrue's worst-kept secret,' Nommo said. 'People have eyes, don't they? No one's going to forget what they saw at the Celebrations.'

Jin scowled. He could remember *that*.

'Come on, sir,' Meek pleaded. 'Just a little bit of flying.'

'It's *not* flying –'

'And it's *not* going to happen,' Pago interjected.

'But, sir,' Meek whined, 'you promised you'd tone it down!'

'You did, sir,' Flit drawled. 'I want to see you fly too,' she whispered in Jin's ear.

Pago screwed up his face in indecision.

'Please, sir,' said Nommo, 'the Kahnen said he could use majik if he really had to, and they said it was really important for us to know what he can do –'

'Ugh, you lot are so annoying!' Pago yelled, waving a hand. 'Fine! Jin, just do it.'

'I'm not sure –'

'For fuck's sake Jin, fly!'

'Okay . . . *okay.*' Jin made to stand up, but Flit tugged on his hair. 'Wait!' She reached out and grabbed the sleeve of his shirt, ripping a long strip from it.

'Hey!' Jin protested as he held up his ruined sleeve.

'That's not your shirt,' Meek said. 'It's mine.'

'Oh.'

Flit tied a knot at the end of Jin's thick blond braid. 'Done,' she said proudly. 'Now you can go fly,' she said, throwing out her arms.

'That's not how you do it,' Jin said, making a face at her as he staggered upright. 'You have to lift *up*. Like this.' Jin splayed his hands by his thighs and pulled them upwards, hurling his body skyward. He'd never gone so high so fast before; he'd left his stomach somewhere down below.

This time, there were clouds, the stars obscured. It didn't matter though because Filip wasn't here. Jin had drowned him in ale. He wondered vaguely if Aren might want to see the stars. He looked around for her, but she wasn't there either.

'You don't deserve to be sad about her,' Jin called out to the sky. 'You're the reason she isn't here!'

No one answered him. As he drifted, Jin thought he could vaguely feel his power seeping from him. Maybe. It was hard to tell with all the ale. Maybe he would just float along until he dropped from the sky. Or would he Turn first? Did it even hurt? Or did you die with all the happiness?

He had all these questions, and all the answers eluded him. There was so much about majik he didn't know. So far, his 'training' felt rather futile. He couldn't figure out if Stolt was just witless or had no intention of teaching him anything other than how to boil his own bones.

Jin lowered his hands, dropping himself closer to the city below. He looked down. He could see the bridge, the river beneath it, the lake. He spotted Aren's house, the Bha mansion, dark on the mountainside. He looked away quickly.

He spied the empty brothel, thinking of the women locked in their dungeon cell. Then he closed his fists and let himself fall.

CHAPTER 16:
LOTTIE

Lottie had suffered many humiliations in her life, but none so bad as this. With her hands encased in an iron ball in front of her, she could do nothing for herself that she wanted to. Instead, the women had to do it for her.

Thankfully, there was a female Krijen who seemed to sympathise with Lottie (and Eliza of course, her own hands having been cut off years ago for illegal harnessing), and the female Krijen did her best to give them privacy, moving the men with their leering eyes out of the cell across from the women.

Even though the women had each other, it was hard to stay positive. Twelve whores (plus Mama Hidel) crammed into a dungeon cell for months, all fearing for their lives and loved ones and hearing nothing had left their spirits lower than low. Especially because Maude must be dead.

Jin had never come back.

They knew he was alive because the other Krijen spoke of him. They called him KrijenMayj now though. Lottie wasn't sure what that meant, but it sounded like a good thing.

Lottie knew that Jin wouldn't leave Mama Hidel in the dark like this, not unless he was scared to tell her he'd failed. The women all knew what failure was to Jin. Lottie just hoped he wasn't beating himself up about it (he'd had enough of that from his father). She worried about him endlessly, especially as there was little else to do. She was almost tempted to ask that kind female Krijen if she might find Jin and let him know it was okay to visit even if he'd not been able to save Maude.

That was why it was such a pleasant surprise when Jin himself came stumbling out of the darkness towards them.

'Jin!' Lottie would have run to him, but she was manacled to the wall. The other women squealed and crowded around the cell bars, blocking her view. Eliza stayed back with her, her alabaster skin glowing with excitement.

Jin staggered up to the bars and reached through, smiling as the women pulled at him and ran their hands over his arms and face. He looked more handsome than ever, his blond hair braided back like how some of the Krijen wore it. He wore normal clothes instead of black wraps. One of his shirt sleeves was torn.

'Lottie!' Jin's brown eyes caught hers. They quickly widened in horror. 'No, no, no, no –'

Jin tugged back from the women and flicked his wrist, the lock on the cell door clicking. He pulled the door open and strode inside the cell, staggering over to Lottie. 'That is coming *off*,' he said, pointing to the iron ball. He made a twisting motion with his hands and the ball cracked down the middle, the two halves clattering to the floor.

Lottie cried out in pain, her hands stiff and raw from their extended imprisonment. Jin reached out and gently took her wrists, turning her hands over in his. His skin was hot to the touch (hotter than usual anyway), and they soothed her swollen joints.

'I'm so sorry,' Jin breathed on her. He reeked of ale. 'I should've done that earlier.'

'It's okay,' Lottie said. 'Thank you.' She desperately wanted him to stay, but the Krijen were strict. He would almost certainly get into trouble for talking to them, let alone being in their cell. 'You probably shouldn't be in here.'

'No, he shouldn't.'

The women turned to Mama Hidel. She stood in the corner of the cell, arms folded across her enormous bosom, her eyes on Jin.

Jin let go of Lottie and took a few unsteady steps towards Mama Hidel before stopping. He hung his head miserably, but he still towered over her.

'Mama, I –'

'I don't need to hear it,' Mama Hidel said sharply. 'It was enough that you tried.' There were tears in her eyes. The brothel owner stepped forward and embraced Jin. He was broad enough that Mama's arms couldn't wrap around all the way around him. Jin swayed in her grip. Mama Hidel let him go, stepping back and wiping her eyes.

'Was it quick? She didn't suffer?'

Jin shook his head. 'She wouldn't let me save her,' he said, his voice breaking. 'She *wanted* to go.'

Mama Hidel nodded. 'I know. Thank you for telling me.'

'I took too long to tell you –'

'You took as long as you needed, which is fine by me. I already knew anyway. I just don't know how I'm going to tell her mother.' The women were quiet.

Poor Mama. Poor Maude, Lottie thought.

Jin stumbled to the back wall of the cell and leaned against it, sliding down until he was sitting on the ground. 'I'll stay here for a bit,' he said. The women tittered, excited. Lottie shuffled over and tucked herself in next to him, unbelievably glad he was here and safe, however drunk and unhappy. They would soon fix that.

Eliza sat on Lottie's other side while Dhuna, Sari, and Aubrey settled in front of Jin. Mama Hidel tutted. 'No, Jin, you need to leave before they find you. You'll be in a world of trouble.'

'That's fine,' Jin grinned, his eyes unfocused. 'I don't mind cuts.'

'What do you mean?'

'Oh. These.'

Jin pulled back his torn shirt sleeve, revealing layers of white bandage beneath. His fingers fumbled to untie it. 'I already have a hundred and twenty – no. A hundred and fifty . . . No. I don't know.' He peeled back the bandages.

To Lottie's horror, his entire forearm was covered with deep cross-hatched slits, some of which still oozed blood.

'They just use the tip of a dagger, and . . .' Jin made a jerking gesture with his hand. The women gasped. Then they converged on him, all asking questions at once.

Lottie and Eliza exchanged looks as Jin tugged the bandage back down. He laid his head back against the wall, his eyes half open, looking lazily at Josefina while she spoke.

'That's Krijen for you,' Eliza sighed. 'Awful, isn't it?'

Lottie leant towards her, whispering so Jin wouldn't hear. 'He's not wearing his black wraps. Do you think he's off duty?'

'I hope so,' Eliza whispered back. 'Or he'll get more than cuts for this.'

'*Lottie.*'

Lottie jumped. She looked back to Jin, whose face was so close to hers she almost went crossed-eyed trying to focus on him.

'There is something I need to tell you.' Jin's eyes were shining. 'It's Aren. She's dead.'

Lottie blinked, shocked. 'Oh, Jin. I'm-I'm so sorry. How?'

Jin's face twisted. 'I don't . . . I don't want to say.'

'You –'

'Don't tell the others,' Jin whispered. 'Please, don't tell Mama Hidel.'

Lottie tensed at the sound of Krijen boots padding towards them. A young thick-set Krijen with a snub nose appeared behind the bars of their cell. 'Hello, ladies,' he said, folding his arms as his eyes locked onto Jin. 'Ah, Jin,' he chuckled. 'You haven't changed one bit.'

Jin groaned and closed his eyes, burrowing his face into Lottie's shoulder.

Dhuna got to her feet and sidled towards the young Krijen, her hips swaying. 'And who is this dashing young man?' Dhuna slipped her hands around the bars, running her eyes over him. Sari soon followed, standing up and placing her hands on Dhuna's waist, looking up at the newcomer from under her eyelashes. It always impressed Lottie how naturally they slipped into whoring.

'This is Nommo,' Jin mumbled into Lottie's shoulder before pulling his head back. 'He's a loud-mouth prick.'

'Hey!' Nommo said. 'I'm the loud-mouth prick who's going to save your arse. The only reason I don't strictly have to tell Pago you're here is because you're off duty. But even so . . .' Nommo eyed the open cell door. 'Come on, get out of there. I'm not getting more cuts because of you.'

'*No.*'

'Oh, for fuck's sake. Excuse me,' Nommo said, stepping into the cell. The women trailed their hands over him as he reached through and hauled Jin up by the arm. 'You know, you really shouldn't drink,' Nommo said. 'Though it *is* nice to see you smiling. Mind you, any man would smile surrounded by these beautiful women.' Nommo grinned unashamedly around at them. 'What are you all doing in here anyway?'

'I was hiding mayjen children in my brothel,' Mama Hidel said bluntly.

'Oh.' Nommo's eyebrows pulled together as he looked up at Jin's slack face. 'You really like playing with fire, don't you? Come on.'

Nommo dragged Jin out of the cell and slammed the door behind him. He pulled out a key and turned it in the lock.

Eliza leant through the bars as Nommo lead Jin away. 'You take care of him!'

Nommo didn't look back, but Jin turned and waved, a smile on his face as they disappeared into the shadows.

'I'm worried,' Eliza said quietly as she came back to Lottie. 'Look what they're doing to him.'

'I know. But maybe he'll start visiting now that he's not scared of telling us about Maude.'

'If he even remembers this,' Eliza said. 'That boy is a danger to himself. Let's hope that squad of his doesn't ruin him.'

CHAPTER 17:
SID BHA

'Do you mean to tell us,' Jakki said, her expression a little crazed, 'that there was an enormous mass of power trapped in the crater lake driving away nature? *That's* what caused the Unsettlement?'

Sid had to sit down. They were gathered in the kitchen of Jakki's house, wooden cabinets and a bench taking up one side of the room, a table and chairs in the middle, and a little sofa shoved against the back wall. Sid sank onto the edge of the sofa, placing a hand out to steady himself.

'But-but how?' Sid stammered. 'How could that possibly have happened? Noel?'

Noel looked as equally shocked as Jakki. 'I haven't got a clue,' he said. 'But it certainly explains the extent of the damage. The Deadlands were just so vast . . . And you say it's gone now, Drax?'

'I can't feel it anymore,' Drax said.

Aren sat up next to Drax on the sofa, suddenly alert. It was a relief to see she was getting stronger by the day, now able to get up and dress herself without help. She'd even borrowed a pair of maroon-coloured wraps from Jakki because she'd always preferred wraps to dresses or skirts. It made Sid happy to see her looking like herself again.

'We saw it happen,' Aren said. 'Wren and I, only we didn't know what it was. This surge of water came out of the sky. It must have been the lake exploding.'

Sid's breath caught at the name of the Lost Square, followed by a fresh wave of regret. He should never have told the thing about Aren. He felt sickened to know it had followed him back and snuck into Jakki's home to continue its perversions with his daughter. Aren had been profoundly duped, a victim of her own purity. Of course, Aren was incorrigible, no matter what they said to her.

Mae was understandably furious with Sid. It would have been so easy to leave the Lost Square thinking Aren had died. Aren would have moved on, she always did. She was never down for long.

Mae was struggling as much as Sid was in wondering where they'd gone wrong. They'd never spoken to Aren about Lost Squares because no one ever spoke about them. Acknowledging them gave further credence to their shameful existence. Everyone just *knew* that somehow. Everyone except Aren.

'Who's Wren?'

Sid cringed. Jakki didn't know. No one had been brave enough to tell her. When the Lost Square visited, they bore its presence in silence, their eyes averted. On multiple occasions now, Sid had found it sitting in the bedroom with Aren, indecently close. But nothing could be done. Nothing *should* be done. This inconceivable situation made Sid feel all kinds of wrong.

Aren lifted her nose in the air. 'Wren is –'

'Lost, Jakki,' Noel cut in.

'Lost? Wait. Lost as in *Lost?*' Jakki bristled as she turned to Aren. 'I don't know why you said that name, but I don't want to hear it ever again.' Everyone but Aren pointedly avoided her gaze. Jakki swelled as she looked around her kitchen. 'What don't I know?'

'Wren has been visiting me here,' Aren said brazenly. It amazed Sid that Aren didn't cower away from the murderous expression on Jakki's face. Jakki sucked in a deep breath. 'NOEL!'

Noel jumped as Jakki swung around, advancing on him. 'How *dare* you!' she screeched. 'I'm not having this. First, you bring Mandavar's son into my home, and now a *Lost Square?*'

Noel backed away from her, further retreat thwarted by the kitchen bench. 'Jakki, I'm sorry,' he said. 'We didn't realise Aren was –' he froze. 'Wait. Did you say *Mandavar's son?*'

'Oh, don't pretend you didn't know,' Jakki spat, pointing at Drax, who huddled closer to Aren on the sofa. 'How could you not? He's the spitting image of him!'

Noel looked stunned. 'I-I thought you were upset about Drax being here because he's wanted by the Krijen!'

Jakki gave Noel a withering look.

'I'm *so* sorry, Jakki. Truly, I didn't know.' Noel put a hand to his forehead. 'By the Great Kahn, how did I miss that?'

'I have no idea,' Jakki said snidely. 'And here I was thinking you were intelligent.'

Sid vaguely knew the name, but he didn't know why. 'Mandavar,' he said, 'who is that?'

Jakki backed down from Noel and folded her arms, leaning against the kitchen bench. 'Mandavar was a KahnenMayj. He was stupidly powerful with a matching ego and more arrogance than anyone has a right to. He hated the rest of us mayjen and treated us as inferior. Before the Unsettlement, in just a few short years as a KahnenMayj, Mandavar single-handedly turned even the most sympathetic of the People against us. He was a despicable, selfish man,' she added, looking over at Drax, who blinked back at her.

Mae folded her arms and frowned at Jakki. 'Us? You're a mayj?'

Jakki rounded on Noel again, who flinched. 'You never told them about me?'

'I wanted to protect you.'

'Oh please. Didn't they ever ask why you keep that dirty beard?'

Noel glared at her. 'Few people are so bold as you, Jakki.'

Aren was practically bouncing on the sofa. 'I asked!' she said. 'But Noel refused to tell me. Why do you have a beard, Noel?'

'Because –'

'Because I threw one of my pots at his face when he said he was leaving,' Jakki said loudly, 'which he sorely deserved. He's got a scar on his chin to prove it, but he hides it beneath that hideous beard because he hides everything.'

Jakki ignored Noel's warning look.

'Jakki, I have *so* many questions for you,' Aren said eagerly. 'Are you himajik?'

'Ugh, that word is infuriating. I'm a Builder, an average one at that.' Everyone looked at her blankly, except Noel, who shook his head. Jakki glowered at him. 'Have you told them *anything*?'

'No,' Noel muttered. 'Like I said, I wanted to keep you and them safe. You've always been too open about your majik.'

'That's because I'm not ashamed of what I am.'

Noel's face darkened, but Jakki had already looked back towards Aren. 'So there are actually different types of mayjen. Different expressions, I think, is the official term. Most people know mayjen can move things with majik because all mayjen do that, but Builders are mayjen who also create majikal bonds between matter. It means we can put things back together after Breaking or manipulating the bits of them.' She shrugged. 'So that's what I do. But don't bother asking me more. I know the basic jargon but not enough to explain anything to you properly. I was never formally taught anything about majik, unlike Noel, so everything I know is just down to him and my own experimentation.'

Sid met Noel's eyes, who gave him an apologetic look. 'I know I never told you much about my past,' Noel said quietly.

'Your life is your business,' Mae cut in. 'But it makes me sad to think you're ashamed of what you can do.'

'You're brilliant, Noel,' Aren said with a smile. She turned back to Jakki. 'So what are the mayjen types? Or expressions, did you say? Are they something to do with harnessing ability? Or is it do with power?'

Jakki opened her mouth to reply, but Noel cut across her. 'Not today, Aren,' he said. 'We will talk about majik another time. I promise.'

Aren gave him a sour look. 'How about Mandavar then? I don't think

Drax knows anything about him.'

'He wouldn't want to, either,' Jakki said. 'Mandavar slept happily in his bed in the KahnenKeep, shoving his superiority down our throats while the rest of us lived in fear of being attacked in the streets. I was a part of a group of activists –'

'Extremists,' Noel said under his breath.

'– who fought to maintain peace between the majikal and non-majikal community. This was before Noel joined me, of course.' Noel winced, and Jakki ignored him, continuing her explanation. 'Any progress we made to relieve the tensions, Mandavar would tear down in seconds. He had a real talent for it.' Jakki had an ugly look on her face. 'It still makes me angry to talk about it though it doesn't matter anymore. Mandavar disappeared a few years before the Unsettlement. He's long gone.' Jakki looked over at Drax. 'Just to be clear, I like Drax much more than his father. But *no*,' – she directed a vicious look towards Aren – 'to go back to the original issue at hand, I'm not having a Lost Square here. You invite that thing back again, that's it, I'm kicking you all out.'

Sid watched nervously as Aren snapped her wrist wraps, clearly agitated. He closed his eyes, wishing that just this once Aren would listen.

When Sid opened them again, to his immense relief, Aren was nodding. 'Fine,' she said. 'But I don't have a way to tell him not to come, he just shows up –'

'It will not come into my house,' Jakki said. 'No excuses.'

Sid didn't envy anyone being on the wrong side of Jakki, but if he had to wish it on anyone, it would be the Lost Square.

'Going back to majik,' Jakki said, making Noel groan softly, 'Drax, what are you going to do about Aren?'

Drax tucked his head into his shoulders. Other than by Aren, he was rarely asked questions. 'I don't understand,' he said.

'Once she's healed, you still have to keep her heart going, right?'

'Yes.'

'So what? You're going to follow her around forever?'

Aren looked taken aback. 'What? Drax, you can't do that.'

'Yes, I can.'

Aren's jaw dropped. 'Absolutely not! You can't be stuck with me forever! You need a life. *I* need a life –'

'I agree,' Jakki said. 'Noel, any ideas?'

Noel shook his head. 'I don't know how to fix this. I'm telling the truth,' he insisted as Jakki made a tutting sound. 'You overestimate me. I don't even know how Drax is doing what he's doing.'

Jakki turned back to Aren. 'Well, in that case, you need to go to the University. They'll be your best chance –'

'*Jakki!*' Noel cried. 'Don't! Please, just . . . don't.'

But Aren had already latched on. 'The University? You mean a place where people go to learn stuff? Like in your books, Noel?'

Noel looked furious. 'Yes, that's what a university is.'

Sid was confused. 'There is no university in Valrue. I remember the Kahnen discussing it once, years ago, but with the worsening Unsettlement, we weren't able to source the resources required to build one –'

'I didn't mean a university in Valrue,' said Jakki. 'I mean *the* University in Holu Mon.'

Oh, Sid thought. It had been so long since he'd heard that name. He wondered why Jakki bothered mentioning it. The suggestion of leaving Valrue was preposterous. For starters, it wasn't possible.

Aren's head was whipping between them. 'Holu – what? Hold on. I know that name . . .'

'It's another city,' Sid explained. Aren would have likely read of it in Noel's books. She seemed to remember everything she read.

Noel was glaring at Jakki once more. 'Don't be ridiculous, Jakki. I can't believe you would suggest such a thing.'

'You want us to go to Holu Mon?' Aren's face lit up with excitement. 'You want us to *leave* Valrue? I didn't think that was possible!'

'It's not –'

'Yes, it is,' Jakki said.

Noel turned to her. 'Oh yes? And how do you propose we do it? The journey would take *months*. We'd be lucky not to die in the Deadlands, and that's only if we even get out of *Rue* because we'd be travelling with the most wanted person in the city –'

'You don't have to go through the Deadlands,' Jakki said. 'The Bhouli can send you by river.' A ringing silence followed these words. 'That's right,' Jakki said, 'I've learned a few things since you walked out on me, Noel.'

'What river?' Aren cried. 'How do we find it? Where are the Bhouli?'

Sid whimpered at the look on his daughter's face. There would be no stopping her now.

CHAPTER 18:
JIN KANJU

It had been eighteen days or twenty-three days or something like that since Jin had killed Aren. His arm was smarting where, at some point, he'd earned himself thirty more cuts for being late to his post outside the KahnenChambers. Pago was livid.

'What the fuck, Jin? Look, I know you're hurting and all, but you've got to pull yourself together. This isn't like you.'

Jin barely heard him. That endless ringing in his head was particularly bad today. He was hungry all the time too because he was harnessing so much more with his majik training, and that was making him vile towards everyone.

The worst thing was that Jin didn't care because Aren kept coming around in her midnight-blue wraps, the ones she'd died in, right when he didn't expect it. So he spent his days in a constant state of apprehension, dreading her appearance, which may or may not leave him gasping on the floor.

Last night, he'd gone down into the dungeons intending to see Mama Hidel's women, so desperate to speak with them he'd literally been standing around the corner from their cell, tensed on the balls of his feet to take that next step into the light, the selfish temptation unbearable. He had a vague feeling he'd stood in the same spot before.

After a few torturous minutes when he'd finally worked up the courage to take a step forward, Filip started yelling at him and wouldn't let up until Jin had turned away. Because of Maude.

After that, Jin returned to the bunkroom and stalked past his squad, brushing off their concerned looks as they got ready for bed. He threw himself down on his bunk, fully clothed, not bothering to underdress because there was no point; he wouldn't sleep.

Time wasn't linear anymore either. Jin swore it jumped from night to day in an instant, and the only way he could tell how many days it had been since he'd killed Aren was that he gouged a little notch on the underside of the bunk above him whenever he lay down under it. It was a terrible measure of time, but it was the best he could manage.

'You're a mess, Jin,' Filip kept telling him. But once Jin thought he heard Jokah say it though it didn't seem right to hear that from Jokah. Jin wasn't sure of himself after that.

One time – like now, perhaps – when he was vaguely more aware of his surroundings, he noticed it was dark outside. Flit was there, standing next to him in the corridor outside of their bunkroom. One of her eyes was still black and purple and yellow after Jin had knocked her out. He thought it had been weeks since then but maybe not. Unless he'd punched her again during his training. He couldn't remember. He'd never apologised for the first time, but he figured it was too late now had he felt inclined.

'Jin, I have news,' Flit said.

Jin was staring out the window at the city. He wasn't sure where he was supposed to be, so he'd stopped here, and that seemed good enough. When Flit spoke, Jin grabbed his daggers from his thigh wraps, turning around, ready for whatever she had to say. Flit eyed them for a moment, then reached out and took them from him, prying his fingers off the hilts. 'I'm not going to attack you. Look at me.'

Jin returned his gaze to her, having looked away when she'd taken his weapons.

'What's wrong, Jin?'

Filip laughed. 'How long does she have?'

Jin said nothing.

Flit took a step closer. 'What do you need then?'

'Nothing. I'm fine.'

Flit folded her arms, eyes flashing. 'I'm trying to help you. Do me the courtesy of telling the truth. Just give me something. *Anything.*'

'Why do you want to help me? I don't deserve it.'

'Don't I know it,' Flit said, pointing to her eye. 'Nommo too. His arm is going to take weeks to heal.'

Jin frowned. He didn't remember what happened to Nommo's arm. 'Sorry.'

'Are you? Because I think you did it on purpose.'

'They're figuring you out,' Filip said.

'Shut up,' Jin snapped at him.

'I will not!' Flit shoved Jin in the chest. 'I guess that's sixty cuts for me then,' she said loudly. Jin looked down at her and frowned. Her hands had felt cold against his chest.

After a pause, she shoved him again, harder this time, so he had to take a step backwards to keep his balance. 'Sixty more,' she said.

'You're making her crazy, too,' Filip said, staring at Flit.

When Jin didn't respond, Flit raised her hands again. Jin held his hands up in surrender. 'Flit, *stop*. What are you doing?'

'Finally! A normal response!'

'I'm not telling Pago you pushed me,' Jin said stubbornly.

'No, I'll do that, thank you,' Flit said. 'But I'm going to keep doing it until you tell me one *fucking* thing you need.'

'Don't make her hurt herself, Jin,' Aren said, stepping from nowhere to stand next to Flit. 'Please.'

All the anger and heat and fight in Jin left him at Aren's expression. His arms sagged, and he looked at the ground. 'I'm sorry,' he said to Aren. What he needed, he couldn't have. And it seemed unfair for him to ask when she was standing right next to him. The fact that Jin had any kind of Aren at all was definitely more than he deserved.

'What I *want* is to talk to Aren's father,' Jin said to Flit.

'Sid Bha? The Weapon's Master who escaped with Oji's murderer?'
Jin swallowed. 'Yeah.'

'Jeez, Jin.' But Flit was giving him a curious look. 'Why?'

'To say sorry.'

Flit was quiet. Jin had no idea what she was thinking. 'Just that you're crazy,' Filip said again. He was trying to make Jin angry. He wanted Jin to keep his shell.

'It's funny you've said that,' Flit said, 'because what I came to tell you was that we know where Sid Bha is.'

Jin was astonished.

'I don't know quite where you've been lately with your head and all,' Flit went on, 'but the Krijen have been scouring the city for him since he escaped with Oji's killer. Jokah and Pago have been helping the city roamers. They mentioned today that Sid Bha was spotted recently.'

Flames roared up in Jin's chest at the thought of catching the skahk. His hands shot to his thighs, but Flit was still holding his daggers.

'We've not seen the mayj who killed Oji,' Flit said, 'nor anyone else who was with Sid Bha that night. Just him. We wanted to inform the FaKrijen before saying anything, but he's still out in the Deadlands, and we've had word that he's not coming back anytime soon. So that's why I'm telling you.'

Jin's restless hands twitched. 'Well?' he demanded. 'What are we going to do?'

'That's Pago's call. He's not wanting anyone to go, not yet. We don't know what we are up against.'

'Where is he? Where is Sid?'

Flit didn't reply.

'Please, Flit, where is he?'

'If I tell you, you'll go. And you'll get worse than cuts for that.'

'She's right,' said Filip.

'Come on,' Jin pressed. 'You asked me what I need? I need this.'

'Look,' Flit said, 'I won't *tell* you. But if it helps you get out of this' – she waved her hands at him – 'muddle that you're in, I'll lead you there.'

'How is that better? That just means we will both get in trouble.'

'Someone has to have your back.'

'No, they don't. I don't want you to get in trouble for me.'

'I don't care. You're not going alone. I won't let you.'

Jin ran his fingers through his hair. Flit was so much braver than he was. It wasn't brave if you truly didn't care about what happened, like how he felt. And even though Flit said she didn't care, she clearly did.

'Oji should have picked you,' Jin said.

'Picked me for what?'

'To lead.'

Flit shook her head. 'No, not me.' Then she gasped, and her eyes twinkled. 'By the Great fucking Kahn, maybe *that's* the problem.'

Flit held out Jin's daggers. He took them and slid them back into his wraps, giving her an accusatory look. 'When you took these, you said you wouldn't attack me,' he said, thinking of how she'd kept shoving him.

Flit shrugged. 'I lied.' She grabbed his hand. 'Come on!'

Jin went willingly this time, his arms and chest aching at the thought of seeing Sid. His thoughts were screaming at each other, all clamouring to know what to say to him. But Jin soon realised they weren't heading to the city. Flit was leading him further into the KahnenKeep. 'Wait,' Jin said, pulling back on her, 'you said you would take me to Sid –'

'I will! But we need to do something first.'

Perplexed, Jin let Flit tug him along to the dining hall of all places. He'd thought it was night-time because of the darkness outside, but the smell of shitty breakfast maize wafting from the dining hall proved him wrong; it must be early morning. Several Krijen were already there, including the rest of Jin's squad. Flit dragged him over to where they were sitting.

'We wondered where you two were,' Nommo said, eyeing their clasped hands. As Flit had said, his arm was splinted. Jin still couldn't remember when that had happened.

Flit let go of Jin's hand and pointed to the bench. 'Sit down. I'll get you food.' As she trotted off, Nommo wiggled his eyebrows at Jin. 'Flit to the rescue, aye?'

'Don't,' Jin warned. 'I'm not above punching you again.'

Nommo laughed. 'Wow, a joke? What did Flit say to you?'

'That wasn't a joke. It was a threat.'

Flit shoved an enormous bowl of maize under Jin's nose. He was growing impatient. 'Flit, you said you would take –'

'And I *will*. Everyone,' – the others looked over to her – 'I vote to change squad leader.'

'FINALLY!' Pago yelled, making everyone in the dining hall look around at him. Pago closed his eyes, a massive grin on his swollen face. Maybe his nose was still healing from when Jin had broken it. Or maybe something had happened more recently than that.

'I've been squad leader for *eight months*. Seriously, guys? Jin, *eat*,' Pago snapped. 'I'm still leader for the next minute at least, so that's an order.'

Jin threw him a salty look and obeyed. He *was* hungry. Filip sat down opposite Jin and watched him shovel in food. 'Flit said she would lead us to Sid,' Filip said. 'Does she need to do this *now*?'

'Be patient,' Aren said from next to Filip. 'I trust Flit. As soon as she's voted in as squad leader, we can go without fear of being reprimanded under her command. It's a good plan. It'll save you some cuts, Jin,' she added. It was the most that Aren had spoken since Jin killed her. Jin stopped eating for a second, staring at her.

'Everyone in favour of making Jin squad leader, raise your hand,' said Flit.

Distracted by his name, Jin glanced up at his squad. They were all looking at him. They all had their hands up too, appearing mighty proud of themselves.

'Wait,' said Jin. 'What? *No* –'

'Sir,' they chorused, raising their hands to their clavicles in salute.

'Oh, fuck no,' Jin said, dropping his spoon. 'You can't –'

'You can't *not,* sir,' Jokah said. 'It's discourteous to decline squad leadership.'

'You can't deny a one hundred per cent win,' Meek grinned.

'I didn't vote!'

'You don't count.'

'Take it, Jin,' Pago said. 'For fuck's sake, take it. I'm sick of cutting you.'

'Jin, don't you see?' Flit smiled at him. 'Oji wanted you to lead. You haven't been leading. You've been trying to follow. This feels right, doesn't it?'

Jin shook his head as everyone nodded in agreement.

'Jin,' Filip said, leaning forward across the table, '*do it,* you idiot. You can go to Sid now.'

Jin stood up. 'Take me to where Sid is.'

'Absolutely, sir,' Jokah said. 'But please, can you finish that bowl of maize first?'

***

The run into Rue was the longest of Jin's life. He imagined this is what it felt like to go to the gallows, or to be strung up, or to be beheaded. You could try to escape the inevitable, but eventually, it caught up with you. So you just had to go.

It was also over far too quickly.

They were almost there; the sun was well up now. Jin still didn't know what he was going to say to Sid. He expected Mae would be there too, and Noel, and maybe even Bish. And if he could catch them without that skahk, then maybe he could help them. He hoped his squad would understand.

'They don't have to understand,' Filip reminded him. 'You are squad leader now. You can order them away, and they won't get in trouble for it. You know that's why they did this, right? So you're responsible for your own mistakes?'

Yes, Jin thought. For once, he was glad to be squad leader. The only person he was going to make suffer was himself now. Flit was brilliant.

'When was Sid last seen?' Jin asked his squad as they ran.

145

'A few weeks ago,' Pago admitted, 'but we monitored the tower closely. He's not left. We think it's him based on the description, but the Krijen who saw him weren't certain because they'd never seen him up close. The Weapon's Master kept to himself a lot.' Pago scowled. 'I guess now we know why. You can't recognise someone if you don't know what they look like.'

Jin stayed quiet. He didn't like the way Pago spoke about Sid. Sid wasn't like that. Well, he hadn't been.

Nommo read Jin's mind. 'You think you know Sid Bha, Jin, but that skahk got to him. You can't trust him anymore.'

People watched them suspiciously as the squad made their way down the street. Knowing their black wraps would draw attention, they'd dressed in plain clothes, but Jin still felt glaringly obvious. They moved in a way that was undeniably Krijen, impossible to untrain. The least they could do was split up.

He slowed to a stop, his squad with him. 'Meek and Nommo, come in from the north streets. Flit and Pago, take the east. Jokah, west. I'll cover the south. It won't take me long to get there, so just give it a few minutes, then move in.'

Jin's squad nodded. Jokah looked up at the buildings stacked towards the sky. 'We know which one it is, sir, but that's as far as we got. I'm not sure if you've been inside the towers of Rue before, but they are a right nuisance. You can get lost quickly.'

'I won't,' Jin said. 'I was born in one.'

'What? I thought you were from Val?'

Jin shook his head. 'I moved there later.'

'You made the Cross? Jin, that's incredible.'

'I was seven. It had nothing to do with me. My father did it.'

Jin saw Nommo tighten his grip on his daggers. He knew what Nommo was thinking – that Jin's father didn't deserve the respect he got for that.

Jin ran his hands over the hilts of his own daggers, this time tucked in at his wrists. He had scoured the streets on the way here, and there had been no Krijen roamers, their numbers spread desperately thin since the

Unsettlement. After only a few months in the city, Jin understood that was part of the reason Rue was the way it was. No matter how many years they trained and how hard they were to kill, there simply weren't enough Krijen to meet the demands of the population anymore.

Not enough to fight fair with the streetlings either.

Pago said the Great Kahn had requested the city-based squad leaders increase Kahnen protection. It was a valid request, considering the threats made against them at the Celebrations, but to do so, they had to pull Krijen out of Rue. Jin didn't like it. It seemed wrong to subject the citizens of Rue to the whims of the streetling gangs so the Kahnen could sleep in their beds at night.

'Fraught with naughty thoughts, are we?' Filip was giving him a sly look. 'You're quick to criticise the Kahnen now.'

'This is the People's fault,' Aren said, 'isn't it? For voting them in?'

Jin shook his head. 'No,' he said quietly. 'It's the Krijen's. For letting the Kahnen do this to us.'

Having forgotten where he was, Jin looked around at his squad, amazed his mind had wandered so far with the possibility of the skahk being so close. His squad frowned at him but said nothing. They were probably used to him talking to himself.

'Stay outside,' Jin commanded. 'Monitor the exits. I'll be fine in the tower.'

Jokah and Flit gave him hesitant looks, but they nodded along with the others.

'Go,' Jin said. His squad took off in their allocated directions. Jin began to run, slipping through archways and between alleyways and through doors he knew would lead him somewhere. It had been fifteen years since he'd lived in Rue, and it wasn't the Left South Side where he'd grown up, but it all came back to him anyway as though it were only yesterday he'd run through these streets with no shoes on.

Jin slowed as he approached the south side of the tower, eventually stopping in front of the open doorway at its base. He could see the spiralling staircase beyond.

'What are you going to say to him?'

Jin glanced sideways at Filip. 'I don't know,' he said. He looked to his other side, searching for Aren. She wasn't there. Maybe she didn't want to see this.

Jin closed his eyes, feeling for the skahk. There was no antipathy, no familiar dread. Not from the skahk, anyway. Just the regular kind that made his veins burn.

Jin opened his eyes and walked into the tower.

CHAPTER 19:
PYRA

Eventually, Pyra stopped procrastinating. It probably had something to do with the fact her sixteenth birthday was looming, a jarring reminder that time was passing faster than she realised.

Earlier that morning, she'd told Rifter everything. He took it well, even better than Juno. Pyra hoped she could trust him. Even if he wasn't completely convinced, she was confident Rifter would go along with it, at least for a bit just to see how things played out.

So with Rifter, Barrett, and three other streetlings in tow, they headed towards Turning Point.

As Rifter predicted, the girl was not there. *It* was. The Lost Square was leaning against a wall looking into space with that perpetual scowl it wore. Its hair was stupidly long, long enough that it had to tie it up in a knot. It had also let the hair on its face grow out since she'd last seen it, which made it even ickier than Pyra thought possible. Other than the haughty, stuck-up look and the boots it wore, the Lost Square barely looked like a Square anymore. Pyra wondered if it had done that on purpose to stop people from knowing what it was.

As if *that* was ever going to happen.

It reeked of disgrace. It rolled off it in waves, festering in the streets of the Lower West Side.

Pyra had expected fewer people would go to the Point with the girl gone, assuming her disappearance would help the problem. Then once the Turners all accidentally offed themselves, the Lost Square would have no one left to save, and he would soon be gone too. But the idiots still came, desperate as they were. So Pyra decided it was best not to wait any longer.

Pyra and Rifter chose to execute their plan mid-morning, so the Lost Square would be tired. Pyra had sent some of her gang to pester the residents during the night, so the thing had spent the last eight hours fending off over-excited streetlings. They'd left the Point a while ago now, so the Lost Square would be thinking about taking a nap, assuming Pyra's minions were done with their fun. The Turners were more alert during the day and more able to defend themselves while it slept. The Lost Square wouldn't be worried about itself. No one dared look at it, let alone *touch* it, which was why Pyra was certain it wouldn't see them coming.

Ugh. This was going to be so unpleasant.

It was a credit to Pyra's vicious character that the streetlings she'd gathered for phase one of the plan agreed to go along with it, no questions asked. They must *really* like their tongues.

Pyra waved her hand behind her. Barrett and two of the bigger streetlings, both ladened with lassoed ropes and belts, hurried down the street and disappeared around the corner, hunkering into the shadows.

The youngest streetling, Ala, trotted off after them, stopping just outside the mouth of the Point. She didn't hide but stood slightly out of the Lost Square's line of vision at the ready. Pyra was certain it wouldn't recognise her. They'd even stuck Ala in a pink dress and wrestled her knotted blonde hair into two bunches atop her head so that she looked less like a streetling. She looked ridiculous.

Pyra pulled her floppy black hat from her head and rolled it up, shoving it into the back of her pants under her shirt. She didn't want to lose it.

Pyra nodded to Rifter, who backed against the wall. She crouched down beside him, rubbing her wrist where she'd tucked an old horseshoe into her red wrist ties, its end filed down to points. She thought longingly of her crossbow, which that stupid KrijenMayj had exploded into tiny pieces. Ah well. It wasn't likely to be helpful here anyway. Pyra had agreed specifically *not* to injure the Lost Square, which was going to make this even harder. She hoped the others would get carried away. Then it wouldn't be her fault.

Pyra peered around the corner at the Lost Square. It was still gazing at nothing, like a moron. She gave Ala a big thumbs up. Preluded by a scarily wicked grin for a seven-year-old, Ala opened her mouth and let out a high-pitched scream.

The Lost Square's head snapped up. It pulled a dagger from inside its sleeve and sprinted towards the street mouth where they stood. As it ran, Ala zipped backwards down the street, her footsteps purposefully loud as she pounded away from them. She screeched to a stop in the distance and dove down the alleyway where Barrett and the others were waiting. She let out another scream just as the Lost Square skidded around the corner of the Point.

What a sucker, Pyra thought, watching from the shadows as it took off after her voice.

Pyra and Rifter ran after it, matching their light steps with the soft sound of its boots to cover their pursuit. Squares could sneak, but so could streetlings. They were right behind it when it stopped just ahead of them, staring down the empty alleyway after Ala.

'Now!' Pyra screamed.

A wide loop of rope sailed over the Lost Square's head and snatched tight about its torso, locking both arms by its sides. Barrett leapt from the shadows and dragged a black hood over its head, throwing his whole body down onto it. The Lost Square swore, stumbling under Barrett's weight. Another streetling threw himself at the Lost Square's feet, looping a belt buckle around its ankles and yanking it tight. The Lost Square toppled to the side with a beautiful crunch, tangled in streetlings.

Then to Pyra's fury, it kicked a foot free of the belt and somehow got its dagger under the loop of rope, slicing right through it.

Bellowing commands, Pyra threw herself forward and pinned the Lost Square's dagger-wielding arm to the ground while Barrett wrestled with the other. The burly streetling boy slammed both knees down onto its shoulders, pressing them into the dirt so it couldn't get momentum to swing itself upright.

'Get its leg!' Pyra screeched.

The streetling holding the cut rope tossed it aside and threw himself down onto the Lost Square's unbelted leg, promptly earning himself a knee to the face. However, he was a determined little sucker, and the streetling wrapped himself around tightly about the leg as it kicked furiously.

Pyra was attempting to pry the Lost Square's fingers from its dagger, but the thing was holding on with superhuman strength. Snarling, she dug her nails into the quick of its fingers until the Lost Square swore again and let go. Pyra tossed the dagger backwards into the street, out of reach. She nodded to Rifter who raced forward, more rope in hand. But he was too late.

The Lost Square had gotten its arm out from under Barrett and thrown a blind punch, clocking him on his chin and knocking him sideways. Quick as a flash, Ala leapt forward and grabbed the Lost Square's fist in her hands, biting down on its knuckles. It howled and flailed its fist, but Ala didn't let go. Pyra felt a spike of pride, impressed and a little disgusted by Ala's dedication. There was no way Pyra would put any part of that thing in her mouth.

With a yell, Barrett righted himself and grabbed the arm that Ala had latched onto. He pulled it around, trying to lock it in behind the Lost Square's back as it twisted in their grip. Rifter stood at the ready, holding more rope, but the Lost Square was thrashing madly, throwing the streetlings around while they clung to their respective limbs.

Pyra was pissed.

She wished she had Trigger back, their little streetling mayj. He would sure come in handy right now. The Lost Square had *five* streetlings on it, and it was all they could do to keep it pinned. It was too strong. They needed to fight dirtier.

Pyra sat down on the Lost Square's forearm and held out an empty hand. 'Throw me the belt!' she yelled. The streetling clinging to the Lost Square's leg snatched the belt from the ground next to him and tossed it to her.

'Rifter! Hold this arm down!'

Rifter dived down beside her, trapping the arm as ordered.

Pyra had no qualms about what she was about to do. Normally, doing such a thing to a living, breathing creature would sicken her, even just a little, even if it was necessary. Like the tongue thing.

But Lost Squares didn't count.

Pyra threw the belt around the Lost Square's neck, sliding the leather tongue through the buckle and pulling it tight. She heaved backwards. The Lost Square thrashed even harder, straining against the streetlings.

Pyra wasn't really sure how long she needed to hold on for. The idea was to make it dizzy so that it wouldn't struggle so much. She wondered where the line was, between it passing out and it dying on her. Hopefully she wouldn't miss the line, or she was in for a lot of grief.

After a crazy long time, its silent thrashing weakened.

'Now!'

Barrett and Rifter leapt to their feet. They dragged the Lost Square's arms behind its back and tied its hands together. Once they were knotted tightly, Pyra loosened the belt.

The Lost Square coughed and gasped and wheezed under the hood for ages before choking out a few well-thought-out words. 'What the *fuck*, Pyra?'

Squares and their foul mouths.

For good measure, Pyra wrapped another loop of rope around the Lost Square's torso to lock its arms by its sides and tied more rope between its ankles, so it could walk but couldn't take big steps. Eventually the Lost Square was nicely trussed. The streetlings all stood around it, panting and beaming at each other.

'Search it,' Pyra ordered.

They pulled a large collection of weapons from under its shirt, more daggers from its pants, and knives from down the sides of its boots. Pyra loaded herself up with them, using her red ties to strap the weapons to her forearms. Lastly, she picked up its dagger from where she'd tossed it into the street.

Barrett and Rifter hauled the Lost Square to its feet. It had stopped coughing and gone quiet but stood on its own, which was a good sign she hadn't killed too many brain cells. Not that killing off its brain cells would bother her, but she wasn't sure if it counted as hurting it or not because you couldn't see stupid. The only real injury they'd given it was a bloody, toothy half-moon across one of its knuckles. Ala's fabulous work.

Pyra shooed away the other streetlings so it would just be her, Barrett, and Rifter. As they left, Ala skipped over, leaning up on her tippy toes to whisper in Pyra's ear. 'Did I do good?'

'You did good. I said go away.'

'Where are you taking it?'

Pyra grabbed the little girl by one of her blonde bunches. 'I don't care how pretty your hair is, Ala. If you ignore an order one more time, I will scalp you, understand?'

Ala scarpered off after the others. Pyra would have to watch her. Ala was too ambitious for her own good.

Pyra jerked her head towards the Upper West Side. Barrett and Rifter grabbed the Lost Square by the shoulders and steered it forcefully after Pyra.

They caught a heck of a lot of attention on their march through Rue, but it was the good kind. Pyra had a reputation to maintain and leading someone hooded through the streets as though bound for execution looked great in her opinion. The People and the other streetlings didn't know it was the Lost Square, not with the cover over its face. Pyra didn't know how people would react to that, but she was pretty sure it would help their cause. The Lost Square had been undermining her authority after all. But she was smarter than to test her theory, especially without discussing it first.

It was about an hour's walk to their destination. Pyra fell back to trail behind the two other streetlings and their captive, watching the Lost Square scratching at the ropes at its wrists. Its fingers were slowly turning blue. Ah well.

They ducked into one of the innumerous rickety towers of Rue. They had to drag the thing up the steep spiralling staircase mostly because it kept tripping. It was rather annoying but partly their fault. The Lost Square might not trip so much if it could see where it was going.

They headed off onto a landing and through a maze of doors and rooms, passing more curious faces. Eventually, they came to the faded door with the old knocker. Pyra stood close to the door and surreptitiously pulled a key from her red wrist ties, sliding it into the lock. It was so well-oiled it didn't even click as she twisted it.

The door swung open into a small, circular room. It was warm, the sun streaming in through the open windows and lighting up the low wooden table in the middle and the cushions snuggled in their chairs. A woman – Pyra's partner – was sitting in one of them, looking rather regal in her silk robes, still dressed to impress despite not being in character. Pyra had already given her a heads-up about Barrett and Rifter, and the woman ran a critical eye over them as they pulled their captive into the room.

Pyra was just about to close the door behind them when the Lost Square stomped a foot down onto Barrett's. The streetling howled and let the Lost Square go to grab his foot, hopping on one leg. The Lost Square shouldered into Barrett, sending him sprawling over the low table. Rifter threw himself at the Lost Square and knocked it into the wall, but Rifter wasn't nearly as burly as Barrett and his own momentum sent him bouncing backwards. The Lost Square stuck out a foot and Rifter tripped over it, landing in a pile at the Lost Square's feet.

Pyra slammed the door shut and leapt forward, yelling as she flung herself against the Lost Square, which crunched back into the wall.

'Oi!' Pyra yelled at it. 'Will you quit being a dick for just *one second*?' She reached up and ripped the hood off its head.

The Lost Square's bloodshot eyes darted about the room, taking in the open window, the woman sitting on the couch, and the closed door to its right. Then it hoicked up a loogie and spat it right in Pyra's face. She screamed and smacked it upside the head.

'Pyra! Stop that right now,' her partner rebuked. 'You don't need to be in character!'

'I'm *not*,' Pyra hissed, not taking her eyes off the Lost Square. Using her sleeve, she wiped its saliva off her face, shuddering.

Rifter and Barrett dragged themselves to their feet and edged towards the Lost Square. 'Don't you fucking come *near* me,' it snarled. Rifter glanced at Pyra, who shook her head.

Her partner stood up, walking slowly towards the Lost Square, watching its expression change from murderous to one of shocked recognition. 'Hello,' she said to it with a grimace.

Pyra understood. It wasn't a pleasant experience feeling the eyes of a Lost Square on you. It was violating.

'I would say it is a pleasure to meet you,' Pyra's partner continued, 'but I think you would see through that. Do you know who I am?'

The Lost Square ran its eyes over her. Pyra could see the cogs turning, trying to figure out what was going on. 'You're one of the Kahnen,' it said in a voice that sounded like grinding cobblestones. Its throat was probably swelling from being strangled.

'That's right,' Pyra's partner said. 'I'm a member of the Eighth House. My name is Lady Hia.'

CHAPTER 20:
SID BHA

Sid's heart stopped. Somehow, Jin was standing in the doorway leading from the tower stairwell, looking at him. His tall frame blocked the exit.

'Jin? What are you doing here?'

'Sid, I'm so sorry.'

Noel had been speaking to Jakki by the kitchen bench. Sid saw Noel turn his head, then leap back in shock.

Sid had expected to hate Jin or at least feel angry at his appearance, but Sid couldn't see past the memory of the little boy with the bruised face that Aren had brought to their doorstep seventeen years ago. That was how scared Jin looked right now.

Mae slowly stood up from her chair, her whole body trembling. Jin turned to her. 'Mae, I didn't mean to do it. Please believe me.'

Mae said nothing. She looked as shocked as Noel. Sid's thoughts whirred. Jin was an enemy now, wasn't he? Was he here to arrest them? He wasn't wearing Krijen wraps, and he appeared to be alone. But that didn't mean he was.

'Jin?' Aren appeared in the bedroom doorframe, wearing Jakki's maroon wraps. Sid closed his eyes, hoping Drax wouldn't follow her.

Sid didn't know what Jin would do if he saw Drax. The last time, he'd tried to kill him.

Thankfully, Aren didn't run to Jin. She stayed where she was, her hand clutching the doorframe, a barrier, perhaps to stop Drax from coming through. Her other hand floated down to rest lightly on her thigh. She'd taken to carrying her daggers again, saying she felt strange without them. Sid recognised the gold and black hilt of the cardonite one he had given her.

A disturbing thought crashed into Sid. Aren had begun sparring after the rally, after meeting the Lost Square. Was the Lost Square the reason? Had she been frightened of it, and learning to fight properly had been a plight to protect herself before it had gotten to her? But right now the Lost Square wasn't the problem. It was Jin who was scaring his daughter because he wanted Drax dead. Sid held his breath, terrified of how Jin would react when he saw Aren.

But Jin didn't look at Aren. Instead, he took a step towards Sid.

'Sid, it was an accident, I swear it. Please say you understand.'

'I-I don't . . .' Sid stuttered, unsure what Jin meant. He must be talking about killing Aren, which made no sense because she was standing right there.

Jin took another step forward, his expression tortured. Out of the corner of his eye, Sid could see Jakki slowly reaching for one of her kitchen pots. Noel's eyes flickered to and from the bedroom door, clearly sharing the worry that Drax would show his face and that Jin would see him. But Jin had eyes only for Sid.

'What did he say to you?' Jin pleaded. 'Why are you helping him?'

'Who?'

'*Him.*' Jin pointed behind Sid, a red gleam in his eye, the monster that Sid had seen before rearing its head again. Sid spun around, clutching at his chest.

Drax had edged into view, his dead blue eyes peering out from underneath Aren's arm. The boy rarely showed emotion of any kind, but Sid could tell he was afraid. Even so, Drax shuffled forward, placing himself next to Aren.

'You fucking skahk,' Jin spat. 'What did you tell them?'

Sid held his hands up. 'Jin, please, listen –'

Without warning, Jin lunged towards Drax. Sid yelped, surprising himself by diving in front of Jin and pressing his hands against Jin's chest. No sooner than he'd touched Jin, he snatched them back. Jin's skin was burning hot, even through his clothes.

'You,' Jin breathed, his red eyes locked on Drax. 'You're the reason that *Aren is dead*!' He screamed the last few words over Sid's head, making Drax sink to the ground at Aren's feet. But the little mayj stayed where he was.

'It's okay!' Aren cried. 'I'm right here!'

Jin's eyes flickered to Aren for the briefest moment before going back to Drax. Sid could see his fingers twitching, the veins standing out on the tops of his hands.

'Jin, look at me!' Aren entreated. 'What's wrong with you?'

Jin pointedly ignored her. She started towards him, but Noel stepped right in her path, holding his hands up towards Jin, mirroring Sid. 'Don't hurt the boy, Jin. There is a lot you don't know. Please sit down. We will explain everything.'

'Whatever that skahk has said,' Jin spat, 'he is *lying*.'

'He's not lying, and he doesn't deserve to be hunted like this. He's not what you think –'

'He murdered Oji! He's going to get what's coming to him!'

Before Sid could even think of a way to stop him – let alone muster the courage – Jin thrust out a hand towards Drax just as Jakki hurled a pot straight at Jin's head.

There was a crack and an explosion, the force of which knocked Sid to the ground. He threw his arms over his head, curling into a ball as chunks of wood and stone rained down. He could hear Noel yelling next to him.

Coughing, Sid battered away the dust, peering through the blur of his vision at the destruction. The bedroom doorframe that Aren and Drax had stood in had been replaced by an enormous jagged hole. The surrounding walls and ceiling were obliterated as though Jin had intended to rip Drax apart. Like what Drax had done to Oji.

'No!' Sid pushed himself to his feet and stumbled through the ruined doorframe into the bedroom, his heart thundering in fear for his daughter. Jin had torn right through the far wall, leaving a gaping stone mouth with crumbling teeth through which Sid could see the other towers of Rue.

Aren and Drax were gone. An awful thought caught Sid. Had the explosion thrown them from the tower? Just as he made to move forward, something grabbed him from behind, wrenching him around. Sid found himself face to face with Jin, who had a trickle of blood running down from his hairline. Jakki had hit true with her pot.

'Sid, are you all right?' Jin asked. 'Where did he go? You can tell me! I can help you!' His words were kind, but Sid only saw the red-eyed monster. The little boy with the bruised face was hiding now.

'Sid,' Jin repeated, his voice now changed, dripping with scorn. '*Why are you protecting him?*' He shook Sid so hard that his head snapped back and forth. Noel came barrelling out of nowhere, covered in white dust, with a kitchen knife in his hand.

Reacting, Jin threw Sid to the ground. Sid hit the floor hard and scrambled away, twisting around to watch as Jin grab Noel's wrist, stopping the knife that had been spearing towards his gut. 'Noel, *don't*,' Jin warned. He ripped the knife from Noel's hand and tossed it aside. 'I don't want to hurt you, I *don't!*'

Jin dragged Noel over to the hole in the wall. Sid endured yet another moment of terror in thinking that Jin was about to toss Noel through it, but Jin only clung to Noel's wrist, stopping him from running while his eyes combed the streets below.

'He's still in the tower, isn't he?' Jin asked. He turned back to the room. 'Stay here,' he warned them. 'You'll be safe in the tower. If you leave and my squad see you, they'll have no choice but to arrest you.' Then he flung Noel towards Sid as carelessly as if he were tossing aside a rag doll, as though he didn't realise how rough he was being. With a grunt, Noel landed next to Sid, hitting the floor on all fours.

Jin strode past them both, heading back into the kitchen. Sid watched from the floor as Jin shoved past the kitchen table now lying on its side, a leg missing from it. The table that Mae had been standing right next to before the explosion.

But she wasn't there anymore.

CHAPTER 21:
JIN KANJU

Jin had crossed the kitchen and was almost at the stairwell when a dust-covered figure erupted from the rubble on his left. A powerful tug on his clothes wrenched him backwards over the edge of the broken table that lay on its side, and he landed in a heap on the floor behind it, his ribs smarting, body smouldering with adrenaline.

'Stay down!' yelled an unfamiliar voice. It was that woman who'd been standing next to Noel in the kitchen.

'She's a mayj,' Filip said, looking down at Jin where he lay on the floor. 'Be careful. She could be as dangerous as that skahk.'

Jin felt for her, her power. This close, the repulsion was there but barely. She was weaker than Stolt. Nothing at all like the skahk.

But I could be wrong, Jin thought. He didn't understand why, but this time he'd not felt the skahk until he'd seen him in the doorway. It was as though he'd suppressed his power somehow. This woman might be able to do the same, especially if she'd learnt her tricks from him.

Jin moved quietly, rolling up into a crouch but staying low. The table blocked his view of Noel and the woman, but Jin could see Sid perfectly now, right in front of him, crawling on his hands from the bedroom into the kitchen and shoving aside chunks of wall and broken furniture as he went. He looked terrified. And sure, Sid usually looked terrified, but there was something else in his expression that had Jin instinctively reaching out a hand to help.

He snatched it back as Sid gave a yelp and hauled a coughing, debris-covered Mae from the wreckage.

'You could've killed my mother,' Aren said suddenly.

Jin flinched. He'd been so absorbed by Sid he'd not seen her appear. She crouched beside him, back in her midnight-blue wraps, which was strange because he could've sworn they were maroon a second ago. It was as though his brain couldn't decide what she should wear because in Jin's memory, Aren had only ever worn her favourite green ones. But she'd not died in those.

Her words dragged a wave of guilt over him. He hadn't meant to hurt Mae. He'd been aiming for the skahk, who – as Jin sat moping on the floor – was getting away.

'Sid,' Jin said. 'Mae.' They both jumped, looking startled to see him only a few feet away. 'Just tell me where he's gone,' Jin begged. 'I can help you. You don't have to protect him.'

'Please, Jin,' Mae begged, 'don't kill him!' She tried to crawl towards him, but Sid grabbed hold of her skirt, holding her back. 'You can't kill him,' Mae repeated, coughing as she tried to shove Sid off. 'Drax is keeping Aren alive!'

Drax? Jin never expected the skahk would have a name.

'Ah, I get it now,' Filip said. 'The skahk's blackmailing them. He's told them he's got Aren alive somewhere. They think by protecting him, he'll spare her life.'

That's why they were so desperate to keep Jin away.

'It's a *lie*,' Jin said to Mae. 'You know that as well as I do!' They'd seen it themselves, seen their daughter die. *Because of me,* Jin thought. *They must hate me.*

Jin glanced to the side to see Aren scowling, and his ears were ringing, and Filip was steadily getting louder. 'Do you want to kill this skahk or not?' the dead Bhouli kept asking.

Mae said something then too, but Jin missed it, distracted by Filip.

On top of everything else, the pain in his forearms was burning him, his bridled power blistering his wrists.

Sid's kind face was dragging on Jin's attention, too. 'It's okay,' Sid was saying to him. 'We know you didn't mean to do it –'

'You're going to miss your chance!' Filip yelled.

'Everything is going to be okay –'

'What the *fuck* are you waiting for, Jin?'

Jin's head twinged painfully and he hissed, shaking his head, trying to clear it. Between the constant ringing, Sid's hollow words, and Filip's relentless nattering, Jin couldn't find his own thoughts in all the mess. He could only feel the heat rising, the pain rising, his power wrestling its way up his throat, cutting off his air, like it did when he'd pressed it down for too long.

'Leave, now!' Filip bellowed at him, drowning out Sid's voice. 'They'll never give up the skahk if they think there's a chance to save Aren! Stop cowering behind that table and go after him!' Because, of course, Jin was hiding like he'd done when he was a little boy. Like when he'd first met Aren behind that wooden cart.

And the skahk was still getting away.

Jin stood up, turning away from Mae and Sid towards the stairwell. The mayj woman moved quickly, planting herself right in front of the exit. She had her arms out threateningly towards Jin, her grey curls flaring out from her head, having come loose from her headband. Noel was at her side, looking panicked.

'*Move*,' Jin snarled at her.

'Not a chance,' the woman said.

Noel tentatively held his own hands held out towards Jin. It was hard to see Noel looking at him like that.

'Don't you do that,' Jin said to him, his teeth gritted back against the flames in his throat. 'Get out of my way.'

'We can't let you go after Drax,' Noel said. 'You can take us in if you need –'

'*It's not you I want!*' Jin gasped as his power seared a path into his fingertips. He clenched his fists tightly, his whole body shaking with the effort of keeping it in.

'Don't hurt them,' Aren begged beside him.

'I'm trying not to,' Jin ground out, hoping she believed him. 'I don't want to hurt them!'

'He's getting away!' Filip reminded him, right in his ear. 'The skahk is getting away, *again!*'

The others were yelling now too, but Jin couldn't tell what they were saying. Their voices were just noise resounding violently in his skull, deafening him. He put his knuckles to his temples, trying to concentrate. 'Stop,' he said, but their voices kept crashing over one another, growing so shrill that Jin felt like his head was splitting.

'STOP YELLING AT ME!'

Jin reached and grabbed the table with his hands, hurling it towards the voices. But there was no booming crash, like Jin expected. Instead, the table hurled back towards Jin. Without thinking, he flared his fingers, and the whole thing exploded into brown dust.

Jin dove through it, racing towards the doorway to the stairwell, but something snatched at his clothes again and Jin snapped around, throwing a hand out as he went, knowing it was that woman. He grabbed onto her with majik and flung her back into the wall, indulging in the brief release that came with it. He didn't care if Stolt said he shouldn't harness like that; it felt insanely good.

On cue, Filip was right in Jin's ear. 'I thought *you* were the one who didn't like harnessing people, Jin?'

'Fuck off, Filip!'

The woman contorted her hands, and the wall behind her melted and raced in a torrent towards Jin. He threw his own hands up, catching it just before it smothered him. It reminded him of the melted daggers from his training. *She fights like Stolt*, Jin thought.

'You can too,' Filip said in his ear. 'Try it.'

Jin obeyed. With both hands, he ripped the liquid wall from the woman's grip and flung it back at her. It enveloped her body, and Jin stared down the length of his outstretched arms, satisfied, watching while she drowned in it –

A blade sung past his nose. Jin jerked his head back from it, but he didn't let go of his majik; nothing was going to stop him from killing this mayj. There was movement to his left, and Jin glanced to the side to see Mae swinging a snapped-off table leg towards him.

'Mae, no!' Jin yelled, ripping one of his hands free and grabbing a hold of Mae instead, intending to nudge her away, but with all the heat coursing through him, he got it wrong. There was too much power in it. Mae flew backwards and hit the far wall with a sickening crunch. Sid cried out and scrambled over to her.

'Be gentle,' Aren pleaded in Jin's other ear. 'They're breakable.'

'I didn't mean to –'

Jin felt a drag on his power, and he turned to see Noel harnessing his way through the shimmering mess of wall to the woman, whose knees were buckling under the slurry as she suffocated.

'Noel, don't!' Jin yelled. 'She's with *him*, we need to stop her!'

'Jin, you *moron*,' Filip said. 'Stop letting them distract you, and GO AFTER THE SKAHK!'

Roaring in frustration, Jin let go, dropping the liquid wall and sprinting across the room into the stairwell. With a flick of his wrist, he slammed the door behind him and clung onto it as he ran down the steps, wondering just how far away he could go before he couldn't hold on to it anymore.

Jin shoved through doors and ran across landings, twisting down through the maze of the tower, eventually feeling a slight tugging, but he wasn't Turning, he wasn't even close, so he just kept on harnessing. It was probably that woman or Noel trying to get through the door.

Aren was gone again, but Filip was running behind him. 'Jin, why are we spiralling down in endless circles? Just blast your way out, like you did at the Keep!'

'No! I might bring the whole tower down.' It was true. The Rue towers could not withstand that sort of destruction. Aren would hate him forever if he brought one down, filled with people. He'd already put Noel and her parents in danger, blasting through the room they were standing in when he'd seen Oji's killer standing there. That skahk brought out the worst in him.

'I don't care if we bring the towers down,' Filip whined. 'That skahk is getting away –'

'I CARE!'

Filip quietened, leaving Jin with only the sound of their footsteps thundering down the stairs and the ringing in his head. Eventually, he let go of the door. The tugging had stopped, and it was getting harder to concentrate on holding the door shut anyway, as far away as he was. He kept running.

The top of the tower was silent, but, as with all Rue towers, the stairwell burst out intermittently onto an endless number of landings, the stairs taking invasive turns and twisting down through the rooms of people's homes before narrowing back into another tight stairwell.

As Jin descended, he startled people: exhausted-looking women carrying things along the hallways, little children screaming with glee as they played, and lovers shouting at each other over meaningless things. They all leapt back in shock as Jin burst forth into their lives for just a second before he was gone.

Too soon, Filip was whining again. 'Where are you even *going?* How do you know you're heading in the right direction? You can't feel him!'

'I know!'

'Stop then,' Filip commanded. 'You're chasing him blind. What if he went up to the rooftops, not down to the street? Try again.'

'Fuck!' Jin came to a halt in the next stairwell, grabbing onto the wall to steady himself against the sudden change of pace. He closed his eyes, trying to feel. The sound of his own breathing was getting in the way. He wasn't puffing from exertion, but anger. He took a deep, shuddering breath, and waited. There was nothing, no creeping aversion to anything. He opened his eyes.

'Nothing. I can't feel anything. I'm going to lose him *again!*'

'I told you so.'

Jin smacked his fist against the wall, cracking the stone and splitting the skin on his knuckles.

'You should've listened to me,' said Filip. 'Maybe your squad will get him.'

'They can't even take *me* down,' Jin spat. 'There's no way they'll get *him*!' He sat down on the stairs. Filip made a disgusted sound and bent down to him. 'What are you doing? Get up!'

'No,' Jin said.

'You're going to let him get away?'

'He's already gone. We both know it.'

'What about Sid and the others?'

'What about them?'

'They're in on this with him! And you've left that woman with them!'

'You told me to leave.'

'Because I wasn't expecting you to give up on the skahk and have a sulk in the stairwell!'

Jin said nothing. Instead, he chewed on the inside of his cheek, trying to figure out what had just happened. How had he managed to fuck it up so profoundly again? It was like in the Deadlands when he'd gone and harnessed in front of the Krijen because there had been a mayj, and he'd had no choice but to use majik to save them. He'd been treated like he was all but Lost for a while until Oji pardoned him.

And now, Jin had gone to apologise to Sid, to do the right thing, even though he should've known that was impossible because he couldn't do anything right, not even when he tried. Then that skahk had shown up, and everything had gone *wrong*.

It was clear now just how deep that skahk had his claws into Aren's family and into Noel with all his lies. Noel had always been the cleverest too, and he'd been the one to carry Aren's body away; he would have felt the death of her in his arms. Noel should have known better.

'They wanted to stop me,' Jin said bitterly. 'And that woman, Noel tried to *save* her. And did you see the way Sid and Mae looked at me? Like they were scared –'

'Of course they were scared,' Filip scoffed. 'You killed their daughter. And yeah, maybe you would've been able to change their minds about the skahk before that, but you're never going to convince them otherwise now. They'll hate you forever for what you did. You did this Jin. Don't try to blame anyone else.'

Jin put his head in his hands.

'Look,' Filip went on, 'if you won't go after the skahk, then at least go back and arrest the others. You can't let them go.'

'No,' Jin said, looking up again. 'Like you said, this is my fault. They don't need more punishment.' He swallowed. 'Losing Aren is enough.'

Aren sat down next to Jin in the stairwell, back in her midnight-blue wraps from the night she died. 'I'm right *here*,' she said. 'You really need to stop talking about me as though I'm not here.' Jin looked sideways at her, a slight twitch in his fingers. Nerves.

'Are you going to stick around, though?' he asked her. 'You keep leaving me.' He knew he sounded pitiful. But it was Aren. Unless he said it out loud, she wouldn't know.

Aren had a hint of a smile on her face, her brown eyes bright. 'I'll stick around if you want me to.'

'You're not lying to me?'

'When have I ever lied to you?'

Jin didn't know of a time. Aren never lied to him, not that he knew of. She always said exactly what went through her mind, which was what he loved about her. It had always seemed fair to him because he couldn't lie back. He'd never been good at it.

Aren's words calmed him. Jin took a deep breath.

'Better?' Aren asked.

Jin gave her a weak smile. It *was* better. 'What do I do now?'

'Don't give up,' Aren said. 'That skahk is quick, but you'll catch him. You just need to be smarter about it. Use your squad. Don't waste their skills, use them.'

And just like that, Jin had an idea. It seemed strange that no one had thought to do it before, stretched thin as the Krijen were. Then again, Krijen stayed away from things they'd not done before, lest it lead them astray from the safety of conformity.

But Jin didn't care so much for that. If they weren't willing to bend a little, the skahk and his tricks might just break them.

Jin stood up and started down the staircase again. He could hear both Aren and Filip behind him, Filip nattering once more. 'Why do you listen to her, but not me?' he complained.

'Because it's her.'

As Jin ran down the tower, Filip and Aren tight on his heels, his power nudged at him. It wasn't strangling him like before, but he allowed it to spill from his chest into his arteries, and he pushed it into his muscles, using it to quicken his pace. He reached the bottom of the tower in moments.

Jokah met him as soon as he stepped into the street. 'Sir! What happened? There was an explosion –'

'The skahk was there,' Jin said. 'He got away. Alert the nearest roaming pairs and tell them to meet me at the Square's training grounds.'

Jokah looked confused. 'The Square's training grounds? Not a perimeter, sir?'

'No.'

Jokah dashed off.

A crowd had gathered around the base of the tower, people looking up and pointing at the hole near the top of it.

Jin flexed his fingers. Was the skahk on the rooftops after all? The Kahnen hadn't wanted the People to know about him yet, but how much did he care if people saw?

'Don't lift yourself,' Filip said. 'The skahk will spot you a mile away. It's not worth trying to get a better view.'

'Fine,' Jin said. Instead he pulled out his daggers from their snug spots at his wrists. Filip eyed them up. 'Do you honestly think you'll catch him?'

Jin shook his head. 'No. But I'm going to make him run. I want him fearing for his fucking life.'

Jin had found a clarity that had evaded him for weeks. He didn't know where the skahk would run to, but Jin would make relentless waves with the Krijen. The skahk would run from them until his feet bled.

Jin started towards the crowd, and they parted before him, hushing as they spied his daggers. Up ahead, he saw Flit and Pago sprinting between the towers. Soon they stood before him.

'Sir?' Pago asked.

'Come,' Jin said. He broke into a run, and they spun on their heels to follow. They passed a roaming pair of black-wrapped Krijen who raised their fists to salute him. Jin waved them over and they fell in next to him as he ran, curious looks on their faces.

'Sir?'

'Come with me. I'll speak to your squad leader later.'

'Yes, sir,' they replied.

They collected more Krijen roamers as they ran, eventually coming to the gates that marked the entrance to the Square's training grounds. Jin slowed to a walk, leading them inside. Jin doubted they would guess why he'd led them here, but they didn't ask either.

The training grounds were back to how they'd been before the Celebrations. A row of fifteen barracks stretched into the distance, each fronted by an enormous empty square marked on the sandy ground. The Geni hid their bemused expressions well as the Krijen marched past them. The Squares did not. The Firsts, the five year olds, stared with open mouths.

The second square was empty, but Jin could see a larger gathering up ahead, an enormous group of tiny children seated in neat rows around the thirteenth square. It was common for the younger Squares to observe the older ones. Jin headed towards them.

As the Krijen passed, the older Squares stared too, but with more subtlety than the Firsts, and only when they were sure their Geni weren't looking.

Geni Igna glanced up as Jin approached. The tall Krijen looked exactly the same as Jin remembered, his expression as severe as ever. Geni Igna's Squares were Seconds now, the Geni having started anew after Jin and his victorious fellow Fifteenths had become Krijen more than a year ago. Geni Igna stood next to Geni Lupo, a stocky Krijen with a bald head. Geni Lupo raised his hand, and the Thirteenths slowly lowered the krije swords they practised with, turning to watch the arriving Krijen.

'Jin Kanju,' Geni Igna said as Jin stopped in front of him. 'This is rather unprecedented.' Despite his unimpressed tone, Geni Igna lifted his hand to his clavicle as did Geni Lupo. The Seconds and the Thirteenths followed suit. Jin found it strange to have his former teacher saluting him, but it was an appropriate gesture. As a squad leader, he was their superior.

'Geni Igna, I have a request.'

'A rather important one, I hope, to interrupt training.' Geni Igna was a stickler for rules. As were they all.

'I have a training exercise for the older Squares,' Jin said. 'I was hoping you might speak to the relevant Geni for me.'

'What training exercise might this be?'

'Catching the late FaKrijen's killer.'

Geni Igna raised his eyebrows. It was possibly the most overt display of surprise Jin had ever seen from the man.

Geni Igna observed Jin for a moment longer, and then slowly turned to Geni Lupo. 'What say you?' he asked.

Geni Lupo frowned. 'I agree with Geni Igna. This is unprecedented. You are not the FaKrijen.' He wasn't saying no, Jin noted. He was just pointing out that it had never been done.

'No, I'm not the FaKrijen,' Jin replied. 'I'm asking you for help, not commanding.'

The two Geni shared a long look. Geni Lupo shrugged. 'I do not see why not. It seems relevant to their training and a respectful endeavour.'

Geni Igna nodded and turned back to Jin. 'Very well. We will speak with the relevant Geni. The Elevenths and up, I presume?'

Jin nodded.

'Give us a moment.'

Jin watched as Geni Igna headed down the row of barracks to the Elevenths and Twelfths, and Geni Lupo went up to the Fourteenths and Fifteenths.

'Sir?'

Jin looked back at Flit.

'Are we really doing this, sir?' she asked.

'Do you have any objection?' Jin trusted Flit's judgement.

Flit shook her head. 'None at all. You've just surprised me.' The other Krijen nodded. Aren was smiling at him.

Geni Igna and Geni Lupo returned shortly with four more Geni and an army of Squares in tow. There must have been three hundred of them. They all stopped and saluted as one, sending a chill down Jin's spine.

'They are yours for as long as you need them,' Geni Igna said to Jin. 'Within reason,' he added. 'We want to catch the late FaKrijen's murderer as much as you do.'

Jin nodded. He looked over the Squares. They looked shockingly young, but they all stood bolt upright, ready to obey, like the perfect Krijen that Oji hadn't wanted.

'All right, Squares,' Jin called. 'Listen up!'

CHAPTER 22:
PYRA

Four years and three months ago

'I got another notice,' Polly said. Pyra looked up at her older sister from where she lay on the floor, stringing beads. Polly had started selling Pyra's bracelets in their shop, and Pyra was so excited she'd started making more. Now there were hundreds of them in a scattering of beautiful colours around her.

Polly stood by the door, looking glorious in her red dress with her obsidian skin. Her black hair was pinned back, falling in tight spirals to her waist. Pyra was so jealous of Polly's hair. Pyra could never seem to keep hers on her head, especially now that she was growing up, having just turned eleven. She'd wrapped a satin scarf around her head to cover the bald patches.

'Did it say anything different?' Pyra asked.

'Only that we need to vacate the property or the Krijen will forcibly remove us.'

'What?' Pyra cried. 'They can't do that!' She scrambled up from the floor and hurried over to her sister.

'Sure they can,' Polly said. 'The Krijen will do whatever they are told.' She looked around at her little shop, also their home. It was filled with silks and ribbons and buttons and jewellery and anything and everything required to make oneself feel pretty.

Polly had done it all on her own too. She'd started by stitching holes in clothing for people who couldn't afford to buy new ones, using a needle and thread borrowed from a friend. With the coin earned from that, she'd bought wool and knitted quilts, and with the coin earned from that, she'd bought leather and punctured belts. Eventually she'd bought a shop in the Upper West Side of Rue because her tiny stall at the markets in Val had been overrun with customers.

And now Lord Reider wanted her shop for himself.

Pyra was pretty sure she knew why. Lord Reider was a Kahn, and the Kahnen were bullies. They did what they wanted simply because they could without a thought for anyone else. Polly didn't think that was the reason, but she was too nice to think badly of anyone.

'What are you going to do?' Pyra asked.

'I'm going to speak to Lord Reider himself,' Polly said. 'I think he'll do me the courtesy of an audience, given he's so keen to have my shop.'

Lord Reider had sent a stream of people to their doorstep over the last few weeks, trying hard to buy the shop from Polly. At first, she'd been interested, but Pyra was glad when her big sister eventually said no. The shop was Polly's. It seemed wrong to sell it to someone else.

Sure, the coin would be nice, but they didn't have a bad life, and Pyra wanted her sister to be happy more than she wanted to be rich. The Kahnen were rich, and they still weren't content with what they had.

'So you still won't sell?' Pyra asked.

'Do you want me to?'

Pyra shook her head. 'No. I like living here.'

'Me too,' Polly agreed. 'I'll see if I can find out why Lord Reider wants it so badly. He's not yet given me a reason. I'll go tomorrow. Can you keep an eye on things? I'll be gone a few hours, and it's a long walk to the Keep.'

'Of course!'

Polly smiled at her. 'What would I do without you, Pyra?'

'You'd have a very tidy shop.'

Polly laughed, looking at the beads that Pyra had left on the floor. 'I can live with a little mess if it means I can keep you around.' She pulled Pyra into a sideways hug and gave her a squeeze. Then she raised a hand, tugging gently on Pyra's satin headscarf. 'Can I take this off?' Polly asked.

Pyra didn't really want her to, but she nodded anyway. Her sister pulled the headscarf off her head, revealing the bald patches.

'You're beautiful Pyra. You shouldn't cover yourself.'

Pyra looked up at her. 'I'm not as beautiful as you though.'

Polly gasped. 'That's not true! What makes you think that?'

Pyra blushed and looked down at her feet, suddenly self-conscious.

Polly squeezed her again. 'Well, you know what? I wish I had your nose. It's like a perfect little button. Mine is far too long.'

Pyra looked back up at her sister and made a face. 'That's so silly! I love your nose!'

'And I love your hair,' Polly said, kissing the top of Pyra's patchy head.

'Okay, okay, I get it,' Pyra said. But Polly was still more beautiful, regardless of the fact she preferred Pyra's nose. Pyra's mind wandered back to Lord Reider again. 'Why do *you* think he wants the shop?'

Polly quietly pondered the question. 'It *is* rather strange for a Kahn to covet a trinket shop in Rue,' she said. 'Maybe he likes sparkly things.'

'But the Kahnen already have sparkly things!' Pyra complained. 'They wear so many glittering gowns, every time I see them it makes my eyes sore.'

'When did you last see one of the Kahnen?'

'I walked by a rally the other day. I was just curious.'

'A rally?' Polly crossed her arms. 'And what did you think?'

'I mean, the Kahn was saying a lot of things really loudly, but they didn't mean anything. Everyone liked it though.'

Polly nodded grimly. 'Sounds about right. But that's politics for you. Don't bother getting mixed up in all that. It's full of people pretending to be something they're not.'

Pyra shrugged. She kind of liked the idea of pretending to be someone different than she was even if just for a day. It could be fun. Then again, that was something she hadn't liked about her parents. They were nice to Pyra and Polly, but they weren't nice to other people. That was why Pyra found it hard to make friends. Everyone had been scared of her parents and still seemed to be, even though they were dead.

Pyra looked up as the doorbell chimed and Polly stepped aside, smiling at her customer. It was early, and the sun was barely up. The shop would soon brim with customers.

Pyra scooped up her beads from the floor and trotted over to the shelves, straightening things that were already straight and listening absentmindedly as Polly chatted to the woman who'd walked in the door. She was after a new hat by the sounds of it.

Polly led her to the hat stand and selected a round ladies' cap. She held it out to the woman, who placed it on her head. It would do nothing to keep off the sun; it was purely decorative. Pyra thought it interesting that this woman had plenty of hair yet still felt the need to cover her head. It made her feel better about her patchy scalp.

'Pyra?' Polly called. 'Can you get the petty coin? I'll need change.'

Pyra dashed down the stairs to the basement. It was far too cluttered for Pyra's liking. Polly had pushed shelves of things to the walls to allow room for the mess in the middle. There was still some order to it, thanks to Pyra. Even though Pyra had called herself the untidy one because of her beads, it was Polly who left the most chaos in her wake.

Pyra carefully stepped over a barrel of spindles and made her way to the far wall. Once there, she dragged a shelf out of the way, revealing a round tunnel that sloped slightly downwards. Like many places in Rue, the tunnels went a little way underground, but they never went anywhere. Although this tunnel was as high as Pyra's shoulder, it only went in about twelve feet before it ended abruptly in black mountain rock. It was small and shallow compared to most, perfect for hiding coin in.

Pyra ducked into the tunnel and dragged a little wooden chest towards her. Slipping a hand into her sock, she hooked her fingers around a small key she kept there and pulled out it, using it to open the chest. The lid fell back to reveal a modest amount of coin with a little silk purse sitting on top. Pyra filled the purse with coin and closed the chest, locking it again. She pushed the chest back into the tunnel and slid the shelf back into place.

As Pyra made her way back upstairs, the doorbell chimed over her head once more, followed by footsteps and Polly's cheery welcome, announcing that the day had properly begun.

CHAPTER 23:
PYRA

The Lost Square kept looking between Pyra and Lady Hia, its surprise quickly dissolving into an ugly sneer as it tried to piece everything together. 'What the fuck do *you* want?' it asked Lady Hia, still with a voice like grinding cobblestones.

Rifter and Barrett moved to stand next to Pyra, taking wide stances. The Lost Square's dark eyes flickered over them, too. 'And since when have the Kahnen been cosy with streetlings?' it added.

'Not the Kahnen, per se,' Lady Hia replied. 'Just me.'

It narrowed its eyes suspiciously. 'Why? They tried to kill you all last year.'

Lady Hia eyed up the thick bruise forming around the Lost Square's neck, her gaze trailing to the ropes around its torso and feet. Then she clasped her hands before her, turning to Pyra. 'I find this situation a little perverted. Pyra, untie him please.'

Him? Like it was an actual person?

Pyra gave Lady Hia her best are-you-kidding-me face. 'No way! Do you know how hard it was to catch?'

'I am sure it was difficult, but I do not want him under duress. That is not what we do, Pyra. We are not like them.'

Pyra folded her arms stubbornly. 'Nope. Give it something to chew on first, and then I'll *think* about untying it. Otherwise, it'll jump straight out that window. You know I'm right.'

Lady Hia sighed, clearly exasperated. But she nodded. 'Fine, fine.' She turned and sat back down in one of the plush chairs around the low table.

'Tell me what you *want*,' the Lost Square repeated rudely.

Lady Hia eyed it for a moment. 'Pyra is not what she seems, and neither am I,' she began slowly. 'Before I became a member of the Eighth House, I lived a normal life in Rue. By normal, I mean one of poverty and desperation. Everyone was suffering under the rule of the Kahnen, though others had it worse than I did.'

Lady Hia paused as though waiting for Pyra to speak. Pyra glowered at her. She didn't want this Lost Square to know her life's story.

Lady Hia noticed Pyra's look. She sniffed before continuing. 'As soon as I was old enough, I began advocating to improve life for citizens in Rue. I made a name for myself and became involved in the political side of things. I even became a Kahn, though for the Second House, not the Eighth. It did not matter. Every attempt to do something worthwhile was thrown back in my face. I quickly realised if I was to have any impact, I needed to get into the ruling house. To do that, I needed to be something the Great Kahn was missing. A type of puppet he had yet to collect. So I became Lady Hia, a pathetic character who bowed to the whims and opinions of others. I tempted the Great Kahn with false insights into the sentiments of mayjen citizens, and when I got voted in, he was content for me to stay.

'But, of course, my great plans to save Rue from itself quickly came to nothing. Even though I was finally privy to the inner workings of the Eighth House, the Lady Hia I became was inadequate; too weak-willed to catalyse change. The Eighth House were beyond corrupt. I soon learned they had no intentions of improving the lives of the People, only their own.

'There was also the problem of the Krijen. They would do anything commanded of them, no matter how criminal. I could not play this game cleanly if I wanted to rid Rue of corruption. I needed pressure from the outside, I needed to beat them at their game. I needed an army to match the Krijen. And where, you might ask, was I going to find a ready-made army, vicious enough and willing enough to take down a government?' Lady Hia rose from her chair again and walked over to Pyra, putting a hand on her shoulder. 'The streetlings.'

Pyra ground her teeth. Lady Hia was spilling all their secrets so readily to the vulgar Lost Square. Then again, if the Lost Square ever tried to tell anyone, no one would listen to it.

When Pyra didn't speak, Lady Hia gave her a stern look. 'Your turn, Pyra.'

'Fine,' Pyra snapped. But she still didn't agree with this plan. She turned her head pointedly away from the Lost Square. She wouldn't give it the satisfaction of looking it in the eye when she spoke to it. It didn't deserve it.

'The streetlings run Rue,' Pyra said, 'but they are so distrusting. The only way to infiltrate the gangs and get them onside is to become one of them. So Lady Hia approached me one day with a plan. I agreed. So I became Pyra, the streetling girl who cuts out tongues. It wasn't long before I was a gang leader. My reputation preceded me,' Pyra said, baring her teeth at Rifter, who grinned back. She had her parents to thank for that.

'Pyra earned the respect of the streetlings on every side of Rue,' Lady Hia said, nodding her thanks at Pyra. 'She gathered the gang leaders and made them work together. It was not as difficult as we expected –'

'Easy for you to say,' Pyra muttered under her breath.

'They all loved the idea of taking down the Kahnen. A little too much even. On the day of the Celebrations, we only wanted to scare the Eighth House and give them a chance to step down to reclaim some of their decency. But that day did not go as planned.'

Lady Hia and Pyra exchanged looks. The stupid KrijenMayj had nearly ruined everything. That, and the streetlings had got a bit overexcited in all the fighting and killed Lord Oman.

'It was not much of a loss though,' Lady Hia said, looking back to the Lost Square as she sat back down. 'The only Kahn who died that day was a gossip and a drunk, a detestable man. I cried no tears over him. And that, I believe, is everything,' Lady Hia concluded.

Pyra snuck a peek at the Lost Square, reluctantly curious to see its reaction. Its sour expression hadn't changed, and it remained backed against the wall. 'So,' it said, 'you want to take down the corrupt Kahnen using streetlings. What the fuck does that have to do with me?'

Lady Hia glanced at Pyra. 'Do you agree that is enough for him to chew on?'

No, Pyra thought. But Lady Hia had that face on her where it was stupid to keep arguing.

Grumbling, Pyra pulled the Lost Square's dagger from her wrist tie. 'Don't try anything,' she warned it.

Rifter and Barrett flanked her as she walked towards the Lost Square. 'Well? Turn around,' Pyra ordered. It threw her a scathing look and then did as she asked. Quick as a flash, she slit the rope from around its arms, not caring that she left a long cut right through its filthy shirt. Then she grabbed its tied wrists and sawed through the knotted rope, jumping back as the rope fell to the floor.

The Lost Square did nothing at first. She'd expected it to leap at her and swipe its dagger from her hands the second it was free. Instead, it kept the hand that Ala had bitten behind its back and slowly squatted down to untie the rope from around its ankles with the other, its eyes trained on her.

Satisfied it wasn't about to attack her, Pyra stalked away and threw herself down into one of the chairs around the low table. Rifter and Barrett followed, coming to stand on either side of her.

Lady Hia gestured to the chair opposite her own, looking at the Lost Square. 'Do you want to sit?'

Pyra laughed at her efforts to be polite; they would be futile.

The Lost Square completely ignored Lady Hia. Instead it walked over to the window and looked out. They were nine floors up, but Pyra wouldn't put it past the Lost Square to jump. Pyra would probably do it. There was plenty to grab onto on the way down. If they were lucky, the

Lost Square would slip and fall. The thought made Pyra grin mischievously. It would be rather satisfying if it broke a leg.

'You have become a bit of a problem for us,' Lady Hia said to the Lost Square.

It looked back over its shoulder at her. 'How?'

'You are detrimental to Pyra's reputation. It is hard to keep control of the streetlings with you treading over her authority, thwarting her attempts to clear the Point. You protect the scum of the Lower West Side, the creatures that give our cause a bad name.'

'Your cause?'

'We want the citizens of Rue to work with us. To keep my position in the Eighth House, I need to keep their votes. We promised to clean up their streets and ensure they feel safe. You are making it very difficult for us to maintain their trust.'

The Lost Square scowled. 'I don't give a shit about your cause. Anyone who comes to the Point willing to accept my help will get it.'

Pyra's hands clenched into fists. 'Oh sure, you're *helping*,' she snarked. 'All you're doing is collecting a bunch of lowlives and skahks!'

'*Pyra*,' Lady Hia warned.

Pyra glared at her. It wasn't like she thought all mayjen were skahks. Just the Turners, the ones that got their kicks off the back of everyone else's suffering. They weren't harnessing with any purpose other than to have a good time, and since that Lost Square had shown up, they'd been over-doing it less. They weren't dying at anywhere near the rate they used to.

The Lost Square frowned at Lady Hia. 'Don't you see the hypocrisy here?' It jerked its head at Pyra. 'She and her streetlings are the ones terrorising Rue citizens, not the Point residents. Maybe you should reconsider working with this psycho. She's taking her acting too far.'

'I'm working on that,' Pyra snarled. 'The gang leaders and the citizens are coming to an understanding. They'll let us do what we need to do, and we stay out of their way because we all want the same thing, to make life better in Rue. This is bigger than you realise. So if you get in the way, I will *end* you.'

Lady Hia rolled her eyes, which peeved Pyra. It detracted from her threat.

'Look,' Lady Hia sighed, 'all we need you to do is back off from Turning Point. Let us clear the alleyway, let the visitors move on, and let the residents move on. They will find somewhere else. Either that or help us.'

'What?' Pyra was out of her chair in an instant. 'Help us? How can a Lost Square possibly *help* us?'

'Bring him to meet the gang leaders,' Lady Hia said. 'He has fifteen years of combat and strategy training. He could have a useful take on things.'

Pyra's jaw dropped. 'That's a terrible idea! That thing is not *useful,*' Pyra said, pointing at the Lost Square. 'If I try to bring it to a gang meet, everyone will turn against us!'

Lady Hia gave Pyra her stop-acting-like-a-child-we-will-discuss-this-later look. 'Everyone will see his value even if they do not like it. You of all people should know that to achieve our goals, we need to do things we do not like.'

Pyra could tell Lady Hia was angry, but the Kahn kept her composure like a champion. Pyra had not yet mastered the art.

'Now please, give him back his weapons,' Lady Hia said.

Aggravated, Pyra flicked the Lost Square's dagger at it so fast that Lady Hia cried out in alarm. The thing snatched it from the air a split second before it hit his face.

Stupid Lost Square, Pyra thought. She pulled out the rest of its knives from where she'd tucked them and tossed them onto the ground at its feet, then she sank back into her chair, slouching with her arms folded.

Lady Hia shook her head, appearing embarrassed on Pyra's behalf. Pyra knew it was a show. Lady Hia was a politician, and they could lie better than anyone. The Lost Square would know it too, so it was all wasted effort.

The Lost Square slid its weapons neatly into its clothes and boots with one hand, the other one still held loosely behind its back. Then it crossed the room and leapt straight out the window.

Lady Hia gasped and jumped up, running over to look down into the street.

'Did it break a leg?' Pyra asked.

'What?'

Guess not then, Pyra thought disappointedly.

'Don't worry,' Rifter said to Lady Hia. 'We know where to find it.'

As Lady Hia turned back to the room, Pyra threw her a dangerous look. 'Why did you suggest it get involved? Are you insane?'

'You two, out,' Lady said to Rifter and Barrett.

Rifter wrinkled his nose, his eyes creeping to Pyra's. 'Go on,' Pyra said. She would tell him something afterwards to make him think she would pass on the important stuff. It would also make it seem like she had no qualms about double-crossing Lady Hia, which the streetlings would like.

Rifter and Barrett left.

Lady Hia sat back down, bringing her fingers together in front of her. 'I do not think the Lost Square realises how many people now rely on him and that girl,' she said. 'It will not be good for us when he figures it out. But if we can get him on our side first, it will not matter.' She sent a patronising look Pyra's way. Lady Hia was good at those.

'Fine,' Pyra said. 'I see your point. If we can't get rid of it, we have to use it. But I wish you'd told me first that you were going to ask for its help. Don't blindside me like that.'

Lady Hia pursed her lips. 'I am doing what needs to be done,' she said, sounding bitter. 'And you need to as well.'

'What do you mean?'

'Seriously, Pyra?' Lady Hia raised an eyebrow. 'You need to sort your turf out. The things I have been hearing . . . Did you know that streetlings have been lining up for food at the Point? That includes some from the Upper West Side!'

Pyra stiffened. She hadn't been aware of that.

'I have too much to deal with without worrying about your streetling gang running rampant as well,' Lady Hia snapped. 'Deal with it.'

Pyra pouted. It looked like she was going to have to cut out a few more tongues after all. Maybe she could catch some of the traitorous streetlings who'd been taking food from the Point.

Pyra left the room and closed the door behind her, walking right past Rifter and Barrett, who waited in the hallway. Barret was sucking on his teeth, bored. Rifter looked sour, still angry at being dismissed by Lady Hia.

As Pyra led the way down the stairs, she let out a shout of frustration. After *everything* they'd worked for, how far they'd come, how could they be in this position, bargaining with a Lost Square? Pyra wanted it to decline Lady Hia's offer to join them, so she didn't have to degrade herself by working with it. But that was really their only option, short of killing it, and Lady Hia wouldn't allow that. And even though it was Lost and therefore not the same as killing a real person, Pyra tried not to do things like that, not unless she really, *really* had to. It was tedious being good, but she would be better than *them,* those contemptible Kahnen and the murderous Krijen.

For now, Pyra would wait and see what happened. But she wasn't dumb. She'd make sure she had a plan B, just in case the Lost Square said no and refused to 'help' them.

Pyra wasn't about to let it spoil her shot at revenge.

CHAPTER 24:
AREN BHA

Aren couldn't run anymore. Neither could Drax, it seemed. They dove into a little stone archway under some steps and collapsed on the cobblestones, gasping. Aren's heart beat in fits and bursts, sometimes stopping completely. That was when her world would blacken at the edges until her heart jerked back to life again.

Drax clutched at her, burying himself into her chest, trying to get close. She tried to stay still for him, but fear was taking over, making her shake, her poor heart run ragged with adrenaline.

Jin had attacked her *again*. She didn't understand what had just happened; he'd completely ignored her while begging her parents for forgiveness. It made no sense. And he wasn't ready to listen to them, still hurting after Oji's death, still wanting Drax dead.

Aren would not let that happen. She knew the safest place for her and Drax would be with Wren, but she decided against it. She could never live with herself if she drew the Krijen to Turning Point. There was only one other option, assuming it was even a real option.

'We have to get out of Valrue,' Aren whispered to the top of Drax's head. 'We have to find the Bhouli, like Jakki said.'

Drax still has his face pressed into her wraps, his reply muffled. 'This is hard, Aren.' He meant the majik.

'I know, I know. But we can't stay in the city. There is nowhere to hide. We can't go back to the others, not with the Krijen looking for you.'

Drax slowly looked up at her, his face as blank as ever. 'Okay, Aren.'

Aren wracked her brain, thinking. Jakki had said the Bhouli were underground, in tunnels. Were they the same tunnels as under the brothel? They were closed off, but perhaps they would lead somewhere if Aren and Drax could get through, assuming they were the right ones.

Aren bit her lip. She could so easily be wrong, but she couldn't think of anything else, and they didn't exactly have time to mull it over. 'We've got to get to Val,' she said. 'Just follow me and concentrate on doing what you need to do. Don't worry about anything else.'

'Okay, Aren.'

She took a step forward and then stopped. 'Wait, one more thing. If we get caught, you need to leave me behind and run, like at the KahnenKeep. Understood?'

Drax didn't reply immediately, but Aren could tell he was thinking because he went impossibly still. Then –

'No, Aren.'

Aren reeled. 'Wait-what? But-but you have to!' she sputtered, shocked by his sudden disobedience. 'I won't have you die because of me!'

'You died last time I ran,' Drax said.

'I . . . but, well *yes*, but –'

Drax had never said no to her before, and it worried her that he couldn't shake the obedience trained into him. Except for this time. This time, it was ridiculously important he obeyed.

'Drax, please,' Aren begged. 'If I tell you to run, you run. *Okay?*'

Drax slowly shook his head. 'No.'

Frustrated, Aren let out a strangled yell, making Drax cringe away from her. 'Why *not*, Drax? You can't risk yourself for me, not again!'

'You are kind,' he said simply.

Drax had said that before, about Sid. It was the reason he'd followed Sid back to their home in the first place.

'That's not a reason! There are lots of kind people!'

'No,' Drax said. 'There are not.'

Aren was puffing, growing dizzy. Drax edged closer to her, closing his eyes. 'It's harder when you are upset,' he said. 'Please don't be so upset.'

'Ugh,' Aren moaned. If only it were that easy. 'If we survive this, Drax, you and I are having a proper talk.'

'Okay.'

Once her dizziness had passed, Aren stood up, pulling Drax with her. Then she stuck her head around the archway they'd tucked into, trying to get her bearings.

Aren didn't know where they were. After Jin had torn Jakki's house apart, they'd just run, Aren following her nose as they pounded down through the tower. They'd dived through hallways and sprinted past windows and bedrooms and kitchens before they'd hit the ground floor, bursting into the streets. Then they'd raced up random alleyways, taken shortcuts through shops and backtracked on themselves, purposefully tying their journey in knots to muddle anyone pursuing them.

They'd certainly muddled themselves.

Based on the towers above them, Aren guessed they were somewhere in the Upper West Side, having come from the Lower East. Technically, they weren't far from Val, but right now, knowing the Krijen hunted them, Mama Hidel's brothel and its underground tunnels seemed impossibly distant.

Aren couldn't see any black-wrapped figures around, but that didn't mean they weren't there, undercover. Wren was particularly good at spotting them. Aren didn't have the same knack for it, but she remembered him saying they would come in pairs. They wouldn't stand together, but they would stay close, not leaving one another's sight.

From their nook, Aren scoured the many faces passing by. The streets were so narrow and crowded that a moving wall of people hemmed them in. Anyone walking by the archway could see them clearly, which made Aren nervous, but that wasn't the real problem. There were so many beggars and streetlings in Rue that seeing people crammed into crannies wasn't unusual by any means.

The problem was Drax.

He drew attention because he simply didn't fit in. Up close, it was obvious he wasn't a streetling or a beggar, and his lifeless blue eyes, stark-white face, and bizarre gait had left a trail of curious glances behind them. She turned to see him blinking at her.

'Drax, when we go out again, you need to stand up straight. As straight as you can. And keep your eyes down.' That, at least, she knew Drax could do well.

Drax nodded.

'Let's go,' Aren said.

Aren stepped out from under the stairs and slipped into the crowd. As she'd asked, Drax walked ramrod straight, his head down. Even though she knew it was his best effort, it looked almost as unnatural as when he ambled along. But it wouldn't do to make a fuss.

They wove through the crowd, keeping to the walls. Aren's eyes flickered from doorways to faces to people's hands in their pockets. There was so much activity it scared her; she could easily miss something.

She was on such high alert that when she saw her father's face in the crowd, it startled her. She hastened towards him before stopping, quickly realising it was nothing but a life-sized poster stuck to a tower wall. The likeness to Sid Bha was astounding. Aren edged closer. Beneath the poster, words boasted the promise of a reward of more coin than even Aren could imagine. She stared at it, entranced and horrified until she felt a gentle tug on the back of her wraps.

'Aren?'

Aren glanced at Drax, who was looking to her right. A little ways down the street was another poster. It depicted a small, angular child with black hair and blue eyes. It was clearly meant to be Drax, but they'd got him wrong. He looked far too young with a stern look on his face instead of the blank one he always wore.

'Let's keep moving,' Aren said, hurrying them away. She was thankful no one, not even the Krijen, had got a good look at Drax at the

Celebrations from which to draw a decent likeness. But the poster might still be enough. The blue eyes alone could incriminate him, as rare as they were. Almost everyone else in Valrue had a shade of brown.

Aren moved through the crowd with new haste, now and then turning to make sure Drax kept his head down. No one stopped them. No one yelled out or asked them what they were doing or even spared a second glance at Oji's killer and his accomplice as they made their way through the Upper West Side.

There were more posters of Sid and Drax on the route they took. Aren half expected to see Noel and her mother leap out of the crowd at them, as Sid had, but they didn't. Only now did Aren realise the danger she'd put her father in when she asked him to go find Wren. Aren didn't regret asking because she couldn't bear thinking about what Wren would have done otherwise, but she was angry at herself all the same. She was perilously close to slipping back to being that ignorant little rich girl from not long ago.

But maybe her thoughtless request helped explain why everyone hated Wren so much. Frankly, their response to him had shocked her. She'd expected them to be uncomfortable with the Lost thing, but their outright revulsion had thrown her. They'd come around to Drax so quickly, and in Aren's eyes, what he'd done was more worthy of their hatred.

Soon Aren and Drax were back at the same square where Wren had first saved her, opposite the bridge leading to Val. It looked so different from the day of the rally, and Aren choked on the view.

Down the whole length of the bridge were the dried bodies of children, strapped to the crumbling black stone walls overlooking the river. Aren had not been over the bridge in months, not since the aftermath of the Celebrations and the Krijen purge of mayjen youths.

None of the strung-up children had hands.

Did *Jin* do this? Aren thought with horror. It was incomprehensible. She turned to Drax. He was looking at the bodies with his usual dead expression. She wondered if he knew why they were there. 'Let's go,' she said, eager to get the next part over with.

They crept closer to the bridge, hugging the towers for as long as they could. It was the middle of the day, and there were hordes of people crossing to and from Val.

Aren scoured the square, reluctant to step into the open even though she knew they were no safer by the towers than in the crowd, their reassuring shadows nothing but false comfort.

Aren spotted two black-wrapped figures on the far side of the square, far enough away that she couldn't see their faces clearly. They'd have to have impeccable eyesight to recognise Drax from that distance.

'Okay, Drax,' Aren said, 'we're going to cross. Keep your head down.' She reached back and took his hand, and he immediately snatched it away.

Aren stared, and Drax's head sank into his shoulders. 'Sorry, Aren. I wasn't ready.'

'You don't like me holding your hand?'

'It's okay. Again.'

Aren held her hand out to him, and he took it without hesitation. His grip was limp, and she squeezed it gently. 'I'm sorry,' she said. 'Next time, I'll ask. Ready?'

Drax nodded. They stepped out from the cover of the towers, and Aren glanced over at the Krijen as they started across the square. Their attention was elsewhere.

It was an agonizingly slow journey through the swarm of people. With every person who got in their way, Aren felt her anxiety mounting despite her pulse keeping a steady rhythm. Their short break had allowed Drax to catch up, and he was holding her heartbeat well.

Above them, the sun blazed so intensely its rays were burning the parting in Aren's hair. She was hot and sticky in her borrowed maroon wraps; the heat from the people pressing in on them was suffocating.

They were only feet from the bridge when a horribly familiar, girly voice floated out from behind Aren.

'How funny to see *you* here.'

Aren spun around and swallowed a scream. The sight of the streetling girl with patchy black hair and red ties at her wrists struck terror into

Aren's already delicate heart. How could she have forgotten they were in Pyra's territory?

The streetling gang leader had two others with her, a burly, brutish-looking one and a tall, lanky one. The burly one cracked his knuckles.

Aren gently tugged Drax behind her, placing herself between him and the streetlings.

'I just caught up with your . . . thing,' Pyra said, her nose wrinkling as if in disgust.

Aren's blood ran cold. 'Wren?'

Pyra pulled her teeth back from her lips, hissing softly at the name. 'I thought you might be dead,' Pyra said, running her eyes over Aren. 'You haven't been around to watch its back. Did you have a falling out or something?'

'Where is he? What did you do to him?'

Pyra's smile widened, her lips squeezing over surprisingly white teeth. 'I throttled some life out of it,' Pyra admitted wickedly. 'But it'll live.'

'You –'

Drax tugged on Aren's wraps. They'd stopped at the beginning of the bridge, their huddle drawing wary looks, people doing their best to give them a wide berth in the crush. Pyra stood out like nobody's business, and everyone knew who she was.

Aren didn't know what to do. Of all the people they could have run into . . .

'Oh? And who is this?' Pyra peered around Aren at Drax. She pulled a face. 'You don't look right.'

Aren let go of Drax's hand and gently stepped backwards into him, nudging him onto the incline of the bridge. 'It's okay,' she whispered out of the corner of her mouth. 'Keep moving,'

'Who is he? What's wrong with him?' Pyra asked. She followed them onto the bridge. 'Where are you going?

The two streetling boys were close behind Pyra. The burly one pulled out a little ball on a chain punctured with nails while the lanky one twiddled what looked like an arrow shaft between his fingers, both ends sharpened to points.

'Stay away from us,' Aren warned, doing her best to sound threatening. 'There are Krijen in the square. If you come into Val, you know they'll follow you.'

'That's true,' Pyra said, tilting her head to the side. 'And that makes me wonder . . . Why haven't you called them over?'

That was when Pyra's expression suddenly changed. She looked up to her left, staring up at the dried body of a little boy strung to the crumbling bridge wall, one shoe still on a shrivelled foot. Her head snapped back to Drax.

'Well, well, well,' Pyra said slowly. 'String me up, Salli. He's that mayjen boy, isn't he? The one they say killed the FaKrijen.'

Aren's breath caught in her throat at Pyra's shrewdness.

Pyra bared her teeth again, this time without a smile. '*He's* the reason the Krijen are being so intolerable to us poor streetlings. They think he's one of us.'

Pyra was still stalking towards them, her outrage visibly brewing. Aren's thoughts were tripping over themselves, all clamouring to be heard, none of them giving a viable way out of this trap. She and Drax could turn and run, but in their current state, Pyra and her streetlings would outstrip them in seconds. Drax would refuse to leave her, and she knew he couldn't harness properly unless he let go of her heart. He'd undoubtedly refuse to do that.

Aren thought of her cardonite knife tucked into her thigh. It would also be useless. Drawing a weapon here surrounded by people – the Krijen would be alerted in an instant. She also couldn't talk Pyra down; the streetling gang leader wasn't known for clemency.

So for the second time in her life, Aren found herself completely at Pyra's mercy.

This time, Wren wasn't around to save her. She resisted the urge to rub the spot on her arm where her Bhouli tattoo was. Maybe her luck had finally run out.

Aren and Drax were still backing slowly up the incline of the bridge. It was in such a state that entire chunks of its walls had fallen away. Aren could hear the river rushing below them, and she had to be careful where she placed her feet. Drax trembled behind her, but she didn't dare look around at him. She needed to keep both eyes on Pyra.

'How come he looks so pathetic?' Pyra asked. 'He looks nothing at all like the posters.' Her strides were wider than Aren's, and she was easily keeping up with them as they backed up the bridge.

'Did he tell you why he did it?' Pyra asked. 'Why he murdered the FaKrijen?' She was so close, close enough that Aren had to crane her head back to look up at the girl.

'And why, of all people, are *you* with him?' Pyra reached out and prodded Aren in her sore chest. Aren slapped her hand away.

'In fact, *why* is it,' Pyra pestered, incessant, 'that every time I come across trouble, *you* are there?' Without warning, she snatched Aren by the front of her wraps, pulling her face up to hers. The streetling girl's eyes were such as dark brown they were almost black. Aren could see her own warped reflection in them.

'I'm not as cruel as people think I am,' Pyra hissed so quietly that only Aren could hear. 'I give people chances sometimes. This is your last one. I hope you can swim.' Then she shoved Aren sideways, sending her tumbling through a gap in the bridge wall.

Aren heard a scream that wasn't her own as she plummeted through the air, desperately grasping at nothing. She hit the river so hard it was like a giant hand had smacked across her back. Immediately, water consumed her.

The river was powerful, tearing at her limbs and hair and sending her swirling around. She kicked hard and just as her head broke the surface, something heavy crashed into the water next to her. Before she could take a breath, a weight grabbed her shoulders, pulling her back under.

Everything was going black, and far too quickly. She wasn't out of air, but her body wasn't working. Her limbs were heavy, her heartbeat sputtering. Something was holding her down; a bony body flailing on top of her. Aren thrust away from it as hard as she could, and she came gasping to the surface.

'Drax,' she choked, her voice was barely audible. 'Stop –'

Water cascaded into her throat, and she was under again. Aren's feet scraped the bottom, and she danced briefly on her tiptoes, pushing off as best she could to return to the surface.

Finally, she found air, and it whistled into her throat. It was not enough to stop the endless spinning, but it was enough to help her think.

Aren snatched at the body next to her and wrapped her arms around it, clinging on as it fought against her. 'Drax!' she coughed. 'Calm down! *I've got you.*'

Drax stopped struggling, blessedly succumbing to his inclination to obey, still strong enough to override the fear of drowning. Even when the bottom of the river disappeared from beneath Aren's feet and water rolled over their heads again, Drax stayed still in her arms. Aren kicked upwards, bringing them back to the surface again, her heart stumbling all the way.

The river was brutal with them. It took all of Aren's strength just to keep her legs moving. She tried to steer them to the side to grab onto the wet stone walls, but the current was too strong and the water tugged at her, constantly threatening to pull them back under. She tucked herself in behind Drax, wrapping her arms around his chest to keep his head up.

'Drax,' Aren said weakly. She wasn't sure if he could hear her over the sound of the water. 'We're going to go over the edge . . .'

Drax responded by wrapping his limp arms around hers, clutching her closer to him.

'Please,' Aren begged, 'please, let go of my heart!'

The ends of the stone walls were coming up fast. Aren could see the far side of the mountain, blurrily distant, the edge of the river frothing up ahead of them.

'Let go, so you can do something –'

His nails bit into her arm.

'Drax, please! We're both going to die –'

Aren's strength was suddenly gone. Her grip on Drax slipped and he was ripped away from her, the river triumphant as it dragged her back under. Her heart sputtered, and she felt a sense of weightlessness, followed by a sickening drop. Even in her vague consciousness, Aren knew they'd gone over the edge of the waterfall.

Then there was nothing.

The Founding of Valrue (Excerpt 3)

The Bhouli treat the chest area with reverence though only for non-mayjen. The skin is kept blemish-free and untouched by the sun, reserved specifically for either the first pattern or the tattoo completing the definition of the first purpose, depending on the preference of the individual.

It has long been speculated why the careful treatment of the chest pertains to non-mayjen only. Below is the theory that has the strongest evidential foundation and is supported, though not in so many words, by Gosha the Bhouli mayj, who was referenced earlier in this volume.

It is well understood that power, one of the two pillars of majik, originates in the chest. It is stimulated consciously by the mayj or in response to the release of adrenaline. It travels through the nervous system of the body until it is released, typically from points near the nerve endings, more specifically, the fingertips.

Because the Bhouli believe the chest is already 'inhabited' by power, they consider mayjen to have a partial purpose at birth and therefore do not need to preserve the skin of the chest.

According to Gosha, the purpose, or purposes, of mayjen are strongly influenced by their power and majikal abilities.

In addition, the writings of the early settlers state that Bhouli mayjen of significant power had more selfishly-inclined purposes than other mayjen. It was originally thought that purposes were altruistic in nature (perpetuated by the misconception around the Pledge Against Violence discussed later in this volume). In actuality, the Bhouli have given no indication that the morality of a purpose affects its worthiness of realisation.

CHAPTER 25:
AREN BHA

Aren's first thought was that death was very, very cold. And sore. Her throat ached, and her lungs hurt, and her eyes watered. In fact, she was drenched, and shivering as a result. She could hear the thunder of rushing water and the tinkle of droplets too. The ground beneath her was hard, and even colder than her. There were voices speaking quietly close by.

Aren opened her eyes.

A face was right above hers, just visible in the dim. The woman had deep-taupe skin and a shaved head; she wore no headscarf. White swirling tattoos covered her face, trailing down her nose and spreading over both cheeks. Most strikingly, a large tattoo enwrapped her neck, raw and swollen around its white edges; it was new. Its shape was reminiscent of a winged insect, one that Aren couldn't remember the name of right now.

'She is awake,' the Bhouli woman announced.

Aren slowly sat up, fighting the dizziness that came with it. She lay on the edge of a stone lip within an enormous cavern. On her left, across a dark pool of water, a small waterfall cascaded. A wet streak shined on the rock leading from the water's edge to where Aren sat, lit by tiny lanterns that dangled from the arms of shadow-cast figures. Their white tattoos stood out in the darkness. They must've dragged Aren from the water.

Aren blinked droplets from her lashes. Altogether there were six Bhouli, not a single one of them wearing a headscarf. Two stood over Aren while another four surrounded a small figure covered in a blanket a short distance away. With a jolt, Aren realised who it was.

'D-D-Drax!'

Aren scrambled over to him, scraping her hands and knees on the stone. The Bhouli stepped aside to let her through. Aren threw herself down onto Drax, pulling his limp body up to her chest, gritting her teeth as her stitches pinched. He was so, so cold.

'Get her warm,' said the Bhouli with the insect tattoo. Someone threw a blanket around Aren and vigorously rubbed her shoulders. Aren's teeth were chattering, but she clung to Drax, trying to share whatever tiny amount of body heat she could.

'I am sorry,' said the Bhouli with the insect tattoo. 'We thought you were dead. Your heart was not beating.'

'Th-th-that's ok-k-ay.' Relief flooded Aren. If her heart was beating, it meant that Drax was alive. She thought she could feel his heart beating too, but she was shaking so much it was hard to tell. She lowered her ear to his chest.

Yes, there it was.

Aren looked up at the Bhouli standing around her. 'Wh-wh-what happened? D-d-did you s-s-save us?'

'You came through there,' one of the Bhouli said, pointing to the waterfall. 'You do not remember?'

'N-n-no –'

Drax suddenly stiffened in Aren's arms, and she cried out as his body contorted and twitched. One of the Bhouli leant down and placed his hands on either side of Drax's head. 'He is having another seizure,' the Bhouli said. 'We do not know why. Is he unwell?'

'N-n-no . . .' Aren chattered, clutching at Drax, trying to still him. What was wrong with him?

'D-D-Drax? Are you ok-k-kay?' Drax went limp once more. Aren swayed, her own heart faltering. Aren gasped. 'Oh, oh no –'

'What is it, child?'

'He's going to T-T-Turn!'

Another Bhouli leant down. 'He is harnessing? It is not possible. He does not use his hands.'

'He d-doesn't need to! What do we do?'

The Bhouli standing closest to Aren – a tall broad-shouldered man – frowned. 'What is he harnessing? He should not be using majik.'

'It is okay, Natoni,' said the Bhouli with the insect tattoo. 'You forget my new purpose. Majik is not the problem it once was.'

Aren frowned. Did the Bhouli know the Unsettlement was over?

'Let us take him back and get him warm. That is the best we can do.'

The Bhouli called Natoni reached down and gently pulled Drax away from Aren. 'No!' she cried. 'I have to stay close –'

'I must carry him, child. You may walk with me.'

Natoni reached down and picked up Drax like he weighed nothing. He waited while Aren scrambled to her feet before he turned away from the water, leading the group towards a dark tunnel that came off the cavern.

Aren clutched the blanket around her shoulders with one hand and took one of Drax's limp hands in the other, hoping he would know it was her and that it wouldn't upset him. He didn't like people touching his hands; she remembered that. Aren remembered Pyra too and being pushed off the bridge before going over the waterfall. Beyond that, she couldn't recall anything.

'D-Drax must have saved us,' Aren said.

'What are you calling him?' Natoni asked.

'D-Drax,' Aren chattered. She clenched her teeth still. 'Sorry. His name is Drax.'

The Bhouli murmured quietly behind her.

'What? What is it?' Aren asked.

Natoni spared a glance at the Bhouli with the insect tattoo who walked beside them. She shook her head. 'It is but a name.' She turned to the other Bhouli. 'It is but a name,' she repeated. They silenced.

'What is it?' Aren asked again.

Natoni shook his head. 'Something of no consequence to you. You say he saved you?'

'Yes,' Aren said. 'I don't know how, but he did.'

'The waterfall you fell through is fed from the bottom of the lake,' said Natoni. 'I am surprised neither of you drowned. In fact, we thought that *you* had,' he said, looking down at Aren. 'He is harnessing *you*, I think.'

'Can one harness people?' one of the other Bhouli asked.

'Yes,' the Bhouli with the insect tattoo replied, 'though it is not common knowledge.'

'Yes, Ruha speaks the truth,' Natoni nodded. 'But Drax does not use his hands, and I do not understand how.'

They walked on through the darkness, their way dimly lit by the Bhouli lights. Aren stumbled along next to Natoni, barely keeping up with his long strides. A few times, she had to grab at his arm to steady herself when her knees buckled or if she missed a breath. Drax was struggling.

'Can you please slow down?' Aren puffed. 'It's harder for him if I'm moving quickly.' Natoni frowned down at her but slowed his pace.

The tunnel they walked was wide and above them twinkled tiny lights, different to the ones the Bhouli carried. At first, Aren thought they were stars, and she kept looking up, thinking that couldn't be right because she was certain they were underground. That, and sometimes while she was looking at them, they would disappear.

'They are glow-worms,' one of the Bhouli said, noticing her curiosity. 'They do not like sound.'

'Glow-*worms*, did you say? They are animals?'

'Of sorts,' came the reply. 'They returned quickly.'

Aren was fascinated. She leant towards Drax, still in Natoni's arms. 'You were right,' Aren whispered to him. 'I think the Unsettlement is over.' She wondered if Drax could hear her. And why the Bhouli were so disturbed by his name.

Suddenly there was a light up ahead, so bright it hurt Aren's eyes. They continued towards it. As her eyes adjusted, Aren could see the end of the tunnel opened out into a cavern even larger than the first.

They stepped out into it, and Aren leant her head back, staring up in awe. A little city was carved into the mountain stone, sprawling up and all around the sides of the cavern. Stone rooms stacked atop one another as they curved up the walls, and columns of stabilising stone twisted up between the rooms, denoting glorious swirls of brown, red, and black that appeared to move under the firelight, burning from braziers and brackets scattered across the city.

'This is amazing,' Aren said as they walked by. 'Drax,' she said, squeezing his hand, 'you'll never believe this.'

He did not stir.

More Bhouli looked down on them from various fire-lit rooms as the group made their way into the city.

No one wore a headscarf here either. Aren remembered Maude saying she wore her white headscarf to stop the sky from tempting her. There was no sky here, just blackness above them. The glow-worm lights were gone now too.

Aren tried not to stare at the Bhouli as they made their way around along the perimeter of the cavern-city. Some had so many swirling white patterns it made Aren dizzy to look at them.

Aren spotted a young girl, probably fourteen or fifteen, her shaved head smeared with white ink. The sight of her made Aren miss Maude terribly. She wondered if Maude was here somewhere. Bish had said she wasn't in the dungeon with the women. Maybe because she was a child, the Krijen had let her go?

Aren shivered, thinking of the children on the bridge. *No*, she thought. *Krijen were not so merciful.*

As they walked through the city, the other Bhouli in their group peeled off until it was just Natoni left with Aren, still carrying Drax's limp form.

They passed black stone walls, stepping up off the cavern floor onto a smooth walkway which wove around the outside of stone rooms. There were no doors in sight, only open archways. Now and then, when they walked past, Aren could see straight through into the depths of the mountain. There was nothing other than black stone at the other end that wavered under flickering orange light as though there was a fire there, just out of sight.

It was warmer than Aren expected, given how deep underground they must be.

Natoni led the way up a flight of stone steps, through an open archway, and into a square room with half a dozen other archways leading off two of its four walls. Empty cots lined the room, punctured by a fireplace glowing with embers. Natoni walked over to a cot and gently laid Drax down.

A new Bhouli woman appeared through one of the many archways. Her face and head were free of tattoos. Instead, they wound all down her bare arms, tracing the veins under her skin. 'Remove his wet things,' she said.

Natoni unwrapped the blanket from around Drax and peeled his wet clothes off him. Aren wasn't sure if she should look or not, but her curiosity got the better of her. She'd never seen Drax's body before. The white cross-hatched scars covered every inch of skin.

Natoni paused after removing Drax's shirt. 'Asha?'

The Bhouli woman came over and looked down at Drax. She leaned closer, inspecting the scars that speckled his bony ribs. 'Krijen' was all she said. Then she pulled the blanket back over Drax. She glanced up at Aren. 'You too. Clothes.'

Feeling rather self-conscious, Aren slowly removed her wet wraps underneath the blanket she wore. Natoni reached out a hand and took them off her, unfazed by Aren's discomfort. 'I will leave you with Asha,' Natoni said. 'She heals.' He left.

Drax was shivering under his blanket. Aren climbed onto the cot and lay down beside him against the pillows, tugging her blanket over them both.

Asha nodded in apparent approval before disappearing through an archway. Almost immediately after she left, the Bhouli woman with the insect tattoo on her neck reappeared through another archway, carrying a chair. She placed it next to the cot and sat down. Up this close, and with better bearings now, Aren could see the Bhouli woman looked tired, her white tattoos curling beneath dark-ringed eyes.

'I am Ruha,' she said. 'He is Drax. Who are you?'

'I'm Aren. Thank you for rescuing us.'

Ruha shook her head. 'I was there, but it was not me. Ester found you. That is her purpose.'

Aren frowned. 'Her purpose?' Maude had said something similar once.

'Yes. Ester seeks for new.'

Ruha did not seem to have anything to add to this. The Bhouli were a strange people. From her many conversations with Maude, Aren knew that further questioning wouldn't help her understand any better. 'What is this place?' Aren asked. 'It's incredible.'

'It does not have a name,' Ruha said. 'It was here well before names were given though we have added to it somewhat.'

'No name? Then how do you refer to it?'

'That is exactly the point. We do not.'

Asha was back. She swept over to Aren, holding out a small spoon with red paste on it. 'This will warm him and give him strength,' she said, indicating to Drax.

Aren took the spoon from her and sniffed tentatively at the paste. It smelled like nothing. 'What do I do with it?'

'Rub it on his lips and chest,' Asha said. 'I see him now. I do not think he would want strangers touching him.'

Aren looked down at Drax. She wasn't sure if Drax would want her to touch him either. She dipped her finger into the paste and carefully dabbed it on Drax's freezing lips. As she was rubbing it onto his bony sternum, she noticed a slight warmth coming from it.

'That should be enough,' Asha said. 'His . . . colour is returning.'

Aren knew why Asha had hesitated. Colour wasn't quite the right word for Drax, given he'd never been anything other than bone-white. But he certainly looked less dead than before. 'Drax?' Aren asked gently.

'Can you hear me?'

'Yes, Aren,' came the reply. Drax's blue eyes opened the tiniest bit. Aren yelped in delight and threw her arms around him, pulling him into a hug. 'Thank the Great Kahn!'

'Do not thank the Great Kahn,' Asha said coldly. 'Thank me.' She turned and walked out of the room.

Aren's jaw dropped. 'But-but that's not what I . . . Thank you!' Aren called after her. Nervous, Aren looked to Ruha, but Ruha's expression gave her no reassurance. Feeling decidedly unsettled and unsure what to do about it, Aren turned back to Drax. 'How do you feel?'

He blinked blearily at her. 'Hungry.'

Aren could have cried with happiness. Drax was going to be okay.

'Asha will bring you food,' Ruha said to Drax. 'Now, you do not seem surprised to be here. You knew you were coming to us.'

'Well, sort of,' Aren said. 'We were looking for you. For the Bhouli, I mean. We just didn't find you in the way we expected.'

'What do you want?'

It sounded rude, but Aren was sure it wasn't intentional. 'We need to get out of Valrue,' she explained. 'We were told you can help us?' She wouldn't mention Jakki just yet, in case it wasn't okay for Jakki to be spouting Bhouli secrets.

Ruha's brows pulled together. 'You did not say it, but I think I know what you want. You want to travel down the river.'

Aren sat up, tugging her blanket with her. 'Yes! That's right!'

'I cannot help you.'

Aren's excitement extinguished in an instant. 'You can't?'

'I cannot. Natoni can.'

'Oh! Is he coming back? Can I speak to him?'

'He will return.' Ruha was looking at Aren with a peculiar expression on her face. 'I know of you,' she said.

'You know *of* me?'

'Yes. Your auburn hair, your freckles, your heart-shaped face. I have heard talk of you.' Ruha pointed to the inside of Aren's wrist where her white tattoo was now visible, having removed her wraps. 'May I see?'

Aren slowly held out her arm for Ruha. Even though Maude had said the white-ink patterns and tattoos were not specific to Bhouli, she couldn't help but feel like she'd stolen it.

Ruha leant forward in her chair, inspecting the tattoo. 'This explains why Ester found you,' she said.

'I was told it means lucky,' Aren said quietly.

'And happiness.' Ruha looked up at her. 'Maude had a gift.'

Aren felt her heart thump harder at Maude's name, and Drax shifted in the cot next to her. 'You know Maude?' Aren asked. 'Is she here?'

'No. She is not.'

Aren was disappointed. 'Do you know where she is?'

'Yes.'

Aren waited, but Ruha did not expound. Aren could feel herself growing irritable. Bhouli did not make conversation easy. 'Where can I find her?'

'Maude is with the stars, my child.'

'With the stars?' *No*, Aren thought. *No, that can't be what she means.* Aren always misinterpreted what the Bhouli said.

'When is Maude coming back?'

'She will not return. She has no need to.'

'Oh really?' Aren couldn't keep the scathing tone from her voice, angry that Ruha wasn't giving her a straight answer about something so serious. 'Did Maude send some cryptic message telling you that?'

'No,' Ruha said. 'We found her body floating in the water, in the same pool we found you just now.'

We found her body floating in the water.

'Wait,' Aren said. 'You mean . . . you mean Maude is . . .'

'She is gone from this world. She is dead.'

Aren felt dizziness take her again, and she fell back against the pillows, Drax letting out a little cry as she did so. Her heart must've done something it shouldn't have.

'You seem upset, child,' Ruha said blandly.

Aren couldn't believe what she was hearing. 'Of course, I'm upset!' she yelled. Tears welled in her eyes, and she brushed them away angrily.

She did not want to cry in front of this heartless woman. 'Maude was one of my friends, and you've just told me she's dead!'

Ruha did not say anything.

'How did she die?' Aren demanded.

'Fulfilling her purpose.'

'That is *not an answer*! What does that even mean?'

Ruha's face darkened. 'A purpose is what we spend our lives striving for,' she said. 'It gives meaning to our existence. Maude sacrificed herself to rid the city of majik.'

'She sacrificed herself? You mean like . . . like a saviour?' That had been the meaning of Maude's tattoo, the one Aren had watched the Bhouli girl ink onto her chest. Aren thought of Mika, the mouse that Maude had saved.

'Oh no,' Aren said. 'No, no, no –'

Everything was falling horribly into place. Maude had an arcane ability; mayjen couldn't harness around her. It was as though her presence inhibited majik. The Bhouli had found Maude's body in the pool of water, which Natoni said fell from the lake. The power in the lake was gone now, and the Bhouli knew that too.

Could it be? Had Maude discovered the trapped power was causing the Unsettlement and somehow sacrificed herself to its depths in the hope her ability would put a stop to it?

'Yes, like a saviour,' Ruha said, nodding. 'That was Maude's purpose. Her patterns were ever so meticulous.' She frowned. 'Not that I could ever see them up close.'

'So . . . *wait*,' Aren said, placing her hand on her chest. The air was not coming fast enough into her lungs. 'You're saying you knew what her patterns meant, and you let her ink them onto herself? You *knew* what she might do?' Aren wanted to yell at the Bhouli woman, but she was trapped against her pillows, her body inexplicably heavier than it had been only moments ago. She couldn't tell if Drax was struggling to deal with her body in its shock or if he was doing it on purpose.

'Your anger is misdirected,' Ruha chastised. 'Maude chose her own path. She was self-assured with a noble purpose.'

'Maude was fourteen!' Aren choked out. 'She shouldn't be saving cities! She should be worrying about things like what colour to wear, or . . . or what she wanted to be when she grew up. *That* kind of purpose!'

'Be careful with your words,' Ruha warned. 'You have some ill-conceived notion that Maude was too young to know what she wanted, but you are wrong. Maude was eight when she prevented her own death and the death of her father with her unique ability to stymy majik. Maude interpreted this as her first step towards meaning. Her sense of purpose was enviable.'

'What kind of adults are you?' Aren cried. 'How could you let Maude hurt herself like that?'

Ruha's voice rippled like thunder. 'Your criticism of Maude's purpose shows your ignorance.'

'But –'

'Do you think your opinion matters? It does not.'

'You –'

'Do not seek to blame me. I had as little say as to Maude's purpose as you did. Less even, given how much she spoke of you. I think she considered you an inspiration, but after this conversation, I cannot fathom why.'

The thought made Aren feel sick to her stomach. 'I would *never* encourage her to fulfil that kind of purpose! What a sick and twisted expectation to put on a child!'

'That is not what I meant. You are determined to not hear me.' Ruha pinched her lips together. Aren could hear her breathing through her nostrils. 'However, I can see you are upset, so I will forgive your belligerence on this occasion. I will come back when you have had time to reflect. I have many more important things to do than pander to you.' Ruha stood up and walked out of the room.

Aren snarled, deep at the back of her throat, trying to scare away the tears that threatened again. She'd never felt so angry, so *useless*, in her whole life. It hurt to know that Maude had been happily plotting her own death, right in front of them. Aren had suspected there had been more to that tattoo, and she'd done nothing about it, never dreamt of what it might mean.

Aren also hated that Maude had been right. The Unsettlement was really over. Her death had done that apparently.

Aren felt another tug on her arm. Drax was trying to get her attention. '*What?*' she snapped. His face immediately became a mask, dragging on her guilt.

'Sorry,' Aren said quickly. 'I know I'm making it hard for you.'

'You are crying.'

'*Ugh.*'

Drax watched drowsily while Aren dried her eyes on the blanket. She dropped it quickly, her arms too heavy, and looked down at him next to her. 'How did you do it?' she asked, desperate for a distraction from the horrors of Maude. 'How did you save us?'

Drax blinked slowly, once. 'When we went over the edge and went into the water, I kept the air around us.'

'Like a bubble?'

'I think so.'

'How did we end up where we did? Did you know where to take us?'

Drax shook his head. 'You said we were looking for tunnels. I could feel space beneath us that wasn't filled with water, so I took us there. But it got too hard, the water was heavy, and you were heavy. I had to let you go for a bit.' He looked unhappy about this.

Aren shook her head in disbelief. 'You're amazing. You know that, right?'

Drax gave her one of his tiny frowns. 'Amazing is good?'

'Yes,' Aren said, rubbing his arm affectionately. 'Amazing is good. Really, *really,* good.'

CHAPTER 26:
SID BHA

For the first time in his life, Sid wondered if fear was going to be the death of him. As in if you lived in a constant state of stress, one where your heart beat too fast for too long, would it eventually kill you? Sid knew that animals, especially birds, used to die that way. Why not humans?

It was bad enough to live like this, constantly fearing for Aren and thinking of all the things that might have happened to her. But then it got *worse.*

On the same day that Jin tore through Jakki's home in the Lower East Side tower, Jakki insisted they move back in. Sid felt like bait for the Krijen, but once Noel and Mae were convinced, that was that. He tried to fight back, but no one listened.

'We can't possibly risk this,' Sid said, his voice wavering in terror.

'The Krijen won't return here,' Mae said. 'They'd never dream we would come back.'

'Have you all gone mad?'

'Let the Krijen come,' Jakki growled. 'I'll rip them limb from limb if they turn up on my doorstep again. Especially the one that came here, that so-called friend of Aren's. Jin, did you say? He needs a proper smack around the head if you ask me.'

'Don't say that,' Sid said sharply.

Jakki looked affronted. 'Backlash from *you,* Sid?' She frowned, looking around her destroyed kitchen at everyone's sombre faces. 'What did I say?'

'Jin has an abusive father,' Noel said quietly.

After that, everyone got on with moving back in. It took the better part of three days for Jakki to harness her kitchen and bedroom back together. She grumbled the entire time, saying how hard it was to build all the tiny bits of rubble back into wholes. But at least she made no more snide remarks about Jin.

Sid still needed to work through how he felt about that. Sometimes he caught those red eyes staring at him when he wasn't concentrating on much else, but they were quickly replaced by Jin's brown ones, along with that cheeky smile Aren loved. Sid wondered how she felt about the whole thing. Her best friend had killed her, after all.

Sid wished he could talk to Aren, wished he'd spoken to her about it when he'd had the chance. He missed her sorely. Thinking of his daughter sent him into a whirlwind of worry once more.

On the fourth day after Aren left, Sid's fragile nerves finally got a moment of reprieve. Jakki came running in, her face flushed and her grey curls in disarray. 'I have word from the Bhouli!' She flapped a piece of paper at them. Mae snatched it and read it out loud.

'"J. There is a young woman here who says she knows you. She is with a young man. I assume you know who they are. We will send them where they need to go. This is the last time. You know I am not meant for this. R." Oh, it's them, it's Aren and Drax!'

'How did they do it?' Noel asked. 'How did they find the Bhouli?'

'Who knows?' Jakki shrugged. 'The Bhouli never tell me anything. Aren and Drax must have really offended Ruha. It's a rather harshly worded letter.'

'The Bhouli are easy to offend,' Noel said.

'Not if you know what to say,' Jakki replied. 'You just need a bit of tact, that's all.'

'You think you are tactful?'

Jakki sniffed. 'I can be.'

On the fifth day after Aren left, Sid was fearing for his life again. He'd been the first one up and had walked into the kitchen. He was pulling pots from the cupboard to prepare breakfast when someone spoke behind him.

'Where is she?'

Sid nearly jumped out of his skin. He spun around, hefting the pan over his head to find the Lost Square standing behind the door, a dagger hanging from its hand.

Sid quickly averted his eyes. In that briefest of regretful moments, Sid saw how frightful it was. Its clothes were ripped and filthy, its hair matted. There was a black and purple ring around its neck as though it had survived a hanging. Maybe that explained the new roughness of its voice.

Sid couldn't believe Aren went near the thing. How it had convinced her to, he couldn't bear to think about. Sid turned away and began preparing breakfast, his hands shaking.

He yelped when the Lost Square grabbed the pot from his hands and placed it on the bench. 'Come on, Sid,' it said, 'tell me where she is.'

Sid turned away. Doing his best to stay calm, he started back towards the door to the other room. If he could just get there in time, he could lock it out, but the Lost Square was too fast. It was already in the doorway with its dagger. 'At least tell me if she's okay,' it said. 'Just give me a yes or no, that's all I'm asking. Then I'll leave.'

Sid couldn't help but glance at the dagger in the Lost Square's hand, which sent another tremor of fear through him. The Lost Square must have seen him look because it quickly tucked the dagger behind its back. 'Shit, sorry. Look, I'm not going to hurt you.'

Sid could feel its eyes on him. He felt exposed.

'I know you'll talk to me. You did it before.'

Sid cringed. He would not make the same mistake again. He still didn't understand what had possessed him to go to the alleyway. Aren had wanted it so desperately, but she hadn't known she deserved better.

Sid should have been a better father and said no.

Sid retreated towards the kitchen. He didn't want to turn his back to the Lost Square, but he couldn't look at it either because that wasn't right. He didn't know what to do. He was trapped.

'I'm not leaving until you tell me,' it said.

Sid sucked in a few deep breaths, trying not to panic. But it was very hard not to look at something that leered at you, watching, waiting for you to crack under the strain of it.

Sid sensed more movement, and he couldn't help himself. He peeked at it again, and his heart skipped a beat. It had shifted to lean against the wall beside the door, arms folded. It was looking right at Sid, menacing even with its dagger now tucked out of sight.

'You're not welcome here,' Sid said to it. Unfortunately, it came out strangled.

'No shit,' the Lost Square replied. 'Come on. Where is she? She's not here, and she's not dead.' Despite its bluntness, Sid sensed a lack of conviction in its words. The Lost Square didn't know the truth. It was hunting for it, hoping to squeeze it from him. Sid looked away again, lest his face give it away.

There were quiet footsteps, and the newly repaired door from the bedroom opened. Jakki emerged, now having reclaimed her room with Aren gone. She yawned, throwing her arms wide, then gave Sid a curious look, most likely wondering what he was doing.

In his attempt to escape the gaze of the Lost Square, Sid had edged to the far side of the room and was now huddled against the wall. Sid threw Jakki a pleading look, jerking his head towards the opposite wall where the Lost Square stood, desperately hoping she would see it.

'Sid?' Jakki asked. 'What are you –' Her eyes narrowed to slits. She'd seen it. 'Oh, no, you don't,' she said dangerously. 'Get *out* of my house!'

The Lost Square quickly stood up from the wall. It seemed startled at her directness, likely not used to anything other than cold dismissal. Slowly, it tucked a hand behind its back, no doubt wrapped around the hilt of its dagger. 'Jakki,' it began –

'Get my name out of your shameless mouth!' Jakki spat. 'What Aren was thinking when she brought you here, I have no idea. Let me make it very clear. I will *not* have you in my house!'

The Lost Square didn't so much as tremble. 'I'll go as soon as someone tells me –'

'You want to know what happened to my daughter?' Mae stepped into the room. There were real tears rolling down her cheeks, and her voice shook with sorrow, genuine enough that Sid almost fell for it himself. Mae was always the strong one in their relationship. She would say what needed to be said.

'My daughter,' Mae continued, 'is *dead.*'

Sid looked pointedly away, so he did not see the look on the Lost Square's face in the deafening silence that followed.

'You've got what you came for,' Jakki spat at it. 'Now get out.'

Sid watched from the corner of his eye as the Lost Square crossed the room, pulled open the door to the stairwell, and disappeared into the tower.

Mae hurried over to Sid and took his hand. 'Are you all right?' she asked. 'It didn't hurt you, did it?'

'No, it just gave me a fright.'

'I hope that's the last we see of it,' said Jakki. 'I usually consider myself above murder, but I've never been more tempted. That thing shouldn't exist.'

'You shouldn't engage with it,' Noel said, also stepping into the room. Sid saw Mae raise her eyebrows. He'd come out of Jakki's bedroom.

'I'll deal with it how I see fit,' Jakki snapped. 'But it won't come back now. Mae, I'm rather impressed.'

Mae lifted her chin; the change in her demeanour striking. Her eyes were bone dry. The whole thing had been an act. If Sid was honest with himself, he felt rather unsettled by how calculated it had been. He'd not realised Mae was capable of that.

'No more talk of this,' Jakki said. 'My morning was just ruined. I need to salvage the rest of my day.' With that, she crossed the room and disappeared into the stairwell of the tower.

Sid vaguely wondered what would happen if Jakki caught up to the Lost Square on her way out. No one would raise a finger to save it from her. Whilst it had spent fifteen years training to be Krijen, Sid would put money on Jakki winning that fight. And Sid had never gambled in his life.

CHAPTER 27:
AREN BHA

It took two days before Drax could get out of the cot by himself without both he and Aren collapsing to the floor. Aren itched to explore the Bhouli city, but Drax clawed at her if she so much as walked to the far side of the room. So she sat at his bedside, doing her best not to sulk.

The Bhouli weren't at all interested in their visitors. Now and then, an unfamiliar face passed by the archway nearest to their cot, but no new ones ever looked in. Only Ruha and Asha came and went, spending as little time as possible with Aren and Drax before disappearing again. Their visits were brief and tense.

For starters, Ruha and Asha didn't understand the concept of privacy and weren't in any hurry to get Aren and Drax's clothes back from Natoni. When Asha appeared one morning and saw Aren had tied a bedsheet around herself, she kicked up the most enormous fuss, insisting that the sheets weren't intended for that purpose.

Drax lay in his bed looking blankly bewildered while Aren tried to explain, as calmly as possible, why she didn't want to be naked. 'But you wear clothes!' Aren insisted. 'How can you wear clothes, yet not expect us to want to wear them?'

'That is not the problem,' Ruha said in the low, steady tone she now used when speaking to Aren. 'Your clothes are not ready, and our clothes are not meant for you.'

After a very circular argument that achieved nothing, Aren threw up her hands and lay down on the cot because *apparently,* it was okay to wrap a bedsheet around oneself when one was horizontal. However, the message must have sunk in because a few hours later Asha appeared with Aren's borrowed maroon wraps and Drax's shirt and trousers, clean, dry, and folded. She left with her lips pressed together.

Unfortunately, their differing opinions on clothing were not the only issue. While Aren was dressing one morning, Asha became unreasonably upset when she noticed the enormous wound on Aren's chest. She disappeared into an archway and returned quickly with a foul-smelling ointment, waving the little bowl in front of Aren's face. 'Please, you must rub this onto your chest,' Asha said.

'Why?' Aren asked, wrinkling her nose. 'What's it for?'

'To stave off the scar.'

'It's a bit late for that, isn't it? It's almost healed.'

Asha looked horrified at this, which only made Aren more confused. 'Why are you bothered if I have a scar on my chest?' she asked. 'Drax is covered in scars – sorry, Drax – and you haven't asked him to use it.'

'He is a mayj,' Asha replied, as though that explained it.

The one thing that Aren and the Bhouli didn't argue about was food. At first, Aren was worried they wouldn't be able to keep up with Drax's insatiable appetite. Since harnessing Aren's heart, he'd spent almost every waking moment eating. However, to Aren's surprise, the Bhouli seemed to have an endless supply of food and kept it coming without prompting or complaint. It was strange food too, all of which Aren had never seen before. There was a grain resembling tiny white beads with black centres smothered in a salty red sauce. There was a brown drink with little bubbles in it that made your tongue and lips numb if you had too much of it. Drax refused to drink it, but Aren thought it delightful, apart from the taste, which was like dirt. The best food they ate were these paper-thin squares that melted into nothing on your tongue but left an aromatic sweetness that lasted for hours.

Even though Aren asked countless times, the Bhouli never told her what the food was or where it came from. She couldn't help but feel a little resentful towards them for hoarding their secrets, thinking of all the people living above their heads who were starving, though she wasn't sure if that was fair or not. There had to be a reason for such selfishness.

Within only a few days of arriving in the Bhouli city, Aren became nothing but a ball of pent-up frustration, having spent the whole time bickering with them. Despite her best intentions, everything she said caused offence. Eventually, she gave up and shut her mouth, letting them get on with whatever it was they came to do.

As Drax spent most of his time sleeping, Aren was left with little other than her thoughts to preoccupy her. She spent hours thinking about the other city that Jakki had mentioned, Holu Mon, dreaming up its walls and buildings and the people in it who looked like her but different. Well, she expected they would be different, as different as the Bhouli were to them. But it was hard to imagine how different because the Bhouli were technically from Valrue, were they not? The question stumped Aren. Even before the expanse of the Deadlands left it completely isolated, Valrue had little to do with the surrounding cities.

Aren couldn't recall ever meeting anyone who wasn't from Valrue, and Noel's books that detailed life outside the city were cumbersome to read. They mostly spoke of old trade routes and boring politics concerning people of no significance to Aren. Far more interesting were the books on living things, how the world was strung together, and the exciting history of the Krijen and the stories of their bravest warriors.

When she was younger, Aren had been enamoured with the Krijen, back before Jin became one. She'd loved his stories about being a Square, jealous as she watched him grow into the warrior she'd wanted to be, but also proud of what he was to become. Then she'd seen actual blood spilled at his Dancing Ceremony, and it had all changed.

Aren hated the Krijen now. Not only did it make her nauseous to think Jin killed Filip to become one, but she also despised what the Krijen did to Wren with all their expectations.

Aren bit her lip. Pyra hadn't properly explained what she'd done to Wren. She'd said he wasn't hurt, but would Pyra tell her the truth? Probably not. Then again, Pyra would've got a kick out of telling Aren if something awful had happened to him. The fact that she hadn't surely counted for something.

But if Wren was okay, he would return to the tower to see her, and Aren didn't know how that would play out. Her family had been so harsh, so unwavering in their opinion of him. For the first time, Aren didn't trust them to do the right thing. The most likely scenario would be that they would completely ignore him, and if Jakki were there, she would chase Wren out of the house. It hurt to think that he wouldn't know what had happened to her. She just had to hope that he would be all right.

On the fourth day after entering the Bhouli city, Drax seemed to come right again, and the Bhouli quickly sent them on their way.

Just after they woke up, Natoni appeared for the first time since their arrival. Lights dangled off his torso, sending flickering shadows over two large backpacks slung across his shoulders.

Eager to leave, Aren was up and dressed in a heartbeat, trying not to snap her wrist wraps impatiently while Drax slowly pulled on his clothes. When they were ready, Natoni lead them down through the city, backtracking the same path they walked in on. Aren wondered if he did that on purpose, to stop her curious eyes from wandering more than necessary.

It wasn't until they were at the very edge of the city that they met Ruha. She, like Natoni, was strung with glowing lights. She led them down a dark tunnel along a different path this time, which wound along the side of a gentle river.

The walk was rather cathartic. The only sounds were their rhythmic footsteps and the quiet bubble of water. Up above them, glow-worms reappeared like tiny stars above their heads, flickering as the Bhouli lights passed beneath them.

They walked down and down and down, and it grew so cold that Aren started shivering again. Natoni glanced back at her. He stopped and dropped the backpacks on the ground, bending down to open their straps.

He pulled a thick blanket out of one and gave it to Aren, then pulled a second blanket from the other and laid it wordlessly on Drax's outstretched arms. Natoni closed the buckles, hefted the packs back over his shoulders, and continued on.

Grateful, Aren wrapped her blanket tightly about herself, glancing at Drax. 'Do you need help?' she asked.

Drax shook his head. 'You are not so heavy now.' As though it had a mind of its own, the blanket in his arms unfolded and draped itself about Drax's shoulders. It was a wonder to watch. So much of the majik he did, Aren couldn't see. Like keeping her heart going. This time, it hadn't missed a beat while he harnessed. He was definitely getting stronger again.

Ruha and Natoni were watching Drax with the same expression. 'You are a marvel,' Ruha said. Drax blinked at her.

They carried on down the tunnel. Despite the bone-deep chill, neither Natoni nor Ruha seemed cold. 'We are used to it,' Natoni said, knowing Aren's question before she opened her mouth.

'Do you take other travellers through here?' Aren asked. 'Do other people know about this place?'

Natoni didn't look back as he answered. 'Some.'

Aren wasn't sure which of her questions he was answering, but his tone made it clear he wouldn't indulge her further.

After an age, the gentle slope became wet stone steps, chiselled right into the curve of the rock. The river beside them disappeared into the belly of the mountain; she could hear rushing water below.

The glow-worms faded as they circled deeper and the water grew louder, drops speckling them through the gaps in the stone walls worn away by the current. The steps elongated and straightened, eventually becoming a massive tongue of smooth stone that expanded before them and came to a sudden stop. The way beyond was nothing but river, which flowed down the dark throat of another tunnel.

A wooden contraption floated at the edge of the stone tongue. Thick ropes were tethered around its bow and stern, pulled taut by the strong current.

'A boat?' Aren asked.

There had been no need for boats in Valrue since the Unsettlement had stripped the lake of life. It looked different to the abandoned ones she remembered floating by the docks. It was small, barely two lengths of her, half of the deck occupied by a little cabin. Even though Jakki said they would travel by river, Aren hadn't quite believed her until now.

'Where does it go?'

'To the edge of the Deadlands,' Natoni answered. 'When you arrive, you will need to walk a little way, but it is not far to the forest.' He shared a glance with Ruha. 'It may even be closer now.'

Aren's jaw dropped. 'The *forest*?'

Natoni frowned. 'You wish to leave Valrue, yes?'

'Yes,' Aren breathed, 'but . . . I didn't expect –' She broke off. She had no idea what she'd expected. It all seemed so easy, so terribly simple to get out of Valrue after all this time spent assuming it was impossible.

'It will take you six days,' Natoni explained. 'The current is strong, but it will be a gentle journey from here. We are lucky that mayjen of long ago used this river and smoothed the path.'

'Six days? To cross the *entire* length of the Deadlands?'

'Yes.' Natoni walked up to the boat and stepped onto it, opening the cabin door. He pulled the backpacks off his shoulders and put them inside before stepping back off the boat. 'I packed enough food for your journey and blankets to help you stay warm. You may drink the river water. It is safe.'

Ruha gestured to the boat. 'Take a look.'

Aren rushed forward and stepped onto the boat, which tilted slightly underfoot. It was the strangest sensation. She grabbed a hold of the wooden sides to steady herself and stuck her head into the cabin. It was empty save for a mattress and their packs. She and Drax would both fit, but it would be snug.

Aren looked behind her towards the stern. A wooden frame with a thin curtain partitioned the very tip of the boat from the rest. Aren stepped closer to it and pulled the curtain aside. At her feet was a wooden bucket. 'What's this for?'

'Relieving yourselves,' Ruha said unabashedly. 'You will not be stopping, and it is better not to risk falling in.'

Aren grimaced. Of course, they wouldn't want to hang over the edge. Thank goodness the Bhouli agreed on needing privacy for this sort of thing. Or as much privacy as one could get using a thin curtain and a shared bucket on a tiny boat. At least her inability to stray too far from Drax over the last few weeks had somewhat prepared them for this.

'You must hope neither of you get sick,' Ruha said. 'Some people find the journey unpleasant.'

'Sick?'

'The movement of the boat can unsettle your stomach.'

Drax stepped onto the boat to join Aren. There wasn't much room with both of them on board. A little wooden bench ran around the inside of the boat. Their knees would almost touch if they sat opposite each other.

'What do we do when we get there?'

'There will be people waiting. I know little of what they do; I am not meant for that. But they will help you as much as they are able.' Ruha slid the lights from her arms and held them out to Aren. 'We will leave you these as most of the journey will be in darkness.'

Aren leant over the side of the boat and carefully took the lights from her, wobbling as the boat tilted.

'When you see the crack in the sky above you, you must be quiet,' Ruha went on. 'The river travels the length of the Crevasse. While it is not possible to be seen from up above, you can be heard. You do not want to risk a Krijen roamer listening over the edge.'

'They won't find us when we arrive?'

'Those who wait for you have the means to hide from the Krijen. You will be safe.'

Aren settled back down onto the wooden bench, clinging to the edge as Drax carefully moved to join her. As she watched him ease himself down, a thought struck her. 'Why are you helping us?' she asked the Bhouli. 'I mean, we're strangers. I know you know Jakki, but –'

'This is what I do,' Natoni said simply. 'I help people find their way.'

'It just seems like such a lot . . .' Aren trailed off at the Bhouli's stern looks. 'And we are really grateful!' she added quickly. 'How do we thank you?'

'You do not,' Natoni said. 'Likewise, we will not thank you for fulfilling your purpose.'

'Right,' Aren said, though she had no idea what Natoni meant. She didn't have a purpose, not in the way the Bhouli did. Nor did she *want* one, not after what Maude had done in pursuit of fulfilling hers. Sure, Aren wanted to do something meaningful with her life, and she'd let Maude ink happiness and luck on her arm, but that didn't mean she'd committed herself to some higher purpose.

Aren felt a tingle of adrenaline creep through her. Maude had always said the ink wasn't permanent until it was under your skin. It was certainly under Aren's. She couldn't take it off.

Aren squirmed, uncomfortable for the first time that she'd let Maude tattoo her arm. She'd not really thought of the tattoo as significant until recently; she just liked the pattern. As she thought about it, she remembered the tingling warmth it had left on her skin – even just the temporary ink of it – as though it meant something.

Aren couldn't deny she'd been exceptionally lucky, more than any person had the right to be. As she'd told Marigold, Wren had saved her not once but twice since Maude had first inked the temporary pattern on her arm. Aren had also been much happier since.

But she'd been happy and lucky before then, hadn't she? Being born into wealth with a family that loved her, however suffocating their love was, should be plenty enough. So perhaps the tattoo hadn't caused luck and happiness. They'd already been there.

'Are you ready?' Ruha asked, pulling Aren from her thoughts. Natoni and Ruha had each drifted to where the ropes tied the boat to the rock.

Aren looked at Drax, who blinked at her. 'I am ready,' he said. Aren placed the little lights on the seat next to her and sat down. Drax settled opposite her, his feet tucked up on the seat.

Aren turned to the Bhouli. 'I know you don't want it, but thank you,' she said. 'We are ready.'

Without another word, Natoni and Ruha untied the ropes. The current took the little boat swiftly away from the stone lip.

The Bhouli didn't bother waiting. They turned and headed back towards the steps. As she stared after their retreating backs, Aren felt a surge of guilt. They had dismissed her gratitude, but she and Drax had taken so much from them and given so little. Yet she'd still called them selfish in her head. She was disgusted with herself.

'Wait!' Aren's voice echoed back to her.

The Bhouli turned around.

Aren gaped, unsure what she'd intended to say. She floundered for a question. 'Do you at least get the boat back?' she called.

'We have our ways,' came Ruha's reply. With that, the Bhouli turned and disappeared up the stone staircase into the mountain.

CHAPTER 28:
PYRA

Four years and three months ago

Polly was away at the Keep, and the shop was empty. Pyra took the opportunity to sort through their leftover materials in the basement, figuring out what they could salvage and create into something lasting. Waste was not a thing in Rue.

Pyra heard the doorbell chime above her head, and she left her neat piles and dashed up the stairs. 'Hello, how can I help –'

Pyra stopped dead in her tracks. Two black-wrapped Krijen stood by the shelves closest to the window. Pyra was certain they weren't interested in the jewellery they were running their eyes over. Her parents would have said they were looking for hidden weapons. Polly would have said they were looking for something nice for their promises.

The Krijen turned to Pyra as she approached, their faces calm, their hands relaxed at their sides. They both seemed vaguely breathless, though Pyra wasn't sure why. Neither of them had reason to be nervous around a child.

Pyra, however, was shaking. 'C-can I help you?'

One of the Krijen held up a scroll. He thrust it at her, and she took it with trembling fingers.

'This property now belongs to the Kahnen by the decree of Lord Reider,' the Krijen said. 'You are trespassing. You are to collect your belongings and leave at once.'

Pyra unrolled the scroll and looked at the words, but her brain wasn't working, and the black lines just blurred together on the page. She rolled the scroll up and looked up at the Krijen. Pyra was tall for her age, but the Krijen were huge. She swallowed at the sight of the dagger hilts at their thighs, the necks of the blades glinting at her.

'Please, can you wait until my sister gets back? She's gone to see Lord Reider. He might change his mind.'

'Lord Reider sent us not an hour ago,' one of the Krijen replied. 'Your sister will have nothing to add. Now leave.'

'B-but –'

They ran here, Pyra realised. That's why they were breathless. They'd been told to arrive before her sister returned to take the shop with as little fuss as possible.

Pyra swallowed. It was up to her to stop them, but she didn't know how. She couldn't force them out; she wasn't strong enough. There must be something she could say.

'But this is our *home*,' Pyra said. 'You can't take it.'

Wordlessly, one of the Krijen stepped forward, grasped her by the arm, and began pulling her across the room. Pyra shrieked and clawed at the shelves, trying to grab onto something. Her hand caught the corner of a table laden with trinkets, and she clung onto it desperately. The Krijen tugged harder on her arm, and the table screeched across the floor, sounding exactly like Pyra as she strained to keep hold.

'Stop, *please!*'

'Let go, girl.'

The Krijen prised her hand off the table and grabbed her around the middle, lifting her off the ground. Pyra kicked and screamed uselessly, flailing her legs as the Krijen carried her to the door. Just as they reached it, the door banged open, and the bell chimed madly above their heads.

It was Polly. She wore her best red dress, and she looked flustered;

her hair had come loose from its pins. She leant over, gasping and clutching at her side, a shine of sweat on her face. 'Pyra!' she cried. 'No! Please, don't hurt her!'

Polly dashed forward, her arms outstretched towards her little sister, who squirmed in the arms of the Krijen. The second Krijen stepped between them and shoved Polly roughly aside. She stumbled backwards, tripping on the hem of her red dress.

As Polly fell, her arms windmilled, and a little 'o' of surprise appeared on her face.

As Polly fell, Pyra let loose a blood-curdling scream.

As Polly fell, her head came down onto the corner of the jewellery table with a sickening crack.

Polly tumbled to the floor, her body limp.

'POLLY! POLLY, NO!'

No matter how loudly Pyra screamed, the Krijen did not let her go. Instead, he carried her out the door and dumped her on the cobblestones outside.

She scrambled to her feet and lunged back towards the door. Blinded by tears, she almost collided with the second Krijen as he came outside. Polly's limp form was in his arms. He gently laid her on the cobblestones, then both Krijen headed back into the shop and slammed the door.

Pyra fell to the ground beside Polly, lifting her head and placing it on her lap so it wouldn't hurt more when she woke up on the ground. 'Polly! Polly, it's okay, you're okay!'

Polly's beautiful hair was wet with blood. It was like the red dye that Pyra used to colour their clothes. The very same colour as Polly's dress.

'Pyra? What's happened?'

Pyra looked up, blinking away tears. It was Tiju, the old shoe cobbler who owned the shop next door. Other people were gathering around now. Everyone knew Pyra and Polly.

'The Krijen,' Pyra wailed, 'Lord Reider sent them to take the shop!'

'Oh!' Tiju cried. 'Great Kahn, save us!' He knelt next to Pyra, taking Polly's wrist as people crowded around, hands over their mouths and shock on their faces. A few heads turned towards the shop, and Pyra followed their gaze, looking through the window at the two Krijen who watched them with impassive expressions.

Tiju turned to Pyra with a sad look in his eye, his hand still tight on Polly's wrist. 'Pyra . . .' he said gently.

But Pyra stopped listening after that. She was watching the blood as it soaked into her sister's red dress at her shoulders, spilling out over the cobblestones in a puddle that was growing too big, too deep, to be okay.

'Pyra –'

'No,' Pyra said. '*No.* Polly! *Polly –*'

A hush fell upon the street, silent except for Pyra's anguished screams as they echoed up to the bright blue sky.

CHAPTER 29:
PYRA

'We will do Lady Elira's Reckoning first. We have got her Pyra, we got her!' Lady Hia was so excited her composure was slipping. Not that it mattered because they were alone in the tower room again.

Lady Hia had come to Rue in her Kahn clothes. She looked so out of place. She didn't bother changing anymore, saying it was important for the People in Rue to recognise her. It must be working, because her votes were climbing.

Pyra didn't understand how flashing your riches about could earn you votes in a place where people were so desperate they ate the scum off their shoes. Then again, Pyra didn't know much about politics; that was Lady Hia's area of expertise.

Pyra's skill-set in this twosome was bossing the streetlings around, threatening the streetlings when they didn't do what she asked, and then, when it got really bad, getting Barrett to hold them down while she scratched her name into their foreheads with her horseshoe. The tongue thing was old news, she'd decided.

Pyra growled. 'I want to do Lord Reider's Reckoning first.'

Lady Hia gave Pyra a sympathetic look. 'I know you do. But we have no proof. Starting rumours will only make us look bad, and we need to be smart about this. Right now, Lady Elira's popularity is plummeting. It is no surprise why, and we will be much more likely to sway the People's opinions with her.'

'But Lord Reider's the worst one!'

Lady Hia sighed. 'I know. But the People trust him too much. We need irrefutable evidence to take him down, or we could turn the whole city against us. Lady Elira will be easy, especially given what we have on her.' Lady Hia's tone softened further at Pyra's expression. 'I *am* sorry,' the Kahn said gently. 'The second you bring me something tangible on Lord Reider, we will do his Reckoning. But until then, our hands are tied.'

Pyra sniffed. Lady Hia was right. How Lord Reider managed to get away with what he did to her and Polly, with so many witnesses, she had no idea. Even though she hated them, the Krijen weren't to blame, Pyra knew that. How could you blame something that had no ability to think for itself? It was Lord Reider who deserved to die for what happened to Polly, not them.

But Lord Reider was slippery, smart, secretive. Pyra knew what he was doing at the KahnenCull, but for the life of her, she couldn't get the evidence even with the help of her filed-down horseshoes pressed against the throats of the workers. Lord Reider continued to best her. He was a treacherous piece of –

'Pyra, you are ruining my chair.'

Pyra blinked. She had her horseshoe in her hand, and she'd speared it straight through the soft arm of the chair. She pulled it out and stuck it through a hole in the belt slung across her torso.

'So you will set up a gang meet?' Lady Hia asked.

Pyra leant back on the cushions, lounging in the sun that streamed through the window, her feet resting on the low table around which they sat. As raucous and unpredictable as they were, Pyra was glad she was in charge of the streetling meets and not the Kahnen ones in that Red Room that Lady Hia spoke of. It sounded creepy and *super* boring from how Lady Hia described it. At least no one could ever accuse the streetlings of being boring.

'I'll set up a meet,' Pyra said.

'And you will bring the Lost Square?'

Pyra kicked out at the table harder than she intended, knocking it over. 'Do I have to? I *hate* it,' she said viciously.

'I know it is unpleasant, but getting the Lost Square onside will be easier than getting rid of him, especially now that half of the West Side is flocking to the Point.' Lady Hia gave Pyra a sharp look.

'What?'

'If you had simply done something about him when I first said it –'

'I know, I know!'

Pyra had stubbornly refused to acknowledge the Lost Square until the thing had literally thrown her from Turning Point. Apparently, it didn't like Pyra and her streetlings garrotting the residents. Personally she'd thought they'd been doing Valrue a favour.

Pyra swung herself out of the chair and picked the table up, placing it back on its feet and making sure it was perfectly centred in the little space. 'Why don't the Krijen do something about it?'

'You know why. He is unworthy of their attention. Can you imagine what message it would send if the Krijen went after one of their own Lost Squares? That all they have to do is cause a little trouble for some acknowledgement? And if the Krijen attempt to string up the residents, the Lost Square will try to stop them. No, they will ignore him.'

Pyra sat down again, slumping into the cushions with her arms folded. 'So the Krijen are too good for it, but you still want me to drag it to a gang meet?'

'*Yes*, Pyra. Stop arguing with me on this. And use *him*, not *it*, when you are around him. It is not much to sacrifice to get him onside.'

'But –'

'It is not like I am asking you to say his name. For goodness' sake, be more tactful.'

'But –'

'Enough!' Lady Hia snapped. 'You knew when we started this you would have to get your hands dirty! You are acting like this is the most difficult thing I have asked of you. You would rather eat tongues than fake a little propriety?'

'Calm *down*,' Pyra said even though Lady Hia wasn't looking all that crazy. She was insanely good at keeping it together. 'You know I never *actually* did that. And I'm trying to ask you something, but you won't let me finish!'

Lady Hia pursed her lips. 'Sorry. Go on.'

'*But*,' Pyra continued, 'won't this look just as bad for us? You want the People to vote for you, and you want the streetlings to do as I say, but what happens when they think we've teamed up with a Lost Square?'

Lady Hia shook her head. 'I thought that too, to begin with, but life in Rue has become so bad that the People will accept any help from anyone, no matter who it is. If he continues to gain loyalty like this, particularly from streetlings, we *need* him onside. If we try to remove him now, we will lose more votes than we would gain. I *cannot* lose the Lower West Side. It is too big of a voting base. Anyway, I am not worried about how the streetling gang leaders will react to him. You will handle them well.'

'Pff,' Pyra said. 'I'm glad you have so much faith in me.'

'You have never proven me wrong. Has the Lost Square said he will come?'

Pyra locked her jaw. It was the only way to stop herself from grinding her teeth at the thought of going near it again. 'I haven't asked yet,' Pyra gritted out.

'Do not procrastinate. We missed out on quashing this at the start. Do not let it fester further.' Lady Hia frowned when Pyra made no move to get up. '*Today*, Pyra –'

'All right, all right! I'm going.' Pyra pushed herself out of the chair and tugged her floppy black hat out of the back of her trousers, cramming it onto her head. The sun was blistering today; she didn't want a burnt scalp. The night had been cold though. Strange. Valrue was never cold.

'Oh and Pyra,' Lady Hia added, 'please be careful. There are Squares roaming with the Krijen now. It was the KrijenMayj's idea, though I doubt he realises how politically savvy the move was.'

'What do you mean?'

'Historically, the Kahnen have preferred Krijen numbers to be tightly controlled. Enough to manage the city's population, but not enough to threaten the government if the FaKrijen was ever dissatisfied. A necessary precaution because despite the Krijen's reputation for unwavering loyalty, there has always been tension there. Of course' – a slight frown punctured Lady Hia's expression – 'the Kahnen used to have the protection of their KahnenMayjen, who also acted as a deterrent to a Krijen uprising. However, with the KahnenMayjen gone now – and I still do not understand *how* we let that happen – the Kahnen have only the Krijen for protection. That is why the Eighth House are quite happy for the Squares to join the Krijen numbers, completely ignoring the fact that the late FaKrijen, Oji, proved that the Krijen *are* capable of rebellion. But no one listens to me, given the pathetic Kahn I am playing. They are just happy there will be more Krijen around to protect them.' Lady Hia made a face. 'Well, that and the Eighth House are desperate to keep the Krijen's loyalty. That was part of the reason they created a KrijenMayj. They wanted to reassure the Krijen that the Kahnen still respect them. That is why they are letting Eden out on a very loose leash . . .' Lady Hia shook her head. 'Why they think surrounding themselves with more Krijen is a smart idea, is beyond me.'

Pyra chewed on that as she left the room and spiralled down the staircase. By the time she reached the bottom of the tower, she was in the foulest mood.

Lady Hia was right. The Krijen had been annoying before, but with the Squares bolstering their numbers, they'd become *insufferable*. The Krijen were stringing up streetlings left, right, and centre, especially the mayjen ones, meaning the army that Pyra and Lady Hia had spent the last four years nurturing was slowly being picked off. That's why they needed to get the Reckonings underway. They needed the People behind them and fast.

Pyra started off down the street, Rifter and Barrett falling into step beside her. They must've noticed her aggravation because they stayed silent. However, once they got to the rooftop overlooking the Point, they began making indignant noises.

'That thing *again*?'

'Just deal with it, Barrett.'

Rifter looked at Pyra sideways. 'I thought with the girl gone, we'd fixed the problem.'

Pyra grumbled an unintelligible reply. She stepped up to the edge of the roof and looked down over Turning Point. 'What's going on?' she asked.

People crowded the middle of the alleyway, the usual line of hungry visitors having dissolved into a bulging mess. Part of the wall across from them had collapsed, and people stood around the fallen rubble. There was a fair bit of yelling going on, which was unusual for the daytime. The Turners tended to get rowdy at night.

Pyra crouched down to get a better look. It looked like the visitors to the Point were having a go at two of the resident Turners. A woman lay on the ground opposite from the rubble, slack-faced and limp. A man tugged on her arm, trying to get her to move. The visitors surrounded the pair, fury on their faces and their fists raised.

'Huh,' Rifter said, 'the Turners must've harnessed the wall onto them. The idiots.'

Pyra grinned at that. 'Ooh, this should be good,' she said, eager for a show. 'Any sign of the Lost Square?'

'No,' said Rifter, who settled down on the rooftop to watch, swinging his legs over the edge. Barrett stood on Pyra's other side, his arms folded.

The Lower West Side visitors weren't people that Pyra would willingly mess with. Sure, she had enjoyed plaguing the Turners before the Lost Square showed up, but she wasn't about to go down there and start taunting angry, starving people that still had all their faculties, or near enough to it. Several visitors had no hands or were missing legs or eyeballs, but they still had that look about them that said, 'If you have something I want, I'm taking it.'

'There it is,' Rifter said, pointing.

The Lost Square parted the crowd simply by running through it. No one wanted to touch it. It put itself right in front of the Turners, and immediately a large chunk of the visitors turned away with murder on their faces, but a few stayed and looked at it. One even got up in its face, waving his arms around and yelling at it. It was proof of what Lady Hia had said. People were acknowledging the Lost Square now. Pyra didn't like that.

Eventually, the rest of the visitors turned around and reformed a semblance of a line. The de-escalation was disappointing. Pyra had been hoping the Lost Square would get stabbed or something. But it was too much to wish for.

The Lost Square squatted down over the limp Turner, whose friend was tugging harder on her arm to no avail. The scrawny man didn't have enough strength to move her.

Pyra stood up from her crouch and pulled her floppy black hat off her head, shoving it into her trousers for safekeeping. There was no sunshine in the alleyway; her scalp wouldn't burn. She walked along the edge of the rooftop and dropped to the one below it, quickly making her way down into the alleyway. Rifter and Barrett stayed close behind.

Pyra landed lightly on the cobblestones before the line of people, who hissed and jumped back from her. Pyra ignored them. She headed towards the Lost Square, slipping her belt from over her shoulder as she walked. She plucked her horseshoes from it and tucked them into the red ties at her wrists for easy access.

As they got closer, she caught some of what the Lost Square was saying to the woman on the ground. It sounded angry. 'I told you to wait for me!' it yelled, its voice no longer sounding like grinding cobblestones. 'You can't keep doing this!'

The woman had a trickle of blood running down her chin, but she had a dopey smile on her face, her eyes unfocused.

Her scrawny friend spotted Pyra. He stopped tugging on his friend's arm, and to Pyra's disgust, began pulling at the Lost Square's shoulder. She couldn't believe the Turner was *touching* it.

'Benny, get *off*!' The Lost Square flung his arm back, trying to shove the Turner off him while he tended to the woman on the ground. Benny tugged more forcefully, his eyes widening as Pyra approached. Finally, the Lost Square glanced over its shoulder. It leapt to its feet when it saw Pyra, pulling its dagger out.

It looked like a right mess in Pyra's opinion. Worse than usual. Its stubbly face was grubby, and the shirt it wore was just threads now, the grey of it gone black with filth. It had clearly given up on trying to keep clean. Pyra stopped before it, her nose wrinkling.

'Fuck off,' it hissed.

'You know, you really need to expand your vocabulary,' Pyra replied. 'There are some truly fabulous words you could use, like vamoose, or skedaddle –'

The Turner on the ground started coughing, curling into a foetal position at the Lost Square's feet. The Lost Square glanced down at her before looking back at Pyra. It actually seemed worried about the woman. How pathetic.

'I'm serious,' it said. 'Not now –'

'Yes, now,' Pyra said, stepping towards it. She folded her belt over in her hand and tapped the buckle threateningly against her palm. Barrett and Rifter stepped in beside her, holding up their own weapons, looking menacing. The Lost Square's eyes flicked to the belt in her hand. Maybe it was remembering the time Pyra had wrapped the belt around its neck. The memory made her smirk.

Suddenly the Lost Square lunged forward, snatching the belt from her hands. Pyra screeched and swiped at it, but the Lost Square lifted the belt out of reach and snapped a dagger tip up to her gut.

'I said, *not now.*'

It didn't even flinch as Barrett and Rifter raised their own weapons, pointy bits towards its face. It kept its eyes on Pyra. She gave it her most scathing look. The one that made her streetlings run away from her, screaming.

'You *moron,*' Pyra snarled. 'You need to stop messing with my authority.'

'Then stop trying to fuck with me,' it said, lowering the belt but keeping the dagger between them. 'Go away. I'm busy.'

'I imagine it's harder to control this lot now that your little friend is gone, aye?'

It was oh so satisfying to watch the Lost Square's reaction. Its face went this lovely pallid colour beneath the grime.

Aha, Pyra thought. She had it now. 'You're wondering where she is, aren't you?'

'I said don't fuck with me.'

The dagger nudged the spot just between Pyra's ribs. The Lost Square looked angry, but she could smell the panic underneath. It made her grin.

'Let's make a deal,' Pyra offered. 'I'll tell you what I know if you come to a meet.'

'A – what?'

'A meet! A streetling meet.'

The Lost Square's nostrils flared. 'Why?'

'You know why!' They'd told it everything it needed to know the other day.

The Lost Square narrowed its eyes at her. 'I'm not stupid. The streetlings would murder me on the spot.'

Pyra shrugged. They'd certainly try.

'I'm not doing that,' the Lost Square said. 'And you don't know a thing about what happened to Aren.'

'You're willing to bet on that, are you?'

The dagger dug in a little farther, enough that Pyra sucked in a breath. She refused to back away, but she was loath to let the thing draw her blood. 'Say you'll come to the meet, and I'll tell you what I know.'

The Lost Square looked like it wanted nothing more than to rip her head off. But it hesitated. It was thinking.

'Say it. Or you'll never know.'

The Lost Square sneered at her. 'Fine. I'll come to your meet.'

'I pushed her off the bridge,' Pyra said with a smile.

The Lost Square didn't react. It just kept its dagger pressed to her ribs, its filthy face on hers. Pyra couldn't tell if it believed her or not. But it wanted to hear more.

'It's okay though,' Pyra continued in her sweetest, mocking tone. 'It turns out that your friend can swim.' Pyra paused, then frowned for dramatic effect. 'The boy couldn't swim though. He kept climbing on top of her, trying to save himself. Actually, I was pretty sure he was trying to drown her, which might have ended up better for her anyway because they went over the waterfall, and if you hit the water from that height, you'd probably explo – OW!'

The Lost Square had snatched the front of Pyra's shirt and wrenched her forward with enough force that her heels pulled off the cobblestones. She scrabbled around on her tiptoes, feeling the belt loop in its hand tickling her chin. Its dagger came up too, nicking the skin on her neck. It was breathing all over her, which was so gross. She wanted to scream at it to let her go. But gang leader Pyra wouldn't do that.

Instead, gang leader Pyra cackled and wrapped her wrist around its neck, dragging its face to hers until their noses touched. She made sure to scrape the sharp edges of her horseshoes along the skin by its collar.

'You stab me, I'll slice you,' Pyra threatened.

Rifter and Barrett moved in; she could feel the heat from their bodies pressing into her back.

After a few tense moments, where all Pyra could hear was the blood pumping in her ears, the Lost Square slowly lowered its fist until Pyra's feet found purchase on the cobblestones again. But it didn't let go. Its dagger was still at her neck; her horseshoes likewise pressed against its jugular.

Normally, Pyra loved a good stalemate. It was, in a way, a rite of passage for new gang leaders when they came across the more established ones. It proved them worthy. That was why this particular stalemate pissed Pyra off to no end. The Lost Square wouldn't even know the significance of it. And she *hated* that it was happening.

'Don't lie to me about this,' the Lost Square whispered.

'I'm offended you would accuse me –'

'Is she alive?'

Pyra shrugged again, acting aloof even though she was all tensed up. 'Like I said, I didn't see what happened after they went over the waterfall –'

'I said don't fucking *lie* to me, Pyra!'

Something had changed in the Lost Square's expression, like it might just kill her if she said the wrong thing. Best not to taunt it anymore.

'I didn't see what happened,' Pyra repeated carefully. It was the truth.

'You said she was with a boy. What did he look like?'

'Weird,' Pyra said. 'He looked all warped and wimpy –'

The Lost Square shoved her away, lowering its dagger, relief on its face. 'Drax,' it said. Whatever that meant.

'Happy, then? Good,' Pyra said. 'We're done here. I'll send someone to tell you about the meet. If you don't come, you'll regret it.' Before it could say another word, she turned on her heel and stalked back down the Point towards the mouth of the alleyway.

Rifter and Barrett shadowed her as usual. Curious faces followed them the entire way, the line of visitors having watched the interaction from afar. Pyra didn't know what they would think. No one had been standing close enough to hear, so it probably just looked like a streetling scrap. Apart from the fact it was with a Lost Square. And it had walked away from her unscathed yet again.

Ugh. Pyra hated the association with it, the whispers she would hear in the streets and when she walked down the corridors of the towers. Her authority was under enough scrutiny as it was. She was already pining for her belt, furious that the grubby Lost Square had it; she'd never get it back now.

That Lost Square was turning into an absolute *nightmare.*

CHAPTER 30:
AREN BHA

'Can I ask you something?' Drax whispered.

Aren looked up at him from where she sat cross-legged on the mattress in the boat cabin. Drax huddled against the opposite wall under his blanket, but their knees touched as small as the cabin was. The little Bhouli lamps gave off a dim light, but no heat came from them. Aren could see her breath puffing out in front of her.

Six days was a long time to spend on a boat in the cold and the dark, where all you could take was three steps in one direction before you hit a dead end. The forced quiet of it was suffocating too.

After what Aren presumed was the first day – because the days were impossible to tell in the darkness of the Crevasse – Aren had stepped outside, and a jagged strip of light had appeared in the distance above their heads. From that point on, they'd kept their voices low like the Bhouli had advised them. Drax wasn't much of a talker anyway, so Aren had spent most of the time talking in hushed tones *at* him. She'd only stopped recently, worried her constant chattering was a bit much.

Drax didn't like being on the boat. Aren imagined it was scary for him despite his majik because he couldn't swim. She knew her heart kept him trapped more than he would admit to even though he was regaining his strength and getting better at keeping it beating.

'Sure,' Aren said quietly, eager to break the silence. 'What do you want to ask?'

'Are those children on the bridge dead because of me?'

It horrified Aren to think how long Drax had been sitting on the question. 'Oh, Drax. Is this because of what Pyra said? The streetling girl on the bridge?'

'Yes. Did I kill them?'

'No, you didn't. The Krijen did that.'

Drax actually frowned. Aren watched his eyebrows come together in a little *v* shape. It was a strong reaction.

'Can I ask *you* something?' Aren asked.

Drax nodded.

'When we first spoke, you said that the Krijen hurt you.' Aren wasn't sure how Drax felt about discussing what had happened to him. He'd spoken little about his life with Felle and Pakker after his escape from the Keep and nothing of his life before when he'd been a prisoner there.

'You said it was to do with your father?' Aren prompted carefully.

'Yes,' Drax said without hesitation. 'Felle said the Great Kahn told them to hurt me because he hates mayjen. But the Great Kahn said it was because my father scared the Krijen, so I scared them too.'

'You said your grandmother gave you to them?'

'That's what the Great Kahn told me.'

'Do you think she knew what was going to happen to you?' Aren asked, afraid of the answer.

'I don't know.'

'Did your father know about you?'

Drax was quiet for a moment. 'Maybe. The Great Kahn knew about me because he had my father followed. That's how he heard rumours about me. I don't see how my father wouldn't have known about me if he were still in the city.'

'So he left you?'

'I think so.'

From what Jakki had said, Mandavar had been an awful man. But could anyone be so cruel as to leave their son behind, knowing what might happen to them? From what Aren had heard of Mandavar, it was possible.

Something else had been bothering Aren. Mandavar had been this big shot KahnenMayj, yet Jakki said he'd disappeared a few years before the Unsettlement. But the Unsettlement had happened so slowly, it was hard to tell when it really began.

'Do you think Mandavar had something to do with the Unsettlement?'

Drax's eyes were like orbs.

'I have a theory,' Aren said, 'but I don't know enough about majik to know if it could work. Maybe you do?'

Drax blinked at her.

'I mean, there are things other than people that contain power that are created by mayjen, yes? Like my dagger.'

Aren reached over to her backpack and tugged out the cardonite dagger. Her father had given it to her when she'd begun sparring daily. She slid the dagger from its sheath, the dark green blade appearing black in the dim. 'You said you can feel this, right?'

'A little.'

'Does that mean that power is trapped in this, somehow? Is that what you're feeling?'

'Yes. But I can't feel it right now. I could feel it before I started harnessing your heart.'

Aren frowned. 'Has its power gone?'

'No,' Drax said. 'When I am weaker, it feels weaker too, even when it's not.'

Aren wasn't sure what to make of that.

'But the power in the dagger feels different to how the lake felt,' Drax went on. 'Not as big, but also . . . different.'

'Different?'

'The dagger does not feel . . . good. But not bad either.'

'What do you mean by bad?'

'Jin feels bad.'

'Oh.' It was hardly surprising, seeing as Jin seemed intent on killing Drax, but it still made Aren cringe. 'You think Jin is bad?'

'I do not think it is the right word,' Drax mumbled. 'I could feel Stolt too, though he was not like Jin. He was easier to be around, but still not nice.'

'Okay.' Aren wasn't sure how she felt about that. 'But the lake *didn't* feel like that?'

'No. The lake felt . . . like . . . like . . . me.'

'Like you?'

'Familiar. Nice. And it grew.'

'It *grew?*'

'The power in the lake grew. Even if I wasn't harnessing, I could feel it getting bigger.'

Aren's jaw dropped. 'But that explains why the Unsettlement kept getting worse! As the power in the lake grew, it pushed nature further away!'

Drax sank into his neck. 'I'm sorry,' he said.

Aren's excitement disappeared quickly at Drax's reaction. 'Whatever for?'

'I knew that. I didn't say anything. I didn't know the power in the lake was bad. It didn't feel bad to me.'

'That's not your fault!' Aren said quickly. *'None* of this is your fault. But I need to know what more you know, just in case there is something else important. Like I don't understand why the lake feels nice to you, but my dagger and Jin don't?'

Drax shifted under his blanket. 'Well . . . I can feel if people are mayjen if they're strong enough. There aren't many people like that. I don't like being close to them. Like their power upsets me.'

'It's their power doing that?'

Drax nodded. 'I think so. Your dagger has trapped power, which is why I feel it sometimes. Jin has *lots.*' Drax cocked his head. 'If you think my father started the Unsettlement, then maybe he put his power in the lake. Maybe that is why I don't mind it, because it's like me.'

Aren leant back, stunned. 'Wow. Okay, so if that's true, then

Mandavar had to have done it on purpose, right? That's why he disappeared without a fuss. He put some of his power in the lake, then . . . then left us all to suffer the consequences.' Aren could taste something bitter in her mouth. The more she learned about Mandavar – or what they suspected to be true about him – the more Aren hated him.

Aren looked down at Drax's hands, which peeked over the top of his blanket, resting on his knees. His loose sleeves had fallen down, and even in the dim light, the white-crossed hatched scars were visible, as were the raised purple rings at his wrists.

'What happened to your hands?' Aren asked.

Drax sank his head a little in his shoulders, making Aren cringe. 'Sorry, I shouldn't have asked.'

'I don't know if you want to hear it. It's not happy.'

'I didn't think it would be,' Aren said quietly. 'But I'd like to know if you're okay to tell me.'

'Okay.' Drax's face became his usual blank mask. 'The Krijen came to my cell one day. They had a new kind of knife. It was big and square, not like the daggers they usually used to make their cuts, so I didn't know what it was for. They took me to this little place with a wooden block, and I put my arms on it when they asked –'

'*Stop!*' Aren's voice echoed out into the Crevasse, making her jump.

Drax had got there so fast, and she found she couldn't bear to hear it. 'Sorry, I . . . what happened after that? I mean, how did you . . .' Aren didn't have the words. She gestured to his hands.

Drax understood what she meant. 'I didn't know why they cut them off,' he said. 'I needed my hands. I needed them to do majik, and if I didn't do majik when they asked, they would hurt me. So I tried to put them back on. It didn't work. My chest was cold. Everything was cold.' Drax blinked. 'I think my power was gone.'

Aren didn't understand. 'But . . . but you can still do majik . . .'

'Yes. The Krijen left just after they did it. They were called away. Then a KahnenMayj came in. He harnessed my hands back on. Well, he tried to.'

Drax held out his hands, and they fell limply from the wrists. Aren watched as he slowly moved his fingers, one at a time, curling them into his palms.

'It wasn't nice. But it sort of worked. They went back on. But I couldn't harness. I was still cold. It wasn't until a little while later the warmth in my chest came back. I think my hands needed to heal a bit first on the inside.' Drax dropped his curled hands back onto his knees. 'Later, the Krijen came to my cell. They wanted to see if I could harness again. I tried. I sort of could even though it was so hard, but I kept on trying because they were very pushy, you know?'

'I know,' Aren whispered.

'I thought maybe if I healed my hands a bit, it would help. So I tried to heal them on the inside. I didn't do it very well. I couldn't see inside.' Drax frowned again, the little *v* back between his eyebrows. 'I think the KahnenMayj had not put everything back together properly. I tried to fix it and make it all fit, and I pulled some bits apart, and moved them around, and pushed the blood through. But it wasn't quite right.

'You know how there are scars on the outside of me? I think there are scars on the inside because I kept trying to fix my hands, and it kept on scarring, which is why my hands don't work well. But it was okay. I knew I needed to be able to harness for the Krijen, so they wouldn't hurt me. I tried very hard and realised I could do majik without my hands. I can't really explain it, though.' Drax turned his palms up, his fingers still curled in. 'It doesn't come from here anymore. It comes from . . . here.' He raised a limp wrist to his lips. 'And . . . everywhere. But if something is difficult to harness, using my hands helps. Just a little.' Drax looked pointedly towards Aren's chest. 'That's why I didn't try to Build your heart. I just held all the torn bits in place, so it would heal on its own and you wouldn't get so many scars.'

Aren realised her mouth was hanging open and she closed it quickly. 'Thank you, Drax.' She flushed, feeling like her thanks was woefully inadequate. 'Why . . . um . . . why don't you harness your hands to make them work the way you want?' Aren assumed he didn't bother because he got by perfectly well without them even if it looked awkward, like when he was eating. But she needed to stop assuming things.

'I could,' Drax replied. 'But I don't like using majik on myself. It reminds me of all the bad things.'

Aren nodded in understanding. 'Did the KahnenMayj who healed your hands ever come back?'

'Yes, he did,' Drax said. 'Just one more time. The first time, when he healed my hands, he never said why he did it, only that if I told anyone, he would hurt me. The second time he came back, he told me that if anyone asked, I needed to say the Krijen cut my hands off a second time and that he saw me harness my own hands back on.'

Aren's breath caught in her throat. 'The Krijen didn't, did they? They didn't cut them off again –'

'No, they didn't. And I never harnessed my own hands back on. I didn't understand why the KahnenMayj wanted me to lie. The first time he came, he sounded so angry. The second time, he sounded angry too, but he also looked scared.' Drax cocked his head. 'I think he was trying to be kind to me but also needed to keep himself safe.'

Aren nodded. As horrible as it sounded, she suspected Drax was right. A KahnenMayj had taken pity on him perhaps and done his best to help. Even if he'd fixed Drax's hands poorly, tried to lie his way out of it, and then abandoned Drax in fear, at least he'd tried.

'How long ago did this happen?'

'A few years. I don't know exactly. And the Krijen stopped coming. So I was alone for a long time.'

It was hard to know what to say after that. Aren picked at her wrist wraps, trying not to look at Drax's hands. Another question quickly floated to mind, one less morbid. Sort of.

'So my heart is healed now? You're not having to hold it together anymore?'

'Yes. That's why it's getting easier.'

'And it definitely won't work on its own?'

Drax shook his head.

'Have you tried?'

'I don't need to. It won't feel good.'

'For me?'

'Yes.'

'That's fine. Please? I want to see.'

Drax gave her a look that was just a little exasperated, which made her smile. She liked it when she knew his opinion.

'Okay, Aren.'

A few seconds later, her breath caught and the world spun and she threw out a hand to catch herself before she fell sideways. Her vision quickly righted itself.

'Ugh. That felt so gross.' At least now she knew.

'I don't want to do it again.'

'I won't ask. I promise. But why won't my heart work?'

Drax gave another little frown. 'You ask lots of hard questions.'

'I'm sorry. You don't know the answer?'

'I don't know how to say it.'

So he did know. He seemed to know everything about majik even if the explanation eluded him.

'It doesn't matter. But can you tell me how you got so good at majik? I mean, people are born with harnessing ability and power, but no one knows how to use it.'

'The Krijen wanted to know what I could do.'

Of course. Aren felt bad for asking.

'Felle wanted to see majik too,' Drax added. 'And Pakker. You did not. I thought you were strange.'

Aren stifled a laugh. She'd thought Drax rather strange too when she'd first met him.

'Can you tell me more about Felle and Pakker?'

Drax's face darkened. 'Felle was not kind. She made me do things I did not like. Different to the Krijen.'

Aren wouldn't press him on that. 'What about Pakker?'

'Pakker was strange, too. But in a different way to you.'

'How so?'

'He made me do majik. But I didn't mind that so much.'

'You said he made you harness the power from the lake?'

'He wanted me to use all of it. Not in bad ways though, just as much as I could at once in the ways he told me. And I tried, but there was too much. It was confusing because he and Felle were together, but they didn't want the same things. I don't think Pakker liked Felle. He did some things she asked, but he also kept things from her.'

'Hmm,' Aren said. It sounded like Pakker had his own agenda. 'How did you end up with them?'

'Pakker found me after I escaped the dungeons. Felle was with him.'

'How long ago?'

'I don't know. A long time. A year?'

'How did you escape?'

'I thought they wanted me to leave. The cell door was open.'

'Wait-what? The Krijen just left it open?' That seemed an outrageous accident. So outrageous it had to have been purposeful.

'Not the Krijen,' Drax said. 'A KahnenMinder. I saw him when he opened it.'

'A *Minder* let you out?'

'Yes.'

Aren's heart was suddenly pounding, enough that a touch of worry crossed Drax's face.

'And then . . .' Aren's mind was whirring. 'And then Pakker found you? How long after you escaped the Keep did he find you?'

Drax looked upset now. 'Time was hard to tell, Aren.'

'I know, I'm sorry. Can you guess, though? I think it's important.'

'Maybe a few days. The sun came up a few times.'

Aren felt a tingle all down her spine. Something was *not* right. 'Minders are really obedient, and they're loyal to the Kahnen. Unless the Minder was acting of his own accord, the Kahnen gave the order to set you free. And in that case, they *must've* been working with Pakker. It's too much of a coincidence that he found you so quickly.' Aren gasped. 'Is it possible the Kahnen knew there was power trapped in the lake causing the Unsettlement?'

Caught up in the revelation, Aren's thoughts were tripping over each other, spilling from her mouth. 'But did they know about the lake this whole time, or did something happen a year ago when you were set free?

And why hide it? Why did they want *you* to do it? They have KahnenMayjen – well, one anyway. Why didn't they get the KahnenMayj to fix it? Unless it wasn't possible? Because you said it was too hard to use all the trapped power, didn't you?' Aren stopped talking when she noticed Drax's face. He looked miserable. 'That's a lot of questions,' he said.

'It's okay, they aren't for you. I'll figure it out.'

Without warning, the boat jerked to a stop, and Aren cried out, throwing her hands out to catch herself. 'What was that?' She scrambled over to the cabin door and opened it. It was pitch black outside, the jagged strip of light gone from above them. They were underground again.

Aren clung onto the door frame and held up the Bhouli lights. They were in a little cave, the walls dark and wet. There was a flat lip of rock next to them. The water bubbled along its edge, indicating the river dove under the lip, where the boat could not follow. Across the cave were more stairs carved straight out of the stone, disappearing upwards.

Aren stuck her head back inside the cabin. 'We've reached the end of the river! Come on.' She shoved her blanket inside her backpack and tugged it onto her back, then helped Drax with his backpack so he wouldn't have to harness to put it on. She gathered the Bhouli lights in her arms.

The boat was jammed tight up against the rock. Aren carefully stepped from the boat onto the rock lip. She felt a swooping motion, and she stumbled sideways, reaching out to brace herself against the rock wall. At first, she thought Drax was struggling with her heart again, but Drax had done the same thing and staggered sideways into her, his eyes wide. The sensation was as though they were still moving down the river. Aren figured they weren't used to being on solid ground after so long on a boat.

Without her blanket on, it was freezing cold. Aren was keen to start climbing the steps. 'Do we just leave the boat here?'

Drax looked towards the boat. 'I don't know.'

'It's not going anywhere, I guess. Ruha said they could get it back.'

What Aren wouldn't give to know *how*. 'Let's go.'

Aren led the way up the staircase. They climbed and climbed, and Drax fell behind. Aren's heart didn't falter once, but he was clearly struggling. She stopped.

'Do you want a break?'

He shook his head. 'No, we are close now. There is not much rock above us. I can feel space.'

Aren nodded and they carried on up the stairs. Despite her efforts, Aren's thoughts floated back to Drax's earlier comment on Jin. She knew Drax didn't mean Jin was a bad person, but she was stuck on it.

Jin wasn't bad, he *wasn't*. He'd just done bad things because he was confused. The way he'd reacted in Jakki's house, Jin must *actually* think she was dead even though she'd been right in front of him. He'd been so distracted he hadn't been paying attention. She just needed to speak to him, to tell him she didn't hate him. She needed to explain about Drax, too. Jin just needed to *listen*.

Distracted, Aren stumbled when they reached the landing of the steps. There was a dark wall in front of them, and Aren held up the Bhouli lights. 'Look! It's one of those round plate things.' The same ones they'd seen in the tunnels of the Keep where her father had been imprisoned.

Drax nodded. 'It feels as heavy as your dagger,' he said.

'They contain trapped power, you mean?'

'Yes.'

Aren strung the Bhouli lights over Drax and grabbed a hold of the plate with her hands, turning it. There was a gentle resistance. Her chest had healed, but it still ached with the effort.

A slither of light pierced the cave, so bright that Aren had to look away from it for a moment. Once her eyes stopped watering, she went back to twisting the plate until the strip of light was big enough for them to walk through. With her arm raised against the glare, Aren walked forward into the light.

The scene she stepped out into was so outlandish, so obscenely green and shimmery with dew that at first, she didn't know what she was looking at. She rubbed her eyes, then rubbed them again, just to be sure she wasn't dreaming.

'Oh, my . . . Drax, come look! It's a *forest.*'

CHAPTER 31:
JIN KANJU

The Squares had taken Valrue by storm. They'd purged the streets of streetlings so effectively that, for an entire week, Jin saw none.

Not that he was stupid enough to think they'd got them all, not even close. There were thousands of them, and they'd only killed hundreds. You could barely walk over the bridge anymore for all the bodies. But the Krijen had them running scared. Jin knew they hadn't got the skahk, but that hadn't been the intention. Jin hoped he was cowering somewhere, afraid and regretting what he did to Oji.

When Jin let the Squares return to their usual training, the Geni thanked him though he wasn't sure why. He was the one who had asked for their help, after all.

The Eighth House said they were appreciative, and Jin could believe it after the streetling antics at the Celebrations, but overall, Jin suspected he was a disappointment to them. They'd yet to announce him as their KrijenMayj despite their initial excitement. Not that he cared about the title, but it made him nervous to think they might be regretting their decision. They didn't think he was good enough.

The People voiced their thanks to the Krijen too, which he hadn't expected. Sometimes, when Jin and his squad were in the streets, citizens came up to them to say how safe they felt without the streetlings terrorizing them. But that happened in Val, where the streetlings rarely crept. And they didn't know he was a mayj; he'd not used majik in the streetling purge because the Eighth House had yet to give him their go-ahead. That would probably change the People's minds.

Rue was a different story. Occasionally people nodded to the Krijen as they walked past, but most stared, or hissed, or ran. Jin kept thinking back to Crushed Foot, the swiftrunner who told Jin had dehumanised himself by tearing holes in men in front of them, no matter that the men were bandits. Jin worried he'd done the same again with the streetlings. Perhaps the Krijen were taking it too far now.

Jin knew he'd not been himself lately. But whatever had taken over him that day he'd seen Sid and the others was gone, ebbed away to nothing. He suspected it was to do with Aren because now that she stuck around, everything was a little more bearable.

Jin still hurt, his power still scalded. He felt like he wanted to explode most days. But he was finally *present* for the first time since he'd killed Aren. He was aware of what life was like at the KahnenKeep. He'd paid so little attention before.

Being a Krijen in the city wasn't the same as being in the Deadlands. It was not as liberating. Sure, there was more downtime because he wasn't spending a week at a time on roaming missions or supply runs, but that wasn't necessarily better.

Between his trainings, roaming the streets, and guarding the Keep and its corridors, his duties were more varied if not always pleasant. There was more food even if it wasn't as nice, and for the last few days, it hadn't tasted like ash in his mouth. Krijen whispers still followed Jin though his squad insisted they were good whispers this time, not like after the bandit attack last year.

There was also news from the Deadlands that animals had been spotted and that the trees were growing back towards the Fourth Bases, instead of fleeing from it. The rumour that the Unsettlement was over spread like wildfire through the Krijen, and there was a sense of excitement in the Kahnen too, mingled with apprehension. Jin didn't know when the Eighth House would tell the city. He suspected it would be a while because they wouldn't risk being wrong even though Jin knew they weren't. But he wasn't *supposed* to know that.

Jin suspected another reason they were so hesitant was because the second they announced it, the city would flood with majik once more. All the mayjen that had been cooped up, fearing for their lives should they risk harnessing, would do so again.

Or maybe the Kahnen would never tell the People outright. Maybe they would just let the rumours flow because eventually word would get out, and some mayjen would harness and others wouldn't. Maybe the balance would come naturally.

Would they free the mayjen locked in the dungeon, if that were the case? Would they free Mama Hidel's women if their crime was no longer relevant? Jin was still raw with guilt over Maude. He was ashamed he'd not told Mama Hidel. It was so pathetically cowardly of him, which is why he thought it odd that Filip was so against him telling her because Filip despised the coward in him.

'She'll hate you for it,' Filip reasoned. 'Don't do it.'

Filip was often right, but Jin didn't know what to think. He turned to Aren, who'd not yet given her opinion on the matter. 'What should I do?'

'Tell her,' Aren said. 'It's Mama Hidel. She'll understand. And you need the women.' Aren gave him a sad smile. 'You know you need them.'

Jin ran to the dungeons. He felt breathless as he approached the cell, and the women turned to him, smiling and reaching out to him and saying his name. He stopped just out of their reach, wanting to go to them, but now that he was here, he was terrified of what he had to say. What would they think of him? They'd never judged him before, but surely even they would have their limits.

'Jin? What are you doing? Come here.' Eliza pressed forward to the front, her wrist stumps hooking around the bars.

'Eliza,' Jin breathed, moving towards her. Of all of them who would understand, it would be her. 'Eliza, I –'

Lottie stepped forward to join Eliza. Jin stared at her hands as she wrapped them around the bars. They were unmanacled. 'Thank fuck,' Jin said, reaching through the bars and taking her hands in his. 'When did they take those off?'

Lottie frowned. 'You don't remember coming here, do you?'

'What? I came here? When?'

All the women tittered, and Jin's palms flared with heat. Lottie squeezed his hands gently. She could feel his stress.

'When did I come?'

'Forget *when*,' Filip said. 'What did you *say?*'

Oh no, Jin thought, hot air catching in his throat.

'It's all right,' said Mama Hidel as she pushed to the front. 'I know about Maude.'

Jin flinched.

'You were in quite a state about it, so let's leave it be.'

'But I –'

'Enough. There is nothing more to be said. Now you may stay, but you'll not come this side of the bars again. I won't have you getting more of those cuts.'

Jin blinked at her. His cuts were all but healed now. He must have visited *weeks* ago. Beside him, Aren shook her head. 'How did you forget so much, Jin? Was it because of me?'

All the women were talking now, a few of them reaching through the bars to tug on his wraps, wanting his attention. Lottie's hands were still clasped in Jin's. Her hands felt cold. Jin searched her face for answers.

'I'll tell you what happened,' Lottie said quietly to him. 'Don't worry now. We can talk about Aren.'

Jin's palms burned hotter.

'Oh *shit*,' Filip said.

'What did I say?'

'You said Aren died,' Lottie admitted sadly, squeezing his hands once more. 'We're here for you. But you must come back when you need us, okay?'

Relief flooded Jin, dousing the flames again. He'd not said it had been him who'd killed Aren. He was so glad he'd listened to her and come to see the women.

'Sir!'

Jin spun around, letting go of Lottie's hands. Pago jogged towards him, his face carefully blank. 'Nommo mentioned you might be here, sir,' Pago said. 'You've got training, remember?'

'I do,' Jin said. He'd not forgotten this time though it spoke volumes that his squad felt the need to remind him.

'I'll come back,' Jin said to the women.

Lottie smiled and nodded. 'You better.'

Pago fell in beside Jin as they headed back up into the Keep, towards that horrid webbed-wall room. Pago was usually quiet, but Jin wished he would talk. It scared him to think how much his squad had seen of him when he hadn't been paying attention.

'Pago,' Jin began slowly, 'I'm sorry for hurting you. During the trainings, I mean.'

'It's nothing, sir. We get it.'

'Get what?'

'Nommo . . .' Pago looked uncomfortable. 'Nommo told us a few things.'

Heat stung Jin's veins, and his hands twitched over his dagger hilts.

'Don't blame him, sir,' Pago said. 'He didn't give it up easily. Flit bullied it out of him.'

Fucking Flit and her meddling, Jin thought. 'What did Nommo tell you?'

'About your father, mostly. You should've said.' Pago hesitated. 'It explains a lot.'

'Maybe it's better they know,' Aren said. She walked briskly beside him, taking two steps for every one of his. 'You want to hide things, but I don't think that's helpful.'

'If you don't mind me saying, sir,' Pago said after an awkward silence, 'what you did with the Squares was brilliant.' He was trying to make Jin feel better.

Jin was glad for the change of topic, albeit one that made him nervous. 'I'm not sure. I'm worried about what the People think. The streetlings are just children, after all.' It seemed like the right thing to say even if Jin felt no conviction about it.

'Streetlings don't count as children,' Pago said coldly, surprising Jin. Pago was the gentlest of all of his squad. 'They're little murderers. They killed Oji. They killed Vulmin. You remember the streetling girl at the Celebrations with the red wrist ties?'

'I'm not likely to forget.'

'Apparently, she used to eat people's tongues. For *fun*. And then she got bored with that, so she started carving her name into their foreheads. I mean seriously? That's just sick.'

'Yeah . . . I worry that the People think the Krijen are going the same way. Becoming too ruthless, I mean.'

'*You* are worried about being too ruthless?'

Jin didn't reply. He didn't want to know what that meant.

'You don't need to worry, sir. The People are glad to be rid of the streetlings, they've made that clear. The Eighth House too, especially after what happened at the Celebrations.'

'What about FaKrijen Eden? What if he thinks I overstepped by recruiting the Squares?'

'He won't. He'll just be annoyed he didn't think of it himself. Besides, it sounds like he's been busy out in the Deadlands. He probably appreciates someone taking the lead here. You know they're thinking the Unsettlement might be over? There are plants sprouting up around the Fourth Bases, now.'

'I heard.'

'I can't wait, sir. But you need to stop worrying. Everything looks good, for once. The streetlings are under control, the Unsettlement's on its way out. We'll get that skahk who killed Oji too. I'm sure of it.

'And the Kahnen are excited about you. I can tell. They've been running scared without the KahnenMayjen and with the Krijen numbers being so dire. They know you're a game-changer even if Stolt is doing his best to prove otherwise. They can all see how much you scare him, and they're smart enough to know why. And if something goes wrong, sir, the squad's got your back.'

'Thanks, Pago,' Jin said even though Pago's promise was hollow. Just because he was squad leader, it didn't mean they would be loyal to him. He was squad leader the last time they turned on him. At the end of the day, his squad answered to the FaKrijen, and something told him that FaKrijen Eden wouldn't be as forgiving as Oji if Jin were to make a mistake.

CHAPTER 32:
AREN BHA

Drax slipped through the rock and came to stand by Aren's side, his eyes wide. Together, they took it all in.

Green spread all around them as far as the eye could see. But there was almost as much brown as there was green.

Aren dashed to the nearest tree. She leaned in close, in awe of it. The thick bark of its trunk was cracked and imperfect, nothing like the smooth stone of Valrue. Aren ran a hand along it. It was rough under her touch, catching on the pads of her fingers. She looked up into the leaves that glistened above her head, never having seen anything so beautiful.

The forest smelled like nothing that Aren could put words to, other than fresh and earthy and damp, which were nowhere near sufficient.

'This is amazing! Drax, come here –'

But he was already right behind her, keeping close for her heart.

'Sorry, sorry I'll calm down a bit,' Aren said, sucking air into her lungs and closing her eyes.

'It's okay, Aren,' Drax's voice floated out to her. 'Remember, now you've healed, you aren't so heavy.'

Aren opened her eyes again, the green blinding her once more. It was wonderful. She looked around, searching for something that would tell them what they were supposed to do next.

'I thought Ruha said someone would meet us here?'

Drax edged closer to her, looking uneasy.

'Maybe we need to walk a bit,' Aren suggested.

'Okay, Aren.'

Aren looked behind them. The hole through which they had come was in the side of a small cliff face. The trees were somehow growing up the sides and over the top of the cliff, right into the rock. It would be a good viewing point at the top.

'Let me get our bearings,' Aren said. 'I'll only be up there for a minute. Then I'll come straight back down. Is that okay? Or is that too far?'

'It's okay, Aren.'

Aren walked to the base of the rock, dropped her pack, and began to climb, using the tree roots as footholds. She made her way back up the rock face, glancing down at Drax now and then to check he was all right. Her heartbeat was steady. She got to the top quickly and held up a hand against the glare of the sun.

They were at the very edge of the Deadlands.

Through the trees, Aren could see the mountain containing Valrue, a triangle on the horizon. From its feet came the dark bolt of the Crevasse, stretching into the barrenness towards her.

Aren could see where nature sprang to life. It was a hazy line in the distance, too far away to see properly, but it didn't matter because Aren could picture the details clearly in her mind.

Closest to the mountain there was dirt, and sand, and more dirt.

Then came the sticks, skeletal shrubbery that had tried and failed to survive.

Then full bushels popped into existence like the drawings in Noel's books, only more vibrant.

Then came the trees, and Aren didn't need to picture those. She stood amongst them.

They'd come so far from home.

Aren turned around. Compared to the sparse view towards Valrue, the trees were so thick and tall she couldn't see through them or above them. The forest was quiet, save for the rustling of the leaves. That was where they had to go.

Aren quickly scurried down to Drax and slung her backpack over her shoulders. 'We should keep going east, the same way the river was taking us.'

'Okay, Aren.'

'Let's close the door in the rock.'

It took Drax only a few seconds to find the plate on the outside, subtle as it was against the surrounding rock. He must've felt it there. Aren wrapped her hands around it, twisting it until the rock slid back into place. She took a step back to admire how well it was hidden. The outline of the door appeared like a natural crack in the rock.

'We'll have to remember this spot,' Aren said. 'Just in case –' She froze. She could hear voices. Drax blinked at her, fear on his blank face. He could hear them too.

'It could be the people the Bhouli said would be waiting for us,' Aren whispered.

Drax shrank into his shoulders in reply. Aren wasn't ready to take chances either. She grabbed Drax by the hand and led them behind the nearest tree. Nerves jangling, Aren peeked around the trunk, searching for the people in the details of the forest.

Finally, she spotted them in the distance, wading through the trees towards them. It was a man and a woman wearing grey shirts and trousers. They both had their sleeves rolled up, black material peeking out at their wrists, dagger hilts tucked in snuggly. It was the way they moved that gave them away. They walked like Wren, smooth and silent. Like Jin, too.

'Drax,' Aren hissed, 'they're Krijen!'

She pulled her head back and pressed herself against the bark of the tree. She breathed deeply, trying to settle her heart, which had begun to beat frantically. Drax huddled into her side.

It was incredibly lucky the Krijen were talking; Aren wouldn't have heard them otherwise. If she and Drax stayed out of sight, the Krijen should walk right past them, completely unawares.

Aren gripped Drax's hand tighter as one of the Krijen spoke, close enough now that they could hear every word. His voice was rough and gravelly.

'Do you miss being Base Master?'

'Nah, I needed a change,' the Krijen woman replied. 'Twenty years of the same shit, you know? And I was sick of saying goodbye to everyone. Even the roamers never stayed longer than a few months. It's nice to have a squad again.'

'You don't miss bossing people around?'

'Nah. Could you imagine missing out on *this?*'

Aren didn't know what she meant.

'Nope. I can't believe it,' the Krijen man replied. 'They must've been stealing supplies right from the farms. How did we miss them?'

'Because they were *underground*. These mayjen and their stupid love of digging holes in the earth! By the Great fucking Kahn, if we hadn't learned our lesson from the last bandit attack –'

'We still should've found them earlier.'

'Fourth Base East never had enough Krijen to cover the area, you know that.'

'At least it's not my fault this time.'

'*Enough* with the self-pity, Myles.'

'Yeah, all right.' He paused. 'But I don't envy those underground bunker bandits if that's what they are.'

'You feel sorry for them?'

'Fuck no! I've got more reason than any of us to hate bandits. I meant the FaKrijen. He's . . . '

'He's what?'

'He's not like Oji.'

'No. He's something else.'

The Krijen fell silent. Too silent. Aren couldn't tell if they'd stopped walking or not. Drax was growing more unsettled next to her, responding to the hastening beats of her heart.

They waited, scanning their surroundings. *I'll count a few seconds and then look again,* Aren decided. Once she got to ten, she slowly eased her head around the tree.

She stifled a squeal. The Krijen were walking right past the rock face, terrifyingly close. The man was tall and gruff-looking, and the woman had wide-set eyes and a long black braid which trailed down her back. The Krijen weren't looking at them, but Aren could see their eyes roaming the tree roots and skimming the top of the cliff, on the alert.

Aren ducked to the other side of the tree and watched them disappear into the forest. She felt a gentle nudge on her shoulder and looked back at Drax, who blinked at her. 'Do you think the Krijen got them?' he asked in a whisper. 'Did the Krijen get the people who were supposed to help us?'

Aren swallowed. It sounded like they had, but the Krijen had called them bandits. Was that right? She couldn't imagine the Bhouli working with people who stole things. Then again, the Bhouli were a mystery to her. And bandits or not, they must be doing some good. They were helping people get out of Valrue.

'I hope not,' Aren replied. She'd heard rumours about the new FaKrijen, none of which she wanted to believe. But knowing the Krijen, they were true.

'Let's go,' Aren said. 'We won't know if the Krijen got them unless we look.'

She stepped out from behind the tree, Drax trailing close behind. They pushed on through the wilderness as quietly as possible, on the lookout for roaming Krijen. Aren couldn't comprehend how Drax must be feeling, knowing they were so close to them. In saying that, it had been his idea to go back into the KahnenKeep for Sid, the place where the Krijen had committed all kinds of horrors on him.

Aren watched Drax amble ahead of her, his laborious gait making her cringe. How had he turned out so gentle, so sweet, considering what had been done to him? Aren slowly breathed in to stay calm. One day, she wished she could meet the Krijen who'd done it so she could punch them all in the face.

And Felle. Aren wasn't sure about Pakker. He didn't seem as bad.

And Mandavar. In fact, Drax's father seemed the most monstrous. Both nature and nurture should have been against the little mayj. The thought prompted a question.

'Drax, do you know who your mother is?'

Drax stopped and turned back to Aren. 'My mother –?'

A blood-curdling scream split the air.

Aren threw herself at Drax, knocking him straight into the ferns. They hit the forest floor and lay there in fraught silence, the smell of crushed plants floating up around them while the seconds ticking by.

Aren's poor heart pounded. To her relief, no daggers whizzed over their heads. They hadn't been spotted.

Another scream cut the air, even more piercing and drawn out than the first. Aren wanted to run towards it, to stop it, to rescue whichever poor soul was enduring enough agony to make such a sound.

'I want to see what's happening,' Aren whispered.

Drax nodded, but he was shaking violently.

Aren hesitated. 'Is it okay if we go look?'

'It's okay, Aren.'

They picked themselves off the ground and stayed low, heading in the direction from which the screams had come. Soon they heard muffled conversation. The forest wasn't so thick this way, the ground more trodden. Aren stopped behind a patch of dense shrubbery, and Drax tucked himself in behind her. Together, they peered through the leaves.

In a clearing, four grey-clad Krijen stood with their daggers out. The tall, gruff Krijen man and the Krijen woman with the long black braid were there.

Before them knelt a short row of bedraggled-looking people, three men and a girl who looked, at most, sixteen years old. Each captive had their hands splayed on the ground in front of them. Their clothes were torn, and they were covered with leaves and dirt as though they'd been dragged across the clearing.

Indeed, there was a path scraped in the earth before each captive to a small opening in the ground, maybe thirty feet away. Piled next to the opening was a mound of wooden crates filled with waterskins, and food sacks which had split, their contents spilled on the ground. A few green limes had rolled free.

Next to the strewn supplies was a fifth captive, a limp figure lying on his stomach, whimpering softly. Two more grey-clothed Krijen knelt over him, each with a cleaver in their hand. Red leached into the surrounding ground.

Above them lorded another Krijen in traditional black wraps. He had a pointed chin and prominent cheekbones and jet-black hair. He held a dagger hilt up to his face, the blade of it gone, his wrist stained red.

Aren didn't need to know his face to know who he was.

'You melted my blade,' FaKrijen Eden said to the limp figure at his feet. 'I've not seen that before.' He sounded excited.

The FaKrijen bent down and picked something up off the ground from next to the limp figure. 'Now,' he said as he rose again, 'that wasn't so difficult, was it?'

'No, sir,' the two Krijen next to him replied, both rising to their feet.

The FaKrijen tossed what he was holding towards where Aren and Drax hid in the shrubbery. A pair of severed hands smacked into the dirt before them, the white bone visible at the wrists. Aren raised a hand to her mouth, turning to Drax in horror. He stared at the hands, his face back to the blank mask.

The limp mayj at the FaKrijen's feet groaned and rolled over. Aren could see a puddle of silver on his chest, the shiny substance dripping down his front to join the red on the ground.

The FaKrijen dropped his useless dagger hilt onto the ground and stepped over the mayj, striding towards the four kneeling captives. He smiled a smile so vile that Aren's stomach twisted at the sight of it.

The FaKrijen stopped in front of the captives. 'Kill the mayj,' he said to his Krijen. 'Put these ones back where they came from. We will bury them.'

The gruff-looking Krijen stepped forward, lifting his blade towards the captives.

'No, Myles,' the FaKrijen said. 'Alive.'

Myles slid his dagger back into his wrist wraps and grabbed a captive by the scruff of the neck, hauling him towards the opening in the ground while the man kicked and pleaded.

Another captive cried out and lunged after them, earning himself a sharp blow to the temple from the Krijen who stood behind him. The captive pitched forward into the dirt, clutching his head. The Krijen who'd struck him cleared his throat. 'Sir, these don't seem like typical bandits. Perhaps you want to –'

'I want them in the ground.'

The other Krijen followed Myles' lead. They moved together, pulling the captives to their feet and hauling them back them across the clearing.

'You can't do this!' one of the captives yelled. 'We haven't done anything!'

'You've been stealing supplies,' the FaKrijen said.

'No, we haven't!'

'Lies,' the FaKrijen replied, pointing to the pile of food next to the opening in the ground. He turned to his Krijen. 'We will set up camp here. It's a good spot. I see why they chose it.'

'Drax,' Aren whispered, shaking him gently. 'Drax, please, we . . . we have to do . . .' The words died in her mouth. It would be utterly selfish of her to ask him to do something, especially considering she couldn't do anything herself. Sure, she could handle streetlings and a few overenthusiastic visitors to the Point, but she could not take on Krijen. Drax couldn't fight them either, not while her heart was beating. She couldn't ask anything more of him.

Aren twisted her wrist wraps furiously in her fingers, aching to help. *No*, she told herself, hot tears welling in her eyes. They couldn't do anything.

The captives fought hard, but they were unarmed, outnumbered, and their mayj protector was all but dead. They screamed as, one by one, the Krijen wrestled them back into the earth, helped along by a dagger hilt to the head or a fist to the face, sending them toppling into the dark hole.

The Krijen woman with the braid had the girl in her grip, the last of the captives above ground. As her imminent grave loomed, the girl shrieked louder, pressing her feet in front of herself and shoving backwards. The Krijen woman pushed her relentlessly forward, indifferent to the girl's pleading. Just as the Krijen woman raised her fist to strike the captive, there was a flash of a blade, and the girl suddenly had a Krijen dagger in her hand.

'She's a mayj!' Aren hissed, feeling a spark of hope.

The girl swung the blade wildly at the Krijen woman, who twisted to the side and dodged the attack, lashing out like a whip and smacking the girl upside the head. The girl staggered and dropped the weapon, but she threw her hands out towards the Krijen woman's boots. The girl jerked her hands, and the Krijen woman smacked onto her back, her feet dragged out from under her.

The girl took off running, but the Krijen woman was already back on her feet. She sprinted after the fleeing captive, throwing her arms around the girl's neck and bringing them both crashing to the ground. The rest of the squad raced towards them.

'No!' the FaKrijen ordered. 'Leave them. I want Kimjit to do it.'

The squad skidded to a stop, their hands twitching atop their daggers, surrounding the wrestling pair.

The girl had managed to pry Kimjit's arms from around her neck, her strength no doubt bolstered by her power. But fighting with majik could be as exhausting as fighting without it, and Aren could see the girl's fatigue setting in.

The girl rolled onto her stomach and clawed at the dirt, kicking out at Kimjit as she tried to pull herself away. Her cries dissolved into tears as Kimjit hauled her back.

The girl screamed and twisted on the ground, throwing a handful of dirt into Kimjit's face. Kimjit spat out a mouthful of brown saliva, and in one swift movement, she grabbed the girl by the face and slammed her head into the ground.

The girl moaned, struggling until she had strength for nothing other than swatting uselessly at Kimjit. Kimjit straddled her, trapping the girl's arms beneath her knees.

'No . . . please,' the girl begged, dazed. 'Please, we weren't stealing . . . we weren't . . .'

One of the other Krijen stepped forward with his cleaver, but the FaKrijen held up his hand. 'I said Kimjit will do it.'

Wordlessly, Kimjit took the cleaver. She looked up at the FaKrijen.

'Go on.'

'Please,' Drax whispered to Aren, 'can we go?'

Aren quickly took Drax's limp hand in hers, leading them back from the clearing. As they moved, a dull thud vibrated through the ground towards them. The girl's scream split the air, echoing through Aren's head, through the guts of the forest. It stretched out to the Deadlands, covering the sound of their footsteps as they slipped away.

CHAPTER 33:
THE GREAT KAHN

The Great Kahn felt the KrijenMayj's skahk eyes follow him as he crossed the room. The Great Kahn didn't know why he himself was there, only that his feet had taken him. Maybe it was Luka trying to tell him something. It had been weeks since Sid Bha's escape, and the Great Kahn had promised himself he would repent.

Stolt had failed to fix the webbed cardonite walls. Sure, the skahk had left the Keep in such a state that the clean-up had kept Stolt busy, but the Great Kahn thought it strange that Stolt hadn't at least tried to hide his inadequacy. No one need know he hadn't Woven the cardonite walls back together, so long as he filled in the cracks. Then again, maybe even that was too much to expect from Stolt.

The Eighth House respectfully stepped aside, the Great Kahn taking his place in the centre while they waited for the training to begin.

The Krijen squad stood around their skahk, a new obeisance to their stance. The Great Kahn wondered if it were because of the skahk's growing majikal prowess or simply because they'd made him squad leader. Perhaps both.

Mandavar always had a commanding air about him that no one else could replicate because of his power. This skahk had something similar. The Great Kahn tried not to let his lip curl as he looked at him. He would be civil to Oji's spawn, he told himself. For Luka.

Stolt stepped up to the Krijen squad. 'Are you ready?'

The skahk – *no,* the Great Kahn silently corrected himself. The *KrijenMayj* nodded.

Then he attacked.

It had been years since the Great Kahn had seen a mayj fight with majik and never against a group of Krijen. It was not the walkover it should have been, nor was the KrijenMayj struggling. A contradiction.

The KrijenMayj seemed to toy with his squad, letting them get close before picking them off, one by one. But what was so odd was that he would occasionally let a blow glance off him, or take a kick to his back, or a dagger slice to the arm.

It didn't seem fake when this happened, but it must be because it made no sense. It took a few minutes, but eventually the KrijenMayj had his squad all tied up in knots using their own wraps. They fell over, wriggling pitifully on the ground and yelling obscenities at him, having forgotten their audience.

'He has not broken any of their bones for a while now,' Lord Reider said quietly to the Great Kahn. 'He is restraining himself.'

'Yes,' the Great Kahn agreed. 'He certainly is.'

Stolt spoke some nonsense as the squad picked themselves up off the floor. While they mightn't have had their bones broken this time around, they still looked in a sorry state. One of them had a bandaged hand, another a splinted arm. It displayed carelessness on the KrijenMayj's part, another mystery, given Krijen were not known for that. Quite the opposite. The Great Kahn almost regretted not having come to the earlier trainings. There was a lot about this young man he did not understand.

After an hour or so, Stolt dismissed them. The Eighth House led the way out, glancing back at the Krijen, some of whom were lying on the ground again, still recovering from their latest round.

They all threw loathsome glances towards Stolt as he walked past with his chin in the air. He was too arrogant and too stupid to know he shouldn't make enemies of the Krijen.

The Great Kahn watched as the KrijenMayj helped his squad up off the floor before turning to leave. 'Jin, wait,' the Great Kahn called.

The KrijenMayj looked back in surprise. His squad hesitated too. 'Go,' he said to them. They saluted him and left, throwing glances over their shoulders as they went. That was not very Krijen either, but the Great Kahn wasn't sure if it was curiosity or something else.

As the KrijenMayj walked towards the Great Kahn, he pushed his hair back from his face, a few blond strands having escaped his braid. He stopped before the Great Kahn, thumbing the hilts of his daggers. He was very tall. The Great Kahn barely came up to his nose.

'May I call you Jin?'

'That's your prerogative, my Great Lord.'

He looked rather restless, the Great Kahn decided. His gaze was steady, but he was constantly moving, his fingers twitching. His eyes were bloodshot.

'You are holding back.'

'My Great Lord?'

'You are not harnessing how I would expect someone with your power to harness.'

The KrijenMayj looked taken aback. 'I'm doing what Stolt tells me to.'

'You should not listen to Stolt.'

The KrijenMayj stared at him. 'He is my teacher –'

'And a terrible one at that,' the Great Kahn said. 'He is a jealous man. His ego gets in the way, and he is too thick to comprehend your abilities. Not that he is honest with you about what he *does* understand.' The Great Kahn didn't know why he said it. It was too honest with too much feeling.

The KrijenMayj looked shocked. 'And what . . . what do you know about my abilities?'

'Enough that I find myself intrigued by your performance just now. For example, you are an Influencer, which is to your great advantage, yet you do not Influence. While there is an obvious need for mayjen to conserve power, you are clearly an exception.'

The KrijenMayj was silent for a moment, thoughts battling behind his eyes. 'If I may, my Great Lord,' he said tentatively, 'you seem to know a lot about majik.'

'I knew an exceptional mayj once. I learnt a lot from him.'

The KrijenMayj frowned. 'I thought . . .' He stopped.

The Great Kahn waited. As the ruler of Valrue, there were certain things people were reluctant to say to him. It was irritating, to say the least.

'Speak your mind,' the Great Kahn said. 'I am not here to chastise you.'

'I thought you hated mayjen,' the KrijenMayj said slowly. He paused. 'You particularly seem to hate *me*.'

'You are very perceptive. I do hate you.' The Great Kahn's eyes flickered to the KrijenMayj's thumbs as they stilled over the hilts of his daggers. 'When threatened, you still react like a Krijen,' the Great Kahn said, looking back up again. 'We will make a proper mayj of you yet.'

The KrijenMayj looked perplexed. 'But if you hate me, and you hate mayjen . . . why would you want to?'

'I recognise what is important, even if I do not like it.' The Kahnen had to be placated. The books would still burn, of course, but as a Breaker, this KrijenMayj posed little threat to the balance anyway. He could not Weave.

'May I show you something?' the Great Kahn asked.

'Okay.' The KrijenMayj was thumbing his daggers again. He was a bag of nerves.

'I noticed you harness only one thing at a time.' The Great Kahn slowly pulled off his many rings. He held them in his closed fists, three in his left, four in his right.

The KrijenMayj frowned. 'Yes, Stolt keeps telling me –'

'I already told you that Stolt is an idiot,' the Great Kahn said. 'How he expects you to master challenging majik whilst your squad attack you is beyond me. What I am going to show you is a simple concept but difficult in practice. Stolt may have called it cognitive dexterity.'

'He mentioned something like that. I don't know what it means.'

'It means multitasking.'

'Oh.'

The Great Kahn kept his left fist clenched but held out his right, revealing the four rings nestled in the centre of his palm. 'Lift one ring,' he said.

The KrijenMayj raised an eyebrow. 'One?'

'Yes.'

Wordlessly, the KrijenMayj held out a hand and flicked a finger upwards. A single ring leapt into the air and hovered just above the Great Kahn's palm.

'Good. Lift another to join it.'

The KrijenMayj flicked another finger. A second ring floated up to the first.

'Now the remaining two, together.'

The other two rings floated into the air.

The Great Kahn nodded, and then lifted his other fist and unfurled it, revealing the other three rings. 'Now these.'

The KrijenMayj lifted his free hand.

'No,' the Great Kahn said. 'With the same hand.'

The KrijenMayj gave the Great Kahn a long look before focusing on the three rings, his free hand moving back to a dagger hilt. His harnessing hand drifted in the air, fingers twitching. His lips parted as he concentrated, his head tilting to the side. Slowly, the three rings floated upward to join the others.

'Huh,' the KrijenMayj said. 'It's not hard to do. It just took a while to think of how to do it. Like it's teasing my brain.'

'Precisely.'

The Great Kahn watched as the KrijenMayj splayed his fingers wider. The rings floated away from each other and began swirling around the air above their heads, all in different directions, following a gentle stirring of the KrijenMayj's fingers.

'You picked it up quickly,' the Great Kahn said.

'I've done it before,' the KrijenMayj said. 'I think. In the Deadlands.'

The rings slowly floated back down to the Great Kahn, who scooped them from the air and placed them back on his fingers.

'The Deadlands?' The Great Kahn couldn't keep the venom from his voice. The reminder of the bandit attack only made him think of Oji, who had thwarted him. His nostrils flared, and he shook his head, trying to clear it.

The KrijenMayj noticed. 'Thank you for pardoning me,' he said, bowing his head. 'I know I put you in a difficult position –'

'Let us move on,' the Great Kahn said coldly. He did not want to talk about this. 'Tell me what you did when you harnessed like this before.'

The KrijenMayj folded his arms, trapping his twitching fingers. 'I created a sandstorm. That counts as moving lots of things at once, doesn't it? But once it got going, all I needed to do was . . . stir it, I guess.'

His words gave the Great Kahn pause. 'Did you move the sand? Or the air?'

The difference was huge. If he moved the sand, it was simply an exceptional demonstration of cognitive dexterity. But if he moved the particles in the air, it was atomik majik. Good enough for Mandavar, even.

'I . . . I don't know,' the KrijenMayj said, his brow furrowing. 'I can't think of what I grabbed hold of.'

'If you remember, let me know. Either way, you are correct. You would have been moving millions of things at once. Their negligible mass is what would have made it easier than lifting these rings. That, and dare I say it, you have a natural flare for majik. It is remarkable what we can conjure up when in need, without knowing what we do.'

'I think I understand.' The KrijenMayj didn't acknowledge the praise. 'What about moving liquid?' he asked instead.

'Talk me through what you are thinking,' the Great Kahn said. It was a logical leap but not one that the Great Kahn would expect a novice mayj to make.

'Well, it's easy to move solid things because they hold their shape,' the KrijenMayj said. 'But I've been able to move liquid too with relative ease. Isn't liquid more like air?'

'Somewhere in the middle. Liquids have stronger bonds between their particles than air, so they are easier to manipulate as a whole.' The Great Kahn waited, but it seemed the KrijenMayj had no more questions.

'We are done here then.' The Great Kahn swept towards the door.

'Wait!'

The Great Kahn turned back, surprised to see how pale the KrijenMayj had suddenly become, the fear making his bloodshot eyes stand out. He was easier to read than a book. 'Can *you* teach me,' he asked with a hint of desperation, 'instead of Stolt?'

The Great Kahn had suspected this question was coming. 'No.'

'Why not?'

'Because I do not want to.'

It was too soon, far too soon for him to do such a thing. Even speaking of majik still made him shudder. *But you spoke of it today,* the Great Kahn thought to himself. It was one more step in the right direction. Back to Luka.

He left the KrijenMayj standing alone in the training room.

CHAPTER 34:
PYRA

The tower room was filled to bursting with streetlings. The noise was unbelievable; they were screeching and squabbling, hurling things, and spitting at each other.

It was almost peaceful for once.

Pyra narrowed her eyes, scanning the grubby faces. For the streetling meets, the gang leaders were allowed to bring whoever from their gang wanted to come, and their seconds, of course. The seconds were the top picks of the toughest, grossest, or meanest streetlings in Rue. Perhaps there were even a few here that could do majik despite the Krijen's best efforts to string them all up. No one needed to tell Pyra to be careful. This was the most dangerous room in the city.

The gang leaders stood on tables at the back of the room with their streetlings crammed into the space in front of them because they weren't stupid enough to stand in the middle.

Each gang leader represented a side of Rue. Pyra was Upper West Side, the best of the lot. The four others present covered the Upper East, Lower East, Left South, and Right South Sides. The Lower West was missing. They'd not had a gang leader for a while now. A proper one anyway.

Pyra ran her eyes around the room once more. The Lost Square's scowling face was not here. Pyra was pissed off about that.

'ALL RIGHT, LISTEN UP!' she screeched.

The noise died away instantly, save for some quiet hissing where the streetlings stood next to members from another gang. Pyra trusted they were excited enough about this meet that they would eventually shut up and listen.

That, and Pyra's new crossbow was pointed at them.

Rifter had loaded a thick bolt and balanced the contraption on Barrett's shoulders next to the table on which Pyra stood. It calmed the streetlings enough that this time, Pyra was confident they could get through the pertinent bits without interruption. Even so, she needed to be quick. Streetlings had shockingly short attention spans.

'I know the Krijen and their Squares got us all good,' Pyra began, 'and we've had to lie low lately. But you know what? It's a good thing. They think they've got us spooked. But they don't know that streetlings don't spook. Isn't that right?' Pyra grinned as gleeful shrieks clattered around the room. 'Those Kahnen think they have us trembling in our towers, but really, they just gave us more time for scheming. And a scheme is exactly what I have for you. Our first Reckoning is upon us, my friends.'

Pyra gave them a moment to hoot and scream, then raised her arm for silence.

'Before I share the plan for the next few weeks, I want reports. Now, don't give me shifty stories. If I find out you're lying, you know what to expect.' Rifter paraded his fingers against the side of the crossbow, to make the message clear.

The meet went as expected. Every side of Rue was down on numbers, especially of mayjen, and ready for retaliation, enough that they were just as likely to turn on each other like they used to. But it would do no good for them to waste their efforts on petty outbursts in the streets. The gang leaders had learnt from the Celebrations that if they held back and bided their time, the bloody reward was worth the wait. The promise of the first Reckoning was enough to keep thirsty streetlings in line. Until

Pyra said go, at least.

'What do you want, Toot?'

The Lower East Side gang leader had dropped down from his table and stalked through his sea of streetlings to the edge of Pyra's gang. Pyra could see Ala with her blonde bunches at the front, snarling at Toot as he stopped in front of her.

Toot had a mean face and a sharp wit. He was known for shoving nails through the eardrums of creepers, streetlings who strayed across their boundaries. A rather respectable pastime in gang leader Pyra's opinion.

'They never strung up that Krijen after the Celebrations,' Toot said. 'The one who was a mayj. I've been waiting for it.'

'No, they didn't,' Pyra said bitterly. 'Instead, the Kahnen gave him an honorary title for his efforts. The KrijenMayj.'

The room hissed.

Pyra *would* have mentioned he was the same Krijen who sicked the Squares onto them, but they'd go out of their minds at the news. It would be more trouble than it was worth to bring that up at a gang meet.

'What do we do if he shows up at the Reckoning?' Toot asked.

Pyra had thought of this. They couldn't afford for him to get in the way, so Lady Hia said she would deal with this if needed. 'He won't,' Pyra replied. 'We've got eyes on him.'

After the meet, Pyra stood on the rooftops of the Upper West Side in the sun, grinding her teeth. That bloody Lost Square had not shown its face. Not that she wanted it there, but Rifter and Barrett had been present when she'd made her demands at the Point. Their loyalty to her, and to their cause, wouldn't stretch so far as keeping the slight against her silent. *No one* fell through on a promise made to a gang leader. If Pyra didn't deal with it in the appropriate fashion before everyone found out, her reputation would take a hit.

Rifter came to stand next to her, wrinkling his nose at the expression on her face. 'We're going to the Point, aren't we?'

'Duh,' Pyra said. 'Who'd you ask to pass on the message about where the meet was?'

'Ala.'

'Did she have anything to say?'

'Just that it said it would come.'

That blasted Lost Square.

'Get Barrett,' Pyra snapped. 'Tell him to bring the crossbow.'

Rifter slipped away.

This was going to be tough. Pyra needed to convince the streetlings the Lost Square had been adequately punished for disrespecting her. At the same time, she had to make sure it would agree to come to the next meet, or Lady Hia would have her head. Being in charge was not all it was cracked up to be.

Pyra spotted Rifter and Barrett wading through the street below her, the crossbow loaded on Barrett's shoulders. She pulled her floppy black hat from her head and tucked it into her trousers for safekeeping, then jumped down the rooftops to meet them. They wound their way to the Point.

The line of visitors was longer than ever. Pyra walked the length of it, leaving silence in her wake as the hungry eyes spied the crossbow.

Several visitors turned to leave, mostly the mothers with clinging children, their innocent eyes wide as their mothers whisked them away. They weren't stupid enough to stick around when the gang leaders were out for vengeance.

The residents watched from their dark shadows. There were so many of them now that Pyra had a rare strike of nerves. After all, they *were* mayjen, even if they were the ones that had given up, the ones with no fight left. A lot of them looked like they'd recently been Turning, their hollowed eyes unfocused.

Strangely, two of them had a small circular patch of blood on the front of their clothes, as though they'd been stabbed in the chest and left to bleed. It didn't seem to bother them. They slumped against the walls of the alleyway, giving Pyra dopey grins as she passed.

Once again, the Lost Square was nowhere to be seen. 'It's hiding,' Pyra said to Barrett and Rifter. 'It knows we're here, and it's just too scared –'

'I assume you're talking about me,' said a voice behind them. Pyra whipped around.

The Lost Square appeared out of a stone doorway, stepping between a small haunt of residents who looked up at it with slack expressions. The Lost Square had Pyra's belt slung across its torso, a bloodied knife shoved through it, smearing red all over the leather. Pyra felt a surge of anger at the sight of it.

'Barrett, get *down*,' Pyra commanded. Barrett knelt and braced himself on the ground as Pyra stepped in behind the crossbow. The Lost Square paused on its walk towards her, scowling as Pyra aimed the bolt at its head.

'What the fuck are you doing?' it asked, articulate as ever. 'Give it a rest, won't you?'

'You really had me going for a minute,' Pyra spat. 'I don't know why I expected a dirty Lost Square to keep its word. So that's my bad. I won't be making the same mistake again.'

'I don't know what you're talking about.'

'You didn't come to the meet!'

'You had it already?'

The Lost Square put on a good act, that was for sure. Pyra wouldn't fall for it. 'You think I'm stupid?'

The thing snorted. 'No, I don't. But you're doing a fucking good impression of it right now.'

Pyra screeched, and her finger hovered dangerously above the crossbow trigger. But she knew she couldn't because she'd promised Lady Hia. The Lost Square knew it too, or it wouldn't be looking so bloatedly smug with her bolt trained between its eyes.

Pyra stepped out from behind the crossbow and treaded slowly towards it, pulling out her horseshoes from her wrists as she went. 'You were told about the meet –'

'No, I wasn't.'

'And *that's* a fib if I ever heard one.'

The Lost Square barked a laugh. 'A fib? Isn't that a bit hypocritical? All you are is one, great, dirty lie.'

Pyra stopped just in front of the Lost Square, eyeing it up. It glared back at her as ugly and stubborn as ever.

Shoving down her repulsion, Pyra leaned in towards it until she was just close enough that the others couldn't hear. 'I told you the truth about that friend of yours, you know,' she said quietly. 'You *owe* me for that.'

It wasn't what gang leader Pyra would say. It was what Polly's Pyra would say. But she didn't know what else to do. This thing had her at *another* stalemate.

'I said I would come,' the Lost Square said coldly. 'I meant it. No one told me about the meet. Now get out of my face. I don't have time for this.'

Blast it, Pyra thought as she stared into the Lost Square's dark eyes. It was telling the truth.

Ala, the little villain, had lied.

This was going to be bad.

CHAPTER 35:
AREN BHA

Aren wanted to go back. She wanted to go back and dig out the bandits who weren't bandits from the black hole in the ground. If that young mayj girl was still alive, Aren wanted to wrap her stumps in bandages and tell her it was going to be okay even though it wasn't, and Aren knew she couldn't, because the Krijen were camping on top of the grave.

After hours of fighting their way through the forest, its foliage thickening the further they pressed, she and Drax sat down on a log and drained their waterskins. Drax looked exhausted, and he was moving slowly, but Aren's heart kept its rhythm. She'd given him the rest of her food that Natoni had packed for them, including a few strips of dried meat and some hard squares of what she thought was cornbread. She wasn't hungry, but Drax must be starving.

'Aren? Are you okay?' Drax's eyes pleaded with her.

'Yes! I'm *fine.*' Aren's voice came out in a snarl though she hadn't meant it to. She felt like a weak little rich girl all over again. 'I'm fine, other than being completely and utterly *useless.*'

'You're not useless.'

Aren snorted, a perfect rendition of Wren. 'Oh, but I am. Especially compared to you.' Aren folded her arms to stop herself from snapping her wrist wraps in frustration. It irritated people, but try as she might, she couldn't kick the habit.

Drax frowned at her. 'You lied,' Drax accused. 'You're not okay. You're angry with me. You wanted me to do something.'

'I'm not angry with you!' Aren's anger melted away at the look on Drax's face. 'No, I'm angry with *myself.* I'm the reason you couldn't do anything to help those people. You might've had a real chance of saving them if it weren't for me and my stupid heart.'

'I should've tried –'

'No. It was horrible, but we had no choice. I've seen something like that before.'

Drax cocked his head. 'What do you mean?'

'Last year, the Krijen caught a mayj and cut off her hands, right in front of me. Wren held me back because there was nothing I could do. But now it's happened *again* even though I swore I wouldn't be so useless the next time –'

'It's okay, Aren.'

'No, it's not okay! And the *worst* part is that those people were supposed to be helping us, and we just left them to die –' Aren stopped talking abruptly. Drax had leant over and settled his arms around her, his limp hands flopping together.

'What are you doing?' she asked. 'Are you *hugging* me?'

Drax quickly let go, cringing away. 'I'm sorry, I'm sorry. You hugged Bish when he was sad.' His head sank into his shoulders at her silence.

'You're right,' Aren said, remembering the moment. 'I did.' She reached out and took Drax's hands in hers. 'You don't need to be sorry. I was just surprised. It was a really nice thing to do.'

'You feel better then?'

Aren gave him a weak smile. 'Yes, a little.'

'Do you want to go back to the Krijen? I'll try to fix it for you.'

'No, but thank you.'

Aren gave his hands a gentle squeeze and stood up off the log, staring into the depths of the forest. She could feel Drax's eyes still on her. He couldn't be tricked.

'You're still sad.'

'I'll be all right. I promise.'

'Okay, Aren.'

The light was fading quickly. *This is a disaster*, Aren thought. They had no idea if they were going in the right direction, and they were in a forest with Krijen, who they might walk into at any moment. They had no water, no food. Drax needed more than what he'd just eaten even though he wouldn't say it. Aren thought of the mound of food supplies back in the clearing. It made her sick to her stomach, but she wished they could've taken some. At least she trusted the Krijen would send it to Valrue and not let it go to waste.

Or maybe that sick, twisted FaKrijen would leave it there to rot for the pleasure of it.

'Aren?'

Aren realised she'd been silently staring into the trees for far too long. 'Let's rest here. It's as good as any other spot, and it'll be dark soon.' The bush was so thick that no one would see them unless they were practically on top of them.

Aren tugged open Drax's backpack for him and pulled out a bedroll and a blanket. The air was a little cool but nowhere near as cold as in the Crevasse.

'You sleep first. I'll keep watch,' Aren said. 'Then we can swap. Sound good?'

Drax nodded. He fell asleep immediately, leaving Aren to her thoughts. Her mind was racing, tired as she was. She was thinking over the endless books Noel had shoved under her nose that had been about fishing and farming and all those boring things she'd never felt the need to learn about because there had been no reason for it. Perusing the markets was about as close as she'd ever gotten to foraging for food in Valrue.

Aren stood up. She wanted to be moving, but she couldn't go far, or she would wake Drax. So she paced up and down in front of the log, grinding the plants before her into nothing as she rummaged through her brain, trying to drag out anything she could remember that might be useful.

She knew there were berries you could eat, and roots, and grasses, though she remembered them all looking the same or similar, and Great Kahn only knew if they even grew here.

As for animals – Aren stopped pacing. Speaking of, where were all the animals? They'd heard them at night, but they hadn't *seen* one, not even a bird in a tree. Then again, they hadn't been looking.

Aren stepped over the log and slowly crept down its length, running her eyes over the rough bark, struggling to see in the darkness that had settled.

There was nothing.

She kept moving, edging a little further, stopping only when Drax began twitching in his sleep. It prompted a thought. Were there no animals around because of Drax? Were they running from his power?

Something moved at Aren's feet. She squatted down, peering into the dirt. *Aha,* she thought.

There, trekking in a row, were little creatures. They were bright green and looked like someone had pinched the tops of their bulbous little bodies, making them look like tiny leaves. In fact, had they not been scurrying away from Drax as though their lives depended on it, she might not have spotted them.

It could be a coincidence, sure, but it made sense.

Aren watched the little creatures curiously for a while and then walked back and settled down next to Drax. She leant against the log, looking up at the night sky beyond the tips of the trees. The twinkling stars made her think of Maude. They seemed a long way away.

Aren hoped the Bhouli were happy up there. Not that Aren believed it, but it seemed a nice idea to live among the stars.

Aren looked down again and pulled back her sleeve, exposing the tattoo she had on her wrist. It was a circle with two pinched edges that curled. The circle was filled with swirls of different weights that seemed to revolve as Aren looked at them.

They'd been lucky, maybe. But she'd not felt happiness today.

It seemed hard to believe that Maude had put this on her arm with so much conviction. Maybe it was meant as a reminder that it was important to look for the good in things. There was so much bad in the world, it was easy to get swamped by it.

Holding onto that thought, Aren closed her eyes not to sleep but to listen to the sounds of the forest as it came alive around her.

***

Aren woke to her heart fluttering. From the look of the light, it was very early in the morning.

'Sorry. I think I woke you,' Drax said. He'd taken over watch in the middle of the night. Aren didn't even remember falling asleep. She sat up, dizziness fading as her heart picked back up its rhythm.

Next to her, Drax had the waterskins resting upright against the log with their caps off. He had a vague look of concern on his face. 'Normally, this would not be so hard,' he said. 'But I need food.'

Aren rubbed sleep from her eyes before peering at the waterskins. 'What are you doing?'

'Filling them.'

Aren leant forward and picked one up, incredulous. It was heavy with water. 'How did you do this?'

'Everything was damp this morning, so I pulled some of the water into them. Is that okay?'

'That's . . . that's brilliant, Drax.'

Aren slowly screwed the caps on, frowning. That was one problem down, only a few more to go.

They rolled up their bedrolls and blankets, strapped their packs on, and took off into the forest. 'So you need food,' Aren said. 'If we're lucky, there might be some fruit, or leaves we can eat.' Aren swallowed. Assuming they didn't pick the poisonous ones. Her knowledge of plants was dangerously lacking. Anything they ate would be a gamble. And plants certainly wouldn't be enough to sustain them, especially not if Drax was harnessing. She remembered being a little girl and watching Noel cook an enormous bunch of green leaves, thinking him silly as he shoved them into the pot because surely they couldn't all fit. Then they shrank away to nothing, leaving Aren wondering why Noel had bothered in the first place if he'd known the food was going to disappear on him.

What they needed was meat.

The thought of killing something brought a warm wave of bile into Aren's mouth. But she would do it. She'd sat on it all night, wrestling with herself. But she wouldn't be useless anymore.

'I think it's best we find animals,' Aren said. 'They'll feel you coming though, which is why we haven't seen any. But that's okay,' she went on hurriedly as Drax ducked his head, looking guilty. 'I think I know a way around this. If you're harnessing *me*, will *I* scare the animals off?'

'No,' Drax said, 'you're not a source of power. And you use what I give you too quickly.'

'What about my cardonite dagger? Can they feel that?'

'I don't think it will be enough to scare the animals.' Drax paused, frowning like he did yesterday. 'Why do you want animals?'

'To hunt them. How far do you think I can move away from you before it becomes too hard?'

'You want to go away?'

'Not for long.'

Drax's face had become a blank mask again. 'I don't like this idea.'

'Why not?'

'I don't know.'

'I think it might work though. And I can't think of another way to do it. Unless you can catch animals using majik? But are they hard to harness, like people are? I thought maybe you had to see them to use majik on them, but now that I think about it, you keep saying you feel things even when you can't see them, so maybe that could work –'

'I don't want to kill things.'

'No, it's okay, I'll do that bit –'

'Please, Aren. I can't, *I can't.*' Drax stopped and looked back at her. 'I can't hold them while you hurt them.'

Aren stopped too, noticing the look on his face. 'All right,' she said softly. 'I won't ask you to do that.' So it was back to plants then.

They walked on.

Aren desperately scoured the greenery for anything which looked vaguely edible, a seed of worry growing in her gut. Hours later when the sun had crossed the sky and it was getting dark again, they'd collected only a few berries, one of which Aren had sniffed and taken a tiny nibble, hoping it wouldn't kill her.

When she'd survived another hour, Aren had given them all to Drax, refusing to eat any more herself. She'd not had any food since before they'd got off the boat, but apart from her stomach gnawing on her insides, she felt okay.

Drax, on the other hand, was shaking so much that Aren worried he might start Turning. She knew from watching people starve to death in Valrue that humans could go a few weeks without food, but not while doing majik, and especially not while keeping someone's heart beating. Drax was deteriorating so quickly it scared her, and it was all her fault.

As Aren crawled into her bedroll that night, the guilty thoughts followed her into her sleep, nagging at her and making her dream bad dreams.

CHAPTER 36:
PYRA

Pyra *hated* the Lost Square. This was its fault. If it wasn't so odious, so undeserving of existence, then maybe Ala would have done as she was told.

But the little streetling hadn't. She'd disobeyed.

'ALA!'

Pyra stormed through the tower, one of her horseshoes clenched in her hand.

This was the part that made her feel sick, like, for *real*. It was the part where the two sides of her collided, Polly's Pyra and gang leader Pyra, each of them thinking that the other was right. Every single time, Pyra pleaded for a compromise even though she knew there wasn't one because streetlings did not deal with shades of grey, only black and white.

'ALA! I KNOW YOU'RE HERE!'

And if there was one thing that streetlings expected Pyra to do, the *one freaking thing* that she couldn't back down from – not ever – was following through on her threats.

'ALA –'

'It was too yucky, Pyra!'

Pyra spun around in the corridor, making the streetlings around her flinch into the walls. Their morbid fascination tempted them to watch because it had been so long since anyone had disobeyed Pyra.

Ala stood in the corridor, her cheeks red, her tiny hands squeezed into fists. 'I shouldn't have had to do it!' she cried.

'Come. Here.'

The little streetling took a few steps forward, then stopped, her face indignant. Pyra snapped out an arm and grabbed a hold of Ala by one of her blonde bunches, which she'd worn since they'd duped the Lost Square. Ala must've liked the disguise despite how much she'd whined about it.

Ala squealed as Pyra dragged her forward. 'You remember what I said I'd do if you disobeyed me again?'

Ala burst into tears, slapping at Pyra's wrist. *Great Kahn save me*, Pyra thought. She'd never used that expression before, but it seemed perfectly fitting right now. She needed more than human strength for this.

'No, don't do it!' Ala cried. 'Don't do it!'

'It's too late, Ala,' Pyra said. She had to. Gang leader Pyra had no choice. She looked down at the weapon in her hand, staring at the tiny sharp point. *Who am I kidding*, Pyra thought. She couldn't do this with a filed-down horseshoe. She dropped it on the ground.

'Give me your knife, Ala.'

Ala squealed louder, tugging backwards with all her might, but Pyra held on tight. Ala was so small and skinny that Pyra could have picked up her in one hand if she'd wanted.

A blade appeared in the air beside Pyra's head. 'Here, take mine,' a streetling said. Pyra took it.

Then she forced Ala's head to the floor, kneeling on her chest to keep her still as the little girl writhed.

While the streetlings looked on in silence, Pyra held the blade against Ala's hairline, gritted her teeth against her revulsion and Ala's screams, and began to slice.

An hour later, Pyra stood outside Polly's shop. Pyra couldn't see what was happening beyond the dirty windows. Lord Reider wasn't taking care of it, this shop that he'd wanted so badly.

Pyra was glad it was dark and raining because there were tears streaming down her face. If anyone saw gang leader Pyra crying, the rumour would beat her back to the tower. She didn't wipe the tears away though. She let them fall down her cheeks onto the cobblestones. It would be best to get them all out now.

Maybe some people would think her tears silly, and that the things she cried over were trivial. *How can you cut out tongues without tears, Pyra, but not take off scalps?* they would ask.

Well. She supposed she'd accepted the tongue thing was a necessary evil back when she'd started it. She'd been angrier then, Polly's murder still fresh, and she'd not cared all that much about the streetlings. Like the older folk always said, they were just another type of city rat.

But Pyra cared about them now.

Never again would Pyra be so stupid as to threaten a scalping. The words had left her mouth without any thought because people said stuff all the time that they didn't mean. She'd just momentarily forgotten who she was supposed to be, and it had come back to bite her.

'Pyra?'

Pyra jumped and looked up, quickly wiping her eyes on her sleeve.

It was Tiju, the old shoe cobbler from the shop next door. She'd not seen him for years. 'Get away from me,' she said, holding up one of her horseshoes. 'Get away from me or I'll . . . I'll . . .' She couldn't think of a threat. There was nothing that would make her hurt Tiju.

'Pyra, come now. Come inside.' He put an arm around her shoulders, and Pyra let him steer her towards his shopfront, the bell dinging just like Polly's used to as they stepped over the threshold.

Tiju locked the door after them, then took her through to the back and led her up the stairs into the little home he shared with his wife Nellie.

Nellie was stirring something on the stove when Tiju pushed Pyra gently into the kitchen.

'Oh, Pyra! Oh, I can't believe it!'

Nellie ran forward and threw her bony, withered arms around Pyra. 'Oh, my dear, how are you? Goodness, you look like you need a good feed! We don't have much, but I'm just making some tea now and I can give you biscuits.' She grabbed a tin from the cupboard and came hurrying back as Tiju settled Pyra into a chair.

Everything was the same as Pyra remembered. The room was beautifully clean and starkly empty, apart from the necessities. There was a little dining table in front of which Pyra now sat. A thread-bare sofa occupied a corner of the room, a colourful quilt folded over the back of it. Pyra recalled that Nellie liked to knit. Polly had liked some of Nellie's creations so much she'd started selling them in her shop, giving Nellie all the profits and taking none for herself. Not that she'd ever told Nellie she forfeited her cut.

Pyra blinked, and the memory was gone. Nellie was rattling the biscuit tin in front of her. There were three biscuits left. Tiju and Nellie never had much, but what they did have, they shared. Pyra was horrified to feel herself welling up again.

'I'm sorry,' Nellie said, quickly pulling back the biscuit tin. 'I thought you liked these?'

Pyra stood up from her chair, threw her arms around Nellie, and began sobbing uncontrollably on her shoulder.

'Oh, my dear! There, there, it's okay!' Nellie said.

'No, it's not! It's all *wrong . . .*'

Pyra cried and cried and cried, letting out years of horrors, and when she was finally done, she let go of Nellie and slowly sat back in her chair. Tiju wordlessly held out a handkerchief, and Pyra took it, blowing her nose.

Nellie tentatively held out the biscuit tin again. Pyra took one and bit into it, busying herself with chewing. She was already ashamed of her outburst. If any of the streetlings saw her now, she'd be dead meat. Pyra quickly came back to herself at the thought. 'Thank you,' she muttered.

'I don't mean to intrude.'

'You're not intruding,' Tiju said. 'We've been watching you from the window. I thought it kinder to bring you inside than let you get yourself into trouble. We know what streetlings are like.' It was like they'd read her mind.

'I guess you know what I've been up to then since Polly died,' Pyra said.

'I don't think there is a soul in Valrue who doesn't know what you've been up to,' Tiju said quietly. 'Unfortunately, few of them have the pleasure of knowing you the way we do.'

'I'm not the same girl you remember.'

'I beg to differ. I think you're the same girl, just with a meaner exterior. If you were really as nasty as you pretend to be, I wouldn't have found you crying on the street.'

Pyra sniffed. 'So you don't think I've gone the same way as my parents?'

'Oh, Pyra,' Nellie said gently. 'You're better than your parents. There's too much of your sister in you. You do bad things, but we know you have a good reason for doing them.'

Pyra frowned up at them. 'How are you sure it's for a good reason?'

'Everyone in Rue knows the Kahnen are corrupt,' Nellie said. 'You made it clear at the Celebrations that you and your streetlings won't stand for it.' Tiju and Nellie shared a knowing look.

Pyra tensed. 'Do you . . . what do you know?'

'Don't worry, my dear,' Tiju said. 'We don't know your secrets beyond there being more to your agenda than pleasurable terrorising.'

Pyra wasn't convinced. But even if they knew about Lady Hia, they wouldn't tell. But that wasn't what was bothering her.

'So you're not disappointed in me?' Pyra asked. 'I didn't mean to become this bad, honestly. I just didn't realise what I would have to do to get things done.'

'We are not so naïve as to expect a more righteous way would work,' Tiju said. 'Fight fire with fire, my dear.'

Pyra blinked at them. 'Really?'

'Really. You're ever so brave for doing what you do. I don't know any other souls who would dare try to win over the streetlings, let alone survive it. And people are noticing they aren't as bad as before. The folks in the Upper West Side have hope that life might soon get better, rather than worse, for once. I mean, that's not to say they aren't terrified of you and your gang, but at least they understand what you're about.'

Pyra nodded. 'Good. I've been trying to rein the streetlings in a little, but it's hard to do without blowing my cover. Gang leaders aren't known for their mercies.'

'No, they certainly aren't,' Nellie said, giving Tiju another look. Pyra assumed she meant the tongue thing, or the carving of her name onto foreheads thing. Maybe the scalping thing would get back to her too. Pyra wondered if they would still think her a good person when they heard that. She hoped so. She liked to think Polly's Pyra was still in there, regardless of what gang leader Pyra did.

Tiju gave a gentle cough. 'On the topic of mercies, could we bother you for a small favour?'

Pyra sat up straight, intrigued. 'What is it?'

'I mean, I understand the need, but could stop your streetlings from stealing so many shoes from the shop? We're struggling as it is.'

Pyra felt a wave of hot anger flare inside her. She nodded. She'd not known her streetlings were menacing Tiju and Nellie. 'I can do that.'

'Thank you. Is there anything more we can get you? Anything at all?'

'No, nothing,' Pyra said. 'You've given me everything I need.'

CHAPTER 37:
AREN BHA

Drax barely had enough strength to refill their waterskins the next morning. His body shook as she screwed the caps on, and when he wasn't looking, she snuck a few things from his backpack and shoved them into hers, hoping to lighten his load. He was carrying far too much already.

After that, Aren ripped up some questionable-looking roots, and they chewed on them. They were bitter and tough, and Aren had to force herself to swallow them down. It was enough to dull the pains in her own stomach, but she could hear Drax's growling even after they'd eaten. It was nowhere near enough.

They set off into the forest again, hungry and tired and still unsure if they were going the right way. Aren's dark thoughts from yesterday had followed her through her dreams into the new day, and they'd barely been walking for an hour before her melancholy got the better of her. She stopped and turned on Drax. 'That's it! You're *done*,' she snarled. 'There is no reason for us both to die. Let go of me.'

Drax took a step back from her, his eyes widening in shock. 'No,' he said.

'*Yes!* I'm sucking the life out of you. I will *not* be the reason you die.

Now let go!'

'No.'

Aren screamed in frustration. 'If you don't let go of me *right now*, I'll make you!' She pulled her cardonite dagger from her wraps and swung it up to his face.

Drax flinched and cowered into the ground, his blue eyes fixed on the dagger tip as it quivered between his eyes. 'What will you do?'

The question caught Aren off guard. She had no idea. She'd hoped her threat would scare him enough that he would let go of her heart, but it still beat in her chest, mocking her efforts.

Drax's gaze flickered to hers, his eyes still wide with fright. But clearly not enough. And there was no way Aren was going to take her blade to him.

Perhaps a change of tact.

'I take back what I said,' Aren snapped. 'You need to obey me. Stop harnessing!'

Drax stared at her, then slowly shook his head. 'You're sad,' he said. 'That's why you are pretending. This is not you.' He moved closer, shuffling around Aren's dagger, his limp hands reaching out to her as if to embrace her. 'It's okay, we'll find food –'

'No!'

Desperate, Aren turned and ran, shoving through the bushes, which hurt because they tore at her face and hands, but she kept going anyway. If she got far enough away, Drax would be forced to let go.

She made it about ten steps before her heart buckled and her breath caught. The ground whipped up to meet her. She heard quick, ambling footsteps before Drax crash-landed on top of her, his limp hands weakly gripping her wraps as he pulled himself closer to her heart.

'Let go! *Let go of me!*'

Aren wanted to push him off, but she wasn't sure which way was off because her world was a whirl of colours, so she just shoved at him and smacked at his scarred hands.

'Don't do this!' Drax cried, clutching her tighter. 'Please, don't! I'll hunt for you. I'll catch an animal! I'll kill it for you, so we can eat it!'

His pleads went bone deep.

'That's not what I want!' Aren choked out. 'I'm trying to *save* you!'

'Don't leave me, Aren. Please don't leave me!'

It was a mess, everything, all of it. How could it have gone so badly wrong in a day? Drax's breath was coming in gasps, and Aren could feel blackness looming, but Drax still held on. He would never let her go.

For the longest time, Aren had energy for nothing other than to just lie there, listening to Drax sobbing. She didn't feel guilty for running because even though it hadn't worked, at least this way the end would come sooner instead of drawing out Drax's suffering.

But Aren regretted not having enough breath in her body to say sorry. Sorry that after Drax had finally escaped from the KahnenKeep and from Felle, Aren had only trapped him again. Drax thought this was freedom, but it wasn't. And now he would never know what it felt like.

Eventually, to Aren's relief, Drax quietened, and he let go of her wraps, tucking his head down by her heart. Together they listened to the sounds of the forest.

After a few minutes or an hour or maybe most of the day, Aren could tell Drax was close to Turning because birds were singing right above them. His power was ebbing away, enough that it didn't bother them anymore, and they'd come to see these strange new beings.

Maybe they're wrens, Aren thought. She'd never asked Wren if he knew he was named after a bird. Aren smiled at the thought of him and at the birdsong which sounded like lots of little bells tinkling together in a peaceful melody that was so beautiful it didn't seem real.

Maybe it wasn't. Maybe it was her dying mind giving her some peace, some happiness before she went. Aren had stalled death long enough that she knew it would be the end this time. No one would be lucky enough to come back from the dead twice, not even her.

Drax wasn't dying just yet, but it wouldn't be long. Aren's eyes drifted down to him, still curled into her chest, looking so serene he could easily be sleeping. Maybe he was. Either that or he was enjoying the bliss that came with Turning. *That would be a nice way to go*, Aren thought. She couldn't remember dying last time, but she didn't think it hurt. She just remembered Jin's terrified face, floating above hers.

There was something next to her face again, Aren could sense it. She opened her eyes, not sure when she'd closed them.

A little brown head had crept up to her and was snuffling around, its whiskers grazing the tip of her nose. It had bright eyes in which Aren could see her reflection. It didn't seem worried to be so close, distracted by the smell of these strange things and wondering what they were.

Aren still had her dagger in her hand. She clenched it tighter. Then, with all the strength and speed and stoicism she could muster, she pulled up her arm and plunged her dagger down through the soft brown fur, through spine and sinew, until her blade speared the earth.

The animal screamed and bucked and jerked and died. Aren stared at it, the dagger hilt protruding grotesquely from its tiny body.

'Drax?'

Drax slowly raised his head, his blue eyes half closed. 'Aren?' His voice was barely audible.

'We need to start a fire.'

CHAPTER 38:
JIN KANJU

Seven years ago

Jin threw the door open to Josefina's room. She'd been standing over by the window, and she shrieked when he entered. 'Great Kahn save me!' she exclaimed, a hand going to her chest. 'Didn't the other women ever teach you to *knock*?'

Jin paused in the doorway. He *had* been told off for not knocking before. 'Mama Hidel said you weren't with a client.' Jin looked around the room. 'And you're not.'

'My client isn't long gone,' Josefina growled, 'and I don't appreciate you bursting in. There are certain things you shouldn't see.'

'Don't worry, I've seen it all before.'

'Jin,' Josefina said, looking cross, 'you are a *very* young man.'

'Right, okay,' Jin said, not listening. He shut the door, pulled off his Squares' boots and sat down cross-legged on the bed. 'I need to ask you about a girl.'

Josefina swept over to join him. 'You want to talk? Nothing else?'

'Not today,' Jin said. He wasn't in the mood, not after what had just happened.

'I'm still charging you.' Josefina lowered her hands from where they'd sat expectantly on the silk strings of her gown.

Jin dug in his wraps and dropped some coins on the bed. Then he sat back, doing his best to keep his hands in front of him and not on his dagger hilts. Geni Igna hated it when he fidgeted.

Josefina scooped the coins up and counted them carefully before placing them onto her bedside table. 'Okay. What do you want to ask me? Is it about Aren?'

'No, it's about someone else. Her name is Linija. She's in the Tenths with me. Or . . . she was.' Jin frowned. 'I don't know what happened. But I think' – Jin dropped his voice lower – 'I think she left the Squares because of me.'

'Why do you think that?'

'Because she said so. In front of *everyone*.'

Jin could still see Linija standing alone at the other end of the barracks, her bag slung over her shoulder. Ten years of her life packed up ready to go. Tears streamed down her face as she screamed at him. It had been so humiliating. Jin didn't even know what he'd done wrong.

'All right,' Josefina said. It was her kindest voice, but it sounded more exasperated than anything else. Josefina wasn't as patient as the other women, and she would be brutally honest with him, which was why Jin had come to her. He wanted honesty right now.

'So what happened with this girl? From the beginning, please.'

'The beginning, beginning?'

'Whenever you think it's important to start from.'

Jin wracked his brain. Linija had *always* been there, like the rest of the Tenths. The only thing that set her apart was that she was the last girl. The others had left for a multitude of reasons.

'Maybe a few months ago? She started being around more. Well, more than she used to.'

'Oh, yes?'

'Yeah. She would come and chat. She was fun.'

Josefina nodded. 'What else?'

'I don't know. She kissed me once.'

'And what did you do?'

Jin shrugged. 'I kissed her back.' None of this seemed important to Jin, but Josefina had a frown on her face that said otherwise.

'Do you like Linija?'

'Yeah, she's nice.'

'No, what I'm asking is do you like this girl the way you like Aren?'

Jin made a face. 'Of course not. Linija is nothing like Aren.'

'Did you tell Linija this?'

'Yes. After a while.'

Josefina raised an eyebrow. 'And how did she react?'

'She was okay with it. Well, that's what she said.'

'Hm.' Josefina clicked her tongue. 'You said you kissed. What else did you do with this girl?'

'Nothing!'

Even so, Jin was beginning to feel like he'd done something wrong. Against his best efforts, his rebellious thumbs had snuck to the dagger hilts at his thighs, and he pressed against them nervously. 'We just fooled around a bit. The usual stuff, you know.'

Josefina shook her head.

'*What?*'

'Oh, Jin,' Josefina sighed. 'It seems we women have done you a disservice. Not all women treat sex the way we do.'

Jin's thumbs paused on his dagger hilts. 'What do you mean?'

'Some women only do it with people they care a lot about. Not with so many strangers.'

'You're not a stranger.'

'No, I'm not. But that's not what I mean. Linija liked you the way you like Aren.'

'So? It's not like I said I liked her back.'

'But to her, you *acted* like you did. She thought that what you were doing with her was special.'

Jin was shocked. '*Special?* Why?'

'Gosh, let's see.' Josefina tapped her chin, looking up at the ceiling in thought. 'Because sex makes people feel vulnerable? Because it's the most intimate physical thing you can do with someone? Because you bare your soul and all its flaws to the person you share it with?'

'I've never felt *any* of that,' Jin said.

'That's because you haven't had sex with anyone you care about.'

'That's not true,' Jin said, a little offended. 'I care about you, and Eliza, and Dhuna. And there's that new girl, Lottie –'

'No, Jin. We are whores.'

Jin didn't like that word. 'You shouldn't call yourselves that,' he muttered.

Josefina ignored him. It didn't bother the women like it bothered him.

'Do you understand me now?' Josefina asked.

'Not really.'

'Imagine what sex would be like with Aren. Would it be different or better than with someone else?'

Yes, Jin thought. It would be nice, *really* fucking nice. But scary too because he wouldn't want to mess it up, not with Aren.

Jin frowned. Sex hadn't been scary for a long time. 'Okay, I think I get it,' he said. 'So what do I do about Linija?'

'You have to find her and apologise.'

'But-but it's too late! She's gone!'

'This is *Valrue*, Jin. She'll be in the city somewhere.'

'No, I mean gone from the Squares. Once you leave, you can't come back.'

'Without exception?'

Jin nodded miserably. The Geni did not allow take-backs.

'Well, there's nothing you can do about that.'

That was not what Jin wanted to hear. 'So you're saying that I ruined her whole future for a bit of fun? Why didn't anyone tell me this stuff before?'

'It's not really something people have to be told.'

Jin moaned into his hands.

Josefina gave him a piteous look. 'Go speak to her,' she suggested. 'I suspect she didn't leave the Squares just because of you. It would be an incredible overreaction, even for a fifteen-year-old girl.'

'She told *everyone* that she left because of me! She said I was selfish, and-and conceited –'

'People say all sorts of things when they're angry, especially things they don't mean. But listen to me, Jin. This is an important lesson. You need to be careful. Some people use sex not just for pleasure or for love but for control too. Or to hurt people. It's not something that should be pursued thoughtlessly.'

Jin swallowed. 'I didn't realise it was so complicated.'

'More than it needs to be,' Josefina nodded. 'Us whores know that more than anyone.'

Jin left her room quickly. He was glad he'd spoken to Josefina, but he felt terrible now. He spiralled down the stairs, looking at his feet and thumbing his daggers. He could feel Mama Hidel's eyes on him as he crossed the main room of the brothel. 'Is everything okay?' she asked.

'Fine,' he said though he didn't know why he bothered. It wasn't a good lie.

Jin stepped out onto the porch. He had no clue where Linija's family home was. He'd never asked her. Unless Bish knew, Jin would have to go door to door to find her. He'd rather not ask the other Tenths. They'd want to know why, and he was sick of them knowing his business.

Jin was so angry at himself for not knowing about sex being special. He was used to the women at the brothel, where it had always been so transactional, so explicit. He'd assumed it meant the same for everyone. So if some women thought sex was special, then maybe what happened with Linija might happen again. He couldn't trust that a girl meant it when she said it didn't matter if he didn't like them the same way or that he didn't want anyone other than Aren.

I'm not making the same mistake twice, Jin thought. Mama Hidel's women were okay because they didn't expect anything from him other than coin.

But other girls, other women – it wasn't worth it.

CHAPTER 39:
JIN KANJU

'Is there a Krijen called Jin here?'

Jin looked up. He'd been staring into empty space, thumbing his daggers and thinking about Mama Hidel's women still locked in the dungeons.

'I'm Jin,' Jin said. He waved to the KahnenMinder from his post outside the Red Room. The Eighth House were in session, and both he and Meek had been guarding the door for the better part of an hour.

Standing still was hard work today. Jin was restless, and he knew why. It had been almost a week since he'd harnessed, and his power was catching up with him.

The Minder bustled over. 'You're the KrijenMayj?'

Jin glanced at Meek. He wasn't sure if that was common knowledge or not. Meek looked as bemused as Filip, who stood next to him. Aren was on Meek's other side, her eyes on the Minder.

'There's a woman asking for you,' the Minder explained, not waiting for an answer.

Aren frowned. 'Who could that be?'

Jin had absolutely no idea. 'I'm on duty,' he said, inclining his head to the heavy door of the Red Room.

The Minder nodded. 'She said she would wait.'

Meek smirked. 'I wish women would wait for me. How do you do it, sir?'

Jin ignored him. 'Fine. Where can I find her?'

'The sitting room of the KahnenChambers,' the Minder said.

'Oh?' said Meek. 'Is she a Kahn from one of the other houses?' His grin was infuriating.

'No,' the Minder said, 'but it seemed appropriate.' He turned and left, leaving Jin thumbing his daggers once more.

Meek snickered as the Minder walked away. 'Don't look so tense, sir. I know it's been a while, but I'm sure you'll remember what to do.'

'Not another fucking word, Meek.'

'Yes, sir.'

***

An hour later, the Eighth House and a smattering of Minders filed out of the Red Room, the Kahnen giving curt nods to Jin and Meek as they passed.

The Great Kahn was the last to walk out. He and Jin hadn't spoken since that last training session and seeing the Great Kahn up this close ignited Jin's nerves, sending little spasms of heat surging to his fingertips.

Jin had no idea what to think of the man. He'd been certain the Great Kahn hated him, but after their last interaction, he wasn't so sure. He even wondered if the Great Kahn was avoiding him now, but perhaps he was overthinking it.

Jin nodded to the Great Kahn as he passed. To Jin's surprise, the Great Kahn stopped and nodded back before continuing on, his robes blustering about him as he walked down the corridor.

'He makes me nervous,' Jin said.

'Yeah, me too,' Meek said, making Jin jump. He'd been speaking to Filip and Aren.

'Are you going to go see your mystery woman, sir?'

'I guess so.'

'You'll tell us about her later, right?' Meek waved Jin off, looking delighted.

'He's so vulgar,' Aren said as she trotted down the corridor next to Jin.

Jin agreed. 'He and Nommo are a dangerous pair.'

He started up the staircase towards the KahnenChambers, Filip leading the way. It didn't take long to get there. When Jin opened the door to the sitting room, his visitor immediately stood up to greet him. Normally, Jin would do a visual sweep of the room, take in the exits and the distances to them, but this time he forgot all of that.

His visitor was incredibly distracting.

The woman eased herself off the sofa, sweeping her long dark hair over her shoulder as she went. Her figure was outrageously feminine, artfully contouring underneath her purple wraps. Even Lottie would be envious. The woman's cheekbones were high, her eyes intense, her lips rounded. She wasn't far off perfection, really. 'You're the KrijenMayj?' she asked. *Fuck*, even her voice was like honey.

'I'm Jin,' Jin replied, avoiding the question. 'Can I help you?'

'I certainly hope so,' the woman said, a stunning smile lighting up her face. She gestured to the empty armchair across from where she stood. 'Sit down,' she said as though the chair and the room were hers.

Jin hesitated. He didn't enjoy sitting on soft furniture. Krijen weren't meant for that.

'Please,' the woman insisted.

'You're off duty now,' Filip said.

Jin looked at Aren. She was watching the woman with mild curiosity. 'Go on,' Aren said finally, without looking at him.

Jin sat, hoping the cleaver strapped to his back wasn't digging into the velvet.

The woman sauntered over. She circled him, trailing a hand over the back of the chair as she did so, and Jin had to crane his head back to keep her in sight. Then she stopped and perched on the armrest, so close that

Jin had to lean back to give her space.

'You're not what I was expecting,' she said. 'You're very handsome, you know.'

Fuck, she was forward. Jin's immediate thought was that she was a prostitute. He thought back to Meek's glee as he'd waved him off. Had Meek and Nommo sent her here as joke?

'No,' Aren said, 'they wouldn't do that. That would mean cuts.'

If I gave them, Jin thought.

He was aware the woman was watching him, the tiniest of frown lines appearing between her dark brows, which disappeared the second he brought his focus back to her. She smiled down at him again, trailing the tips of her fingers across his knees before shifting herself from the armrest and coming to stand between his legs. She leant over him, running her hands up his thighs.

Jin's brain wasn't working. He had no idea what to make of this woman, nor an inkling of what was going on. All he knew was that he was suddenly full to bursting with desire, on top of everything else. He hadn't had sex in over a year. With the women from the brothel locked up, he'd accepted it was just another punishment he had to live with.

This woman in all her carnal furor was obscenely tempting. It was obvious that she was no Linija either, but through his daze, Jin knew she was one of those women he needed to be careful of. That, and Aren was standing *right there*. It was not something Jin wanted her to see. His sense came crashing back.

The chair legs screeched across the floor as Jin shoved it backwards, standing up, and the woman quickly leapt back, looking startled. Filip and Aren came to stand on either side of Jin, both of them looking disdainfully at the woman.

'Look,' Jin began, 'you seem . . . nice.'

Anger flashed plainly across her face.

'But who are you, and what do you want?'

The woman eyed him carefully for a moment, then she strolled back to the sofa and sat down again, crossing one of her legs over the other. 'I am Felle,' she said. 'I know something I think you'll be interested in knowing, too.' Despite the scowl on her face, her eyes kept running over him, lingering on places that left no doubt as to what she was thinking.

But Jin suddenly felt colder than he had for a long time. 'Sure, you came to tell me something,' he said slowly. 'So what was with all the preamble?'

'I liked what I saw. Maybe next time,' Felle said with a sudden sweet smile, the scowl vanishing. 'So don't you want to know what I have to say?'

She's definitely one to use sex for control, Jin thought grimly. And he'd been so close to ripping her wraps off despite the promise he'd made himself. Thank fuck for Josefina.

'What do you have to say?'

'You're hunting the mayj who killed the late FaKrijen.'

'That's no secret,' Jin replied. 'Krijen have been hunting the skahk since the Celebrations.'

'And more recently, they've been joined by Squares,' Felle said. 'I heard that was your doing. Clever. There have never been enough Krijen to keep control of this city.'

Jin waited, but Felle said nothing further. 'Is that what you came to tell me?' he asked. 'Some shit I already knew?'

'Easy now,' Filip warned.

Jin hadn't realised his fingernails were cutting lines into his palms. He took a deep breath and relaxed his hands.

Felle smiled wider. 'You think the skahk, as you call him, was a streetling, acting of his own accord. You are wrong.' The smile slid off her face. 'He was *sent* to murder the FaKrijen.'

Jin hesitated. He knew he couldn't trust the woman, but she'd caught his attention. 'Sent by who?'

'The Great Kahn.'

Jin's heart smacked against his ribs.

'Bah,' said Filip, 'she's lying.'

'I agree,' said Aren.

'Be careful what you say,' Jin warned Felle. 'I could execute you for that.'

'I wouldn't lie, not to *you*.'

Jin frowned. Her contrition was convincing, but what she said made no sense. 'The Great Kahn wouldn't have the FaKrijen killed,' Jin said. 'He *commands* him.'

'I'm not saying I know why he did it,' Felle said. 'Only that it's true.'

'Right. And how do you know that?'

'Because Drax used to be *mine*,' Felle said.

Oh, fuck.

'Ah, you know who I'm talking about,' Felle said, leaning forward on the sofa. 'So you must know I'm telling the truth.'

Jin was shuddering now, the heat inside him swelling.

'It's okay, stay calm,' Aren said softly.

'You've proved nothing other than you know his name,' Jin said. 'How?'

'Because I named him,' Felle said. 'I found Drax. He looked injured, starving, so I took him in. He was incredibly shy and scared of everything. I never thought of him as dangerous until I caught him harnessing. I hadn't realised until then he was a mayj. I was upset, of course, but he seemed genuinely repentant, and I cared about him too much. I agreed to let him stay, so long as he didn't harness anymore. I thought I was doing the right thing in being kind. But it wasn't long before he started doing things he shouldn't.'

Jin couldn't help it. He was intrigued. 'Go on,' he said.

'For both of our sakes, I warned Drax to not be seen, to stay away from people. I feared what my neighbours would do if they learned I was harbouring a mayj under my roof. Drax was also young and fallibly innocent. He could easily fall victim to someone's manipulations. So when Drax started disappearing for hours on end, I grew worried.

'When I asked him about it, he insisted he never left the house, but I could never find him when I went looking. When the hours eventually became days, I confronted him and accused him of abusing our trust. He was distraught, and he cried, but he never conceded and I had no evidence. I left it alone after that, thinking that perhaps I was just going slightly mad with worry.

'Not long after that, Drax came to me one night. He said he was sorry and that he was leaving to see the Great Kahn. I was shocked. Drax said he wanted me to know the truth. I demanded he tell me why, but he refused to say. I begged him not to go, but he went anyway.

'Drax never came back. When FaKrijen Oji was killed at the Celebrations with majik, the rumour went rampant. A streetling boy had murdered him. Of course, I knew Drax had done it. But I didn't tell anyone. I was terrified at what it meant, that the Great Kahn had given the order, and Drax had been tricked into it. And I'd not stopped him.' Tears were welling up in Felle's eyes.

Jin felt no sympathy. There were some gaping flaws in her story. 'How do you know it was the Great Kahn who ordered it? How do you know that's not a lie, and it was really the streetlings the skahk was plotting with?'

'The streetlings were preaching for a fair democracy. It would have made more sense for the Great Kahn to be their target, not the FaKrijen.'

'The Great Kahn was protected by KahnenMayjen.' Felle didn't need to know there had been only Stolt left, at the time. 'The FaKrijen wasn't.'

'The KahnenMayjen wouldn't have been a match for Drax.'

True, Jin thought. Stolt would have been worse than useless. 'But the Great Kahn would never work with a skahk. He hates majik.'

'Do you think that would stop him from using it to his advantage?'

'Huh,' Filip said.

Jin couldn't help but look at him. 'It makes sense,' Filip shrugged. 'The Great Kahn showed you how to harness those rings. He helped you even though he admitted he didn't want to.'

It was a fair point. Jin thought back to the words that the Great Kahn himself had used. *'I recognise what is important, even if I do not like it.'*

Fuck.

Jin was growing annoyed. 'Why did you come to me?' he asked Felle. 'What makes you think I'm not going to go running to the Great Kahn with all this?'

'Because I hoped that as a Krijen, you'd want justice for the late FaKrijen. Because as a mayj, I hoped you wouldn't fully trust the Great

Kahn and that you'd be willing to listen. Because I think you're the only person who can help me,' Felle said. 'I need you to read this.' From her wraps, she pulled out a crumpled envelope. She held it out to him.

Jin eyed it suspiciously. 'What is it?'

'A letter,' Felle said, closing her eyes as though in pain. 'A letter which reveals what caused the Unsettlement –'

Jin snatched it from her and tore the envelope open.

Jin read it, then read it again, his heart thudding behind his ribs.

It was a love letter of all things. He choked on the bit about the power being trapped in the lake. That was exactly what Maude had said before she'd thrown herself into it. The mercenary had told her that.

And the torn-out page that was mentioned . . . could it be? Was it the same torn-out page that Jin had taken from the mercenary? *It had to be.*

Jin's blood was pumping in his ears, so loud it drowned out the ringing.

'Mandavar,' Jin read out loud. This Mandavar had trapped the power in the lake using the Du Bellor Spell.

Jin shook as he lowered the letter. 'Are you telling me,' he hissed through clenched teeth, 'that the Unsettlement, the last quarter of a century of suffering, was because of a fucking *love feud?*'

'I believe so,' Felle said. 'Did you see the bit about the power –'

'Where did you get this?'

'Dijak, the man who wrote this letter, raised me. I found it in his study after he disappeared.' Felle wiped a tear from her cheek. 'He left one night and never came home. I fear this Luka person killed him when Dijak went to tell him Mandavar's secret. I think they were still in love despite what Dijak wrote.'

'Where is Mandavar?'

'I-I don't know.' Felle slowly sat back down on the sofa.

'You don't know who Luka is?'

'No, I don't. But I'm certain Luka hurt Dijak. Dijak was like a father to me. I know he made a mistake, but he was a good man, trying to do the right thing. I need to know what happened to him.'

'What does this have to do with the Great Kahn and the skahk?'

Felle shook her head, tears dripping onto her lap. 'Nothing. I hoped that by telling you what I know about the FaKrijen's death that *you* would help *me*.'

Jin felt hot and breathless, his temper knocking at his chest. He sat down hard in the chair behind him.

'Will you do it?' Felle asked. 'Will you help me?'

Jin looked at Aren and Filip, wanting them to tell him what to do, but they both shook their heads at him, lost for words.

Felle was properly sobbing now, her breath coming in gasps. She staggered up off the sofa and fell to the ground at Jin's feet. 'Please, Jin! Think of all the hatred, the shame that you've endured because of the Unsettlement, of being born the way you were. Don't you want to find the people responsible? Don't you want to find Luka too? Don't you want to find *Mandavar*?'

Jin's veins burned at the thought. Felle was right. He wanted to know.

It was hard to watch her sobbing at his feet, pleading with him. Her hardened shell from before had broken down completely. Maybe her attempts to seduce him were just that, a wall to protect her from her suffering. But he couldn't be sure, and he was not in any state to make decisions.

'I'm sorry,' Jin said, struggling to keep his voice steady. 'I need time to think this through.'

And if anyone ever found out he'd had this conversation –

'No, I understand!' Felle exclaimed, lifting her head, her face just as beautiful with her lower lip quivering and tears staining her cheeks. 'This is huge, what I'm telling you. It's unthinkable that the Great Kahn would be a part of the FaKrijen's death.'

Jin's stifled power was crushing his lungs.

'Get out of here,' Filip warned.

Jin shoved Dijak's letter into the folds of his wraps. He leapt out of the chair and ran across the room, wrenching the door open. He tore down the corridor and up the stairs, dashing around shocked KahnenMinders. He reached the solid wooden door which led to the outside and burst out onto the stone ramparts. It was the middle of the day, the light of the sun blaring down on him, taunting him.

'It doesn't matter if you're seen,' Filip said. 'Everyone knows about the KrijenMayj. Felle knew. The Kahnen are kidding themselves if they think you're a secret.'

'Just go,' Aren agreed.

That was good enough for Jin. He harnessed himself up into the air, dragging himself into the sky so fast that he was already in the clouds, the wetness of them cooling his hot skin, and then he kept going until he couldn't breathe not because of his power but because the air was so thin that there simply wasn't enough of it.

It was about then that he began wondering when, if ever, the bliss would take him.

CHAPTER 40:
AREN BHA

Life in the forest got easier. They had good days and bad days, and today was a good day. Aren and Drax came across a shallow river, and Drax stood in the middle of it, watching with fascination as all the fish turned around and tried to swim upstream away from him.

Aren speared a row of them with her dagger, and they feasted until their bellies were full. Then they bathed for the first time in weeks, and Aren scrubbed the muck from her body, laughing as she unearthed her freckles beneath the grime. She hung her wraps out to dry and walked around naked beneath her blanket, whistling the tune that she'd heard the birds singing on the day they'd almost died. The melody had stuck.

After a few verses, she looked up to see Drax blinking at her. 'What?'

'You're happy,' he said.

'For the most part,' she said, smiling at him.

Aren missed her family. She missed her friends. She missed Wren. She missed sleeping in a bed, and she missed the residents at the Point. She missed not worrying about what the next day would bring and if they would ever find Holu Mon and its University and be able to free Drax from the burden of keeping her alive.

But there was nothing she could do but get on with it. So that was what Aren did.

They quickly settled into a routine. Drax ensured they had water, lit the fire, and once Aren had figured out what to look for, he helped her gather fruit and dig up edible roots.

Aren navigated their way as best she could, and she did the kills. She'd made a mess of the rabbit that had saved them, but she'd quickly learned how to cut the animal to bleed it right and remove the guts before ripping the skin off. It was gruesome work, but Drax harnessed the blood off her when she was done. She was grateful for that.

Aren wasn't exactly sure how long they'd been in the forest. All the days seemed to string together even with the changing scenery reminding them that they were moving.

The forest and everything in it was getting bigger. It was as though their surroundings feasted on life itself and doubled in size since the edge of the Deadlands. Aren couldn't remember what was normal, but from her memories of the sketches in Noel's books, she was certain flowers shouldn't all be the size of her head.

It was disconcerting at first, but it made foraging more fruitful, and even though Aren's hunting attempts weren't always successful, one kill soon lasted them a few days instead of barely being enough for a meal. Drax constantly needed to eat, so it helped that he could harness the meat dry, so it lasted longer.

Unfortunately, the growing enormity of the trees made it harder to find their way. Before, Aren could climb to the treetops to get a good look at their surroundings and pick out landmarks to follow if she felt they were going off course. Drax didn't like her being up so high for so long. He waited anxiously at the bottom while Aren scaled up and down with increasing confidence.

However, when the trees became so large that their roots reached waist height and it hurt to look up at them, Aren grew nervous about making it to the top. The branches were so far apart she often had to jump to reach them, and if she fell, Drax would kill himself to catch her.

Eventually, Aren gave up on climbing to get their bearings and instead lay down at night, looking up at the tiny patch of stars she could see through the tips of the trees, trying to find a pattern that might guide their way. She knew it was possible because she'd read about it. She just didn't know how it was done.

'Come on, Maude,' Aren muttered quietly one night, stranded in the worry that she was leading them in circles. 'Help me out a little. Are we going the right way?'

It came as no surprise that Maude didn't reply.

'Aren?'

Aren sat up, looking over towards the fire to where Drax crouched on his bedroll. His eyes were bluer than ever, standing out against the red of the flames, but the shadows that danced in the hollows of his face made him look gaunt, just like when Aren had first met him in her sparring court back home. He'd lost the weight he'd gained in the months spent living with the Bha family. Aren wondered if she looked like that too or if it was the constant harnessing that was taking its toll.

Aren got up and walked over to Drax, settling down beside him on his bedroll. 'What is it?'

'It was the Great Kahn who sent the Minder to leave my cell door open.'

'What? How do you know?'

'He wasn't surprised when I went to his room. It was as though he knew I was coming. And I think he knew Mandavar.'

Aren had not gotten used to Drax springing information on her like this. 'As in, the Great Kahn knew Mandavar as more than just one of the KahnenMayjen?'

'Yes.'

'What makes you think that?'

'The Great Kahn talked about how much I look like my father. How he could draw Mandavar's face from memory.'

'He said that?'

Drax nodded. 'I've been thinking about it for a while. I wasn't sure what it meant. And the Great Kahn knew Felle,' Drax added. 'He said her name.'

'*What?*' Aren suddenly sat bolt upright on her bedroll. 'Then it must have been him who released you! It's too much of a coincidence that Pakker and Felle found you!'

Drax nodded slowly. 'Yes.'

'You don't think' – Aren gasped – 'you don't think the Great Kahn knew it was Mandavar who caused the Unsettlement?' Aren could feel the adrenaline pulsing in her fingertips. The only thing keeping her calm was Drax's steady hold on her heart.

'Then again, if the Great Kahn knew Mandavar had done it, why did he keep it a secret all these years? Unless . . . unless he was in on it?' Aren frowned. 'But that doesn't make sense. The Unsettlement started after the Great Kahn came to power. Why would he ruin his own reign?'

Drax shook his head. 'Maybe he knew it was Mandavar who did it, but I don't think he knew how. Not until he asked Pakker to get me to fix it.'

Aren pondered this. 'And you're sure he wanted you to fix it? What did Pakker ask you to do?'

'He took me to the Deadlands. He asked me to do majik.'

'What kind of majik?'

'He wanted me to harness the earth from far away, using the power in the lake. I think he hoped the distance would help me use more power.'

'And did it?'

'Yes, but not enough.'

'What else did he ask you to do? Surely the best way to use lots of power is to harness people?'

Drax shifted where he sat, clearly uncomfortable. 'Yes. When we were out there once, he led us to some people at a camp. He called them bandits.' He met Aren's eyes with his icy blue ones.

Oh no. 'He . . . he didn't ask you to hurt them, did he?'

Drax sank into his shoulders. 'That's what he wanted at first. But then he changed his mind, and he hurt them instead. He said he had to because they'd seen us. He killed them all. And then we went back to the city.' Drax looked away. 'I think maybe he was trying to be kind.'

'Oh, Drax.' Aren didn't know what to say. There was so much he'd gone through, so much he kept in his head, and she only got the smallest parts of it. The parts he thought were important enough to share.

After a while, Aren realised Drax was nudging her gently with a limp hand.

'What is it?'

'The Great Kahn hid a lot of things,' Drax said. 'He hid me. He hid that he knew about the power in the lake. But I don't understand why he hid that he was trying to fix it because that would make him good, right? Because the power in the lake was a bad thing. And when good people hide bad things, they . . . they are . . . I don't know the word –'

'Ashamed,' Aren said. 'The Great Kahn is ashamed of something. Something to do with Mandavar.'

CHAPTER 41:
PYRA

The First Reckoning was now.

Pyra and her streetlings had been ready for two months. Given how long it took, Pyra had briefly worried that Lady Elira was smarter than she'd realised and decided against hosting another rally despite how desperate the Kahn must've become. But finally, the rally was announced, and the streetlings started a riot in the Left South Side in their excitement. It had taken a few days to calm them and get everything in order.

Pyra had to admit she was a little nervous. It wouldn't have been so bad if her charges weren't the scoundrels they were, but you had to work with what you had. At least news of Ala's scalping had spread and put off the creepers for the time being, so Pyra could concentrate on what needed to be done, rather than carving her name into foreheads.

Despite their usual wayward antics, the streetlings came together on the day of the Reckoning, just like they had at the Celebrations. Porge and his gang agreed upon a day's reprieve for the event, so for the first time ever, Pyra stood on the main street that cut through the Upper East Side with Porge standing calmly by her side, both of them watching Lady Elira as she strolled up the way.

The Kahn was smiling and waving, appearing comfortable in the midst of her voting base. It was all fake, of course. She would say anything to please the crowd, intent on clawing back the supporters she'd lost. She must've run out of metal.

The idiot.

The Upper East and West Sides of Rue were the most dangerous places for her to be. Here she was surrounded by the shrewdest of citizens, smart enough to be on the edge of Val, but not stupid enough to Cross. They were the ones who would want to pick holes in what Pyra said because they hated streetlings, but at the same time, these citizens knew what she was about.

Well, that was what Tiju and Nellie had said.

Perhaps the people here would respect the streetling cause just enough to listen. Unlike the citizens of Val, who would turn a blind eye to anything so long as they were kept in the manner to which they were accustomed, the citizens of Rue would turn to Lady Elira demanding answers. She would have nothing but lies to share.

And lies were what Pyra thrived on.

Six Krijen flanked Lady Elira, a whole squad, which was rather naïve of her. The Celebrations had been months ago and with streetlings lying low like they were – well, apart from the single recent riot – it only made the Kahn look scared. Lady Elira's voters would suspect she didn't trust them.

Although that was good thing, Pyra ground her teeth. Six Krijen was a lot to handle, especially having so few streetling mayjen now. But they would do it. At least the KrijenMayj wasn't there. Lady Hia must've done her part.

Pyra stepped out into the street behind Lady Elira with Porge at her side. A crowd of streetlings fell in behind. She could hear them hooting softly, jostling each other.

Now that it was happening, Pyra was a little excited. This First Reckoning was almost as anticipated as the Celebrations had been, and that had been fun, right up until the point when the Great Kahn had lost his mind and attacked her. Perhaps something unexpected would happen today too. Pyra would be ready for anything.

They made it to the open square where the rally would take place. Pyra looked up from under her floppy black hat as Lady Elira climbed the stairs to the stage. Four of the Krijen flowed to the corners of it while the other two stayed at the base of the stairs.

The square in front of the stage was packed with people, and Pyra made sure she and Porge were right in the middle of it with their streetlings. The other gang leaders would be somewhere, probably on the rooftops for the best view and where they could jump down and join the fray if they felt so inclined. She knew they would.

The Krijen watched them all with wary expressions, their hands resting on the hilts of their daggers. It was not unusual for streetlings to be at rallies. In fact, it would be strange if they *weren't* there. Perhaps these Krijen still had night terrors from the Celebrations, assuming Krijen could feel such emotion. Pyra had yet to see any proof that they did.

Lady Elira started speaking, and the crowd settled down to listen. Pyra didn't take in a word of it. It was all lies, anyway. She let Lady Elira get to the heart of her speech, then Pyra began pushing forward, a few of her streetlings moving with her, Rifter and Barrett included. Barrett dragged the crossbow across the cobbles behind him so that it made a loud screeching sound, which Pyra loved. It really drew attention.

She pulled off her floppy black hat and tucked it into the back of her trousers. She wanted Lady Elira to see her face, her patchy hair, the skin of her scalp. If she didn't already, Lady Elira would know her after today. Pyra would make sure of it.

'Excuse me,' Pyra said as she pushed through. '*Excuse* me.'

People turned and let loose little screams, and news of Pyra spread so fast that soon people were yelling out and squashing themselves out of her way, clearing a path.

'My lady,' Pyra called. 'My lady!'

Lady Elira stopped in the middle of her speech, her disgruntled expression turning to horror when she saw who it was. Maybe she remembered Pyra from the Celebrations after all.

The Kahn quickly recovered her composure, but Pyra had seen the fear in her eyes. It was *thrilling*.

'You!' Lady Elira cried. 'How dare you show your face here!' She turned to the Krijen, who had already drawn their daggers. 'Arrest her at once!'

Pyra feigned offence, throwing a hand to her chest and gasping loudly. 'On what charges?'

'Murder! Insurrection! Sedition!'

'Well, I can't argue with that,' Pyra shrugged.

The two Krijen stationed at the base of the stairs shoved through the crowd towards her. 'But I think you should reconsider, my lady,' Pyra continued, unfazed. 'I'm not here to steal your thunder. In fact, I'm here to talk about *you*.'

She snapped her fingers, and Barrett stepped forward, swinging the crossbow onto his shoulders. Rifter swiftly loaded a bolt and aimed the weapon at the two oncoming Krijen. They both froze, daggers raised defensively in front of them.

The crowd screamed and pressed further back, but there was nowhere to go. That was okay though. Pyra would give them a good show.

'Now,' Pyra said to Lady Elira in her best little girl voice, 'I can imagine you're thinking I'm going to shoot you. But honestly, I just need your help. I'm a poor, benighted streetling after all. This politicking is beyond me, and I have three conundrums if you please.'

The four Krijen on stage had moved to stand directly in front of Lady Elira, and Pyra could see how much it irritated her. She'd come to her rally to be seen. This was her last chance to redeem herself, and hiding would not endear her to voters.

'Move aside,' Lady Elira ordered. The Krijen shared nervous glances. One of them spoke quietly in her ear. The squad leader, Pyra presumed.

'I said *move aside*,' Lady Elira retorted.

The squad leader nodded and the Krijen stepped back, their faces carefully blank. Pyra grinned. You could always count on Kahnen to dig their own graves.

'Oh, good –'

'Get on with it, girl,' Lady Elira interrupted.

'That's rude,' Pyra said. 'But I agree, no one likes a dallier. Here is my first conundrum. Do you know what *this* is?' From her sleeve, Pyra pulled out a slip of paper. She waved it in front of the two Krijen in front of her, still paused in the line of fire.

'Bring it to me,' Lady Elira called to them.

One of the Krijen slowly stepped forward, keeping his stance low. Pyra was a little impressed. It took a brave man to walk towards a crossbow wielded by a streetling. Or a brainless one, which, truth be told, seemed more likely. He was Krijen after all.

The Krijen took the paper from Pyra's outstretched hand and dashed up to Lady Elira, who snatched it off him and ran her eyes over it. Even from where she stood, Pyra could see Lady Elira's face lose colour.

'What is this?'

'Now, you see, that's what I asked *you*,' Pyra tutted, making the streetlings cackle.

'You have been in my private chambers!'

'No. I assure you I have not.' Pyra grinned. It had been Lady Hia. 'Now please, can you explain what this bit of paper is?'

There was a pause. 'It is a purchase agreement.'

'Oh! It means you've bought something? Because that's your signature right there, isn't it? What does it say you bought?'

Lady Elira said nothing.

'You don't know? That's a shame. Oh, I have more of these, by the way.' Pyra pulled out a whole stack of folded papers from her other sleeve. 'Here is one for – oh? Copper? What a strange purchase. And here, another one, for zinc? And here –'

'What does it matter what I have bought? These questions are fatuous, a pathetic attempt to disrupt my rally! Krijen! Arrest –'

'Now, now,' Pyra said sweetly as Rifter tapped the side of the crossbow. 'You forget we already did that. But just for argument's sake, let's play it out, shall we? For fun?'

The streetlings squealed and clapped, a gentle hoot stirring up from their midst.

Pyra gestured to Rifter. 'Rifter here has pretty good aim. I think he's got a decent chance of killing at least one Krijen with that crossbow, probably two. If, after that, another Krijen manages to get around him to arrest me, I'll be sure to keep them busy. Then you're left with only three Krijen to protect you, against about say . . . a few hundred streetlings? And I think we still have a few mayjen, isn't that right?'

The streetlings screamed with mirth, leaping and raising their hands, all claiming to be majikal. The beautiful little liars.

'And I feel like that's a *very* favourable scenario for you,' Pyra said to Lady Elira. 'So all I ask for is a little patience.'

Pyra could see the Kahn's eyes darting around, looking to escape. Behind her was a stone wall, and in front was a sea of voters. Pyra could hear mutterings in the crowd, many of them cussing the streetlings. Despite that, they seemed intent on staying. And they would soon change their tune.

'I'm curious, my lady,' Pyra continued, 'and I'm sure your voters are too, astute as they are, as to why you made these purchases. According to this one' – Pyra flapped another piece of paper in Lady Elira's direction – 'you've been buying up steel, in ludicrous quantities. What could a lady such as yourself possibly want with steel?'

'I am a Kahn,' Lady Elira snapped, a lie prepared this time. 'We employ blacksmiths and have a demand for weapons.'

'Ah, but your Weapon's Master is in charge of those purchases, is he not? And if I recall, you haven't had a Weapon's Master in months.' Pyra frowned. 'Is this what you do with your precious time? Are your voters happy you've dedicated yourself to purchasing metal for the Keep?'

Fresh whispers broke out amongst the crowd.

'This has nothing to do with my duties as a Kahn,' Lady Elira snapped. 'Is this your best attempt to discredit me? It is failing!'

'Let's explore my second conundrum then.' Pyra opened her mouth as if to continue, then paused for dramatic effect. 'Actually, I don't need you for the next bit.'

She spun around, her eyes roaming the crowd. 'You, sir! You look like a learned man.' Pyra strolled over to a man in the crowd she'd selected at random. The man jumped and began to sweat, his eyes flickering between Pyra and the streetlings who stood behind her, licking their lips. 'Never mind them,' Pyra said to him. 'They rarely bite. Tell me, sir, do you know what a coin is made of?'

'A – a coin?'

'Yes, a coin. What is it made of?'

The man just gaped at her. *How useless*, Pyra thought. He wasn't playing along at all –

'Coins are made from steel.'

Pyra whipped around to see a burly man, his face and clothes bearing black smudges. He folded his arms, looking rather grouchy. 'Steel typically plated with copper.'

'Aha! I think you are right, my good sir. And how, may I ask, do you know this?'

'I am a blacksmith,' the man said. 'I used to work at the Keep mint. Before they no longer needed me.'

Pyra's grin widened. This was going even better than expected.

She spun back to Lady Elira. 'Do you know what I find with people who are in positions of power, like yourself? They rather like themselves. They get caught up in having their names plastered on things, shoving their presence down our throats, oozing their way into every facet of life just so that when we come to vote, you expect us to tick the first name we recognise because it's easier for us that way. You think us so *simple*, don't you?'

Lady Elira looked down at Pyra, a smile now playing around her mouth. It would have made Pyra nervous, had she not known how devious politicians could be. They could look confident while peeing down their legs.

'You have nothing,' Lady Elira said. 'You are resorting to putting words in my mouth. A weak trick. Child's play.' The Kahn smiled at her own joke. A few of her voters laughed.

Well, there would be a few imbeciles here, Pyra thought. It was Rue, after all.

'Quite the opposite,' Pyra said. 'I'm giving you a chance to admit, for yourself, what you've done.'

'I have done nothing,' Lady Elira said. 'You have claims against me? Make them! I want to hear them, not this blithering nonsense. What say you, my People?'

The crowd cheered. Some of them even spat at the streetlings, who shrieked and lobbed loogies right back at them, gnashing their teeth. They were getting riled up, fast. Pyra had to hurry, lest they let loose before the truth was out.

'You really don't know what I'm getting at? You can't figure it out?'

'No,' Lady Elira said loudly. 'I will not entertain the words of a murderous little streetling any longer. My People, I apologise profusely for this tedious interruption. I am leaving. Let me just say that if you give me your next vote, I will unleash the most abominable punishment upon this streetling. You have my word.'

The crowd cheered as Lady Elira began to walk down the steps, the four Krijen on the stage moving tight to her, daggers out. The two Krijen before Pyra backed away slowly, their eyes still on the crossbow, which Barrett swivelled around at a sharp whistle from Pyra, focusing it on Lady Elira.

Pyra pointed a finger straight towards the Kahn. 'You've been forging coins and paying for votes. You're nothing but a fraud.'

The crowd stopped cheering as Lady Elira stumbled on the steps, shock on her face. Then she laughed. '*Forging coins*? From the metal I purchased? And how do you suppose I did that? There is not a blacksmith in this city who will back up your story!'

'You don't need a blacksmith,' Pyra said. 'And I know that because you've been doing it yourself. You're a mayj. And a very naughty one at that.'

CHAPTER 42:
AREN BHA

Drax was fussing in the morning when Aren woke up. She blinked at him blearily from her bedroll. 'What's wrong?' His head sank into his shoulders. 'We're almost out of food.'

Drax didn't like asking her to hunt, but he needed it, and she didn't mind the excuse for them to stay where they were for another day. She could put off telling him they were lost, without making it worse. 'That's okay. I'll find something.'

Aren took a freshly filled waterskin from him and tucked it into her wraps, out of the way. She tapped the outline of her cardonite dagger at her thigh, now so used to the weight of it she had to check it was there. She would leave her backpack here. It would only slow her down.

'You ready?'

Drax nodded grimly.

'I'll be back as soon as I can.'

'Okay, Aren.'

Aren headed into the forest, another unspoken worry on her mind. Hunting wasn't difficult for the reasons she'd expected. The killing was unpleasant at first, but after a surprisingly short time, she'd grown used to it. She knew how to make it quick now, so the animals didn't suffer.

What was difficult was the strain of leaving Drax alone in the forest with only the rhythm of her heart to tell her if he was coping.

That, and in the past week or so, many of the animals had become so big that Aren was reluctant to kill them. There were copious amounts of deer, but even the smallest of them were now too large to butcher by herself, and she'd promised Drax he wouldn't have to help with that. There was no way they could carry all the meat, and Aren didn't want to waste a life by leaving half of it behind.

She wouldn't try for boar. Even when they were smaller, she'd been nervous to attempt to kill one. Their necks had looked so thick she was worried her dagger wouldn't go through it. They'd easily been double the weight of her, and their tusks were terrifying, so she'd stayed away. Now they were twice as big.

Rabbits were still okay, even the biggest of them, but she couldn't always find them.

Maybe it was time to make a trap, Aren thought. She had an idea of how it might work though she felt bad to ask Drax for help, given what it was for. It would also mean more harnessing. She would try making a trap herself, but what Drax could do in a few minutes with majik would take her hours. Surely it would be easier than hunting these ridiculous beasts with nothing but a dagger?

Aren walked for a few minutes before settling down under the cover of some bushes. This seemed to be about the distance it took for the animals not to be disturbed by Drax. She could prowl a perimeter if nothing came by, but she had to take care not to wander too far, or her heart would falter and Drax would come running in a panic.

Now came the wait.

Unfortunately, Aren's thoughts were poor company. After an hour, she was immensely bored, and her muscles were stiff from sitting still. Drax needed a break too; her heart was fluttering. She needed to go back.

Just as she was about to move, something rustled in the bushes close by, and the plumpest bird Aren had ever seen scrambled through them, pecking its way towards her. It scrounged around, kicking up leaves over its spotted brown body and flicking its green head, oblivious to her presence.

Normally, Aren didn't bother hunting birds as they were hard to catch and had more bone than meat, but this one seemed worth a shot. Surely it couldn't fly, it was that round.

Aren waited for it to come closer, easing herself up out of her crouch, as silent as the unhelpful sky. She slowly pulled back her arm, eyes on the bird. After a breath, Aren sent her dagger snapping towards it.

A split second after the weapon left her hand, a mountain of a creature sprang from the greenery to her right, and her dagger plunged straight into its enormous shoulder. A roar erupted from the creature's maw, so loud that Aren screamed, her bones rattling.

The bird took off squawking into the forest, and Aren scrambled backwards, tripping over thick roots in her haste.

The black creature roared again and turned its massive head towards her. She froze.

It was a cat, but it was nothing like the cats Aren remembered. It was *huge*, larger than the oxen that used to heave carts over the bridge. It was entirely black with a foot-high fin of pricked fur arching between its shoulders and tapering down the length of its back. Its swishing tail ended in a point like an arrowhead, and black claws glinted on its paws. Every edge of the creature was designed to pierce its prey.

Its orange eyes were on Aren. Her heart began pumping wildly in her chest.

Aren could see the black and gold hilt of her cardonite dagger lodged firmly in the creature's shoulder. It took a step towards her, hissing as its muscles rippled around the blade. Then it sank down into a crouch, the way cats did when they were about to pounce.

No, no, no, Aren pleaded. She could think of a million ways she would prefer to die over being ripped apart. She'd been given plenty of opportunities too and thwarted them all. Maybe this was death laughing at her, for evading it for so long. She took a tentative step back.

The creature roared and its mountainous haunches gathered, its fur rolling into a bulging wave which amassed on either side of the fin on its back. Then it leapt forward, and in two bounds, it was upon her.

A black paw blurred past her face as Aren threw herself to the side, scrambling to stay on her feet, slipping on leaves and dirt. The cat howled as it hit the ground beside her, its wounded shoulder buckling. It spun itself around and came screaming back to her.

Aren flung herself over the thigh-high roots of the nearest tree. The mass of the cat hurled over the top of her, and she heard it roar in pain and felt the thud through the earth as it landed, but she didn't have time to look –

Aren took a running leap and sank her fingers into the grooves of the next enormous tree root, hauling herself over the rough surface, panicking as the bark snagged at her wraps, threatening to trap her. She slid down and landed roughly on her feet, but her heart staggered in her chest and she fell between the roots, clutching at fingerholds to keep herself upright.

Everything was blurry now, probably from fear, or maybe it was Drax struggling because surely the power needed to fuel her terror and adrenaline was churning through his reserves.

Aren stumbled her way up the length of the tree's roots towards the dark hole beneath the trunk. If she could get herself into it, the cat, as big as it was, might not be able to follow.

A snarl ripped through the air above Aren, and she looked up; the sky was suddenly filled with black fur and claws. Aren shrieked and threw her arms over her head. Something heavy caught her between the shoulder blades and ripped down the length of her back, the weight of it knocking her onto all fours.

Gasping for breath, Aren curled her fingers into the dirt and scrambled towards the dark gap under the tree, crying out as something pierced her boot. It yanked her backwards, dragging her down onto her stomach. She kicked out and dug in her elbows, pulling herself deeper into the narrowing fork of the roots.

The roar of the cat was all around her, and she closed her eyes because for some reason she thought it might hurt less if she couldn't see her death coming. The cat had her trapped, but she kept pulling and dragging herself forward because she knew Wren would be furious if she gave up with safety this close. Then the earth disappeared under her ribs and she fell forward, toppling down the tiniest of slopes into something hard and damp. She opened her eyes. A wall of grey clay greeted her.

Aren twisted around and snatched her legs out of the way as a black paw swiped across the space they'd just been in, leaving deep gauges in the earth. She dug in her boots and pressed backwards, forgetting she couldn't go any further and shrieking as the forest floor crumbled beneath her feet. She slipped forward, the cat's claws inches from her boots. It threw itself against the trunk of the tree which groaned in protest, its roots cracking as the creature tore at it.

The cat screamed again. Its paw retreated from the gap between the roots, quickly replaced by its huge head. Its ears were flat in anger and its molten eyes were on her, a guttural sound echoing from somewhere deep in its throat. The bulk of its shoulders were the only thing stopping it from clawing its way into the space. Aren could see her dagger just visible through the gap, the hilt ringed by bloodied fur. The gold spirals of it were coming back into focus. Aren's heart was growing steadier.

Oh no.

'Aren!' Drax's distant cry sounded petrified.

The cat snatched its head back, its vast chest filling the gap. Maybe it would run. Maybe Drax would scare it off because of his majik. But something told her Drax's power was running a little low for that.

'Aren? Aren, where are you?' Drax's voice was growing louder.

'Don't come any closer!' Aren yelled as loudly as she could, terror making her voice waver.

'Aren?'

'Stop! I don't need help –'

The cat roared and sprung away from the tree trunk.

'No!' Aren threw herself towards the gap, crying out as her injured back scraped against the bark above her. She crawled up and out from under the tree just in time to see the giant creature lunge at Drax. Aren's heart stopped, and her lungs snagged, and the world fell into browns and greens. Then the ground hit her.

The cat screamed, and suddenly she could breathe again. Sucking in glorious air, she staggered to her feet just as Drax came barrelling out of nowhere and crashed into her, sending them both stumbling over tree roots.

'Run, Aren!'

Aren turned and ran, doing her best to follow the blur ahead of her that was Drax, but she couldn't see properly, and she'd barely made it a few steps before something caught her foot and the ground came up to meet her again.

'I'm *sorry*,' she choked into the dirt, 'I can't –'

The earth and leaves slipped away beneath her, and she was upright again.

'Run!'

Aren obeyed. She focused on putting one foot in front of the other, steered by a tugging on her wraps that led her onwards. The ground shook underfoot, and the roar behind them was so close that Aren was sure the creature was upon them, but they kept on running and running until the roar was joined by a cacophony of booming barks and yelling and the next time Aren tripped and fell, instead of seeing colours, everything went black.

CHAPTER 43:
PYRA

The look on Lady Elira's face was priceless. Her composure slipped enough that Pyra briefly saw the terror underneath. Then the Kahn quickly hoisted on a look of amusement. 'Me, a *mayj?* What a farcical accusation and unfounded at that. You cannot prove it!'

Pyra pulled something from her red wrist ties and threw it at the Kahn, who flinched as a Krijen plucked it from the air in front of her.

'Tell me,' Pyra called to him. 'What is strange about that coin?'

Lady Elira snatched the coin from the Krijen and tossed it back into the crowd. 'Do not listen to her! I have had enough of this –'

'What's strange about it?'

A young man in the crowd had caught the coin and pushed forward to the front. He held it out to Pyra. 'Tell us.'

Pyra gave him her best smile. 'You recall I said that Kahnen like to impose themselves upon us. If you look closely, my friend, you will see there is an *E* on that coin, where there shouldn't be.'

The young man frowned at the coin. 'I can see it,' he said. He held it to the person next to him. 'Look.'

People began digging in their pockets, muttering and calling out to each other. Pyra grinned around at them all. 'Ah yes, Lady Elira couldn't help but plaster her own initial onto the face of each coin. A subtle yet daily reminder of *her*.'

'This is a joke,' Lady Elira scoffed. 'How is having an *E* on a coin any proof that I put it there?'

'You just said yourself that no blacksmith in Valrue would claim you ordered the making of these coins. So how, may I ask, did your initial end up on them?'

'It is a coincidence! It is an *E*, nothing more!'

Everywhere people were inspecting their coins, pointing and frowning. The young man looked up from his own handful and called out to Lady Elira. 'Some of these coins look different from the others. The ones with an *E* don't look right.'

Lady Elira grabbed on to the Krijen closest to her. 'These are lies,' she cried. 'These coins have been planted!'

The crowd began to rumble.

'Why did you order all that metal, Lady Elira?'

'Are you really a mayj? The Krijen strung up my niece for that.'

The questions came thick and fast, and Pyra closed her eyes and listened to them, enjoying the sharp tongues, the needle jabs, and the piercing words as they sliced into Lady Elira's façade.

This was it. It was time for the final blow.

'Do you know what happens,' Pyra called loudly, turning around and spreading her arms wide, 'when you put more money onto the streets? Do you know what happens to your coin if there is too much of it? It becomes worth *less*.' She pulled out her horseshoes and pointed their filed ends towards the Kahn. 'Lady Elira has deceived you! She's been paying for her votes, pouring countless coin into Valrue to fund her political campaign. She's been robbing you of your rights, all the while making the rich richer and the poor poorer!'

The crowd were turning to each other, their faces red, their expressions angry.

'And you know I'm right,' Pyra added. 'Because some of you are in on it.'

There was a bellow from behind Pyra, and she spun on the spot, expecting an attack. The blacksmith who had spoken earlier lunged forward from the crowd, but instead of running at Pyra, he charged right past her and shoved Rifter aside, smacking his hand onto the trigger of the crossbow still mounted on Barrett's shoulders. The bolt tore from the weapon and speared right into the shoulder of a Krijen as he dived in front of Lady Elira. The force of it threw him backwards.

Screams split the air as chaos erupted, and the People converged on one another, throwing punches and hurling shoes into the fray, the only weapons at their disposal.

In the midst of the mayhem, Pyra stood watching it unfurl. She'd not expected the People would be the first to attack. It was almost as much of a shock as when the Great Kahn had swung his sword at her at the Celebrations. Anyhow, she may not have started it, but she would not miss an opportunity to take a stab at a few Krijen while she had the chance.

Pyra charged towards the squad of Krijen who had swallowed Lady Elira into their protective circle. The Krijen with the bolt through his shoulder was still standing, his dagger out, a grimace twisting his face as he battled against the surge of people. With their combined efforts, the circle was moving through the crowd despite the mountain of citizens clamouring around them. Lady Elira was getting away.

That was not what Pyra had planned.

Lady Elira had her chance to turn herself in, and she'd thrown it back in Pyra's face twice now. As per their agreement, Lady Hia wouldn't begrudge the streetlings this murder.

Pyra screamed and slashed at the nearest Krijen, who retaliated so fast his dagger sliced a deep cut right through her upper arm, making Pyra screech and drop one of her horseshoes. The Krijen stepped away from his squad and darted towards her, bringing up his fist up and around to hit Pyra in the jaw so hard she swore her neck snapped, and she saw stars as she twirled and fell.

She smacked onto the cobblestones, and luckily enough, sense came with her. She rolled to the side just as a dagger-blade came tearing down through the space where her head had been; the tip dinged as it glanced off the cobbles.

Pyra scrambled up and made to dive away, but the Krijen wrapped a hand around her foot and yanked her back. Pyra dug her fingers into the cobbles, but her nails skidded over the smooth stones, and she couldn't find purchase as the Krijen dragged her towards him, towards impending doom, towards the death that Pyra had not expected to come so quickly with so little warning. The shock of it tore straight through gang leader Pyra to Polly's Pyra, who let out an ear-splitting scream as she twisted around to see the Krijen raise his dagger, the blade flashing clean in the light the way they do before they get bloody.

Pyra was ashamed to say she even closed her eyes, and she felt a shadow fall over her and heard the clang of metal, expecting something to skewer her. But nothing happened.

So Pyra peeked to see why she wasn't dead yet.

The Lost Square stood in front of her. It had its dagger raised, its stance identical to the Krijen in front of it, who looked like he was having a seizure. He kept looking at the Lost Square and twitching, then looking down at Pyra, then back to the Lost Square again.

It was almost comical to watch.

Pyra wished the Krijen would take a swipe. It would solve so many of her problems if he cut the Lost Square down, but Pyra could tell he wasn't going to do it.

Like Lady Hia said, it was beneath him to touch it.

Pyra snatched her dropped horseshoe from the ground and pushed herself to her feet. She turned her back on the pair and shoved through the crowd, hunting for Lady Elira. To her fury, the Kahn was almost at the edge of the square, having been successfully smuggled away by the rest of her Krijen guard.

The severe lack of streetlings was also cause for concern. Pyra spun on the spot, looking left and right. *Where were they all?*

'Oi!'

Pyra stiffened. It was that stupid Lost Square. It was in her way again, and she cursed the Krijen for letting it get away. She tried to sidestep it, but it just moved with her, looking angry as usual. 'What are you playing at?' it snapped.

The stupid thing was trying to talk to her in *public*. Pyra darted to the side.

'Oh no, you don't!'

It got right in her way again. Pyra bared her teeth and spat at it, but it kept blocking her exit. It was so bloody *quick*.

Pissed off, Pyra couldn't help herself. She finally lifted her chin and looked the Lost Square right in its grungy eyes. Her mouth turned up in disgust. She'd not seen it for months, and even by streetling standards, the thing was a mess. It was filthy; its hair was in knots, and its shirt was so shredded it may as well not have bothered with it.

'Get out of it!' Pyra snarled.

'You think I don't notice when all the streetlings suddenly disappear from the Point?'

Pyra threw herself backwards, ducking down between a stream of legs, losing the Lost Square in the crowd. Why did it care where the streetlings were? It had made it pretty clear it didn't want to be a part of what they were up to. It had better not ruin this Reckoning like it ruined everything else.

Where *were* all her streetlings?

To Pyra's amazement, she found them right back where she'd left them in the middle of the square. They'd waited, trembling with anticipation, nail-punctured gloves at the ready, frothing to be unleashed. Their desperation to join the fight was such that Pyra almost felt bad for leaving them there. She was a little proud they'd restrained themselves but mostly amazed. Of course, she'd not given the word, but she didn't think she'd need to. Streetlings did not typically wait for permission.

Porge stood at the ready, his eyes locked on her face, waiting for her lips to move. She grinned at him and opened her mouth to call the attack, but a rough hand clamped hard over her mouth.

'Don't do it!'

Pyra let loose a muffled scream and twisted, wrenching herself from the grip of the Lost Square. 'GET OFF ME!' She spat onto the ground, feeling nauseated. She couldn't believe it had put its dirty hands on her *face*. 'You do that again, and I'll put my horseshoe through your eye!'

So it shoved her instead, its face even angrier than before. 'Are you insane, Pyra? Do you *want* a massacre on your hands?'

'THAT'S EXACTLY WHAT WE WANT!'

'More Krijen are coming! If you let the gangs attack, you'll only give the Krijen a reason to kill them!'

Was it for real? 'We are *streetlings*,' Pyra hissed. 'Krijen don't need more of a reason than that to kill us!'

'But your plan already worked! Lady Elira is ruined –'

Pyra let out a scream of frustration and turned away from the Lost Square, infuriated she was letting herself get caught up in its logic. How dare it question her authority so brazenly? She knew what gang leader Pyra *should* do. Gang leader Pyra should call the attack and unleash the streetlings on the Kahn like she'd promised them.

But there was a stupid voice in her head telling her that the Lost Square was right. This Reckoning had already worked, and with Ala's scalping so raw in her mind, Pyra didn't have it in her to let her streetlings die needlessly simply because the fiendish little idiots wanted a bit of fun and didn't know what was good for them.

But Porge was watching.

Pyra couldn't imagine the backlash from the streetlings if they thought her to be backing down from a Kahn killing at the word of a Lost Square. She needed to do something drastic to fix this.

With a yell, Pyra lifted her horseshoes, spun on her heels, and lunged at the Lost Square. It startled and brought its dagger across to meet her horseshoes with a loud clang, knocking her attack to the side.

'Are you *kidding me,* Pyra? I just saved your life!'

Pyra screeched and lashed out again, driving towards the Lost Square. It swung back from her attack, raising its dagger between them.

The streetlings *loved* this. They gathered around, hollering and hooting and egging her on, pulling out nails and belts and shaking them enthusiastically at the pair. But the Lost Square wasn't stupid. It was backing up fast, and the streetlings squawked as they scrambled away, not wanting it to touch them.

Pyra pressed forward with her horseshoes again, licking her lips because she knew her streetlings would lap it up. As expected, they screamed in mirth.

The Lost Square had had enough. 'Fuck you, Pyra,' it said. Then it turned and ran from her, and the streetlings cackled and spat at its back as it disappeared into the crowd.

Feeling triumphant, Pyra raised her hands, a wicked gang-leader-grin on her face. 'Back to the towers!'

Wails of disappointment rang out. Pyra signalled to Rifter and Barrett, who nodded their heads and readied her crossbow, aiming it at her constituents. 'Back to the towers or I'll put a bolt in your brains!' She meant it this time too. Either way, they'd be dead because the Krijen would get them. At least this way, it made her look tougher. But still, she hoped her show with the Lost Square had placated the streetlings enough to listen even if they weren't getting what they wanted.

Pyra nodded to Porge, then swung in a circle and marched back down the street towards the towers. To her relief, the streetlings followed, pulling faces at the crowd as they went and swiping coins from people's hands.

Porge forked off when they got to the edge of the square, his Upper East gang zipping after him.

Trailing streetlings, Pyra led the way up to the rooftops and looked down at the mess of citizens scattering as Krijen reinforcements arrived to clear the square. The blacksmith had been arrested. The admirable man was probably going to be strung up for his efforts, so Pyra would be sure to bow to him when she passed him on the bridge. But he seemed tough. Maybe he would survive.

Lady Elira was gone. She was alive, sure, but her lies were exposed. Pyra didn't expect the Kahnen would do anything about it, but maybe this time, it didn't matter. The citizens knew, and word would spread, so regardless of what happened, Lady Elira would eventually get what was coming to her because she would spend every night for the rest of her life lying awake in terror, knowing there was something out there worse than streetlings.

    Voters wanting vengeance.

CHAPTER 44:
THE GREAT KAHN

Now that he'd burned the contents of Mandavar's study, the Great Kahn felt lighter than air. He'd not realised how much it had been weighing on him until he'd seen it all go up in flames. He'd salvaged only Mandavar's copy of *The Founding of Valrue* for its excerpts on the Bhouli. It had been dreadfully wearisome trying to read the copy from the KahnenLibrary given its frequent mentions of majik. Half the book had been redacted.

Slowly, Luka was coming back. The Great Kahn could feel him every time he thanked a KahnenMinder for doing some menial task, every time he said yes to the Eighth House when they asked something of him with fear in their eyes.

But it wasn't enough. He'd been avoiding the main problem.

In the distance of the corridor walked the KrijenMayj, the older squad member at his side. They were recognisable by their long braids, one blond and the other white. The Great Kahn recalled that the older squad member was called Jokah. He'd made an effort to remember the Krijen who guarded the KahnenKeep. It seemed important now. It was something Luka would do.

The pair wore Krijen black, daggers at their thighs, krije on their backs. They were heading off on some duty, no doubt, where the People would see them, and they needed to look like the warriors they were.

'Jin,' the Great Kahn called.

The KrijenMayj turned around, a hand going to the hilt of a dagger.

'Wait, please.'

Maybe the Great Kahn was imagining it, but there was something different in the young man's posture while he waited for the Great Kahn to approach. He was tense, like always, but it was more than that. There was a wariness or a suspicion that wasn't there before. It had been two months since they'd spoken during the training session, so it wouldn't be surprising if the KrijenMayj had forgotten the Great Kahn's attempt at kindness. Or perhaps he just needed to harness.

'What is it, my Great Lord?'

'I want to speak with you.'

The KrijenMayj didn't look pleased. 'Will it take long? Lady Hia is waiting for us. She asked us to escort her into Rue.'

'Send someone in your place. She does not need you for that.'

The KrijenMayj did not drop his hand from his dagger. He turned to Jokah. 'Take Nommo. He's in the bunkroom.'

'Yes, sir.' The older Krijen saluted his young squad leader and left.

The KrijenMayj turned back to the Great Kahn expectantly. The Great Kahn didn't know what to say to him; he had nothing prepared. But he was sick of his own excuses. He needed to get over his hatred of mayjen, particularly this one, if he wanted to give Luka a chance.

After an extended silence, the right words still eluded him. However, it was an interesting exercise in itself. The KrijenMayj's agitation was becoming more apparent. There was a twitch in his jaw now. The Great Kahn dropped his gaze and looked pointedly at the KrijenMayj's fist, still poised on his dagger hilt.

The KrijenMayj saw him look and dropped his hand. But he didn't apologise, which the Great Kahn found rather poignant. He longed to know what was going on inside the young man's head.

'My Great Lord, what do you want?'

It wasn't rude as such, just unnecessarily terse.

'How are you?'

The KrijenMayj blinked in surprise. The Great Kahn was rather disappointed in himself. He'd expected something better too.

'Fine, my Great Lord,' came the reply, though the KrijenMayj's hands flared briefly, and his eyes flickered to a spot just to his left, lingering there for a moment before coming back to the Great Kahn. Something had distracted him.

'You do not lie well,' the Great Kahn said.

The young Krijen looked annoyed. 'I'll lie better next time then.'

The Great Kahn laughed, genuinely amused. He missed these kinds of interactions, where someone dared to challenge him. So few had done it since Mandavar, and nearer the end, those challenges had always turned deadly, going beyond the banter the Great Kahn had wanted. Eventually there had been no pleasure it in at all.

The KrijenMayj did not smile back. 'Why do you ask? You've been avoiding me for weeks.'

So he noticed, the Great Kahn thought. 'Valrue demands much of my attention,' he said, making his voice sharp. 'I do not have time for the pleasantries and attention you suggest.'

The KrijenMayj flushed.

Good, the Great Kahn thought. It would not do for the young man to know he had any kind of influence over him.

'In any case, I am asking now. We pushed a big responsibility on you just after your mentor was killed, and you have yet to catch the mayj responsible. I imagine it has been a difficult time.'

'What did you care about Oji?'

That daring brusqueness again, so soon after his sheepishness. Great Kahn hesitated. Perhaps he should not have brought up the late FaKrijen. He must tread carefully.

'Oji and I did not always see eye to eye, but I respected him. He was a powerful ally, and I regret his death,' the Great Kahn lied. 'I am haunted by the Celebrations and how the streetlings got away with what they did. It is terrifying to know they have a mayj that powerful amongst them.' It was the mercenary who suggested they play on the assumption that Drax was a streetling. Streetlings were easy to blame, and the boy looked the part. It was a more believable lie than Felle, now.

'So the mayj was definitely a streetling?'

The Great Kahn felt a strange swooping sensation in the pit of his stomach. Nerves, he realised. This was very dangerous territory. But he needed to entertain this line of questioning, lest he appear to be hiding something.

'You think otherwise?'

'I don't know what I think,' the KrijenMayj said. The Great Kahn waited, but the young man didn't have more to add.

The tension was still there, taut in the air. Was it possible that the KrijenMayj knew something?

No, the Great Kahn thought, pushing the idea away. He would not let paranoia fester where there was no cause for it. This was just the power pressing on the KrijenMayj, fuelling his suspicion. He was just testing boundaries, like Mandavar used to.

Even so, the Great Kahn had to do something. This tension was not helping Luka's cause.

'How are you progressing with your training?'

'Better since you explained the multi-tasking thing.' The KrijenMayj's tone was accusatory. He wanted more. 'I mean what good is Stolt, really? He hasn't even fixed the walls in the room we train in. Is it because he can't?'

The Great Kahn suppressed a smile, impressed that the KrijenMayj had noticed Stolt's failings. He was learning quickly despite his shocking teacher.

'Why do you think that?'

'There is something about those walls. I don't know why, but I don't think Stolt can harness them back together even though he made out like he could. He says he doesn't harness for the sake of the Unsettlement, but that's a lie. He doesn't strike me as a man who wouldn't flaunt his talent if he had it. He must be powerful because I can feel him, but he does *nothing.* It's almost like he doesn't know what to do. Why do you keep him around if he's so useless?'

They still stood in the corridor, and the KrijenMayj was not speaking quietly. The conversation was teetering towards topics that would not be wise to continue when so many ears could be listening. But this was Luka's chance.

'Come,' the Great Kahn said, inclining his head down the corridor. 'I will not talk about this here.'

'Why not? Because it's about majik? The Unsettlement is over, isn't it?'

So *brazen*.

'It seems that way,' the Great Kahn said noncommittally. 'But we lack proof. Now, if you want to talk, you will follow me.' He turned and started down the corridor from which he'd come. Only a backward glance told him the KrijenMayj was following, his boots silent on the stone floor.

The Great Kahn's own chambers weren't far away, but the Great Kahn did not want the KrijenMayj in his personal space, nor would that be appropriate. Instead, he led them to the nearest windowless room.

It was a smaller version of the Red Room, velvet lining its walls. Tables crammed it, papers strewn over every surface. Six KahnenMinders walked up and down the rows, musing over the documents. They were reviewing accounts for the running of the KahnenKeep.

'Out,' the Great Kahn said to the Minders. It came out more harshly than he intended, the way he'd been saying it for the past quarter of a century. They scurried past him and closed the door.

The KrijenMayj walked up to one of the tables, running his eyes over the documents. The Great Kahn let him look; there would be nothing in there of interest for him.

'The walls in the training room are made of cardonite,' the Great Kahn said, finally answering the KrijenMayj's question. 'You are right. Stolt cannot fix them.'

'What's cardonite?'

'Matter bound together by a most arcane kind of majik. It requires a very specific type of harnessing ability, and a lot of power to create. Stolt may have the ability, I do not know, but if he does, he does not know how –'

The Great Kahn stopped mid-sentence, suddenly angry with himself. Why bother burning the books if he was only going to blab about Weaving later? It didn't matter that the KrijenMayj couldn't do it; the knowledge was dangerous.

'Do you know how it works?'

'No,' the Great Kahn said truthfully. Mandavar had tried and failed to describe Weaving to him on many occasions. It was something you felt, he said. There were no words.

'I can pull the cardonite apart,' the KrijenMayj said. 'Could I put the training room back together, if I knew how?'

'No. You are a Breaker. No matter how powerful you are, you are limited by your harnessing ability. It is why you are struggling so much with your power. You do not have a good outlet.'

The KrijenMayj was quiet, thumbing the tops of his daggers. 'You know it's difficult?'

The Great Kahn raised an eyebrow. 'You think you are hiding it?'

'I guess not.' The KrijenMayj's thumbs froze on his daggers, and he quickly dropped his hands. 'Does cardonite always look like that? With the webbing?'

'Not always, but most of the time it does. Mayjen do it on purpose when they want people to recognise their work. They tend towards arrogance.'

'No shit.' The KrijenMayj was no doubt thinking of Stolt. 'Sorry,' he added quickly as though remembering who he was speaking to. 'I've just seen it around, the webbed stone. The Split in the Deadlands looks and feels the same. I don't like it.'

'Of course not. It is another mayj's concentrated power. Powerful mayjen have an aversion to one another. It is supposed to stop them from congregating, to prevent imbalances.' The Great Kahn cursed himself silently. What was it about this young man that made him say things he shouldn't?

The KrijenMayj nodded slowly. 'Your sword is made from cardonite too? I noticed the webbing at the Celebrations.'

The Great Kahn did not reply immediately. He did not want to talk about Mandavar's sword. 'Yes,' he said in a clipped tone.

'I don't think I *felt* the sword though, not like I can feel the cardonite walls in the training room. I don't know why.'

The Great Kahn had suspected as much. At that time, the lake had still been full of Mandavar's power, which would have overwhelmed the sensation of the sword, both having been wrought by the same mayj.

'You don't have it on you?' the KrijenMayj asked. 'The sword? I can't feel anything.'

'No.' At least the Great Kahn had not been that stupid. If the KrijenMayj made the connection between the sword and the lake, it could expose him. No, it could ruin him, ruin Luka. He'd been foolish to carry it around like he had.

The Great Kahn should never have kept it. Worst of all, he couldn't even explain *why* he'd kept it. It had not been something to remember Mandavar by, no. Most likely it had been because he'd wanted something that Mandavar had loved in his possession, something to keep from him. How thoughtless his anger had made him.

The KrijenMayj regarded the Great Kahn silently, a ponderous expression on his face. His thumbs were already back on his dagger hilts. 'Why do you use the sword,' the KrijenMayj asked, 'if you hate majik?'

The Great Kahn couldn't stop his lip from curling at the question.

The KrijenMayj noticed. 'Sorry,' he said quickly. 'I don't mean to pry.'

'Yes, you do,' the Great Kahn said through clenched teeth. He could feel his hackles rising above the disappointment. He'd been doing so well for Luka –

There was a commotion outside and a frantic knocking at the door.

Seething, the Great Kahn strode over and pulled it open, glaring down at the Minder panting before him.

'*What?*'

'My Great Lord, it's Lady Elira,' the Minder puffed. He flinched at the Great Kahn's expression.

'What about her?'
'She's been attacked.'

CHAPTER 45: ARENBHA

Aren could feel a heart beating, but she was pretty sure it wasn't hers. Firstly, it was by her face, and that was not where hearts were. Then again, if that creature had ripped her heart from her chest, it was entirely possible that it was sitting by her face, and Drax had just kept it going because he had an irksome habit of holding on when he shouldn't.

Secondly, there was a heavy weight on top of her. Now, she was *fairly* certain it was Drax because he had a tendency to do that when he was trying not to Turn. After a little more pondering, she noticed a soft thud growing under her ribs.

Ah, Aren thought. *That beat must be mine.*

Sure enough, after that realisation, the pain quickly came, searing down the slices in her spine, made worse by the fact her back was pressed into the dirt. She was awake enough to feel all of it now.

But there was something else going on that was really, really out of place. It made her consider that perhaps she'd dreamt the whole thing: the fall from the waterfall, the Bhouli underground, the forest, the Krijen, the giant cat. That out-of-place thing made her almost certain that she was still in bed because she'd woken up feeling much like this before.

It was the sound of people talking.

Aren opened her eyes, seeing nothing but white scars above her. She was staring at Drax's neck.

'Drax,' she said, 'I'm okay.'

'You're hurt,' came his voice.

'Not badly.' She hoped it wasn't a lie. It *really* hurt. 'Can you let me up?'

'No, Aren.'

'Why not?'

After a strikingly long pause, a strange male voice boomed down to her out of the sudden silence, the sound of people talking having stopped.

'*You*,' the voice said. 'You brought that unbalanced creature straight into our camp, and now you lie here, flaunting indecency itself! Explain yourselves!'

Aren pushed Drax off and slowly sat up, wincing as her back came off the ground. Immediately, the tip of a sword appeared between her eyes. She looked up at its bearer, a young man with shoulder-length brown hair in hundreds of little braids and a braided beard. His demeanour made him seem like the leader. There were other men standing beside him, encircling her and Drax, each tentatively holding their weapons out. Their hair was all braided in a similar fashion as the first, and they wore black and white trousers and tunics, and heavy black boots. At their feet were five regular-sized dogs with brown fur and white tips on their tails, gently growling their displeasure at Aren and Drax.

Aren blinked rapidly a few times, just to be sure she was actually seeing what she thought she was.

'Tell Donna to hurry up,' the leader said to a pair of his companions. 'Before Gi smites us all.' A pair of men turned and ran off.

'You're injured too, I see,' the leader snapped at Aren. 'Serves you right. What in Gi's holy name were you doing, going after an Edgecat? And with a party of two? It's a stack of slights!'

The way he spoke sounded odd. Aren was sure she understood but still couldn't make sense of it, especially with all the strange words. 'An . . . an Edgecat?'

'Yes, an Edgecat! Do you think feigning ignorance will see us forgive your recklessness? You could have got us all killed!'

Drax cowered into the ground. Aren's heartbeat was strong, so she knew Drax was okay, if scared. 'What happened?' Aren muttered to him. 'Did these people save us?'

Drax nodded, blue eyes locked on the dogs, whose heads were turning towards him. They were no longer growling.

'Oi! Did you hear me, slighters?'

The leader's sword sailed so close to Aren's face that she was forced to lean back from it.

'I said *explain* yourselves!'

'We didn't mean to lead the – um – the Edgecat to you,' Aren said. 'I was hunting, and the Edgecat and I went for the same rabbit . . .' She trailed off at the look on the man's face. If Aren wasn't wrong, he looked a little disturbed.

'Who in Gi's name *are* you?'

Aren opened her mouth, a lie on the tip on her tongue. She hesitated. What could it hurt to tell the truth? These people clearly weren't Krijen. She and Drax been wandering the forest for weeks, and they were lost. This might be their only chance at help.

'I'm Aren,' she said. 'This is Drax. We're from Valrue, and we're trying to find Holu Mon. Do you know where it is?'

The men all stared down at them, looking stunned. Then the leader's face grew angry once more. 'You think we're going to believe *that*?'

Aren paused. 'Which part don't you believe?'

'That you're from Valrue. You think that'll justify your actions, do you? That we'll fall over ourselves trying to save your slightful souls?' The leader scoffed.

Aren looked at Drax, alarmed. What more did they need saving from?

'Please,' Aren said nervously, the tip of the leader's sword still between her eyes, 'we don't mean you any harm. We're sorry about leading that cat here. If you let us go, I promise we'll stay away.'

'Absolutely not,' the leader said. 'You're not going anywhere in your state. Gi would never forgive us if we let you.'

Aren swallowed. 'What are you going to do?'

'Send you back to the city. You've not exactly given us a choice.' The leader grimaced down at them as though the sight of them caused him great pain. 'We've got a party going back in a few days. You can go with them.'

'Wait.' Aren could hardly believe her ears. 'By the city . . . do you mean to Holu Mon?'

'Where else?'

Being sent to Holu Mon as a prisoner was better than being stuck indefinitely in a forest.

Aren twisted, trying to see Drax's face, sucking in a breath as a sharp pain ripped down her back. Wetness had soaked into her wraps at her lower spine. She was glad she couldn't see the damage.

The dogs began to whimper. They had their tails between their legs, and they inched slowly away from Aren and Drax. They must be feeling his power as it returned.

'What's wrong with the dogs?' one of the men asked, sounding worried.

The leader frowned at the dogs. Then he whistled, and the dogs all sat down on their haunches, still whimpering.

'Olmonon . . .' one of the men said. He was speaking to the leader, using his name. Olmonon leant over to him, his face stern as the man whispered something in his ear. Olmonon's eyes widened at Aren and Drax. To Aren's surprise, he slowly lowered his sword from between her eyes.

'Hang on.' He reached up and ran a hand through his braids, then whispered something in reply to his neighbour, who reeled back, startled by whatever had been said.

'You're sure about that?' his neighbour asked. 'That just seems so *unlikely* . . . but . . . well . . .'

Aren was straining to hear. She thought she heard the word 'Edgecat' once or twice but couldn't make out anything else.

Eventually, Olmonon turned to them, slowly raising an eyebrow. 'Is one of you a mayj?'

Drax flinched and Aren's heart skipped a beat before it began pounding with renewed vigour in her chest. Would they hurt Drax if they knew what he was? Everything in her screamed yes.

Aren quickly scanned the circle of men. If she was fast enough, maybe she could grab one of their swords. Only Olmonon had lowered his weapon, so the rest were up for grabs. She'd not had much practise with a sword, but it couldn't be that different to a dagger, could it? It was better than nothing. Drax wouldn't be able to harness more than her heart, so it would be up to her to get them out of there.

Just as Aren gathered herself to attack, Olmonon squatted down in front of them. 'Gracious Gi, I'm right, aren't I?' he said, looking incredulous. He whistled sharply and waved his hand. The dogs took off running, glad to have been let away. All the men abruptly lowered their weapons.

Perplexed, Aren froze, her legs still tensed to spring. She glanced at Drax, unsure of what to do.

'Please,' Olmonon said earnestly, 'which one of you is a mayj?'

Aren eyed him suspiciously. 'You had your sword pointed at us only a second ago.'

'I'm so sorry.' His forehead crinkled in concern. 'But you should have said!'

'Why does it matter if one of us is a mayj?'

'Are . . . are you serious?'

When Aren didn't reply, his jaw dropped. 'Oh, gracious Gi,' he repeated. 'You *are* from Valrue, aren't you?'

Muttering broke out around the circle of men.

'Which one of you is a mayj?' Olmonon pressed. 'I promise we won't hurt you. In fact' – he gulped – 'I'm surprised you didn't hurt *us* –'

'Me,' Aren said loudly. 'I'm the mayj.' She ignored Drax's blank stare. It was a good thing he shut down when he heard things he didn't like. 'And again, why do you care?'

Olmonon clapped his hands together, a grin spreading across his face. 'I can't believe it.' He stood up, looking over the shoulders of the men circling them. 'What's taking so long? Where's Donna?'

'I'm here!'

The circle broke apart and two women immediately appeared in the gap, one in her teenage years and one middle-aged, led by the pair of men who'd been sent to summon them.

Olmonon turned to the middle-aged woman whose braided blonde hair was tied in a giant knot behind her head. She looked down at Aren and Drax sitting on the ground. 'What in Gi's holy name is going on?'

'Donna!' Olmonon flung out a hand, excitedly pointing a finger at Aren. 'This girl was wounded by the Edgecat. She's a mayj!'

Donna gasped, her hands flying to her mouth. 'Olmonon, do not fib about such things!'

'I'm not! I swear on life itself!'

Donna knelt on the ground and held out a trembling hand to Aren. 'May I help you up?'

Aren hesitated. The woman looked kind enough, her face full of wonder and worry. Aren reached out and gently grasped her hand. The woman's soft hands curled around hers, and she stared into Aren's eyes for a moment. 'Sola, help us.'

The younger woman rushed to Aren's other side and put an arm under her. Together, the two women helped her to her feet.

Aren bit down on her lip, every movement like a spike down her spine. She swayed, lightheaded, not because of Drax. He was right behind her, breathing down her neck.

Donna and the other woman were both staring at him. 'Move away,' Donna said sharply. 'You know better than that.'

Drax shook his head.

Donna's nostrils flared. 'What do you mean, no?'

'Leave it, Donna,' Olmonon said. 'He's with her. And they aren't from Holu Mon. They are from Valrue. They don't do things like we do.'

'Valrue?' Donna whispered. 'Gi, spare me from those abhorred slighters! Come quickly,' she said to Aren, 'before you bleed to death. Gi would never forgive us for that. Olmonon, chaperone the boy, please. He may accompany her, but his slights are not so easily forgiven.'

The men hastened out of their way as Olmonon led them out of the circle, Aren clinging to Donna and Sola for support. Drax ambled so close behind Aren that he kept standing on her heels. The women from Holu Mon took turns throwing him accusatory looks over their shoulders.

As they walked, Aren did her best to take in their surroundings. They were in a section of the woods where the trees were sparse, and there was nothing but earth at their feet. The ground was well-trod.

Spaced between the trees were six enormous tents. As they made their way towards one of the tents, they passed a great many people, all of whom wore the same black and white clothes. They wore their hair in hundreds of tiny braids, and all the men had beards. They stopped and stared. Some mouths were agape while others had pursed lips, accompanied by flashing eyes of steel, but most wore soft *O*'s as though they didn't know what to make of the newcomers. More dogs hunched at the feet of the befuddled audience, whining pitifully as Drax passed.

Someone rushed forward to open the tent flap for them. Aren peered up in awe when they stepped inside. The makeshift room was exquisite. Thick wooden poles spaced the length of the tent, supporting the dark brown canvas. From each pole hung a bundle of lanterns, their hexagonal prisms like a grouping of glowing berries, casting a speckled light across everything. The floor had rugs, and there were red lounge chairs with plush cushions not unlike what Aren's father had in his blacksmithy, in the room he called Day.

In contrast to the eye-watering grandeur was the barbarity of a giant black-furred head which adorned the middle of the room. It hung on a pole, its jaw wrenched open, exposing yellow teeth. Its eyes were glassy, empty. But it was not the head of a cat. Its ears were rounded, its jaw longer.

A bear, Aren remembered. A bear without its body.

Olmonon marched them past the bear's head and pulled back a partitioning into a separate, simpler room. A row of beds lined the back canvas wall, interspersed with shelves loaded with supplies.

'Over here,' Olmonon said, stopping and gesturing towards a waist-height table on the left side of the room. Behind it was a bench, upon which lay a few scary-looking instruments. Aren eyed them warily as they approached. She could feel Drax trembling behind her.

'Let's take a look at you,' Donna said, helping Aren ease herself onto the table. 'It's a miracle you got away alive. Gi has eyes on you.'

Sola began unfolding a wooden screen around them. Olmonon quickly stepped behind it, out of sight.

'You too,' Donna said, scowling at Drax. Drax shook his head and stepped closer to Aren.

'He can stay,' Aren said quickly. 'I don't mind.' Drax was still recovering from holding onto her heart. He needed to stay close. That, and she didn't trust these people, not yet.

'It's not about whether you mind,' Donna said. 'It's *most* inappropriate. Olmonon, come get him.'

Olmonon appeared from behind the wooden screen and reached a hand towards Drax, who edged away from him, shaking his head, pressing his back into Aren's knees.

'Please,' Aren said. 'I want him next to me.' She didn't get it, but she didn't want to argue either. Her back hurt too much.

Olmonon, Donna, and Sola shared another look. 'Fine,' Donna said. 'Gi, forgive us all this slight. But he needs to stand *back*.'

Olmonon disappeared behind the screen again.

'Lie on your front,' Donna said to Aren. 'I need you to relax.'

Wincing as she went, Aren lay down, feeling strange exposing her wound to this stranger. She already felt so vulnerable, and Drax's distress wasn't helping her nerves.

Donna picked up some scissors, and Aren tensed at the sight of them despite Donna's request.

Drax stood by Aren's head, visibly squirming as Donna stepped forward. Aren shivered as cold metal tapped the base of her spine, travelling upwards as Donna sliced through her wraps. Drax's blue eyes followed the sensation, something lurking in his blank face that Aren couldn't quite read.

After a long minute and feeling slightly more reassured that Donna was not going to stab her while she worked, Aren rested her chin on her hands and looked off to the side, watching Sola prepare something on the bench. A drink of sorts. Sola kept glancing back and shaking her head at Drax, making soft tutting sounds.

Aren sucked in a breath as Donna peeled the wraps off her sliced skin. Drax whined like the dogs outside.

'You're lucky,' Donna said. 'These cuts are deep, and the wounds will need a good clean but I am deft with a needle. We have some tonics to aid the healing. Unless . . .' she moved around the table so that Aren could see her. 'Unless you would like to deal with these yourself?' Her eyes were expectant. 'If you want to harness, I can get you a mirror?'

There was no way Drax could do that kind of harnessing right now; healing her would surely require an extraordinary amount of majik. Aren wracked her brain, trying to come up with a believable reason to refuse, staring at Drax's scarred hands as they sat limp on the table in front of her. She remembered something Drax had said.

'Please do the stitches,' Aren said to Donna. 'I don't want the scarring from using majik, and I'd rather not spend weeks holding the skin together.' Aren looked up at Drax. His eyes were wider than ever.

Donna nodded in understanding. 'Of course. Sola, the tonic.'

Did she actually know what I meant? Aren thought. *Or was she pretending?* The fact that she'd suggested Aren heal herself implied that Donna knew more about majik than most people in Valrue. In Valrue, it was an accepted truth that majik didn't work on people. But it wasn't the truth at all.

Sola swept over, holding a cup out to Aren. Aren tentatively took it, looking down into its clear liquid. 'What's this?'

'Lunilum. It stops it hurting so much,' Sola said. 'We've got better stuff, but I can't rub a numbing salve on a dirty wound, and it's going to hurt to clean it. Unless you'd prefer a sedative?'

'No,' Aren said quickly. 'Not a sedative.'

Drax's eyes pleaded with her above the edge of the cup, but she wasn't sure what he was trying to say.

Aren was tempted not to drink it and just deal with the pain, but that sounded like a bad idea, especially if Drax would be around to watch. It seemed unlikely that Donna and Sola wanted to poison her, so Aren tipped the cup back and drank it down. It tasted like mildly sweet water. Her lips immediately went numb, not unlike that drink the Bhouli had given her.

'It will need a minute or two to work,' Donna said. She turned back to the bench with Sola, both of them busying themselves with something Aren couldn't see.

Aren gently flicked her wrist wraps, waiting. Already, the pain in her back was subsiding. She felt herself relaxing, not realising she'd scrunched herself up as much as she had. She slowly lowered her chin back down onto her hands once more, keeping her eyes on Drax's. 'What sort of camp is this?' she asked.

'A hunting camp,' came Olmonon's voice from behind the screen. 'We set up a few weeks ago. The Edgecreatures were getting out of control.'

'You mean that thing that attacked us?'

'Yes, it was an Edgecat. You really don't know about them?'

'No,' Aren replied, 'we don't have animals in Valruc.'

'Oh. Right.'

Aren wondered what Olmonon was thinking. Now that he thought her to be a mayj, she got the feeling a lot was being left unsaid, perhaps out of politeness. Aren hated that, and she hated being this ignorant again. She'd thought the days of making a fool of herself were behind her.

'We're Valruean,' Aren said. 'Just assume we know nothing about anything. It will make it easier.'

There was a pause. 'Okay, then.'

'So can you tell us about Edgecreatures?'

'Edgecreatures are animals that inhabit the Edge,' came Olmonon's voice. 'The Edge is the bit between Valrue and Holu Mon where the majikal imbalance caused everything to grow way too big.'

'Why?'

'We aren't sure just yet. It's likely related to the excess power, but the research is ongoing. Everything in and around the Edge is perverted.

The animals are really violent and dangerous, and even Gi can't save them, so we hunt them to keep their numbers down.'

'You-you killed that creature? The Edgecat?'

'Sure did,' Olmonon said, a smile in his voice. 'You know, we seemed angry before, but really we should be thanking you for leading the Edgecat to us. We just weren't prepared when it came right into the camp. It was quite impressive really . . . I couldn't figure out how you managed to keep ahead of it. But it makes more sense now, knowing you're a mayj.'

Before Aren could answer, Donna came back over to her. 'Can you feel that?' she asked. There was a gentle pressure on Aren's spine, but nothing else. 'Not really,' Aren replied.

'Good. We'll clean it out and stitch you up.'

Donna and Sola set to work on her back. Aren rested her forehead down on her hands. Because she was skinnier than she'd ever been before, the wood of the table was pressing into her hips though it didn't hurt with the numbing drink. Her stomach rumbled. She could only imagine how hungry Drax was. It had been hours since they'd eaten.

'Our backpacks,' Aren said suddenly, lifting her head again. 'Drax, we left our backpacks behind!'

'We've got them,' came Olmonon's reply. 'We found your campfire, too. How long have you been travelling for?'

'I don't know,' Aren said. 'Maybe a couple of months?'

'How did you get out of Valrue?'

Aren was silent. She didn't have a lie prepared.

'Sorry,' Olmonon said, 'it's none of my business. I'm just so curious. I've never met a mayj before, let alone one from Valrue –'

'Olmonon,' Donna warned. 'Don't pester the poor girl. She's had her back sliced open by an Edgecat, and she's full of lunilum.'

Aren jumped as Donna's needle went through her skin. It surprised her far more than it hurt, but Drax made a sharp noise in the back of his throat that Aren had never heard before. 'I don't like this,' he said. 'I don't like this.'

Donna's hands paused above Aren's back.

'It's all right,' Aren said gently to Drax. 'Noel gave me stitches before, remember? This is normal.'

'It didn't hurt when Noel did it,' Drax said.

'I wasn't conscious when he did it.'

Drax stared at her.

'It's fine. It doesn't hurt. It just surprised me, that's all.'

He didn't look convinced.

'Here,' Aren said, 'hold my hand.'

Sola let out a little scream as Drax slipped his limp hand into Aren's.

'Of all the unbalanced indecencies!' Donna cried. 'What do you think you're *doing?*'

'What?' Aren asked, shocked by their reactions.

'Do you wish to bring Gi's tears down upon us all?'

Olmonon's voice floated to them from behind the screen. 'Are they doing it again?'

'Doing *what* again?' Aren asked.

'Touching,' Sola whispered, looking at Aren and Drax's clenched fists as though it were truly the worst horror she'd ever seen.

'Touching? We're holding hands!' Aren said exasperatedly. 'Is there something wrong with that?'

'*Very,*' Donna said emphatically. 'He is a boy and you are a girl. I know you are a mayj, but for his sake, you mustn't touch each other!'

Aren quickly let go of Drax's hand. 'We didn't mean to offend you,' she mumbled.

'He was *lying* on her before,' Olmonon called from behind the wooden screen. 'In front of everyone!'

Sola gasped and put her hand to her chest. 'Gracious Gi, *really*? How slightful!'

'He travels with a mayj though,' Olmonon said. 'Gi will forgive it?'

'Perhaps,' Sola breathed. 'Perhaps Gi smiles on both of them. They've not only escaped Valrue but an Edgecat too!'

'You're right,' Donna said. 'We must remember ourselves. It's not for us to judge Gi's choices.' She sucked in a deep breath, holding up the needle. 'Shall I continue?'

Aren nodded. Her head was exploding with questions, but for once in her life, she waited. She locked eyes with Drax, returning his icy blue stare with a gentle smile, hoping to calm him even though the rapid beat of her heart gave her away. They needed to figure these people out and fast. If holding hands was enough to cause mortal offence, who knew what other seemingly trivial thing might send them over the edge.

But Aren was determined. *This will not be like the Bhouli*, she thought. These people were being good to them – like the Bhouli had been – even though they were strangers and did things differently. Aren felt like she'd been given another chance to do it better this time.

Aren would make sure she did.

CHAPTER 46:
THE GREAT KAHN

'Tell me what you know,' the Great Kahn demanded of the KahnenMinder.

'There was a disturbance at Lady Elira's rally, my Great Lord,' the Minder said in a rush. 'The People are in an uproar.'

'Where is Lady Elira? Was she harmed?'

'On her way back to the Keep. We believe she is unharmed –'

The KrijenMayj darted over to them, making the Minder yelp. He'd not seen the young man standing behind the door.

'She has her Krijen guard?' the KrijenMayj asked.

'Yes –'

'What happened?'

The Minder swallowed. 'I don't know the full details, but someone fired upon Lady Elira with a crossbow.'

'A crossbow?' The KrijenMayj's eyes flickered to the Great Kahn's. Then the KrijenMayj spun in a circle and began pacing the room, his fist clenching and unclenching at his sides. 'I know who this is,' he spat. 'It's that fucking streetling from the Celebrations. I shattered her crossbow before.'

The Great Kahn remembered the crossbow too, and the streetling girl with the red ties at her wrists who accused him of running a corrupt democracy.

'So,' the Great Kahn said, turning back to the Minder, 'the streetlings attacked Lady Elira?'

'I-I don't know, my Great Lord, I didn't hear that –'

The KrijenMayj turned on the Great Kahn, his expression ugly. 'Of course, it was the streetlings! It's the skahk, isn't it? He's shown his face again!'

The skahk? the Great Kahn thought. For a moment, he thought the KrijenMayj was speaking about himself. Then it clicked. He was talking about Mandavar's son.

The Great Kahn had not expected the KrijenMayj would use such a word.

He stared at the KrijenMayj, carefully reassessing. Heat broiled off him, and the Great Kahn could see the twitch in his jaw as he struggled to keep control.

Perhaps it was in defiance of the KrijenMayj's transparent fury, but a sense of calm was coming back to the Great Kahn.

'I want to know exactly what happened,' the Great Kahn said. He thought quickly. *Teal would know.* 'Go find the KahnenSpeaker and bring him to the Red Room.'

The Minder dashed off immediately. The KrijenMayj made to go after him.

'Jin, wait.'

The KrijenMayj paused mid-stride, and his shoulders tensed. 'Why am I waiting?' His voice was so sharp. Enough to make the Great Kahn hesitate.

'Because good decisions are not born of anger and ignorance,' the Great Kahn warned. 'We will speak with our eyes and ears first, and then we will act. Lady Elira is in good hands.'

'But –'

'You do not trust the Krijen?'

'I'm going after the skahk!'

'If he was at the rally, he will be long gone. Come with me to the Red

Room.' The Eighth House would want the KrijenMayj there. No, they would *demand* his presence, especially in the absence of the FaKrijen.

'Fine,' the KrijenMayj snapped.

The Great Kahn swept into the corridor, leading the way to the Red Room. The KahnenKeep corridors were suddenly full of people running, ringing with news of Lady Elira's attack as word spread.

'Gather the Eighth House,' the Great Kahn called to another Minder who'd begun trailing them. She bowed hurriedly and ran off in the other direction.

They'd just turned the corner when a black-wrapped figure appeared in the distance, some papers clutched in his hands. The KrijenMayj sprinted ahead of the Great Kahn to meet him, and their raised voices echoed back to the Great Kahn over the noise in the corridor.

'Sir!' the Krijen began breathlessly. 'I was at the rally –'

'Any dead or wounded?' the KahnenMayj asked.

'Of the People, I cannot say. Of Krijen, no deaths, one wounded.'

'How badly wounded?'

'A crossbow bolt to the shoulder, sir, but he'll be okay.'

The KrijenMayj swore. 'Reinforcements have been sent?'

'Yes, sir.'

'Why are you here and not with them?'

'My squad leader sent me to you.'

'Me? Why?'

'We need to know what to do. But it's –'

The Krijen stopped, looking startled as the Great Kahn reached them and stepped up beside the KrijenMayj.

'Speak,' the Great Kahn said.

The Krijen looked around, his eyes running over the bustle of the corridor. 'My Great Lord, there is more to say but not here.'

'Come then.'

They kept moving down the corridor, and the Great Kahn could hear the KrijenMayj firing further questions at the Krijen as they followed behind. It did not escape the Great Kahn that in the absence of the FaKrijen, the Krijen went to the KrijenMayj. It was not wrong, but Krijen procedure did not demand it.

Lord Salli was already in the Red Room when they arrived, standing beside the stone slab. He'd barely opened his mouth before the Great Kahn raised a hand. 'Let us await the rest of the house.'

Lord Salli nodded and sat down in a chair, his eyes narrowed at the sight of the Great Kahn's Krijen companions, who moved to the far corner of the room. The Great Kahn did not suggest they take a seat. Krijen did not like to sit, not when they wore so many weapons.

The Great Kahn did not sit either; he could not. Instead, he stood at the front of the stone slab, arms clasped behind his back.

The heavy door to the Red Room opened and Lady Macey, Lord Flynn, and Lord Bajeridine filed inside. Teal, the black-haired KahnenSpeaker, followed a respectful step behind. Another Minder scurried forward. 'My Great Lord, Lady Hia is in Rue, and Lord Reider is not in his chambers. I have sent someone to find him.'

The Great Kahn nodded.

The Minder backed out the door and the members of the Eighth House hastened forward. They bowed their heads to the Great Kahn as they took their seats. Lord Flynn perched on the edge of his chair. He shot a quick look towards the KrijenMayj, who was staring somewhere to the left of himself. At nothing apparently.

'My Great Lord,' Lord Flynn said, looking towards the Great Kahn, 'what has happened?'

'Let us find out.' The Great Kahn turned to the Speaker. 'What do you know about Lady Elira's rally?'

'Much already,' Teal replied, 'though it happened less than an hour ago. I came immediately to the Keep. The streets are raucous with rumour, but I have word from my keenest eyes.'

'I would expect nothing less. Go on.'

'In the midst of her speech, Lady Elira was interrupted by the streetling gang leader of the Upper West Side, who made a number of sordid accusations against her ladyship.'

'We know of whom you speak. What were the girl's accusations?'

'That Lady Elira forged coin to pay for votes.'

There was a collective gasp around the room.

'That is not all,' Teal continued, 'the streetling gang leader accused her ladyship of being a mayj, that she was harnessing the coins herself.'

It was a shocking statement. The Great Kahn took a moment to think. It seemed the streetling girl was following through on her promise to unveil corruption within his Kahnen.

'Lady Elira, a *mayj?*' Lord Salli rumbled. 'What an outrageous claim!'

'Sordid indeed,' Lady Macey said, her hands gripping the stone slab. 'But from the mouth of a streetling, it carries no merit whatsoever.'

Lord Flynn and Lord Bajeridine were carefully silent, watching the Great Kahn.

The Great Kahn needed to hear the rest. He looked back at Teal. 'How did Lady Elira respond to this?'

'She said it was an attempt to discredit her, my Great Lord. However, the streetling girl had some papers which, regretfully, backed up her claim. I believe the papers are clutched in the hand of that Krijen over there.'

Heads snapped around.

'Yes, I have them,' the Krijen said, walking forward. He held the papers out to the Great Kahn, who took them and read carefully before passing them to Lord Salli.

'Lady Elira recognised them. She says they are from her private rooms,' Teal said quietly.

'Lady Elira admitted she signed these?' the Great Kahn asked. 'They have not been forged?'

'She confirmed the signature is hers, my Great Lord. She said the metal purchases were expenses of the Keep.'

Lord Flynn frowned. 'I do not believe so. I am across our accounts. And if they were purchases of the Keep, they would not be in Lady Elira's private chambers.'

A silence fell upon the room, all eyes on the Great Kahn with the exception of the KrijenMayj. A quick glance confirmed that the young man remained in the far corner. The light from the candle next to him was not enough to brighten the shadows across his face.

'It is out of the ordinary,' the Great Kahn said, bringing his attention back to the Eighth House, 'but not enough to incriminate her. Let us deal with each of these claims. Firstly, what proof do we have that she was forging coin?'

'An *E* is detailed on each, my Great Lord,' Teal replied.

'An *E*? How is that proof?'

'By her own admission, there is not a blacksmith in Valrue who would claim to have made these coins.'

'Why would she say such a thing?'

'This was before she was accused of being a mayj,' Teal said. 'And my ears tell me the mint has not required the services of a blacksmith for a number of months because there is too much coin in Valrue.'

The Great Kahn frowned. 'Lord Flynn, is this true?'

Lord Flynn had a deep frown on his face. 'It is hard to say,' he said. 'Prices are higher than ever, but the Unsettlement has put a strain on our resources.'

'The Unsettlement is over,' the KrijenMayj snapped.

The Great Kahn looked back to him in shock.

The KrijenMayj had stepped forward. His face was red with heat, his veins visible on the backs of his hands which strangled his dagger hilts.

'For *months* the Krijen have reported seeing animals on roaming missions,' the KrijenMayj growled. 'Plants are breaking through the ground at the Third Bases. Runs have been smooth, packed with more supplies than ever. The Unsettlement is *over*.'

The Great Kahn flinched, and a surge of anger flooded him at the KrijenMayj's words, at the audacity of his statement. But it would not do to lose his temper because the evidence was such that there was no denying it now.

'Yes,' the Great Kahn said. 'The Unsettlement is over.' He turned back to his Kahnen, who gaped at him. 'So prices should *not* be rising.'

Lady Macey was the first to recover. 'Let me hear this again,' she said to Teal. 'You say that Lady Elira is a mayj, so effective in her method of bribery that she has forged enough coin to inflate our economy yet conceited enough that she risked harnessing onto each coin a means to identify her?'

Teal nodded. 'The People believe it, my lady. That is why they attacked her.'

'*What?*'

'I speak the truth, my lords, ladies, and Krijen. A citizen commandeered the streetling's crossbow and fired upon Lady Elira. The streetlings did not take part.'

The Great Kahn looked up at the Krijen who stood next to him, rod-straight. 'This is what you wished to tell us earlier?'

'Yes, my Great Lord. We arrested the blacksmith who fired the weapon, but as for the rest of the citizens who were part of the attack . . . we were even more uncertain as to what to do.'

'Uncertain?' demanded Lord Salli. 'What possible uncertainty is there? Citizens or not, they attacked a member of the Eighth House! They must all be strung up, along with the blacksmith!'

The Krijen hesitated before he spoke. 'Forgive us, my lord. If you recall, the Krijen were ordered not to interfere against the will of the People regarding attacks upon mayjen.'

The Great Kahn took only a moment to remember. Last year, after the Krijen intervened at an execution resulting in the deaths of a number of citizens, he'd ordered the Krijen to stand down against attacks on mayjen. He'd not retracted this. Nor did he want to. But Luka would never forgive him if he didn't. And now he wasn't sure who he hated more, mayjen or traitorous Kahnen.

'Go,' the Great Kahn said. 'Arrest any citizens involved in the attack.'

The Krijen glanced at the KrijenMayj, who gave a terse nod. The Krijen saluted him and ran from the room.

The Great Kahn walked up to his dais and sat down in his throne-like chair, looking down at the surface of the stone slab. 'How did the streetling girl get her hands on the papers?'

'I do not know,' Teal said. 'I will find out.'

'There is still something not right here,' the Great Kahn said. 'It is not in the nature of streetlings to stand by and watch a riot unfold.'

'I agree, my Great Lord. But although they did not attack, the streetlings provided the means and the excuse. The People are vulnerable, and they played on that.'

The Great Kahn worked hard to hide his anger. It was difficult to believe that Lady Elira was a mayj even with the proof before him. It was harder still to believe that *streetlings* had discovered a secret that had slipped under his nose.

But it was pride that stood in the way of his belief, nothing more.

The Great Kahn stared around at his Kahnen. Did he trust them? Did he know their characters enough that he would vouch for them, faced with evidence that screamed otherwise?

No, he did not. He had been somewhere else in recent years, having grown obsessed with being the puppet master, all the while being played by Mandavar, by Oji, and by Sid Bha. By his own house. If Lady Elira had duped him, the others could too. She was not the smartest of them, not by a long way. He must send a message to his Kahnen.

The Great Kahn turned to a Minder. 'When Lady Elira arrives, request the Krijen take her to her chambers and keep her there until I speak with her.'

The Minder gulped. 'And if she resists, my Great Lord?'

'Tell her she is under arrest. Take the gloves with you. Give them to the Krijen guarding her.'

The faces of his Kahnen paled. Lady Macey stood up from her chair, shaking. 'My Great Lord, consider how it will look when we are seen to believe the streetlings above our own house member.'

'Don't worry about that, my lady,' the KrijenMayj said, his poisonous tone drawing the attention of the room. 'The streetlings will be dealt with as well.'

The Great Kahn stood up from his chair and stepped off his dais, walking slowly over to the KrijenMayj. The young man's eyes had grown red in the space of the meeting, their fine blood vessels having burst.

The Great Kahn stopped before him. 'Could you feel Lady Elira?' he asked quietly. 'Could you sense her power?'

'No,' the KrijenMayj replied, 'but that doesn't mean shit, apparently.'

The Great Kahn pondered this, knowing what the KrijenMayj meant. He did not believe Lady Elira was smart enough to deplete her majik before every audience, and if she were, it would be impossible to maintain it low enough to evade discovery for so long.

She is not powerful, the Great Kahn concluded. Stolt may be close to useless, but he wouldn't be stupid enough to let a majikal threat linger untamed. He would have felt her and said something, especially if he considered her a threat to himself.

The Great Kahn ran his gaze over the young man in front of him. He'd never really noticed how young the KrijenMayj was before now. There were no lines around his eyes, no slackening of the skin under his chin. He had slight hollows in his face but not from age. No, they were from hunger, a different kind than what the citizens of Rue were used to.

The Kahnen think he can be controlled, the Great Kahn thought. But they didn't know Mandavar. The Great Kahn would not make that mistake again.

'I care nothing for the streetlings,' the Great Kahn said. 'Do what you want with them. I am no fool. You are no secret.'

The KrijenMayj left the Red Room without a word.

'My Great Lord,' said Teal, 'what would you have the People know?'

'Everything,' the Great Kahn said. 'But first, we will hunt the coins engraved with the letter *E* and arrest any citizens with them in their possession.'

Lord Flynn looked nervous. 'You would have the Krijen take coin from the People?'

'I would. I suspect those who resist will be the ones we need not worry about. Those in the know will want to be rid of the evidence.'

'My Great Lord,' Lady Macey said, 'what is to be done with Lady Elira?'

'I will speak to her. Unless she can provide me with a satisfactory explanation, I will have her executed.'

The room was silent.

The Great Kahn looked towards the single remaining Minder. 'The FaKrijen is on his way back from the Deadlands. Tell him to find me when he arrives.'

'Yes, my Great Lord.'

The Great Kahn was moving towards the door when Teal spoke again. 'My Great Lord, there is something else.'

The Great Kahn stopped and suppressed a shudder. 'What?'

'They are calling it the First Reckoning, my Great Lord. The People, in echo of the streetling girl.'

'The First suggests there will be a Second.'

'Yes, My Great Lord.'

The Great Kahn slowly turned to face the room. His Kahnen were looking at him like they'd done the last quarter of a century, their renewed confidence in the wake of his recent efforts to rule without fear, smote.

'If there is to be a Second Reckoning,' the Great Kahn said, 'I hope to be invited to watch.'

CHAPTER 47:
JIN KANJU

Jin couldn't breathe again.

As he rounded up his squad, he could feel his power choking him. These days he simply couldn't get rid of it, no matter what he did, and spending the last few minutes in that Red Room with its padded velvet walls had nearly been the end of his sanity.

He'd experimented, trying to find ways to escape it. Lifting himself wasn't enough. Even if he stayed at it for hours, he'd barely grounded himself before he was twitching again.

He'd tried not eating. At the end of a whole day of consuming nothing but water, he'd got some mild relief from the crushing sensation in his chest. But after he relentlessly snapped at his squad the following morning and collapsed on the ramparts when on duty with Pago, his ex-squad leader had promptly dragged him to the dining room and stood over him until he'd eaten four plates of food.

'Starving yourself won't do any good,' Aren had said from across the table, her freckled face screwed up in concern.

'It sort of worked,' Jin had muttered back.

'I don't understand what's happening, sir,' Pago had said, looking worried. 'You were never this bad before. Back in the Deadlands, we didn't even know you were a mayj until the bandit attack. Why is it getting worse?'

Jin had a theory, but that theory came from the torn-out page he shouldn't have. He wouldn't tell a soul about it. It would only lead to questions that would incriminate him. He wished he could go back to when all it took was ripping apart the belly of the Deadlands, but that was no longer an option. The amount of damage he would need to do to feel even a touch of relief scared him shitless. Valrue might tumble into the mountain if he tried.

There was only one thing that would work.

He'd tried to ignore it but knew that if he wanted to escape his power, even just for a day, he needed to Influence. It was the most repulsive thought. He hated that he'd done it to Bish and to Meek, who hadn't asked for it, and he hated how *good* it felt.

Ah, fuck. He'd done it to Flit too. But he'd been drunk. That didn't count.

If Jin *had* to do it, he could do it do streetlings. He'd tried it on their skahk the day he'd killed Aren and almost Turned, but that was before his power had grown to the point of strangling him. He reckoned he could do it now.

This time Jin didn't need to ask the Squares for help. The Great Kahn had made it very clear he could do whatever he wanted. That included using majik.

'Let's go,' he said to his squad. They took off running, black wraps, boots, daggers, and krije at the ready, tearing down through Val and making people stop and gasp as they passed.

Jin poured power into his legs and ran on ahead so he could talk to Filip and Aren without the others hearing. Filip and Aren kept pace next to him. He didn't understand how Aren managed. She was so small, but she had no trouble keeping up.

'Felle is pissing you off,' Filip said.

'What she said makes no sense,' Jin growled. 'There is no reason the Great Kahn would want Oji dead.'

Jin had been tempted to question the Great Kahn outright when he'd had him alone, but there were so many things that didn't add up about Felle's story.

That skahk was too powerful to be a pawn. Felle said he was innocent, but he'd ripped Oji apart, and innocent people did not do such things. The skahk could have easily been playing Felle. And the Great Kahn still had *no reason* to kill Oji. The streetlings did.

'You're forgetting that Oji criticised the Kahnen once,' Aren said. 'Remember? In the Deadlands?'

Aren had not been there at the time.

'He criticised the Kahnen, not the Great Kahn,' Jin replied.

'They're the same,' Filip said.

No, Jin thought, *they were not.* The Great Kahn seemed different to the Kahnen somehow. Better maybe.

'You just want him to be better than them,' Filip said, 'because he's being nice to you.'

Jin didn't like that.

'I think he *is* better,' Aren said. 'At the Celebrations, the streetlings didn't threaten the Great Kahn with a Reckoning like they threatened his house. Either they were too scared to threaten him directly, or they have nothing on him. Maybe he isn't corrupt, like they are.'

'Impossible,' Filip said. 'He's a politician. He's corrupt by nature.'

'Poor choice of words,' Jin muttered.

'Maybe you should speak to the women about Felle,' Aren suggested.

'You think so?'

Jin felt strange that Aren knew about the women. He'd always hoped to keep that from her.

'They've never put you wrong before,' Aren said.

Jin led the way across the bridge and stopped in the middle of the square beyond, his squad gathering around him. Under his feet, crimson streaks darkened the cobblestones, and splinters of wood signalled the remnants of the stage Lady Elira had stood on. Save for Jin's squad, the square was deserted.

The streetlings knew what was coming; they'd gone to hide in their towers. The People of Rue knew what was coming too, and enough of them had been involved in the riot today that they'd all run, lest they be accused of the crime. Thank fuck for that. Jin shouldn't do this with them watching, not if he were to be harnessing before they knew the Unsettlement was over or before he'd been properly announced as the KrijenMayj. They'd hate him. They'd probably still hate him afterwards too.

Then again, it was so *hard* to care about being hated right now.

Jin flexed his hands, feeling his power travel from his heaving chest, down his arms, and into the tips of his fingers, burning them.

'Pair up. Jokah, with me.' Jin turned to the serious faces of his squad. 'Go, find streetlings. Do what you think is right.'

The others nodded and took off down the quiet streets. Jokah pulled his dagger from his wraps. 'An interesting choice of words, sir,' he said.

'What do you mean?'

'"Do what you think is right"? You mean us to kill streetlings.'

'Yes. They're murderers.'

'Except they didn't do it this time,' Jokah said. 'It was the People who attacked Lady Elira.'

Jin stared at the clean, sharp edge of Jokah's blade.

'I know you want an excuse to hurt them because of what happened to Oji,' Jokah said, 'but this is wrong.'

'We can't just do nothing,' Jin retorted. 'Even if they didn't do it this time, it doesn't mean they aren't guilty of a million other crimes.'

'True. But you seek vengeance for one crime, from one streetling. Are you going to hold all of them accountable for what their mayj did?'

'They were all in on the plan.'

Aren gave Jin a knowing look. Assuming he was their mayj, it said. He turned away from her. He didn't want to hear that right now.

'You were there at the Celebrations,' Jokah said. 'You heard the streetling girl and her intentions. Death is a high price to pay for wanting to end corruption.'

Jin turned on him. 'Oji wasn't corrupt! Why did they have to kill him?'

'You know why. The FaKrijen protects the Kahnen and everything they represent.'

'But Oji wasn't like them! He was a good man!'

'Oji owed a debt for a lifetime of horrors, and he accepted that. Don't turn this into a personal vendetta in his name. It's not what Oji would've wanted.'

'I don't have a choice! We've been ordered to kill the streetlings!'

'You're lying. The FaKrijen isn't here. He didn't order this purge. You have no obligation to follow through with the Kahnen's wishes.'

Jin bellowed in frustration. He badly needed *out*. His power scalded as it climbed up his throat.

'Easy, Jin,' Jokah said. 'Easy now.'

'This fucking *hurts*.'

'I know it does. But this isn't the way to solve it.'

'Of course not, talking never is,' Filip said. 'You just need to rip a few heads off.'

Jin was shaking. Ripping off heads sounded so *good* right now.

'No, Jin,' Aren said, throwing Filip a sharp look. 'Listen to Jokah, listen to *reason*. Don't do something you're going to regret because you're angry.'

'Fine,' Jin said. '*Fine!*'

'Come,' said Jokah, sounding far away. 'Let's get the others.'

They found the rest of the squad before they'd gone too far. They slid their daggers away with bewildered looks on their faces. Nommo appeared the most confused. 'You *don't* want us to kill streetlings?' he asked. 'Are you sure?'

'No,' Jin muttered under his breath. Filip looked as thunderous as Jin felt, but Aren chased his eyes with hers until he felt the pull on the guilt beneath the fury.

Then to Jin's surprise, Flit saluted him. 'I think it's good you changed your mind, sir.'

'Why?'

'Because, for once, I'm not angry with the streetlings,' she said. 'I'm angry at Lady Elira. Do you honestly think she was a good person? I know everyone wants to think the coin thing is just some wild story the streetlings concocted to frame her, but I don't believe that for one second. The evidence against her is overwhelming. It's pretty clear she was fucking everyone else over for her own gain.'

A throbbing silence fell at her words. Krijen did not criticise Kahnen.

Jin's squad tucked their chins, watching him with tight expressions. Flit should get cuts for that. Many, many cuts.

But Jin didn't give any.

Because at Flit's words, beneath the crushing weight of his power intent on tearing him in half, stirred the *reason* that Aren spoke of. His decisions had not been his own today. Maybe he didn't actually want to kill streetlings this time; he was just chasing a moment of reprieve. And he agreed with Flit. He didn't trust Lady Elira, not one bit.

'I need to harness,' Jin choked out.

'Yes, sir, you do,' Meek said. 'I'm surprised you're not bursting into flames. I can *feel* the heat coming off you.'

'Come, sir,' Jokah said. 'I think that room we train in might be able to handle a bit of destruction. What do you think?'

Of course, Jin thought. *The cardonite.*

They began their run back to the Keep. Flit fell quickly into step beside him.

'Sir? I'm not sorry for what I said. I understand if you –'

'Next time you disagree with me, tell me.' He said it through clenched teeth but only because he was wrestling fire back down his throat.

'If you want me to, sir,' Flit said.

'The same goes for the others. I don't care what any of you say about the Krijen or the Kahnen or any of that. I need to know what you're thinking.' Jin couldn't trust himself anymore, not if this is what his power did to him when he couldn't get rid of it.

Flit's face broke out in a grin. 'Yes, sir,' she said. 'You know, I hope you don't think we just made you squad leader so you wouldn't get into so much trouble.'

'But that's why you did it.'

'Sure, but it's not the *only* reason. I said it before and I'll say it again, you're actually pretty good at leading.'

'How do you figure that?'

'Because you expect your squad to have minds of their own. This is what Oji wanted.' She sounded excited. But she had it all wrong.

'Jokah just stopped me doing the exact *opposite* of what Oji wanted.'

'No one's perfect, Jin. You're going to fall down a few times, right?'

'Krijen aren't supposed to make mistakes.'

'Despite what we are taught, Krijen are human. You are human.'

'You have too much faith in me,' Jin snapped.

'Yeah well, you deserve it.'

No, Jin thought, *I really, really don't.*

CHAPTER 48: AREN BHA

The hunters of Holu Mon were nothing but generous. After they'd stitched Aren's wound, they fed them and returned their belongings.

Aren was overwhelmed with gratitude in getting her cardonite dagger back, one of the hunters having pulled it from the body of the dead Edgecat. They'd left the creature in the forest, saying they would never bring something so perverted back to Holu Mon despite it being their most impressive kill yet. They'd offered to take Aren to see it, but she declined despite being morbidly tempted. Drax would have to come, and he wouldn't want to see that.

Aren was careful not to touch Drax in front of the hunters, which was hard because he stayed closer than ever, probably scared they would try to keep her from him, given their earlier reaction. He seemed so stressed that Aren worried he was reverting to the version of himself she'd first met in her sparring court. It was made worse when the hunters expected Drax to sleep in the tent with the men, and Aren with the women. It would've been do-able, had the tents not been at opposite ends of the camp.

'It's okay,' Aren whispered to him as he huddled behind her, 'we'll figure this out.'

Aren hated how unreasonable she and Drax appeared for refusing to comply with such a simple request, especially after Aren's promise to herself that this would go better than it had with the Bhouli. But she didn't yet trust the hunters enough to tell them the truth.

So to save the hunters the slight of Drax sleeping in the women's tent, Aren suggested they both sleep outside under the watchful eye of those who stayed up late talking around the campfire. Despite Aren's worry that this would cause some other offence, the hunters rather liked the compromise. In fact, several of them dragged their bedrolls outside to join her and Drax, including Olmonon and Sola. At first Aren wasn't entirely sure why, but the reason became clear when Olmonon requested to see some majik. Aren was surprised they hadn't demanded it sooner, but Olmonon and the others seemed to ask out of genuine awe, as opposed to wanting proof that she was a mayj.

'I hope you don't think me rude,' Olmonon said, the blush on his face odd under the orange light from the fire. 'I've never seen majik up close.'

'It's not rude,' Aren said. She sent a nervous glance Drax's way. He gave her the tiniest nod.

Hoping it looked right, Aren slowly lifted a hand towards the fire and flicked her wrist like she'd seen Jin do. A smoking log leapt into the air and hung there, suspended. She quickly lowered her hand, and the log fell back onto the fire with a little spatter of flame.

It was the most meagre demonstration, and Aren expected they wouldn't be satisfied, so she was pleasantly surprised when everyone around the fire yelled and pointed in excitement. 'That was amazing!' Olmonon cried.

Aren shrugged, grinning despite herself.

Drax didn't smile. He shifted where he sat, edging close enough to Aren that Olmonon's smile wavered.

'It's okay, Drax,' Aren whispered. 'They like majik. It's not like Valrue.'

'I know, Aren.'

Aren couldn't interpret the new tone in his voice. 'Are you okay?

Was that too much for you?' Her heart hadn't skipped a beat.

'No, that was okay.' He was clearly upset, and it frustrated Aren that she couldn't talk to him properly, not in front of the others.

They settled down to sleep in their carefully separated bedrolls. But when the fire died to a dull glow and there was nothing but stars above them to see by, Aren reached out a hand in the darkness and slipped it into Drax's. She gave it a gentle squeeze, feeling relieved when he squeezed gently back.

***

Three days later, Aren watched in astonishment as two horse-drawn wagons rolled into camp. The horses were huge, their hooves as big as dinner plates, and they tossed their heads about, their manes woven into hundreds of little braids, just like the hunters' hair.

Aren could barely contain her excitement. She fought the urge to run towards the horses to get a better look, remembering that she was supposed to be a mayj and it would be suspicious if the animals didn't panic when she came near. This was especially the case now that Drax didn't stick so desperately to her side.

After enduring nothing but kindness and endless meals from the hunters, Drax had recovered and relaxed to the point of allowing Aren to wander around the camp unaccompanied for a few hours. She went back to him when her heart grew weary.

So when Aren had buckled their backpacks shut and readied them to leave, it was with a touch of disappointment she learned that most of the hunters were staying behind.

Olmonon and Sola wandered over to see them off. Sola had brought a little collection of bottles for Aren. 'This is more lunilum,' she said, handing two bottles over. 'I've diluted it, so it won't make you so drowsy, but it will help with the pain in your back.' She handed over two more bottles. 'This is antiseptic. They'll have plenty more at the University, and far better healers than myself if you need them. They'll be able to help you with dressing changes, too.'

'Thank you,' Aren said, knowing perfectly well that Drax would do a better job of that than any healer.

'It's only a day's ride to Holu Mon,' Olmonon said. 'You'll be there before the sun goes down.'

'You're not coming either?' Aren asked.

'No, I've got a few more months out here yet. But if you're still in the city when I come back, maybe I'll come find you at the University?' He looked hopeful. Aren suspected Olmonon wanted an excuse to see more majik.

'Yes,' Aren said, 'come find us.'

'I will,' Olmonon said. 'Oh, and I sent word ahead, so I'd be surprised if someone from the University isn't waiting for you at the gates.'

Aren found it hard to believe the University would take the word of a hunter, given what she'd heard about the scholars there. They sounded like a rather prestigious lot, and in Aren's experience, prestige was a synonym for snobbery. Then again, that was what people frequently assumed about *her* for being a Bha. Wren had when he'd first met her. A small smile crept onto her face at the thought of him.

Aren caught herself and pushed her attention back to Olmonon. 'You think the University will take us in?' she asked.

'Without a doubt. I don't think you realise how few mayjen there are in Holu Mon. I know that's not the case in Valrue because of the Unsettlement as you call it, but you're special to us.'

'Really?'

'*Really.*' Olmonon laughed.

Aren turned to Drax, who ducked his head. He was nervous about Holu Mon and the University in all its majikal eminency.

'They will like you, Drax,' Olmonon said kindly. 'And they will *love* you, Aren.'

Aren bit her lip, feeling guilty about the lie. But she wanted to wait until they got to the University before they let everyone in on the truth in case they didn't react how Olmonon said they would. She also suspected the hunters might completely lose the plot if they learned Drax could harness without his hands, especially if lifting a log impressed them.

'You have nothing to worry about,' Olmonon said to her. 'Gi smiles on you.'

Okay, Aren *really* needed to know. 'Who is Gi?'

Sola gaped at her. 'You're serious?'

'Sorry. I should have asked earlier, but I wasn't sure if I should. But you all keep saying it, so I figure it's important . . .' Aren flushed, embarrassed.

'No, that's all right,' Olmonon said. 'I guess it makes sense that you don't know, given where you're from. Gi is life. Gi is everything, really.'

Aren wasn't sure what he meant. 'Gi is everything?'

'Sure, that's why balance is so important. And why Valrue has been such a problem,' he added with a frown. 'When you go to Holu Mon, make sure people know you're a mayj. That way it won't matter if you accidentally slight and do things you shouldn't.'

Aren had learnt enough in the last three days to know that slights were bad, like touching the opposite sex or wearing maroon wraps apparently. The hunters had politely offered Aren and Drax fresh tunics and pants – everything in black and white – and a pair of heavy boots. They'd obligingly worn them.

'Why does being a mayj exempt me from slights?' Aren asked.

'Because you're a gift from Gi,' Sola said.

Aren was only more confused. 'How can *everything* give a gift? It sounds more like Gi is a person –'

Just then, one of the hunters yelled that it was time to go.

'I've never met someone who doesn't know who Gi is, so I'm not so sure how to explain it to you,' Sola said as they headed towards the wagons. 'Maybe ask about it at the University.'

The wagons were uncovered with a partition between the occupants in the back and the driver's box, blocking the occupants' view of the horses.

'You can sit on the back with the others, so you don't need to walk,' Olmonon said, looking pointedly at Drax, who was ambling awkwardly alongside them. 'And don't worry about frightening the horses,' he said to Aren. 'They're trained to tolerate mayjen.'

'Thank you,' Aren said. 'I hope you do well with your hunting.'

Olmonon grinned at them. 'Me too. Wait, Aren no!'

Aren paused, her hand resting on the back of the wagon, about to climb up into it. The men sitting in it turned to her in surprise.

'What?'

'Not that one,' Olmonon said. He looked ever so uncomfortable. 'You must sit in a wagon with at least one other woman. It's for the balance.'

'Oh.' Aren dropped her hand from the wagon. '*Oh,*' Aren repeated, realising something. 'Is that why you kept running over whenever we were in big groups with all the hunters?' Aren asked Sola.

Sola flushed red. 'Yes. Gi frowns upon a single person being surrounded by only the opposite sex. It's so unbalanced, you know?'

Aren was annoyed. The rules seemed arbitrary, but at least if they knew what they were, they could try to follow them. She didn't want to go around offending people without knowing it.

'Why didn't you say so earlier?' Aren asked.

Olmonon looked rather sheepish. 'Sorry. You're a mayj, so it doesn't matter for you, only for the others involved in the slight . . . But mostly we didn't know if you knew or not.'

'You thought I was just being rude?'

'Not rude. Slightful.'

Aren wasn't sure of the difference. Either way, they were both bad.

She scanned the wagons. There was one with three women and two men. 'That one, then?'

'That one is good. Let me go speak to the driver, so he knows he's got you.'

They made their way over. Olmonon and Sola disappeared around the front of the wagon while Aren led the way to the back. She climbed up, greeted by cries of delight from the wagon's occupants as they recognised her and shuffled up to make a space. Drax followed somewhat awkwardly, sitting down next to Aren, leaving a small but obvious gap.

Olmonon and Sola reappeared at the back of the wagon. Olmonon gave them a thumbs up. Sola waved as the horses dug in their hooves, and the wagon rolled away from them. Soon, they turned back towards the camp. Aren felt a strange sadness come over her. She'd not known them long, but she hoped she would see them again.

The sadness didn't last long.

As it turned out, riding by wagon was very bumpy and uncomfortable. It even hurt Aren's back a little, but she relished every minute of it. She chatted to the other hunters from Holu Mon as they bounced along, happily answering their questions about Valrue. Curiosity was a trait that had always got her into trouble, so it was a pleasant surprise to learn that certain probing questions were okay, if not actively encouraged.

'"Knowledge is power" is a saying they use at the University,' one of the women said. 'Though it referred to majikal power, initially,' she added unnecessarily with a nod in Aren's direction.

'You all seem to know about majik and how it works,' Aren said. 'How come? None of you are mayjen, and Olmonon said he'd never even seen it up close, so I don't understand.'

The woman laughed. 'He probably meant that he never got a front-row seat. The University holds open lectures on majik. Anyone can attend, but they are so popular you can't always get in the room. I've been to a few myself. They are fascinating.'

'Anyone can go and learn about majik?'

'That's right. But I can't imagine we know anywhere near as much about majik as you,' she said. 'Valrue must be full of mayjen, what with the power imbalance. You must have seen it all.'

Aren shook her head. 'No, majik is condemned in Valrue. The government cuts off the hands of people who harness. Either that, or they kill them.'

The hunters all gasped, looking around at each other. 'Oh gracious Gi,' the woman said, placing a hand on her chest. 'I mean, we've all heard the rumours, but I didn't realise they were true. The Devoutists said them after all. Is that why you left?'

Aren glanced at Drax. 'Yes.' It wasn't entirely a lie. 'What are

Devoutists?'

'Extreme believers,' said a man sitting opposite Aren. 'They take Gi's expectations too far.'

'But they are important, nonetheless,' the woman said curtly to him. 'They help right the wrongs of the slighters, who don't take them far enough.'

Aren shared a look with Drax. His head sank into his shoulders.

There were a few shouts in the distance that echoed up the row of wagons to where Aren sat.

'Ah,' the woman said. 'We have arrived.'

Aren and Drax's Journey to Holu Mon

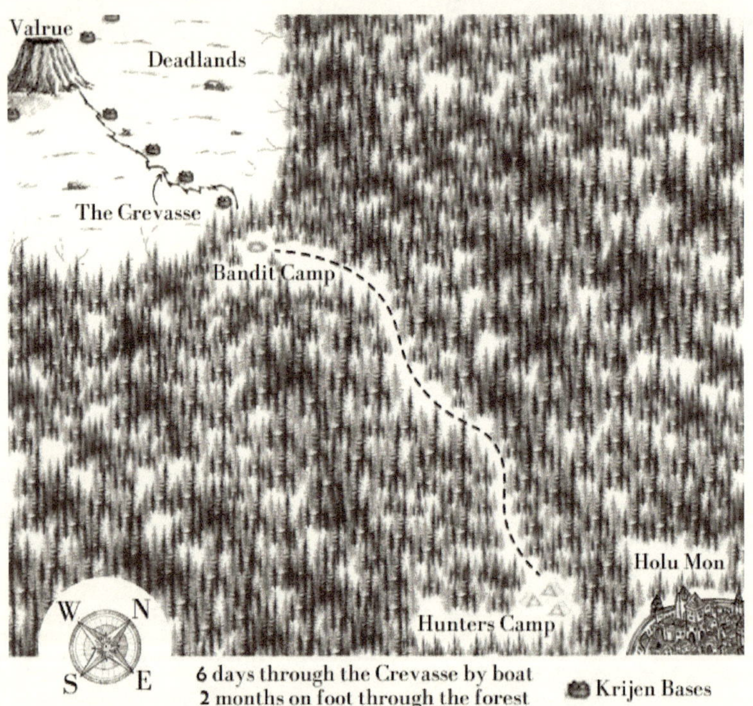

CHAPTER 49:
PYRA

Lady Hia was impressed by the success of Lady Elira's Reckoning, which pissed Pyra off to no end.

'It could not have gone better,' Lady Hia said. 'You completely discredited Lady Elira. She has been arrested, you have terrified the Kahnen out of their wits, kept the streetlings from getting violent *and* brought them some credibility! This is such a key event for our cause!'

Of course, Pyra had failed to mention that the so-called success was because the Lost Square had got in the way.

'It was stupid,' Pyra snapped. 'The streetlings were looking forward to that Reckoning for months. I promised them a fight, and they didn't get one. I'm going to pay for this.'

'What are you worried about? You kept them under control at a *Reckoning*, of all things.'

Lady Hia didn't understand what it meant to be a streetling gang leader.

'Stopping them from attacking might be a smart move for *us*, but to the streetlings looked like weakness. They'll want to test me now.'

Pyra was furious she'd listened to the Lost Square. It could easily ruin everything they'd worked for. So much for the terror-induced obedience resulting from Ala's scalping. It had been the shortest-lived of the lot.

'You will find a way to fix it,' Lady Hia said. 'But remember, the whole reason we are doing this is to end corruption. We cannot keep letting the streetlings have their way with the citizens. If we want our cause to be successful, we need to move forward like this.'

'I get that. But the streetlings will try to kill me now.'

'Oh, stop being so dramatic.'

'You're not listening,' Pyra said. 'To them, there is no good reason I wouldn't let them loose at the Reckoning. I've got to prove to them again that I'm not weak. To do that, I need to go after the Krijen. *Properly*, I mean.'

By the look on Lady Hia's face, the message was finally sinking in. 'Krijen? Surely there is another way.'

'That's the only way to give the streetlings what they want without hurting citizens.'

'We cannot do that. It is too soon. Granted, the Krijen are losing support under FaKrijen Eden given they have been unjustly intolerant, but too many of the citizens still view the Krijen as their protectors.'

'Yeah, well our army is made up of streetlings. Were you expecting to win this war without letting them fight a battle or two?'

Lady Hia was quiet for a moment. 'You are right. I just got my hopes up in thinking we might get away with less violence.'

Pyra made a face. Lady Hia was getting too cosy up in that Keep.

'Did the Lost Square go to the Reckoning?' Lady Hia asked.

Pyra ground her teeth.

'I only ask because if you are going after Krijen, maybe ask the Lost Square for some advice.'

'I will not.'

'He has no loyalty to them. He might be willing to help.'

'I doubt it.'

'Why not?'

Pyra was silent.

'Pyra, what did you do?'

'It got in the way. At the Reckoning.'

'*Pyra –*'

'I didn't kill it,' Pyra snarled. 'I just scared it off.'

'How could you be so short-sighted? We *need* him –'

'I had no choice! It forced my hand, and you know why? Because it's too stupid to understand the consequences of what it was doing! I refuse to work with it, and you can't make me!'

Pyra didn't care to see the look on Lady Hia's face. She got up and stalked to the door, ripping it open, and the walls of the tower shook as she slammed it behind her.

CHAPTER 50:
FAKRIJEN EDEN

Eden was in a good mood before he entered his chambers. As he approached the open doorway, he spotted the black-wrapped figure waiting for him. His day was about to get even better.

'Ah. Word has already spread about my return.'

'Yes, sir.'

Eden entered the room and closed the door. 'The Deadlands is an interesting place, isn't it?'

'Yes, sir.'

'A shame to leave it, especially with the forests. And the deer. Hunting is such a fun venture.'

There was no reply.

'I said hunting is fun, isn't it?'

'I haven't hunted deer before, sir.'

Eden smiled. 'No. But as Krijen, you hunt criminals, streetlings, mayjen. You know the thrill.'

'Yes, sir.'

'The dungeon is full, I see. The Krijen have been doing well in my absence.'

'Yes, sir.'

'Though I do have one question, and I know you'll have the answer. Or you'll find out for me anyway.'

Silence.

'I was in the dungeons earlier,' Eden continued. 'Being so full, I thought it best to make a start on emptying it. I noticed a cell full of whores, a cracked iron ball on the floor. An iron ball meant as a restraint for a mayj. I asked the Krijen on duty about it, and he insisted that all the prisoners are accounted for.'

'They are, sir.'

'So this mayj whore is still in the cell?'

'Yes, sir. She couldn't get past the Krijen if she tried.'

'How did she get out of the restraint? Is there another mayj in there with her?'

'The only other mayj in the cell is already without hands, sir.'

'So who took off her restraint? It had to have been a mayj. The ball was split down the middle. But there have been no visitors to the dungeons.' Eden tapped his chin in thought. 'Unless it was a Krijen. A naughty one too.' Eden rather liked the idea of a naughty Krijen. That was what cuts were for.

'Was it you?' Eden asked.

'No, I'm not a mayj, sir.'

'Who did it then?'

There was a pause. 'The KrijenMayj, sir.'

Eden smiled even wider. This day was getting better and better.

'Why?'

'I don't know, sir.'

'Find out.'

'Yes, sir. Did you want the mayj restrained once more?'

'No,' Eden said, 'leave her for now.' He sucked on the inside of his cheeks in excitement. 'You shouldn't startle the deer before the hunt.'

CHAPTER 51:
JIN KANJU

J in had shattered the cardonite training room. He'd sent his squad away because he didn't want them to watch and turned to the goading webs of cardonite that pressed in on him. He'd ripped it from the walls, moulding it, stretching it, tearing it into nothing, bit by bit until he collapsed on the floor, laughing at how tired he was.

Near the end, he'd even found a touch of bliss where the ringing in his head stopped, and the heat in him died, and Aren and Filip disappeared for a moment. But as he lay gasping amongst the dust with tears tracking down his face, his ecstasy turned melancholic.

No one could put this room back together.

It terrified him to think of what he would have to do next time his power took him. Hopefully, he would have some time to figure it out before it happened.

But thank fuck, he could think clearly again. He'd remembered Aren's suggestion, and he'd gone to speak to the women about Felle after he'd finished with the room.

Jin felt guilty asking for their help. He still wanted to set them free. To him, it would be worth whatever punishment the Kahnen could dream up for a rogue KrijenMayj who freed a bunch of prostitutes from the dungeons. But he knew the women wouldn't leave at his word.

So a few days later, with their reassurances that he'd done the right thing about Felle still resounding in his head and his chest feeling pleasantly cool, Jin felt better than he had in weeks.

He smiled as he harnessed yet another nail into what felt like the hundredth wooden slat before him. But it wasn't a bed slat this time. The bridge was so full of strung bodies that they'd needed something for the overflow, so they'd been put to work making crosses.

Jin's squad worked in one of the outdoor courtyards in the shadow of the Keep. Jin's hands were busy, so his mind was free, and he used the time well, his thoughts looping frequently back to the women.

They'd seemed more than happy to see him when he'd shown up in the dungeons again. Exuberant, in fact. They'd even let him inside the cell, for which he was grateful. It had been so long since someone touched him; their soft caresses had felt incredible.

He'd not mentioned Felle's accusations about the Great Kahn; he spoke only of her advances on him, but both Eliza and Josefina agreed she sounded like one of those women best avoided. Jin was tempted to tell Lottie the whole of it because Lottie always said the right things back. It was nice to speak to her again even if he couldn't have her in all the ways he wanted to. It brought him back to the first time he'd met her –

'Hey, sir? You've got that look on your face again. You're thinking about your women, aren't you?'

Fuck, Nommo was annoying.

'Ignore him, sir,' Pago said. 'He's just jealous. He got turned down again last night.'

Nommo's expression grew sour. 'I mean, what's the point of being Krijen if you can't get the women you want? I didn't sign up for this so I could spend my days building crosses with four blokes.'

'Excuse me?' Flit held her hammer above her head, poised for another pound. 'Am I invisible or something?'

'You don't count. You're practically a man, anyway.'

'Why, you little –'

Jin flicked his fingers and the piece of wood Nommo held snapped upwards, smacking him across the face.

Meek and Pago burst out laughing. Even Jokah entertained a small smile. Flit was grinning from ear to ear.

'I think you owe Flit an apology, Nommo,' Jin said.

'It's okay,' Flit said. 'He's still bitter because I beat him in that arm wrestle.'

Nommo muttered something unintelligible under his breath.

'Hey, sir, how come you're making us do this?' Meek piped up. 'Now that you're no longer a secret and all, surely you could harness these things together in about five minutes?' He grinned cheekily. 'I can think of plenty of better uses for that time.'

The Eighth House had indeed made the announcement in the wake of what had happened with Lady Elira. They probably hoped the threat of a KrijenMayj would deter future Reckonings.

Lady Elira was still imprisoned in her room. The Krijen had yet to learn what was to be done with her, but when on guard, they could hear her screaming obscenities behind the walls. She'd not harnessed yet, but it might only be a matter of time, given her mounting frustrations.

'And make Jin do all the work, you mean?' Flit asked. 'Where is the squad building in that?'

'What, we don't spend enough time together already?' Meek whined. 'Come on, sir, Nommo's got the right idea. You can let us off duty early.' He looked imploringly at Jin. 'We all know you, sir. Wouldn't you rather spend this time getting –'

'Don't say it, Meek.'

'But you could go back to your women!'

'They're not *my* women,' Jin said, growing annoyed by Meek's persistence.

'No, sir, they're anyone's women,' Nommo said, chuckling.

'And that's why I'm rather baffled,' Meek said. 'I don't understand why you'd pay for whores when –'

'*Don't use that word.*'

Meek's smile faltered at Jin's tone. 'Sorry, sir.'

Nommo was looking curiously at Jin. 'Actually, Meek mentioned a woman came looking for you at the Keep a few months back. You never said what she wanted.'

'Stop nosing, Nommo,' Flit warned.

'Oh, give over. I've known Jin since he was five years old. He'll tell me to shove off if he wants. You just don't want to hear it because you're worried you won't like the answer.'

'What's *that* supposed to mean?'

'Oh come on, it's so obvious –'

'I despise the insinuation,' Flit said, her cheeks reddening, 'that because I'm a woman surrounded by men, I must be besotted by one of them!'

'That's not a denial –'

'Shut it, you lot,' Jin snapped. Their relentless bickering was quickly adding fuel to the recently smothered fire in his chest. 'Flit, don't lean into it, you know he's just winding you up. Nommo, if you're so starved for sex, stop harassing us all and go contribute a coin or two to the cause. And, Meek, if you only need five minutes, then I don't envy the poor woman you've got your eye on because you'll need to invest a *lot* more time than that if you expect her to promise herself to you.'

His squad was silent.

Jin turned back to the cross in front of him, the nails half-harnessed in. He reached out a hand, letting a trail of heat drip down his arm, forcing the metal deeper into the wood.

'Sir –'

'I said *enough*, Meek.'

'No, sir . . .'

An off note in Meek's voice made Jin look up.

FaKrijen Eden was watching them from across the courtyard. Jin snapped upright, his hand racing to his clavicle. His squad already stood around him, saluting their FaKrijen.

The FaKrijen did not cut the strident figure that Oji had, but there was something about him that set Jin on edge as he strode towards them.

Maybe it was the fact that, in his absence, Jin had been forced to fill his boots, and he did not know how the FaKrijen would respond to that.

The FaKrijen stopped in front of Jin. He smiled but it was a sharp, pointy smile that looked hooked in place. 'KrijenMayj,' he said. 'I don't believe I've had the chance to introduce myself properly.' He held out his hand.

Tentatively, Jin shook it.

'I know shaking hands is not the traditional way of it,' the FaKrijen said, 'but then again, I feel you don't mind breaking the rules.'

Jin stilled.

'With regard to being the first KrijenMayj, I mean,' the FaKrijen explained. He looked around at Jin's squad, his eyes drifting to the pile of crosses beside them. 'I hear you've been busy,' the FaKrijen continued, 'with streetling Reckonings. And Squares.' His gaze flickered back to Jin.

'Uh-oh,' said Filip, making Jin jump. He'd almost forgotten the dead Bhouli was there. Aren was there, too. She was watching the FaKrijen with narrowed eyes.

'Yes, sir,' Jin said, 'the Geni generously permitted the Squares to assist with getting the streetlings back under control.'

'Generous indeed.' The FaKrijen still wore that stretched smile. 'I heard it was your idea?'

Jin could hardly deny it. 'Yes, sir.'

The FaKrijen lifted his chin. 'A good idea. I'll remember that.'

Jin said nothing, resisting the urge to look at his squad.

'You already know the Eighth House made the announcement about you,' the FaKrijen said. 'I just had an audience with them. They wish to formalise it. A parade of sorts. I gave my permission.'

Jin's stomach dropped out from beneath him. 'A parade, sir?'

'Yes, a parade. To celebrate you.' The FaKrijen slowly tilted his head to the side. 'It's important to reassert Krijen authority in these troubled times, isn't it? What a perfect way to do it by walking it through the streets for everyone to see.'

Aren's eyes narrowed further. 'Surely not,' she said.

But Jin was hopeful. 'Will this mean that the Great Kahn will announce the end of the Unsettlement, sir?'

Jin's squad whipped their heads around to him. He'd forgotten he'd not mentioned it.

The FaKrijen was still smiling. 'The Great Kahn wasn't there, and the Eighth House had nothing to say about it. Regardless, you'll attend the parade. It's a good idea.'

Jin wanted to disagree, strongly. He did not think the People would appreciate the flaunting of a KrijenMayj, not while they still believed themselves to be drowning in the deep of majik. But he didn't know if he could disagree with this particular FaKrijen.

'Yes, sir.'

'Very good. And call me Eden,' the FaKrijen said. 'Oji did away with all that formal nonsense. In case I wasn't clear at the start, I have no issue with lack of tradition.'

With that, he turned and walked back across the courtyard and into the Keep.

CHAPTER 52: AREN BHA

Coming into Holu Mon was queer for many reasons. For one, there was no barren ring of nothing. Instead, when the trees stopped a ways before the city walls, vivid green grass and tiny white flowers paved the rest of the way to the gates.

The Gates of Holu Mon were so captivating that they would forever be etched into Aren's brain. Two colossal golden pillars erupted from the earth, their tops disappearing into the blue of the sky. As the wagon trundled between them, Aren craned her head up the length of the thick golden bars that formed the gates, suspended from the pillars. They must be immensely heavy. 'Did a mayj make those?' she wondered out loud.

Drax looked in awe too, his blank face turned up to the sun so that Aren could see the white scars under his chin.

Ten oddly dressed men lined the mouth of the city. They wore white jackets with enormous cream-coloured feathers sticking out the tops of their cube-like hats. Aren couldn't imagine the size of the bird they'd been plucked from. The men held golden spears in one hand, waving with the other as the wagons rolled past, smiles on their faces.

'What are these men here for?' Aren asked the woman next to her.

'Protection, of course,' the woman said. 'You have soldiers in Valrue, don't you?'

'Yes, but not like these.'

These soldiers hardly seemed comparable to the threatening presence of the black-wrapped Krijen with their stiff stares and glistening dagger hilts.

'They aren't going to stop us and ask our business here?'

'No need,' the woman replied, 'they know us hunters well. We trek in and out of the city all the time throughout summer.'

'Summer?'

The woman raised an eyebrow. 'You don't know what seasons are?'

'I know what they are,' Aren said, feeling silly. She'd just never experienced any season other than blistering heat with the occasional downpour of warm rain and thunder that quickly disappeared back into a cloudless day. Majik brewed that sort of weather. The Unsettlement was over, but they'd not had the chance to see the sky turn before they'd left.

The trees reappeared on the other side of the city walls, weaving flourishing green lines between the buildings. Aren had never seen plants and stone collide like they did here. It looked as though each was trying to trump the other with green creepers climbing never-ending walls of light brown stone, which sprawled endlessly before them, forming houses and shops and neatly cut curbs that all met at perfect right angles as though whoever built them had never heard of a curve.

'This is *incredible,*' Aren gushed, her head revolving on her shoulders as she tried to take in everything at once. 'I mean, look at this place!'

Drax cocked his head, looking around. 'It's nice.'

Up ahead was a large grouping of stables, identified as such by the monstrous beasts that peered out from them, and the yellow hay scattered in and around the stalls. Young boys darted around with armfuls of leather and carried wooden buckets, slopping water over their feet as they went.

Other wagons had already arrived, their occupants spilling out onto the surrounding ground, rubbing sore bottoms and shaking out their legs.

Their wagon rolled to a stop, and Aren was just standing up when the driver trotted around to the back of the wagon leading a man that Aren could only describe as swollen. It was as though his body had been filled with water, stretching his skin taught and oozing through as beads of sweat that glistened on his forehead. He had only half a head of hair, a semi-circle of baldness from which grey braids burst and flowed down his back. He had on a dark blue jacket and trousers, not unlike the style worn by the soldiers at the gates, but it stood out because it was the first colourful clothing Aren had seen. The dark blue jacket had a golden trim, and a belt strained around the man's midriff which preceded his arrival in front of their wagon.

Aren caught herself staring, and she quickly brought her eyes to his face. She knew what too much food did to people, and some of the long-serving Kahnen kept little bellies, but food was such a scarcity in Valrue that she'd grown used to seeing people that resembled pins. It was a shock to see a man who looked like he'd eaten another.

The driver pointed at Aren excitedly, and the enormous man in dark blue rocked on his heels and clapped his hands as he approached her and Drax. He must be from the University. Olmonon had been right; someone had come to greet them.

The other occupants of the wagon were packing up their belongings with exaggerated slowness, their hands resting on straps and buckles for much longer than necessary, watching the man in dark blue with rounded eyes. A commotion behind him drew Aren's gaze back to the street.

People were gathering, a swarm wearing black and white, braided hair brushed back over their shoulders. Many whispered to one another behind their hands, nodding their heads at the man in dark blue. He was someone important, and because he was watching Aren, the people were watching her too.

Aren jumped down from the wagon, careful not to tear her stitches.

'You must be Aren!' the man in dark blue said breathlessly, bouncing on his heels as she descended. 'We received word you were coming! Please, please, come . . .' He stepped back to give her space. Drax huddled close behind, barely giving an inch of room between them.

'I am Mo Nu,' the man in dark blue said, his words quick with excitement. 'I beg you excuse my tardiness. I would have met you at the gates, but I am not so light on my feet these days.' As if to prove the point, he pulled a little handkerchief from inside his pocket and dabbed at the beads on his forehead. 'You must be tired from your journey. Rest assured, the University is but a short walk, and I have brought a chaperone who will take your belongings.'

A woman stepped out from behind Mo Nu, having previously been hidden by his massive form. She was almost comically thin by contrast, and she wore a similar outfit to Mo Nu with the gold-trimmed jacket, apart from the fact it was black and white.

'I am Fom,' she said, holding out a spindly arm. 'Please give me your backpacks.'

Aren handed over Drax's backpack but declined the second proffered hand. 'I'll carry mine,' Aren said as she hefted it over her shoulder. It was uncomfortable with her stitches, but the woman might snap if she carried two.

'As you wish.'

'Wonderful!' Mo Nu said. 'Let us go!' With that, he flourished his hands and held them out ahead of him, and the gathered audience hurried to make a path.

'Bye, Aren! Bye, Drax!' the occupants of the wagon called as they walked off through the crowd, Fom falling in behind.

Aren felt most uncomfortable with so many eyes on her. She was grateful when Mo Nu flapped his hands and people quickly scattered, going back to their bustling and throwing glances back over their shoulders until they disappeared around the corner.

'I must apologise, I tend to draw quite an audience as I do not often step outside the University,' Mo Nu said. 'People have a tendency to follow me about when they get the chance, knowing what I do. That and the obvious, of course.' He gestured down at himself, as though Aren would know exactly what he meant.

'Um . . . what do you do?'

'Oh! I am the dean of the University. But I am smart enough to know that it is not me that the crowd want. No, it is who I spend my time with that people find most alluring.' He gave Aren a broad smile. 'It is you they wish to see. Once we get to the University, there will be fewer ogling audiences, I promise. That is, until word spreads. So enjoy this walk, where we can skirt the eager eyes. You will get little peace after this.' He looked delighted at the thought.

Aren was quiet for long enough that Mo Nu squinted at her, his brow furrowing. 'I am sorry. I hope I have not scared you already. Everyone will be curious, but rest assured, you are perfectly safe.'

'No, I . . .' The unexpected attention worried her, given such scrutiny would push Drax to his limits, but that wasn't what was bothering her right now. 'The hunters took our word for it that I was a mayj. We harnessed for them anyway, but . . .' she hesitated. 'You're the University. Don't you want some proof?'

Mo Nu laughed. 'I have plenty of proof. The hunters sent word about having seen your majik, and the word of anyone from Holu Mon is enough. Lies are slights, you see. You will not catch a liar here. Not unless they are mayj.' He gave her a cheeky grin. 'You see what I am saying?'

Aren glanced back at Drax. It was obvious what he was thinking despite his blank face. By Mo Nu's logic, Aren was a walking impossibility, being a liar who was not a mayj. She bit her lip. Surely these lies would catch up with her soon.

Aren forgot her concerns as they walked through the city. There was so much to look at, and everything was so different from Valrue. For starters, the streets were flat, without a slope to say whether you were walking north or south. The buildings didn't devolve from sweeping webbed mansions into rickety towers but remained stubbornly square and brown and rarely went over two stories high despite the sky-high pillars that fronted the city.

Blossoming flowers gave colour. Pink and yellow blooms burst out at Aren as they turned corners, her eyes drawn to beauty that did not exist in Valrue. She even thought she saw a few marigolds, which made her twitch in discomfort. She wished she'd not left things so tense with her friend, but she could not forgive the things Marigold had said about Wren.

A rat suddenly ran across their path, and Aren pointed at it in delight, prompting a strange look from Fom.

'Your city is beautiful,' Aren said.

'I cannot imagine what you must be used to, for you to describe vermin as beautiful,' Mo Nu replied, but he smiled at her all the same. Then his smile faltered. 'No, let me correct myself. I can imagine. We know what majik has done to Valrue.'

'You do?'

'To an extent. I hope you will not feel disquieted when I tell you that I have a morbid fascination with what has happened to your city. Majik is both elusive and enthralling to me. I have dedicated the last ten years of my life to learning more about it.'

'You are not a mayj?'

'Oh. Yes, I am,' he chuckled. 'I apologise. I thought you knew that from my blue clothing.' That explained his earlier gesture to himself. 'I am a Breaker of minimal power. In other words, I am useful for nothing more than basic classroom demonstrations.'

'A Breaker?'

'Yes. May I ask what you are?'

Aren opened her mouth and found the lie easier than expected. 'I'm a Builder.' Aren remembered that Jakki had called herself a Builder, mayjen who create bonds between matter. Aren still wasn't sure what that meant.

Mo Nu clapped his hands. 'Brilliant! Such a rarity! Oh, Gi is smiling on us today! And of your power, may I enquire? Am I to push my luck in hoping you are an Influencer?'

'Um . . .' Aren looked at Drax for help, who did nothing but sink further into his shoulders.

'Look,' Aren said, thinking that some truths couldn't hurt. 'I don't really know all the jargon. If I'm honest, I can't explain how majik works . . . I just know how to do it.'

Mo Nu shook his head, neck rolls jiggling. 'My deepest apologies. I forgot myself in my excitement. I know of the oppression that mayjen in Valrue face because of the majikal excess.'

'How?'

'Because I have met some of them,' Mo Nu said. 'Far fewer in recent times, but there were plenty who ventured through Holu Mon when I first became dean. They never stayed long and were understandably reluctant to harness or share their majikal knowledge, so many of my conclusions are drawn from my own studies.' He fixed Aren with a knowing look. 'It would be hard to live in a city where you are blamed for an unspeakable crisis, especially when it is so unclear as to where the fault lies. But let us save that conversation for another day. We have arrived.'

They'd stopped before what Aren could only describe as a city within a city, complete with a towering brown wall separating it from the streets of Holu Mon. They stepped through a gateless break in the wall, and Aren stared up the curving path that wound into the city within a city. Further up, the path split into tendrils, each heading towards a different round building made from what looked like condensed sand. The buildings had enormous tree trunks twisting between them, blocking off pathways so that the black-and-white-clad students walking on them had to duck under stray branches.

The students themselves were fascinating. They all seemed to have such a sense of *purpose*. Some were in pairs, hurrying along the pathways with books and scrolls piled in their arms while others lounged in groups on the grass between the buildings, chattering animatedly to one another, their arms gesticulating widely.

There was a lone young woman lying on her back in the grass, her head resting against a satchel, her eyes closed, and her face to the sun. Her braided blonde hair fanned out from her head. Despite the relaxed appearance of her body, there was a deep line between her eyes, and her lips moved rapidly in a silent rehearsal of something of great importance. Her tunic was dark blue.

She's a mayj, Aren thought.

'Welcome to the University,' Mo Nu said, throwing his arms wide as they strolled up the path. 'We have six thousand students enrolled though that number has grown every year since I became dean,' he said proudly. 'We offer sixty-seven courses on a broad range of topics. Lectures are open to the public, so anyone can attend. However, depending on the course, it can be difficult to find a seat. Particularly for our lectures on majik,' he added, wiggling his eyebrows at Aren. 'The campus stretches from here all the way into the centre of Holu Mon and contains the lecture halls and housing for the students. As you can see,' he said as they passed under a particularly thick tree branch, 'we like to let nature take the lead, and for the sake of the balance, we weave ourselves in around it.' He chuckled again. 'Get it?' he said, looking at them expectantly.

Aren stared at him blankly. She didn't understand what was funny. Drax's expression was the same.

'No? We *Weave* ourselves – oh, never mind,' Mo Nu said. 'It is not quite the same when one has to explain their own joke.' However, he looked more disappointed than Aren would have expected. He kept glancing back at her as he led them onwards, his eyes darting between her hands and her face.

'So shall we settle you into your rooms, and then I can take you on a tour?'

'Sure,' Aren said. She turned to Drax. 'What do you think?'

Drax nodded.

With that, Mo Nu led them into one of the buildings. They entered a round foyer with wooden panelling and corridors branching off from it. They strolled down one of the corridors. There were giant windows spaced down the walls, yet strangely, there was no roof above them, so the sun streamed down onto Aren's shoulders. Beneath her feet were black and white tiles. They were so shiny she could see her reflection when she looked down.

Her surroundings were so distracting it took Aren a while to pull a much-needed question into her head. 'Excuse me, Mo Nu, what is it you think we're doing here?'

'You are seeking our help, yes?'

'Yes, that's right.'

'Then we are here to help.'

'But we haven't told you what it's about.'

'No, you have not, but that is not your fault. I have not asked.'

'Why not? We are strangers.' These were exactly her thoughts with the Bhouli. 'Don't get me wrong. We appreciate it, we really do. But you seem willing to do anything, offer anything, without knowing what we're actually here for. The hunters were the same.' Aren tried to keep an accusatory tone from her voice. It was hard to not be suspicious of something that seemed too good to be true. At least with the Bhouli, Aren understood they were driven by purpose. What the people of Holu Mon were driven by, Aren had no idea.

Mo Nu slowed to stop. Drax came in close to Aren's side, watching Mo Nu. Fom stopped behind them, not having said a word since they left. Aren had almost forgotten she was there.

'Please know there is nothing sinister in our actions,' Mo Nu said. 'We expect nothing from you, I promise.'

'I still don't understand.'

'I worry the explanation will make no sense to you, not while you have such little knowledge of Holu Mon. May I ask that you settle in and allow us to show you something of ourselves before delving into that topic?' He looked earnestly at them.

Aren chewed on her lip. So there was something in this for them, as she suspected there would be. Despite that, her gut said she could trust them. If Mo Nu was willing to offer help and put a roof over their heads and food in their bellies in the meantime, surely the least they could do was be patient.

Aren turned to Drax with the unspoken question. *What do you think?*

Drax's icy blue eyes bored into hers. He nodded.

'Okay,' Aren said, turning back to Mo Nu. 'We'll wait.'

Mo Nu smiled at her. 'Thank you. Now, would you like to see your rooms?'

The Founding of Valrue (Excerpt 4)

It was within the space of a few years that Val and Rue became known collectively as Valrue as the population of the town blossomed. At this point, a further note is warranted on the crater lake.

Upon arrival at the mountain, the crater lake was described as being 'of colossal size and depth.' It was large enough to sustain life, and therefore, part of the appeal of settling within the crater itself. Efforts were made by the townsfolk to ensure the fishing stock flourished, and the lake quickly became a valuable source of food.

However, the size of the crater lake was highly unusual. To maintain such a large volume of water, there would have to be an extraordinary amount of rain, which was simply not the case in the mountain, where rainfall was minimal. Additionally, the encouragement of harnessing resulted in warmer weather, which further increased the rate of water evaporation. Thus, an adept-minded townsman pointed out that there was something unnatural about the lake, given its water level never dropped.

Due to a lack of any other reasonable explanation, the people of Valrue concluded that the lake volume was being sustained by majik even though the townsmayjen denied harnessing its waters.

The ponderments of the townsfolk reached the ears of their Bhouli visitors, and Gosha, having since formed a close relationship with some of the townsfolk, explained that there was a Bhouli mayj whose sole purpose was to give life. Eventually, the townsfolk understood that the Bhouli mayj maintained the lake by drawing water into the crater from the surrounding ground and air.

Whilst a fascinating discovery, it also gave cause for concern, given the townsfolk depended on the lake as a food source. The townsfolk requested to meet the Bhouli mayj.

Gosha obliged and arranged the meeting, and the first active collaboration between the settlers and the townsfolk began. Several of Valrue's more powerful mayjen set to further bolstering the lake's waters to support the Bhouli mayj, eventually taking over when the mayj passed away the following decade.

CHAPTER 53: THE GREAT KAHN

The Great Kahn stared down at the page in horror.
He read it again.
And again.

Several of Valrue's more powerful mayjen set to further bolstering the lake's waters to support the Bhouli mayj, eventually taking over when the mayj passed away the following decade.

'FUCK!'

The Great Kahn slammed the enormous book shut and dashed to the wardrobe, digging right to the back to the things he no longer wore.

His wardrobe had grown garish with time. He ripped blood reds and stark whites out of the way, instead pulling out an old grey cloak. The decorative trim was faded enough that it wouldn't draw attention. He dragged it over his shoulders and pulled the hood forward, tying it with fumbling fingers.

How could he have been so negligent?

How could he have forgotten that the KahnenMayjen were responsible for maintaining the lake?

And that last year, he'd had that mercenary kill all of them!

All but Stolt.

The Great Kahn paused, his hand on the door handle to his chambers. But it was a wasted pause. There was no way Stolt could maintain the lake. It was not a job for an imbecile.

The Great Kahn yanked open the door and swept into the corridor. It was the middle of the day; he'd garner more attention as a grey-cloaked and hooded man walking through the corridors than as himself.

Cursing himself again, he rushed back into his chambers, snatched a hateful blood-red cloak from his wardrobe and threw it on over the grey one before dashing back into the corridor. He left the hoods down and hastened along, hoping to appear as though walking with purpose, not panic.

But of course, Minder after Minder approached him.

'My Great Lord –'

'Not now,' he said to each of them with forced calm, waving a hand. One by one, the Minders dipped their noses to the floor and scurried on.

He passed patrolling Krijen and Kahnen too; Krijen hands going instinctively to their hilts yet making no further move when they saw who it was, and Kahnen following him with prying eyes.

It was going to take the Great Kahn hours, but he needed to get to the docks. They were at the far end of the city, the winding path down to them starting on the border between the Left and Right South Sides. He'd prefer to go to the ramparts or the low city wall overlooking the waterfall – both much closer – but he'd see poorly from either. The lake's surface would be too far below him, and he wouldn't be able to tell if the water level had dropped, not unless the lake had already shrunk to the size of a puddle. He was at least sure *that* hadn't yet happened. Teal would've told him because news of it would have flooded the streets. The lake mightn't contain the fishing stock it used to, not since the Unsettlement, but it still fed their entire plumbing system. Without the lake, the city would have no source of water.

The Great Kahn wracked his brains, trying to understand how this could have happened. How he could have *missed* this. He vaguely remembered reading about the maintenance of the lake in one of Dijak's letters, in looking for clues of Mandavar, but that was almost a decade ago now, and he'd brushed the mention of it aside. They'd had KahnenMayjen to do that job. Sure, their numbers were dwindling, but at that time, the KahnenMayjen had still been somewhat capable, and none of them had voiced concerns about the lake. It was no wonder it had slipped his mind.

But had the KahnenMayjen not mentioned the lake because there were no issues with maintaining it? Or because they *hadn't* been maintaining it?

Ah. Mandavar's spell worked by Weaving power between particles, binding them together. From the time it was cast, the power from the spell would've kept the water of the lake trapped. Its particles would move around one another and flow, but they wouldn't evaporate. It made sense that the lake didn't require a mayj to maintain it, not after the Du Bellor Spell.

But which KahnenMayj was responsible for maintaining the lake *before* Mandavar wove the Du Bellor Spell into it? Which KahnenMayj had failed to mention that, all of a sudden, his power was no longer needed?

But, of course, it would've been Mandavar. Mandavar, and whichever KahnenMayj he'd deemed powerful enough to assist him. And Mandavar would've made sure to take full control of the lake's maintenance before setting about Weaving the spell so that none of the KahnenMayjen would grow suspicious.

And sure, the KahnenMayjen had felt it, the power growing in the city. They had said as much. But given the lake's size, the sensation of it swamped them. It had been impossible to tell where the excess power had originated from, hence why the mayjen population of the city bore the blame.

But perhaps some of the KahnenMayjen had suspected it was Mandavar? Would they have recognised the feel of his power even though he'd disappeared five years before the Unsettlement truly began?

If they had, they would've been too scared to say it. Those who had worked with Mandavar knew what he was capable of, the monster he could be. Even more terrifying would've been their failure to understand what was happening. Weaving was something that Mandavar alone did. To the other KahnenMayjen, if they even knew the term, it was but an incomprehensible dream.

So instead of exposing Mandavar, the KahnenMayjen who might've put a stop to it left instead, saving their own skins and leaving the city to suffer.

That is exactly why the Great Kahn *hated* mayjen. They were selfish, arrogant, pieces of –

The Great Kahn stopped, puffing before the gates of the Keep and out of sight of the guarding Krijen. He pulled the blood-red cloak off his shoulders and bundled it up, tucking it under his arm. He pulled his grey hood forward as low as it could go and took off into the winding streets of Val.

At least it was downhill. The Great Kahn was not unfit, but the running of a city took an extraordinary amount of time, and he'd not had the chance to spar nor exercise for far too long.

He'd not brought Mandavar's sword either, or any means to protect himself. Perhaps he should've brought one of the Krijen with him. Then again, that meant a witness, however obedient or trustworthy. And the Great Kahn did not want witnesses. He was done having to dispose of them like he'd used to with the Minders when he'd told himself he had no choice.

He would not do that again. Luka deserved better than that.

But it meant he needed to do this alone. He didn't plan on drawing anyone's attention. He'd only have to hope that no one would see a mysterious hooded stranger and be tempted to try their luck. If he stayed on the borders of the streetling territories, it would be safer. Not *safe*, as streetlings weren't the only dangers out there, but they were the ones who were impossible to reason with, the ones tending towards humiliation as their means of punishment. The Great Kahn would rather be blackmailed than strung up on the bridge for streetling entertainment.

He continued down through the city streets, stepping around strangers with his head tucked, acrid smells hitting him. A sudden rogue thought punctured his mind.

Valrue wasn't so hot anymore. There was even a slight chill in the air, and the sky was clouded over such that wisps of it could still be seen in the streets, as high as they were in the mountain. Surely the People knew that meant the Unsettlement was over, the ones who were around when it began at least. Everything was happening again, simply in reverse.

The Great Kahn knew he was being stubborn about not announcing it, but he wasn't ready. He certainly wouldn't announce it until he was sure the lake wasn't going to dry up and kill them all.

Then again, he would have no choice when the animals started arriving.

When the Unsettlement began, the smallest animals – the mice, the cats, the birds – had been the first to go. It was not because they were the ones most affected but because the larger animals like horses and oxen had been locked in stables, and the dogs were too loyal to their owners, their distress visibly growing until one day they died. The circulating majik had strained the bonds holding their bodies together to the point that they could no longer survive.

Those creatures less sentient, such as the spiders and the insects, had been the last to leave, less consciously affected by the power but still overwhelmed by it in the end. Viruses, bacteria, and other such things, they'd mostly gone too unless they'd had a human host on which to survive. At first, the Great Kahn had thought that not so bad, but then he realised infection and disease had kept the city population under control. Without it, the population boomed while the food supply shrank. The forests died, the farms failed, and the fishing stock faded to nothing.

Humans themselves tolerated the power, with non-mayjen particularly immune to the harmful sensations of majik. Before they understood that, the Great Kahn remembered the terror of it; everyone thinking they would be the next to die. The Eighth House had nearly turned on him while the People had turned *to* him, and Luka had never wished more in his life that Mandavar would return because he would've known what to do. Or even if he didn't, at least Luka would get to see him again.

That was before Luka finally admitted to himself that Mandavar had done this to him. And that was about the time that Luka started losing himself.

***

The Great Kahn blinked.

It was hours later. He stood before the abandoned docks, perspiring beneath his cloak, the late-afternoon sun dappling the lake through the clouds.

There was no one around.

The docks were strange to look at. Still free of lichen, they stretched out into the lake from the stone edge on which the Great Kahn stood. Some had collapsed after years without maintenance. A few boats remained tied to them though most had their cabins caved in or their hulls punctured, so they sat, half-drowned, in the shallower waters. No doubt the streetlings or other young hooligans had done it and moved on when the fun was done.

It was quiet; the bustle of the city behind the Great Kahn, gone. He hurried to the dock before him, the sound of his boots changing as he moved from the echo of stone to the dull knock of wood. He slowed and looked down at the water. It was brown with muck, the run-off from Rue pungent enough that the smell burned his nostrils. The water level was as high as the Great Kahn remembered it being. It hadn't dropped.

In relief, the Great Kahn sucked in a deep breath of air, coughing on the stench that came with it. However, it was a tense relief. The People were not due imminent death from dehydration, but *why?* If not Mandavar, then who was maintaining the lake? Was it another city mayj? Or possibly the KrijenMayj? No. The KrijenMayj was capable and he certainly had the power, but he was too young to know about the

416

maintaining of the lake. He'd yet to understand his abilities enough to do such a thing anyway. No, someone else was harnessing it.

Perhaps it was the Bhouli.

The Great Kahn mused on that while he stared out over the calm waters of the lake. If it were true, then he owed the Bhouli more than he realised, that Bhouli girl having also been the key to freeing them from Mandavar's spell. The Great Kahn felt bad about that now, no matter that it had been worth it, and he didn't regret it. She'd been an innocent after all, and the last few moments of her life would've been terrifying. If only she'd known she was to save thousands more.

But just in case he was wrong and the Bhouli weren't looking after the lake, the Great Kahn resolved to check it again soon.

He turned back towards the city to begin the long walk up to the Keep, thinking of a lie to tell should anyone ask where he'd been.

CHAPTER 54:
SID BHA

Sid had never met anyone so restless as Jakki. Aren perhaps rivalled her tenacity, but even Aren could sit down and ponder the world for a time.

Jakki had already left the world well behind.

A month after Aren left, Jakki had snapped at Sid. 'Sid! Whatever are you doing? Stop moping about my house, I won't have it! You're supposed to be good with your hands, aren't you? Do something useful!'

Noel had attempted to come to Sid's rescue, but Jakki had fired back at him before he'd even opened his mouth.

'He doesn't have to leave the house! He just has to stop being part of the decor. I don't like clutter. Anything in my home *will* have a purpose!'

Jakki bustled in and out of the tower, always in a flurry of movement. She often left before anyone else was awake, came back late at night, and rarely said where she was going. It wasn't long before Mae joined her. Sid did not ask what they did. Instead, he busied himself as ordered. He found rattling door handles and loose nails and shelves that leaned. He dug to the backs of cupboards to board holes and filled cracks that spidered across walls, the strain of the tower having left many rooms in a perpetually precarious state.

Sid fixed everything in Jakki's house until it was perfectly straight again, realising after a time that Jakki must have left these things undone for the sake of giving him something to do. Being a mayj, she could have done it all with a flick of her wrist.

Another month after that, when Sid was busy sanding down the table to remove the stubborn stains on its surface, he felt movement behind him. He leapt around, raising the hand holding the sanding paper, his other held out in front of him, braced for attack.

But it wasn't that Lost Square this time. It was Noel.

'My apologies,' Noel said. 'Do you know what Jakki and Mae are doing?'

Sid slowly lowered the sanding paper, nervous already. 'No, I don't.'

'Aren't you worried?'

Sid inspected Noel's face. He had wrinkles now, making him look old when he hadn't before despite his white hair and beard.

'I always worry,' Sid said carefully. 'But I would never try to stop Mae from doing what she wants.'

The lines of Noel's forehead deepened. 'Isn't that the attitude that got you into this mess in the first place? If Mae and Mama Hidel had not been so persistent with caring for those mayjen children, the women wouldn't have been arrested, you would still be in your home, and Aren would still be here.'

It was unlike Noel to be so harsh. The words hurt.

Trembling, Sid slowly sat down in one of the chairs. 'You think this is my fault?'

Noel gave him a long look and sighed. 'No.' He sat down opposite Sid. 'I'm sorry. I didn't mean it like that. I feel guilty about letting Jakki and Mae go about their mysterious business, and the consequences of doing nothing. I know Jakki too well; she will take risks. It wasn't her that wanted the quiet life.'

'No?'

'No.' Noel shook his head. 'That was me.'

Sixteen years ago, Noel had shown up on the Bha doorstep in answer to their advertisement for a live-in tutor for their little girl. Since that day, they'd never asked him questions about his past, and they'd accepted the story he'd told them about wanting to Make the Cross, and this being the only opportunity he could ever hope to have.

Young Aren had been delighted by Noel, the strangeness of a new person, the wrongness of his beard, and that he seemed to know the answer to every question she could think of, no matter that he wouldn't always give it. Noel had impressed the Bha family enough that after his month-long trial, they'd allowed him to move in.

Sid had never discussed Noel's past with him because when Sid and Mae got to know Noel well enough to ask those sorts of questions, they respected him too much to pry into a life he so clearly wanted to leave behind.

'Jakki and I were heavily involved in the activist movement in the beginning of the Unsettlement,' Noel said. 'At the time I joined, Jakki had already been a part of it for years. She convinced me we were doing the right thing.'

Sid said nothing. He didn't know if he wanted to hear this. These sorts of conversations led to the bringing up of truths that were better left buried. He didn't want to learn things about Noel and Jakki that might disturb his thoughts about them. But Noel seemed intent on telling him, and it would be too telling of his spinelessness for Sid to get up and leave. He had no choice but to endure it.

'I wanted to teach non-mayjen about majik,' Noel said. 'I thought if more people understood it, it would help calm the fires between the two sides. But not all mayjen agreed. Many of them thought non-mayjen were lesser than us and wanted to feed their fear of inferiority. Instead, in our arrogance, we fostered a divide within the mayjen community itself, and Jakki . . . she was willing to go further than I was.'

Sid looked down at the tabletop, wishing he could sink into the swirls of the smooth wood and escape Noel's worried gaze.

'You don't need to say this,' Sid said quietly. 'We know it.'

'How could you possibly know it?'

Sid paused. 'Jakki is not shy.'

'No, she isn't. But she hasn't told you the whole story, has she?'

Sid grimaced. 'She hasn't.'

'You don't want to hear it?'

'Like Mae said before, it's your business, Noel.'

Noel looked disappointed, but he leaned back in his chair, nodding. 'Okay.'

Silence fell.

Sid didn't know what to do. Noel clearly wanted to get involved in whatever Jakki and Mae were doing, but the thought terrified Sid. He'd barely escaped one prison. He didn't think he was quite ready for another.

The main door opened, and Jakki and Mae entered, their arms loaded with bags. Noel quickly got up to help. Mae eyed up the sanding paper in Sid's hand. 'You're still finding things to do, then?'

Sid avoided looking at her.

'Mae's right,' Jakki said, 'that's enough fixing for now. It's been months. You need to get out of the house.'

'I-I really don't think that's a good idea,' Sid said. 'The Krijen are still looking for me.'

'That wasn't a problem when Aren asked you to go the Lower West Side only a week after your escape,' Jakki snapped. 'And unlike what everyone in this city seems to think, the Krijen aren't faultless. If you grow a beard and put on a hood, they wouldn't have a hope of recognising you. The posters of you have all been torn down now anyway.'

Sid wasn't convinced. He looked to Noel, desperate for help.

'If you're bothered about the beard, he's the wrong person to speak to,' Jakki barked.

'It's just . . . I don't think there'd be much point in my leaving the house . . .'

Mae placed the rest of her bags on the ground and walked over to Sid, taking his hand. She led him up out of his chair to the corner of the room. Noel and Jakki turned away, busying themselves with whatever Jakki and Mae had purchased.

Mae pulled Sid's face up to hers and put a hand on his cheek. 'I know you're scared,' Mae said. 'And I know it's not the same without Aren. But you've got to keep living. Jakki is right. It wouldn't take much to disguise you. All I've needed is a hood, and I've got around just fine. You might even look nice with a beard.'

'A beard would attract attention.'

'You'd be hard-pressed not to find a beggar in Rue without one,' Mae said.

'You'd have me look like a beggar?'

Mae pursed her lips. 'You're not a vain man. Why these excuses? Jakki is right. You went to that dreadful alleyway for Aren.'

'And look what happened,' Sid said. He'd brought that Lost Square back into his daughter's life.

'That thing is gone.' Mae held Sid's gaze. She knew him too well to know when he wasn't saying something.

'Noel is worried about you,' Sid said. 'I am too.'

Mae dropped her hands from Sid's face. 'What is it you think Jakki and I are doing?'

Sid nervously twisted his hands in front of him. 'Apparently, Jakki tempts trouble,' he said quietly. 'Perhaps you shouldn't go out with her anymore.'

Mae's anger flared quickly, clashing with her kind face. 'You know nothing about Jakki because you're too scared to ask.'

'I don't want to pry.'

'That's a lie! And you're not worried about me, you're worried about yourself! You've always been a careful man, and I've done my best to pander to your precious heart because I love you. But your daughter *died* to get you out of that prison, and now here you are, putting yourself in another one. I've had *enough*.'

Mae spun away from him, crossed the room, and strode into their bedroom, slamming the door behind her.

CHAPTER 55: AREN BHA

When Mo Nu said rooms, Aren had not expected the grandiose suite he led them to. She gazed up at the ceiling that arched high above her head, glittering stones embedded along its surface. The room was round, as was everything in it: the rug on the floor, the little wooden table in the centre, the cushioned stools encircling it. Even the bookcase curved along the circumference of the walls at the long end of which was a similarly curved desk.

'Are all your rooms like this?' Aren asked.

Mo Nu laughed. 'No, this room is reserved for scholarly guests. However, we have no one visiting at present and given it is more private than our student rooms, I thought it more appropriate for you.' Indeed, there were no windows in the walls, only strips of glass in the ceiling that allowed the sunlight to soak through.

Mo Nu pointed to a door across from them that dissected the curved bookshelf. 'The bedroom and washroom are through that door. You can leave your things there. Then we will go to . . . to *your* room . . .' The dean flushed as Drax gave him a blank stare. 'I am sorry,' Mo Nu said. 'What did you say your name was?'

Drax's eyes darted to Aren. She nodded encouragingly.

'Drax,' Drax said quietly, tucking his chin.

'Drax, it is a pleasure to meet you. Your room is further along –'

'Please,' Aren interrupted, 'would it be possible for Drax to stay in this room with me?'

There was a loud bang behind Aren, and she whipped around, her hand flying to her cardonite dagger.

Fom, the quiet, near-invisible chaperone had dropped Drax's backpack on the floor. The noise had been its buckles smacking into the wood.

'I'm so sorry,' Fom said, quickly scooping up the backpack.

Mo Nu gave her a stern look but turned to Aren with a slightly paler face. 'You wish to stay in the same room?'

'Please.'

'I-I . . .' He cleared his throat. 'That will be fine. My apologies.' His face twitched, but he quickly smiled at them again. It was only slightly alarming. 'In that case, we will allow you time to freshen up. I will come and get you in an hour, if this is suitable? We have much to show you. Fom? Let us go.'

Fom was standing by the bedroom door, staring at Drax.

'Fom? Fom!'

Fom jerked towards the sound of her name, eyelids fluttering. 'Sorry, I'm coming.' She hurried forward and placed Drax's backpack at his feet, looking up at him as she did so before walking back into the corridor. Mo Nu followed, and with a little flourish in the doorway, turned to nod at Aren and Drax. After the tiniest pause, he closed the door.

Aren let out an enormous sigh of relief and lowered herself onto a cushioned stool. Her legs were wobbly, and it had nothing do with Drax's hold on her heart. 'Wow,' she said. 'Just – wow. This place is . . .' She wasn't sure how to describe it. Not just the room but all of it. And if it was a lot for her, it would be a lot for Drax. Aren looked over at him. 'Are you okay?'

Drax peered around the room. He shuffled over to the bookcase and looked down the rows of innumerous volumes. 'I'm okay,' he said.

Aren could hear something in his tone. 'But?'

His blank expression was vaguely tortured as he turned to her. 'I think they expect big things from us,' he said. 'But we need a big thing from them. Do you really think they can help?'

'Jakki said they could,' Aren said. 'And I trust Jakki. I don't trust Mo Nu yet, but I believe him when he says they have no sinister intentions. He's right, too. There are things about them we don't understand. We need to settle in, see what they do here, and figure out if they can help us or not. Then maybe we will know what we can offer in return.'

Drax sank into his shoulders. 'They still think you're the mayj,' he said. 'Are you going to tell them the truth?'

'I'll have to eventually. But let's wait a touch longer, okay?'

'Okay.'

Aren stood up again and walked over to the bedroom door. She carefully opened it. The room was dark beyond, but she could make out a round bed in another smaller, round room.

'They really have a thing against us sharing a room,' Aren said. 'The hunters didn't like the idea of you coming to sleep in the women's quarters, which I can sort of understand. I assumed it was to do with the balance more than anything else. I can't imagine why what we might do in private bothers them so much.'

'It's a slight, I think,' Drax replied. 'They allow it because they think you're a mayj. The woman, Fom, she is worried for me. She thinks Gi will not forgive my slights.'

Aren agreed.

'I don't like making them uncomfortable,' Drax said.

'I don't either. But with any luck, it won't be for long.' Now that they were here, Aren was itching to get out and explore. She didn't need time to settle in.

As she turned back to the main room, her eyes travelled to the curved desk. Next to a neat ream of paper and a quill was a tiny pot of ink. No matter that it was black instead of white like the Bhouli ink, it reminded her of Maude.

Aren crossed the room and picked the ink pot off the desk. She slid a book from the shelf and shoved the ink pot deep into the gap. She pressed the book back into place. The book's spine stuck out a little, but at least the ink pot was hidden. It made her feel better.

'Do you think they would mind if we had a look around without them?' Aren asked, turning back to Drax.

'I don't know.'

'Let's do it. Give me one second.' Aren dug into her backpack and pulled out the bottles that Sola had given her. She took a quick sip of the lunilum to dull the growing burning of her back, her last dose having worn off.

Drax led them back into the sun-soaked corridor, and Aren closed the door behind them. They began walking opposite to the way they'd come, farther into the building.

The corridors connected the large circular rooms that Aren had seen from outside. Her boots made squeaky sounds on the black and white tiles. She adjusted her footsteps to quieten the noise, her gaze drifting to a tree branch outside that wound the length of the corridor. Nature still claimed this place. And the people of Holu Mon let it.

Aren wondered if there was a point where there was too much nature, like when there was too much majik. They always talked about a balance, but it only ever seemed to swing one way.

Considering how busy it had been when they'd first walked through the University gates, the corridor was empty. It was so quiet that when she and Drax rounded the corner, the abrupt crash of noise nearly sent Aren into a panic. Her heart leapt in her chest as she came to a halt, feeling Drax cringing into her back at the swarm of people filling the space ahead of them.

Hundreds of black-and-white-clad students all with braids cascading down their backs babbled excitedly as they filed through two open doors set into a curved wall. Each student kept a perfect inch of space between them and the person they followed.

Aren was desperate to see where they were all going.

'Excuse me,' she said, stepping up to a girl with dark hair and a satchel over her shoulder who stood at the tail of the line. 'What's going on?'

The girl raised her eyebrows. 'You're new here?' She ran her eyes over Aren, then they passed slowly over Drax. She frowned. Drax's scars were visible at his neck where his white shirt hung off him, his collarbone poking through.

'Yes,' Aren said, recapturing her attention. 'We're new here.'

'This is the lecture on genetics,' the girl said. 'Is this what you want?'

'I've no idea,' Aren said. It sounded fascinating. She turned to Drax. 'Shall we see what it is?'

Drax had shrunk into his shoulders again, but he nodded.

Aren stepped forward into the throngs of people, keeping a careful space. She could feel Drax at her back, but he did not touch her again.

The influx of students slowed, and people craned their heads to spot a space they could squeeze into. Eventually, Aren and Drax made it through the doors into a massive round lecture theatre with tiered stone seating leading down to an empty circular depression in the floor. Every other inch of space was occupied; people stood in the aisles.

The lecture theatre thrummed with excitement. Students pulled out scrolls and writing pens and filled tables with books and little pots of ink, the sight of which made Aren ache inside again, thinking of Maude. At least she'd hidden the one in their room.

The noise died as a woman swept into the lecture theatre. Gold trim glittered on the lining of her white jacket, and she wore her braided grey hair in a neat little bun. 'Good afternoon,' she said loudly as she navigated her way down the stone tiers, stepping around students. 'I have to say, I am humbled by the turn-out today. My classes are not usually so popular. I do hope you get from this what you expect to.'

The woman stepped off the final stone tier into the empty space of the circular depression, looking around at the hundreds of faces with her hands on her hips. 'Today we will discuss gene expression. Note that I use the word *discuss*. I want you to listen, not write, while I speak. How can one possibly expect to understand a new concept if distracted throughout the explanation . . .'

The woman spoke with a potency that left Aren enthralled. Not that she understood much of what was said. She couldn't catch most of the words; they were too foreign.

'. . . And thus, we have alleles, which are found in the same loci on homologous chromosomes, which make up a genotype, which as you recall . . .'

The other students nodded and murmured along. This was not their first lesson in genetics, it seemed. With a rush of heat to her cheeks, Aren was suddenly jealous of their understanding. Not once had Noel spoken of this topic. The lack of mention was needling at her because he'd tutored Aren on just about every topic under the sun, except for those relating to majik, so she couldn't understand why he wouldn't have taught her –

'. . . Some perfect examples of recessive traits are those pertaining to harnessing ability.'

Aren bolted to attention.

'You may have guessed that we refer to the different types of harnessing ability as expressions because it is a reference to the phenotypic expression of those genes. The dominant nature of the non-harnessing allele explains why the vast majority of people are non-majikal. The rarity of certain alleles explains why some expressions of harnessing ability are more common than others.'

There was an outbreak of whispering around the lecture theatre, prompting a smile from the woman. 'Ah. So this is why my class is full today. Some of you actually completed the pre-work and knew we would touch on majik. I *am* impressed.'

This explains why Noel never mentioned genetics, Aren thought sourly. He knew it would lead to too many questions.

A hand shot into the air on the far side of the room. 'What about power? Are there recessive traits for power too?'

'Not so much. Power is a spectrum of expression as opposed to one allele dominating another. However, we believe the genes for power are carried only on the X chromosome, which is why males tend to have more *extreme* expressions of majikal genes, for want of a better word.'

There was more muttering. Someone sitting in the row beside Aren raised their hand. 'So you're saying that because there is only a single X chromosome in males, there is no competing allele like there is in females, so the trait *must* be expressed?'

'A nice way to word it,' the woman replied. 'You are correct. However, that is not to say majikal traits cannot be inherited from the father . . .'

'Aren,' Drax whispered.

'What?' Aren couldn't take her eyes off the woman.

'Mo Nu is at the door.'

Aren turned to see the expanse of the dean, indeed taking up most of the doorway at the top of the stairs. Students had crammed into impossible spaces to give him room, all the while managing not to touch their peers. Aren was learning that this was quite a skill in Holu Mon.

Mo Nu beckoned Aren and Drax with his finger.

Aren nervously wove her way up the steps towards him, Drax close behind, hoping the dean wouldn't be upset that they'd left their room.

Mo Nu shuffled back into the corridor, giving them space. Fom stood diligently behind him, her stick-like body blocked by his massive figure.

Mo Nu waited for the doors to close before speaking. 'You have been enjoying our teachings already, I see?' He said it with a warm smile, and Aren's worry quickly vanished. This man was not like Noel. He *admired* her curiosity.

'Yes,' Aren replied, 'I can't say I understood much of it, but it was fascinating.'

'Oh? Which parts did you not understand?'

'Well . . .' Aren couldn't help but feel a little self-conscious. 'Most of the words, really. But I think I got the gist of that last bit. That woman was saying that males are more likely to be himajik, wasn't she?'

Mo Nu opened his mouth as if to reply, then closed it again. 'Himajik? What do you mean by that?'

'Himajik mayjen are . . . um . . .' Aren frowned, unexpectedly stumped by the question. She didn't really know what himajik meant, just that in Valrue, the himajik mayjen were harder to capture and were considered more dangerous. Now that she thought about it, she remembered that both Noel and Jakki had criticised the term. Noel had called it 'preposterous', and Jakki had said it was 'infuriating'.

Mo Nu was regarding Aren silently. 'Tell me,' he said gently, 'what do you understand about majik?'

Next to Aren, Drax shuffled his feet, clearly uncomfortable.

Mo Nu noticed. 'Please, I am not here to judge. As both a mayj and a scholar myself, I appreciate what it is like to know how to do something even if I cannot find the words to describe it.'

'Well,' Aren began nervously, 'majik is what you get when you harness your power. The amount of power and harnessing ability you have determines if you are nomajik, lomajik, or himajik.' Aren couldn't help but cringe. It didn't even sound right when it came out of her mouth.

Mo Nu nodded. 'Okay, you have used some terms that I am not sure about –'

'We know some proper terms,' Aren said quickly. 'We know Breaker and Builder.'

'Yes, you said you were a Builder.' Mo Nu paused, looking uncertain. 'Forgive me, but do you understand what it means?'

'It's got something to do with matter and bonds,' Aren mumbled. She folded her arms, glancing over her shoulder at Drax. He'd moved to stand behind her, but Aren's skinny frame failed to hide him from Mo Nu's questioning gaze. 'Do you want to add anything?' Aren asked.

Drax shook his head.

Aren swallowed. This didn't look good. Here she was claiming to be a mayj, and Drax was one himself yet neither of them could explain it in any meaningful way.

But the dean gave them a sympathetic smile. 'Gi, save you, you poor things,' he said. 'To wield so much goodness, yet not know what it means . . . Please, follow me.'

Mo Nu led Aren, Drax, and Fom a short way down the corridor to another pair of double doors. He threw them open, leading them into a round lecture theatre even larger than the previous. Open windows spaced along the curved white-washed walls, letting in a gentle breeze.

The room was empty. Aren could see each tier of stone steps, their rings growing smaller as they descended towards the centre. In the middle of the floor, snuggled in a stone ring, were a number of transparent glassy orbs of all different shapes, sizes, and colours. There were about thirty of them.

'This is one of our largest lecture theatres,' Mo Nu said as he led them down the stairs. 'Typically, we use it for our introductory courses on majik, which are very popular. For anything beyond the introductory course, we offer exclusive classes for mayjen students only. It is not that we would deny people the opportunity to learn, but we have so few professors with the skill required to *teach* it. We need their attention focused on students who can actually apply the learnings.'

They reached the bottom tier, and Mo Nu stepped into the centre, walking towards the orbs. 'If you will allow me, I will explain majik to you in a more . . . academic fashion.' He gestured to the empty stone tier just in front of him. Aren and Drax obliged and sat down, Aren twitching with excitement. Fom stood off to the side, her hands clasped before her, watching Drax.

Mo Nu cleared his throat. 'Majik is the manipulation of matter and of the bonds that bind matter together. Matter makes up everything; the building blocks of the world, if you will. Matter makes up a rock, and a grain, and a person. Matter makes up living and non-living things. You, my dear, are made of matter,' Mo Nu said to Aren. 'Majik allows us to alter matter from its natural state. As you said, majik comprises two components called pillars, which work together: harnessing ability and power. People find power easier to comprehend, so let us start there. Put very simply, the more powerful you are, the more majik you can do. If you try to use power beyond what you have, it can kill you. I assume you know this?'

'Yes. When you start running out of power, we call it Turning,' Aren said. 'When you've died, that's when you've Turned.'

'We use those terms too. Now, power follows certain rules of physics. If you are further away from something, it requires more power to harness it. If you are attempting to harness something on a larger scale, or with a larger mass, it requires more power. If you are particularly powerful, you can exert your power over other people because, just like everything else, we are made of matter. We call this Influencing.'

'Influencing,' Aren breathed. She couldn't believe it had a name. 'What makes it more difficult to harness people compared to objects, if we are all made of matter?'

'A good question. It is because every person has an innate power, even non-mayjen, whereas objects have none. To harness someone, you must override their innate power. Technically, any mayj can attempt this. An Influencer is simply the term for a mayj who can achieve it without Turning.'

Aren nodded furiously. 'And that's why it's even harder to harness a mayj? Because they have more power to overcome?'

Aren sensed, rather than saw, Fom perk up at her words.

'That is right,' Mo Nu said with a knowing smile. 'So you know about Influencing, save for the terminology?'

'Not much. But I'm a fast learner,' Aren said quickly.

'You are lucky. That will serve you well.' Mo Nu tucked his chin so that the rolls of skin bunched together. He looked up from under his brows at them. 'Shall we discuss harnessing ability?'

'Yes,' Aren said eagerly.

'Right then. It is fortuitous that you happened upon our genetics class because it is our genes that determine not only if we are a mayj, but what kind of mayj we are.

'There are three types of harnessing ability, also known as expressions. You, like most people, are familiar with Breaking and Building. However, all expressions share one similarity: they can move matter. For example, regardless of what harnessing ability a mayj expresses, they will be able to lift one of these orbs should they have sufficient power to do so without Turning.'

With that, Mo Nu raised a hand, and one of the glassy orbs gently rose into the air in front of them, coming to a stop at shoulder height.

'The differences in harnessing abilities lie in how mayjen create bonds *between* matter. For example, Breakers cannot create bonds between matter at all. All they can do is tear the matter itself apart, so the bonds are broken through force.'

Mo Nu raised his other hand, and with a violent twisting motion and a crack that made Drax flinch, the floating orb split down the middle, separating into two halves. Mo Nu slowly lowered his hands until the halves touched the ground. Mo Nu dropped his hands, and the two halves lolled around on the floor before they stilled.

'Breaking requires the least amount of power. Even I can snap a stick in half without majik. For this reason, we consider Breaking the elementary expression. Naturally, this causes conflict between our scholars.' He chuckled. 'Now, to put something back together, you must recreate bonds between the matter of it. This is called Building. Breakers cannot do this. It is important to remember that the bonds created are not the original bonds but majik *mimicking* the natural bonds. If done well, the object you are Building back together should appear whole and unbroken, and the strengths of the bonds would reflect those of the original, natural bonds.' Mo Nu indicated to the orb halves. 'Would you mind?'

Aren glanced at Drax, who blinked at her. *I'm ready*, he meant.

Aren slowly raised her hands out towards the orb halves and brought her fingers together, unsure of the motion required. The two halves soundlessly rolled together, forming a perfect whole on the floor at Aren's feet. She dropped her hands. The orb stayed as a whole. Aren picked it up. Its surface was perfect, unblemished.

Fom clapped, and Mo Nu began bouncing on the balls of his feet again. 'Marvelous!' he said.

Aren was enraptured. It all made so much *sense*. She wanted to know what Drax was thinking, but his face was as unreadable as ever. Aren couldn't tell if he understood or not. Regardless, he was most definitely a Builder, and she knew he was powerful; her beating heart was proof. She carefully put the orb back into the ring, wedging it between its glassy peers.

'We are only beginning to understand majik and all its complexities,' Mo Nu said. 'Its rarity makes it difficult to study, of course. We encourage all mayjen to attend the University but not everyone enjoys sitting in a classroom. However, we are lucky to have a particularly skilled mayj with us in present times, despite his classes being rather challenging. Even our most talented Building students find the teachings frustrating, particularly regarding chemical manipulation. Then again, it is difficult to know if they simply require more practise, or lack the required cognitive dexterity . . .'

Aren was digging deep to recall Noel's teachings about science, but she still couldn't follow Mo Nu's new tangent. Drax was staring out the window.

Luckily, Mo Nu sensed he was losing his audience. 'Perhaps that is enough for today. Let us take you back to your rooms.'

The foursome left the orbs on the floor and headed back up the steps into the corridor, Mo Nu and Fom leading the way. Drax and Aren trailed behind.

'Aren,' Drax said quietly, 'I don't know what he was saying.' He looked terribly dismayed.

'That's okay,' Aren whispered. 'It was hard to understand. And you know it all already. It's just the words that you're missing.'

'I want to know the words.'

'Me too. We'll go over what he said when we get back to the room.' Aren frowned. 'Wait a minute. Mo Nu said there were three expressions of harnessing. He talked about Breaking and Building, but did he mention the third –?' Aren broke off at an exclamation from Mo Nu.

'Oh, how serendipitous! Look who it is! Professor! Professor, a moment please!' Mo Nu called after a tall figure who had stepped out of a room up ahead. The figure paused in the corridor, then strode back towards them.

It was a handsome man with shoulder-length black hair, two regal streaks of grey flowing from his temples. The dark blue university jacket he wore was so perfectly unwrinkled it was reflective. He had purple rings of fatigue under his eyes, which looked rather out of place in all the perfection.

Mo Nu rushed forward to introduce them. 'Aren and Drax, I am very excited for you to meet our most *prestigious* mayj scholar.'

The man had looked almost bored as he'd stepped up next to Mo Nu, but his expression quickly became one of intrigue. Even though Mo Nu had gestured at Aren, the man wasn't looking at her. He was looking at Drax. His lips parted ever so slightly, and a slight crease appeared between his eyes.

Aren suddenly realised who he was. He might be taller, and older, and straight-boned where Drax was twisted, but she could see it in the curl of his black hair and in the blue of the man's eyes. The same blue as his son's.

With all the strength she could muster, Aren pulled back her fist and punched Mandavar squarely in the mouth.

CHAPTER 56:
PYRA

'I still cannot believe we are doing a *parade,*' seethed Lady Hia. 'How vulgar, especially when we have yet to announce the Unsettlement to be over. And in the name of the KrijenMayj! He is a walking, talking, *harnessing* contradiction of everything the Eighth House has been trying to achieve for the past twenty years. I am rather shocked to say I agree with Lord Salli on this matter.'

They were in her usual room, in the usual tower, in the usual chairs. Pyra perched on hers, her feet tucked up under her. 'I don't understand why you're so worried. The People will love it,' Pyra said bitterly. 'They love parades, especially ones complete with a hero to save them from the streetlings.'

'That is not what irks me. It is the principle of the thing!'

'You're a politician. You're not supposed to have principles.'

Lady Hia leaned back in her chair, huffing. 'You are a streetling. You are not supposed to have smarts.'

'Some streetlings are smart.'

'Some politicians have principles.'

Pyra grinned. 'Fine. Are we going to do this thing or what? Don't you have to be up the front waving or something?'

Lady Hia sighed and pressed herself out of her chair. Her gown glittered in the sunlight streaming in from the window. *She looks ridiculous*, Pyra thought. Then again, that was what the Kahnen wore to parades, and Lady Hia always made sure to dress the part.

'You will keep the streetlings at bay? I cannot have them ruining this for the People. It would be terrible for our image.'

Pyra shrugged. 'Sure.' There were no specific shenanigans planned for today. And although they were definitely showing the warning signs of rebellion against *her* with the Krijen out in force and rumour of an upcoming execution of Lady Elira, the streetlings would be content with lobbing spitballs onto the crowd today.

'Good,' Lady Hia said. 'And regarding the KrijenMayj, he will almost certainly grow more troublesome now that he can carry on with his duties without needing to . . . restrain himself.' Lady Hia hesitated. 'It got me thinking about the Lost Square.'

Pyra growled.

'I know you do not want to talk about him,' Lady Hia said carefully. 'But hear me out.'

'Fine,' Pyra replied through clenched teeth. 'What does that *thing* have to do with the KrijenMayj?'

'If I am not mistaken, they were in the Squares together. In the same year, even.'

'So?'

'They know each other, Pyra. The Lost Square might have insights about the KrijenMayj we could use to our advantage. I know you do not want to involve him, but you cannot deny he could be valuable –'

'*No*,' Pyra said.

'But –'

'I SAID NO!' Pyra's voice rang out beyond the tower windows.

Lady Hia did not respond immediately, but when she did, her voice was disturbingly soft. 'Pyra, look at me.'

Pyra leaned her head back so she could look down her nose at Lady Hia, who stood over her.

'I am worried about you,' Lady Hia said.

'Why? Because I won't do what you want?'

'Do not bait me. I worry because I know what happens to streetlings when they get too old. It must be playing on your mind. I cannot think of another reason you would be so disagreeable.'

Despite the patronising answer, Pyra's anger evaporated. She slowly sat up in her chair. She'd wondered when this would come up. She'd had so much going on that she'd pushed the problem aside. But she couldn't ignore it any more than she could stop time.

'*They* don't know how old I am,' Pyra said.

'That girly voice will not last forever. You are tall too, and growing taller.'

Pyra didn't like to hear it, but it was true. She'd gotten away with being a girl for far too long. Womanhood was screaming up at her, and she'd not prepared herself for what that meant. There weren't any grown-up streetlings for a reason. Sure, some of them grew out of it, but not everyone, and *especially* not the gang leaders.

'I'll deal with it when it becomes a problem,' Pyra said stiffly. 'You need to go,' she said, changing the topic. 'Stop procrastinating.'

Lady Hia held her gaze for another long moment. Then she sighed. 'Fine, fine. Can you tell I am just *dreading* this?' She crossed the room and placed a hand on the door handle before turning back. 'Oh, and I know you will go to the parade for appearance's sake, but please stay out of sight of the KrijenMayj. He seems very unstable. If he recognises you, I do not trust what he will do.'

Pyra nodded with no intention of doing as Lady Hia asked. She wanted to get another look at this KrijenMayj. She'd not seen him since the Celebrations and only down the distant end of her crossbow. If she was to come up with a plan to take him down, she needed to know exactly what she was dealing with.

CHAPTER 57:
JIN KANJU

For the first time in his life, Jin had vomited up his nerves. He'd not even done that on the day of his Dancing Ceremony. Since he'd woken, his stomach had been taunting him, and rolling waves of nausea left him hanging his head out of a KahnenKeep window on the way to breakfast.

Nommo and Meek had been worried when they'd first seen his pale, sweaty face, but when he explained the problem, in between swallowing down bouts of bile, they both burst out laughing. 'You're *nervous,* sir? What the fuck are you nervous about? The People are going to love you!'

That was when Jin threw up.

Howling with glee, his squad members had smacked him on the back and shoved their waterskins at him while he wiped his mouth. Luckily, he'd not had much in his stomach to bring up.

So to no one's surprise, Jin turned his nose up at his breakfast, feeling queasy while Nommo and Meek waved mocking spoonfuls of odious maize under his nose until Pago had told them to pull their heads in, sensing that Jin was reluctant to open his mouth to tell them to stop.

'But they *are* right,' Aren had said to Jin. 'You don't need to worry. The Kahnen are confident you'll be well-received.'

'The Kahnen just want to show me off,' Jin had mumbled. 'Why did I agree to this?'

'Even you're not dumb enough to ignore a direct order from your FaKrijen,' Filip had drawled. 'Now stop whining and get on with it.'

So now Jin stood at the end of the bridge, staring across its length into the mouth of Rue, fighting the burning heat from his power that always brewed alongside his fears and hoping with all his might that today wouldn't be the day he finally burst into flames. Not with everyone watching.

The Eighth House were already up ahead, leading the way. Jin could see them waving to their admirers, gowns glittering in the sun. The light from them seared his eyes as though he wasn't hurting enough already. A blood-red robe marked the Great Kahn at the very front. He wasn't waving, but Jin imagined he was smiling.

And of course, Jin had to walk next to Stolt. The repulsion Jin felt towards the KahnenMayj was almost enough to make him forget the heat melting the skin from his fingertips.

'Don't you dare make me look like a fool,' Stolt shot at him. 'Get yourself under control. I can see you twitching from here.'

'You're right,' Jin snarled back, squeezing his hands into fists. 'Smashing the cardonite training room didn't quite do the trick.' Jin was pissed off about that. All it had taken was a week before he was climbing the walls again, the anticipation of the doom-filled parade sending his power into overdrive. 'Maybe I should crack your bones instead.'

Stolt narrowed his eyes at Jin. 'You disrespectful little shit. You forget who you're speaking to –'

'Trust me, I know *exactly* who you are. You're the reason the Kahnen were so eager to make me a KrijenMayj. You failed so miserably at being a mayj that they needed someone else to do the job –'

'You know nothing about me!' Stolt screamed.

Jin had hit a nerve. Thrilled at his unexpected triumph, he opened his mouth, ready to prod further, but he felt a firm hand on his arm. It was Jokah.

'Sir, it's time. Are you all right?'

'Yes,' Jin growled, sick of Jokah's concern.

Jokah quickly let go of him, probably because Jin was burning hot. 'This will be over soon,' the older squad member said calmly, moving to place himself between Jin and Stolt. 'We'll watch your back.'

'I don't need my back watched,' Jin snapped, turning away.

A sharp look from Aren made Jin immediately regret his harsh words, but the drums had started, and they'd begun to move.

Flit ducked to Jin's side. He was grateful that Eden had allowed his squad to join him for the parade. He still didn't know what to think about the FaKrijen. Eden's antics the other day had left him uncertain. Despite Eden denying it, Jin felt like he'd offended the FaKrijen, and the man made him nervous. Flit's clear hatred for Eden also pressed on his worries.

'Remember to smile, sir,' Flit said under her breath.

'It feels wrong to smile.' Normally Jin wouldn't admit to that, but he was so on edge. His eyes roamed of their own accord, his subconscious looking for something to leap off, to escape.

'I know,' Flit said. 'But you've got to play the part. This is politics, remember?'

They stepped onto the bridge and passed the first bodies, some of which were moving. The weather had not been so hot lately, so more of the strung-up criminals survived. Their eyes followed Jin.

Jin and his squad crossed slowly, skirting the holes in the stone. The jagged sides of the bridge had crumbled so that Jin could see the river below, the water gushing with more fury than he remembered. It rained more often these days.

The weather was turning. It was because the power in that lake was gone, and the skies were free once more. Not that the People knew that. They still thought majik was throttling the life from their city. They still blamed the mayjen. They would blame Jin. Yet here he was about to stroll through their streets, lording the hypocrisy over them, and the Kahnen expected them to fall at his feet.

That's what this is, Jin suddenly realised. *A trap*. His throat closed. 'This is it,' he gasped. 'They're going to kill me.'

Flit looked up at him. 'Don't let the bodies worry you, sir.' She hadn't heard him properly.

'They *hate* me, Flit. How can they not?'

'What? You mean the People? You're Krijen. They don't hate you.'

'But they don't know the Unsettlement is over!'

Flit frowned. 'Well no, but –'

'What's going on?' Pago had moved up to join them.

Jin span to him. 'They hate me, Pago,' he said.

'Who?'

'The People!'

Pago gave him a strange look. 'Are you serious, sir? Can you not hear them?'

Jin couldn't hear beyond the ringing in his ears.

They stepped onto the stained cobbles of Rue. Jin watched his boots as he walked, one foot in front of the other, the pulse of his footsteps matching the pulse in his head. His squad flanked him. A cool hand pressed at his back, and he responded, pushing forward, certain that was the intention, but then a hand snatched at the wraps by his elbow as though to drag him back. He hesitated, unsure of what they wanted. He kept walking.

'Jin,' Aren said gently in his ear, 'you need to look up.'

He didn't want to look up. He didn't want to see the rake-thin bodies of the People or the teeth gnashing at him in hatred. But it was Aren asking, so Jin looked up.

The crowd strained towards him, their hands outstretched and their mouths moving, their screams silent to Jin. As he expected, they looked hungry, desperate to claw off a piece of him and slowly tear him apart for how long they'd been starving because of majik, and Jin couldn't help but stagger back from them before he caught himself, remembering that he was Krijen, and if this was what the People wanted, he had no choice but to let them kill him –

'Ho, Jin!'

The voice was familiar, but it did not belong to anyone in his squad.

'Ho, Jin! It's me! By the Great Kahn, didn't I tell you? Didn't I say the Kahnen would want you?'

Finally, Jin found the owner of the voice and shoved around his squad to the man in the crowd. He couldn't believe his eyes.

'Crushed Foot?'

The swiftrunner from the Deadlands burst out laughing. 'Crushed Foot did you say? Ho, I'm *No Foot* now!' Indeed, the man leaned on crutches with nothing but an empty trouser leg dangling from his left knee. 'But you remember me! I knew you would! And all the others said there wasn't a chance of that. I proved them wrong!' The swiftrunner cackled once again, then closed one beady eye, squinting up at Jin. 'Maybe you should take one of my crutches. You look like you're about to topple over.'

Jin grabbed the proffered crutch in one hand, but instead of leaning on it, he wrapped his other arm around Crushed Foot, lifting him clear off the ground.

'Woah, Jin! What –'

'I need your advice,' Jin said, ignoring the baffled faces of his squad as he carried the swiftrunner into their midst. Nommo was immediately in Jin's ear. 'Sir! What are you doing?'

'I need to talk to this man.'

'*Now?* Have you lost your mind?'

'Leave it,' Jokah said, pulling Nommo away.

Jin leaned his head towards Crushed Foot, glad the noise of the crowd would cover their conversation.

'How's Darli?' Jin asked, remembering he needed to do the courteous thing.

Crushed Foot gave him the most enormous grin. 'Ho, he remembers! Darli, my darling girl is doing just fine –'

'You told me to humanise myself,' Jin interrupted. 'After that bandit attack in the Deadlands. Do you remember that?'

'Well, sure!' Crushed Foot leant his head back from Jin, a few beads of sweat dripping from his forehead. 'Jeez, you're *warm*, son. Are you sick or something –'

'How do I do it?' Jin begged him. 'How the fuck do I do it?'

'Er . . . Humanise yourself, you mean?'

'Yes!'

Crushed Foot looked around. 'Is this really where you want to have this conversation?'

'*Yes!* Please, help me!'

Crushed Foot blinked back at him. 'Well, all right then.' He waved the crutch he still held. 'For starters, you can put me down. Not many men can carry another with one arm, you know.'

Jin quickly placed Crushed Foot down and gave him back his second crutch. Despite his short stature, the swiftrunner had no trouble keeping up with him on his one powerful leg as they continued along.

'Please,' Jin said, bending down to him, 'something's wrong with me. I can't . . . I can't . . . I don't know if I can do human anymore.'

Crushed Foot didn't laugh at him. Instead, he gave Jin a searching look. 'What makes you think that?'

'I keep overdoing it. You told me that's what I did after I ripped a hole in that mayj in the Deadlands. But I couldn't help it. I . . . I did it again,' Jin said, thinking of the mercenary.

'You ripped a hole in another mayj?'

'This one wasn't a mayj.'

'Right . . . Did he need a hole ripped in him?'

'No! Well – *yes*, he needed to die – but that's not what I mean! It just happened! And now when I get upset, I just want to rip things apart because it feels good. It's like I crave it, you know? But it scares people! I need to figure out how to stop it. I can't have people hating me!'

Crushed Foot looked around them. 'Son, I don't think you've got anything to worry about there.' He looked back to Jin. 'I know my advice back in the Deadlands was to humanise yourself, but that was then, and this is now. I don't think that's what the People want anymore.'

'What do you mean?'

'The People love you *because* you're something special. You amaze them! Lean into it!' Crushed Foot made a face. 'Though just make sure if you're ripping holes in people that they deserve it.'

'But you said –'

'That was back when being a mayj was going to get you killed. Look at you now! A Krijen doing majik, endorsed by the Kahnen themselves! You've got nothing to worry about.'

'But that makes no sense!'

'People are fickle, what can I say.'

Jin couldn't believe what he was hearing. 'So-so you think I should embrace it? Just do what I need to do, and not worry?'

'That's why they made you the KrijenMayj, right? The People are in awe of you. Go. Enjoy it. The Great Kahn knows you deserve it.'

With that, Crushed Foot stepped back into the crowd and called through a cupped hand, 'Remember to wave!'

Then he was gone.

CHAPTER 58:
PYRA

Pyra twirled her horseshoes in her hands all the way down the staircase of the tower, then tucked them into her wrist ties, tugging her floppy black hat onto her head as she stepped out into the sun.

Barrett and Rifter were nowhere to be seen. Pyra had asked them to stay away this time. If they followed her around too much, the streetlings might assume Pyra was running scared, and that simply wouldn't help the whole them-trying-to-kill-her situation.

She also needed to blend in a bit more if she was going to attend this parade. The streetlings would recognise her, but she needed to make sure the Krijen wouldn't.

There was a new dress shop up ahead choked with customers. Pyra ducked in and quickly lost herself among the messy stacks of clothes. She swiped at a grey dress as she went by, tucking it under her arm, keeping her chin low so that her face was hidden. She quickly sidled back out the same door, snatching a yellow scarf from another rack as she went.

It was shamefully easy to steal these days. All it required was a touch of gumption and a sly hand. And this store owner deserved it. Anyone who kept their shop in such a dreadful mess clearly had no respect for their wares or customers. Sometimes Pyra returned her stolen goods when Polly had been playing on her mind, but mostly she kept what she took. How else were people supposed to learn important life lessons?

Pyra stopped in an alleyway, pulled off her hat, and then dragged the dress on over her shirt, which bunched uncomfortably and left her looking much more buxom than she was. Pyra shoved her floppy black hat down the front of her new bosom, along with her horseshoes, their silver tips peeking out at her. She untied the red strips of material from her wrists and shoved them down beside the hat before wrapping the yellow scarf tightly around her head, hiding the bald patches. Then she joined the crowds as they filed towards the main street of the Upper West Side that cut through from Val.

Krijen lined the cobblestones, creating an empty strip for the parade. People squabbled and craned their heads over each other, trying to get a good view.

Pyra looked up at the rooftops, seeing the jagged zags of grubby streetling faces watching from their perches. It would be Pyra's preferred place from which to view the parade too, but the Krijen would be much less likely to see her if she was right in front of them. She stood only a few feet from one now, his hand resting on his dagger hilts and his head tilted up towards the streetlings.

Pyra squeezed over to him and stuck her head out into the empty strip between the crowd, looking up the way. People were growing restless from the wait, and the drums beat in the distance, announcing the imminent procession. The excitement of the crowd was disturbing.

Pyra wondered what would happen if she flicked one of her horseshoes at the KrijenMayj when he came past. Would he be prepared for it? Or would it slide through his jugular and that would be that? The idea was appealing, no doubt. It would certainly solve a lot of their problems. But the risk was enormous, and Pyra would be strung up by end of the day, if not lose her head on the spot. So she settled into place among the masses, wondering how the KrijenMayj was feeling as he walked over the bridge full of mayjen bodies the Krijen had strung up.

Then again, Krijen didn't feel feelings. What a wasted thought.

It was entertaining when the Eighth House came by. Pyra waved and cheered with the rest of the crowd, sticking her hands out to touch their gaudy gowns, and Lady Hia's falsely terrified eyes drifted right over the top of her, utterly oblivious.

Pyra was mildly surprised that the Krijen let the People get that close, but she supposed elections were coming up and the Eighth House wanted to please. The whole point of this parade was to show off their KrijenMayj, their new indomitable toy.

And there he was.

He stood out like buckteeth on a beauty, like something that looked all kinds of wrong, and you couldn't help but stare at it. He wore Krijen black, like the rest of his squad, who surrounded him. His head stuck out of the top of their circle because he was stupidly tall, even for a Krijen. Six-foot-five, maybe.

He had long blond hair which fell in a thick braid down his back, though his hair was cut so short around the ears that he was almost bald there. The others in his squad had this hairstyle too. They all matched. It was weird.

Below his blond hairline, veins bulged at his temples as though the blood was ready to burst from his face.

His eyes were brown. Pyra thought they would be red.

He just seemed so *tight*.

He didn't smile, he didn't wave, he just stared ahead while his thumbs pressed on his dagger hilts so hard that the tips of their blades speared through the fabric on his thighs.

Given the KrijenMayj's striking appearance, Pyra was shocked she hadn't remembered him more clearly. She watched with interest as one of his squad members, a brown-haired and freckle-faced female, craned up her head to say something in his ear, and he bent down to humour her.

Pyra watched his lips.

I'm okay. Yes, I'm okay.

Pyra had never spotted a more obvious lie in her entire life.

Finally, the KrijenMayj's eyes roamed instead of staring dead ahead, and Pyra sucked in a breath as they travelled across the rooftops and settled on the faces of her streetlings.

Don't you dare, Pyra thought. *Don't you dare.*

The KrijenMayj's hands twitched on his dagger hilts.

Just then, another squad member, an older one with a white braid, came up and put a hand on the KrijenMayj's arm. He smiled, and the KrijenMayj's fingers flexed instead, coming off their daggers. But his eyes stayed on Pyra's streetlings.

Pyra had seen enough. She turned and pushed back through the crowd, away from the KrijenMayj. Lady Hia had mentioned a few times that she was worried about him and how he was a growing problem for their cause. Pyra thought she'd understood what the Kahn had meant.

How wrong Pyra had been.

CHAPTER 59: AREN BHA

'You *murderous* piece of shit!' Aren bellowed as she wrestled against Fom. The woman had grasped her around the waist, desperately trying to tug Aren backwards as she clawed at Mandavar. Aren couldn't believe how strong she was, for a stick.

Drax hadn't moved.

Mandavar had cursed and taken a step back, rubbing his jaw, his eyebrows raised in astonishment. Aren was thrilled to see blood welling from a split in his lip.

'You monster!' she spat. 'We know what you did! We know it was you who put the power in the lake!'

'Aren, please!' Mo Nu cried, sounding close to tears. 'What is the meaning of this?'

'That man is *evil!*'

'Professor,' Mo Nu pleaded, watching helplessly while Fom made a pitiful noise, still straining to hold Aren back. '*Do something*!'

For another few seconds, Mandavar watched Aren calmly while she wrestled against her scrawny captor. Then he held up his hand, his digits curling in.

Fom leapt back as an invisible pressure forced itself up Aren, dragging her arms down to her sides, and her feet together, locking her in place. 'No!' Aren screamed. 'No –'

'Let her go.'

Aren clammed her mouth shut. The tautness of Drax's voice was shocking, filled with a darkness Aren had never heard before.

Mandavar paused with his hand still outstretched towards Aren. He looked at Drax, slowly cocking his head to the side, his gaze hovering over Drax's near-translucent skin, the stark cheekbones, the white crosshatched scars. Aren could see thoughts whirring behind his eyes.

Then Aren's heart stopped.

Mandavar choked. His throat contracted and his free hand slipped to his throat. Aren felt the pressure against her release and her legs buckled, and she fell into stick-thin arms. As blackness swooped in around the corners of her vision, Mandavar flicked out a hand. Aren didn't see what happened, but she heard Fom squeal and drag her backwards, and Drax let out a strange cry. Suddenly Aren's heart was pounding again.

Aren took a few gasping breaths as her vision returned, realising she had slumped into Fom's arms. She fought to stand up out of them. Fom quickly let go and took a step back, leaving Aren on wobbling legs, her heart picking up its usual rhythm. Her back didn't hurt, but she noticed a wetness at the base of her spine again. She had split her stitches, probably from punching Mandavar. It had been worth it.

Drax stood in front of Aren, using his body as a shield. Before him, Mandavar was bent forward, his hands on his knees, coughing. Mandavar slowly brought a hand up to rub his throat, his icy blue eyes turning up to Drax. Then Mandavar started to laugh. The raw, hacking sound echoed through the empty corridor as Mandavar pressed himself up off his knees and flashed his teeth in a handsome smile. 'Gi have mercy,' he said to Drax. 'I know who you are.'

Drax didn't react in the slightest. He only continued his dark stare, chilling enough that Aren felt a crawl of nerves down her back. She'd never seen Drax look so dangerous.

Mo Nu looked like he was about to faint. 'Y-you know each other?'

His head twisted between Drax to Mandavar, his cheeks wobbling back and forth.

Mandavar didn't answer Mo Nu. His eyes were locked on Drax. 'I can't believe it,' he breathed. 'And I can already tell you are incredible. Of course, you *would* be incredible. But there is something that I don't . . . I don't understand . . .' Mandavar stepped towards Drax, who shoved backwards into Aren, prompting another shriek from Fom.

'You're harnessing without your hands,' Mandavar said. 'How?'

'Get away from him,' Aren spat at Mandavar. He turned his icy blue eyes on her. 'Who are you?'

'I'm Aren. I'm from Valrue. You know, that city you *ruined*.'

Mandavar's mouth twitched.

'Why did you do it?' Aren demanded, knowing in the back of her mind that this was probably not a man to further antagonize. But she was just so *angry*. 'I mean, what *possessed* you to do something so cruel, so calculating?'

'I don't know what you're talking about,' Mandavar said, his expression now infuriatingly blank.

'YOU LIAR!' Aren screamed.

'Aren, please!' Mo Nu cried.

'It's okay,' Mandavar said, holding up his hand and making Drax flinch. Mandavar's eyes flicked back to his son. He slowly dropped his hand. 'You've come from Valrue, you say?' Mandavar asked as though he didn't already know. 'You must have some stories to tell.'

'Oh yeah?' Aren challenged. 'You want to hear some horror stories, do you?'

But Mo Nu stepped between them with his hands up, looking at Mandavar. 'Professor, please,' the dean whimpered. 'I do not understand what is going on here, but I would rather you not upset our guests. You should know that Aren is a mayj –'

'She's no mayj,' Mandavar said softly. 'But he . . . he is something else.' Mandavar paused. Then he jerked his head towards Aren. 'Is this the reason you are here?' he asked Drax. 'To save the girl?'

How he'd known that, Aren had no idea.

'Yes,' Drax said. 'I want to save Aren.'

Aren whipped her head around to Drax, shocked at his candour. 'Drax! What're you *doing?*'

'Drax? That's your name?' Mandavar asked.

'Yes. I want to save Aren,' Drax repeated. 'Can you help me?'

Aren's jaw dropped. 'Drax, don't –'

To Aren's horror, Drax took a step back towards Mandavar. 'You will help me. You have to.'

Mandavar raised an eyebrow. 'I have to?'

'Yes.'

'And what makes you think I can?' But Mandavar was smiling, and Aren could smell the arrogance leaching from him.

'Drax, stop it.' Aren tugged on Drax's arm and pulled him away, ducking her head towards his. 'What're you doing?' she hissed. 'Why would you ask for his help?'

Drax stared back at her, a little frown on his face. 'This is why we're here, Aren.'

'But why did you ask *him*? There must be others we can ask! This is the University, for goodness' sake! There must be other mayjen –'

'He's the only one who can help.'

'What? That's ridiculous, you can't know that!'

'I'm right, Aren.'

Drax wasn't looking away. He wasn't cringing into his shoulders or shuffling his feet. He was confident in this.

'I don't want you doing this for me,' Aren said. 'Please, can we talk about this?'

'I will do anything for you, Aren.'

'Oh, Drax, no –'

Mandavar's voice cut across her. 'I have a class tomorrow,' he said. 'You should attend. And you,' Mandavar said, waving a hand at Fom. 'They'll need to share a room.'

With that, Mandavar turned and strode down the corridor, leaving ringing silence in his wake.

CHAPTER 60:
BISHINROJAK LONLI

One and a half years ago

Wren stood across from him, his outline doubled. The Fifteenth's krije was slung over his shoulders, the point of the blade spearing towards the sky.

Bish knew there weren't two of Wren. But that didn't help.

Bish's head pounded from where Prinn had punched him, and the screaming of the crowd was like a distant rumble as though Bish had stuck his head into the sand, and the sound had to wrestle through the grains to get to him.

Bish closed one eye, and Wren's double-form became one. It was not smart to dance with only one eye open, but Bish didn't have a choice. He did his best to focus as Wren slowly slid the krije from his shoulders, bringing it before him and slipping into a crouch.

Wren never fought like the others. He had his own style of things, and it had always thrown them. Fuck, it had even thrown Jin. Of course, Jin always beat Wren but only by sheer brute force.

Jin always beat everyone.

It wasn't until today that Bish admitted to himself that he never would have made it through the Squares without Jin. That was why Bish had to win this dance, to prove to everyone that he could do it, that he was worthy of being Krijen, because he'd not won against Prinn. No, Prinn had harnessed and cheated and lost his head. But he'd not lost. He was not Lost. So now it was Wren or Bish.

'You may begin,' Teal called to them, his voice hoarse.

Bish attacked. He staggered forward with his krije and jabbed the blade before him, and Wren darted back, whispering out of the way.

Then Wren returned like lightning, sending his krije tip towards Bish's throat.

Bish couldn't bring his arm up in time. Instead, he flung himself backwards, the movement sending his vision whirling. But he tucked his blade to his chest, the weight of it steadying him, and then he twisted round, snapping his weapon back towards Wren.

Their blades met with a crack of steel, and then they were locked into their dance, an endless fury of swings and parries.

Fuck, Wren was fast. He fought like the wind when it whistled in your ears and made them hurt, and it was all you could do to clamp your hands over them, desperately trying to keep it at bay, but you knew that eventually it would win because it was the wind.

Bish held Wren off for now, but it was only a matter of time because Bish couldn't see; he could barely think. It took every ounce of his will to fend off Wren's attack, and Bish could feel himself being pressed back, and Wren advancing, pushing and pushing and *pushing* –Until Bish slipped.

Bish couldn't believe it. Squares didn't slip. Krijen didn't slip. Yet here he was, smacking into the ground and rolling to the side as Wren's blade punctured the sand where he'd been only moments before.

Wren ripped his krije free, stepping forward, and as Bish squinted with his one eye up at Wren's dark form, Bish saw him hesitate.

'No!' Bish yelled at him. 'Don't! Don't do that, Wren!'

'This isn't right –'

Bish wasn't having it. He whipped his krije across the ground, forcing Wren to jump over it. Snarling, Wren sent the tip of his blade back down towards Bish.

Bish felt a burst of energy whip through him, and he rolled onto his back, bringing his krije up. The crack of his blade against Wren's sent tremors up his arm. Bish yelled out, his arms straining as Wren pressed down on him, the blade inching closer and closer to his face. Bish was so sure his grip would slip, the hilt of his krije hot under his sweating fingers.

But somehow, Bish held. Then with a roar of strength Bish didn't know he had, he jerked his blade to the side, catching Wren's and smacking it away.

Immediately Bish was back on his feet, parrying Wren's next attack. Bish saw the surprise in Wren's dark eyes. Bish could hardly believe it too.

Bish unleashed a flurry of tight stabs, and it was his turn to push, and push, and push against Wren, and his opponent took a step back, and then another, and another.

Fear filled Bish's veins, fear that if he didn't win this fight, he would lose Marigold, and his family, and Jin, and most of all, he would lose his life because everyone knew what was expected of Squares who Lost.

Bish feinted to the side, which he never usually did, but something was telling his body to move that way, and Wren realised a second too late as Bish stepped in next to him, grabbed Wren by the front of his wraps and wrenched with more strength that he knew he had.

Wren felt light, and so fuelled by fire was Bish that he sent Wren whirling off balance. He grabbed Wren's fist as it sailed past, the one that held his krije, knocking it out of the way and bringing his own blade up to kiss Wren's throat.

Wren froze, his dark eyes dropping to the steel sitting beneath his chin. 'No,' he said. He lowered his arms, and his krije thudded into the sand at Bish's feet. '*What?*' he cried as realisation sunk in. 'No! NO!'

Bish slowly lowered his krije.

Wren was white as a sheet, a strange contrast to the sweat that ran down his temples. There were two of him again. Bish had opened his bad eye.

'I'm sorry,' Bish said to him. Then he remembered he wasn't supposed to speak to Wren. He was Lost now.

Bish turned away to see Jin sprinting towards him across the arena, the other victorious Fifteenths close behind. Then Jin smacked into him like the mountain he was, and he pulled Bish off his feet, crushing him in his excitement. Bish got a mouthful of metal; the taste of Filip's blood was still on Jin's wraps.

'You did it!' Jin yelled. 'You won!' He was laughing, and the other victorious Fifteenths were all around them, laughing as well, and when Jin finally put Bish down, they smacked him on the back and shoulders so hard that his legs buckled, and his knees hit the dirt.

'Woah, hey –' Jin dragged Bish back to his feet as Teal sprinted over to them.

'Come!' the Speaker said, grabbing Bish's hand and thrusting it into the air for the audience to see. 'Bishinrojak Lonli has won his *second* dance!'

The crowd screamed, and Bish heard them as though the sound came through the sand once more, the grit of it sticking in his ears.

So that was it.

'Fuck, I've never been more ready to celebrate,' Jin said, his eyes roaming the crowds as they spewed from the arena, crushing towards the exits. Bish knew he was searching for Aren. Aren, or his father.

Bish hated Jin's father, hated what he'd done to Jin. Jin couldn't lose because of him; Jin had to be the best at everything, but he still didn't realise that the best would never be good enough for his father. So in a strange way, Jin always lost.

Bish looked behind him.

Wren was still there. He was sitting on the sand, his face slack, eyes on his krije which lay on the ground before him. Legs surrounded Wren, their owners not bothering to look down at the forsaken warrior in their midst.

Bish took a step towards him.

'Bish,' Jin said sharply, tugging on his wraps. 'Come on. Marigold's waiting.'

Right. Bish tore his eyes off Wren, turned his back on him, and strolled after Jin towards Marigold's beautiful face in the crowd.

458

CHAPTER 61:
BISHINROJAK LONLI

'Y ou no longer want to be Krijen?'

Bish sat in his wheeling chair before the FaKrijen. It had been a long way to the Keep, and going up the slope of Val hadn't been easy. Bish wasn't as strong as he used to be. He hated that. But it was self-inflicted, so he could hardly sulk about it.

'That's right, sir.'

'Well. That's certainly new.' The FaKrijen looked at Bish's limp legs. 'You were in the bandit attack in the Deadlands last year, weren't you?'

'Yes, sir, that's how I broke my back.'

'The KrijenMayj saved you.'

Bish couldn't help it. He grimaced, just a little. 'Yes, sir.'

'Oh? You hold it against him?' The FaKrijen looked sideways at him. 'And here I thought the KrijenMayj could do no wrong.'

'Trust me. There's plenty wrong with him, sir.'

Bish didn't know what made him say it. *Well no, that's not true*, he thought bitterly. He knew exactly what made him say it. He'd just not intended to say it in front of the FaKrijen. But then again, he was sick of everyone loving Jin. They didn't know the real Jin. Not like Bish did.

The FaKrijen smiled but it wasn't a warm one. It didn't meet his eyes, and it looked painful. Stretched.

'You were on a swiftrun, right?'

Bish shifted in his chair. He didn't particularly want to talk about it, but he could hardly deny the FaKrijen.

'That's right, sir.'

'I remember hearing that the bandits didn't go for the supplies. Instead, they attacked the Krijen. Do you know why?'

'No, sir. We never figured out why.'

'FaKrijen Oji went to join you at First Base East in the aftermath. He never investigated?'

'He was busy with Jin, sir.'

The FaKrijen's lips pulled tighter. 'I'm tempted to deny your request. We need more Krijen like you.'

'I don't deserve to be Krijen.'

'What makes you say that?'

Bish couldn't say it, even though he knew the FaKrijen would love it because Eden so clearly disliked Jin, probably because Jin had done what Jin always did. He'd shown the FaKrijen up and acted like he didn't know what he was doing when really the whole thing was calculated as fuck because Jin never did anything by accident. Jin was too smart to make mistakes.

But as much as Bish hated him, he wouldn't tell the FaKrijen the truth about what Jin did at the Dancing Ceremony. Bish wasn't going to sink that low. And this wasn't about Jin, anyway.

It was about Wren.

The memory of him wouldn't leave Bish alone. He strolled in and out of Bish's dreams and spent every waking hour dragging him back to that moment during their dance, where Wren had hesitated for half a second in the biggest fight of his life because he felt like the fight wasn't fair. He could've won in that half-second.

And Bish had been okay to beat Wren because Bish thought he'd won, fair and square. It was shit for Wren, but that was how it worked. Wren knew that.

But then Jin had told Bish the truth, and since then, Bish couldn't get Wren out of his head.

Marigold was convinced it was something she'd done. Bish hadn't yet told her the truth, so she still hated Wren. The way she'd reacted to him after learning about Wren and Aren being a thing was completely rational. Anyone in their right mind would be just as horrified to discover their friend had been seduced by a Lost Square.

Apart from the fact that Wren wasn't like that. And he didn't deserve to be Lost because if it weren't for Jin, *Bish* would have lost that dance.

And if Wren could never be Krijen, then Bish couldn't either. Now *that* was fair.

Bish refocused on the FaKrijen. 'I can't walk. I can't fight. What good am I? I haven't been part of a squad for months.'

'I can give you a squad.'

Bish shook his head. 'No, sir. Thank you, but I don't want one.'

The FaKrijen rubbed his chin. 'You're still wearing black.'

'I have nothing else. I'll fix that.' Bish pulled his daggers from his wraps and held them out to the FaKrijen. They hadn't felt right for months. 'Please, take these, sir.'

'You're sure?'

Bish nodded.

The FaKrijen took them from him and looked down the length of the blades. 'I can hardly deny you this,' he said. 'But I resent your decision. You showed so much promise. Not many Squares win twice at their Dancing Ceremony.'

Bish dug his nails into the arm of his wheeling chair. He said nothing.

'All right.' The FaKrijen slid Bish's blades into his own wraps. 'You're now stripped of your duties and your Krijen title. You're forbidden to wear black or carry a krije or a Krijen blade.' He paused. 'I guess you don't need to call me sir.'

Bish nodded. 'Thank you.'

The FaKrijen lifted his head. 'You can go.'

Bish wheeled himself into the corridor. Strips of warmth landed in his lap as he rolled past the windows of the Keep. At least the trip home would be a breeze. He would barely have to push.

He dreaded it a little though because he'd not told Marigold where he was going. She would have tried to convince him otherwise, and he wasn't having that. She thought that if he stayed Krijen then it gave him something to hold on to. But she was wrong. Being Krijen just made Bish hate himself.

Now Marigold's tears would go nowhere. Bish couldn't renege on this decision. He knew Marigold was scared because he'd not been himself for a long time, but he was getting closer now. They were going to be okay even if she was worried they weren't.

Bish may have lost his self-respect, but he would not lose Marigold.

He was done letting Jin take things from him.

CHAPTER 62:
AREN BHA

After seeing Mandavar, Aren and Drax had gone back to their room, escorted by a thoroughly shaken Mo Nu and pale-faced Fom, neither of whom had spoken another word.

Drax had doused her Edgecat wound with antiseptic and redone the dressing. To add to her burning back, Aren's hand ached from punching Mandavar after the lunilum wore off, so she'd taken a few more sips of it and settled in to wait for the ache to subside again.

Shortly after that, there had been a knock on their door. Aren had opened it to see two dinner trays laden with food on a little table with wheels, and no one in sight.

After she and Drax had eaten it all, still making up for their months of near-starvation, Drax had fallen asleep in their bed. Aren spent the rest of the evening and most of the night lying awake on her belly next to him, thinking of all the sadistic ways to kill someone, wondering if any of them were as bad as Mandavar deserved.

When a knock sounded at the door the next morning, she was already up.

It was Mo Nu again. He appeared without Fom by his side with two tall silver cups in his hands. He held one out to Drax, who'd wandered out of the bedroom, rubbing the sleep from his eyes with his wrists. 'This is for you,' Mo Nu said.

Drax stared at the cup, then awkwardly wrapped his wrists around it, spilling some onto the floor.

'Oh, I am sorry!' Mo Nu cried. 'I did not think –'

'It's okay,' Drax murmured.

Mo Nu turned to Aren and wordlessly held out the second silver cup. She took it from him. 'Thank you, but . . . what's this?' she asked. 'We've already received our breakfast trays.' She pointed to the two trays on the table left outside their room this morning. Hers was empty; she'd already eaten it all, and Drax would no doubt finish his.

'It will help replenish Drax's power more quickly,' Mo Nu said, not quite meeting Aren's eyes. 'If he is harnessing the way the professor tells me he is . . . he will need it.'

Aren nodded. Drax needed all the power he could get right now.

Drax tentatively lifted the cup to his mouth and took a sip. Aren was full from breakfast, so she placed hers to the side. Mo Nu's eyes followed it. Then they darted back to Aren and Drax. 'Are you ready?' the dean asked.

'Yes,' Drax said before Aren could open her mouth.

'Follow me.'

Mo Nu led them down the hallway, Drax ambling just ahead of Aren. The dean still seemed a few degrees colder than his friendly welcome of yesterday. Fom's absence also played on Aren's mind. She'd thought Fom had been there to maintain balance, given they had more men than women in their group. Aren didn't understand what had changed.

'She will no longer be attending us,' Mo Nu said when Aren asked. She was right. His tone was definitely off.

'I'm sorry,' Aren said, already worrying she'd ruined everything. It hadn't even been a day. 'Did I upset Fom? Is it because of yesterday?' On reflection, maybe she shouldn't have punched Mandavar. At least not in front of their hosts.

Or maybe it was because they now knew she was a liar.

Mo Nu sighed and shook his head. 'Forgive me. I owe you an explanation. Fom is very conscious of her spiritual well-being, and considering you seem less' – Mo Nu cleared his throat – 'concerned than most about slighting, I thought her chaperone services would be better used elsewhere.'

So it *was* about the lie. Aren felt horribly guilty. But Mo Nu's voice was kinder than before, so she let it be. Instead, she worried about Drax. He'd said almost nothing since their unexpected meeting with Mandavar yesterday, and despite her gentle pressing, he'd not given her much more than a blank expression. He was definitely upset. Aren bent her head towards him as they followed Mo Nu, careful to keep an inch of space.

'Are you sure you want to do this?'

'Yes.'

'Are you absolutely sure?'

'Yes, Aren.' He blinked at her. 'It's okay.'

So that was that.

Mo Nu led them into yet another round lecture theatre with the usual stone steps falling into the floor. It was much smaller than the last one and completely empty.

'We are early,' Mo Nu explained. 'The professor asked that you arrive before the rest of his students.'

Aren folded her arms. 'Why? For the pleasure of having us wait on him?' She quickly stopped herself, biting back a further and fouler retort. She didn't want to upset Mo Nu again.

'He's here,' Drax said.

Aren turned as Mandavar's tall frame appeared in the doorway. He swept down the stairs, his eyes on Drax. The rings under his eyes were gone. 'I'm glad you came,' he said as he reached the circular floor and stopped before them. 'Mo Nu, you may go.'

The dean hesitated, glancing at Aren. 'I'll behave,' she said quietly, feeling a touch of heat in her cheeks, embarrassed that he was so clearly nervous about what she might do if left unattended.

Mo Nu gave a clipped nod and puffed up the steps. Mandavar waved a hand, and the doors closed behind the dean.

'Sit,' Mandavar said, pointing towards the bottom-most stone tier.

Drax carefully sat, awkwardly putting his empty silver cup down beside him. He'd finished it quickly. *Good*, Aren thought, though she wished he'd eaten breakfast too.

Aren sat on Drax's other side, crossing her arms and legs and glaring up at Mandavar. She still couldn't believe they were here, sitting in his classroom, having done as bidden. Of course, Mandavar would have a knack for making people run around after him. She just never expected to be one of them. But she would keep calm. She *would*.

Mandavar flicked and rolled his wrists, and a little seat of stone flowed up out of the floor at his feet. He sat down, facing them. He observed Drax silently for a moment, eyes lingering on the purple rings at his wrists, and on the white cross-hatched scars that crept up his neck and over the backs of his limp hands. 'Those scars are from Krijen,' Mandavar said quietly.

Drax blinked at him. 'Yes.'

Mandavar's eyes flickered to his son's. 'I didn't mean for that to happen to you.'

Aren's resolve to stay calm evaporated instantly. 'So why'd you do it, then?' she snarled. 'Why'd you leave him?'

Mandavar had the gall to stay silent.

Aren's anger exploded. 'You owe him an explanation!' Her voice echoed so loudly in the empty room that Drax cringed away from her.

Mandavar's mouth twitched.

'We know you put the power in the lake,' Aren spat. 'We know you did it on purpose.'

Mandavar gave her a stare as blank as his son's. Then slowly, he lifted his hands. Drax tensed beside Aren, but all Mandavar did was flex his fingers, forming and re-forming fists in front of him. 'He's still in power, isn't he?'

Aren couldn't help herself. 'Who?'

'Luka.'

'*Who?*'

'The Great Kahn,' Mandavar said simply. 'Of course, no one would know him as Lord Li anymore. How long has he reigned now? Twenty-five years? Twenty-six?'

Beneath her anger, Aren felt a thrill. She'd been right. 'What happened between you and the Great Kahn?'

Mandavar lowered his hands. 'Nothing of consequence.'

'You smothered an entire city because of him,' Aren said, her voice trembling. 'Don't you dare tell me it was nothing.'

Mandavar gave her a long look. 'Fine,' he said. 'The Eighth House were scared of me, scared of the majik I could do. Scared of what my children might be capable of doing should I father any. So in a transparent attempt to control *me*, they passed a law requiring all KahnenMayjen be sterilised. Luka wanted me to be his castrated dog when he became the Great Kahn. I refused.'

Aren was shocked by his sudden candour. Not that it was the answer she was expecting. 'His *castrated dog?*' She turned to Drax, but she could see in his face that he didn't understand. She was glad he didn't. Mandavar was admitting, in not so many words, that he fathered Drax out of spite. Then left him to the whims of the man he hated.

'You are *sick*,' Aren whispered, 'sick and twisted!'

'I didn't know what Luka would do,' Mandavar said. 'What amazes me is that he stayed in power all this time. The People did not tear him from his throne for his failings?'

'The People didn't blame him for the Unsettlement,' Aren spat. 'They blamed mayjen.'

'Ah. They do not know the truth then. So the power remains in the lake?'

'The power is gone,' Drax said.

'You could use the power then? That was the theory of course.'

'I could use it. Not all of it.'

'But you say the power is gone?' Mandavar frowned. 'You broke the spell, somehow? Impossible, I made sure there was no way –'

'*What is wrong with you?*' Aren cried, riding over the top of him. 'All you care about is Luka, and the power in the lake, and the majik! What about Drax? What about the son you abandoned? Don't you want to know about *him*?'

Mandavar turned his blue eyes on Aren. 'When I left Valrue, Drax was not yet born. How was I supposed to know what would happen to him?'

'BECAUSE HE'S *YOUR* SON!' Aren stood up off the stone bench, her hands balled into fists. 'You were the most powerful KahnenMayj in Valrue! You defied the orders of the Eighth House, and then impregnated some poor girl, doing the very thing they were scared you would do. How could you *not* expect the Krijen to come looking for the baby?'

'Sit down,' Mandavar ordered. But he didn't raise a hand to her.

Trembling, Aren sat.

Mandavar turned back to Drax. 'I know you're angry with me, but I never imagined Luka would do what he did. Then again, he sounds rather different now from the man I knew.'

Drax cringed deep into his shoulders. But it wasn't anger. It was fear.

'What is it?' Aren asked. 'What's wrong?'

'My students are here,' Mandavar said, looking up towards the doors of the lecture theatre as they opened.

Down the steps walked two young men wearing dark blue tunics. One was tall and darkly tanned, his midnight-coloured hair braided in the Holu Mon style, with a neatly trimmed beard. The other was shorter, well-muscled, with short black hair. He stood out to Aren. Other than Mandavar, it was the first time she'd seen a man without a beard or braids in Holu Mon.

Not far behind them followed a young woman with blonde braids, the front bits twisted and pinned back from her face. She seemed strikingly familiar until Aren realised that she'd seen her yesterday, lying in the grass when they'd first walked into the University. The young woman wore the same dark blue as she had yesterday but this time as a dress, and she had red on her lips and coal around her eyes. She reminded Aren of Marigold.

Aren winced, still raw about how she'd left things with Marigold.

Although the mayjen students had arrived together, there was no chaperone with them, no Fom trailing quietly behind. They kept an unnatural distance from one another as they walked down the steps. Each of them wore a curious look on their face, their heads turning to Aren and Drax as they sat down at equal distances from each other on the bottom stone tier, forming a square with Aren and Drax.

Drax had edged so close to Aren that they were almost touching. 'You can feel them?' Aren whispered to him.

Drax nodded. 'A little. That one the most,' he said, his eyes darting towards the tall one with the neat little beard. The student was looking at Drax with the deepest scowl on his face, his eyes flickering between Mandavar, Drax, and Aren. His hands slowly curled into fists.

'We have some guests with us today,' Mandavar said without prelude. He stood up from the stone seat and waved a hand at it. It melted into the floor at his feet. Then he strolled to the middle of the room, his head rotating between each of his students.

'This is Drax,' Mandavar said, gesturing to Drax. 'And Aren.'

Aren hated her name in his mouth.

'They are from Valrue,' Mandavar finished.

'You're kidding,' the blonde woman said.

Mandavar gave her a stern look. 'When have you ever known me to kid, Narium?'

'Not once,' Narium said.

'Now,' Mandavar continued, 'can anyone tell me what's going on?'

Silence rang around the room. Aren wasn't sure what Mandavar meant, but she didn't care. Drax was still tensed beside her, and she could feel her heart picking up a pace it shouldn't be as though he was preparing her to run.

Aren's eyes darted to the exit. Not that she thought they had a chance of escape. If these mayjen were putting Drax on edge like this, she very much doubted he could take on all three at once. And that wasn't counting Mandavar. It was highly unlikely that they would attack, but it was hard to remain calm with Drax pumping her heart the way he was.

'He's a mayj,' said the tall one with the beard suddenly. 'He's a mayj and she's . . . not.' He frowned at Aren. 'I don't understand.'

Mandavar stood up from his seat and walked over to Drax, who looked up at him with his usual blank expression.

'You're right about Drax, Demison,' said Mandavar. 'A lucky guess. His empty cup was a hint.'

More silence.

'He's not powerful,' the shorter, beardless young man chimed up. 'I can't really feel him.'

Narium rolled her eyes. 'That's meaningless, Bodin. He could be running his power down to throw us off.'

'So why's he drinking that then?' Bodin replied, pointing to the empty cup.

Narium rolled her eyes. 'It's obviously to *teach* us something,' she drawled. 'We're in a lecture theatre, are we not?' She missed the dirty look Bodin gave her as she turned to Mandavar, an eyebrow arched. 'Am I right? He's actually powerful, isn't he?'

'You want me to give you the answer?' Mandavar said. 'Not what I expect from one of my students.'

'No,' Narium grumbled, 'that's not what I meant.'

'Take care with what you imply then.'

Narium pinched her lips together.

'Don't worry,' Mandavar said after more silence. 'I don't expect any of you to figure it out. Let's move on. Today we are revisiting atomik majik. You will recall from our last lesson the theoretical aspects of this and how limited they are. Atomik majik is an innate skill, not as definitive as harnessing ability but something that if *I* cannot teach you, then it's unlikely you'll ever manage it. Bodin, you're first.'

Aren couldn't believe that Mandavar had just launched into his lesson. It was as though the conversation he'd been having with his tortured, abandoned son hadn't happened. As much as Aren wanted to storm out and leave, Drax was watching intensely as Bodin stood up and came to stand next to Mandavar. He'd relaxed; she could feel it in her heart. It looked like they were staying. She bit down on her tongue, reluctantly curious to see what this atomik majik stuff was about.

Bodin was waiting for instructions. Mandavar pointed to the empty space before him. 'I want you to create water,' he said. 'Right here.'

'Using the air?'

'I'll not answer that.'

'I'll use the air.'

'Why?'

'Because it's got hydrogen and oxygen.'

'Go on then.'

Bodin rolled his shoulders, then slowly raised his hands before him, lips parted in concentration. His fingers flared around an invisible circle, curling and twitching.

'Using more power won't help,' Mandavar said. 'Feel for the particles.'

Bodin grimaced and refocused on his hands. A minute passed. A little trail of sweat etched its way down his face.

'Well, he's doing it,' Narium said. 'Just not well.'

'Hush, Narium,' said Mandavar, 'you're next.'

Another minute passed, and Bodin's breaths grew laboured, his chest heaving.

'I said you don't need more power,' Mandavar said. 'You'll only warp the particles. Take a break.'

Bodin dropped his hands. 'I think I'm getting closer,' he said.

'Possibly,' Mandavar said. 'The trouble with atomik majik is that unless you are overwhelmingly successful, we'll not see it.' He turned away from Bodin to Narium. 'Your turn.'

Bodin took a seat, a scowl on his face.

Narium stood up and rubbed her hands together. Then she threw them out, and with a twirling of her fingers, a tiny glassy bubble of water sprang into the air before her.

'Good,' Mandavar said. 'More.'

Narium waved her hands wide and brought them together again, and the bubble grew to the size of her fist.

'More.'

Narium's face became serious. Aren watched as delicate blue veins raised themselves from her temples as the ball doubled, then tripled in size.

'You're also using too much power,' Mandavar said.

'It's getting heavy,' Narium replied, her voice tight.

'Would you always use this amount of power to lift that volume of water? Adjust your focus.'

Aren could feel the dryness in the room, the scraping of the air as she breathed it into her lungs.

'Break it,' Mandavar said.

'It will take more power to pull the molecules apart again –'

'You wanted to use more power. Break it.'

Ever so slowly, the bubble of water shrank, tiny wisps of vapour drifting off it into the surroundings. Eventually, it was nothing again. Narium let her arms flop down by her sides, a grin on her face.

'You were close to Turning?' Mandavar asked.

'You told me to do it.'

'I did. But I also expect my students to be more than mindless sheep.'

Narium slumped down into her seat.

Mandavar turned to his final student. 'Demison?'

Demison stood up. He was the same height as Mandavar but much slighter. He had that look young men got when they'd finished growing but before they'd filled out. Aren had thought all three students were about her age – in their early twenties – but now that she focused on him, Demison barely looked out of his teens even with the little beard.

Without a word, Demison shot one hand out towards the floor and then dragged the hand back towards himself. Droplets coalesced and streamed through the air, chasing his hand as he raised it up to the ceiling, bringing his other hand up to meet it. Then he slowly pulled his hands apart, and a pane of water stretched between them, shimmering.

'Pass it here,' Mandavar said.

Demison's eyes flickered to his teacher. With a twist of his hands, the pane became a ball, and he threw it at Mandavar.

Mandavar raised his hand, and the ball stopped before him. Mandavar held it suspended in the air for a second, his hands moving around it, pressing in places. Then Mandavar splayed his fingers and the ball promptly burst into nothing.

'Well done,' Mandavar said. 'Where did you pull the particles from?'

'The stone,' Demison muttered.

'I see. Though the hydrogen would've been easier to extract from the air, having already been concentrated from Narium's efforts.'

'I know.'

Mandavar nodded. 'That's all for today then.'

'What?' Narium stood up, looking unsteady on her feet. 'That was the shortest lesson ever!'

'And whose fault is that?' Bodin asked. 'You want to Turn, is that it?'

'Shut up, Bodin.'

A shadow darkened Demison's face. 'What about Drax?'

Aren felt Drax stiffen next to her.

'Drax won't be harnessing today,' Mandavar said. 'He's observing only.'

'Why?' Demison pressed.

Mandavar fixed him with a stare. 'Because he's not here for your entertainment.'

Aren scowled. No, he was there for Mandavar's. All he'd done was use them as part of the lesson. Sure, the majik had been interesting. It had made *sense*. Noel had at least made sure that Aren had a rudimentary understanding of the elements, and she understood how water boiled. What they'd been doing in the lesson was pretty much the reverse of that. But Aren wasn't about to sit through Mandavar's little games for the sake of learning how majik worked. Drax certainly didn't need to. He knew all of it already.

She stood up, eager to leave, before Mandavar could come near them again. But Mandavar stepped ahead of her and strode up the stone steps. He stopped at the door, looking down on them all. 'And Demison,' Mandavar called, 'I can see you twitching from here. I don't teach fools. Don't come to my class like that again.' He left the room, the heavy door closing behind him.

Aren shot Mandavar a hateful look he didn't see. It gave her some satisfaction, at least.

Drax stood up next to her, his eyes on Narium as she strolled over. Narium stopped before them, hands on her hips. She still looked a little dazed from her near Turning experience. 'So you're from Valrue?' she asked.

'Yes,' Aren said, her eyes following Bodin's well-muscled figure as he walked over to Demison. Demison stood in the corner, inexplicably glaring at Drax.

'That's amazing. How did you get out?'

'Oh, um, it's a long story,' Aren said. She wasn't about to share Bhouli secrets with a stranger.

'I'd love to hear about it sometime. How long have you been here?'

'A day.'

'Well, welcome to Holu Mon. So you're not a mayj yourself?'

Aren paused. 'No.' She felt self-conscious about that, given her lie to Mo Nu.

'Take care then. It's easy to offend people in Holu Mon.'

'I . . . I know what you mean.'

Narium smiled at her, and Aren relaxed a little. Narium seemed friendly, if too inquisitive. But it was nice to come across someone who understood.

'You came in without a chaperone,' Aren said. 'Is that because you're a mayj?'

'That's right. So you've learnt something already.'

'Why are mayjen exempt from slights?' The explanation from Sola and Olmonon hadn't really made sense.

Narium rolled her eyes. 'Because the people of Holu Mon think we are gifts from Gi, put here to correct imbalances and carry out Gi's will. To be honest, I'm not sure I believe it myself, but I can hardly complain. It makes life easier, not having to worry about slighting all the time.'

'About that,' Aren asked quickly, noticing an opportunity, 'is there a list of slights I could read, so I know what *not* to do? I'd rather not go around offending people. I have trouble with that.'

Narium laughed. 'No, we don't have a list. It's just stuff we know, you know?'

Aren was disappointed.

'But if it helps, I can make you one?'

'Yes! Please.' Aren was warming up to Narium quickly. Even though the relationship with her teacher came across as rather tense, Narium seemed just as kind as the rest of the people from Holu Mon and less easy to offend.

And Mandavar would bring out the worst in people.

Narium pointed to the empty silver cup next to Drax. 'Did you like it? Shall I get you another? I think I'll need one anyway. Class took it out of me today.' She ran her eyes over Aren. 'You didn't get one?'

'I'm not harnessing,' Aren said, wondering why Narium would ask that when she knew she wasn't a mayj.

'It's not just for replenishing power. Your body is *so* out of balance. I'm surprised Mo Nu didn't give you one too.'

'My *body* is out of balance?'

'Sure. You're too skinny. You're both too skinny. The drink will help you gain weight.'

Aren stared. 'Excuse me?'

'It's another slight.'

Aren gaped at her. 'You've got to be joking.'

'Not at all.'

Aren groaned, realising what she'd done. 'Mo Nu gave me a drink too, but I was too full to have it. He didn't say anything!'

Narium shrugged. 'He was being polite because you're a guest. But if he could, I'm sure he'd be shoving food down your throat.'

'Is that why he's so . . . um . . . big?'

'Oh no, Mo Nu is way out of balance too. But he hangs around with Fom, and she's skinnier than a stick insect, so they balance each other out.'

Aren's brain jammed with questions.

Just then, Bodin came over to join them. Demison trailed up the stairs, throwing a loaded glance at Drax over his shoulder before disappearing through the doors.

'Hey, I'm Bodin,' Bodin said, smiling at Aren. Up close, she noticed his eyes were bright green. Aren didn't think she'd ever seen green eyes before.

'I know,' Aren said. 'I'm Aren.'

'I know,' Bodin replied with a chuckle. 'Aren is a beautiful name.'

'Oh.' Aren hadn't expected a compliment. 'Thank you.'

Drax was shuffling his feet. He wanted to leave.

'Excuse me,' Aren said to Bodin and Narium. 'Thanks for the offer of the drink, but there is one back in our room. We might see you later?'

'Sure!'

Aren led the way back up the stairs into the corridor. Drax ambled along behind her in silence.

'Drax, what's wrong?'

Drax dipped his head. 'Being around them is hard.'

'Because of their power?'

Drax cocked his head. 'No, that's not why. I know I can't feel them properly right now, but even if I could, I don't think Narium and Bodin are so powerful. Even Demison is not so bad. It's worse because they are all together, but they aren't like Jin.'

Aren didn't like that Jin had become the new standard. But it made it easy to understand what Drax meant.

'Mandavar's power doesn't bother you, then?'

Drax shook his head. 'I think it's because he is my father. Our power is similar.'

'But you can still feel him? Like the others?'

'Today, I can feel him, yes. Yesterday, no. It's okay, Aren,' Drax added. 'I'm not worried about them.'

'I'm glad. They seem kind. Well, Narium and Bodin, anyway. Demison not so much.'

Drax didn't say anything in response. He seemed distracted, staring outside at the trees along the corridors. Aren let him be, holding her questions in tight, knowing that he must be getting tired. It wasn't until they got back to the room, and Drax curled up on the round sofa and fell asleep that Aren realised that he'd not really answered her initial question.

CHAPTER 63:
JIN KANJU

It was a miracle that Jin made it through the parade. The stress of it had aroused his power and left his nerves rattling about his body, bouncing off his bones and leaving sparks of adrenaline in their wake.

Maybe he'd overreacted in thinking that the People wanted to kill him. Maybe not.

They had screamed his name and climbed over one another trying to get to him. Sure, his squad insisted it was because the People wanted to touch him and not because they wanted to rip him to shreds. Crushed Foot had pretty much said the same. But if that were the case, Jin knew it was only temporary. The excitement of the day had got the People carried away, and Jin had gone too many rounds in life to know that their shallow infatuation with him wouldn't last.

As Crushed Foot also said, the People were fickle.

But for now, the happiness of Jin's squad in the wake of the parade was infecting him. For the first time, Jin walked through the corridors of the Keep devoid of the dread that usually accompanied him to training.

With cardonite shards still threatening to pierce any visitors to the cardonite training room, training had been moved into one of the outside courtyards.

Jin arrived alone today, save for Aren and Filip, and he couldn't help but notice Stolt's thunderous face when the KahnenMayj stormed into the courtyard.

'I'd love to know what's wrong with him,' Filip snickered.

Jin didn't know either, but right then, he didn't care because the Eighth House had walked in behind Stolt. Lady Elira was not with them, still shrieking away at her indifferent Krijen guards. She was now imprisoned in the dungeons, having finally harnessed in frustration.

The Great Kahn was not with the Eighth House either.

'Why does that bother you, Jin?' Aren asked. 'Did you want him to come?'

'It doesn't bother me.' But of course, there was no point lying to Aren.

But Jin didn't know why it bothered him. The Great Kahn hated him. He'd made that clear. He helped Jin only because that was what he needed to do for his Kahnen and for his city.

Jin had not forgotten Felle's accusations about the Great Kahn plotting with the skahk, but since speaking to Mama Hidel's women about her, Jin no longer felt any inclination to believe the weeping seductress. For starters, Felle hadn't returned to the Keep. She'd been so desperate to find out what had happened to Dijak, her supposed father-figure, yet she'd not come back to see if Jin would help.

Not that Jin had a clue what Felle expected him to do about it.

And Jin didn't really want to save Dijak if he were still alive. From the way the letter read, he'd spent years doing nothing but protecting Mandavar, who'd started the Unsettlement. So if this Luka person had hurt Dijak, Dijak deserved it.

Jin had decided it was nothing but a convoluted plot to make him suspicious of the Great Kahn, and Jin would not fall for that. Sure, Jin would love to find Mandavar and drown him in the lake, but no one smart enough to concoct a spell that could destroy a city would be stupid enough to stick around. No, Mandavar would be long gone, and Jin would not waste time looking for him.

Aren and Filip had carried on their conversation without him.

'Jin is upset the Great Kahn isn't here because he's the only one who actually knows anything about majik,' Filip said.

'But isn't it strange that the Great Kahn knows so much about it?' Aren asked. 'I mean, he said he knew an exceptional mayj once, but what does that mean?'

'He was the Great Kahn before the Unsettlement,' Jin said, turning away from the Eighth House so that they wouldn't see his lips move. 'He probably learned about majik from the KahnenMayjen before it was suppressed.'

Well, actually, it was the Great Kahn who suppressed it.

But there was no point getting wound up about the Great Kahn not being at training. Jin already had enough heat in his hands. He'd done a little harnessing since the parade but nowhere near enough. He flexed his fingers, feeling the nerves pinch. At least he was about to get some relief.

Jin's squad arrived. He strode over to where they huddled in a circle on the opposite side of the courtyard, wondering why they had stopped so far away. They quietened when he stepped up to them, looking up from their circle.

'What's going on?' Jin asked.

'Just some pre-training tactics, sir,' Pago said innocently.

The comment begged a smile from Jin. 'You're plotting against me?'

Meek grinned back. 'How else do you expect us to win?'

FaKrijen Eden stepped into the courtyard. Jin saw Flit tense, her fingers splayed above her dagger hilts.

'Sir,' Jin called, respectfully raising his hand to his clavicle. His squad did the same.

The FaKrijen strolled over to them. 'Jin,' he said, stopping in front of him. 'I've come to watch. I've been looking forward to seeing what you can do.'

'Yes, sir.'

Eden nodded. 'Carry on.' He walked over to join the Eighth House.

'I don't like him being here,' Aren said.

'You're just anxious because Flit hates him so much,' Filip snapped.

'Isn't that reason enough? Don't you trust Flit?' Aren rebutted.

'Flit scares easy. Eden does what needs to be done. What's wrong with that?'

'Shh, stop it,' Jin muttered to them. He moved to stand in the middle of the courtyard, his squad circling him like they always did, pulling their daggers out. The gleam of metal in the sun sent an unexpected shiver down his spine, but it had been a long time since he'd feared a blade; it was merely his power stirring at the prospect of release. It had a mind of its own, these days.

'Are you ready?' Stolt drawled from across the courtyard.

'Yes.'

'Then what are you waiting for?'

Jin's squad attacked in a fury of movement; all five of them sending their daggers screaming towards him at once. They'd not done that before, probably concerned that Jin couldn't escape ten Krijen daggers. Clearly, they'd moved past that.

Jin threw out his arms and spun, swiping the daggers from the air with majik and sending them spearing between the columns of the courtyard, taking care to avoid curious KahnenMinders who had paused in their daily scurrying to watch. A few of them still shrieked and covered their heads.

With another whip of his hands, Jin tugged on the wraps of his squad, stepping to the side, out of the way. He dragged them together, and they yelled in protest as their black wraps unwrapped from their limbs and twisted tightly about them, winding and weaving between his squad until they were left trussed in the middle of the courtyard.

It had only taken about ten seconds.

'You call that an attack?' Jin asked, lowering his hands and walking up to them. 'I'm rather embarrassed to call you my squad.'

'That was hardly a fair fight,' Meek whined from the back.

'Yeah. You should be blindfolded,' Nommo said. He wriggled furiously, making Flit titter. '*Stop* that,' she snapped. 'You're digging your elbow into my back!'

Jin waved his hands, and the wraps loosened from around his squad.

'I think we should set some rules in place,' Pago said darkly as he pulled his wraps back around himself, Jin having almost completely ripped them from his torso.

'I agree,' Meek said, also tying his wraps back together. 'Jin should be expected to fight half-naked too.'

'Nah, that would only be more distracting,' Nommo said, sending a sly grin towards Flit. Flit made a rude gesture with her hand.

Remembering their audience, Jin quickly turned to face the FaKrijen, worrying about what he might've heard; he didn't want Eden to think his squad were disrespectful. But the FaKrijen was clapping as were the Eighth House, the sound of which drowned out anything else as it echoed around the courtyard.

Stolt stepped forward. 'Again,' he said.

'Is that all you've got to say?' Jin asked. But Filip gave him a warning look. He had to take care not to goad Stolt in front of the FaKrijen.

'*Again,*' Stolt said.

Jin sighed. He flexed his burning hands and was about to give the command to his squad when Lady Maccy cleared her throat. 'To what end?'

Stolt sneered at her. 'The purpose of this training is for your KrijenMayj to get better at majik,' he said. 'To *that* end.'

'Improvement requires a challenge. That was not a challenge. Jin's abilities far outstrip those of his squad. I think it is about time *you* fought him, Stolt.'

Jin couldn't keep the smile off his face. Now *that* sounded fun.

'A valid point,' said Lord Reider. 'He needs practice fighting mayjen, does he not?' The other Kahnen nodded in agreement.

Jin smiled wider. Stolt would not get out of this one.

'I'm up for it,' Jin said.

'No,' Stolt said. 'It is wasteful.'

'That's not an excuse anymore. The Unsettlement is over. You don't need to preserve your power anymore.'

'You idiot,' Stolt said. 'There are only two of us. If we deplete our power during training, who is going to protect the Eighth House in the days while we recover?'

Days? Jin would barely need an hour. 'I've got enough power for both of us,' he said.

'And if one of us is injured?'

'I'll be gentle,' Jin purred.

The look on Stolt's face was *priceless*.

'No,' Eden said, stepping forward. 'The KahnenMayj is right. It's an unnecessary risk, and I'll not compromise the safety of the Kahnen.'

Disappointed, Jin stayed silent.

'I appreciate your caution,' Lord Reider said to Eden. 'But how else can we hope to train Jin or future KrijenMayjen if we are unwilling to accept a little risk? The Squares do it all the time in their bid to become Krijen, do they not?'

'They do.' The FaKrijen tapped his chin in thought. Then a smile stretched across his face. 'I've an idea to give Jin a challenge that doesn't require compromising the strength of both mayjen. If you'll allow me?' he asked Stolt.

Stolt gave a terse nod.

Eden waved over a Minder.

'Yes, sir?'

'You know the weapon's chamber in the KahnenKeep dungeons?'

The Minder swallowed. 'Of course, sir.'

'Go there. Bring me the gloves.'

The Minder ran off.

'The cardonite gloves?' Stolt asked. 'What would be the purpose?'

'Like I said, a challenge. Let's see if Jin can escape them.'

'He won't be able to,' Stolt said. 'He'll not be able to harness.'

'Lord Flynn?' Eden span to face the young Kahn, who looked surprised at being addressed by the FaKrijen. 'You like experiments, don't you? Aren't you interested in seeing this?'

'I guess so,' Lord Flynn replied. 'But like Stolt said, nothing will come of it. The gloves are designed to prevent even the most himajik mayjen from harnessing.'

'That was the theory but to what extent have the gloves been tested?'

'We've used them on three, perhaps four, himajik mayjen.'

'Successfully?'

'Of course.'

'I'm glad. But can anyone speak to the skill of these mayjen? Do we trust the gloves will continue to work as we need them to?'

'Surely, you are the best person to answer that,' said Lord Flynn. 'They are your creation.'

'Hardly,' Eden said. 'I provided the idea, but you' – Eden nodded his head to Stolt – 'you manipulated them into Sid Bha's design. They used to be armour, I believe.'

Stolt nodded.

'But Sid Bha showed little enthusiasm for this design, nor a willingness to stress the mayjen he tested them on,' Eden said. 'So this is the perfect opportunity, isn't it?'

Jin didn't like the sound of that, but the Kahnen nodded their heads in agreement.

Jin looked over at his squad. They were calmly watching Eden, save for Flit, whose tension Jin could see from the way her knees were slightly bent, and the purse of her lips.

The Minder returned quickly with a pair of metallic-looking gloves which were crossed at the wrists. They didn't look particularly intimidating, but Jin remembered the discomfort when Stolt had clamped his hands in the steel from the Krijen dagger blades.

This was cardonite.

The FaKrijen took the gloves from the Minder and walked up to Jin, popping the clasp and swinging the top half of the gloves open. Their black surface flashed dark green under the light as Eden held them out. 'Put them on,' he commanded.

Jin felt a slight discomfort from their proximity already, though much less than how the webbed walls of the cardonite room made him feel. The concentrated power of another mayj.

Jin looked up at the FaKrijen's pointed face.

'You asked for a challenge, Jin,' Filip said.

This wasn't what Jin had had in mind.

'You have to do it,' Filip retorted. 'This is your FaKrijen asking. The fucking *FaKrijen*.'

Filip was right. Jin had no choice. He gingerly placed his hands into the gloves, each finger nestling into a groove. The gloves were cold against his hot skin.

The FaKrijen closed the gloves over his hands, and they made a gentle clicking sound as they locked. It didn't feel so bad. Jin could still wiggle his fingers.

Eden looked over at Stolt. 'Would you mind?'

Stolt stepped forward, making Jin grimace at his closeness. The KahnenMayj held his hands over the gloves, his face slowly turning red. Jin could feel the gloves moving, melding to his hands, his wrists. Stolt dropped his hands and stepped back, breathing deeply.

'Now,' the FaKrijen said, 'let's see if you can get out of them.'

Jin pulse pounded through his fingers. Already his hands were hot to the point of discomfort. He tried to move his fingers. He couldn't. There wasn't a whisper of room.

'I can't,' Jin said, hating the satisfied smirk on Stolt's face.

The Eighth House edged closer to stand alongside Jin's squad, forming a wall around him.

'Take your time,' the FaKrijen said. 'I want you to try properly.'

Jin tried again. It was pointless. His fingers were well and truly immovable; there was no way he could harness with these on.

Still the gloves were heating up. The attack from his squad had stirred his power, and the usual waves of heat rolled down his chest, catching in his hands. It hurt.

'I *can't*,' Jin said again.

'Stay calm,' Aren warned, 'or it will get worse.'

'There, you see?' Stolt said. 'He can't do it.'

Jin couldn't stop his anger from flaring at Stolt's words, and the responding flash of fire in his chest left him gritting his teeth against the fresh sear of it.

'Are you going to let Stolt win this one then?' Filip asked. 'Is that it? You're going to give up?'

'Don't, Jin,' Aren said, 'don't listen to him. If you try harder, it's only going to hurt.'

It already fucking hurts, Jin thought.

'Coward,' Filip muttered.

Jin shook his head. *No. No, that's not what this is.* He wasn't being a coward. He'd dealt with pain before. This was just actually impossible.

'You can push power through your body, correct?' asked Lord Flynn.

Jin looked up at him.

'Oh no,' groaned Aren.

'You can't move your fingers on their own perhaps, but you could bolster them with power,' Lord Flynn suggested. 'Would that give you enough strength to move your fingers under the gloves?'

'I could try it,' Jin said tentatively. It just meant more power, which meant more heat.

'*Don't*,' Aren said. 'Please don't.'

But Jin had to. The FaKrijen, his squad, the Kahnen, and Stolt were all watching. Jin steeled himself. Then he gathered the power that was boiling his chest and slammed it down into his hands.

He nearly screamed. Immediately the pain was so intense, so far beyond what he'd been expecting, beyond what he'd realised was even possible, that Jin's instinctive reaction was to stop.

'You can't stop!' Filip yelled. 'You've started now, you can't stop!'

So Jin rode over instinct and shoved more power down his arms, willing his fingers to move, but the rivers of fire channelling from his chest did nothing but build in his hands, the heat spilling back up his arms. A strangled moan escaped him.

Still the cardonite didn't budge.

'Jin, stop, *please*,' Aren begged. 'It's not possible!'

'I know, I know!' Jin cried, his voice rising; his panic laid bare. 'I can't do it, I can't do it!'

'Take them off him,' Jokah said to Stolt, stepping forward.

'Not yet,' the FaKrijen said, holding up a hand.

'But, sir –'

Fear was shuddering down Jin, making him pull against the gloves and whimper despite himself. He felt the FaKrijen press in closer to him.

'How are you not curious about this?' Eden said quietly in his ear. 'Don't you want to know if you can do it?'

The Eighth House were muttering incoherently around them.

'How can you call yourself a KrijenMayj,' Eden went on, 'yet let a pair of gloves best you?'

And so, even as a scream threatened in his throat once more, Jin pushed harder, forcing out more power, feeding the agony in his hands until the monster in his chest roared.

Vaguely, in the background, Jin could hear yelling.

'Sir, please!'

'We need to do something –'

'Stolt –'

'*Someone get them off of him!*'

'What is going on here?'

And even though Jin knew he shouldn't, that tiny bit of faulty human still left in him tried to make him stop. But it was no use. Power was erupting from him, the pain was pressing on it, and Jin was caught up in its waves but this time he couldn't turn it off, he couldn't end it, and the bliss didn't come to save him because he'd given up like the coward that his father always told him he was –

'STOLT, DO SOMETHING!'

Someone else was screaming now. Or maybe it was Jin. He staggered into someone, and hands grabbed at him and he fought back because maybe if he hurt them enough, then someone would take a dagger and shove it through his heart.

But then Jin remembered he'd tossed the daggers all away into the depths of the courtyard, and he'd left his squad weaponless, and he shouldn't expect that someone would want to save him anyway because after what he'd done to Aren, and Bish, and Wren, and Filip, and his mother, that sort of mercy was far more than he deserved.

And with that, Jin sank beneath the black waves, a roar tearing from his throat.

CHAPTER 64:
AREN BHA

Wren's hands were so gloriously warm. They were sliding down the curve of Aren's spine, his thumbs trailing her hips. Aren wanted him to go further.

But Wren was teasing her.

His hands dropped away, leaving cold spots on her skin. Aren fussed, delightfully annoyed. She grabbed at him, wanting to drag him back and have his hands on her again.

But Wren wasn't there.

Aren reached out, feeling for him. She tried calling his name, but he didn't answer. That wasn't like Wren. He never kept her waiting. Try as he might, he never could tease her for long because he gave into her almost as fast as she gave into him. This was something else. There was something wrong.

'Wren,' Aren said. 'Wren!'

'Aren,' came a voice. It wasn't Wren's. 'Aren. Aren, wake up!'

Aren opened her eyes and sat up.

It was a week after they'd arrived at Holu Mon, and they were in their round bedroom at the University. Aren was tangled in their bedsheets, and Drax was tugging at her with limp hands. 'Aren!' Drax said, his eyes wide, panicked. 'Aren, you're bleeding!'

'Huh?'

Aren looked down. There were smears of blood all over the sheets. She quickly stood up, stepped onto the floor, and pulled around her nightdress, spotting the evidence.

Drax was beside himself, his hands all over her, looking for the wound.

'You're hurt, Aren! Where are you hurt? I will help –'

'It's okay, Drax,' Aren said. 'It's just my monthly.'

She'd been a little worried, she had to admit. She and Wren had done their best to be careful. Wren was fastidious with proper precautions, even that first time when he'd spent a painful number of minutes digging through the first-aid kit under her bed to find something, *anything*, that they could use, while Aren lay naked on the bed wondering if this was what all romance was like.

The last time they'd had sex hadn't been long before she'd left Valrue, so it was a relief to know a pregnancy wasn't the culprit behind her missing monthly. No, it had been stress.

'Shh, Drax, I promise it's all right,' Aren said gently. 'It's completely normal.'

'You're bleeding!' Drax cried.

'Yes. Give me a minute and I'll explain.'

Aren grabbed a pile of clean black and white clothes from the bedroom shelves and ducked into the bathroom, stripping off her nightgown and underwear. She rummaged through the drawers in there, finding a stash of cloths that surely could serve no other purpose.

'Aren?' Drax's voice floated from outside.

'Almost done,' Aren replied. She padded fresh underwear and pulled on the clean clothes, before gathering the dirty ones into her arms and opening the door.

Drax flitted around her while she walked to the bed, intending to strip the sheets. But the blood was gone. 'Did you harness these clean already?' She turned to Drax. He cringed into his shoulders. 'Was I not supposed to?'

'No, it's fine,' Aren said. 'It's just that you didn't have to. I was going to deal with it.'

'What's happening, Aren?'

Aren dropped the dirty clothes into the hamper in the corner of the room and then sat on the edge of the bed. 'Sit down, Drax,' she said, patting the bed next to her. It felt like a sitting conversation.

Drax sat.

Aren wasn't sure where to start. Drax hadn't exactly gone through the normal stages of growing up, so she wasn't sure what he knew.

So she started from puberty. She watched as Drax's expression changed from concern back to his usual blank state.

'So the blood is good?'

'It means I'm not pregnant. So yes, it's good,' she reassured him.

'How do you get pregnant?'

Aren gaped at him.

For the first time, Drax's white cheeks tinged pink.

'Sorry, sorry,' Aren said quickly, berating herself. He couldn't have been expected to learn that during his years imprisoned in the KahnenKeep. But he must know something about it because she remembered his reaction back at her family home when they'd agreed Drax could stay with them.

'I remember you offering to sleep in my room when we first met,' Aren said carefully. 'But you didn't seem to want to.'

Drax's face darkened. 'You're talking about sex,' he said.

'Yes,' Aren said, feeling the heat rising in her own cheeks. 'Well, sex is how you get pregnant.'

Drax said nothing.

'You . . . you know what sex is, right?'

'Yes. I don't like it.'

'Oh.' Aren suspected it was because of Felle.

'You like it?' Drax asked.

'Um, well yes, I think most people do.'

'Am I supposed to like it?'

Aren reached out and took Drax's limp hands in hers. 'I think that would be nice. But I understand why you don't.'

Drax cocked his head. 'You did it with Wren?'

Aren nodded.

'If I do it with Wren, I will like it?'

Aren burst out laughing. 'I'm sorry Drax,' she said when she finally caught her breath. 'It's a fair question. You might. But I'm not sure if Wren will agree to it.'

'Because he's yours?'

It was a blunt way to say it, but Aren knew what Drax meant. 'I want him to be.'

'He is. You want to get back to him, don't you?'

'Very much.'

'Then we need to go speak with my father.'

Aren's good mood evaporated instantly. She dropped Drax's hands. 'Fine.' She couldn't put it off any longer. This is what they came for, after all. She was being selfish in procrastinating. Drax needed to be free of her. 'Let's go find him.'

Aren stood up and waited while Drax pulled on his own set of black and white clothes. The neckline gaped wide on his scarred skeletal frame, and it sent a fresh wave of hatred rolling through Aren, a reminder of the role that Mandavar had played in allowing the mutilation of his son.

It wasn't hard to find Mandavar. Mo Nu had pointed out the building containing the staff offices a few days ago. Aren led them out through the doors into the green grounds of the University. They wound down a path and merged with a flow of students, keeping a careful gap as they headed into the round building.

Word had obviously spread of her and Drax because Aren could feel eyes on her, and she could see them on Drax, who took it in his stride. He was more familiar with being stared at.

Thankfully, they quickly left the crowds and passed through a pair of massive double doors, where Drax closed his eyes, concentrating. 'I think . . . I think I feel him now.' He walked them down one more corridor, around a corner, and stopped abruptly.

'Are we here?' Aren asked. They were standing before a large wooden door with a gold handle.

'Yes, but someone else is here.'

Aren paused, listening. She could hear more than one voice on the other side. She pressed her ear up against the door.

Suddenly she heard footsteps, and Aren leapt back as the door burst open, startled to see Demison standing in front of her. His eyes narrowed and flickered to Drax. Aren was impressed that Drax didn't cower into the floor at the vicious look on Demison's face.

After a tense few seconds, Demison stepped out of the doorframe and swept away down the corridor.

'Come in,' came Mandavar's voice.

Aren followed Drax inside.

Mandavar's office was large and spacious, and of all things, square. Bookcases lined the shelves, laden with volumes so enormous that surely their only purpose was to intimidate.

To Aren's surprise, the office was a mess. Scrolls were strewn across the room, and the desk in front of Mandavar had black ink spilt across it, dripping down the sides of the wood onto the floor.

Mandavar stood behind his desk. He flicked his wrist as Aren and Drax stepped inside, and the door closed behind them. Then he waved his hands, and the mess tidied before them. Aren watched, reluctantly fascinated, as the ink seeped back up the desk into its pot, which had righted itself.

Mandavar lowered his hands and rested his knuckles on his desk. 'Take no notice of Demison,' he said. 'He's upset with me.'

'What did you do?' Aren asked, unable to stop herself.

'I told him something he didn't want to hear. But he's not listening. He's young and arrogant.'

'Youth doesn't determine arrogance,' Aren said. 'You're the perfect example of that.'

Mandavar raised an eyebrow. 'You've taken quite a disliking to me,' he said. 'I don't care.' He stepped out from behind his desk and approached them. Drax moved to stand in front of Aren. Mandavar stopped. 'You don't trust me, son?'

'No.'

'So why are you here?'

'We need your help,' Drax said quietly.

Mandavar leaned back against his desk, folding his arms before him. He waited.

Aren kept her jaw clenched firmly shut. She didn't trust herself to say anything.

Eventually, Mandavar spoke again. 'Typically, when people ask for help, they explain what it is they need.' He gestured to Aren. 'Something to do with this, I assume?'

Aren's simmering anger quickly boiled over. '*This?* How dare you!'

'You are very loud, for a cadaver,' Mandavar said.

'A cadaver?' Aren scoffed. 'Is that your best attempt at an insult?'

'It's not an insult. It's a statement of fact. You are dead, so I've no other name for what you are.'

Words were momentarily lost on Aren. She soon found them. 'Are you *insane?*'

'So you didn't know you were dead,' Mandavar said. 'Your innate power is gone. I noticed when I harnessed you.'

Aren spun to Drax, hoping for support. To her horror, his head slowly cocked to the side and his eyes widened as though he'd come to a sudden realisation.

'Drax?' Aren asked, her voice faltering. 'Is . . . is this true? Am I dead?'

Drax's head shrank into his shoulders. 'Maybe.'

'*Maybe?*'

'Mo Nu mentioned innate power before. I wasn't sure what he meant.'

Aren swung back around to Mandavar. His expression hadn't changed, and he didn't reply immediately, clearly brewing on some thought. Aren longed to know what was going through his head.

'Innate power is something that every living thing has,' Mandavar said finally. 'Animals have more than plants. Humans have more than other animals. Mayjen, of course, have more than non-mayjen. They use the excess for majik, and some mayjen have a greater excess of innate power than others.' He looked pointedly at Aren. 'You have none. Therefore, by definition, you are no longer a living thing. So if I'm not wrong, you died at some point.'

Aren ogled him. 'How do you know that?'

'I felt resistance when I harnessed you, but not enough that I would consider it Influencing. You know the term?'

'Yes,' Aren said stiffly.

'It was rather like pushing against a small tree. There was something there, but nothing noteworthy. I soon realised I was feeling Drax's power as he transferred it to you. I could feel him too but only just.'

Drax blinked at him.

'Your power is dulled, spent on her,' Mandavar said. 'But still, I felt you. So not only does that suggest you have substantial power' – the corners of Mandavar's mouth pulled up a little – 'but the fact that you're harnessing without your hands displays an enviable grasp of cognitive dexterity. It threw me, at first. I've never seen that before.' In a strange juxtaposition to his smile, Mandavar sounded vaguely annoyed.

'Wait,' Aren said, thinking about the majik that had ravaged Valrue. 'About the innate power thing. I thought humans didn't run from an excess of majik because they were the source of power themselves, but if all living things have it, why did only humans survive in Valrue?'

'That is an old and thoroughly disproved theory,' Mandavar said. 'It sounds like something the KahnenMayjen of Valrue used to spout.'

Aren frowned. Noel had told her that theory.

'The truth about why humans survive an excess of majik is not known. Humans are an anomaly in that way as we are in many other ways. Probably a mutation of sorts,' he added dismissively. 'Now, I've answered your questions. And if you want my help, you'll answer mine. Firstly, I want a full explanation of how you're doing *this*.' He gestured to Aren again.

'I thought you knew what was going on?' Aren snapped.

'When did I say that?'

Aren ground her teeth.

'Come,' Mandavar said, inclining his head to a door just behind his desk. He looked at Drax's hunched stance. 'I imagine it's not comfortable for you to stand for long.'

Drax followed him, Aren trailing reluctantly behind.

The door led into a square lounge. The ceiling glittered just like the one in Aren and Drax's room. *This man left a city to rot while he enjoyed these riches*, Aren thought viciously. She hated him. Hated him, hated him, hated him –

They settled on the couch across from Mandavar, who occupied an armchair, crossing one leg over the other in a regal fashion.

'So tell me –'

'So yeah, I died,' Aren interrupted, sick of Mandavar's voice. 'I got slashed with a dagger, deep enough that it got my heart. Drax harnessed me back together, and now he keeps my heart going because apparently, I don't have any *innate power*, so it can't beat by itself anymore. We needed to find a way to make my heart beat on its own again and were told Holu Mon was the place to go.'

Aren expected Mandavar to ask who told them to come to Holu Mon. Instead, he looked to Drax. 'How long have you been doing this?'

Drax shuffled his feet, glancing at Aren.

'Maybe two or three months,' Aren replied for him.

'And how are you doing it?' Mandavar asked.

Drax blinked.

'What do you mean?' Aren asked.

'How are you making her heart beat? Are you actively compressing the muscles?'

Aren had no idea. She looked at Drax, who cocked his head in thought. 'No,' he said.

'Then how are you doing it?'

Drax hesitated. 'I don't know how to say it.'

Mandavar raised an eyebrow. 'You don't understand what you're doing?'

'He understands it,' Aren retorted. 'He just struggles with the right words.'

Mandavar stared at Aren, a line of concentration between his eyes. Then he stood up from his armchair and knelt in front of her. Horrified, she pressed herself back into the couch. 'Get away from me!'

'I can tell you exactly what he's doing if you'll allow me to touch you.'

'I'd rather die!'

'You might get your wish,' Mandavar said dryly.

Aren felt a tug on her arm. 'Aren,' Drax said. 'Please?'

Her resolve withered as she looked at his blue eyes, begging her. She turned to Mandavar. 'Why do you need to touch me?'

'I'm not like my son. I need my hands.' His lips twitched again. 'I imagine that is how you are harnessing her heart while you sleep, yes? You do not need your hands to direct your majik, unlike the rest of us.'

That was exactly what Noel had said. Aren didn't miss the bitter tone that Mandavar had used again. 'What are you feeling for?' she asked sharply.

'I doubt you'll understand the explanation.'

'Try me,' Aren snarled.

'I am feeling for the strength of the bonds between the atoms of your heart.'

'Atoms? You mean the matter?'

'Yes.'

'And what will that tell you?' Aren asked suspiciously.

'What kind of bonds they are and therefore, what kind of majik it is.' Mandavar glared at her. 'Trust me. I get no pleasure from this.'

Aren glared back. 'All right. Fine.'

Mandavar reached out his hand and carefully placed it on Aren's chest. He was unnaturally warm. It might've even felt pleasant, except for the fact it was Mandavar.

Mandavar closed his eyes. Aren watched the back of his eyelids as they moved. She could feel his fingertips twitching on her collarbone.

Drax had edged so close to Aren on the couch that he was leaning on her, tensed into her side. He suddenly flinched, and there was the tiniest skip in her heartbeat. Drax gave Mandavar another dark look that he didn't see, his eyes still closed.

'What was that?' Aren asked.

'I had to push,' Mandavar said.

Aren wished she knew what that meant.

After another minute, Mandavar opened his eyes, pulling his hand back from Aren. Then he looked at Drax. 'You really don't know what you do?'

Drax shook his head.

'You are Weaving.'

Drax stared at him blankly.

'Well,' Mandavar went on, 'it is Weaving done in a way that I've never seen before. Who taught you that?' His voice was suddenly sharp.

Drax blinked. 'I was not taught.'

'Not possible,' Mandavar said. 'You can't simply discover something like this.'

'Don't you *dare*,' Aren hissed, her anger flaring again. 'Drax doesn't lie!'

'Everyone lies,' Mandavar said. 'Even in Holu Mon, as slightful as it is. They have simply learnt how not to get caught.'

'*No!*' Aren was on her feet, raging. 'Drax doesn't lie! You think someone taught him? Who do you suggest did that? You realise that after you trapped your power in the lake, the Eighth House burned all the literature on majik? That they strung up anyone who dared to so much as mention the word? That all the KahnenMayjen left the city?'

Aren was breathing hard with exertion, wishing with all her might that she was a mayj like Drax and she could smite Mandavar as he deserved.

Mandavar was quiet. He stared at Drax for a long time, who stared back. Aren was so proud of him for not looking away.

Then Mandavar gave a gentle chuckle and stood up. He crossed back to his chair and collapsed into it, running his hands across his smooth face and gazing at nothing across the room. 'Oh, Luka,' he muttered, 'and you tried so hard to ruin my son.' He looked back to them again. 'So, Weaving. You understand the concepts of Breaking and Building, at least?'

'Yes, Mo Nu explained them the other day,' Aren said shortly, carefully settling herself back down on the sofa. 'He said there were three expressions of harnessing, but he only explained two. Is Weaving the third?'

'Yes,' Mandavar replied, 'Weaving is the third and the rarest. The one that eludes our full understanding. You recall that Building is the creation of bonds between matter that mimic natural bonds?'

Aren nodded.

'Weaving is the creation of special bonds that defy the normal rules of nature. As an example, cardonite is infinitely harder than diamond, yet diamond is the hardest natural substance. It is astounding majik. I think the skill of a Weaver is required to fix your heart.'

'Okay then,' Aren said. 'Are there any Weavers in Holu Mon?'

'Yes, one,' Mandavar replied. 'Me.'

Of course. 'So,' Aren said, a bitter taste in her mouth, 'can you help us?'

'Yes,' Mandavar said. 'I think I can.'

CHAPTER 65:
THE GREAT KAHN

It had been a long time since the Great Kahn had been this angry; it was as though he'd taken Luka and throttled him, and every Minder in the KahnenKeep could sense the murder. So again, they fled before him, like they used to.

But Luka was not dead. No, Luka was very much alive.

And that was part of the problem.

The Eighth House sat in their seats in the Red Room, silently watching while the Great Kahn paced. For reasons unknown, Lady Macey had taken to wearing a floral scent, and the stench burned the Great Kahn's nostrils. The wasteful expense of it was unseemly, especially in the wake of Lady Elira's Reckoning. So far from reality, his Kahnen sat.

That was about to change.

'I have made up my mind,' the Great Kahn said to them. 'It must be done. Lady Elira shamed herself and shamed us. She admitted to her crimes, but her repents are insincere. She thinks I will provide an exception because she is a Kahn. I will not.'

'You made an exception for Jin,' Lady Macey said. 'Before he was the KrijenMayj.'

Except that he had not. Oji had done that.

'Jin saved my citizens,' the Great Kahn said. 'Lady Elira mocked them.'

'She has been loyal to the Eighth House for many years,' Lord Reider said. 'Surely she deserves –'

'If you call what she did loyalty, I cannot help but question your understanding of the word. Or do you consider this loyalty in comparison to something else? Is there something I do not know, Lord Reider?'

'No, my Great Lord.'

Lord Salli was unusually silent today. The Great Kahn turned his gaze to the heavy-browed man. 'You have no comments on this occasion?'

'No, my Great Lord. Lady Elira all but demanded this pyre.'

Lord Flynn shifted in his seat. 'Pyre?'

'Fire is one of the few substances a mayj cannot control,' Lord Salli said. 'FaKrijen Eden thought it a fitting way to carry out the execution.'

Not true, the Great Kahn thought. A mayj could pull the oxygen from the air around the fire to starve the flames. But he doubted anyone in the city would know that, and it would likely be beyond the capabilities of any mayj who did. It was atomik majik, after all.

'That seems unnecessarily cruel,' said Lord Flynn softly.

'I agree,' the Great Kahn said. 'I will not have that. I will speak with the FaKrijen.' He had once considered Eden nothing but an interesting pawn piece given his sadistic tendencies, but with Jin's screams still ringing in his head and the smell of burnt flesh lingering in the corridors, the Great Kahn had taken an intense disliking to the FaKrijen.

The Great Kahn shuddered to think what might have happened had he not been called by a traumatised Minder to that courtyard to see Jin writhing on the ground, his squad holding him down in their desperation to get the gloves off him. Stolt had stood there, pale-faced, the horror of the scene having wiped all sense from him until the Great Kahn bellowed a command.

That was the problem with Luka. He tempted the Great Kahn's pity for the KrijenMayj. The Great Kahn did not overly like it. Sympathy was a weakness, especially sympathy for a mayj. But a necessary burden to get Luka back.

'The gloves are ruined,' Lord Salli was saying. 'Stolt tore them in his panic, and apparently he does not have the means to fix them. How are we supposed to restrain Lady Elira?'

'In the usual fashion,' the Great Kahn said. 'She is not himajik. Clamp her hands in iron.' *How do they think the Krijen have kept her imprisoned thus far?* he thought. Their ongoing ignorance of majik astounded him. Even watching Jin's training sessions every week, they took nothing from it but entertainment, other than perhaps Lord Flynn. But he was too terrified to speak on the topic since the Great Kahn had warned him off it in the KahnenLibrary all those months ago.

'How is the KrijenMayj?' Lord Bajeridine asked. 'How are his hands?'

'It is hard to say,' the Great Kahn said. 'Everything has been done that can be done, at this stage.'

'Surely Stolt can use majik to heal –'

'*No.*'

'Will Jin still be able to harness, my Great Lord?' Lady Macey asked.

So long as the nerve pathways in his hands healed, then yes. But the Great Kahn had to be careful. If he entertained too many questions about majik, they might start asking how he knew all the answers.

'Possibly. Time will tell. But it will be difficult for him to grip a weapon.'

The room fell into silence with nothing but the Great Kahn's pacing footsteps. A Krijen unable to wield a weapon was no Krijen at all.

'It is a good thing he is a mayj then,' Lord Reider said. 'Where is he now?'

'A room near the KahnenChambers to allow more space for his cares. As KrijenMayj, it is fitting for him to have a larger room anyway, not sharing a bunkroom.'

'And nothing is to be done about the FaKrijen, my Great Lord?' asked Lord Flynn.

The Great Kahn stopped pacing. He slowly turned to face the young Kahn. 'What is it you would have me do?'

Lord Flynn shrank into his chair. 'I-I do not know, my Great Lord. I just expected there would be repercussions for this.'

'Repercussions? For the FaKrijen, who gave an order to one of his Krijen, who willingly obeyed?'

'But what he did was wrong.'

Yes, the Great Kahn thought. *It was very wrong.* And it was this that made him even more furious, on top of the actions of Lady Elira, because this wrongness had been orchestrated by the Eighth House.

'We knew what Eden was when we gave him this position,' the Great Kahn said. 'I am not pleased by his actions, but as FaKrijen, Eden has every right to do with his Krijen as he wishes. That is how the law works. You know that.'

Lord Flynn was silent.

'When is Lady Elira's execution, my Great Lord?' asked Lord Salli.

'A few days away.'

'You do not think we are sending mixed messages to the People?' Lord Reider challenged. 'Forgive me, my Great Lord, but first, you told the Krijen to stand down to the mayjen killings. Since then, we have announced our KrijenMayj, and it is growing clearer that the Unsettlement is over. Is it right to follow all of this with the execution of another mayj?'

The Great Kahn pursed his lips. It was unlike Lord Reider to be so argumentative. 'Lady Elira is not being punished for being a mayj.'

'No, but that needs to be made abundantly clear. Our mayjen citizens have suffered for far too long. This is the perfect opportunity to announce the end of the Unsettlement. The KrijenMayj is right. It is time.'

Lord Reider's words came out with such blunt force that the Kahnen all seemed to hold their breath, the sole exception being Lord Salli, who bristled in his seat. It was a daring statement to make, especially when the Great Kahn was so obviously incensed.

Ironically, the Great Kahn suppressed a smile. His Kahnen were no longer stymied by their fear of him. Luka's efforts were coming to fruition.

'I will not turn Lady Elira's death into a celebration by announcing the end of the Unsettlement in the wake of her execution,' the Great Kahn said. 'But I agree. It is nearly time.'

CHAPTER 66:
AREN BHA

'I don't want to do it, Drax.'

'You don't want to be saved?'

'It's too dangerous. I'm not risking it! If I die, everything we've been through in the last few months has been for nothing.'

'You're lying.'

'What?'

'You're lying. You take risks, Aren. And you tried to die before when you ran from me in the forest. Dying is not what you're afraid of.'

Aren ground her teeth. Since when had Drax become so insightful? Well no, he'd always been insightful. The difference was that now he called her on it when she wasn't being reasonable. She blushed under his gaze.

'What is *actually* wrong?' he asked. If Aren weren't so wound up, the inflection in his voice would make her smile. He was learning fast.

'Mandavar is wrong,' Aren replied. 'Everything about him is wrong. You know how he asked us to come to his class? He wasn't interested in teaching you anything. He just wanted to show you off. And it's horrible how he treats his students, playing them off each other!'

'You're still not saying what you mean.'

Aren sighed and took Drax's hands in hers. They were sitting next to each other on the couch in their room again. They spent far too much time in there, but Aren was nervous to leave, worried she might mess up and offend someone again.

'I can't say it. It's too selfish.'

'Please, tell me.'

Drax had gotten ever so good at the pleading-eye thing. And Aren owed him the truth.

'Well, you know how Mandavar says that he can Weave some power into my heart? Like that spell he used on the lake, the Du Bellor whatsit?'

Drax nodded.

'Doesn't that mean that I'll be walking around with a bit of *him* inside me?' Aren grimaced. 'The idea of it makes me feel disgusting.'

So did her selfishness because she knew this was selfish. It was possibly the most selfish thing she'd ever done, denying them help only because it was Mandavar who offered.

Drax's mouth turned down slightly at the corners. 'It's okay, Aren. I understand.'

'You remember he said he'd have to keep doing it, right? My heart isn't big enough to hold sufficient power for it to be self-sustaining. So once my heart uses up the power, I'd have to come back so he can redo the spell. And how often? Every year? Every month? Every week? I'd be trapped here, Drax!' Aren dropped Drax's hands and moaned into her own. 'I can't do it! I'm sorry, I'm so sorry!'

Drax looked at the floor, his shoulders sagging. 'Really, Aren, it's okay. It's *okay*.'

Aren wiped her eyes. She'd never thought of herself as a crier, but since about a year ago, apparently, she'd become one. And it was getting worse. Maybe it was because, more than ever, she felt like a burden. A useless, pointless, good-for-nothing burden. And now she was kicking up a fuss about how to go about *not* being said burden.

What am I doing? Aren thought. Was this really the person she wanted to be? Because right now she was acting like that stuck-up, spoilt little rich girl she hated. No.

'I take it back,' Aren said. 'I take it back. Mandavar said he could fix my heart, so let's do it. I don't care if I'm stuck here. If you're free of me, that's all that matters.' Aren nodded determinedly to herself. She would live here in Holu Mon alone. She would probably never see her mother and father again. She would never see Wren again, and that *hurt*. But she'd had enough happiness and luck to last anyone a lifetime. It was someone else's turn.

'Aren, you're panicking.'

Aren looked up at Drax, sniffling. 'What?'

'You're panicking, so you're being silly. You feel guilty because this is something you want, not something you need, and you don't think you're being fair to me. But that's okay because I was being unfair in the forest. You had to kill animals alone because I didn't want to help.' Drax nudged his limp hands into hers again. 'But I think there is another way.'

'What do you mean?'

'My father said I was Weaving. That's how I keep your heart going. Maybe he could teach me how to do the Du Bellor Spell. I could Weave your heart properly, then we could leave Holu Mon, and we wouldn't have to come back.'

Aren's heart pounded at the thought. 'You think that's possible?'

Drax cocked his head. 'I think so.' He frowned. A real, proper frown. 'I'd have to learn how to do it, and I don't know how long it will take. Is it okay if we stay longer?'

'If you would do that for me Drax, then of course we can stay longer. But . . .' Aren winced. 'But you'll still be stuck with me because you'll have to regularly redo the spell. Not quite as stuck as you are now, but near enough.'

'I'm never stuck with you.' Drax nodded. 'We will always be friends. And I don't want you to be trapped here. You need to be happy. That's very important.' He cocked his head, giving her the tiniest of real smiles. 'I love you. That's what I say, right? Because I care?'

Aren blinked in surprise. Then she laughed through her tears and pulled Drax into a hug. 'Yes, that's exactly right. I love you too.'

CHAPTER 67:
JIN KANJU

There was a knock on the door.

Jin didn't bother to answer. No one cared what he wanted. People came and went as they pleased. They didn't give a shit that he didn't want to see anyone, ever again.

'Jin? Jin, can I come in?'

But that wasn't the voice of a Minder or Flit or Jokah or even a member of his squad at all. It was Lottie's voice.

The door opened, and Lottie's head peeked inside, her blonde hair lit up by the light streaming in behind her. 'Jin? Are you in here?'

There were no windows in this enormous room. Jin expected they gave this one to him to keep him safe from prying eyes, but despite the empty space the inability to see beyond the walls did nothing but make him feel trapped, adding to the suffocation of being in a body smothered by power that ravaged him any way it wanted.

'I'm coming in.'

The door closed and the blackness returned, and Jin could hear Lottie's gentle footsteps across the floor, approaching the bed.

Jin curled back into the headboard. It was strange. Jin had spent so long longing for her, but now that she was here, he didn't want to be touched.

'Go away, Lottie. I didn't say you could come in.'

'Well, that's hardly fair,' came her voice. 'You always used to burst in on me.'

Jin could sense her by the bed and felt a tug on the sheets, and her cold body slipped in beside him. Well, Jin suspected she wasn't cold. She just felt that way to him.

'I heard what happened,' Lottie said. 'I'm so sorry.'

Jin didn't reply. A lot of sorrys had been thrown around lately. Jin didn't know what people expected it would do. He used to say it too. He'd said it to Bish when he admitted he'd interfered in Bish's Dancing Ceremony. Jin had said sorry to Aren on the day he'd killed her.

It changed nothing. The punishment followed him around regardless, which was nothing more than Jin deserved.

'Aren't you going to ask me what I'm doing out of the dungeons?' Lottie asked.

'What're you doing out of the dungeons?'

'Nommo came to the women. He said you needed help. So he snuck me out and brought me to you.'

It was too much to expect that the women had been pardoned. It didn't matter that the Unsettlement was over. It still hadn't been announced, leaving the People with an excuse to go back to hating him. That way, the Kahnen could get rid of him more easily when they'd had enough.

'That's not right, Lottie. You've just spent months in a dungeon. The last place you should be is with me.'

'Yet here I am,' Lottie said.

'I don't want anything from you right now.'

'No, but you need it. Now shift yourself.'

Jin obliged, sitting up and moving forward so that Lottie could slide herself in behind him, resting against the headboard. Jin carefully leaned back into her, his head tucked below her chin. It felt nice, like it always used to.

Jin was glad it was dark. Aren knew about the women, but she didn't need to see it if Jin could help it. She was in here somewhere with Filip. They'd been quiet lately. They knew Jin didn't want to talk much right now. Maybe that was part of the reason Jin never lit the lamps. He could convince himself he was alone in the dark.

Save for the ringing in his head.

At first, he'd thought maybe the ringing was something to do with majik because it hadn't always been there and had grown worse with time. But that made it sound special, and it certainly wasn't. It was more likely tinnitus, a gift from his father from being hit in the head too many times.

Lottie's cold hands ran over his shoulders and across his chest, but instead of running down his torso like they normally wound, they turned and made their way back up towards his neck, then went through his hair. Lottie's fingers caught in the knots of it.

'Everyone wants to talk to me,' Jin said. 'I don't want to talk.' He didn't want to *think*.

'I know.'

She kept running her hands through his hair, working through the knots. Flit had done that too when she'd braided it.

Aren had never played with his hair. It would've felt too intimate between them for her. But it would've been nice if she had.

Lottie didn't ask about Jin's hands. Instead, she gently trailed her fingers back down his shoulders and towards his elbows. Jin stiffened but pulled his arms back anyway, so her fingertips trailed to the bandages at his wrists.

'They must hurt.'

'No.' It wasn't a lie. They didn't hurt because Jin had melted his nerve endings away. And Lottie wasn't really asking if they hurt. She was asking if she could touch them.

'I missed these hands,' Lottie said as she ran her fingers over the ridge of the bandages. 'You're ever so good with them.'

Jin tried not to shudder away. 'They're ruined,' he said.

'You don't know that yet.'

'I fucking know it, Lottie,' Jin growled.

'Jin,' Aren's voice warned from the darkness. 'Don't be unkind.'

Jin didn't have enough energy to feel guilty about it. But it was okay because Lottie stayed with him.

'Lottie?'

'Yes?'

'You're actually here, aren't you?'

She giggled. 'What do you mean? Of course, I'm actually here.'

Lottie gently kissed the back of his neck and nosed her face into the hollow behind his ear as though to prove it to him.

But after a few minutes of this, Jin turned his head, so his ear was pressed up against her chest because with her silence and the coldness of her touch, the thrum of her heart was the only thing convincing him she was real.

CHAPTER 68:
FAKRIJEN EDEN

'What do you want?'

'Now, now,' Eden said, 'that's no way to speak to your FaKrijen. Come in. Close the door.'

The door closed, and footfalls moved across the carpet.

'Why did you do it? Was it because of the Squares? Or was it because he freed that mayj woman from her restraints in the dungeons?'

'Oh?' Eden asked. 'You're talking about what happened with the gloves?'

'Of course, I'm talking about the fucking gloves!'

Eden tapped his dagger hilts. 'If you raise your voice to me again, I'll give you cuts, and then you'll have to explain them to him. I can't imagine that would be a pleasant conversation.'

Silence.

'But you want the truth?' Eden asked. 'No. The gloves were an innocent experiment. I actually thought he might get out of them.' But he hadn't. Maybe it would help the KrijenMayj finally learn his place. 'But you've reminded me of an intriguing question,' Eden went on. 'What is it about those women?'

Of course, there was no answer.

Eden sighed. 'Look, we both know you don't want to be here,' he said. 'But need I remind you *why* you come?'

'I don't know what it is about the women. They're just special to him.'

'Special? They are whores.'

'He doesn't like that word.'

'Good to know,' Eden said. 'Does he have a favourite?'

A pause. 'The mayj woman. The blonde one.'

'I could've guessed as much. But how do you know?'

'She was in his room the other day.'

'How did she get there, I wonder?'

'It wasn't him, sir.'

'Hm. Well, she can't have got out on her own. Who was it?'

'It wasn't me, sir.'

'I didn't ask if it was you, I asked who it was.'

Another pause. 'Nommo, sir.'

'The one he was in the Squares with?'

'Yes, sir.'

'Hm. Any other favourites of the women?' Eden asked. 'Perhaps the one without hands? I can't imagine she'd make for a decent whore, but maybe he is partial to mayjen?'

'She's not technically a mayj anymore.'

'True, very true. But I trust you'll find out, either way.'

'Yes, sir.' The reply was grating.

'Good,' Eden said. 'You are dismissed.'

CHAPTER 69:
THE GREAT KAHN

Lady Elira's execution had been swift. Eden had received the Great Kahn's denial of his pyre with a stone-like expression, but he was placated later when he cut the woman's head off with glee, spurred on by the roars of the crowd.

They'd done it in the arena, where the Dancing Ceremony was usually held. The Geni were not happy about it, but their FaKrijen insisted and the Great Kahn did not care where it happened. He only wanted the People to see so he could prove to them he still cared.

But it weighed on him, Lady Elira's death, and the weight of it was more than just knowing she'd plotted under his nose. There was something else heavy there, and a strange feeling hung with it, and the Great Kahn wondered if it was guilt, not having felt the emotion in so long. This new goodness in him was unsettling to say the least.

Weeks later, he finally determined a distraction.

'This city is a shambles. I want you to fix the bridge, Stolt.'

The detestable KahnenMayj stood in the Great Kahn's chambers, the bottom of his robes dragging on the ground. He'd always had them cut too long, enjoying how they swirled about his feet as he walked, gathering grime wherever he went.

'What? Do you know how long that will take? And I'm not harnessing out in the open! What if I'm attacked?'

Indeed, the streetlings had returned with a fury to the streets. Perhaps it was because after the long-anticipated announcement of the KrijenMayj, he'd all but disappeared. Either that, or there was a traitor in their midst who had whispered that now was the perfect time to rebel. The Great Kahn disregarded no possibilities. He did not trust his Kahnen.

'Take Jin for protection then. It will be good for you to be seen together.'

'The KrijenMayj will *not* agree to come with me.'

'He will if you ask him nicely,' the Great Kahn said. 'He is not petty like you are.'

Stolt looked like he'd been slapped.

'Now go,' the Great Kahn said. 'I will not have my citizens live in unneeded squalor because of your insecurities.'

The Great Kahn turned away, and he heard his door close, and the sound of Stolt's boots disappeared into the Keep.

The Great Kahn walked over to his desk and dragged open a drawer, taking *The Founding of Valrue* from its depths. The Great Kahn placed it on the desk and peeled open its weary pages, the spine creaking, to the final excerpt on the Bhouli. There were no notes on these parts. Mandavar had not cared for the Bhouli. In his opinion, they'd shown little interest in bettering the skills of their mayjen, and he'd found their obsession with purpose rudimentary. Mandavar never understood how someone could commit to something if it did not revolve around self-elevation, but given what the Great Kahn now knew about them, Mandavar was wrong to brush the Bhouli aside. They knew so much more than the Great Kahn had realised.

He'd checked again on the lake, and its water level was the same as before. The Great Kahn was certain it was the Bhouli.

He'd since delved further into the pages of *The Founding of Valrue*, frustrated at how little time he had to read and how uncertain the writer had been regarding many of the theories about the Bhouli.

Perhaps he should take up the librarian's offer after all and send a scholar into Valrue, to see if there was more to be learnt. Whatever they may be like now, the Bhouli at the time of the settlers seemed to have no qualms about sharing their knowledge. It was more that the settlers struggled to understand it.

Perhaps the Great Kahn would finish the book first. There was only this final excerpt left to read anyway. He was about to make a start on it when he heard footfalls in the corridor, and there was a knock on the door. 'Come in,' he said.

It was Stolt again. 'He won't come, my Great Lord,' Stolt whined. 'He refuses to take orders from me.'

'You are not his FaKrijen.'

'Perhaps not, but as his teacher, I still deserve his respect.'

'You have failed to teach him a single thing,' the Great Kahn said. 'I am not surprised he will not take orders from you. He is wallowing, understandably, but he is far from useless. Show him that.'

'That depends on your definition of useless,' Stolt sneered. 'He is a mess, an *embarrassment*. He spends all day locked in his room, drowning himself in ale. What use to the Kahnen is an invalid who can't even get out of bed –'

'Have you no *shame?*' The Great Kahn slammed *The Founding of Valrue* shut, the crack making Stolt jump. 'You stood by while Jin melted the flesh from his bones trying to escape the gloves *you* locked him into! And now you suggest the Eighth House disregard him because of his injuries when you know perfectly well he can still harness?'

'I didn't mean for it to go that far, my Great Lord,' Stolt said, his voice quivering with forced calm. 'I regret what happened. But that was weeks ago, and his behaviour since has been despicable. He isn't worthy of being called the KrijenMayj.'

'This, from you, Stolt? You have neglected even the most minor of responsibilities since the day we gave you your title.'

'Just because I can't fulfil some duties of the former KahnenMayjen it doesn't make me inferior!'

'By definition, it makes you inferior.'

Stolt took a step back. His fists were clenched, colour rising up his neck. 'Well then, by that logic, I'm at least better than him,' Stolt said. 'He's only a Breaker. But still, you play favourites.'

'Favourites? What nonsense is this?'

'You aren't holding him and I to the same standards.'

The Great Kahn knew what Stolt was referring to. 'Ah, so that is your problem. You are bitter about the choice you made.'

'*Choice?* It was hardly a choice. And I don't understand why your KrijenMayj isn't expected to do the same.'

'The law around sterilisation applies to KahnenMayjen. Jin is not a KahnenMayj.'

'A technicality!'

'No. It is an important distinction that everyone seems to forget! I do not control the KrijenMayj, he belongs to the FaKrijen. You, however, are under the command of the Eighth House, and *your* behaviour is bordering on insubordination.'

'Because you're not listening to me!' Stolt cried. 'I can't understand why the Eighth House obsess over the KrijenMayj! I've said time and time again that he's dangerous, yet you disregard my concerns and force me to train him –'

'I disregard you because you are nothing other than a jealous, self-aggrandising opportunist.' The Great Kahn grabbed Mandavar's sword from its nook under his desk and slid it out from its sheath, holding the tip to Stolt's shocked face.

'You wouldn't dare. I am the only KahnenMayj –'

'But not the only *mayj*,' the Great Kahn hissed. 'Make no mistake, Stolt, you are as expendable as ever. If you ever question me again in the way you have today, I will cut off your hands. Now get out of my sight.'

CHAPTER 70:
SID BHA

'Sid? Bish is at the base of the tower. He's asking for you.' Jakki's voice pulled Sid from his thoughts. He was sitting in her kitchen. Mae was next to him, stitching something. Noel was baking bread, as always.

Surprised, Sid trotted down the staircase, ducking through doors and worming his way through the maze of the Rue tower. It was only recently he'd stopped getting lost on his way to and from the street. He'd braved the city a few times now. He'd not been able to bring himself to grow a beard, but he'd become almost comfortable wearing a brown cloak where at least he could hide in the shadows of his hood. He pulled it up as he went.

Bish was waiting in his wheeling chair on the cobbles outside. He was alone, which Sid thought odd. Normally, Marigold would come with him to visit.

'Bish? Is everything okay?'

Bish turned his face up to Sid, squinting into the light. 'Can you please do something for me?'

'Sure, anything.'

'Can you come with me to Turning Point?'

Sid stared at Bish, his mouth hanging open. 'You-you want to go to Turning Point?' When Sid had said anything, he hadn't meant *that*.

'Please, Sid. I'm going to find Wren.'

Sid jumped at the sound of the Lost Square's name. It made no sense that Bish, of all people, would say it.

'Why would you do that?'

'You'll know soon enough.'

Sid waited, but Bish gave nothing up. He sat there, staring Sid down, not letting him look away.

'You . . . you want to go now?'

'Yes.'

Sid looked around. The streets were busier at this time of the morning; it would be the safest it could be. But no time was a safe time to visit the Point.

'Bish, I really don't think –'

'I'm going whether or not you come with me. I just figured it might be a good idea to have someone at my back.'

Sid cringed. Bish had known exactly what to say to guilt him into it. Of all the people he could have picked, why did it have to be Sid?

'You-you have your daggers on you?' Sid knew perfectly well that Bish wouldn't have Krijen daggers anymore, having denounced his title. It had shocked everyone, to say the least.

'No. I've got some knives instead.'

'Oh,' Sid said, disappointed to have lost a valid excuse not to go. 'Okay then.'

Bish gestured for Sid to lead the way. Sid stepped out onto the street. Bish wheeled along next to him, keeping up effortlessly.

Sid kept glancing sideways at him, hoping for a further explanation of this ludicrous jaunt, but Bish looked determinedly ahead, his mind elsewhere. Sid thought it best not to pester; Bish hadn't been himself lately. Sid had a suspicion he was about to find out why.

It took a long time to reach the Lower West Side. The streets grew dirtier, dingier, more cramped. Sid's skin crawled as they stepped off the main thoroughfare and down a narrow alleyway. Dangerous-looking characters were sitting in shadows, eyes following them all the way.

Before long, Turning Point stretched out ahead of them. Like the last time Sid was here, a line of bedraggled people staggered down the street. There were little old ladies, and beggars, and pregnant mothers with children, and streetlings with belts slung over bare potted bellies. All the skeletal faces seemed familiar to Sid, maybe because they'd been waiting here the last time. It made him wonder if what they had been waiting for had ever come.

Bish wheeled down the line, Sid sticking close behind. Sid felt very out of place. Bish drew attention because of his wheeling chair and the distinctly Krijen air he still had about him, but Sid could also feel eyes on his own clean clothes, free from holes. He tugged his cloak tighter about him.

The Lost Square was not around.

Bish spun in a circle, looking along the rooftops. 'Where do you think he is?'

'I don't know,' Sid admitted. 'Last time it was –'

'*He*,' Bish said.

Sid paused. 'Sorry. Last time he was just over there with that . . . er . . . gentleman.' Sid wasn't sure what to call the man he gestured to. He looked nothing at all like a gentleman with his grubby forehead and knee-length white beard, sitting on a blanket on the ground. But the man was within earshot and his expression a little deranged, so Sid thought it best to be polite.

Bish wheeled over to the bearded man. 'Excuse me,' he said, stopping before him. The man jumped about a foot in the air, then looked dopily at Bish, his mouth hanging open. He was missing most of his teeth.

'Do you know where Wren is?' Bish asked the man.

'Wren . . .' the man repeated. His pupils were huge and unfocused.

'Yes,' Bish said. 'The Lost Square?'

'You want him?'

'Yes.'

The man pointed down the street towards a door that hung off its hinges. Several Turning Point residents sat either side of it, all watching the exchange. Even from where he stood, Sid could see dark shadows of sleeplessness around their sunken eyes. Sid felt another shiver of fear up roll up his spine.

Oblivious to Sid's discomfort, Bish wheeled himself towards the door. Not wanting to be left behind, Sid hurried after him. The residents watched with slack faces as Bish and Sid carefully moved around them, peering into the doorway.

It looked like an abandoned bakery. There were three deep stone ovens spaced along the white-washed wall at the back. The room was completely empty, save for dust and wood shavings on the floor.

'There's no one in here.' Sid didn't know why he was whispering.

'Yes, there is,' Bish whispered back. He pointed. 'Look.'

A few rays of sun had snuck between the Rue towers and crept through the bakery windows. The rectangles of light stretched into the room, allowing them to see the rounded outline of something tucked into one of the oven spaces.

'Come on,' Bish whispered. With a short run up, he manoeuvred his wheeling chair over the tiny lip in front of the door and into the bakery.

Sid sidled in after Bish, wiping sweat from his brow. He didn't like the idea of them being trapped in a room with the only exit surrounded by the nightmarish souls outside. Sid glanced back at the haunted faces gathering by the windows.

As he and Bish approached the oven, it became obvious the shape inside it was a pile of blankets. For a bizarre moment, Sid thought he recognised one of them, its purple pattern distinctly familiar.

There was someone sleeping beneath them.

Bish and Sid stopped next to the oven opening, leaning in together to get a better look at the occupant whose head was at the back. It was the Lost Square. It was fast asleep; the blankets were pulled up high, and its dark hair peeked out the top.

Bish looked at Sid. *Shall we wake him?* Bish mouthed the words.

A little alarmed, Sid shook his head. *No. It-he will attack us,* he mouthed back.

Bish made a face. He clearly disagreed. Then he carefully extended a finger and prodded the blankets. 'Wren?'

The Lost Square didn't stir.

Bish looked up at Sid, who held up his hands, at a loss. 'Let's leave,' Sid whispered.

Bish shook his head, then grabbed a fistful of the blankets and yanked on them. 'Wren!'

The Lost Square sat up so fast it smacked its head on the roof of the stone oven. 'Ow! *Fuck!*' One hand had gone to its head, and the other already held a dagger out towards whoever had said its name. The Lost Square froze when it spotted its visitors, and its jaw dropped. '*Bish*?' Then it wrestled itself free of the blankets and leapt out of the oven.

Sid edged in behind Bish as the Lost Square's head whipped between their faces, dagger still clutched in its hand. 'What is it?' it asked. 'Is it Aren? Is she back?'

Sid had no idea how the Lost Square knew Aren was alive. Perhaps Mae had not lied as well as he'd thought.

'No,' Bish said, shaking his head. 'Sorry, Aren's not back.'

The Lost Square's face fell. It lowered its dagger and slowly sat down on the lip of the stone oven, tentatively touching its head again, looking rather pale.

'Don't worry. You're not bleeding,' Bish reassured it.

The Lost Square slowly lowered its hand. If possible, it looked even worse than the last time Sid saw it, now with the same sunken look around its eyes as the people in the alleyway outside. The shadow of its beard was strangely patchy as though cut with a blade not designed for the purpose. Even after blinking a few times at them and rubbing its eyes, the Lost Square still looked exhausted. 'What are you doing here?' it asked.

'I wanted to talk,' Bish said.

The Lost Square paused in its eye-rubbing. 'Talk to *me*?'

'Yes.'

There was a noise behind them, and Sid glanced back towards the door. More Turning Point residents had gathered around the doorway and peered in at them, their eyes quickly darting away when they saw Sid looking.

'Why?' asked the Lost Square.

When Sid turned back, Bish was looking around the room with a disgruntled expression on his face. 'Is this actually where you've been living for the past year and a half?'

'Well yeah,' the Lost Square said quietly. 'I've not exactly had a better option.'

Sid heard yet another noise behind them, and he spun around again, feeling like a lightning bolt kept striking him.

The residents had inched into the bakery, looking like death warmed up. Maybe they'd come to leech the life from them. Sid gently nudged Bish on the arm, but Bish didn't notice, fixated as he was on the Lost Square.

Sid nudged Bish harder, and Bish finally looked back at him. '*What,* Sid?'

'I-I'm sorry to interrupt. Should we be concerned about them?'

Bish looked over his shoulder, past Sid, at the residents creeping towards them.

'They're okay,' the Lost Square said. 'They're just hungry.' If Sid was not mistaken, there was a guilty tone in its voice. Bish must've heard it as well. 'You feel responsible for these people?' he asked.

'Kind of,' the Lost Square replied. 'That's my fault, I guess. I've not been able to help them as much as I was before.'

Sid blinked in surprise. He wasn't sure what he'd expected of a Lost Square, but a conscience was not one of them, even if misdirected towards the petty criminals crowding the room.

'There's a line of people outside waiting for food,' Bish said.

'I know,' the Lost Square said, annoyance breaking through its subdue. 'But I don't have any food right now. I can't do *all of it.* I need Aren. She did the food and kept them calm. I'm shit at that, and I've got no coin to pay for anything because Aren did that too.'

'So why don't you say that? Just tell them you can't help.'

'I *do.* They keep coming back. They don't listen to me, they don't *hear* me. It's the Lost thing. They would listen to Aren if she were here.' The Lost Square sighed and pushed its long hair back out of its eyes, looking over at the residents who stared back.

Sid was distracted by the mention of his daughter. 'Aren did a lot to help here, didn't she?'

'Yeah. She did.'

Sid did not like the look on the Lost Square's face. Sid knew that look, knew what it meant. He'd seen the same expression on Aren's face when she spoke about the Lost Square, when she'd yelled its name at them, ignoring every warning and rebutting every insult thrown its way. Of course, if anyone could be trusted to defy all reasonable societal expectations, it was Aren.

'Wren,' Bish began in a serious tone, 'I need to tell you something. I hope you'll forgive me for keeping it to myself for so long. I didn't know what to do.'

The Lost Square turned its dark eyes onto Bish. 'Well, that sounds fucking ominous. What is it?'

Bish opened his mouth, then closed it again. Sid could see the anxiety brewing on his face. He hesitated long enough that the Lost Square made a frustrated noise at the back of its throat. 'Come on, Bish. You're killing me here.'

Bish took a deep breath. 'I'm sure you know by now that Jin is a mayj?'

Sid frowned. He had no idea where Bish was going with this. Apparently, the Lost Square didn't either. 'Yeah,' it said slowly. Then it snorted. 'Kinda figures.'

Bish nodded. 'I know what you mean. Well, during our dance at the Dancing Ceremony, Jin did something.'

The Lost Square's eyes narrowed. '*Our* dance? Yours and mine?'

Bish nodded.

'Did what exactly?'

Bish screwed up his face, clearly struggling with whatever he was about to confess. 'Jin used majik on me.'

Sid nearly fell over in shock. 'Jin did *what*?' he cried.

Bish ignored Sid, keeping his eyes on the Lost Square. 'Jin used majik on me,' he repeated. 'My body, my muscles, or whatever. He said it would've felt like adrenalin, so I wouldn't notice. He made it so I was stronger and faster than I should have been. So I could win.'

The Lost Square appeared frozen in place. 'You . . . you're saying you cheated?'

'Not intentionally,' Bish said quickly. 'But-but yes. I'm so sorry. Truly, I am.'

The Lost Square didn't speak for the longest time. Its face was a reel of emotions that came and went so fast that Sid caught barely a flicker of each. Bish was biting his lip, his fingers turning white from gripping the arms of his chair.

'Wren, please,' Bish begged when the Lost Square remained silent, 'I *swear* I didn't know. Jin didn't tell me until ages later.'

The Lost Square's eyes hardened. 'When did he tell you?'

'A few months ago. The night after the Celebrations when FaKrijen Oji died.'

At the mention of Oji's name, Sid suddenly felt very light-headed, but he didn't think it was fair for him to be the one to faint right now. He staggered over to the empty oven next to the Lost Square, easing onto the stone lip.

'I'm sorry,' Bish kept repeating, his expression strained. 'There's no way I would've won if Jin hadn't done what he did. I should have lost that dance, not you.'

Sid was ready for an explosion. But it didn't come. The Lost Square looked up at Bish, its face empty of emotion. 'Well. I guess we'll never know.'

Sid was shocked.

Bish looked devastated. 'It's not right, Wren. But I don't know how to fix it.'

The Lost Square shook its head. 'It can't be fixed. But you shouldn't be sorry. You did nothing wrong. This is on Jin.'

'Fuck Jin,' Bish spat, his voice suddenly bitter. 'I hate him for what he did. I really do.'

'It's funny you say that being one of his closest friends and all.'

'Not anymore.'

For some reason, the Lost Square's eyes shifted to Sid. He felt a bizarre surge of guilt. Sid quickly looked away from it.

'Are you sure Jin did this?' Sid asked Bish. 'You're certain?'

Sid had loved Jin like a son, as had Mae, since Jin was a little boy. He'd been Aren's best friend since she was five years old. But after that day in Jakki's house when Jin had gone after Drax, Sid had seen a monster in there. Jin's anger had been all-consuming, ridding him of reason. But Sid had also seen that scared little boy.

'Jin told me himself what he did,' Bish replied. 'And he can't lie, so I know it's true.'

Sid winced. Jin was the worst liar.

Bish leant forward and grasped the Lost Square by its shoulder. It jumped at his touch.

'Can you forgive me for not telling you sooner?'

'I forgive you,' the Lost Square said without hesitation.

Bish looked uncertain. 'You know,' he began, 'I thought you would be angrier. I brought some knives with me.'

To Sid's surprise, the Lost Square laughed. 'Maybe if you'd told me sooner, I might have tried to stab you. I've held onto a lot of hate lately. It kept me alive, sure, but it took me to a dark place. I don't want to go there again.'

Bish nodded. He seemed to understand something that Sid didn't. 'What will you do now?'

The Lost Square shrugged. 'What can I do? Nothing is going to change. It's not like we know what the outcome of the dance would've been.'

'I won't deny it if you want to tell people.'

'Even if I thought people would believe me, I wouldn't tell anyone. I'm okay, and you've had to deal with enough.'

'Don't downplay being Lost,' Bish said. 'I can't believe what you've lived with. What you're *still* living with.'

'At least I lived.'

Sid shivered. The Lost Squares took their own lives after their dances. Or they were supposed to. Sid didn't like that thought.

'I'll be okay,' the Lost Square said. '*They* won't though.' It jerked his head towards the residents behind them. 'I need help. When is Aren coming back? Where is she?'

'She's gone to –'

'*No*, Bish,' Sid said curtly, surprising himself. 'Don't.' Sid wished Aren was back too. He missed her so much. But he didn't want the Lost Square to know where she was. He didn't trust it.

'Oh, come on,' Bish implored. 'It won't do any harm to tell him.'

Sid shook his head. 'Aren is alive and safe. That's all it needs to know.'

The Lost Square snorted again. 'Oh yeah, sure. And thanks for lying about *that* before. Not that I believed you, but all I had to go on was *Pyra*.'

Sid didn't know what it meant by that, but the strange guilt was back again. Sid didn't know what to do with it, so he just looked away, back towards the residents, who froze again under his gaze.

Bish suddenly sat bolt upright in his chair, a smile on his face. 'You said you needed help,' he said. 'We can help. We can provide food, and blankets, and whatever else you need. We'll find somewhere for you to stay too! You don't need to sleep here.' Bish spun his wheeling chair around to face Sid. 'Can Wren stay with Jakki?'

'Woah,' the Lost Square said. 'No, no way –'

Bish waved the Lost Square's protests aside and glared resolutely at Sid, who baulked. 'I don't think that's a good idea.'

'You want to leave him here? In this shithole?'

Sid made a dubious noise, imagining both Mae and Jakki's rage when he and Bish returned with the Lost Square. Sid definitely did not have the grit to take them on.

'Please, Sid? Wren doesn't deserve this. It should have been me!'

'It's not my decision. It would be up to Jakki, and she was very upset the last time it –'

'*He.*'

'The last time *he* was in the house.'

'Upset to say the least,' the Lost Square added.

But Bish was determined. 'Come on, I'm sure we could convince them!'

'I doubt it.'

'Can't you do this for me?'

'I'm sorry, I can't.'

'Do this for Aren then!'

How Bish always knew what to say, Sid had no idea. At the thought of his daughter, Sid's willpower crumbled in an instant. He knew what Aren would want. 'Okay,' he sighed. 'We can *ask*. But I still think it will be a firm no.'

The Lost Square was shaking its head. 'Look, I appreciate you helping at the Point, but there's no way Jakki will want me in her house. I'd be more comfortable here –'

'Shut it, Wren,' Bish snapped, pulling a knife from one of his wraps and waving it in the direction of the Lost Square. 'Stop being so fucking stubborn, for once in your life!'

The Lost Square leant back from him, holding its hands up. '*Okay.* Jeez, I'll come. But it won't go well.'

Sid agreed with the Lost Square, but Bish was beyond being reasoned with.

'Let's go,' Bish said, jerking his head towards the door.

'What? *Now*?'

'Yes, now! You look like shit, Wren. And these people are hungry, and we've got food. Let's *go*.'

Bish pointed towards the door, glaring at the Lost Square until it stood up off the oven and started walking, throwing accusatory looks at Bish as it went.

Sid trailed behind, already feeling anxious about what was coming next. The residents at the door parted as they approached, their eyes on the Lost Square. It didn't seem to notice. Sid struggled to understand how the residents could look at it like that. He couldn't get over the aversion he felt towards it. It was just so hard to unsee the failure even after Bish's confession. They didn't know who would have won if Jin hadn't intervened.

Then again, maybe this was one of the many failings of the Krijen that Oji had spoken of, their forgivelessness when they made mistakes, as humans do. Sid had made mistakes. And, Sid thought grimly, did he really believe that this Lost Square deserved what it got? His daughter clearly didn't. Sid didn't know what to think.

They were almost back to the mouth of the street when something smacked into the back of Sid's head. Sid cried out and put his hands up defensively as an old shoe bounced across the ground in front of him.

The Lost Square spun around, daggers out. 'Thatcher! What the fuck? Why'd you do that?'

Sid's heart nearly stopped when he saw a little group of streetlings standing in the alleyway, flashing him back to the horrors of the Celebrations when a wall of the violent youths had surrounded them.

A grubby streetling boy stood at the front, his remaining stolen shoe raised in his hand, his little face scrunched in indignation. 'Him,' the boy said, pointing at the Lost Square, keeping his eyes on Sid. 'You're gonna bring him back, right?'

Sid was terrified into silence, but Bish rolled forward in his wheeling chair, his eyes wide. 'You want Wren back?'

'That's what I said!'

Bish grinned up at the Lost Square, who looked bewildered. 'Sure,' Bish said to the streetling. 'I promise you we'll bring him back.'

CHAPTER 71: AREN BHA

There was a knock on the door.

Aren looked to Drax, confused. They weren't expecting Mo Nu today. They'd settled nicely into the routine of going to Mandavar's classes and filling their time with any others on the schedule that piqued Aren's interest, which was many.

Drax joined her every time though he mostly looked out the windows at the trees, making Aren worry he stayed only for her sake because she knew he could wander that far from her if he wanted to. Then again, Drax was very good at listening when he didn't seem to be. His brain seemed to be able to do a million things at once. It was probably why he was so good at majik.

Aren opened the door to Bodin's startling green eyes and smiling face, a silver cup clasped in each hand. Narium was behind him.

'Good morning,' Bodin said. 'Can we come in?'

Surprised, Aren stood back. Narium and Bodin entered the room, necks craned up towards the glittering ceiling. 'Wow,' Narium said. 'This is fancier than my room!'

Aren flushed. 'Yes. I feel like we don't deserve it.'

Aren was certain they were not meeting Mo Nu's expectations, whatever they may be. For a while, the dean had visited daily, a silver cup for each of them, which Aren had drunk obligingly every time. He'd shown them every corner of the University and plied them with questions about Valrue and the Unsettlement, but other than that, he seemed content to let them stay and attend classes. He'd yet to ask them for a single thing in return, and he'd made no comments nor asked any questions about the tension between them and Mandavar.

Aren had tried to apologise for lying about being a mayj, and he'd waved it away. 'We could hardly expect you to know what you'd done,' he said. Aren didn't like the sound of that, but she'd been too nervous to press further.

Narium plopped down on the couch while Bodin walked to the bookshelves, staring down the rows of volumes.

'Why are you here?' Aren asked.

'We thought it was about time we showed you around,' Bodin said. 'You've been here for weeks and not seen the city, am I right?'

'No,' Aren said. 'I'd like to.'

'Why haven't you gone out then?'

Aren pointed to the list of slights on the table. It had appeared under their door the day after their first lecture, Narium having followed through on her promise. This Gi thing, or person, whatever it was, seemed unreasonably hard to please.

Narium burst out laughing. 'You know it doesn't really matter?'

'It does for me,' Aren mumbled.

'Okay well, you don't have to worry about slighting when you're with us because we'll explain what not to do. Where is Drax's room?' At that, Drax ambled out of the bedroom. Narium's eyebrows rose so high they disappeared into her hair.

Drax moved over to Aren, eyeing up the silver cups in Bodin's hands. Aren took them from Bodin, then held one out to Drax, making sure he had a firm grip on it before she let go. Bodin and Narium's eyes hovered on the purple rings at Drax's wrists, the scars from the Krijen cleaver. But they said nothing.

'Shall we go?' Narium asked. 'Drax, walk with me.' She stood up from the couch and waited for him to amble over to her before leading the way out the door.

Bodin stepped in next to Aren, and together the foursome wandered down the corridor, thick trunks of sunlight slithering over them as they passed the windows. Bodin kept up an endless stream of questions, mainly about whether they were enjoying Holu Mon and what they'd learned in classes so far. She wasn't sure if it was purposeful that he avoided questions about Valrue. Maybe he thought it would make her uncomfortable.

'Do you enjoy Mandavar's classes?' Bodin asked. 'You don't get bored?'

It was during their third lecture of Mandavar's that Demison had guessed what was happening with Drax and Aren, that they came in a pair because Drax had to keep her heart beating.

Bodin and Narium's jaws had dropped, whereas Demison's had narrowed. Aren could practically hear him grinding his teeth from across the lecture theatre. Aren couldn't think of what she and Drax had done to upset him.

'Yes, they are fascinating,' Aren replied. 'We know nothing about majik in Valrue.'

'What was it like to die?'

The question threw her off-guard after all his rather light-hearted ones. 'I don't really remember it, to be honest,' Aren said. 'I just remember seeing my friend's face above me. Then I woke up.'

'How did it happen?'

'It was an accident. Just a stupid accident.'

Bodin must've picked up on the reluctance in her voice. 'Sorry, that was rude of me.'

'It's okay. It's just not something I've ever talked about.'

Bodin nodded. 'So Drax saved you by Weaving apparently. Where did he learn that?'

'He just knew it. He knows how to do everything, I think.'

Bodin looked up ahead at Drax and Narium. Narium was gesticulating about something, and Drax was watching her face intently with his usual blank expression.

'I won't ask what happened to him,' Bodin said. 'It looks like he's been tortured. But I assume it was because he's a mayj?'

Aren nodded.

'That's awful. I'm glad you're both here in Holu Mon now. Life's going to be very different for you. People love majik here, and they love mayjen.'

Aren smiled weakly. 'I've noticed.'

It was true. They'd left the gates of the University and people's eyes followed them as they wound through the streets. Not only did the dark blue of Narium and Bodin's clothes give them away, but a stream of animals dashed from them as they walked, fleeing from the combined powers of Bodin, Narium, and Drax.

Drax didn't wear the dark blue. He'd stuck to the black and white.

'Yeah, there are so few mayjen in Holu Mon, and majik is so helpful, you know? That's why we encourage all mayjen to attend the University to learn how to use their majik effectively.'

'How many mayjen are in Holu Mon?'

'Two hundred and six.'

'That's specific.'

'Sure. All mayjen are registered. If they come to the University, they're trained up and allocated to different roles when they graduate based on their skill set.'

'Like what?'

'Well, let me think.' Bodin smiled at her, obviously enjoying himself. 'Breakers typically do things like mining and logging, stuff where brute strength is needed but not finesse. It's rare to get a Breaker who can also do atomic majik, you see. They tend to be bigger-picture people, so they aren't great at dealing with atoms, which are so small you can't see them. They typically have poor cognitive dexterity too.'

Aren remembered the term. 'Cognitive dexterity means how much you can harness at once, right? Like multi-tasking?'

'Exactly. Cognitive dexterity is something you can actually get better at too but only to a point. A Breaker is only ever going to be a Breaker.'

Bodin shrugged. 'There are lots of Breakers as well. Builders are rarer. Of the two hundred and six mayjen, there were only fifteen Builders in Holu Mon, last I checked.'

'And all of you are Builders? You, Narium, and Demison?'

'That's right. Mandavar rarely takes Breakers into his classes. He wouldn't waste his time, not unless they were capable of atomik majik, which as I said is super rare . . .'

As interesting as Aren found their conversation, her surroundings were too distracting. She'd still not got used to the *colours*. Vibrant green leaves popped between explosions of gold and violet flowers. Plants inhabited every street they walked, snaking their way up the brown sides of the buildings.

The contents of shops spilt onto the streets, offering a plethora of fruits that Aren had never seen, let alone could name. The meals delivered to their room at the University contained all sorts of fascinating food but none so aromatic as this.

'Do you want to try something?' Bodin asked, noticing he'd lost her attention. Without waiting for an answer, he darted off to the closest shop, towards fruit-laden wooden troughs. He picked up an orange fruit coated with a light white fuzz and held it out to Aren. 'Peach?'

Aren took it and held it to her nose. It smelled *wonderful*. When she looked up again, Bodin was dropping coins into the hand of the shop owner, who gave a courteous nod of his head and pushed a bag swollen with fruit at Bodin.

Bodin came back over to Aren, bag in hand. 'I've paid for that too,' he said, inclining his head to the peach.

'You didn't have to do that!'

'I wanted to. As much as I would love you to feel flattered, fruit costs practically nothing.' He winked.

Aren flushed. Bodin was forthright, but she wasn't sure if it was just how he was, or something else. To distract from her burning cheeks, she took a bite of the peach. The juice dribbled down her chin onto her hands, making her squeal and laugh.

Bodin grinned as Aren wiped the juice off her mouth. 'That good, huh?' he asked.

'I've had fresh fruit before,' Aren replied. 'I just forgot how messy it was to eat.'

Drax ambled over with Narium in tow.

'Drax, you have to try this!' Aren held out the peach, but Narium stepped between them. 'You can't share food,' she said, shaking her head. 'That's a slight.'

'Oh.' Disappointed, Aren dropped her hand. She'd seen that on the list of slights too. She'd just forgotten.

'Don't worry,' Bodin said. 'You're with us.'

Aren still felt funny about it.

They carried on, Bodin chattering away to Aren once more while she finished her peach. A question floated to her mind, and she worried about the answer.

'Why did Demison not come with us?'

'He's with Mandavar today,' Bodin said flatly.

'Doing what?'

'Mining.'

Aren frowned. 'Didn't you say mining was for Breakers?'

'Not this kind of mining. Breakers will gouge out chunks of rock, sure. But Mandavar and Demison do ore extractions. They separate metals from one another,' he added at Aren's baffled expression. 'Doing it without majik is a tedious and toxic process. With majik, you can do it faster, safely, and on a larger scale.'

'Why Demison? Why not you?'

'It requires a lot of stamina.' Bodin spoke in a monotone. 'You don't use a lot of power at once, but it's a delicate process that takes time, so having lots of power helps, and more so if you recover quickly. And it's atomik majik. I'm not quite as good as Demison at that.'

As he finished speaking, Bodin looked away. Aren wondered if she'd hit a nerve somehow, so she was relieved when Narium stopped ahead of them, pointing upwards. Aren's eyes followed her hand, and her mouth dropped open.

The most colossal statue she'd ever seen mountained above them. It was a red-gold figure sitting on its ankles, its face turned down to the ground. Water cascaded from its eyes, forming rivers that tore down its face and collected in giant pools on the ground before it. Aren didn't understand how she hadn't seen it until it was right in front of her.

Narium turned to them, smiling. 'This is Gi.'

'What?' Aren asked. '*This* is Gi?'

'Well, an embodiment of Gi. Gi is everywhere, you see.'

'Why . . . why is Gi crying?'

'Water gives balance,' Bodin said. 'You give water, you give life. Too much of it, and you can drown. But if you remove it completely, life fades away. When the tears slow or stop, it means there is an imbalance being corrected somewhere.'

'You mean a natural and majikal imbalance?'

'There are many imbalances in the world, rich and poor, sweet and sour, acid and base. You know.'

Aren watched the water in the pool. It was perfectly level, not overflowing or dropping. It must seep into the ground, but then she didn't understand how it got back up into the eyes of Gi. Perhaps there was a pump. But it would have to be the most monstrous pump ever created to push that much water around.

'How does it work?' Aren asked.

'Majik,' said Bodin.

'Oh.' The answer was so obvious. 'So a mayj controls this, somewhere?'

'Sure. It will be one of the University graduates.'

'So they can tell if there is an imbalance? *Any* sort of imbalance?'

Bodin laughed. 'Yeah sure, why not.'

Drax cocked his head and looked to Aren, the little frown back on his face. *I don't understand,* she mouthed at him. He shook his head back at her. He didn't understand either.

Aren didn't want to risk sounding stupid, so she stayed quiet. She was confident that eventually, she would figure out what Bodin meant.

CHAPTER 72:
BISHTNROJAK LONLI

'Absolutely not.'

'Come on, Jakki!' Bish cried. 'You're being unreasonable! It's not his fault he's Lost –'

'I said *no*.'

They stood in the alleyway at the base of the Lower East Side tower where Jakki's home was situated. After much coaxing, Sid had agreed to bring the others down and not tell them why, lest they refuse. So after about fifteen minutes, Jakki, Noel, and Mae had appeared with worried faces in the mouth of the alleyway, but none as worried as Sid, who'd shrank back into the brick wall, doing a poor job of blending into it.

'What is it, Bish?' Noel had asked. 'Is everything all right?'

That was when Wren had stepped from the shadows, his arms folded, his dark eyes slits, looking exactly like the horror they thought he was. But Bish could hardly expect him to look any other way, considering Jakki had immediately raised a threatening hand, and Mae gave a screech worthy of a streetling, restrained only by Noel's warning glance.

Bish had given them the full story about what really happened at the Dancing Ceremony in the hope it would garner some sympathy for Wren, but Jakki remained adamant that 'it' would go nowhere near her house.

'Why not?' Bish asked, exasperated.

'Because it's Lost, and nothing, not even you questioning what could have been, will change that! I appreciate what it's trying to do for the Turners and for those people who come to the Point, and I'm willing to help with that –'

'That's great!'

'But I'm not having that *thing* in my house!'

'Leave it,' Wren said to Bish as he opened his mouth again. 'I told you I'd rather stay at the Point.'

'Fine,' Bish said. 'You can stay with me then.'

Wren snorted. 'Marigold won't like that.'

Bish scowled. Marigold loved Jin, and she didn't understand why he and Bish were no longer friends despite knowing the truth now. Bish had told her before he headed to the Point, loathing himself as he left her in the stairwell with tears tracking down her face. She said she could see Jin's side of things.

It was clear that Aren's mother hated Wren about as much as Marigold did. Mae's rosy cheeks darkened to crimson as she eyed Wren. 'You,' she snarled, 'you sick, twisted fiend.'

'Me twisted?' Wren asked. 'You told me your own daughter was dead.'

'To keep her safe from predators like you!' Mae cried, striding towards Wren, her tiny fists shaking. Bish quickly wheeled himself between them, but Wren had already spun on his heel and leapt up to the rooftops, disappearing from view.

Mae rounded on Bish instead. 'How dare you!' she screamed. 'How dare you bring it here again!'

'He's not what you think he is,' Bish said calmly. Yelling at Mae would get him nowhere. It was strange, understanding exactly how she felt, yet knowing she was wrong. But it was best to leave it for now. It had taken him months to get his head around it. Mae and the others just needed time.

'All right, so Wren won't stay here,' Bish said. 'But you said you'd help at the Point?'

After a long pause, Jakki spoke. 'I said I would, so I will.' Her gaze settled on Mae. 'I know you will too, Mae.'

Mae folded her arms and turned her face away. 'So long as that thing stays out of my way,' she mumbled.

'You sure you want to do this, Jakki?' Noel asked.

'Don't patronise me,' she sniffed. 'But coin is going to be a problem. I can barely feed you lot, let alone another hundred. I've sold what I can, but there is a finite number of things I own.'

Bish saw Sid flush in embarrassment. In pursuit of salvaging their belongings, Bish had gone on a mission to the Bha mansion, only to find it stripped of all coin and cloth. Even the cutlery had been taken, the streetlings having got to it after the Krijen were done. It was almost worse that once they'd gutted it, they'd abandoned the building, scurrying back to their lofty towers. Now the mansion stood empty, a skeleton. Bish hoped that at least the beggars would find it and use it for shelter.

'I've got some coin,' Bish said.

'Not enough,' Noel replied. 'And you'll have even less now that you're no longer Krijen. If we're going to do this, we need to be able to sustain it.'

'That's right,' Jakki said. 'I'm not giving those people hope, only to let them down again.'

Sid shuffled forward off the wall, shooting nervous glances towards the mouth of the alleyway. 'Can we go back inside?' he asked quietly, taking Mae's arm. She snatched it from him and stalked back towards the tower. Jakki followed her.

Noel watched them go, then gave Bish a sympathetic look. 'I think it best if you don't come up.'

'I wasn't going to. I'm going back to the Point.'

Noel grimaced. 'Look, I understand how you feel. If Jin did what he did, that's terrible. But it's too late. It's Lost, and you can't undo something like that. And if it was half as decent as you say it is, it wouldn't have agreed to come here again.'

'I made him!'

'It took advantage of your guilt. That alone speaks volumes to its nature. This is exactly why we shouldn't interact with it. And please,' he added, '*don't* put Marigold through this.' Noel turned and followed the women back towards the tower.

Only Sid was left. Aren's father looked a strange shade of green, probably sick with nerves. But he'd stopped trembling. 'I'm sorry,' he said to Bish.

'They agreed to help at the Point,' Bish replied. 'They'll have to deal with Wren, whether they like it or not.'

Sid gave him a tortured look. 'You really think they'll change their minds about the Lost Square?'

'You heard the streetling at the Point, Sid. They didn't hate him. They wanted him to come back.'

'It was a *streetling*.'

'Exactly. Streetlings love to hate things, they don't need an excuse. If they want him back, why can't the rest of us?'

Sid didn't reply immediately. 'For Aren's sake, I hope you're right.' He scurried back to the tower.

Wren dropped out of nowhere to land beside Bish, slowly coming up out of his crouch. 'I have a question,' Wren said, his voice taut. 'What did Noel mean when he said you were no longer Krijen?'

Bish hesitated. He wasn't sure how Wren would react to this. 'Noel meant exactly that,' Bish replied. 'I went to the FaKrijen and asked to be dismissed.'

Wren looked mildly shocked. Then he snorted. 'That's righteous as fuck, Bish.'

'I'm sorry.'

'Don't be. I respect that.'

Bish looked at up at him. 'Did you hear everything then?'

'Every word.'

Bish cringed.

'Nice work,' Wren said. 'They want to help at the Point.'

'The rest of it was rough though.'

'Yeah.' Wren grinned. 'But we knew I was a Lost cause anyway.'

Bish frowned. 'Was that supposed to be a joke? Are you serious?'

'I've had a long time to get used to this. If you're planning on sticking around, you'll need to get used to it too. I won't hold it against you if you change your mind.'

'Don't count on it. Come on. Let's go the Point.'

They left the mouth of the alleyway and started down the street. Some passers-by gave Bish furtive glances while their eyes rolled right over Wren.

'About the coin problem,' Wren said. 'I think I know a way. Aren had this business going before she . . . left.'

'Really? Aren?'

'Yeah. She got the streetlings to deliver things and collect the payment. She'd give the streetlings a cut of the coin. It was enough to keep supplies up and provide food for the residents and most of the visitors to the Point.'

Bish couldn't quite believe it. 'Streetlings? *Working?*'

'Like I said, Aren did it. Don't tell me how. I tried to keep it going, but the streetlings wouldn't work with me.'

'I reckon they could be convinced to work with you now.'

'Nah. Thatcher just wanted an excuse to throw something at Sid because he looked too clean. I'm entirely serious,' Wren added at Bish's dubious look.

'I still think you should give it a go,' Bish said.

Wren snorted again. Bish didn't remember him being so cynical. Being Lost had probably done that to him.

As they neared the Point, a few hollow-looking people turned to follow them, their eyes brightening when they saw Wren.

'People are looking at you, you know,' Bish said.

Wren glanced around, frowning. 'That's because they're all Turners. Go away,' he said to them. 'Not now. And *not* you, Driana,' he growled. 'You need another day.' One of the Turners flapped her hand at him and staggered away. 'I mean that!' Wren called after her.

'You know them?' Bish asked.

'Most of them.'

Wren led the way down the Point past groupings of bedraggled people, ignoring the bony hands that reached towards him.

'They *really* seem to like you,' Bish said.

'It's because I help them stay Turning for longer.'

'You . . . you what?'

'Turning is where they drain their power right down to the dregs,' Wren explained. 'It feels good, so they chase the sensation. Problem is they overdo it. I've learnt how to help them do it without accidentally killing themselves.'

'All right . . . but is Turning a good idea?' Bish asked, looking around at the glazed expressions and sunken faces. 'It doesn't seem like it.'

'It's not good for them, no, but they do it whether or not I help them.' Wren shrugged. 'At least this way, it seems safer. Less of them seize or die anyway. And they don't wreck things so often because it's easier to control how they harness.'

'How does it work?'

'If you want, next time, I'll show you. But it's not all that pleasant.'

Before Bish could ask what he meant, Wren stopped midway down the Point, next to the line of hungry people, most of whom turned to look at him. Bish stopped beside him.

'All right,' Wren said, 'try giving Thatcher a yell.'

'Thatcher? The streetling from before?'

'Yeah. He might come if you call him. He's nosy.'

'Why me?'

Wren rolled his eyes and cupped his hands around his mouth. 'Thatcher!' he yelled.

Bish's eyes scanned the rooftops, the ground, the line of watching people. The streetling did not appear. 'He didn't hear you,' Bish said.

'Yes, he did. You try.'

Bish tentatively raised his hands to his mouth. 'Thatcher!'

Wren leant down towards his ear. 'Be sure to mention Aren,' he said quietly before straightening again.

There was a scuffle behind them, and a scruffy-looking streetling with impossibly knocked knees and long brown hair pushed through the line. If Bish had to guess, Thatcher was about ten years old, with a bulbous belly protruding beneath a skeletal chest. As he approached, the streetling pulled a sharpened horseshoe from the short silk skirt he wore.

Wren groaned. 'Fuck. He's been creeping.'

'What?'

'He's been crossing boundaries, stealing from Pyra.'

'Who's Pyra?'

'The leader of the Upper West Side gang. That's one of her horseshoes.'

'How can you tell?'

'I've seen them up close.'

Thatcher stopped before them, hands on his hips and knotted hair swinging. 'Who are *you?*' he asked Bish.

'Bish,' Bish replied.

'What's wrong with your legs?'

Bish bit back a smile. *The little shit*, he thought. He quickly slid a knife from his wraps and sent the butt of the hilt spearing straight towards the streetling. The hilt ricocheted off Thatcher's left knee and the streetling's leg buckled underneath him, sending him whumping to the ground.

'I could ask you the same,' Bish said lazily.

Thatcher screeched and leapt back to his feet, gnashing his teeth at Bish, swiping the horseshoe threateningly before him.

'Do you want some coin, Thatcher?' Wren asked.

Thatcher froze, horseshoe outstretched, teeth still bared. Only his eyes rolled until they landed on Wren.

'I'm friends with Aren,' Bish said. 'You know Aren?'

Thatcher's eyes rolled back to Bish. 'Aren's coming?' Thatcher asked, his voice warped through his teeth.

'Eventually,' Bish said. 'She wants to know if you can help her by making some coin, for when she gets back.'

Bish heard hooting above them, and he looked up to see a row of streetling faces leaning out from the rooftops. Bish tapped his hand against his thigh, feeling for his other knives.

Wren, however, looked impossibly relaxed. 'How about it then?' he asked Thatcher.

'Three coin cut,' Thatcher said to Bish.

Bish had no idea what he meant.

'He's bartering,' Wren explained. 'Four coins is the fee we charge for a standard delivery. So *no fucking way*,' Wren said to Thatcher. 'That's an insane cut. One coin cut.'

'Three coin cut or nothing,' Thatcher said to Bish.

'One coin cut,' Bish replied, mimicking Wren.

Thatcher shook his head.

'Fine,' Wren growled. 'Two coin cut.'

Thatcher hummed and looked up at the sky, as though pondering the offer. Then he cackled. 'Three coin cut.'

Bish wanted to strangle him, he was that irritating. But then Thatcher turned his eyes back to Wren and held out his hand, wiggling his fingers. 'Three coin cut and we shake,' he said.

Wren stared, shocked, at the streetling's grubby outstretched hand. Then he narrowed his eyes. 'I know what you're doing,' Wren said.

Bish knew it too. He looked around. The line of hungry people were all watching now, the whole of Turning Point unable to turn their eyes away from the exchange.

Despite that, Thatcher was offering up an alliance.

Shaking the hand of a Lost Square was not something that could be taken back, even for an unscrupulous little streetling. And for streetlings, reputation was everything.

'Take it,' Bish said.

'No.' Wren shook his head. 'It's a shit deal for the Point. We won't get much food with that.'

'Come on,' Bish egged, 'this is about more than just food. And if we don't make a deal, we won't have any food at all.'

Still Wren hesitated.

'Do it, Wren!' Bish snapped. 'And you had the gall to call me righteous? Just take it!'

'Fine.'

Wren reached out a hand and wrapped it around Thatcher's. After half a second, Thatcher quickly snatched his hand back. He ducked down, wiped his palm on the grimy ground, then smiled sweetly up at Wren.

'What's the first delivery?'

The Founding of Valrue (The Final Excerpt)

The most controversial beliefs of the Bhouli are regarding death and violence. The Bhouli refer to death as the privilege of being amongst the stars, and they frequently allude to the temptations of the night sky. This suggests a paradoxical belief that death is so desirable they must guard themselves against it.

For the Bhouli, death is intrinsically linked with the concept of purpose. Upon death, one may only go to the stars if one's purpose has been fulfilled. Thus, Bhouli spend considerable effort seeking and defining their purpose throughout their lives in pursuit of fulfilment.

The Bhouli believe that all individuals, not just Bhouli, should endeavour to reach the stars. On the rarest of occasions where a Bhouli was present at the death of a settler, the Bhouli swept their hands across the ground or body of the deceased and called up into the sky with the intention of leading the deceased up to the stars. This ritual was reserved for the settlers, and likely all non-believers, because they lack a defined and fulfilled purpose.

For Bhouli themselves, there is only a single exception in which Bhouli may go to the stars without having fulfilled their purpose. To understand this exception, one must first understand the Bhouli interpretation of violence.

To begin, it is known that the Bhouli make a Pledge Against Violence. Naturally, one assumes the Bhouli would then avoid harmful or destructive behaviours. Considering this, it is intriguing that the Bhouli are exceedingly overrepresented as victims of violent crime.

Of particular interest in the writings is the description of three brutal murders that occurred a century after the founding of Valrue. Each of the victims had chilling similarities. Not only were they all Bhouli, identified as such by white ink patterns on their skin and their shaven heads, but their headscarves had all been removed.

The killer was not caught, and understandably, a period of terror followed, emptying the streets of Valrue for a time as the People retreated to the safety of their homes.

Inexplicably, several months later, the murderer came forward of his own accord, providing indisputable evidence of each of his three kills. He claimed that each of the victims accosted him in the street and coerced him into the assault that led to their deaths.

He was hung for his crimes. Rumour had it he spent the last few months of his life screaming at the walls of his cell, the guilt having driven him insane.

Naturally, the city of Valrue was shaken by the brutal murders and the startling confession. However, most unsettling was the lack of response from the Bhouli community.

Pre-empting their outrage at the deaths of their people at the hands of a settler, the Kahnen sent their KahnenSpeaker into the streets to gather Bhouli individuals before the ruling house to deliver a formal apology.

However, the Speaker returned alone, reporting that the Bhouli declined the request. The Speaker insisted the Bhouli were both aware of the deaths and disturbingly unperturbed by them, and all but disregarded him.

The Kahnen struggled to accept this. Despite decades of harmony between their predecessors and the Bhouli, the Kahnen's disbelief at the Bhouli's apathy quickly fostered distrust. Under the direction of the ruling house, the abandoned attempts to determine the whereabouts of the Bhouli were re-instigated and grew more aggressive, and efforts to avoid offending the Bhouli less so. Ignoring the concern that the Bhouli would consider it an invasion, the first KahnenMayjen began digging further into the depths of the mountain, carving additional corridors and rooms that formed the KahnenKeep.

It was when the harnessing of the ballroom began that a Bhouli by the name of Osin appeared. Osin was described as old, covered with innumerous tattoos alongside smeared white ink. He tremored with every step he took and every word he spoke. He told the Kahnen that despite his many tattoos, he had yet to fully define a single purpose. However, that day, he said he came to give clarity.

In haste, the Kahnen gathered, eager to finally understand the Bhouli sentiment regarding the murders of their people.

Osin provided no such revelation. In fact, his ramblings only stoked to further infuriate the Kahnen. In a fit of frustration, one of the ruling house members struck Osin. The old Bhouli fell and died.

Few people considered Osin's death a tragedy. Sentiment towards the Bhouli had warped with time, and the People of Valrue had grown intolerant –

CHAPTER 73: THE GREAT KAHN

There was a rapid knocking at the door to his chambers. The Great Kahn looked up from his reading as he stood over his desk.

It was a while before dawn, but the Great Kahn had woken well before then. He couldn't even say what woke him because the Keep was dark and quiet as always.

The Great Kahn had no idea who had come to see him. It was highly unusual to have Minders visit at this hour, and they wouldn't knock quite like that. They'd retained a timidity about them despite the Great Kahn's ongoing attempts at kindness, their fear of him running deeper than he'd hoped.

The knocking returned, growing more urgent.

The Great Kahn slipped Mandavar's sword from its nook under his desk, crossed the room to the door, and pulled it open.

To the Great Kahn's astonishment, it was that sandy-haired Krijen from Jin's squad, the one with the dreary name he could never remember. The Krijen was paler than the moon outside, and he'd been biting his lip, already half-turned to leave when the Great Kahn opened the door.

'My Great Lord!' the Krijen exclaimed, looking relieved. 'I'm sorry to disturb you so early. Is . . .' he swallowed. 'Is the KrijenMayj with you?'

The question wasn't suggestive by any means. No, it was born of desperation, judging by the look on the Krijen's face. Regardless, it left the Great Kahn wondering what had led the Krijen to entertain the possibility that Jin would be with him.

'No,' the Great Kahn replied. 'What has happened?'

'It's nothing –'

'I doubt that. Tell me.'

The Krijen looked over his shoulder before replying, his voice dropping to a whisper. 'I can't find Jin, my Great Lord. I went to his room, and he's not there.'

The Great Kahn frowned. 'You felt it appropriate to come to me about this?'

The Krijen flushed. 'I'm so sorry, my Great Lord. It's just that Jin and I are supposed to be on duty, and it's not like him to neglect his duties. Even after what happened with his hands, he's not neglected his duties.'

'Again, why did you come to me about this? Go speak to the FaKrijen.'

'I won't be doing that.'

It was a blunt, shocking response, for two reasons. One, it was a clear dismissal of what the Great Kahn had said. Two, not informing the FaKrijen was disregarding procedure, an extraordinary display of autonomy from a Krijen. One that would demand an equally extraordinary punishment if Eden were to find out.

Yet the Great Kahn understood perfectly why the Krijen didn't want to go to Eden with this.

'What is your name?'

'Meek, my Great Lord.'

Ah yes, that was it. 'Come in.'

Meek dove into the room, and the Great Kahn shut the door. 'You have yet to answer my question,' the Great Kahn said. 'Why have you come to me?'

'I thought maybe you asked him to do something for you, him being KrijenMayj and all.' Meek said. 'And you aren't his superior, so if he's doing something he shouldn't be and you find out, you can't punish him for it.'

The Great Kahn pondered that. It was technically true but a gamble, considering the Great Kahn could simply inform the FaKrijen. There was something that Meek wasn't saying.

'Are you certain Jin is missing? Has he not left his room before now?'

'Only for his duties. Beyond that, he won't leave.'

'You cannot just wait for him to return?'

'It's been *hours*, my Great Lord. I'm worried.'

'Why? Jin is more than capable of looking after himself.'

Meek stood statue-still, like any good Krijen should, but his eyes roamed as though he itched to say something but knew he shouldn't.

'Speak, please.'

'You see, that's just it, my Great Lord,' Meek said softly. 'Jin's *not* great at looking after himself. And he's been worse since the glove thing, which is why I thought he might've come to you for help.'

That gave the Great Kahn pause. It was obvious Jin was struggling. What he went through would have ruined a lesser man. But the Great Kahn did not realise the situation was as dire as Meek suggested.

'Unfortunately, I am no more capable of finding him than you are,' the Great Kahn said. 'Possibly less so, given you know him better.'

Meek looked crestfallen.

'The KahnenMayj, on the other hand, is perfectly capable.'

Meek's head jerked back up. 'Stolt? Why would Stolt help?'

'Because I am *his* superior,' the Great Kahn said. 'He will do what I say.' He didn't understand why he needed to explain this to a Krijen of all people.

'But *how* can Stolt help?'

The Great Kahn raised an eyebrow. 'You are not aware that himajik mayjen can feel one another? If Jin is close enough, Stolt will find him.'

Meek shook his head. 'I didn't know that. Jin doesn't really talk about his majik.'

The Great Kahn tilted his head, curious about that. He was used to Mandavar, who had talked about nothing but his majik.

'In any case, we can ask the KahnenMayj to find Jin,' the Great Kahn replied. 'It is your choice. I am sure you understand the consequences for yourself and for Jin if Stolt informs the FaKrijen. That is something I will not involve myself in.' As Stolt had said, the Great Kahn shouldn't be seen playing favourites.

Meek understood. 'All right.'

'Follow me.'

The Great Kahn placed Mandavar's sword back in the nook behind his desk and opened the door, leading them into the corridor. Candles burned in high brackets along the walls, so the scarlet carpet was almost black under their feet, interspersed with brazen-red rings every few steps.

Stolt's chambers were not far. It took only a few minutes before the Great Kahn stopped outside the dark oak door. He ignored the crass gold knocker, instead rapping his knuckles on the wood before pushing the door open. He would not wait on Stolt.

As it turned out, Stolt was awake too. He leapt up from a chair on the opposite side of the room, raising a hand defensively. He slowly dropped his hand when he realised who it was.

'My Great Lord? What is . . .' His expression hardened when he saw Meek. 'What is this?'

Meek closed the door, one hand on a dagger hilt. He did not trust Stolt. The Great Kahn didn't blame him.

'Jin is missing,' the Great Kahn said to Stolt. 'I need you to find him.'

'Missing? As in –'

'He should be on duty, and he is not.'

Stolt sneered. 'He's gone rogue, has he? Like I said he would?'

'We know nothing of the sort. Like I said, he is missing.'

Stolt folded his arms, looking suspicious. 'The Krijen can't find him? You can't have been looking very hard. His stench is everywhere. It grows worse by the day.'

'The Krijen do not know he is missing. Nor does the FaKrijen.'

'What?' Stolt's eyes flickered to Meek. 'Why is it *my* problem that this dog has a death wish?'

'Because I thought you might appreciate the opportunity to atone,' the Great Kahn said. 'To show me what kind of man you are. To prove that you deserve an iota of the respect you have demanded all these years by doing something decent that does not revolve around yourself. Take your pick.'

Stolt paled. He leaned towards the Great Kahn to hiss in his ear. 'How dare you say this in front of *him?*' He jerked his head towards Meek.

'Why do you care?' the Great Kahn replied. 'He is nothing more than a dog.'

Stolt's expression didn't change, and neither did Meek's. Meek's hand was still on his dagger hilt.

'Fine,' Stolt said finally, lifting his nose. 'I'll do it.'

'Very good. Tell me when you have found him. And, Stolt,' – it was the Great Kahn's turn to hiss into Stolt's ear – 'if Eden hears about this, it will prove to me *exactly* the kind of man you are.'

The Great Kahn crossed to the door and dragged it open, strolling back through the dark doorway towards his chambers.

CHAPTER 74:
PYRA

The first time her streetlings tried to kill her, Pyra felt strangely vindicated. She'd told Lady Hia it would happen because of the Lost Square's meddling, and now she had proof.

The second time they tried to kill her was too close a call.

And it was as she was dangling yet another murderous culprit out the window of an Upper West Side tower, his nails digging into her skin while he screeched at her, that she knew it had to be tonight. She'd never known anyone to be fourth-time lucky.

Pyra was losing the respect of the streetlings and fast. The only way to get it back was to do something so malignant that even the streetlings felt the ick. That was why she'd brought her most ick-insensitive streetling with her to make sure the job got done.

'Are you ready, Ala?'

That's my girl, Pyra thought as the little streetling nodded her mostly bald head, remnant tufts of blonde hair sticking out above her ears. She'd survived Pyra's scalping and had since been the most belligerently loyal streetling there ever was, taking her rusty nails to each of Pyra's attempted murderers and carving her own name into their foreheads as punishment. Pyra was so proud.

'All right, Ala, you know what to do.'

As Pyra watched Ala scurry away into the darkest part of the night, she wondered if, at any point, Polly might convince Pyra not to go through with the plan. But Polly never had to choose between being murdered by streetlings or saving face by murdering Krijen. Pyra was certain that if given the choice, Polly would have also chosen the latter.

The Krijen barracks were the only buildings that weren't towers in the Left South Side. Instead they sprawled within their compound, the rectangular wooden buildings taking up an arrogant amount of space.

It had taken all Pyra and Ala's streetling stealth to sneak into the compound unnoticed even with just the two of them. First, they'd had to skirt the Left South Side gang because technically they were creepers, and Pyra knew more than anyone what was done with creepers.

Even more difficult to evade were the Krijen. They were irritatingly attentive when on watch at the gates despite it being pitch black and silent, and they knew no one would ever be stupid enough to try to scale the slippery compound walls.

Which was why Pyra and Ala had dug under them.

They'd prised up the cobblestones and wriggled through a bone-scrapingly tiny gap, then stuck their arms back through to drag their heavy sack filled with nails and horseshoes in behind them. Pyra had long since kept a secret stash of tid-bit weapons because, as she suspected they would, the streetlings had begun stealing them, trying to catch her out.

So now Pyra stood in the shadows of the barracks inside which the Krijen squads currently slept, the sack at her feet, watching the moonlight reflect off the water gushing from the fancy fountain in the middle of the courtyard.

As the water bubbled, Pyra ground her teeth, pissed off that it had come to this and that despite everything that she'd done for the streetlings over the last five years, Pyra had to keep on proving that she was the toughest streetling there ever was. But even though it was just her and Ala for now, if everything went according to plan, there was no way the entire city wouldn't know what she'd done by sunrise. Pyra's worthiness would never be questioned again.

Pyra got to it, working her way around all the windows, making sure every shutter was closed, pulling horseshoes from her sack and jamming them into the cracks down the sides. She moved to the second barracks, and by the time she'd finished, Ala was bouncing towards her.

'Doors next?' Ala asked sweetly.

Pyra dug into her sack and pulled out strips of red material, the colour as close as a match as she could get to the ones on her wrists. She gave some to Ala, then stuck her head out from behind the barracks, scouring the area. The courtyard was still dead silent. Not even the wind breathed, which was unusual for mountain air. Pyra had been sure to check with Rifter what times the Krijen changed shifts. As planned, they were smack in the middle of one, so there were no Krijen coming and going from the compound.

Pyra nodded, and Ala scooted off.

Pyra crept around to the front of the barracks. The doors were closed to keep out the cold night air but not locked. Pyra pulled out the first red strip, doubled it over, and slipped it between the metal rings hanging from each of the doors, knotting them tightly.

Everyone underestimated the strength of fabric.

Of course, all the Krijen had to do was stick their daggers through the crack in the doors and slice upwards through the material. But panic was a dangerous thing, and it was even harder to think straight in the dark.

Pyra quickly knotted the other barracks doors and ducked back behind their walls, turning to see Ala already beside her. This time, Pyra ripped two strips of material directly from her red wrist ties, which she'd soaked in oil earlier. With the tiniest hesitation at the ick that was about to be, she pressed the strips into Ala's hand, along with an extra horseshoe.

'It's okay,' Ala said in response to Pyra's hesitation. 'I've been practising.'

Then Ala was gone.

Pyra left the empty sack on the ground, then got down on her stomach and crawled into the space underneath the barracks until she got to the middle. She slowly undid one of her wrist ties. It dropped onto the dirt, wet with oil. 'I'm sorry, Polly,' Pyra whispered. But there was some poetic irony to it that the fabric from the dress Polly died in would feed these particular flames.

Pyra dug into her boot and pulled out a rectangle of flint. She struck her horseshoe down its length, watching the sparks land on the strip of oiled material. It burst into flame. Using her horseshoes, Pyra shoved the burning tie up into the wooden floorboards.

Pyra squirmed her way out from under the barracks and sprinted to the next one and dove under its belly, ripping the second tie from her wrist and lighting it up like the first. Once it was firmly jammed into the floor of the barracks, Pyra crawled out on her hands and knees and ducked into the shadow of the compound wall, inching along until she got to the huge wooden gates that marked the only entrance to the compound.

The gates were ever so slightly ajar, and Pyra could see the two Krijen guards through the crack, looking down the dark streets. Krijen never closed gates because they didn't need to. Their bodies and daggers served a better defence than solid wood ever could.

Pyra pressed her body against the gates, heaving. Luckily, they closed without a whisper of noise. Then she reached up and tugged down the stiff wooden slab, which protested louder than she'd hoped. But it didn't matter. The gates were locked now. It was done.

Pyra hurried back along the wall to the place with the loose cobbles. She shimmied through the tiny gap, replaced the stones carefully, then clambered up to the rooftops to where Ala's tiny frame was waiting.

First, they heard the Krijen guards cursing out the front of the compound, followed by the sound of thudding as they banged on the gates, which, as thick and heavy as they were, the Krijen wouldn't have a hope of budging.

It was a few more minutes before Pyra spotted the smoke, backlit by the stars.

It was a little while after that the yelling began.

Then each of the barracks doors rattled, and the red material strained, and the yelling became screams.

Together Pyra and Ala watched as the orange finally broke free from the darkness to swallow each of the barracks whole, and all the while the water in the fountain bubbled away in the middle of the courtyard.

CHAPTER 75:
JIN KANJU

Jin was drowning. It felt like an age since he'd put on the cardonite gloves, and the only reason he'd made it this long without exploding from lack of harnessing was because he'd discovered that if he drank just the right amount of ale – delivered to his room by obliging Minders – he could keep his power at bay. Sometimes it was enough to keep Filip away too even though it sucked because Aren went with him.

But it also wasn't that simple because if Jin drank too much, then it numbed his mind completely, and as desperate as he was to have them give up on him, Jin's squad were determined to remain his responsibility.

After the initial wallowing, his Krijen duties had dragged him from his bed. While Jin hadn't yet dared to grasp a dagger with his swollen hands, his squad came to him for orders, insisting he join them on the ramparts or in their roaming of the Keep's corridors, providing an intimidating, albeit secretly useless, presence.

Jin wanted to go back to the Deadlands, away from all the curious eyes, but that would require him asking the FaKrijen, and Jin couldn't stand the thought of seeing Eden.

Eventually, Jin's negligence caught up with him. His hateful power built up inside until it plagued him like never before, leaving him crunched over in agony, groaning while he spat fire, and even six or seven or twelve tankards of ale weren't enough to rid him of it.

So at some point, Jin stumbled from his room, shuddering as the ice-cold air screamed into his lungs as he headed towards the dungeons. But it was as he was falling down the stairs towards Mama Hidel's women that he realised he would be a fool to go near them in this state. There was nothing they could do for him, not about this, anyway. This problem was all his own making.

He'd stupidly assumed that his power wouldn't kill him, because it was a part of him, and how could something that was a part of you be the death of you. So he'd let it get bad. Really, really, fucking bad. And now he needed to fix it, because if he didn't, he might just die from how much it hurt, and he didn't deserve that kind of escape.

But to fix it required him to Influence, the one thing he'd promised himself he'd never do again because he didn't want that kind of power over people.

No.

He didn't want to *enjoy* that kind of power over people because it felt *that good*, and Jin knew that if he unlocked that box, properly unlocked it, he wouldn't trust himself to close it again. The other times had been accidents, he swore it, so those times didn't count.

But Jin was running out of the privilege of *choice,* and he was ever so desperate, and he was annoyed at himself that he'd drunk so much ale because it made it impossibly hard to think.

It was as he leant against the cold dungeon wall – or was it the floor – that an idea suddenly came to him. It surely didn't count as Influencing. It *couldn't* count if something was dead. But it was still a part of a person, so Jin hoped and hoped and *hoped* with all his might that his idea would work. He just had to get there.

And so Jin found himself stuck in a loop. Not a loop in his mind but a loop in the tunnels out the back of the dungeons, the ones that he'd stumbled through all those months ago when he was searching for Maude, much like he was doing now.

He was sure he was getting closer to the viewing point that looked out over the lake, but his memory was foggy of how to get there because when he'd first walked it, he'd been muddled by Maude, sucking his power from him. He laughed out loud knowing that he was muddled again right now by the complete opposite problem. That and all the ale.

Another problem was that it was so dark that Jin couldn't see in front of him. He went as best as he could by feel, because all the tiny things that Stolt had once called atoms that made up the mountain rock felt different to the air, and if he concentrated hard enough, he could feel where the spaces were so at least he wasn't walking into walls.

But still he looped.

Because although he could tell the difference between the rock and the air, a tunnel was still very much a tunnel, and so he wasn't sure whether it had been minutes or hours or days when he finally felt something on the ground in front of him that wasn't rock or air but somewhere in the middle.

Bone.

Jin flung himself onto his knees, running his ruined hands through the remains of the mercenary, hardly believing that they were still here and picked clean by mice or rats or insects or some creature of sorts. It was more proof that the Unsettlement was over.

Jin's fingers seared constantly now, the pain of healing a sign his melted nerve endings were coming back to life. The bones felt bizarre in his hands. Their shapes were all so strange too, some long and knobbly, others small, clustered, and irregular.

Jin couldn't sense any power coming from the bones, which scared him at first, but then he remembered he couldn't feel anyone's power unless they were Stolt or that skahk. It wasn't until he harnessed non-mayjen that he *felt* them, their heaviness.

Jin raised a hand above the skeleton. He took a rattling breath. Then he felt for it in the darkness, all the pieces of it with one hand, because he could do that now, ever since the Great Kahn had shown him how.

Jin carefully lifted the skeleton into the air with majik, pressing a little harder than before because his power seemed stickier somehow, like it was jamming in his fingers. It was probably to do with his damaged nerves. He waited, his breath held, for that sensation of bliss he craved. Even just a nudge of relief would do.

But there was nothing.

The skeleton was practically weightless; it was useless to him. There was no essence of life in it, no matter that it was human.

'FUCK!'

Jin slammed the skeleton down onto the floor of the tunnel, and the entire thing exploded into dust. He could taste it.

The sound of the bang continued strangely, eerily, until Jin realised it wasn't the explosion lingering, but the ringing returning in his ears. The ale was wearing off.

'Now you *knew* that wasn't going to work,' Filip's voice drawled in the blackness.

'It was worth a try,' Aren said, from somewhere near Filip. 'I agree you needed to do something, Jin.'

'You *still* need to do something,' Filip said. 'And you won't manage it sitting on the floor. Get up.'

Jin staggered to his feet. He moved forward because he knew there would be light in this direction eventually. But if Filip and Aren and the ringing were back, it meant that his power was climbing too, and that monster would follow, and soon Jin was struggling to stay upright because the weight of it all kept knocking him down, and the whole thing felt so cruelly similar to what had happened all those months ago when he'd last been in this tunnel.

Had he thought that already?

And when Jin finally got to the cliff's edge and saw the dull orange of the pre-dawn light and stars speckled across half the sky, Jin wondered why Maude wasn't there waiting for him. Filip and Aren did nothing but follow him around, and he'd been there when they died too.

'The difference is that you killed us,' Filip said. 'Maude killed herself.'

Maybe that was it.

'To help with the power, you could try lifting yourself again,' Aren suggested.

'He's tried that,' Filip said. 'It's not enough.'

'At least it's something.'

'Oh yeah? What's he going to do? Spend the rest of his life hovering in the air? We all know that he just needs to Influence.'

'What about animals?' Aren offered. 'Does that count as Influencing?'

'If you don't know, how would I know?'

'Maybe it does!'

'The forest is barely at Third Base. Even if Jin ran there bolstered with power, it would take days, and all for a *maybe?* And again, what's he going do? Run out into the Deadlands every time he needs a load off?'

'Why are you always so negative, Filip –'

'Because I'm the only one with any sense –'

'Shut up,' Jin said, his tongue feeling strange in his mouth. He was unsteady on his feet, and the edge of the cliff was right under his boots. Beyond that, it was such a *long* way down. The water of the lake was black, and Jin imagined it would be ever so cold. Cold enough to quench the fire that was him.

Jin threw back his head to face to the stars, wondering if Maude was up there like she said she'd be.

Jin hoped it wasn't so bad up there. Maybe Aren would forgive him for Maude's death if it weren't. Then again, maybe that was why Aren hung around, not to keep him company but to haunt him for not being able to save Maude. It seemed more likely.

But that didn't explain Filip.

Jin remembered how obsessed Filip had been about the night sky too, and how he'd also mentioned it when he'd died. It must be some Bhouli thing, to want to go to the stars as though there was something more amazing there than there was here.

Then again, who was to say there wasn't?

Jin squinted, trying to focus on the stars not yet consumed by the orange dawn. He couldn't lift himself that high; he'd tried once and nearly suffocated. But there was nothing stopping him from bringing a star down here.

Jin raised his swollen hands to the sky.

'NO, SIR, DON'T DO IT!'

Jin paused with his hands still raised, frowning. That sounded strangely like –

Something grabbed hold of the back of his wraps and wrenched him away from the cliff's edge. Jin couldn't keep his feet under himself, and he tripped, smacking onto his shoulder. Something heavy landed on top of him, yelling piercingly in his ear.

'I won't let you do it, sir! I won't let you!'

'Meek?'

Meek was wrestling with him even though Jin wasn't fighting back. His body twitched, but other than that, he kept himself carefully limp, not wanting to hurt Meek. Well, that's if it actually *was* Meek. Jin didn't trust that his brain wasn't tricking him because there was no way that Meek would know he was here. Then again, Meek seemed very real, and very heavy, and his voice was so loud it hurt.

'Stop yelling,' Jin gasped, his lungs crushed against his ribs. 'Get off me.'

'No!' Meek cried. 'You can't give up on us, sir! Jeez, you're hotter than a fucking furnace –'

'What are –'

'I know you're feeling shit right now, but it's only because you've not been harnessing!'

Jin's muddled brain suddenly clicked. 'You . . . you thought I was going to . . . to jump off the cliff?' He asked the question slowly, hoping it came out right.

'You weren't?'

'No. I was going to drag a star down.'

There was a long pause. 'I think this power has driven you a little crazy, sir,' Meek said finally. 'But that's okay. Let's fix it.'

Meek hauled Jin into a sitting position and squatted down in front of him. Meek's face was blurry around the edges, but Jin could see his features, backlit by the rising sun. Meek was drenched with sweat, and his cheeks were pink.

'How . . . how did you find me?' Jin asked.

'Stolt.'

'Stolt? But –'

'Listen to me, sir,' Meek interrupted, 'I know you don't like harnessing people, but it's about time you did because you can't keep this up.'

Jin squinted up at him, his shoulders shuddering.

'And knowing you,' Meek went on, 'you're going to make this difficult, so I'm sorry, sir. I'm going to fight dirty.'

To Jin's bewilderment, Meek stood up and pulled his daggers out of his wraps and dropped them on the ground. Then he tugged off his boots and started untying his wraps.

Surely Jin was imagining this. 'You're . . . you're undressing?'

'Yes, I am. And don't give me that look. It's so that you can't cheat and grab my wraps.'

Jin had no idea what he meant, nor what look he'd been giving. It was his power-addled brain. The monster climbing up his throat was as distracting as Meek's stripping, and it was taking all of Jin's might not to spew fire over himself.

'All right, sir. Are you ready? And please, for fuck's sake, catch me.'

Before Jin knew what was happening, Meek's blurry white form ran from him, and with a bounding leap, Meek sailed over the edge of the cliff.

CHAPTER 76:
AREN BHA

There was a loud knock on the door.

Bleary-eyed, Aren dragged herself out of bed and opened the bedroom door leading into the main room. The knocking hadn't continued, so Aren vaguely wondered if she'd imagined it. Best to check. She crossed the room and opened the door leading into the corridor.

It was Mandavar. He looked like he had on the first day Aren saw him, with dark rings under his eyes. Despite that, he seemed restless; his hands twitched at his sides. Aren looked past him into the dark corridor. It was the crack of dawn. 'What do you want?' she snapped, completely awake now.

'You're a delight,' Mandavar drawled. 'I thought it time my son did some majik that didn't revolve around you.'

'He's sleeping.'

'You know,' Mandavar said, 'I don't need to help you. It fascinates me that despite knowing I'm the only chance you've got, you continue to be so unpleasant.'

'That's because I know your game,' Aren said. 'The only reason you're helping is because you're obsessed with majik, and Drax can do things you can't. You're hoping to learn some tricks from him. Don't make this out to be kindness. This is self-indulgent fun for you.'

'You think yourself so astute. You're not.' Mandavar shouldered past her. 'And you shouldn't answer the door wearing that. You're not a mayj, your slights will not be excused simply because you spend your time with them.'

Aren looked down at her loose sleeping shirt and bare feet. 'What's wrong with what I'm wearing?' she asked.

'You're all in white.'

Scowling, Aren closed the door. She needed to re-read that list of slights. It had said something about the colour of clothing, which explained all the black and white.

Mandavar was already in their bedroom. 'Son, wake up,' Aren heard him say. She stopped at the bedroom door, watching as Mandavar flicked up a hand and the lamps ebbed into life around the room, flames flickering.

Aren had once thought mayjen couldn't control fire. Of course, she hadn't understood that fire was simply heat, fuel, and oxygen. Heat wasn't matter, so it couldn't be harnessed but if you remove the fuel or oxygen with majik, away goes the fire.

Alternatively, if you're stuck in a forest, desperate to cook a rabbit because you're so close to Turning that your life depends on it, you can create fire using majik by rubbing two dry sticks together really fast. You'll get heat, followed quickly by flame. Unfortunately, Drax didn't have the power to show her that at the time. That first rabbit they'd eaten raw. Even so, Aren understood what Mandavar had done in their bedroom just now. Using majik, he'd rubbed the particles of the oiled lamp wicks together at high speed until they produced enough heat for a flame.

Drax sat up in bed, rubbing his eyes with his wrists, peering sleepily up at Mandavar. Then he did a double take, seeing his father standing there.

'Come, son,' Mandavar said, inclining his head. Mandavar strode back to the bedroom doorway, past Aren, and sat down in the armchair in the main room.

Aren hurried over to Drax as he climbed out of bed, awkwardly dragging on black trousers under his white sleeping shirt. 'I'm sorry,' Aren said, 'he just walked in. I couldn't stop him.'

'It's okay,' Drax said. He ambled out into the lounge and stopped in front of Mandavar. 'You feel heavy,' Drax said to him.

'Yes, I need to Weave,' Mandavar replied. 'Sit.'

Drax curled himself onto the couch, his legs underneath him.

Aren stayed standing where she was. 'Wait,' she said. 'Had you been Weaving the day we met? Is that why Drax could harness you?'

Mandavar turned his head slowly towards Aren.

'He grabbed onto you right after I punched you,' Aren said. Even though Drax had let go of her heart to do it, but it had been bothering her. Influencing a mayj like Mandavar should be near-on impossible yet Drax hadn't started Turning when he'd done it.

'Yes,' Mandavar said. 'I'd been Weaving that day. My power was depleted, so I was easier to Influence.'

'But . . .' Aren sensed a flaw. 'But Drax's power was also drained from harnessing *me*. Surely he still wouldn't have enough power to Influence you like that?'

Mandavar hesitated. When he replied, he spoke slowly, obviously taking care with his words. 'He could do it only because we are related. At that moment, Drax couldn't have Influenced any mayj other than myself without Turning. We don't repel one another as unrelated mayjen do, so it doesn't require so much power.'

Ah. Aren saw why he was so reluctant to divulge that bit of information. 'So to Drax, you're weaker?'

'And he to me,' Mandavar drawled. 'Do not look so excited. It is neither an advantage nor a disadvantage. When Drax Influenced me, it only made it easy to guess who he was.' He turned back to Drax. 'Now, son, you've been observing my classes for some time, but majikal theory can only get you so far. To teach you properly, I need to see what you can do, which is rather difficult when you are burdened as you are.'

Aren knew he'd used that word purposefully to hurt her. It did.

'However, that is easily solved,' Mandavar continued, looking back to Aren, 'if you'll allow me to take over from my son. Briefly, mind you.'

'You can do that?'

Mandavar gave Aren a droll look. 'What would be the point of my suggesting it otherwise?'

'I meant that you look exhausted,' Aren said. 'Is now really the best time?'

'Yes,' Drax said, 'now is good.'

Mandavar nodded. 'My power is not depleted now, the very opposite. It's been keeping me awake. I thought it best to let it build for this.'

'Let it build? I thought mayjen couldn't grow more powerful?'

'You misunderstand me,' Mandavar said. 'I become uncomfortable at my maximum power, so I run myself down now and then. But it doesn't keep growing if I don't use it. You're thinking of the Du Bellor Spell, which is fed by its own mass.'

That wasn't at all what Aren had been thinking about. 'What do you mean by uncomfortable?' she asked.

'My power makes me . . . irritable.'

'It affects your emotions?'

'It can. You saw Demison the other day, how reactive he was. Weaving uses the most power, but he cannot Weave, so he needs to Build frequently to make up for it. Breaking is mostly worthless for using power for mayjen like us. Sometimes Demison needs reminding. It can be hard to recognise in oneself when you have let your power run away from you, clouded as you become. However, Demison isn't ignorant of this, so that's no excuse.' Mandavar frowned at Drax. 'You know what I'm talking about?'

Drax shook his head. 'I feel warm when I've not harnessed. But I don't think I feel anything else.'

'That's interesting, given you have substantial power. But perhaps that's Luka's fault. I cannot discount what he did to you.'

Aren knew what Mandavar meant. Drax had particularly good control of his emotions.

'How bad can it get?' Aren asked. 'I mean, can a build-up of power make a mayj do things that are really out of character?'

'That's not an easy question to answer,' Mandavar said. 'Majik aside, anyone can do something that's out of character, given the right circumstance. But if you were to remove those confounding pressures . . . then yes. But you would have to be an exceptionally powerful mayj, and be exceptionally neglectful, to let it warp you from your typical self.'

'What about someone really powerful who knows nothing about majik?'

Mandavar frowned. 'That would be a disastrous combination.'

Aren went silent.

'You're thinking of Jin,' Drax said quietly. He looked sad. Drax thought Jin was a lost cause, but Aren refused to believe it.

'Who's Jin?' Mandavar asked.

'My best friend,' Aren said. 'We think he's a Breaker. Drax says he feels powerful, and when we last saw him . . . he wasn't being himself.'

Mandavar looked at Drax. 'How powerful?'

'He's very heavy,' Drax said. 'Much heavier than you are right now.'

Mandavar frowned. 'A difficult comparison to make . . . You may have noticed that when your power is dulled, it relatively affects your ability to sense other mayjen. So right now, even though I am close to my maximum power, I still feel comparably less heavy to you because your own power is dulled. You see the problem when trying to compare the power of two mayjen. The comparison would only be fair if, when you were with the Breaker, your power was equally as dulled as it is now and the Breaker was at full power, like I am now. Understand?'

Drax nodded.

'This Breaker, he's in Valrue?'

'Yes.'

'If he's had no instruction, which I imagine he wouldn't have in Valrue, then it's cause for concern. Unless he's a KahnenMayj?'

'He's Krijen.'

Mandavar raised his eyebrows. 'Is he now? Well, it'll be interesting to see which wins out, being Krijen or being a Breaker with no decent outlet. You say he wasn't himself. What did he do?'

'He killed me,' Aren admitted.

'Ah.' Mandavar smiled. 'I see. That brings us nicely back to the issue at hand then, doesn't it?' He pointed to the couch. 'I suggest you lie down for this.'

Aren slowly walked over to the couch and sat down next to Drax. 'So you're going to take over my heart? How will this work?'

'I'm not sure exactly, but I'll try to mimic what Drax is doing.' Mandavar stood up and came over to the couch. 'I said, lie down.'

Aren shot him a nasty look and lay down, tucking her feet in behind Drax. Her back didn't hurt anymore but it felt tight, streaked with long ridged scars to remind her of the Edgecat. Not that she would ever forget.

Mandavar knelt beside the couch. 'Son, when you feel me pressing, ease off. There's only so much power atoms can hold before they denature, and that's not an easy fix, especially not for a human heart.'

Aren didn't like the sound of that, but Drax gave a curt nod.

'Are you ready?' Mandavar asked. It took a moment before Aren realised he was talking to her. 'Yes,' she said, taking a deep breath. She squeezed her hands into fists, ready for whatever vile thing Mandavar was going to inflict upon her.

'I going to touch you again.' Mandavar raised a hand, and gently placed it on her chest, just above her heart, which began beating rapidly in defiance.

'Try to stay calm,' Mandavar said firmly.

'I *am*,' Aren said. 'Can you blame me for being nervous?'

'Shh, Aren,' Drax said gently. 'It's okay.'

Aren stayed shushed, letting them concentrate, and waited. After a little while, she thought maybe her chest had grown a few degrees warmer, but she wasn't sure because her nervousness had also sent adrenalin rushing through her body. Her fingers went to her wrists, searching for wrist wraps that weren't there. She dropped them by her sides. She didn't like how close Mandavar's face was to hers. His eyes were disconcertingly similar to his son's with a spark of life that Drax's lacked. Aren closed her eyes, so she didn't have to look at him.

'Ease off now,' Mandavar murmured.

Aren's heart skipped a beat.

'I said ease *off*,' Mandavar repeated. 'I can't take over if you hold on.'

'You don't have her right,' Drax said in an uncharacteristic grumble.

'Yes, I do. Trust me, son. Let go.'

Aren's heart spluttered again. Then it picked up a hiccupping beat that quickly left Aren feeling woozy, but she bit her tongue, not wanting to complain. She peeked open an eye. Drax's nose was right up close to her chest.

'I've got her,' Mandavar said. 'Lean back.'

Drax slowly moved away, watching Aren's face.

'It worked?' Aren asked, opening her other eye. Her heart definitely wasn't beating right, but she was alive and nothing hurt, which was good.

'How peculiar this is,' Mandavar said. He leant back, his palm coming off Aren's chest, but he kept his hand stretched out towards her. 'And dreadfully inefficient.'

Aren sat up, and an unexpected wave of dizziness hit her, so she threw an arm over the back of the couch to catch herself.

Drax flinched. 'You aren't doing it right!' he cried, spinning to Mandavar. 'You have to adjust when she moves!'

Mandavar held out his other hand to Drax. 'Yes, I know, son. You had months to get used to this. Give me a minute.'

Aren didn't like how he kept saying son, but Drax didn't seem to notice. 'How do you feel?' Aren asked him. She wondered what it was like not having to hold on to her after months of continuous harnessing.

'It's . . .' Drax cocked his head. 'Nice.'

'You'll feel even better in an hour,' Mandavar said. 'More so after some food.'

'Our breakfast normally comes about now,' Aren said.

'Mo Nu has not shown you the dining hall?'

'No?' Aren didn't know there was a dining hall.

'That foolish man,' Mandavar said. 'Let's go there first. Then we'll see what Drax can do.'

CHAPTER 77:
JIN KANJU

Fuck fuck fuck fuck fuck –

Jin's lungs had finally collapsed on themselves, and even though it was Meek's yell that echoed around the lake back up to him, it was Maude all over again, throwing herself enthusiastically over the edge of the cliff towards a certain death that Jin never seem to be able to save anyone from.

Aren's petrified voice sliced through his senses. 'JIN! WHAT ARE YOU DOING? GO GET HIM!'

Jin scrambled to his feet and stumbled to the cliff's edge, flinging himself onto his belly. 'MEEK!' he screamed over the edge, for all the good it would do. Meek was already so far away, just a tiny white speck hurtling towards the black of the lake.

'Save him!' Aren cried. 'You have to save him!'

Meek had given Jin no choice. He could barely think, let alone see, and with no time to spare, Jin did the only thing he could do. He threw his arm over the edge of the cliff, concentrating with all his might on the small, screaming, naked thing that was Meek and sank his swollen red fingers into the air, grabbing onto Meek's torso.

Clarity hurtled up to meet him as the weight of Meek wrenched on his power.

And with the clarity came the bottled fury.

'Meek! You arsehole!'

Jin shoved power down his arm, riding the wave of relief that went with it. Then he pulled his arm back towards himself, dragging Meek up through space with an almighty effort until Meek was hovering just below the edge of the cliff.

Jin held him there, revelling in the drain of it. It wasn't enough, not nearly enough to send him to bliss but enough that Jin could finally focus on Meek's pale face.

'Woah, sir!' Meek said, gasping, actual tears rolling down his cheeks. 'For a second there, I thought you weren't going to do it!'

Jin growled as he lifted Meek the final few feet over the cliff and dropped him onto the mountain stone.

'You idiot!' Jin yelled, letting go of his majik and lowering his hand. He stomped towards Meek until he was close enough to spit in his face. 'Are you *insane?* What the fuck were you thinking?'

Meek grinned at him. 'Well, sir, don't you seem better.'

Jin roared unintelligibly back at him, but Meek's grin persisted. Then he looked behind himself at his wraps piled on the ground. 'May I get dressed, sir? Or do we need to do it again?' Meek eyed up Jin's shaking form. 'Once more, perhaps –'

'Don't you dare!'

'Yes, sir.' Meek darted backwards and scooped his wraps off the ground, wrapping them around him quickly, leaving his arms bare. Barefoot and weaponless, he padded back over to Jin.

'Meek! I asked why you did that! Answer me!'

Meek raised an eyebrow. 'You're serious, sir?'

'You just threw yourself off a cliff. You could have *died.*'

Meek shook his head. 'Not with you around, sir. And you say you weren't going to jump, and I believe you, but you can hardly blame me for thinking it. Look at the state you got yourself into.' Meek frowned at him. 'Is it because of the whole Krijen thing?'

Jin stilled as much as he could while still shuddering, his power wrestling in his throat. 'What Krijen thing?'

'Excuse me for saying this, sir, but I haven't seen you touch a dagger since the glove thing. I think you're scared to.'

'I'm not –'

'Don't lie, sir. It's okay. I get it because I'm Krijen too. I know what it took to get here, and what it would feel like to lose the ability to fight, to wield a dagger or a krije. And I know you can't hold your dagger properly anymore. You can't do it without majik. And that's why you've not been harnessing since it happened. You think that having to use majik is like cheating at being Krijen.'

Meek had always been the loud, borderline-obnoxious character that cracked jokes and prodded at people until they snapped. He had no right to be so perceptive.

'You don't think it's cheating then?'

'No, sir. I think you've got this gift that you've been told your whole life is a curse, and you're torn to use it and it's killing you a little. But I don't think needing to use it makes you any less Krijen.'

Jin was finally quiet, save for the growling of the monster in his throat. His squad knew so much about him even though he said nothing about himself, and he didn't like it. But he supposed it helped if they understood him.

Yet there was so much Jin didn't know about *them*. He'd been neglecting getting to know them, and that was wrong of him.

A whirl of heat suddenly surged up from Jin's chest, a ball of frustrated power, making him gag.

'You all right, sir?'

'*Yes.*' Jin shoved it back down. He had a question. 'Meek?'

'Sir?'

'Ages ago, I asked you why you requested to be sent to the Deadlands. I don't think I got the chance to hear your answer.'

'Oh, well . . .' Meek chewed on his lip.

Dragging honest answers from his squad about their thoughts on the Krijen was still harder than Jin would've liked. It made him worry to think what they weren't saying.

'Tell me the truth,' Jin ground out as best he could, still forcing down that ball of power. 'You owe me. I just saved your life.'

Meek nodded. 'Yes, sir. I wanted to leave the city because there was so much more killing than I thought there would be.'

That wasn't what Jin had expected.

'You see,' Meek continued, 'there weren't enough Krijen in Valrue. We couldn't keep up. Sure, we caught criminals and strung up streetlings and did what we had to do. But it was endless, you know? I never imagined that as a Krijen, I'd spend my days hurting people. I wanted to protect.'

'You . . . you thought the Deadlands would be better?'

'Yes, sir, running supplies and roaming the wilderness, you know? And it *was* better. I could tell because everyone seemed so relaxed. Apart from you, of course,' Meek grinned. 'You've always acted like someone had lit a fire up in your –'

'I get it, Meek,' Jin snarled as another whirl of heat strained in his chest, wrapping about his lungs. 'But we've been back in the city for months now.'

'Yeah, and that's okay. I knew we had to come back. The shame of it was that nothing had changed. In fact, it was worse. Great Kahn knows I wanted to throttle the mayj who killed Oji, but we spent three days killing children and we never caught him.' Meek looked at his feet. 'I never thought I would do something like that but I did. And was it even worth it? They don't prepare you for this as Squares. The guilt of it, I mean. They really don't.'

Jin had no idea Meek felt like that. Pago had always been the sensitive one of the group and Jokah with the moral compass. Meek had just diligently done as ordered.

'It sounds like you don't like being Krijen.'

Meek looked up. 'But I do, sir! And that's where you come in.'

'Me?'

'You're not like any squad leader I've had before. Sure, you get angry sometimes or go a little overboard, but that's okay because we know why. And you actually seem to want to do what's right, rather than just follow orders, which the rest of us are too shit-scared to do. You're showing us what Krijen *could* be like. I mean you're not perfect, but who is? I don't know where we would be without you, sir. So please,' he added, 'don't go dragging down stars. That doesn't sound like a good idea.'

Jin didn't know what to say. The ale was almost worn off, which was fucking annoying because Jin could barely think straight again. He let out a low groan, bending over as the flames began to take him once more.

'Sir,' came Meek's concerned voice, 'why don't we go back to the Keep and speak to someone about that? Maybe the Great Kahn?'

Jin huffed but in spite of himself, he was listening. 'What . . . what's the Great Kahn going to do?'

'I reckon he'd have an idea. I know he's intimidating and all, but he'd be good about it. He, um . . . he was the one who made sure Stolt got the gloves off you. I wasn't sure if you knew that.'

No, Jin hadn't known. But he also didn't want to speak to the Great Kahn, not in this state. It was embarrassing, to say the least.

'No. No, I don't . . . I don't want to scc him.'

Jin knew his whole squad would know shortly too because they always seemed to know everything. And Jin was losing control. It was bad enough that Meek was here, standing so close.

'I . . . I just need some more . . . ale,' Jin choked out.

'I'm not sure if I agree, sir. But – what's that?' Meek was squinting out over the lake. Jin slowly stood up and eased himself around.

A plume of black smoke was curling up into the air from somewhere in the South Side of Rue.

'That can't be good,' Meek said. 'Should we go back – sir, wait!'

But Jin had already knelt down and grabbed hold of the rock he stood on with majik. He ripped it from the cliff, and in seconds he was soaring over the lake, towards the plume of smoke, leaving Meek behind him.

The sun was pretty much up when the Krijen crashed through the walls of their own barracks compound to douse the flames, using the water that bubbled up from the fountain. It wasn't nearly enough, but the sand trapped the flames, so once the barracks had finished burning, there wasn't anywhere else for the fire to go.

Pyra and Ala watched from their rooftop as squad after squad arrived to help, as word spread. They were so far from the rest of the city down here, which was one of the reasons Pyra had chosen it. Help was as far as it could be because the rest of the city Krijen were based at the Keep.

Pyra felt a stirring of guilt as the Krijen put their hands to their mouths in horror as they looked upon the smoking ruins, realising they were too late, and there was nothing they could do.

The guilt grew when one of the Krijen dropped to his knees, howling, and Pyra realised he'd been guarding the gates. He probably felt responsible for not being able to save them. His squad would've been asleep in the barracks.

No, Pyra thought. *Krijen don't have feelings. Krijen aren't like the rest of us. Krijen do despicable things because they are told to, morality smacked from them as Squares.* At least Pyra had done what she did to save herself so that, in turn, she could save their cause. There was *goodness* in it, in the end. So she was different.

Pyra was content with that thought, right up until the moment the KrijenMayj soared over their heads on a chunk of stone. That was when Pyra realised she'd made a terrible mistake.

'Pyra!' Ala squealed. 'Pyra look! It's the KrijenMayj! He looks so cranky!'

Cranky did not cut it. Cranky was what your mother was when you didn't go to bed when you were told. Cranky was when your father came home pissed off because someone hadn't coughed up their share of the coin, and he'd needed to break a few fingers.

The KrijenMayj was beyond cranky. He was a broiling tempest of all things violent. He may as well have been breathing fire he looked so ready to explode.

'What happened to him?' Ala whispered. 'What happened to his hands?'

Even from their distant rooftop, Pyra could see the KrijenMayj's hands looked raw and shiny, like they'd been burned. *Burned.* Like what Pyra had just done to the Krijen barracks.

'He shouldn't be here,' Pyra whispered. Lady Hia said he'd been laid up in bed dealing with some injury the FaKrijen had inflicted on him. Lady Hia had said he mightn't even be able to harness anymore, which was another reason Pyra had gone with this plan, thinking the KrijenMayj wouldn't be a problem. But here he was, flying through the air, the very picture of a problem.

The KrijenMayj brought his chunk of stone down before the ashes of the first barracks. He leapt from it onto the ground, and the other Krijen swarmed to him. One of them held out their hand, a tiny red dot hanging from their fist. It was one of Pyra's wrist ties, which she'd left on purpose to leave the city with no doubt as to who'd done it.

The KrijenMayj reached out and slowly took the tie in his hand.

'We need to get back to the tower,' Pyra said. 'We need to go *now*, Ala!'

'But that's where they think you'll be!'

And that had been *exactly* the plan because Pyra was so good at plans. She'd expected a rebuttal from the Krijen, but she'd told no one what she and Ala were going to do. She trusted her streetlings would be prepared for a fight. They spent their days begging for it, and the thought of Krijen unexpectedly storming their tower kept them diligently sharpening their rusty nails and preparing their stores of infamous faecal fireballs with glee. But no streetling, not even the mayjen ones, knew how to fight monsters.

The KrijenMayj took off running, his swarm of Krijen in tow.

'Run, Ala!' Pyra screamed. 'RUN!'

CHAPTER 79:
AREN BHA

The sun was barely up, and the morning dew on the leaves smelled incredible as Aren and Drax followed Mandavar across the University campus, making their way through a maze of corridors to yet another room that left Aren's jaw slack with awe.

The University dining hall was rounded, just like the lecture theatres, but its walls were of seamless carved wood as though some mayj in Holu Mon had found the most gargantuan tree in the world, hollowed it out, then cut it off just above root level to let the light in. It was pleasantly cool inside so early in the morning, but Aren imagined that as the sun climbed, eventually they would roast in this room.

In the middle of the dining hall stood six massive structures. They looked like a bunch of circular tables stacked atop one another, the biggest table at the bottom and each table growing smaller as they neared the top, forming a tiered cone.

Each table tier overflowed with food grouped curiously by colour, size, or by no likeness that Aren could discern at all. The structures teemed with students clambering over them on ladders, each loading a bowl in their hand with food plucked from each tier. It reminded Aren of ants on an anthill not from one of Noel's books but from a lecture on biology she'd attended the other day.

Horseshoe-shaped benches spotted the hall, tens upon tens of them surrounded by rounded seats on which sat students who chatted and laughed together, filling the room with bouncing noise.

At first glance, the dining hall was so delightful that Aren wondered why they hadn't yet been there. Mo Nu had always sent food to their rooms, which Aren had assumed was a courteous thing because they were guests. After so long struggling to find food to stay alive, she'd relinquished that duty with a sigh of relief and thought nothing more of it until now.

And as she thought about it, Aren realised that even before they'd arrived in Holu Mon, the hunters had delivered food to them. She and Drax had yet to procure anything for themselves. Even Bodin had given her a peach and told her to eat it; she'd not chosen it herself.

It was these thoughts, combined with the disquieting sound of retching, that made Narium's list of slights flash through her mind.

Slight #24. Indulgence as the sole driver of consumption without adequate rebalance.

Aren's enthusiasm evaporated as the retching sounded again, somewhere at the back of the room, out of sight. She knew then why Mo Nu hadn't yet taken them to the dining hall.

As Mandavar led Aren and Drax towards the food-laden structures, heads turned and students nudged one another.

Aren quickly realised their trio was unbalanced. 'Wait,' she said. 'Wait, should we . . .' she faltered as students stood up from their chairs to look at them. At *her*.

'They're not worried about you,' Mandavar said. 'They're excited to see majik.' Indeed, Mandavar's hand remained stretched out towards her, a tantalising suggestion that he was harnessing.

'But we still need another woman to balance us –'

'Even though you're not in dark blue, they'll assume you're a mayj,' Mandavar said. 'People would never slight so obviously without good reason.'

'And when they realise that I'm not a mayj?'

'Why do you care? Slighting is meaningless to you.'

'But it's not meaningless to *them*,' Aren hissed back.

Mandavar stopped in the middle of the hall and turned to Aren with an expression Aren thought was contemplative, but it was hard to tell. He looked ridiculously like his son, who'd invented the art of the emotionless stare.

'Fine,' Mandavar said. 'You want to fit in? Touch nothing.' He turned to Drax. 'Go to that food tier,' he said, pointing with his free hand. 'Get whatever you want though I would recommend something sweet. It will replenish your power faster.'

Drax gave Aren a nervous glance before ambling away.

Mandavar turned back to Aren. 'Watch.'

Mandavar waved his hand, and a bowl soared towards him from a stack near the tiered tables. He caught it and gave it to Aren. 'I'm sure you've figured out by now,' he said, 'that the people of Holu Mon value balance above everything else. Regarding food, there are some unpleasantries that have become normalised here, which aren't well received by outsiders.'

Mandavar inclined his head towards the back of the room, where the dreadful retching sound had come from. Thankfully, it had stopped now.

'Mo Nu, being the learned man he is, knows what Holu Mon behaviours might shock you, and so has kept you from them. He can be rather short-sighted, for a scholar.' Mandavar waved his hand again, and a selection of foods soared towards them, landing in Aren's bowl. 'If you want to avoid slighting, you must take care with what you eat. If you mis-indulge, you'll be expected to correct it. I'm sure you've noticed what's involved.'

Aren still couldn't quite believe it. 'People make themselves sick?'

'That's one option.' Mandavar said. 'A popular one too, to correct their perceived imbalance quickly. Otherwise, they may restrict their intake for a while to compensate. Whatever is necessary. We've not had a feast since you arrived, but there will be one soon. You'll see.' Mandavar gave her a wry smile. 'You seem uncomfortable.'

Aren was. Students were still craning their heads to look at them. Aren wanted nothing more than to disappear through her seat into the floor. 'You . . . you brought us here on purpose,' she said to Mandavar. *To play games with us,* she mused grimly. This was entertainment for him.

'I know what you're thinking,' Mandavar said. 'But this is for your benefit, not mine. I don't tolerate ignorance any more than I enable it. I'm not Mo Nu. I don't believe protecting people from harsh realities does them any favours.'

Aren grudgingly agreed with him.

Just then, Drax returned, his arms wrapped tightly around his near-to-overflowing bowl, which he'd jammed against his ribs.

Eyes followed them as Mandavar led them to an empty horseshoe-shaped table and sat down. 'Eat,' Mandavar said, waving his free hand again, so a spoon raced from somewhere towards Aren, landing neatly on the table beside her bowl. 'Then we'll do majik.'

Drax sat down next to Aren and began eating quietly. As usual, he didn't use cutlery; he just dug into the meal with his awkward hands, now and then harnessing food to his mouth, unperturbed by their gaping audience.

Aren had purposefully left a gap between her and Mandavar, but he got up and moved around the table, then sat down right opposite her, so Aren had to look at him.

'Don't look so disgusted,' Mandavar said as he rested his outstretched hand on the table between them. 'I'm going to explain your food to you. Are you listening?'

Aren looked down at her bowl.

'Balance comes in terms of colours, type, taste, acidity, and calorific content,' Mandavar said. 'Colours are easy. Pick a food of each colour at each meal, and you can't go wrong. Type refers to whether it originated from a plant or an animal. Animal foods contribute more weight to the balance, so you'll want less of them. Taste is generally sweet versus sour though be mindful of bitterness and richness too. Acidity plays into taste to a degree though your perception of taste can be impacted by what you've just eaten so it's best to cleanse your palate between foods to ensure you don't overdo one. Finally, you have calorific content, which is the most important if you want to avoid rebalancing. It's also the most changeable as individual calorie requirements vary depending on your age, activity levels, body composition, and whether you're a mayj, to name but a few.' As he finished speaking, Mandavar cocked his head to the side in a very Drax-like fashion, looking amused.

Drax had stopped mid-chew, also staring at Aren's meal. He leaned over to her. 'You can eat mine,' he offered quietly.

Despite her rumbling stomach, Aren didn't feel like eating anymore. It seemed ludicrously complex, made worse by the ambiguity of it all. Aren wondered if Mandavar had made some of it up, just to watch her squirm.

'Well,' Mandavar prompted, 'aren't you going to eat?'

Aren picked up her spoon and scooped a mouthful of something green into her mouth, chewing slowly. 'You make it sound difficult,' she said, 'but I'll learn.' She swallowed, cringing as the lump moved down her throat. It probably tasted delicious as all their food had been, but Mandavar's explanation had somewhat ruined it. He gave her a mocking smile. 'Shall we arrange a chaperone for you too?'

Mandavar's hold of her heart was keeping Aren annoyingly calm. It beat in her chest, refusing to quicken despite his taunts. Drax edged closer to her, his eyes narrowing at his father, whose smile fell from his face as a shout echoed across the hall.

'Professor!'

Aren spun in her seat. Mo Nu was hurrying towards them, his mass parting the students like the sea, the rake-thin Fom following in his wake.

Mo Nu reached their table and leaned against it, gasping for breath. 'Professor,' he puffed, 'you . . . you showed our guests the dining room?'

'Obviously,' Mandavar said.

'I did not realise you ate here . . .'

Mandavar's eyes drifted to the empty spot on the table in front of him, then back up to Mo Nu, who reddened. 'Never mind. Drax, Aren, you . .

. you are all right?' He looked terrified.

Aren nodded, glad to have a distraction from her food. 'Yes, thank you. Though I would appreciate it if Fom would accompany me today.'

Fom beamed at her. 'I'd love to,' she said as she sat down next to Aren, folding her hands neatly in her lap. Her eyes shifted to not so subtly inspect Aren's meal, and she gave a slight nod of approval. So Mandavar hadn't been embellishing after all.

Mo Nu remained standing next to the table, twiddling his thumbs, still looking nervous.

'It's okay, Mo Nu,' Aren said to him. 'Honestly, we're fine.' She turned back to her meal, determined to finish it to prove it to him, but with the combined presence of Mandavar and the dean, every student in the dining hall had left their empty bowls and were gathering around them as though something was about to happen.

Aren put her spoon down on the table. 'What's going on?' she asked.

Mo Nu flushed a deeper crimson. 'They are rather excited about the prospect of majik,' he said, repeating what Mandavar said earlier. 'Myself included. I apologise, it is such a rare thing to see. Word gets around rather quickly.'

'It's my fault,' Mandavar said, without a shred of bashfulness. 'Bring that with you,' he said, pointing to Aren's bowl as he stood up, his other hand still stretched towards her. 'Drax, are you ready?'

Drax looked up from his empty bowl.

'Wait,' Aren said. 'You said he would do majik, but you didn't say anything about an audience –'

'It's okay, Aren,' Drax said. 'I don't mind.'

'Come,' Mandavar said. Drax immediately got to his feet and ambled over to his father.

Grinding her teeth, Aren picked up her bowl and spoon and followed. Fom and Mo Nu were close on their heels.

Students parted before them as Mandavar led them out into the bright sunshine, towards a patterned stone ring on the ground surrounded by benches. There wasn't much space, so the students spilled onto the surrounding grass, settling down with crossed legs to watch. Aren couldn't believe how many of them there were. It was just a wall of black-and-white-wearing, braided-haired people in every direction.

When he reached the far side of the stone ring, Mandavar stopped. He lifted his free hand up to join the other, still stretched towards Aren. Her heart gave a little skip and then picked up its beat again as Mandavar swapped hands. He dropped the hand he'd previously been using and flexed the fingers of it, shaking it out. He'd stopped twitching, but there was nothing to say he was having any trouble harnessing Aren's heart.

'He's more powerful than me,' Drax whispered to her. He was getting good at reading her mind.

'It just looks so easy for him,' Aren whispered back, disconcerted.

'He knows what he's doing.'

Mandavar watched them, a mysterious smile playing around his mouth. Aren didn't think Mandavar would hurt Drax, but she didn't trust him. He always seemed to have an agenda, regardless of what he said.

'Are you sure about this?' Aren asked. 'You don't have to do it. Surely you need more time to recover?'

'It's okay,' Drax said again. 'Food helpcd. And they won't hurt me for doing majik here.'

'No, but I don't want you to feel manipulated into it, either.'

'Don't worry, Aren,' Drax said. 'I'll do only what I want to.'

Aren stepped back. She believed him. He was certainly not the same scared young man she'd met all those months ago.

Still she was surprised when Drax called to Mandavar across the stone ring, loud enough for everyone to hear. 'Promise you won't let go of Aren.'

Mandavar's smile was gone. 'I won't let go of Aren.'

'Good,' Drax nodded. 'What do you want me to do?'

'Whatever you wish.'

Drax blinked. 'Anything?'

'Anything.'

Drax nodded. 'Okay then.'

The students all around them gasped as tiny, dewy droplets of water suddenly cascaded from every stem, leaf, and stone towards Drax. It looked like a million glass ants sprinting all at once to collide at his feet, forming a heavy, shimmering, transparent mass as they morphed upwards into a figure that grew and grew until suddenly a head sprouted from glassy shoulders, and the figure stilled.

Aren smiled. It was a perfect replica of her father, Sid Bha.

Mandavar frowned at the figure.

Then Sid Bha twisted and span and the stone at his glassy feet spiralled up into his form until Sid Bha was gone, and the stone tree that stood in the courtyard of Aren's family mansion was in his place. The glassy parts of it formed webbing along the structure, looking almost exactly like it did back home.

Mandavar frowned, then stretched out his free hand towards the tree. It shattered, and crystals of it bounced over Aren's feet.

'You made it look like cardonite,' Mandavar said. 'But it's not. You copied the webbing. The Valrueans have a deplorable habit of that.'

Most of the mansions in Val were made of webbed stone. To the builders or Builders who made them, the webbed look depicted status, mimicking cardonite. Grandiosity, Mandavar had called it once. Fake majik.

'I can reBuild it,' Drax said, 'and try to make it real cardonite.'

'No, we'll not Weave today,' Mandavar said. 'I'd like to see you manipulate life.'

Drax looked around at the students of Holu Mon. They gazed wondrously back.

Is he going to Influence? Aren thought.

Apparently not. Drax's eyes roamed away from the students, searching for something else. His gaze shifted up.

There was a tree not far from them, an enormous oaky giant of a thing, with low-hanging branches so heavy some of them kissed the ground. Students had climbed onto them to get a better view and sat watching in a row, their feet dangling above the ground.

Drax ever so slightly shrugged his shoulders, slowly turning his wrists out, and lifted them half an inch from his sides.

As he moved, so did the arms of the tree. It groaned as its branches heaved off the ground, and students cried out and leapt off onto the grass. Like a rolling wave, the trunk of the tree stretched up and up and up, thinning as it speared into the sky, its branches reaching higher. No leaves fluttered down from it as Aren thought they might. Drax was keeping every piece of it perfectly intact.

Entranced by the tree, Aren jumped when someone next to her spoke.

'You need to eat that.' It was Narium, her eyes on Aren's half-eaten bowl of food. 'Everyone might be watching Drax, but they're watching you too,' she said.

Aren raised another spoonful to her mouth as the oak tree let out a final groan and stilled, its branches raised straight up to the sky.

Mo Nu began clapping madly, and the sound erupted around them as everyone joined in.

'Impressive,' Narium said, her gaze rising up the tree trunk.

'How so?' Aren asked, genuinely curious as to the answer. 'I know the tree is technically alive, but I thought most of a tree was made up of dead cells?' She'd learnt that surprising fact in a biology lecture the other day. 'Would it be that much harder to harness than say a rock of the same size?'

'Are you kidding?' Narium asked, giving her a withering look. 'You've been spending too much time with mayjen who aren't like the rest of them. That was not at all like harnessing a big rock. A rock you can pull apart the matter of it, make an absolute mess of it, and so long as you've got enough power to Build it back together, you've still got a rock. You're only limited by your power and there is little skill involved.' Narium pointed at the tree. '*That* was infinitely more difficult, assuming the tree survives. Sure, it's got more dead cells than living, but it's still got innate power and it's a huge tree, so it requires considerably more power than harnessing a rock of the same size. What's *really* impressive is that Drax Broke the bonds between every individual cell of that tree, moved them, then Built the cells back together, all without separating each cell from its neighbour. Not only are there more cells in that tree than your brain can conceive, but you can't see them, not without a microscope. He kept the structure of the tree intact through feel.' Narium shook her head. 'I don't know if you remember from class that if you shove too much power into something, you'll break it. The living cells of the tree would require more power than the dead ones, so Drax had to feel for the differences by pressing against each cell and adjusting for it.'

Aren was finally starting to understand the complexity involved in certain types of majik. She knew Drax was extraordinary, but she couldn't explain how beyond seeing him do things that other mayjen couldn't seem to do. 'Can you do what Drax just did?' she asked Narium.

'If I had time. Drax did it all so *fast*. The speed of his majik is incredible. I've got the power sure, but the cognitive dexterity required . . . I'm fairly good at that sort of thing, but it would take me days to get my head around the details of the tree, how to adjust my power to keep it alive.' Narium looked at Aren from under her brows. 'And I'm not a good benchmark. Neither is Bodin, and certainly not Demison. Your average mayj couldn't bend that spoon you're holding without needing to take a break afterwards.'

Aren looked down at her spoon. 'Really?'

'Yeah. Most mayjen couldn't wrap their heads around what Drax did just now. Their brain doesn't work that way. So much of majik isn't teachable. It's something you have. Like with you,' Narium added, 'I *might* be powerful enough to keep you alive without Turning, at least for a little bit, and I know the theory of Weaving, but I just can't do it.'

'That must be frustrating.'

'You've no idea.' Narium frowned. 'Drax is something else. How does he harness without his hands?'

'I don't know. He uses them sometimes if something is particularly difficult. Like just now.'

Drax looked tired. His shoulders slumped, and his arms hung limply at his sides. It had barely been an hour since Mandavar took over Aren's heart, and harnessing the tree seemed to have used up most of the power Drax had replenished in that time.

'Mandavar won't push him too hard, will he?' Aren asked.

Narium shook her head. 'No, Mandavar has a strict rule against Turning. And he's taken a liking to Drax. He won't push him, not with an audience.' There was something tight in Narium's tone. It sounded almost like jealousy.

'You know Drax is Mandavar's son, right?' Aren asked tentatively.

'*What?*'

Aren nodded.

'Of *course*,' Narium said, her head turning between Drax and Mandavar. 'Oh, gracious Gi, how did I not see it?'

'I thought Mandavar would've said something. Or you would feel it,' Aren said. 'I thought their power felt similar.'

Narium laughed. 'I don't have casual chats with Mandavar,' she said. 'As to feeling it, Drax's power has been dulled since you got here. We can feel him but barely. You know, you really freaked us out when you arrived. Mandavar doesn't just invite random mayjen to join our classes. We figured Drax was special but . . . wow, his *son.*' She whistled. 'Someone needs to tell Demison.'

Aren was about to ask why when students began climbing to their feet around them, moving towards their classes for the day. Drax ambled over. 'We're done,' he said. Mandavar was beside him, his arm still held out towards Aren.

'Narium,' Mandavar said, inclining his head in acknowledgement. 'I'm cancelling class for the rest of the week. Tell the others.'

'The whole *week?*'

'Yes.'

'Fine,' Narium said, folding her arms. 'Bye, Aren.' But she left with a smirk on her face, for which Aren had no explanation.

Mandavar watched her go, then turned to Drax. 'Well done. Go rest. Tomorrow we will Weave. You'll need power for that, so Aren will stay with me for the rest of today.'

Darn, Aren thought. She didn't particularly want to spend the whole day with Mandavar, but Drax needed a break.

Drax hesitated.

'I'll not let go of her,' Mandavar said. 'I keep my promises.'

Aren scoffed. 'As if your word means anything.'

'I find it interesting you say that,' Mandavar said, lowering his voice, 'when it's you who was caught in a lie, telling the hunters you were a mayj when you weren't.'

The sudden guilt from his statement smacked the breath from Aren's lungs. 'I did it to protect Drax!' she hissed, glancing around to ensure no one heard. 'It was for a good reason!'

'The people of Holu Mon will not see it the same way. Lying is a very dangerous thing to do here.' Mandavar fixed Aren with his icy blue stare. 'You will do well to remember that. Otherwise, you will end up regretting it.'

CHAPTER 80:
JIN KANJU

It was infuriating how much fucking *time* the Krijen took to get anywhere. At first, Jin had run with them, instead of lifting himself over the city, but he'd quickly left them behind in his frustration. They'd slowed him down so much that now his own squad were running towards him. Meek had returned to the Keep and informed them.

'Jin, sir!' Nommo yelled as he spotted Jin. Jin was tempted to run right past, but Aren's quick, light footsteps were behind him, and she wouldn't approve of that.

'Sir, wait!' Flit called to him. 'Sir, what's happening?'

Jin skidded to a stop before his squad. 'They burned the South Side barracks to the ground,' he said in a rush. 'That streetling gang leader from the Celebrations left her red ties everywhere. They locked the Krijen in the barracks and killed them. All the Krijen!'

'They're . . . they're dead?' Flit asked. '*All of them?*'

'Save the pair at the gates,' Jin said through clenched teeth as fire rolled down his arms, the pain making him tremble. 'Forty-six Krijen dead.'

His squad stared at him, speechless.

'The streetlings didn't even give them a chance to fight back,' Jin hissed. 'They tied the doors shut and locked the gates and ran like cowards.'

Flit's face flushed red. 'That's just . . . that's just so . . . Why are we all standing here?' Her face twisted into a snarl as she pulled her daggers from her wraps. *'Let's go get those little shits!'*

Nommo had done the same. 'Give me orders, sir!'

'Wait for the other squads,' Aren warned Jin, rightly assuming that his power was about to take off with his sense. 'You need backup.'

Furious, Jin turned to look back down the slope of Rue. Krijen were bursting from the arteries of the street, speeding towards him. Squads crowded around Jin again, waiting for orders even though Jin couldn't fathom why because they all had squad leaders.

'Eden's not here yet,' Filip said to Jin. 'They need cohesive orders. They can be useful, make them useful.'

The monster inside Jin roared, and the strangled sound of it escaped him, the heat of hatred and excitement bubbling up and over his lips. But a little note of caution poked through. 'Has the FaKrijen given any orders?' he asked his squad.

'Not to us,' Nommo said with a surprising amount of venom in his voice. Jin nodded. That was enough for him.

Jin turned to the waiting Krijen. 'Surround the Upper West Side tower, you know the one,' he growled. 'Block the exits. Monitor the windows, the rooftops. If you see a streetling, kill it. Stick in your pairs. I don't want to see a Krijen alone. And no one goes into the tower apart from me and my squad.' He didn't want anyone getting in the way.

'Do we need the Squares again, sir?' someone called out.

'No,' Jin said. 'I don't need them. Go!'

The Krijen squads took off around him. *This is it,* Jin thought. Nothing was going to prevent him from getting that murderous gang leader and her horde of shitlings this time. Not unless –

Jin span to face his squad. They waited with their daggers poised. 'You,' Jin said to Meek. 'You stay here.'

Meek looked taken aback. 'What? Because of what I said earlier about all the killing?'

'Exactly,' Jin snarled.

'You don't need to do that, sir. I want to come. I want to help –'

'I said STAY HERE!'

Jin had barely turned away when he felt a forceful tug on his wraps. He looked down to see Jokah holding onto him. Of course. The last time Jin had wanted to go after streetlings, Jokah had stopped him.

Jin dragged his arm from Jokah's grip, expecting the older Krijen would tell him to calm down or have some wise words to guilt Jin out of the bloodlust he had in mind.

Jin opened his mouth to order Jokah away.

'Sir,' Jokah said, 'you have no daggers.' He held out a dagger to Jin, one of his own. 'Do you want this?'

Jin looked down at it.

'Don't leave him a dagger down,' Aren said. 'He needs it. You don't.'

'You're more scared of holding that dagger than storming this building, aren't you?' Filip asked. 'Worried you'll drop it?'

'Sir, take it,' Jokah said. 'Please take it.'

Jin reached out a stiff hand and took the dagger, allowing a sliver of barely bridled power to ease down his arm into his fingers. The dagger didn't seem right in his hand. He couldn't feel it properly. He tightened his grip on the hilt so it wouldn't slip through his fingers.

Then Jin turned and ran, his squad falling in behind him, all apart from Meek, who was left standing alone yet again, his daggers limp by his sides.

Soon they caught up to the other Krijen, their pounding feet creating a cacophonous march that rumbled the People from their beds. Faces appeared in the windows above them. Jin used to worry that he frightened them, but Crushed Foot's wise words at the parade had reassured him otherwise, and the monster inside him had forced any remaining fear from his body. The People liked blood just as much as he did.

Jin and his squad sped to the front of the Krijen, and once more it was an effort to slow himself down enough that they could keep pace.

The Upper West Side tower staggered up before him, washing lines slung between the open windows of the towers on either side, offering little avenues of escape.

Jin slid Jokah's dagger into his thigh wraps and threw up his hands. With majik, he tore down the lines and slammed shutters on windows, flicking catches and stringing snapped ends between the gaps in the wood, knotting them together. He would trap the streetlings inside their safe house like they'd trapped his Krijen in their barracks.

They reached the base of the tower. As ordered, the Krijen fanned out to surround it.

Jin burst into the mouth of the tower, his squad behind him. As he spiralled up the stairs, he could hear screeching above him, and when that first streetling came around the corner, teeth bared and nails out, Jin pulled Jokah's dagger from his wraps and ran it through the little shit.

His power roared in delight, and the momentum carried Jin upwards until they burst through a door onto a landing that rang with more screeches. Jin and his squad smashed through them all.

At Jin's command, Nommo hunkered in the stairwell, while the rest of the squad moved through rooms until there were no screeches left. Jin led them back to the stairwell, and up the next flight of stairs, trailed by Nommo, the impenetrable blockade.

With each floor they mounted, it was as though Jin's power grew and grew because he'd stopped trying to crush it back, but he still wasn't *using* it, not like it wanted, and with a shock, Jokah's dagger suddenly slid from Jin's grasp.

It wasn't because he'd dropped it but because the hilt had warped in his grip from too much heat or power or whatever it was, and so without thinking and with the screeching of the streetlings all around him, Jin reached out and tore at the sounds with his hands, having no dagger to throw.

With every screech that dissolved into the ringing in Jin's head, he got a little closer to that touch of bliss, closer and closer until eventually he was there, and Filip was yelling at him, and Jin fought not to fall off the precipice, teetering between glorious solace and suffering.

After a time, when fatigue worked its way through and Flit's gentle voice replaced Filip's, telling him it was done and they were tired and it was time to go, Jin finally lowered his hands.

CHAPTER 81:
PYRA

Pyra hadn't made it in time. When she and Ala arrived at the Upper West Side tower, the Krijen had blocked every entrance, including the ones that Pyra hadn't realised they knew about.

For the rest of the morning the Krijen sentried it until the sun started its descent, and the streetlings that hadn't been inside the tower gathered on the rooftop behind her in silence, watching. Rifter and Barrett were there, for which Pyra was grateful.

In one way, Pyra's plan had been an overwhelming success. She was now responsible for the single largest killing of Krijen in streetling history, so Pyra's ruthless reputation would, once again, be indisputable. Hence, Pyra felt it ironic that after she'd given her orders and her remaining gang had scarpered off into the streets, Pyra ran to the little shoe shop where she cried her eyes out over hot tea and biscuits and told Nellie and Tiju everything.

Eventually, they coaxed Pyra into sending a message to Lady Hia, and when the Kahn turned up in a black hood after darkness had settled in Valrue, the older couple politely made themselves scarce, disappearing downstairs to potter quietly around their shop. They were trying to give Pyra and the Kahn privacy, but given how loudly Lady Hia was yelling, Nellie and Tiju surely heard every word. Regardless, Pyra was glad they stayed because Nellie and Tiju couldn't be bullied or bought. No, they would be impressively hostile witnesses, should Lady Hia decide to murder her because of this.

'What have you done, Pyra?' Lady Hia cried, her face white with shock. '*What have you done?*'

For once, Pyra had no rebuttal. She had nothing to say to defend herself, to make it any better, or to make her feel as though this time she was in the right, and Lady Hia was wrong.

'Do you have anything to say? *Anything?*'

'I messed up,' Pyra said, which only further incensed the Kahn.

'Messed up? *Messed up?* Not only have we lost a substantial portion of the Upper West Side streetling army, but you have provoked *sympathy* for the Krijen. The People are in overwhelming support of this streetling massacre. They are chanting the KrijenMayj's name in the street!'

'I know –'

'You have just undone everything we have spent the last five years working towards! Any meagre amount of support for the streetlings is completely gone!'

That's an exaggeration, Pyra thought. They hadn't ever expected *support* from the People towards the streetlings. All they needed was for the People to be content to stay out of the way, and they had been after the First Reckoning.

Unfortunately, Pyra had ruined that. In the last few hours before sunset, the citizens had begun picketing the streets, screaming for more streetling blood, all apart from those in the Lower West Side, where there remained an infuriating, peaceful silence.

'There is only one way to salvage this,' Lady Hia said. 'You have left me no choice. I am going to speak to the Lost Square!' The Kahn paused as though waiting for Pyra to challenge her.

Pyra didn't.

Lady Hia harrumphed and stood up, giving Pyra one last seething look before storming out of the door, leaving her untouched tea and biscuits on the table that Nellie had so kindly offered her.

CHAPTER 82:
FAKRIJEN EDEN

Eden sucked on his tongue. Something didn't add up.

The KrijenMayj had beaten him to the burning barracks. But the more Eden thought about it, the more he believed it wasn't possible. Not when the KrijenMayj should have been on duty deep in the bowels of the lower Keep and when the Krijen who delivered the news insisted they had informed Eden first. A few hundred cuts later, they still said the same thing.

Not that they would lie to their FaKrijen.

'Where was the KrijenMayj?' Eden asked. 'Where was he on the morning of the streetling attack?'

The ringing silence was plenty loud.

'Don't bother hiding it,' Eden said. 'I *know* you know. The KrijenMayj was supposed to be on duty in the lower Keep, yet he was one of the first to the barracks. How is that possible?'

A pause. 'Jin moves very fast when he wants to, sir.'

'No,' Eden tutted. 'No, no. No Krijen in the Keep were informed of the fire until after the attack on the tower began.' The FaKrijen was excited about where this was going. 'The KrijenMayj was in the Keep. He couldn't have known about the fire, not unless someone told him when they shouldn't have.'

'No one told him, sir. I swear it.'

'So how did he know?'

More silence.

'Hmm,' Eden mused. 'Have you changed your mind then? You actually *do* want to know what happens to a Krijen who is exposed as a fraud?' He took a step towards the door. 'Shall we find out?'

'No one told him,' came the quick reply. 'Jin saw the smoke.'

'He saw the smoke? From the lower Keep?'

'Not from the lower Keep, sir.'

'Oh?' Eden was enjoying this immensely. 'Are you saying that the KrijenMayj was *not* where he was meant to be?'

'Yes, sir.'

'So where was he?'

'He was outside, sir. Up on a cliff overlooking the lake.'

A strange answer. But it didn't matter. The only thing that mattered was that Eden had caught the KrijenMayj skirting his duties.

'Why was I not informed of this?' Eden raised a questioning eyebrow, another delightful thought coming to him. 'His squad mate should've told me. Who was he supposed to be on duty with?'

Silence.

'Well, it's a process of elimination, isn't it? Was it the same Krijen who let the mayj whore into his room?'

'No, sir, it wasn't Nommo.'

'You really want to play this game? Okay then. Was it the older one?'

'Not Jokah, sir.'

'Pago? It was Pago, wasn't it?'

'No, sir. It-it was me.'

'You?' Eden tutted again.

'Yes, sir.'

'I'm glad we've finally got somewhere. I thought it might be that other one, the one with the dreary name –'

'No, sir, it was me. I was supposed to be on duty with Jin, and when I couldn't find him, I didn't tell you. I worried you might hurt him more.'

Eden smiled. As much as he would have liked to catch another one of the KrijenMayj's squad members out for being rebellious, he was content with two, for now. The way the KrijenMayj was going, it wouldn't be long before he had another. It was like a little collection, and eventually he would get all the pieces.

He couldn't wait.

Eden pulled his dagger from his wraps. 'It's been a while since you've been this naughty.' He licked his lips, salivating over what was to come. 'Give me your arm. Some cuts are in order. What do you think? A hundred? Two hundred?'

'Whatever you think is best, sir,' Flit replied, holding out her arm.

The Founding of Valrue
(The Final Excerpt continued)

Few people considered Osin's death a tragedy. Sentiment towards the Bhouli had warped with time, and the People of Valrue had grown intolerant of the mystifying visitors. Thus, born of ignorance, the divide between the Bhouli and the People of Valrue began.

The diaries of the Kahn who struck Osin dead were discovered shortly after his own passing. Surprisingly, the Kahn wrote almost daily of the old Bhouli, dating from only a few months after the incident. The Kahn described in disturbing detail the many conversations had between them over the years as though Osin had kept his acquaintance after his death.

The Kahn initially referred to Osin as an innocuous bystander in his life, quiet and transient. Later on, the Kahn wrote of how Osin became a permanent presence, more provocative, and stimulated contrary thoughts. However, Osin knew nothing more or less than what the Kahn knew himself. Therefore, the Kahn did not believe Osin to be a separate entity, but a manifestation of his own mind.

The Kahn also described a ringing in his head, one such that worsened when he felt particular fear or anger.

He wrote of his stepping down from the Kahnen and his excursions into the tunnels, perhaps with intention of finding the Bhouli and seeking reprieve from Osin. His diaries soon dissolved into commentation on the Bhouli and their beliefs. His understanding appeared such that one could almost be convinced he found them though he never wrote it in so many words. If he indeed found the Bhouli, he never told a soul of their whereabouts, not even in his diaries.

The once-Kahn eventually returned to Valrue, where he became as rambling an old man as Osin had been on the day he died. The Kahn also grew more violent, such that he ended up a prisoner in the Keep, threatened with the gallows. His social status was his only saviour.

Buried among the scribbles depicting his descent into insanity, the

Kahn's diaries contained a revelation of great poignancy, a revelation pertaining to Bhouli violence.

According to the Kahn, the Bhouli interpretation of violence is much narrower than our own. For Bhouli, violence refers solely to the acts of suicide and self-harm, not violence against others. Therefore, the Bhouli Pledge Against Violence is, in fact, a pledge only against harming oneself.

The Kahn wrote that the Bhouli introduced this pledge in the aftermath of the Great Change. He wrote nothing more on the matter.

Remember that the Bhouli believe a person lives not one life but thousands. They believe there are many more lives waiting for them in the stars, each life with a potential purpose or purposes needing to be fulfilled. Therefore, Bhouli who cannot define their purpose in one life will endeavour to move to the next through death.

While a disturbing thought to many, if someone wishes to die before their time, suicide is the obvious solution.

Yet with their Pledge Against Violence, the Bhouli do not condone suicide. Bhouli who take their own lives are no longer considered 'the same', and they do not get a place in the stars. The only exception is suicide in fulfilment of purpose. Therefore, to go to the stars without having fulfilled one's purpose, one must die by another's hand.

Finally, we come to Osin's 'clarity'. On the day of Osin's death when he visited the Kahnen, Osin indeed gave clarity. However, he gave this not through explanation but through demonstration.

He provoked his own murder.

Remember that despite Osin's numerous tattoos, he claimed he had yet to fully define a purpose and thus had not fulfilled it. Having one's life taken by another being the only acceptable death for one without a fulfilled purpose, upon his murder, Osin was free to go to his next life amongst the stars. However, Osin left behind a haunting of himself; a figure that appeared to the Kahn, his killer.

One assumes that Osin knew this would happen.

Recall the behaviour of the murderous settler in the months leading up to his death: screaming at his dungeon walls as though seeing things that were not there. The parallels between his descent into madness and the Kahn's descent into madness cannot be ignored.

It is left to the reader to contest the morality of Osin's actions. In one's musings, consider the following:

If the reader were to accuse the Bhouli of wrongdoing in leaving behind a haunting to torment their murderer, remember that whilst the hauntings of the murderous settler quickly drove him to confession and execution, by comparison, the haunting of Osin merely troubled the Kahn, at least in the beginning. In fact, some of the Kahn's diaries described pleasant, even helpful conversations with Osin. It is unclear if the Kahn's eventual madness was because of Osin, because of the guilt of the crime itself, or some other affliction of old age.

The purpose of the hauntings is unclear if there is any at all. Given their Bhouli counterparts were without fulfilled purpose in this life, one may venture that the hauntings are a final attempt to fulfil a purpose through their killer. However, neither the murderous settler nor the Kahn voiced any definitive purpose of their own after the murders, and throughout the rest of their lives, both killers remained bereft of white ink.

To this day, no Bhouli has ever been convicted of a violent crime. This may be why the People's misunderstanding of the Pledge Against Violence is perpetuated.

To put one final, incongruous thought forward. Although the killer Kahn was convinced that the haunting of Osin was of his own mind's making, and many perceived the haunting as nothing but a benign vision in the mind of a monster, there is no proof that the hauntings are not monsters themselves, full of malicious intent and ready to twist an already vulnerable mind into a most abominable and inhuman thing.

Perhaps these hauntings are yet another Bhouli thing we will never understand.

Or perhaps they are revenge.

EPILOGUE

It was that time again.

Ruha stood on the stone lip under the lake, next to the waterfall that Maude's body had fallen through almost a year ago.

Ruha did not know how long she could keep this up. But she had to. As a mayj, this purpose had been decided for her, and so she'd tattooed the butterfly pattern on her neck. It was permanent; it would do no good to wish it away.

What scared Ruha was that she had other purposes, all yet to be fulfilled. But since Maude's sacrifice, the power in the lake was no longer. With nothing else to keep its waters trapped, Ruha had to give every ounce of herself to fulfil this new purpose, save for a few hours of the day to rest and recover.

This was such a brutal and unkind world. But until death took her, Ruha would give life.

Asha stood beside her, prepared with food, drink, and pillows, for when she fell seizing to the floor. It was inevitable.

'Are you ready?' Asha asked.

'Yes.'

Ruha held her hands out before her and let a slow ebb of power sigh from her chest. The heat of it filled her arteries, her veins, and the capillaries burned in her wrists as the power left her, spreading into the particles of the water, channelling up the waterfall and up into the lake, so vast and so deep that it terrified Ruha because she never failed to get lost wandering it even though she stood perfectly still.

Bit by bit, Ruha turned the tide of the waters that flowed the wrong way, and she drew it back into the crater where it needed to stay, doing her best to close all the cracks in the rocks that she could not see and knowing she would miss some. The water would eventually escape through them once more.

Ruha shuddered as a chill swept through her, starting in her chest, and a slither of bliss sliced into her mind and spread. She couldn't help but chase it, struggling to concentrate on her purpose, the lake.

'Not yet, Ruha,' came Asha's voice. 'Here, sip on this.'

A straw tapped Ruha's lips, and she sucked obediently on the sickly sweet drink, the taste of it nudging away the bliss. It hurt to lose it.

But it would be back.

Because as long as Ruha had to maintain the lake, she would be forced to harness to her Turning point, so she needn't worry about losing it.

The bliss would always come back.

THE END

Second Glossary

This glossary contains all the majikal terms pertinent to both Book One and Book Two of the Valrue Series.

Expressions of Harnessing Ability:

Breaker – A mayj who moves matter

Builder – A mayj who moves matter and uses majik to create bonds that mimic the natural bonds between matter

Weaver – A mayj who moves matter and uses majik to create bonds that mimic the natural bonds between matter and creates specialised bonds between matter

Pertaining to Power:

Influencer – A mayj with sufficient power to use majik on other people without Turning

Pertaining to Cognitive Dexterity (majikal multi-tasking):

Atomik majik – Majik applied to individual atoms

The Spells of Weaving:

The Cardonia Spell – Power that is Woven between matter to bind it into a lattice-like structure called cardonite. Durable, particularly against majik.

The Thorson Spell – Power that is Woven into a bond between objects that can be passed through. The bound objects are called Lockstones.

The Du Bellor Spell – Power that is Woven between matter as a means of storage outside the body. It is leaky and burdensome though if a certain 'mass' of power is obtained, the spell becomes self-sustaining. Woven into the crater lake by Mandavar, the Du Bellor Spell caused the Unsettlement in Valrue.

Bhouli Beliefs in Summary

Pertaining to Tattoos and Purpose:

Bhouli beliefs centre around the idea of purpose. They believe they live multiple lives, each life with at least one purpose which they must define and fulfil. Bhouli may have multiple purposes in a single lifetime, all of which must be fulfilled in order to move to the next life among the stars.

Temporary white ink symbols known as patterns are used to explore and define possible purposes. When an individual is particularly confident with a selected pattern, the pattern is permanently inked under the skin and referred to as a tattoo. Multiple tattoos may be required to fully define a single purpose. The Bhouli will continue to add tattoos until they feel their purpose has been satisfactorily defined, at which point the purpose can then be fulfilled.

Fulfilment of a purpose is not marked on the body in any tangible way. It is up to the individual in question to acknowledge fulfilment for themselves. Unlike in many cultures, for Bhouli, social recognition of one's achievements is not strongly coveted.

Whilst certain patterns have predetermined meaning, most patterns are unique, their meaning determined by the wearer. Therefore, Bhouli with the same or similarly defined purposes, may not share the same tattoos.

Pertaining to Mayjen:

The chest area is treated with reverence for non-mayjen and is reserved for either the first pattern, or the tattoo completing the definition of the first purpose, depending on the preference of the individual.

In mayjen, the Bhouli believe the chest is already 'inhabited' by power, thus they consider mayjen to have a partial purpose at birth and do not need to preserve the skin of the chest.

Pertaining to Violence and Death:

Since the mysterious Great Change, Bhouli make a Pledge Against Violence. For Bhouli, violence refers only to self-harm and suicide. The settlers misinterpreted this as being a pledge against all violence as their interpretation of violence is much broader. This misunderstanding has perpetuated into modern-day Valrue.

Bhouli who cannot define or fulfil their purpose in one life will endeavour to move to the next through death. Death is not considered 'the end' for the Bhouli, simply a means to move to the next life. Therefore, it is not viewed as something to be feared or treated with the same gravitas as it is by the settlers and their modern-day counterparts.

For reasons unknown, since the mysterious Great Change, suicide is no longer an acceptable means of moving to the next life (except for suicide in fulfilment of purpose, such as Maude's sacrifice). Therefore, a Bhouli with an unfilled purpose or purposes must have their life taken from them to move to the next life among the stars. To do this, they will provoke their own death.

A Bhouli killed by another person leaves behind what the settlers refer to as a haunting, a ghost-like apparition sharing their likeness that only their killer can see. This is accompanied by a ringing in the ears of the killer that grows stronger during moments of fear or anger.

The hauntings know nothing more than what the killer knows themselves. Therefore, the hauntings are thought to be a manifestation of the killer's own mind as opposed to an external influence. However, this is only a theory, and it remains unclear as to what the hauntings truly are.

Warning: the following character map contains Book Two spoilers. It is recommended to be read upon completion of this book.

CHARACTER MAP

Blood relative
Unrelated

BROTHEL:
Mama Hidel (Madam)
Lottie
Eliza
Josephine
Dhuna
Named prostitutes

(friends)

BHOULI:
(aunt/niece)
Maude (Deceased)
Ruha
Natoni
Asha
(Deceased) Filip
(haunting/killer)

KAHNENMAYJEN:
Stolton Ono

EIGHTH HOUSE:
Great Kahn (Lord Luka Li)
Lord Salli
Lord Reider
Lady Macey
Lady Elira (Deceased)
Lady Hia
Lord Flynn
Lord Bajerdine

Sid Bha (father/daughter) (Weapons Master)
(promised)
(daughter/mother) Mae Bha
Noel
Jakki
Aren Bha (Deceased)
(student/live-in tutor)
(ex-lovers)
Nellie & Tiju

Wren (Lost Square) (lovers)
(friends)
Bish (promised)
Marigold

KRIJEN:
Jin Kanju (killer/haunting)
Flit
Jokah
Meek
Pago
Nommo
Jin's squad
Oji (Late FaKrijen)
Eden (FaKrijen)

STREETLINGS:
Pyra (Upper West Side gang leader) (psuedo-child/parents)
Rifter (second-in-command)
Barrett
Ala
Porge (Upper East Side gang leader)
(sisters) Polly (Deceased)

HOLU MON:
Mo Nu (University dean)
Fom (chaperone)
Narium
Bodin
Demison
Mandavar (father/son) Drax
(ex-lovers)
(ex-lovers)
Dijak (rescuer/rescuee) Felle

HUNTERS of HOLU MON:
Olmonon
Sola
Donna

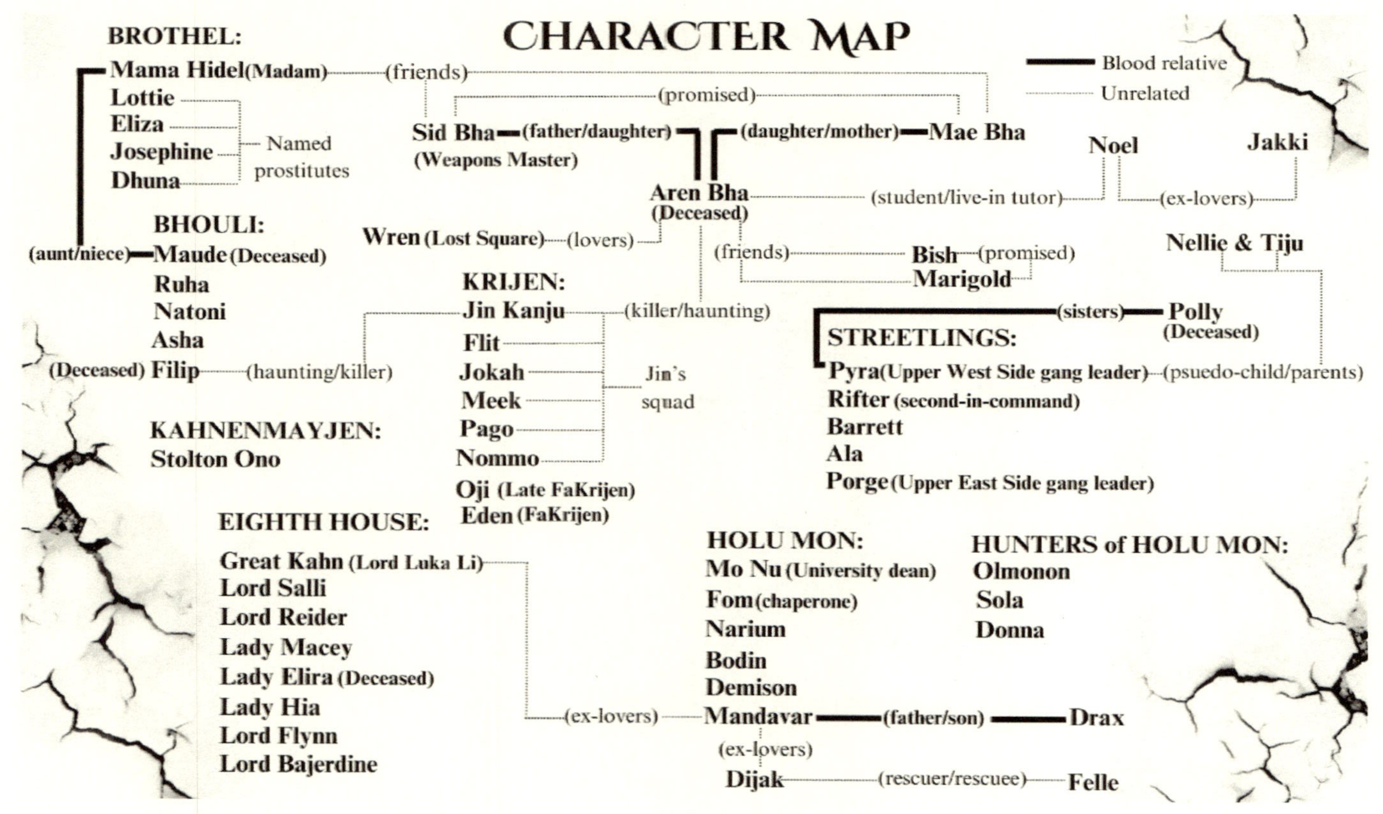

613

Thank you so much for reading *All the Shadows of Death*.

Reviews are one of the most important determinants of a book's success, especially for self-published authors. Please consider leaving an honest review of this book on the platform from which you bought it, and on Goodreads. Thank you.

www.valruefantasyseries.com

Instagram: @ColeyTaylorAuthor
TikTok: @ColeyTaylorAuthor
Facebook.com/ColeyTaylorAuthor